The Last
WALTZ

Marshall Co Public Library
@ Benton
1003 Poplar Street
Benton, KY 42025

Baker & Taylor
MAR 2 1 2012

OTHER NOVELS BY G. G. VANDAGRIFF

The Arthurian Omen
Poisoned Pedigree
Tangled Roots
Of Deadly Descent
Cankered Roots

To the memory of my father,
Robert Valentine Gibson,
who loved this book best

Acknowledgments

To my brilliant daughter, Elizabeth (Buffy) Vandagriff Bailey, for her insightful, thoughtful, and outstanding editing. An added point of interest is that she edited this book at age twenty-seven, which is the same age I was when I began writing it. She had not yet been born.

To my husband, who has encouraged this project from its inception shortly after our marriage. I have lost count of how many versions he has read.

To the lovely Polynesian woman who found the manuscript (and the diaper bag that contained it) in the Los Angeles airport and cared enough to go to great lengths to see that it was returned to me. This was way before computers, so the loss to me would have been staggering.

To my many friends over the years who have read and encouraged me in this project: Ginny, Anna, Sandra, Alana, Rondi, Susan, and my sister, Buffy, to name a few.

To my editor, Suzanne Brady, and product director, Jana Erickson, for their enthusiasm and encouragement.

NORWAY

Stockholm

FINLAND

St. Petersburg

SWEDEN

DENMARK

Copenhagen

RUSSIA

PRUSSIA

Amsterdam
The Hague
NETHERLANDS

Berlin

GERMANY

POLAND

Brussels
BELGIUM

UKRAINE

Paris

AUSTRIA

Vienna

Budapest

FRANCE

Bern
SWITZERLAND

HUNGARY

ITALY

ROMANIA
Bucharest

Belgrade

SERBIA

BULGARIA

Sofia

CORSICA

Rome

ALBANIA

SARDINIA

GREECE

TURKEY

Athens

SICILY

Tunis

TUNISIA

AUSTRO-HUNGARIAN EMPIRE 1913

Pedigree of Amalia Eugenia Faulhaber

Count Franz Herbert von Hohenburg   m.   Elisabeth von Erdmann.

Eugenia von Hohenburg   m.   Johannes Reichart

Lorenz Reichart   Margareta (Gretel) Reichart   m.   Matthaeus Faulhaber

Wolfgang (Wolf) Faulhaber   Antonia Faulhaber   Amalia Eugenia Faulhaber

Part One

VIENNA

DECEMBER 1913

Chapter One

Traveling across the vast imperial courtyard of the Hapsburg Palace, Amalia appeared as a mere speck of green against the snow. The matronly edifice, surrounded by cream pastry monuments, rose as a fantasy out of the white. From here an unbroken line of Hapsburg emperors had ruled over central Europe for half a millennium. This fact was there, buried deep in whatever consciousness of self the nineteen-year-old Amalia Faulhaber had, telling her much more than she realized about who she was—a Viennese.

Eberhard thought these thoughts, striding impatiently before this aged grandeur as he awaited his fiancée. When she arrived and he handed her down from the carriage, he had the familiar sensation of possessing a long-stemmed lily—graceful, fragrant, and pure.

"This is rather melodramatic, darling," Amalia said. Her mahogany red coiffure was capped by a perky feathered hat, hardly suited for the impending blizzard. "A note to meet you alone! I hope you know I had to lie to Mama."

"Let's walk," he suggested curtly. Head and shoulders above his fiancée, who was tall for a woman, he barely tamed his stride to accommodate hers. She appeared to be a typical young socialite in her loden cape, but to him, she was anything but typical. Somehow, in her artless way, she had ensnared a heart that belonged to another life, another world.

Now, instead of speaking, Eberhard studied the snow-darkened horizon that was capped by the ornate roofs of the courtyard buildings, green with age. How could he begin? He must shake off this feeling of being small. This place of doomed decadence had no hold over him. He belonged in the fast-paced Protestant streets of Berlin, where men strode instead of strolling. But there was Amalia . . .

"What's wrong, Eberhard?"

"We're going to have another blizzard," he said, without looking at her. "We'd better get this over with and return you to your home."

"That sounds rather ominous." She drew a little apart. Capturing her arm, he held her to him and guided her down a pair of steps. He was taut all over at the contact.

"Come, tell me what this is about. Why couldn't you call at the house in the normal way?"

"Someone is always hovering. I needed to talk to you alone, and I didn't want you flying off before I'd finished speaking to you."

"It's bad, then?"

"I'm afraid it is." He gazed into her face for the first time.

Amalia withdrew her hand from his arm, raised her chin, and looked him straight in the eye. Eberhard was the first to avert his gaze, running his fingers through his hair. Best to get it over with. "Amalia, I have to leave Vienna."

"Your mother . . . ?" she began.

Cutting her off with a raised hand, he added, "Mother's fine. It's just that I'm afraid it will be impossible for me to marry you."

Obviously stunned, she raised a gloved hand to her mouth. He read the thoughts in her transparent countenance—*He can't possibly be serious! We are engaged! The notice has been published in the newspapers! I am being fitted for my wedding gown! What madness is this?*

He was instantly repentant, grasping her hands and squeezing hard. He had to make her understand. "I've decided I must go back to Berlin to enlist in the army."

She breathed again, and the tension went out of her. "Is that all?" Her lapis blue eyes chastened him. "Then there's nothing really wrong."

"I don't think you understand, Amalia."

"Eberhard, you're making this far too difficult. Soldiers aren't monks."

He felt the lines of his face soften as he looked down at her. Despite her sophisticated air, the milkiness of her skin was that of a child. Her innocence was always refreshing to his spirit in this overblown, world-weary place. "No, of course they're not. But there's going to be a war, you know." He turned his face away. "I may be killed."

"Of course you won't be killed," she said. "If there were a war, which I doubt, it would only be a short skirmish with those devilish Serbs. Germany wouldn't even be involved!" She had recovered her equilibrium now, reminding him that she was the great-granddaughter of a count.

In exasperation, he dropped her hands. They began to walk again.

"There's going to be a blowup, Amalia," he insisted. "This situation can't continue much longer. Russia is Serbia's ally. If she fights, then Germany's bound to. France, too, for that matter."

"Wolf says Russia won't fight over some silly disagreement in the Balkans."

They had had this discussion many times. "Your brother is entitled to his opinion, but that doesn't change the fact that Austria needs to settle things permanently in that part of the Empire. It's a tinderbox. A haven for anarchy. It could ignite all Europe. That's the Kaiser's assessment, and I agree with him." Wresting his gaze from hers, he stared at the horizon and imagined himself in the ceremonial uniform of a Prussian officer with its gold epaulettes, red lapels, and shiny top boots. Memories of his father coming home from the Officer's Club in just such a uniform were as much a part of his childhood as horseback riding, shooting, and . . . violin sonatas.

"But, Eberhard, what does your Kaiser have to do with our getting married?"

"Amalia!" She *wouldn't* see. "Don't you ever look beyond yourself? No. Of course not. How could you? You're a part of this doomed madness." A sweeping gesture took in the overly ornamented buildings of the Hofburgplatz. "It's finished, Amalia, or soon will be. You've got to realize that. You're in moral bankruptcy and decay, hanging on by a fraying thread of tradition. Your emperor is a tired old man, living in the last century. His heir committed murder and suicide, for heaven's sake. Everyone who is anyone in Vienna commits suicide!"

"I don't know a soul who has committed suicide!"

Ignoring her, he proceeded with the speech he had prepared. "Your only prayer is Germany. Our emperor is young, full of fresh ideas. Strength and vision!"

She stood still, studying his face. "Sometimes I think you're quite mad, Eberhard." He heard echoes of her grandmother's hauteur. "You're so passionate about all these things another person can't begin to understand."

"And sometimes, Amalia, you're too Viennese for words."

"Then why on earth do you want to marry me?" she challenged.

"Heaven only knows," he said, the fight going out of him. His heart softened as it did when he lost himself playing his violin. In moments such as these, she sneaked into his breast, bringing her multicolored vitality. It almost blinded him. He had to remind himself that the world was black and white.

"I've got to get away," he said, shaking his head to rid it of her spell. "I should have left weeks ago, but I kept finding excuses to stay."

Amalia stopped. "You make me sound like some impediment to your duty."

A vision, which he had experienced many times—Amalia walking towards him down the aisle of St. Stephen's Cathedral, all trembling and white in her purity—visited him now and wouldn't leave. "Do you think I feel nothing? Can't you see how difficult this is for me?" he demanded harshly.

Shocked into silence, she averted her gaze. Her body suddenly lost its rigidity, and she stumbled to a nearby bench to sit down.

"It's not a good time to be in love, Amalia. I'm sorry."

"So we are expected to turn our feelings off," she said, her voice low. "How *can* you, Eberhard?"

The grandeur around him faded to winter bleakness, and he just managed to cling to the vision of himself in his uniform. "I'm setting you free, Amalia. It's the hardest thing I've ever done."

"You won't even ask me to wait?"

"You weren't made for waiting, my dear."

"You don't know that!"

"I wouldn't ask it of you. I think once I've gone you'll even come to realize you don't actually love me, Amalia." This realization was sudden and came, unwanted, from the deepest part of him.

It stupefied her completely. "How can you mean that?"

"You have never felt for me what I feel for you," he murmured gently, knowing it to be true. He was her mother's catch. A baron. Amalia was too young and inexperienced to feel the agony that was making him tremble.

"Tell me what I've done," she pleaded. "Where have I fallen short?"

Leaning forward, he kissed her forehead. "Someday you will know what it is to love with body and soul."

Her brow furrowed. Flushing, Amalia looked away.

"There are some things that are too big for us, Amalia," he said, his voice suddenly hard as he averted his face. "I have known all my life that I was born to be an officer in the Prussian army. It is simply who I am." He paced two steps away. "Vienna was an experiment I undertook to please my mother. But it is not my destiny to be a dilettante violinist. Nor to marry the Fairy Queen."

She looked up at him, her eyes large and surprisingly angry. "I'm not the Fairy Queen! You're talking like a romantic, Eberhard. You don't even sound like yourself."

He turned his back on her. The move was deliberate, calculated. He couldn't allow her to see inside him to that insecure place he didn't control—the place where the violinist dwelt, where he actually feared

7

for his life, and where he loved her so much that his resolution was nearly gone.

Throwing off these thoughts, he assumed the stance of a soldier while he still could. Innocent she might be, but Amalia Faulhaber was part of this dying city that was threatening to pull him down in its death throes. To fight with the Prussian army was his destiny.

"There isn't anything I can do to make you change your mind?" she asked.

Merely shaking his head, he kept his back to her.

"Eberhard, this is a mistake."

"I'm a soldier, Amalia. That's all I ever was. I'm sorry if for a little while I forgot the fact."

"Yes, it is a pity." He heard the sarcasm in her words and could visualize Amalia drawing herself up. Hers was not a character to be crushed by rejection.

"Well, if you must go, do it now," she challenged him.

He looked over his shoulder, studying her one last time, as she sat there in green, tiny against the immense landscape. Then he turned and walked away without looking back. He knew if he did, he would never go.

Chapter Two

Amalia dismissed the carriage. She could never go home, never face anyone again. Now that Eberhard was out of sight, the spark of anger that had sustained her was gone. Instead, she was numb. Her future had dissolved. It was as though she were suddenly invisible.

Wishing time would freeze like the streets, she knew that now was not the moment for a confrontation with Mama, who would rant at her for letting the Baron von Waldburg go, for not holding him to his promise. Mama would never accept his zeal, his sense of destiny, as a suitable explanation. And while Amalia was feeling so hollow and deserted, so . . . dehumanized, Mama would be too much to bear. She needed time.

Blindly, she walked toward the Ringstrasse that surrounded the heart of her city. Her cape was insufficient covering for her physical and emotional vulnerability, but she was so frozen inside she hardly noticed. She struggled on, small and powerless against the whirling white of the blizzard. If Eberhard had deserted her for another woman, she could have been angry! But to be rejected for an ideal she could not even comprehend left her mystified. Knowing he loved her was inconsequential. No one she knew would ever understand, and the indignity of such scandal was too much for her to consider.

Dimly Amalia became aware of the need for shelter. Her feet were freezing inside her Italian leather boots. She had come out unprepared for a long walk in a blizzard.

After some time, she heard a jumble of voices and laughter rising from a basement doorway, and she smelled the aroma of coffee. "*Der Haushuhn,*" the gold-scripted sign read. Recognizing the name of a well-known student coffeehouse, she saw that she had walked all the way to the university. Amalia felt a stab of curiosity through the numbness. Had Eberhard frequented this place?

The idea offered her a vague idea of sanctuary. Young and unaccompanied, she knew even in her barely functioning state of consciousness that stopping here was not acceptable behavior. She knew she must go home. But that unappealing thought had no power over her frozen limbs and shattered ego. It was easy to rationalize a few more minutes of anonymity. Besides, Eberhard had mentioned that there were a few women students. Maybe she would not be a complete oddity.

Descending the stairs, she wondered why her former fiancé had bothered to come to Vienna to study if he despised it so. A promise to his mother? That was the first she had heard of it. Why had the baroness not insisted on Heidelberg with its solid German tradition?

Amalia pushed open the heavy oak and glass door. The atmosphere of the coffeehouse was pungent with the odors of yeasty bread, beer, coffee, and cigarettes. Unmistakably masculine smells. She felt very out of place in her haute couture ensemble, but the warmth and the babble of noisy students seduced her. Going back out into the bitter winter was not an option.

No one appeared to be taking undue notice of her. They continued their raucous laughter and arguments in small groups all around her. Still feeling invisible, she knew warmth was the closest thing to comfort she could expect at this moment.

*　*　*

Ah! What was this? How had such a lovely creature found her way into this masculine haunt? Looking closer, his professional eye saw evidence of shock, confusion, and utter exhaustion. He stood. "Fräulein! I'd quite given you up."

"You've mistaken me for someone else, I'm afraid." She smiled vaguely and would have gone on, but he touched her arm.

"No, I've been waiting for you half my life, at least. You must have coffee with me."

"No, thank you." She seemed to wilt under the effort of refusal, and he became alarmed. "It would look better if you did, you know. How about some chocolate? You're freezing."

At these words, she looked around her, seeming to realize what kind of establishment she had breached. There were no other women. "But I don't know you," she began.

Could she possibly be as innocent as she looked? Here, in this place, alone? "I'm Zaleski," he told her. "*Doktor* Andrzej Zaleski. Manageable if you don't have to spell it. And it's your health I'm thinking of. As a doctor, you understand."

Her face was so guileless he could read her surrender. She might have said, *What does it matter?* He felt a genuine surge of protectiveness.

"So what is it to be then, coffee or chocolate?"

"Chocolate."

"With whipped cream, I suppose?"

"Yes, please. That would be wonderful." He went up to the bar to get the hot drinks, leaving her as she removed her gloves from trembling fingers.

"What on earth brought you out on a day like today?" he asked upon his return.

She accepted her drink, giving him a brief smile that caused him to forget his question. She was entrancing, whoever she was. Intriguing. Especially in his coffeehouse on a dreary day. He was in need of amusement.

"*Schokolade mit Schlag.* I really don't see how anyone can drink that stuff," he remarked finally.

"I was weaned on it," she informed him, shrugging one shoulder. She surveyed her surroundings now that she was thawing out. He wondered what she made of the fin de siècle posters featuring languid,

11

half-dressed females. The chairs and tables were merely functional, and
the noise and laughter were unrestrained, not like the society chatter
she was undoubtedly used to.

"To me, that is the essence of Vienna," he teased her, seeking
another smile. "Baroque and decadently sweet."

"You're not very original," she told him with a slight touch of hauteur at odds with her seeming innocence. It amused him. "Schnitzler
already said the same thing in a play. Rather a horrid play."

"I'll try not to imagine it. You study literature then?"

"I don't study anything," she returned with a trace of disdain.

"Why don't you take that useless hat off so I can see your hair?"

She looked at him in surprise. Obviously, she really wasn't used to
this sort of badinage and was not certain how seriously to regard it. He
attempted to tease her with his eyes, but she gave no hint of acknowl-
edgment. Then slowly, as if too weak to protest, she removed the small
single feathered thing not selected for warmth.

He grinned at her. "Much better without the hat."

She drank her chocolate.

"You're not an actress?"

Startled, she replied with unexpected force, "No! Did you take me
for a demimondaine?"

He laughed. "No, you're far too young and far too artless, but a
puzzle all the same. As you can see, you're rather an exotic here."

Suddenly suspicious, she looked him straight in the eye. "You speak
more like a German than a Viennese. Where are you from?"

"Posen. Do you know it?"

"It's in Germany, isn't it?"

He felt the familiar stir of hatred and managed to quell it, speaking
lightly. "The Germans say so. We still call it Poland."

She was obviously uninterested in the distinction. "I'm rather tired
of hearing foreigners abuse Vienna. Why do you stay here if you dislike it?"

"I don't really. It's only a pose." He grinned at her again, knowing precisely how engaging his grin was. "I'm here because of one man. The surgeon Theodor Billroth."

She seemed to drift away at that. There was something weighing heavily on her mind, evidently. Women didn't usually react to him in this half-hearted way.

"Tell me," she asked suddenly, "do you think there will be a war?"

No question could have surprised him more, and that pleased him. Turning sideways in his chair, he dropped an elbow over the back and ran his other hand thoughtfully through his hair. "Who says there will be?"

"My fiancé," she replied. "He's German, too."

"I'm a Pole," he reminded her shortly. "Tell me about your fiancé." How could such a lovely young thing be engaged to a member of that monstrous race?

"You're too young to be a doctor," she told him. "You haven't the manner."

"I beg your pardon, Fräulein." He raised an eyebrow at the rebuke. "Surgeons are still the renegades of the profession. But you can ask anyone." He swept the room with an arm. "They'll tell you who I am. However, if you don't want to talk about your fiancé, we can talk about war, if you like. It's a refreshingly novel subject."

"You don't need to entertain me, Herr Doktor."

"But it's you who are entertaining me. You have no idea how unusual it is to find a female with an inquiring mind."

"Are you always so offensive?"

"Women usually find me charming."

The young woman stirred her chocolate without comment. Clearly she lacked the energy for flirtation.

"I repent, Fräulein," he murmured. "Forgive me, and I will cease to patronize you."

Putting his forearms on the table, he leaned forward. "Now, where were we?"

"The war. If it's so imminent, why does no one discuss it?"

13

"I mean no offense, but I presume it's the fiancé who claims it's imminent?"

"His name is von Waldburg," she told him. "Baron von Waldburg. I think he knows what he's talking about."

The doctor puckered his brow. "The name is familiar. Isn't he studying here? Music or something?"

"Yes. I think I must have heard of this coffeehouse from him. I wanted to see it."

"Then why didn't he bring you?"

"He has gone back to Germany on business." She cast her eyes downward as she made this statement, and he guessed it was a sore subject.

"Music seems an odd interest for a warmongering man," he said.

"He's very good at his music. Particularly Bach."

"Forgive me again. Perhaps I only resent the fact that he should have such a redeeming characteristic. Let's return to our discussion of the imminent war." He resumed his pose. "There is hope in some hearts that it might actually happen. The Austrians are inclined to wish it away."

"How do Poles feel about the subject?"

He wondered at her interest in his opinion. Maria would never pursue such a subject with him. She managed to forget most of the time that he was a Pole. Shrugging, he said, "Do you really care? We Poles are liable to be loquacious."

"I've noticed." She smiled, and this time she put more heart into it, charming him still further. An odd flirtation, this.

He looked down into his coffee cup, a lock of his black hair falling over his brow. Raking it back, he said, "Well, first you have to understand that I'm a Polish patriot. Our country is a bit delusional. We still want our twelfth-century borders back. But this war wouldn't really make much difference to us, as far as I can see. If the Russians win—you understand this is to be a war principally between empires—they will take a bit more of my country and the Germans will lose a bit. If the Austro-German alliance wins, they take a little more and the

Russians lose a little more." He stopped to sip his coffee, frowning. Of course, she couldn't understand how deep his obsession went and, like most Viennese, would likely find it boring. "After all this time, it has ceased to matter one way or the other. The only thing that interests me is independence, and your hypothetical war doesn't offer much hope of that."

"No. I suppose not. But how long would such a war last?"

"Ah! The salient question, I presume. I'm no prophet, Fräulein. Have you a name, by the way?"

"I don't usually come out unattended like this," she told him, looking about her as though recalling her surroundings. "Today was rather unusual."

"It must have been. You found your way here to keep our date."

"You are really very impertinent."

"I could find you out quite easily, you know."

Her eyes flashed alarm. "I suppose you could, but I really wish you wouldn't. We won't see one another again."

"You never know." Getting to his feet, he took her hand in his. She had just thrown down a challenge, though she was unaware. "Let me find you a *Fiaker*. You can't walk home in this weather."

"Thank you for the chocolate."

He laughed. "Next time we meet, I'll present my bona fides. I'll have someone introduce us properly."

"I'm certain we move in very different circles, Herr Doktor. There won't be a next time." The attitude of a grande dame descended upon her rather late in the game.

As he saw her off in the hired *Fiaker* a few minutes later, he wondered how long it would be before he could contrive an encounter. Medicine was all very well, but he was bored. Maria had been far too easy a conquest.

Chapter Three

As Amalia anticipated, when she finally arrived home, she was harassed by her maid, Kristina.

"We must get you right into the bath. What was the baron thinking to let you stay out in this blizzard? I knew I shouldn't have let you go. What am I to tell your mother? Your boots are ruined, and the hem of your gown is black with dirt."

Why can't she leave me alone? Why can't everyone just leave me alone until I get my balance?

She spent what remained of the day staring out at the blizzard. Reality simply would not penetrate the world of the practical Faulhaber establishment. Here in her familiar room, it was too easy to pretend the scene in the courtyard had never happened. Kristina informed Amalia's mother that she was suffering from a chill and would be unable to come down for dinner. Amalia went to bed early, glad to escape into oblivion. She dreamed of unrelenting blizzards, scarlet marching parades, and a sleek black cat with green eyes.

The next morning Kristina woke her early. "Your mother has heard that you took the carriage out alone yesterday to meet the baron. I don't know who told her. You had better think of something to take the Frau's mind off it."

The little maid threw back the curtains, letting in sunlight shining off the snow. Amalia was unprepared for the harsh invasion of light. With a grimace she drank the hot lemonade Kristina had brought. "Three times a day," she said. "So you don't catch pneumonia."

Kristina could bully her all she wanted, but Amalia wasn't going to put up with anything of the sort from her mother and sister. The maid was right. She needed to think of a strategy.

As she sat at the ornate vanity table watching Kristina style her hair, Amalia noted her extreme pallor. Normally, she had a touch of rose in her cheeks but not today. Her tortured night showed in the circles under her eyes. No one looking at her today would call her one of society's beauties. She said, "Put out my plain gray dress. I think a visit to Uncle is in order. Mother will see it as penance."

"You want to go out again in this weather?"

"It's not snowing any longer, and if I wear my woolen drawers, I shall be perfectly comfortable."

The maid looked at Amalia suspiciously. "Never have I known you to willingly wear your woolen drawers."

Kristina nodded her head sharply, like a bird going for a worm, and pulled out the plain gray wool dress. Amalia kept it strictly for parish work and visits to her uncle, the radical socialist who lived in the back streets of Vienna.

He was far dearer to her than either her mother or sister, and they could not fathom her willingness to venture into such surroundings. Today he would be understanding. She did not know why, precisely. They had never discussed love, never even discussed Eberhard. But she liked to think that he knew the real Amalia, the Amalia who would exist if there were no such thing as Viennese society.

Standing as he did outside the great social circus, Uncle was an expert on matters of the soul. Of course, he would deny any such expertise. Proper socialists did not believe in the existence of a soul.

Amalia smiled a little grimly. She also wanted to talk to Uncle about the war.

"Eberhard has had to go back to Berlin," she told her mother and sister as she entered the breakfast room. Papa had, of course, left for the warehouse. The sun shone brilliantly through the French doors into the yellow room, reflecting the blanket of near-blinding white inside the

Faulhabers' little walled garden. "Some tiresome business concerning his father's estate."

This piece of news, dropped like a bomb, entirely disconcerted her mother and sister, as she had planned it would. But her mother's formidable expression returned almost instantly. Margareta Faulhaber scolded as she buttered a *Semmel.* "How could you, Amalia? Not a word. Alone with Eberhard! And when, may I ask, does he plan to return?"

The list of her grievances was only beginning. She sputtered on, becoming ever more incensed, while Amalia tried to eat her Semmel with an air of calm. This was more difficult than she had thought it would be. How could she continue to patch her raw wound with lies? She managed to remain detached from her mother's diatribe only by studying the black cat that crept along the top of the garden wall outside. He reminded her vaguely of her dream.

"I'm certain he attributed my behavior to sentiment rather than to lack of virtue," she replied when her mother finally wound down.

Mama's matronly bosom heaved, and she began again. "If you won't think of yourself, Amalia, at least have a little consideration for Antonia's reputation. What if your behavior were to put Erich off?"

The cat, it appeared, was stalking an unwary bird. "Then I shouldn't care very much to have him for a brother-in-law. I would always be making him uncomfortable. Antonia couldn't marry anyone so stuffy."

At this her elder sister stood and pulled her curvaceous self to her full height. She came to Amalia's nose. Her turquoise eyes were narrowed, and she spoke with what Amalia knew to be a dangerous restraint. This was the Antonia that only her family saw. "You think you're quite an original, don't you, Amalia? A cut above the rest of us. But, I'm warning you, I mean to marry Erich if that means locking you in your room to keep you from having any more of these escapades. You know very well we can't afford the license we would have if we were still von Hohenburgs. We must be above reproach or scandal of any kind."

She glided out of the room, her rose peignoir trailing behind her, and Amalia felt a spurt of pity for Erich.

"Eberhard doesn't know how long he'll be gone," said Amalia, answering the other part of her mother's grievance. She lied as though she had been doing it all her life. "He will let us know."

Her mother gave a "humph" and buttered another Semmel. At least she dared not say anything against Eberhard. He was a baron and, therefore, above reproach.

Amalia considered it time to remark, "I thought I'd visit Uncle Lorenz this morning, Mother. He hasn't been well. Would you like me to take him some Christmas breads?"

Her mother snapped, "Of course he's not well. And neither would you be if you'd chosen to live your life in that dark, cold little hole he calls a flat." Amalia knew her mother imagined that Uncle had chosen his living quarters solely to vex her. "And what's to happen to his money when he dies, that's what I'd like to know! I doubt he's given it a thought."

"Uncle has no money, Mama. You know that. He's given almost all of it away."

"Of course. But it's in trust. He's purchased seats on the boards of some very influential charities."

Amalia clenched her teeth. After a moment, she replied evenly, "He hates sitting on those boards. The only reason he does it is that if he didn't, his money would be squandered. He wants to see that it's spent on things that matter. If you have anything to send . . . ," Amalia reminded her.

"Oh, I imagine we can find something." Her mother stood. "But, Amalia, you must be more circumspect. When you take the carriage out this morning, you are to have Hans wait for you and then come home before luncheon. Don't forget we have the von Altwalds' ball tonight."

After a visit to the Faulhaber kitchens, alive with Christmas activity and smelling of strudel and yeast, Amalia secured a basket of breads. She was about to leave when she changed her mind and mounted the stairs back to her room.

She couldn't stand these lies any longer. She must give them some foundation in fact. Taking out pen and paper, she wrote:

Dear Eberhard:

I find I cannot tell anyone your news. It's still too difficult for me to adjust from having everything to having nothing. I am telling everyone that you have gone away on family business. Undoubtedly, you think this very deceitful and unworthy of me. Perhaps it is. I only know that I cannot give it up yet. The future we planned together is still too deeply rooted in me.

Is it really necessary for us to be so brutal to ourselves? I, believe it or not, am possessed of some patience. It is not necessary that we have any definite plans. I can wait.

Mit liebende grüsse,
Amalia

Sealing the letter, she felt far less burdened. She summoned the carriage.

Eberhard disapproved of her uncle, and she imagined that if pressed, her uncle would confess a like disapproval for her former fiancé. She had taken Eberhard to visit only once, and he had not been able to see past the shabby working class neighborhood and the smell of drains. He had not been able to appreciate a man who scorned his birthright, choosing to give it away to the poor. He had despised her uncle's politics as the very opposite of what he himself believed. Driving through the snow-showered city made festive with wreaths, evergreens, and holly, Amalia wondered how she could love two such different men.

"Amalia! You are a brilliant sight in this gloomy old quarter!" her uncle greeted her. Unlike her mother, he was tall with auburn hair like her own. Amalia always thought his elegant von Hohenburg looks made him vividly incongruous in his chosen surroundings. She could not help but be aware that she looked far more like her uncle than her mother.

"And as it happens, I have someone I very much want you to meet."

Ushering her into the small flat, he introduced her to the last sort of person she expected to find there. Of medium height, with a hawklike face softened by warm brown hooded eyes, this man was obviously an aristocrat.

"Amalia Faulhaber, may I present the Baron von Schoenenburg? Baron, my niece, Fräulein Faulhaber."

* * *

Rudolf could never have expected that Lorenz could possess such a stunning niece, who, though dressed simply in a gray gown, was coiffured in the latest mode. She quite obviously adored her uncle, which he found endearing. His heart was not ordinarily open to the wiles of the opposite sex, but she looked nothing like any of the scheming women who had laid their snares for him over the years. She was clearly someone quite out of this world. He knew in an instant she had no darkness in her. Taking her hand, he bowed over it and kissed it gently. Such a long, slim, elegant hand.

"The baron and I serve together on the board of St. Stephen's Orphanage, one of my charities," Lorenz explained to Amalia. "He was kind enough to come here to get my signature on some documents, as I'm afraid I would have nothing to wear should I go calling on him!" He laughed, and Rudolf looked at his friend fondly. He was the heart and soul of the orphanage and many other charities in Vienna. His belief in the essential goodness of man was refreshing, if naïve.

Lorenz turned to Rudolf. "I may have told you before that my mother is the daughter of Count von Hohenburg. She disgraced herself rather badly by marrying a wealthy carriage maker for love. My fortune

 Marshall Co Public Library @ Benton 1003 Poplar Street

comes to me through him. My mother still lives in a grand *palais* in high style, but we are the best of friends." Lorenz Reichart chuckled. "Unfortunately, my sister doesn't hold me in such high regard. I never chose to marry, but she married a prosperous lace importer, Matthaeus Faulhaber. It is her aim in life to launch her son and two daughters back into high society."

"This is one of her daughters, I presume?" the baron asked, amusement tugging at the corner of his mouth. She was shaking her head, rolling her eyes at her uncle.

Amalia made a beautiful curtsey, mocking herself. "As you see."

"I must say that high society, as you call it, Lorenz, is in for a treat."

"Oh, Amalia's spoken for. By a very proper Prussian baron. They are engaged to be married—when is it, Amalia?"

Rudolf was aware of an odd shaft of disappointment. And a Prussian! He couldn't see this gentle, unpretentious woman married to a "blood and honor" Prussian whose soul must be even more twisted than his own.

"Our plans are not yet definite, Uncle. But you're boring this poor man hideously."

"No. Rudolf likes to know about people. They are his specialty. That's why we get along so well."

"You make me sound like a society gossip, Lorenz," he reproached his friend.

"Oh, no, Amalia. I would trust the baron with my deepest, darkest secret. Now, what is it you have in that basket? It smells divine."

"A strudel and some Semmeln."

"We must dine together. The baron has brought me a Christmas ham."

"I'm afraid I can't stay, Uncle. I'm on Mama's black list and must return for luncheon."

"And I must be going and leave you to visit with your niece," the Baron said regretfully. He could see that she had come with a purpose and was anxious for him to be gone. "Don't forget the January board meeting, Lorenz. We need you there badly. We're discussing our appropriations for the year, and you want to make sure your money's spent as you would wish."

As he left the squalid little flat, Rudolf reflected that though she was lovely, Amalia was, after all, a trifle young for him. He sighed regretfully. She was definitely not out of the common mold, stirring feelings in him he had thought deadened by years of cynicism over the deference paid him. Why did she want to marry a Prussian?

*   *   *

As soon as the baron was out the door, Amalia said, "Uncle, Eberhard has broken off our engagement. What am I to do?"

Chapter Four

Lorenz Reichart bestowed a kiss on his niece's forehead. "My poor darling. But what makes you think I can help?" He drew her down next to him on his faded brocade couch. The only ornaments in the room were his floor-to-ceiling bookcases and a cast-off Aubusson rug from his mother's palais. Though he wouldn't admit it quite yet, her news couldn't have made him happier.

"I've lied about it. I've told people he's just gone away on estate business, but he hasn't. He's gone to join the German army. He thinks there's going to be a war. He doesn't want me to wait for him." Her voice rose with each sentence.

"What people?" He asked idly.

"What?"

"What people have you lied to?"

"Mama and Antonia. Oh, and a doctor I met yesterday at the university."

"Well, the doctor sounds like a good story we must save for another time. Now, first things first. I want you to be truly honest. Do you really love Eberhard, Amalia?"

"Of course I do!" she said. Lorenz regarded her steadily, and she lowered her eyes. He knew that from the time she had been a small child on his knee, she had never been able to lie to him. "He doesn't think I do, as a matter of fact, but would I be engaged to him if I didn't?"

Her uncle fixed her with his eyes. "People get engaged for many reasons apart from love, Amalia. You must understand you can give yourself completely to another person only once." He sighed in a manner foreign to him. "It would be a tragedy if you were to marry without having been in love, my dear." He looked at his shelf full of books, trying to summon the memory of Trudi from so long ago. It was growing hazy, but his heart softened nevertheless. He saw her bent over her piano, playing Chopin as though the world were going to end.

"You'll know it when it comes. You see, when you're really in love, you don't have any choice in the matter. You *want* to offer everything you have. Irrevocably. And if you do give it, you never have it to give to anyone else. It's no longer yours to give, you see."

Amalia was sobered. "It sounds very uncomfortable. Is that why you've never married, Uncle? Did you lose someone you loved?"

He felt his chest tighten in that annoying way it had of late. "It was my own doing, but it left its stamp on me. How could I expect anyone to share this life? The woman I loved would have, but her parents . . . you see." He surveyed the room with his arm. The action left him dizzy, and his niece jumped up and assisted him to recline on the couch like the old man he suddenly was.

Pulling a straight-backed chair over beside him, she murmured, "I never meant to upset you, Uncle. We don't need to talk about it."

"As long as we're on the subject, let me say my piece, dear. Do you love Eberhard in that way?"

Amalia appeared thoughtful. She was an honest child. She would give her whole heart and mind to the question. He doubted if his sister had ever discussed love with her daughter in the whole of her life. He seriously doubted whether Gretel even knew what the feeling was.

"I don't know," she said finally. "I think I was on my way to loving him, but we had only been engaged three months. He was like two people. If you could only have seen him with his violin!" Looking down at her slim white hands, she said, "His Bach was exquisite. It revealed a whole different side of him, or I doubt I could ever have contemplated marrying him, no matter what Mama said." She sighed. "I am quite attached to him. It is hard to imagine a future without him."

"I must confess, I've wondered all along how deep your feelings went," he said. "It seemed to me that my good sister was pushing you." He folded his arms behind his head and stretched his slippered feet out in front of him. "If you really want my opinion, I've never been able to see you married to a Prussian. You're far too vibrant and independent. It has been part of my mission in life to teach you to truly assess people, down to their marrow. I have wondered how you could embrace those strange ideas—talk of blood, honor, and glory as though they were some kind of mystical combination." Bringing his arms down, he crossed them over his chest. "I don't understand such ideas." He brooded for a moment, his eyebrows lowered. Prussians!

Without warning he pounded a fist into the palm of the other hand. "Why nationalism? Can anyone tell me why people feel such a need to identify themselves with a spot of ground? Surely it's more natural, more ennobling, to work for the brotherhood of all men. Why fight and die for the rights of just a few?" He knew he was becoming animated and that it wasn't good for him. Instead, he focused on a distant, unhappy horizon. "What will the history of the twentieth century show when it's been written? One of two things: either bloodshed and destruction over this folly, or victory of the brotherhood of man—an international brotherhood where there is no room for petty greed. We have no choice, Amalia. It is either one or the other, and I very much fear we cannot have the second without experiencing the first."

"Not everyone sees as much to love in their fellowman as you do, Uncle. In another age, I believe you would have been considered a saint."

He batted her words away as though they were only an annoying insect. "So. There I've said it. I can't see you married to a Prussian. I think he was very wise to break the engagement."

"Even if I could possibly bring myself to accept that, what can I do now? What about these lies I've told?"

"In a few weeks you can say that you've rethought things and you've decided that you don't want to marry Eberhard after all."

"You make it sound simple enough," she said, and he knew she didn't feel he understood. "I *do* have feelings in the matter, you know.

26

I'm not a political person like you. I expected you to be more philosophical, I guess. More charitable towards Eberhard. He never discussed 'blood and honor' with me. With me he was not a soldier but a musician. A magnificent violinist."

Lorenz felt a moment's repentance. "Forgive me if I've been too harsh. But this is so important. I wanted to speak sooner but didn't think I had the right. Now you have asked my advice. I really don't like the Prussians, Amalia, and you are my jewel. Like a daughter to me. I consider you've had a lucky escape."

"Mama will be devastated if I let a baron go," she gave a brief smile.

"All this inane worship of the three-lettered preposition *von*. It's so absurd I should be laughing if it didn't make me so angry. You can find yourself another one. Von Schoenenburg's available. He seemed quite taken with you."

"Uncle, no matter how you talk about it, I do have feelings for Eberhard. Until yesterday, I thought I would marry him."

"You're only nineteen. Things can change."

He had absolutely no doubt that they would.

* * *

Amalia had never known her uncle to be so obdurate. It troubled her. The rest of the afternoon, she contemplated their conversation. He was usually so cherishing in his manner towards her. Who was the mysterious woman in his past? She wondered if she would ever know. She didn't dare press him about it when it obviously agitated him so.

She had always known that he considered her a daughter. When she was only twelve, he had begun teaching her French by the fire in his cold little flat. He had lent her his Voltaire and even the scandalous *Madame Bovary*. He had also spent many fruitless hours debating Marx and Engels with her at a working man's coffeehouse near his flat. This had had the effect of teaching her to think for herself, for she could not agree with the underpinnings of her uncle's political ideas. He had accused her of being hopelessly bourgeois. She had accused him of being hopelessly utopian. But under his guidance she had adopted his concern for the poor. Very active in her parish, she did what she could in her small sphere.

Her thoughts swung back to her own affairs. There had to be a way to summon up her dreams and plans that were beginning, mist-like, to disperse. Aside from the sapphire ring that Eberhard had chosen because of its likeness to her eyes, the only other evidence she had of her attachment was her journal. Poring over it, she tried reconstructing memories. Was this love? If not, what was?

He had asked her quite suddenly to marry him. It had been a sharp, clear day in late September, and they had been to a matinee performance given by a recently discovered violin virtuoso. Eberhard had been thrown into one of his incalculably poetic moods when his normally impassive face had softened every time he looked at her. It had been those times, and the knowledge of the power she possessed to create this change in him, that had built her feelings into what she knew of love.

They had stood that day in the drawing room, looking out through the French doors at a small whirlwind that swirled through the garden, picking up the varicolored leaves, and then dropping them as it passed up and on.

"I want every day to be like today, Amalia," he had said with a wistfulness she had never before heard in his voice.

They were alone, and she had put her hand on his arm, but he had continued to stare out the window. "Bright," he had amplified.

Then he had turned to her, his light eyes fervent, his color unusually high. "Marry me then, Amalia. Will you please?"

She had been startled. Somewhere inside she had hoped that eventually he might ask her, but aside from these moments of inexplicable softening towards her, he had shown very little evidence of involvement. Until that moment, his attitude had been lofty, correct, and detached. He had never even attempted to kiss her.

But he did kiss her then. It had been a little frightening. She had never been kissed before. It wasn't the gentle, caressing experience she

28

had imagined. It was rough. His beard stubble had scraped her face. She had been glad when it was over, but nevertheless, after a moment she had said yes, she would marry him.

When it was time to dress for the ball, Kristina came to her. Amalia was sitting at her desk, studying the front walk vacantly through her window. "It's no use, Kristina. You'll have to choose something for me. I find everything ghastly."

At length they decided upon the ivory chiffon, with its high pleated neck ruffle and the antique lace trimming, which came straight from the warehouses of Faulhaber and Son.

Mama accompanied her daughters that evening. Hans drove them in the carriage.

Arrayed in vibrant turquoise, Antonia's color was high and her coiffure perfect, for Erich would be there. Beside her, Amalia felt she had all the looks and animation of a Greek statue.

"So tiresome of Eberhard to leave just now," her sister said. "Erich's cousin is visiting from Salzburg. Perhaps he will give you a dance."

"I expect to spend the entire evening standing with Mama and Grandmama."

"But perhaps this cousin will be someone new and interesting. One does get so tired of the same people," Antonia said with complacency.

Inside the von Altwald palais the magnificent chandelier sparkled, and bejeweled guests glittered as they passed from room to room. The familiar magic of the ballroom setting crept over Amalia. Since the time when she, as a child, had watched from her peephole upstairs in her grandmother's house, Amalia had savored the sight of the Viennese in their holiday splendor. Tonight, she was glad to feel that the magic still touched her. With its unique thrill, it overcame her dullness and caused her to feel the old sensation that something wonderful was about to happen.

Filled with the memorabilia of several hundred years, the von

Altwald palais held evidence on every hand of the family's noble lineage—portraits, armor, bric-a-brac, and endless displays of family silver and porcelain. The floor was covered in priceless old Chinese rugs, except in the ballroom, where the fine parquet floor gleamed with high polish. Age and care had bestowed upon the aristocratic dwelling the inimitable patina of antique beauty.

But Amalia knew the family did not restrict its connections to the Viennese upper class. Their taste was varied, and sprinkled among their guests were those of the intellectual community, musicians, artists, and some of the more well-connected burghers like themselves.

Amalia watched as the daughter of the house, Therese, guided them skillfully through the throng. Her trademark was not beauty but rather a disregard of conventional style. Her dress was a curious draped affair in gold lamé, which omitted the obligatory underskirt, showing off her slender legs in silver stockings. Amalia found it quite difficult to keep her eyes off them. There were rumors about Therese.

"Your Erich has arrived, Toni. Mustache perfect, as usual. He's just there," she directed her. Turning to Amalia, she said, "I had a note from Eberhard yesterday saying he'd been called out of town."

Therese raised a questioning eyebrow.

"Estate business," Amalia said unhesitatingly. There, it was out. Soon all of Vienna would know.

"Bore for you."

Amalia shrugged. "I'm sure you can find someone quite amusing for me, Therese, if you put your mind to it. Anyone but Erich's cousin. I'm determined to dislike him."

"Well." Therese's caramel colored eyes lit, and she smiled her odd, triangular smile. "There is someone else. But you'll have to wrest him from Maria."

Therese glided into the crowd, and Amalia followed, curious.

Soon they found Maria, who addressed Amalia eagerly. "Therese tells me Eberhard has gone. She had a note. Is is true? He's left us?"

How am I to face this? It will go on and on, and I will have to tell more and more lies.

Amalia knew that Eberhard had been drawn to Maria for a time just after his arrival in Vienna. A classic golden-haired beauty with an unusual combination of olive skin and honey-brown eyes, she shared his interest in music. The relationship ended badly, for unfortunately either nature or environment had endowed Maria with the disposition of a shrew. When Eberhard began to show an interest in Amalia, Maria blamed her for their falling out. Clearly, Maria's interest in the current turn of events was not merely idle.

"He hopes to return quite soon. But you know what these estate matters are. It could be that he won't be back until spring. But tell me! Therese says you have a new admirer in tow."

Maria ceased her interrogation and smiled like silk. "As a matter of fact, there is someone."

Indicating the corner where several young men appeared to be entertaining one another with political anecdotes and university gossip, she said, "He's the tall, dark one next to Willi."

As though on cue, Maria's new suitor turned and came walking towards them.

"Maria, won't you introduce me to your friend?" he inquired, green eyes alive with suppressed humor.

Maria linked her arm firmly in his. "Amalia, may I present Herr Doktor Andrzej Zaleski? Andrzej, this is Fräulein Amalia Faulhaber, an acquaintance of mine."

Her stranger of yesterday stood politely, his eyebrows raised, his hand extended. In his evening clothes he was transformed—sleek and incredibly handsome with a challenging glint in his green eyes veiled by their long, black lashes. The cat in her dream.

She regarded him for a moment and then gave him her hand. He bowed and kissed it, murmuring "Enchanté," just as she had suspected he might.

Chapter Five

"Where did you meet Maria?" Amalia asked Andrzej boldly. Maria looked from one to the other. Then she answered for Andrzej. "We met at university, as a matter of fact. Why do you ask?"

The doctor rescued Amalia. "Don't you think Maria far too beautiful to be a—what is it the British call it? A bluestocking?"

"Of course she is. But she is a brilliant musician, you know. Have you heard her play the violin?"

"Not yet. She is going to arrange a small recital. Perhaps we could invite the Fräulein, Maria. She seems to be an admirer."

"By all means," Maria agreed. "Amalia's fiancé has just been called to Berlin on business, so she is probably short on amusements."

Amalia smiled, and Andrzej detected a bit of slyness there. "But I can't resist a recital, you know," Amalia told them. "Nor the theater nor the opera. So I imagine I won't be sitting home knitting. As a matter of fact, I don't know how to knit."

Spirit. The doctor laughed and asked, "Would your fiancé permit you to dance at a ball?"

He saw his companion's eyes narrow dangerously, but Amalia appeared oblivious. "He particularly advised me to enjoy myself. He knows how Viennese I am, you see."

"Perhaps we might dance then, later this evening? If your chaperone doesn't object to me, of course."

Maria's mouth set in a thin line.

Amalia smiled slightly. "Perhaps, if the opportunity arises, I'll introduce you. But right now you must excuse me. I see my grand-mother, and I haven't greeted her yet."

"Until later then." He bowed. He was growing increasingly bored at being Maria's captive, lovely though she was. She was far too predictable and had an annoying tendency to cling. He detected a not-so-latent hostility between her and the girl from the coffeehouse. It might be amusing to fan it. Not to mention that he considered the German's fiancée to be fair game.

* * *

As Amalia lost herself in the crowd of guests, she reflected that it was really unkind of her to taunt Maria like that. However, the woman had made her life miserable for a long time with rumors and innuen-dos. Still, she had no intention of partnering the doctor.

Only after a futile search did she remember that her grandmother had planned not to attend the ball. It was the anniversary of Grand-father's death, and she never went anywhere on that night.

She had no choice but to dance with Erich's cousin, Bruno, a stock-ier version of Antonia's beau. "Are you visiting in Vienna long?" she inquired as they began what promised to be an endless waltz.

"Yes, I am," he replied. "Aunt has been good enough to ask me for the winter. She has been very kind to Erich and me. She has no sons of her own."

Amalia listened to the ins and outs of the von Trauenburg family tree and accolades on Antonia, who was surely the "beauty of the sea-son," until at last the waltz ended. When Bruno showed signs of lin-gering near, she excused herself to go upstairs to Therese's boudoir.

"Escaping?" Andrzej Zaleski caught her just as she was about to ascend.

"I thought I might, yes." She stood, poised on the bottom step, her eyes level with his.

"That last one must have been rather a trial. He looked like a team-ster."

"He had fishy hands," Amalia admitted.

"Wherever do you find your beaux?"

"My sister is obliged to find them for me."

"Would she approve of me, do you think?"

"I doubt it. You don't have a title, do you?"

"Alas, no. The younger son of a younger son. But I'm very well connected, nevertheless."

"Yes," Amalia raised an eyebrow, "I can see that." Somehow she must dampen this man's pretensions. She really mustn't slight Maria and make things worse for herself.

"Will you dance with me now?"

"I have no intention of dancing with you."

"The chaperone didn't approve?"

"I didn't ask."

"Could it be the lovely Maria who disapproves? I thought I detected an undercurrent of hostility there."

"We're not on the best of terms. I shouldn't like to put a further strain on the relationship."

He nodded and put his hand on the newel post. "It's rather extraordinary, isn't it, my finding you again so quickly? I thought it might take several weeks, at the very least."

"You never know your luck." She advanced to the second stair, but he followed.

"I had a rather romantic story built around you, you know. A bit like Rapunzel with all that magnificent hair."

"That is absurd," she told him with a short laugh. "In spite of what you may have thought of my behavior yesterday, I don't need rescuing in the least."

"Not even from clumsy beaux? I think you do. You had better dance with me once, just for the experience."

Amalia looked at him steadily for a moment. His eyes were lit with arrogant cheerfulness. Everything else about him appeared relaxed and languorous, except the long fingers that gripped the top of the newel post as though it were a large ball, his fingernails white with some inner tension.

He stretched out his arm. "Come."

Unless she were to deliberately turn her back, leaving him with his arm outstretched, she could not refuse. She allowed herself to be led to the dance floor.

It was another waltz. Eberhard had always performed the dance in a precise, stately manner. But from the very beginning, this was a new experience. This partner swept her with easy grace onto the center of the floor, through the perpetual turns and dips, ever faster, until, in spite of herself, she began to feel an exhilarating sensation akin to flight. She knew that she was in the arms of someone to whom this dance was second nature.

"You make me quite dizzy," she laughed.

"I mean to twirl you until your hair comes down," he replied, his eyes never leaving hers.

"Then I should look like a wanton, indeed."

"No, you would look absolutely entrancing."

His arm tightened about her waist, and she was very aware that she was in his embrace. Their social banter dropped away. The room about them seemed to recede and disappear until they were alone. Slowly, the entire tenor of the experience changed.

Her social persona dissolved in the wake of this new exhilaration, and Amalia felt transparent as glass. This man with the strange green eyes, no longer laughing, was looking straight through to her soul. She felt exposed. Could he see the conflicted woman who loved a ball but was also well-read, despising the sham aristocracy her mother had created around them? Did he even sense the pride of the von Hohenburgs that need offer no excuse for her behavior? She felt he might even envision her girlhood self—headstrong, idealistic, unafraid. Before such scrutiny, she was defenseless. He might even be able to read her thoughts. Eberhard might never have existed.

It never occurred to Amalia that this could be mere flirtation. She had no doubt that they were making this journey together, for she could see into his soul as well.

Amalia sensed this man, oddly vulnerable, opening under her gaze as might a tightly closed bud. With the subtle mockery gone, Amalia saw the possibility of devotion, an old-fashioned chivalry and sense of honor that contrasted absolutely with his outward actions. The arm around her waist tightened, once more pulling her close. A surge of warmth made her ache.

And then it was over. They stood in the middle of the floor, unable to relinquish one another. Amalia actually thought he might kiss her. What was more, she wanted him to.

Finally, with a face utterly serious, he said, "You are completely wasted on that warmongering Prussian. You know very well you were meant for me." Leaving her where she stood, he walked away. His sudden withdrawal left her cold and exposed. After such intimacy, his declaration seemed natural. But his withdrawal did not. He was angry.

And though she looked for him, she didn't see him for the rest of the evening.

* * *

Andrzej retrieved his overcoat and left the ball as though running from fate. What had just happened? The girl-woman had turned the tables on him. Somehow his mask had slipped, and she had got beneath it. In all his vast experience, that had never happened before. Clearly, he must stay away from her. In addition to everything else, she was spoken for.

But a spark of something he recognized as tenderness had worked its way into his heart. Disliking his vulnerability, he wondered how many women it would take to dampen it.

* * *

The following morning Amalia lay under her blue *Federdecke*, pondering on the life-changing event of the previous evening. Lying still, eyes closed, she summoned up the scene, squeezing from it every last nuance. His eyes! She had never known eyes could speak. But a random phrase from her catechism recalled the words of St. Jerome: "The face is the mirror of the mind, and eyes without speaking confess the secrets of the heart." Of course he had been speaking of purity of heart. But she now suspected eyes could communicate anything, if a person allowed it.

And just why had the doctor allowed it? Why did he let her see his vulnerability? She was quite certain he had not meant to. He had meant only to flirt. But something had been stripped away in those few seconds. She had been allowed a precious glimpse. His abrupt departure confirmed that he was aware of it.

How could she let him know that Eberhard was gone from her life? She was free to love. Free to indulge these delicious feelings, to see and be seen. This could be the beginning of the love her uncle had told her of. And Eberhard had known it would happen.

Grandmama advised her to wait. The tall, elegant woman with the silver hair and fine-boned face sat with Amalia in the morning room of her palais. It had always been Amalia's favorite room with its apricot walls and white cornices. Snowy outside, it was sunny within. Unlike her own dark, heavily Biedermeier home, this house was a relic of her grandmother's aristocratic past, with its rococo façade of biscuit-colored plaster ornamented with trim that was like giant dollops of whipped cream. Her grandmother, a *femme formidable*, still slim and beautiful with her rose-petal complexion, was Amalia's accustomed confidante on all that went on in society.

*   *   *

Eugenia von Hohenburg Reichart was impatient with her granddaughter's naïveté. "You have every reason to know that the von Beckhaus girl can be quite dangerous when crossed. If you were to do it twice, she might cause you irreparable harm in society. And how do you

37

know this doctor is anything but a dreadful flirt? At the moment, the world believes you to be engaged, my dear. You must remember your position."

Her grandmother rang for the maid and ordered coffee for them both.

"But what about the way I feel? The way he feels?" Amalia demanded.

"If this is real, which I sincerely doubt, it will endure and grow stronger for the waiting, Amalia. Men don't always act on their feelings, no matter how strong they might be. And at the moment, it appears that Maria's got her talons into him. It's perhaps fortunate that he thinks you're unavailable, because that will cause him not to do anything precipitous."

"But what if he marries her?"

"If he marries her when he's in love with you, then he's not the man you thought him."

"I just don't like living a lie," Amalia said. "What's he going to say when he finds out?"

"He needn't find out. You can just say you've broken off the engagement."

Amalia stood and rearranged the hothouse lilies.

"It seems such a deceitful way to begin a relationship."

"Oh, sometime you should hear all the machinations I had to go through to get your grandfather to marry me! But I was very sure of his feelings, of course, or I never would have attempted such a thing."

Amalia stirred a bowl of verbena sachet, inspecting the flawless needlework on its stand by the window. "Tell me about your machinations," she said. The maid brought coffee.

"I staged a carriage accident, right in front of his house. Did you know that? I nearly killed myself. His housekeeper took me in. I was in residence for two weeks, too ill to be moved." Her heart warmed with remembrance. "I took full advantage of every moment, believe me. Oh, he was handsome, your grandfather! And so full of principle! There was no one like him in the world. Do you know that he read Schiller to me?"

"I'm surprised you didn't find it insupportable!" Amalia laughed.

"No, he had a beautiful voice. Lorenz has it. You can imagine Lorenz reading Schiller, can't you?"

"I don't need to imagine it," Amalia said. "He has often done so. And yes, it was fascinating." Then she said, "Grandmama, you have no idea how grateful I am for Uncle. Without him, I'd probably be just like Toni."

"No, dear," she said. "You've always been just like me. Such a trial to your poor mother." Looking fondly at her granddaughter, she patted her hand. "Just be patient, dear. If this man who waltzes so divinely proves to have any other redeeming qualities, I will be the first to promote the match. I've always detested Eberhard, though I know he was your mother's choice for you."

*   *   *

Why was she just now finding out that those whose opinions she most respected had found Eberhard objectionable? In the midst of this surprise, Amalia received a letter from him that afternoon. Twenty-four hours ago, she would have rejoiced, but now it made her sad. He had been exactly right about her feelings for him.

> I hope you will not mind a letter from me occasionally. I find that I do not do very well without you. It is difficult. But I must not grumble.
>
> If your family does not think too badly of me, please give them my regards. I should enjoy hearing from you, but perhaps I no longer have the right to expect your attentions. I'll abide by your decision in this.
>
> With fond regards,
> E

Chapter Six

Amalia did not know what she had been expecting from Andrzej, but his evident decision to ignore her was a surprise. As the days went by, he didn't call, and the Faulhaber family passed through its annual Christmas rituals—the parish bazaar, the Nativity pageant that Amalia staged every year at Uncle's orphanage, and finally, the trimming of the tree on Christmas Eve.

With plenty of hot *Apfelsaft* available, they began the last task.

"Is your beau going to join us tonight then, Toni?" her brother Wolf asked as he trimmed some ungainly branches. His short, thick frame looked comic perched on the high ladder.

"Yes," answered Antonia, who was sorting candles for the tree. "He'll join us for supper as soon as he can gracefully get away from his aunt and cousins."

"Wolf, darling! Do be careful. I'm certain you're going to fall off that ridiculous ladder," admonished his grandmother.

Wolf turned, his small, shrewd eyes mischievous. "You just want to do this yourself, don't you, Grandmama? Galls you to have to sit and watch others. Here, allow me to assist you." He offered his arm.

"Ridiculous boy!"

Papa arrived late from the warehouse. "You stay later at that wretched warehouse every year. It's after eight o'clock," Mama scolded him. His daughters dutifully kissed his ruddy cheeks. "Toni, you're looking splendid," he praised. "Amalia, you look very nice as well. But what is that you're wearing? Some kind of peasant dress?"

"Yes. I bought it at the Christmas bazaar." The dress had a velvet vest over a loose blouse and a full plaid skirt. It came to just below the knee.

Amalia knelt, trimming the bottom of the tree and imploring her father to help, when Georg, the butler, entered.

"Some young people, *gnädige Frau,* singing carols."

Five indistinguishable people, bundled against the outside weather, strode into the drawing room, singing robustly and harmoniously. The family listened, enchanted as they sang *"Stille Nacht, Heilige Nacht."*

At the conclusion of their song, the madrigals unwrapped themselves amidst much laughter.

"Erich! I didn't recognize you!" reproached Antonia.

"I joined the others on the front stoop. I haven't a clue who they are, but we did harmonize rather well, I thought," he said, unwinding his woolen scarf. His mustache was impeccable under his muffler.

Amalia, who had remained on her knees by the tree, watched amazed as the general removal of overcoats and mufflers revealed Maria, Andrzej, and two others who were vaguely familiar. Aware that her face was growing hot, she bent to continue her task.

Her grandmother was enthusiastic. "What lovely, lovely singing! Maria, introduce us to your friends."

Maria obliged by identifying a small girl in bottle green velvet as Claudia von Eisenburg. The eager bespectacled young man who partnered her was Willi von Neuwald.

Then she turned to Andrzej. "And this is the Herr Doktor Andrzej Zaleski, whose brilliant idea this was. Any complaints should be addressed to him."

She then made the Faulhaber family known to her friends, and Amalia was forced to stand, revealing her stockinged legs. Andrzej raised an eyebrow as he looked at her, his eyes lit, his face sardonic. He was the casual flirt of the coffeehouse. She merely stared back at him. So he meant to play this as though their waltz had never been, as though his words had never been spoken.

Joining the group somewhat reluctantly, she heard Andrzej remark to her grandmother, "Frau Reichart, you are undoubtedly aware that caroling on Christmas Eve is a boorish Polish custom."

"Nothing boorish about it," she pronounced. "The angels sang on that night, after all. Although I've always thought it must be in the spring, really, with the shepherds and the lambing going on."

Mama, quite obviously flattered to be receiving such distinguished visitors, insisted, "Yes. And now, you must have some hot cider and sing some more for us."

"Where in Poland are you from?" asked Grandmama.

"Posen," he replied.

"Ah! I think I must know your grandfather, or could it be one of your uncles? Paul Zaleski."

"Yes, that would be my great uncle. The impoverished count. He finally married, you know, at age sixty. A ravishing Russian ballerina. They have two boys. Ten and eight, I think."

"Not at all incredible. Just what I would have expected of him! Oh! The hearts Paul broke when we were young!"

"But, madam, I am most certain yours was not among them!" Andrzej spoke boldly, his eyes merry.

Grandmama's laughter was gay, and she was plainly enjoying herself. "Don't be too certain! Paul was a very charming young man. Not unlike yourself."

Maria, adorned in claret-colored velvet, was admiring the Faulhaber tree, which Amalia alone was finishing. In her peasant-styled dress, she felt more long-limbed than usual and gauchely unsophisticated next to Maria's expensively scented presence.

"Amalia! What a lovely tree. You are so artistic!" Maria remarked.

"Not really. It's Antonia's creation. I just provide the slave labor."

"And what a charming dress! You remind me of one of those English Victorian greeting cards—'Welcome Home from the Hunt,' or something."

Amalia did not acknowledge what she was sure was not meant as a compliment. She continued hanging ornaments, aware of Andrzej's badinage with her grandmother in the background.

"I hope you don't mind our intrusion. Once Andrzej gets an idea, I find it's best to humor him," Maria continued. "You might be interested to know that I've had a letter from my great friend Lilli. You remember her, don't you? Eberhard's cousin. She's back in Berlin for Christmas with her father."

Amalia's heart gave a nasty jolt. She kept hanging ornaments. "Has she seen Eberhard, then?"

"Yes, and do you know, she told me the most remarkable thing! Her father is trying to get Eberhard a commission in his regiment. Did you know that?"

Now her heart was pounding in her ears, and she held tightly to Wolf's ladder. Then she managed a smile. "Yes, of course." In a lower voice, she continued, "But I must ask you not to mention it. Mama and Papa would *not* approve." That at least was true.

"Here. Let me help you with that," Andrzej insisted, as he approached. He had gallantly assumed that she must be trying to fold up the ladder.

"Just think," he said as he collapsed the ladder effortlessly, "your grandmother was once in love with my Uncle Paul. We could have been cousins if he hadn't been so pig-headed!" Setting the ladder in the corner, he returned. "'Cousin Amalia.' Yes, I like that very much. And I must say that dazzling as Uncle's ballerina is, she can't hold a candle to your grandmother."

"Don't let her mislead you," Amalia returned. "There was only one man in Grandmama's life, and she plotted for years to catch him." She was careful not to look him in the eye. Keeping her voice completely dispassionate, she added, "It's our family disgrace, you know. He had a carriage-making firm, and she was the daughter of a count."

"So how did she overcome his scruples in the end?"

"*His* scruples?" Maria asked.

Andrzej patted her arm. "We're listening to the official Faulhaber version, Maria, please."

"He was rather famous for his driving skill, and so Grandmama practically killed herself staging an accident in his way so he could rescue her. It was all very romantic. She thinks he never knew, but I suspect he thought he had better do away with his qualms before she broke her neck trying it again."

Maria patted back a yawn. "He was one of those muscular, blunt types, I suppose, judging from the look of Wolf." She moved away to visit with Amalia's brother, who had ogled her for years.

"You look a bit harried, my dear. I hope we didn't ruin your evening by coming in bellowing songs like this," Andrzej remarked, his voice showing no trace of concern.

Amalia studied his face. Unused to masking her emotions, she strove, with difficulty to achieve the von Hohenburg hauteur. The humor went out of his eyes, and he brought up a hand to brush her cheek and tuck a stray lock of hair behind her ear. "I had to meet your family or go mad with curiosity," he said.

She batted his hand away. "And now you see us in all our Biedermeier splendor. Pillars of the middle class. Satisfied? I'm sure Maria is."

He propped himself against the wall, keeping his eyes fixed on her face. "You are an intriguing mongrel. More like Grandmama than anyone else, I'd say."

"Are you flirting with me?"

"Attempting to."

"Why do you think it's necessary at all?" she demanded.

"What kind of question is that?"

"A straightforward one. I'm a very straightforward person."

"I believe you are. But how do you expect me to answer? Would you like me to display my true feelings and ravish you openly, right here in front of your family?"

Amalia continued to look him straight in the eye. "It's always seemed to me that flirtation is a man's device for avoiding responsibility. He can say whatever he wants and knows he won't be taken seriously. But I could be wrong. I'm not very experienced at flirtations."

He raised his eyebrows. "So you think men are the only ones who flirt?"

At that moment, Maria chose to rejoin them. She put her arm through Andrzej's and asked, "Having a nice chat, or are you ready to leave?"

He patted her hand, and made a short bow to Amalia. "Debate to be continued, *ma cousine,* but I believe that so far the honors rest with me."

Amalia acknowledged his sally with no more than a polite nod. "Thank you for coming, Maria, Herr Doktor. Happy Christmas."

After everyone had gone, Amalia climbed the stairs to the privacy of her room. She knew now the intimacy that she and Andrzej had experienced on the dance floor might never have happened. For some reason she didn't understand, he had chosen to cheapen it by returning to his flirtations, by purposefully appearing with Maria tonight. The wall of pretense was back in place, and apparently that was how Andrzej wished it to be. She felt as though she had been struck. So much for the great love of her life!

Never would she allow him to know how much he had hurt her! How could she have thought for an instant that he was vulnerable and chivalrous? That he cared for her? He was nothing but a flirt trying to add her to his collection. Without regard for the family gathering below, she stared at the ceiling, dry-eyed, knowing she would never be quite the same innocent again.

Chapter Seven

To no one's surprise, Antonia's engagement was announced at Christmas Eve supper. The couple was the toast of the evening, and Amalia was able to hide her feelings behind a mask of good wishes. "You will have to give her plenty to do, Erich," she told him. "Toni has so much energy, it's tiresome. I don't know how we'll manage without her."

Wolf added, grinning, "It'll be very restful around here. No one to stir things up."

Erich discussed his plans to move Antonia into the family home in Salzburg. His mother was going to their property in the country. Wise woman, thought Amalia.

On the way into the drawing room, her grandmother put her arm through Amalia's. "Why the long face? I liked him very much."

"He's nothing but a flirt after all!"

"My dear," she laughed, "that is the way the game is played. He thinks you're engaged, remember? I think his coming here tonight was a good sign. How is Eberhard, by the way?"

"As stubborn as ever. He doesn't want me waiting."

After the interminable evening finally came to a close, Amalia went to her room and took out the letter that Eberhard had written in answer to her own, torturing herself still more with the details of her predicament. He conceded that his feelings were unchanged, but he absolutely declined to fall in with her plans and bade her to tell the truth before it came out. She envisioned Maria making a discreet disclosure to the doctor. All the more reason to avoid both of them.

Would Herr Doktor Zaleski even bother to flirt with her if he knew she was free? She seriously wondered.

Her uncle remained impatient with the deception. As he shared an orange with her one winter afternoon, he said, "Nothing has ever happened to thwart you before, Amalia, so I don't think you can really take this in. But however misguided his ideals, he is right to keep you out of it. War changes things. I'm not talking abstract politics. I'm talking about men's lives. Husbands' lives. Fathers' lives. It's not just tax money or noble tribute. It's *blood*."

"I know you're right, and I know I'm silly." She smiled at her uncle across the scarred oak table. "I wish you didn't know me quite so well."

By the end of January, she was fast losing her patience with everyone. Toni was redecorating the house. Amalia needed a retreat.

"You could always read to the children at the orphanage," her uncle suggested. "Call there and ask to speak to von Schoenenburg. I believe he's in on Thursdays."

*   *   *

The Baron von Schoenenburg was delighted to see Lorenz's niece again. "That's an excellent plan," he said of her uncle's idea. "And so kind of you to offer us your time. We have some particularly bright children, and all of them love a story."

"I don't have any formal training, you realize."

"That won't be necessary. You have everything I consider essential: affection for the children, good breeding, and the love of storytelling. You will be quite adequate." And what a joy it would be to have her about this gloomy old place!

"I'm glad you think so."

He showed her upstairs into a dim and dusty room with a single bookcase containing a short row of books. "I'm sorry there are not more to choose from. Lorenz and I continually try to persuade the board, but they always have other uses for our money."

"This will be fine to start with," she said. "Just let me look through them. What about the orphanage staff? They'll probably think I'm just a child."

He laughed, and he felt himself shed the years he'd taken on himself too young. Who but a niece of Lorenz would ever think of such a scheme? Maybe there was some hope for the world, after all. "I will do my best to assure them that you are a capable adult. The rest is up to you, Fräulein."

"When shall I begin?"

"It would be nice if you could come on Tuesdays and Thursdays to start with. How about next Tuesday?" He hoped he sounded patriarchal and not like the eager, suddenly young man that he was.

He was only a little taller than she, and she smiled up at him. Her eyes were clear deep blue and her manner totally without artifice.

"That will be excellent. Shall we say ten o'clock? Will that fit in with the schedule?"

"We'll make it fit."

"I'll just show myself out, then, when I'm finished."

Unable to think of a reason to remain, the baron left her after a short bow. But he found himself counting the days until Tuesday. Maybe this would be the woman who could get past the dark, empty room inside him. No. On second thought, he dared not let anyone go through that room.

*   *   *

The following Tuesday, Amalia arrived for her first session with the children and was assailed by the little boys in identical haircuts who clambered up the stairs to the schoolroom.

"Fräulein Amalia," exclaimed little Kurt, who had been Joseph in the Christmas pageant. "Will you read to us a story?"

The request ascended into a chorus, and finally she said, "What shall we have, then? *Die Brüder Grimm?*"

"*Ja, Ja!*"

She removed the dilapidated little volume, began with the first tale, and read on through the fifth, as much under their medieval spell as her listeners. Together, they became possessed by their imaginations, as the tales of enchantment, swift justice, cunning, and avarice unfolded. Because her listeners were children, they were not disturbed by the lack of mercy in this imaginary world. But by the time she had finished, Amalia was acutely aware of it and ready for kinder fare. Promising to herself that she would organize a parish book drive without delay, she took up *Rudolf, the Boy King*, a dragon-slaying fantasy. Wasn't the Baron von Schoenenburg's name Rudolf? Perhaps this had been his book as a boy. Perhaps he had dreamt of becoming a king. Of slaying dragons. What did he dream of these days? It was hard to imagine him as a boy with his grave, hawklike features. She read until it was time for luncheon.

It was only then she realized the baron had entered the room. As the boys scrambled out, she said, "I thought Thursday was your day and so I would be safe."

"Safe from what?"

"Your scrutiny. I am just beginning, you know."

He laughed. "You were enchanting, Fräulein. I found myself very disappointed when the readings were over. By the way, I wanted to tell you, the board has a stipend for an assistant language tutor, which is what we are calling you officially."

"Oh no!" Amalia objected. "If you must spend the money, spend it on new books for the children." Amalia pulled on her gloves.

The baron regarded her ensemble. "I see you came prepared to look the part of a schoolteacher."

"I couldn't have the staff thinking I was one of the children!"

"You look very proper, Fräulein," he said seriously. "I just wish you hadn't been quite so drastic with your hair."

She laughed and wondered for a brief moment if he were flirting with her. Looking at his hawklike face, set in sober lines, she decided not.

*   *   *

One afternoon in mid-February, after a particularly irritating walk with Antonia, Amalia returned home at odds with the world.

"You have a caller, Fräulein Amalia," Georg announced. "A Herr Doktor Zaleski. I put him in the morning room, as the carpet layers are busy in the small drawing room."

Stripping off her gloves, she smoothed her coiffure in front of the beveled looking glass that hung above the table. There was a speculative look in Georg's little eyes as he stood behind her.

"Thank you, Georg." The look was replaced by a blank mask.

Pausing with her hand on the doorknob, she put a smile on her face. She must handle this just right. She had had six weeks to bury her hurt. If he wanted a flirtation, she would give him her very best effort.

*   *   *

Bored beyond tolerance with Maria, Andrzej had finally succumbed to the gnawing desire to see Amalia again. Some part of him had a hunger to be known, to be acknowledged as more than a cheerful, flirtatious doctor. He would risk it for an afternoon.

Whatever he expected, however, it was not the glittering smile of the Viennese socialite with which she greeted him.

"Isn't this a cheerful room? Antonia's been redecorating," she remarked as she entered the bright room with its new flowered chintz upholstery and soft pink walls. "Far too cheerful," she continued, taking a picture of herself in baby ringlets from her guest and laying it face down on the mantle. "I've been thinking of emigrating to Serbia. You could rescue me there, if you like."

He laughed and stood looking at her in her lime green suit with its sashed hips and great fur boa. Though somewhat disappointed, he knew he should be relieved at her attitude. Finally, he said, "You're right. You're wasted here. It's far too tame a setting."

"Something hot to drink?" she asked, ringing for Georg.

"Have you anything really wicked, like a cream pastry? I'm famished. I think I must have forgotten my luncheon."

The butler, whom Andrzej suspected of lingering outside the door, entered and showed the top of his hairless head in the briefest of bows.

"Coffee for Herr Doktor, Georg, and Schokolade mit Schlag for me. And see what pastry Frau Schindler has, will you please?"

"I have a suspicion your butler doesn't approve of me."

"Georg is rather shrewd."

"Ah! You think he suspects me of being about to make off with the plate?"

She studied him for a moment. "Perhaps he senses a bit of what my grandmama would call the adventurer in you. There's always a dark man with green eyes who's terribly dangerous."

"Where is this?"

"In Grandmama's novels. I'm reading one now. *Love in Rio.*"

"*Love in Rio?*"

"Rio de Janeiro. I should like to go there if I don't go to Serbia. It sounds lovely."

"Lovely squalor, you mean. I'm afraid I'd make a very poor adventurer, after all. I like my creature comforts too much to do at all well in an exotic setting."

Was she, after all, just like every other Viennese flirt? Georg entered with an enormous silver tray upon which were two silver coffee urns, a plate of cream horns, a dish of whipped cream, and two flowered Limoges china cups.

Amalia poured out. "You take it black, don't you?"

She must remember from the coffeehouse. That augured well. "Bless Frau Schindler for the cream horns. You must leave me at least two. All this longing for adventure and cream horns paints a picture of abject boredom."

"I have begun a new job. I tell fairy tales at the orphanage. Perhaps that's what's wrong with me. Compared with swordfights and magic spells, my life is far too bland. No knights or dragons, either. I really haven't begun to live."

This both amused and relieved him greatly. She was playing the part of a bored socialite but couldn't hide the rebellious child inside. "What you need is to tempt fate a bit. Come out with me tonight. They're doing Mahler's First at the *Konzerthaus*, and a group of us are going."

"And Maria?"

He hesitated only a moment to invent his lie. "The delicious creature has quarreled with me. Says I study too much. We've exams coming next week."

Looking at him over the rim of her cup, she stared at him piercingly. "Just why do you ask me? To make her jealous?"

For a moment, he felt his mask slip, as he remembered the dance they had shared. "You know why I ask you," he said gravely.

Amalia caught her lower lip in her teeth, and for a moment neither said anything. Then he resumed lightly, "I'm dying to see a tiara in that gorgeous hair. If I must rescue you from something, let it be boredom."

Moving her eyes away from his, she answered, "I appreciate your gallant offer, but even if I wanted to go with you, I must tell you that I couldn't afford to offend Maria."

There was a silence while he ate. He was unused to disappointment where women were concerned. Lifting an eyebrow, he said, "Well, it's your decision of course, but I do think that's rather a cowardly attitude."

"You wouldn't, if you knew what was at stake. And I know Maria very well. You can't tell me she's been the least bit complimentary about me."

"I detect a distressing streak of common sense in you."

"It's called self-preservation. I will probably rot in this house after all, dreaming of Serbian intrigue."

Andrzej stood, impatient with this state of affairs. In a serious tone he said, "I'll call for you tomorrow evening, Amalia. We'll take Grandmama and go somewhere very discreet."

"Don't listen to my silly banter. I don't need rescuing."

"There's my vanity to consider, however. I couldn't bear for you to rot and not dream of me."

He walked to the door. "I'll stop for Grandmama on the way. Shall we say about eight o'clock?"

"What about your studying?" she asked, sounding desperate.

"I'll skip the Mahler tonight."

With that, he left the room and pondered the whole remarkable encounter on the way back to his rooming house. Why did he feel so much like the victorious dragon slayer? Her imagination must be rubbing off on him. He grinned. He had her off kilter. That was good.

Chapter Eight

Amalia awoke the next morning with the clear intention of calling on her grandmother to discuss the evening's planned event. However, with her breakfast tray, came a note in her mother's scratchy hand:

Amalia,

Your uncle is very ill. He collapsed at one of his meetings. Heart, the doctor says. I've gone to the flat. Will send Hans back for you.

Mama

Remonstrating with Kristina for having failed to waken her sooner, Amalia dressed quickly in her gray dress. She bade her maid be swift with her coiffure, which was simple and severe. She knew Uncle must be really ill or her mother never would have gone.

As she went downstairs Frau Schindler met her at the door with a basket. "Your uncle won't have anything in his flat," she said.

When she arrived at last at Uncle's, her mother greeted her. "Oh, Amalia! Why did he never let us know he was so ill? Thank heavens you've brought some food."

"When did this happen?" Amalia managed to ask.

"He collapsed at a meeting last night, else he probably would have died here without a soul knowing. The others at the meeting knew enough about the family to send for me, fortunately. I've never understood why Lorenz couldn't have at least one servant. A man, of course.

And a cook, too. He's shockingly thin, and there's nothing edible in those cupboards. Lentils! Can you imagine living on lentils?"

"But what did the doctor say?"

Finally, her mother stopped going through the basket and passed a hand across her forehead. Then she held onto the sink with both hands, bracing herself. "I'm afraid he's dying, Amalia." She looked up at her daughter, and there were tears in her eyes. "He's been ill for quite a while, the doctor tells me. I've already had the priest."

Not waiting for another word, Amalia turned and went through the flat into her uncle's darkened bedroom.

He lay under a colorful red and blue quilt, a gift from the home for indigent widows he had established, his silvered head shunning a pillow, even in illness. Peering closer, Amalia saw the blue around his mouth and noted gratefully the barely perceptible rise and fall of his chest. One long-fingered, hard-worked hand lay across the top of the quilt, and she reached down to hold it. It felt dry and papery and very cold.

Going into the sitting room, she lifted the wicker chair and carried it crab-wise through the door to the side of his bed. There she settled herself, holding the frail hand and refusing to leave him, even for the bowl of lentil soup that her mother had so laboriously prepared in the primitive kitchen.

"I don't want anything," she whispered. "I'll stay with him. You go rest, Mama. There doesn't seem to be much we can do."

"The doctor said to give him one of those ampoules there on the nightstand when he wakes," she instructed. "I believe I'll just lie down in the sitting room."

He awakened only once, glanced briefly at his niece, and murmured, "Bother for you."

She kissed him on the forehead. "You know how very much I love you, don't you?"

He smiled, and she sensed that a sort of calm had replaced his habitual nervous energy.

"I don't believe you're really much of an atheist, after all, Uncle."

"I do believe in God but not the church. I tell you this only because I'm dying. *We* are God's hands. The modern church has little to do with God."

"I can see where it might not do for one so incorruptible as yourself. But it does do a little good for the rest of us," she chided, holding his hand and massaging it with her thumb.

He looked at her but said nothing more. After a time, he fell back into a slumber and Amalia realized she had neglected the ampoules. She wondered whether to wake him again but felt reluctant to disturb him.

She smiled and stroked his hair. When she was a girl, everyone had told her, "I see you have your uncle's hair." That had puzzled her, for she had never met this dear man. Now she remembered clearly the first time she had seen him. It must have been when she was nearly five years old, for that was the year Grandmama had taken her to the Tyrol for the summer holidays. Uncle had visited them there, on his way to some sort of international meeting in France. He had held her on his lap and she had looked at him very solemnly, unable to take her eyes off his hair, which she could see was the very color of her own.

"Do you want it back?" she had asked finally.

"Do I want what back, you little rogue?"

"Your hair. Everyone says you gave it to me. I don't think I'd be nearly as pretty without it, but you can have it if you like."

He had laughed and laughed. "No, you can keep it, my darling. And the dimple, too."

Sometime later, feeling both melancholy and cramped, Amalia walked in to check on her mother. Mama had fallen asleep with one arm dangling from the tiny divan. Her mouth was open, and she snored loudly. Amalia found a blanket in a cupboard and covered her.

She went into the kitchen, found some Semmeln in Frau Schindler's basket and took them back to her uncle's bedside. After her sparse meal, she dozed uncomfortably and then awoke, startled, unaware how long she had slept. She had no idea what the time was when she heard the front door open.

"Gretel? Amalia?" her grandmother called.

Rising at once to greet her, Amalia halted in surprise at the door to the bedroom. Her grandmother, looking as beautifully groomed as ever in her silver fox coat, was accompanied by Andrzej Zaleski. "My dear child, how is he?" she asked. "Why did no one tell me?"

It appeared that the doctor had called upon Amalia that afternoon and was told only that there was an illness in the family and that she was not at home. He had been alarmed and gone on to Grandmama's, thinking perhaps it was she who was ill, intending to offer what assistance he could. He had found her well, however, still looking forward to their evening together. Upon hearing his news, she had taken the doctor with her back to the Faulhaber residence and demanded to be told what was happening. They had then decided to come on to the flat together. Herr Doktor Zaleski was determined to be of help.

"I'm sorry, Grandmama. I assumed you knew." Amalia put an arm around her grandmother's shoulders.

"Mama! What are you doing here?" her own mother asked.

"Come to nurse my son, Gretel."

"But this is no place for you!"

Grandmama tilted her coiffured head. "Would it surprise you very much, then, to learn that I often come here?"

*　　*　　*

Zaleski removed Frau Reichart's coat and watched the little group, trying not to show how much it interested him. What was Amalia's uncle doing in this wretched flat? Amalia herself looked worn with care, and her hair was straggling down from an unbecoming bun. Her dress was a dingy gray. Did she lead some sort of double life? When her Grandmama had told him of the crisis, he had never expected to be led to such a place as this. Not that his own flat was much fancier, but it did lie in a far better district.

"Now, Amalia, tell me," her grandmother insisted. "Is he dying?"

They both turned to her. Frau Faulhaber retired to the kitchen.

"Yes," Amalia whispered, raw tension evident in her voice. Instantly Andrzej sobered. She was clearly under a terrible strain. This man must mean a good deal to her.

"Thank God you've come," she said.

Her grandmother murmured sadly, "My poor child. You love him so. And you're still so young."

The warm note of sympathy in her grandmother's voice was apparently the last straw. Bowing her head, Amalia choked down a sob. Suddenly Zaleski's gamesmanship fell away. This wasn't a place for flirtation. He sensed that, for Amalia at least, this rude little place was almost holy. He was nearly paralyzed with wonder, humbled by her genuine grief. He dealt so frequently with illness among the indigent, he had become too accustomed to dying.

When finally she was able to look up, her eyes sought his, and he knew that once again she saw inside him. It took the practiced restraint of years to keep him from her side, to prevent him from offering a comforting caress. He was very much *en famille* here. Shedding his overcoat, he assumed his professional manner.

"He's in the bedroom, Grandmama," Amalia said. "We've probably waked him."

Zaleski followed the older woman into the shabby bedchamber. The man lying there was ill indeed. Fleetingly he noted the resemblance to Amalia and then busied himself taking Lorenz's pulse. "Faint and irregular," he pronounced. "I should have my stethoscope." He picked up the bottle of ampoules and examined them.

Amalia's grandmother stood with amazing calm, looking at the bluish pallor of her son's face. Zaleski was privately amazed at the truly tender look on her face. Who was this man who inspired such devotion? It occurred to him at last that Lorenz Reichart was not the down-and-outer he had at first seemed to be. He must be a man of great character to account for the melting of his mother's flinty heart and the adoration of his niece. "There's only room for the one chair, Grand-mama. Perhaps you'd like to sit with him for a while."

"Yes. Yes, I would. Thank you, dear."

Zaleski followed Amalia out of the room into the sitting room, which was by now dark and even grim. She turned up the gas lamp, shivering in the chill of the flat. It was taking every ounce of willpower not to go to her. Finally, he took his topcoat from the chair where it lay and put it over her shoulders.

"Thank you. Uncle isn't much for what you call creature comforts. He spends very little time here, actually."

He examined the titles of the books in the towering bookcases. "Marx? Engels?"

"Didn't Grandmama tell you? Uncle is our black sheep."

"Don't sound so defensive, Amalia. I can see he was no armchair socialist."

"You speak of him in the past tense." Tears began to pool in her great, sad eyes.

"My darling, I'm sorry, but it won't be long." He could no longer keep himself back. She looked like an orphaned waif. Taking one long step he was at her side, pulling her head down to his shoulder. She smelled of gardenias. Clinging to his jacket, she emitted another sob. As he held her, the tenderness he had felt as a boy returned to him. He had once been capable of this kind of devotion. Was it possible to feel real feelings in a world such as this one? A world where every honest emotion had its counterfeit—where society was driven to every kind of excess to feed its jaded appetite? Perhaps Amalia's uncle had the right idea in renouncing it all.

Amalia's mother entered, carrying the breadboard as a tray. On it steamed three crockery cups and a plate of sandwiches.

"Amalia! Herr Doktor!" Outraged, the small, plump woman was turning red.

Amalia did not lift her head, but he could feel her trying to restrain her sobs. He could not bring himself to abandon her to her mother's wrath, but the woman was there in an instant, pulling them forcibly apart. "I know you love your uncle, Amalia, but you must remember who you are! You are the future Baroness von Waldburg!"

A trap closed down on his unguarded tenderness. Thank heavens this termagant had intervened.

"How do you find my brother?" she inquired haughtily of the doctor.

"Weak, Frau Faulhaber. And with his heartbeat so irregular, I'm afraid it won't be long before there's another attack."

"Just as Herr Doktor Straganz said." He swore he could hear some kind of satisfaction in her voice. But then she looked at her daughter, who had collapsed onto the divan and was staring emptily at his feet. "He won't survive another, will he?" Frau Faulhaber asked. To his surprise, he heard real sorrow there.

"It would be very unlikely."

She began to eat a sandwich, but neither he nor Amalia joined her. "Have something to eat, Herr Doktor. I've no idea of the time. This flat gets no sun."

"It's close on four o'clock, I believe. Is there anything you would like me to do, Frau Faulhaber? I can run an errand or fetch my stethoscope and doctor's kit, if you like."

"Why don't you let the Herr Doktor take you home, Mama? You've been here all day and most of the night. Grandmama and I can manage." She looked at him, pleading. The least he could do was take this woman away and leave them alone with their grief.

Frau Faulhaber's face looked suddenly old as she consented. She left the room to collect her basket. He felt Amalia's eyes on him but went to the bookcase and examined titles without seeing them. Soon her mother returned, and they left the odd little flat and the girl-woman who had the almost supernatural ability to see him as he once was.

*   *   *

Amalia sat, relieved and grateful to Andrzej for taking her mother away. Death had never come so close to her before. It was impossible for her to comprehend that the man who inhabited this funny old flat would soon cease to exist. His soul would go somewhere else to dwell, and she would miss him more than it was possible to imagine. Until today, she had not realized that he was the person she loved most in the world.

Chapter Nine

Amalia's uncle died that night. He went peacefully in his sleep, after awakening briefly to acknowlege the presence of his mother. Amalia went home with the waiting Hans to impart the news and retire to her own room.

She waited to feel the thing they called grief, but though earlier, in Andrzej's presence, she had cried freely, now it did not come. She prepared for it, turning out the lamp and sitting in her old rose chair with her knees tucked under her chin. But it seemed her emotions lagged behind her knowledge, as the sense of pain often lags behind a serious injury. Her mind was only dull as she sat there, its sole picture that of her uncle's dear face. Uncle Lorenz alone had required no pretense. Could there ever again be such a person in her life? She very much doubted it. It was impossible not to remember the sweet comfort Andrzej had offered, but she also recalled his withdrawal at her mother's words, and so, sadly, dismissed him.

Kristina forced her to try a bit of soup, some bread, and hot lemonade against the possibility of a chill. But everything turned leaden in her stomach, and she was afraid she would be sick. Next she was herded into a hot bath where she sat, staring until the water turned tepid. Soon after, she was lying in her lilac flannel nightgown under her Federdecke with a hot water bottle at her feet. She fell asleep almost at once.

The next morning she went downstairs after breakfast to find her mother issuing instructions. "Wolf, you will please attend to the newspapers? You grandmother can give you any details you require."

"Don't forget *The Workers' International News*," Amalia interjected.

"No," her mother objected. "I won't have all sorts of riff-raff at the funeral! I won't!"

"Mama, you haven't forgotten we're to have luncheon with Erich's aunt today?" Antonia asked.

"If that's all, Mama, I'll just be going," Wolf announced.

"Why isn't Grandmama doing the funeral?" Amalia asked, stunned at the coldness of the arrangements.

"Your mother has kindly taken the burden upon herself, Amalia, and you will do your best to help her," Papa pronounced.

"Yes, dear. I'd like you to take care of the flowers. It's something you enjoy. I'll be busy with arrangements for the dinner honoring your uncle. So many important charities. We really must make an effort. We'll have the open casket, of course. It's to be at Grandmama's the day after tomorrow, if I can arrange to get Schumanns for the catering. Grandmama is patroness to that marvelous little string quartet that is making such a stir, and they have agreed to play."

Amalia stared at the breakfast table, lips compressed, as she felt the comfort of her simple memories driven out.

"I'm sorry, Mama. I'll not have anything to do with this," she said quietly. "Uncle despised all this sort of *Schmäh*, and well you know it. You're using his death as an excuse to throw a grand party that will bring people you could never get otherwise." She arose from the table, leaving her mother speechless. As she went to gather her loden cape and sable hat, she heard Antonia say, "That was unforgivable, Amalia!"

She headed out the door into the cold of the morning. It was Tuesday, her day for the orphanage. Nothing, she thought, could bring her more comfort.

As Amalia walked through residential Vienna, she saw a carriage or automobile here and there, taking those who worked for a living to their places of employment. Everywhere was the steady drip of melting ice, and water began to flow once again in the gutters. This was the ugliest of seasons in Vienna. Without its blanket of white, winter was a dead, dismal time. In such a setting, the bleak reality of her loss was more immediate. Thank God for the orphanage. It was the only refuge left to her.

"Fräulein Amalia!" they greeted her. "We got some new books today!" Pulling out of the shelves the books she had managed to find among the Faulhaber children's bookcases, they said, "Look! This one is about pirates! And this one is about a shepherd who lives in the mountains who has to battle a troll!"

She found herself laughing with them at their enthusiasm. "Shall we read them this morning, or did you have something else in mind?" she teased as she sat in her accustomed chair. The youngest, Ernstchen, they called him, climbed up into her lap.

"No! Of course we must read them! And look, they have pretty pictures, too."

For the next hour and a half, she managed to laugh and dream along with the children. But then the time came when she must go home. She had nowhere else to go.

When she arrived there, she was told that her mother and sister were out to luncheon and that Herr Doktor Zaleski had called and left a message that he would return later that afternoon.

Amalia, realizing she must eat, tried to swallow some mild fish and potatoes but found that her throat had simply closed up. Going upstairs, she lay fully dressed upon her Federdecke and fell asleep.

Kristina awakened her sometime later with the news that Herr Doktor Zaleski was below in the morning room. "I wouldn't have disturbed you, but he said he was here professionally."

Once Kristina left, Amalia got out of bed and looked automatically at her reflection in the mirror, shuddered, and splashed herself with gardenia scent. Her only black dress was a very severe one she had had made for the orphanage. Its high collar was unsoftened by ruffle or lace, and the color made her skin look dead. She shrugged and went down the stairs.

"Amalia!" Andrzej stood to greet her as she entered the morning room. He looked tired, she thought. The tension that normally dwelt below the surface of his demeanor was obvious. "I'm here to inquire after you. I hope you'll forgive me, but I've checked with the staff and it seems you haven't been eating."

She felt suddenly shy at his professionalism. "No. I'm not interested in food at the moment. You'll have to forgive me. I'm quite dull today."

As she seated herself, he sat in a chair across from her. "Would it help if we talked about your uncle a bit?"

"Why?"

"Because I get the feeling that you are the only one in this house who truly mourns him. You must feel very isolated and depressed."

She regarded him for a moment. This was a different Andrzej. Close to the man she had seen in his eyes. "You're right."

"I feel like I've missed knowing someone important."

She shrugged. "He wasn't important in your sense. He didn't like any kind of public recognition."

A crease appeared between Andrzej's eyebrows. "Your impression of me is rather distressing. But let's not quarrel. Instead, why don't you tell me why he chose to become a socialist?"

"He felt unequally blessed. He couldn't endure his wealth if he had to see others go hungry."

"Then I must disagree with you. A man who has the courage to live by his convictions has my deepest regard. I wish I had his integrity." He stared at the mantelpiece as he said this, and she had the impression he was intentionally avoiding her eyes.

She studied her hands in her lap. They seemed curiously detached from the cuffs of the ugly black garment, the blue veins branching beneath the white skin. For a moment she felt disoriented. "I think I'm going a little mad," she whispered.

He said nothing but rose and came to sit beside her. He took one of the offending hands in his own. Reality swung back into its proper frame, and she looked him in the eye. "He was my touchstone. My grieving is purely selfish."

"If it's any comfort, I think grief usually is. In what way was he a touchstone? That's a lovely word."

"I don't know if I can explain it." Letting go of his hand, she gestured at the walls of the room. "But you see what my life is. Sometimes I feel I'm being smothered in *Gemütlichkeit*—it's like a pillow of goose down. Uncle was different; he made it all bearable somehow. He talked to me as a real person. When I went to visit him, he had a way of making things assume their proper perspective."

"Ah, Gemütlichkeit. Kiss the hand, simper, and then turn up the nose."

She managed a smile. "I didn't always agree with him, but that was half the fun. He taught me French and philosophy. I'm really not the empty-headed child I appear. From the time I was small, I always knew I really mattered to him."

Tears sprang to her eyes, and she wiped them angrily away. Why was it so easy to let go in front of Andrzej?

"Amalia, even though your uncle is dead, you still matter a great deal. You know that. You must."

His earnest manner endangered her composure. She was too close to trusting him. Rising, she went to the window. "Would you like something hot to drink? I'm sorry. I should have asked you before."

"No. I'm just going." He stood and smiled, a gentle smile, free of any amusement. "I won't feel sorry for you anymore, Amalia. You're very lucky to have known such a man. And you know he wouldn't have wanted you to waste away to nothing on his account."

"Then what am I to do with all this grief?" she asked sharply.

Coming up behind her, he put his hands gently on her shoulders. "You will live through it, just as he would have wanted you to do."

Tracing a drop of water with her finger as it slid down the window, she said, "I hope we have an early spring."

"We're certain to, I think. Auf Wiedersehen, my darling."

He left after that, and she stood at the window for some time, watching as he walked away. She would never understand him.

*   *   *

Rudolf attended the dinner in honor of Lorenz with mixed emotions. Such Schmäh was repellent to his nature. The hypocrisy of the ordeal would have turned Lorenz purple and given him a heart attack for certain. Particularly repugnant to him had been the elaborate burial rituals of the Viennese. But Rudolf wanted to see the girl again. He knew she would be distressed.

Amalia was mounting a lonely vigil by the casket, clothed in a black taffeta gown that looked as though it belonged in the last century. Quite possibly it was her grandmother's. Obviously she felt separate from every other soul in the room—all of them indulging in food, drink, and merriment. He imagined everyone's indifference only made her suffering worse.

Before he could get to her, a short, stocky man who looked vaguely familiar approached him, smiling obsequiously and holding out his hand. "Major von Schoenenburg, how kind of you to come. I didn't know you knew my uncle."

It must be one of the men in his reserve regiment. If he was Lorenz's nephew, was he Amalia's brother? "I'm sorry, I can't seem to remember your name at the moment."

The stubby man saluted. "Corporal Wolfgang Faulhaber, Major. Lorenz Reichart was my mother's brother."

How different this fussy little upstart was from his elegant sister!

"Yes, well, Faulhaber, I'm sorry for your loss." As the major approached the casket, the corporal followed him, much to his annoyance.

Amalia kept her distance as he stared down at the remains of his friend. *Well, Lorenz, what do you think of heaven? If anyone deserves it, it's certainly you.*

"Your uncle was an extraordinary man," he said to Faulhaber. "I'm afraid I didn't agree with his politics, but he did a lot of good for the poor."

"He didn't understand selfishness," Amalia said, coming out of her corner. "It mystified him. That's why he could believe in the brotherhood of man." Lorenz's soft champion stood before him, her eyes daring him to debate her words.

"This is my sister, Amalia, Major. Amalia, this is Major von Schoenenburg."

"We are already acquainted," the major told Wolf. "She works for me at the orphanage, telling stories."

Her brother looked from one of them to the other. "She *works* for you?"

"I should have said, 'volunteers.' You have nothing to be ashamed of, Faulhaber. It's a very worthy charity."

Amalia's lips twitched.

"Well," Faulhaber said, "I had no idea." Raising his eyebrows at his sister, he turned back to his commanding officer. "You understand this is a very great shock to the family. Thank you for coming. Be certain to have something to eat. It's the very best. Schumann's." Then, with an insouciant grin and another salute, he left them.

"I hope you don't mind my being here. I wanted to pay my respects," he said to the girl who was looking at her brother's back with a surprising degree of anger in her eyes. "Your uncle will be missed far more than you can imagine."

"You're wrong," she said. "I can imagine it much more than you know." Then, turning, she went back to her corner. He had seen the tears forming in her eyes but had no idea how to manage the situation. With regret, he took a last look at Lorenz's body, replaced his hat, and moved towards the door.

On impulse, he looked over his shoulder at her and was surprised to meet her eyes. Amalia reddened, and he smiled gravely. Tears streaked her cheeks, but after a moment she smiled back and gave him the hint of a wave. His admiration for her took another leap within him. She was the brave soldier standing alone at the last outpost of sanity.

*   *   *

Andrzej arrived late, having with difficulty divested himself of a petulant Maria. He was met at the door by a girl in a half-mourning of lilac, with hothouse flowers woven into her elaborate chignon of unremarkable brown hair. Short and curvaceous, she gave him a ravishing smile. "I'm so glad you could come!" she gushed, offering her hand to be kissed. He recognized her dimly from Christmas Eve. Amalia's sister. "How did you know my uncle?"

Looking past her, he ignored the hand, scanning the room for Amalia. Universal merriment seemed to be in process, and he knew she must be suffering private agonies. He spotted her at last, near the casket, alone and wearing a frightful black gown.

"Doctor," he murmured to the girl. Then, moving past her, he went straight to Amalia.

As he approached, he passed his hand absently over his hair. "What is this?" he demanded. "The Faulhaber social event of the season?"

Amalia smiled grimly as they surveyed the room of social climbers and befurred aristocrats. "Uncle would have hated it." Her voice was low and fierce. "I hate it. I wish I had Grandmama's temperament. I know she can't bear Schmäh like this, but she is perfectly composed over in her corner, receiving condolences."

"You look rather like a nightmare in a Victorian horror story dressed in that thing. No wonder everyone keeps their distance."

"I won't let them even pretend to mourn him."

He took her chin and tilted it up so he could look in her eyes. "Heaven help them if they try." He had meant to be lighthearted, but it fell flat. Amalia was bristling with anger.

Turning her head to the side, she said, "This isn't the time for that."

"You're right. I apologize. It must be the atmosphere. Do you know when I came in your sister gave me her hand to kiss as though it were her wedding?"

"I can believe it."

He waited a few moments by her side, shifting uncomfortably from one foot to the other which was very unlike him. "I'm going to risk your censure by asking you a question."

She turned to face him.

"When's your wedding to be?"

Her eyes searched his, and with some surprise he recognized desperation.

"I don't really know." The words seemed to stumble out. "Eberhard has been held up longer than we anticipated. We haven't even begun to plan anything. And now there's Toni's wedding."

Andrzej looked into the crowd, his heart lightening. Maybe his wasn't a hopeless case after all. "It sounds like you're still not sure of things, Amalia."

"I'm sorry, Andrzej, but this really isn't the time to discuss it." Her voice was suddenly as haughty as her grandmother's. She had regained her poise. He nearly cursed aloud.

"No. It's I who am sorry. No doubt I've been misreading things. Vanity, I suppose."

She searched his eyes again and then said in a low voice, "I would be glad if you would leave me now."

The woman was so appealing with those great, sad blue eyes that belied her words. He had a chance. He *knew* he had a chance.

As he left, he shook his head slightly to clear it. A chance for what? Dalliance? Not Amalia Faulhaber. She was no Maria. No matter what she looked like, she was a daughter of the bourgeoisie. It would be marriage or nothing. And the idea of marriage was unthinkable at this juncture in his life.

Chapter Ten

I
t was her uncle's legacy that saved Amalia's sanity. He had
bequeathed her all his charitable interests. Guided by the baron,
she went over her uncle's surprisingly meticulous records.

Kristina and Antonia had tried to stop her going downstairs in her
black gown and schoolmistress coiffure. Both had remonstrated with
her to no avail. "It doesn't matter. It's business, not a social call."

Now she sat before the fire in the morning room, the baron nearby
in a high wing-backed leather chair. He gazed at her out of hooded
eyes. "The board meetings are held quarterly, so the next ones will be at
the beginning of April. You should have plenty of time to familiarize
yourself with these by then."

"But what about my age? How can anyone possibly take me seriously?"

"If you show them you know what you're talking about, they have
to take your money seriously."

"I don't think I can represent his interests in the Socialist Party. I
don't agree with his politics, you see. Uncle was as blind as a saint. In
my opinion, he was far too optimistic. The majority of us don't really
care about our fellowman."

"I can't believe that of you, Fräulein. You've shown yourself to be
just the opposite."

"I'm grounded in selfishness," she sighed. "I could never rise to
Uncle's heights. And most people are just like me. I used to argue with
Uncle that he would have to find a way to change the basic nature of

man to make his ideas work. People have to change inside themselves. A change in government won't do a thing."

He put his head to one side. "You know, I've never put it to myself just that way, but I think I agree with you. What's to be done about the human condition, do you think?"

Amalia looked carefully to see if he were mocking her. But he seemed genuinely serious. She sighed and shrugged. "I'm no philosopher like Uncle. He was the best man I knew. If everyone were like him, there would be no problem."

"So what do you suppose made your uncle the way he was?"

Amalia had been giving this question a great deal of thought in the days since her uncle's death. At night she had sat in her room, looking at the moon, trying to decipher a path that would lead her to become the person her uncle would have wanted her to become. "When he was dying, he said something that surprised me," she said finally. "I think it may actually have been the key to his character. He must have had some kind of spiritual experience, or maybe it was the influence of my grandfather, whom I never knew." She gazed at the fire. "He said, '*We* are God's hands.' Then he said modern religion had nothing to do with God. His parents encouraged him to be a free thinker. He studied and chose his own road, the one where he thought he could make the most difference. And he did make a difference."

"Yes," the baron agreed. "As much difference as one man can make."

She turned her eyes on him and sat up straighter. "I'd like to make a difference. But I'm only a woman."

He studied her intently before saying, "Women chase away the darkness." Then, as though recalling something unpleasant, he added, "Or they can, anyway. Sometimes. If a man is very lucky."

Suddenly she thought of Eberhard, turning his back on her, going willingly off to war. Studying her hands, she murmured, "Men choose their own darkness."

"Some, maybe," the baron conceded. "But some of us have no choice."

Amalia looked up at him and caught a look of self-loathing on his face. She felt the edges of her world stretch wider as she contemplated what he could mean. That he was talking about himself, she was certain. "You're a good man," she hastened to assure him. "A very good man. My uncle held you in high esteem."

He drummed his fingers on the arms of his chair. "Well," he said, smiling one-sidedly, "There are certain things one is expected to do when one is a von Schoenenburg. Don't make me into a saint, Fräulein Amalia."

Feeling embarrassed, as though she had caught a glimpse of something she shouldn't have, she flushed.

He leaned forward, supporting himself on his forearms, linking his fingers. "I think perhaps you're full of secrets you haven't discovered yet," he said smiling faintly. "Now, what are we going to do about this Socialist Fund?"

He had been invited for luncheon, which Amalia found herself unable to eat. Making himself agreeable to her mother, the baron assured Frau Faulhaber that Amalia's responsibilities would not be seen as unladylike.

"She has her uncle's presence, don't you think?" he asked her.

"Yes. Amalia and Lorenz have always been much alike. They were very close, you know." Mama had evidently decided that anything that threw Amalia together with this baron was a good thing. It had been some time since she'd even inquired about Eberhard.

Amalia spent her evenings poring over Uncle's accounts and many of her days either at the orphanage or with the baron while he explained things to her.

"The soup kitchens for the unemployed were very important to Lorenz. I believe he ate there half the time himself. You will need to make certain you've got a good man there. Someone you can trust. I believe your uncle's choice to have been quite worthy. At least Lorenz never complained. And in his own way, he was very shrewd, you know."

"But how shall I know if someone's cheating me?"

"For the first couple of months, bring the books to me, and we'll go over them together."

It was about two weeks later that she realized she had entirely neglected her grandmother, who must surely be grieving as much as she was.

The baroque façade of the von Hohenburg dwelling welcomed her.

"Amalia! It is lovely to see you my dear. I hear you have been taking over all Lorenz's businesses. But, my! How thin you look. I suspect you haven't been eating properly since his death."

Grandmama rang the bell and firmly ordered breakfast for her granddaughter. "You know you mustn't mourn this way, dear. I have been wanting to talk to you but couldn't do it properly in your home. I'm so glad you came this morning."

"I thought you might be feeling a bit low, actually. I've been neglecting you."

"That's very sweet of you, but I'm older, you see. Death has very little sting for me anymore. It's strange." She gazed into the middle distance and then gave a sudden brilliant smile. "But you feel he was misunderstood, don't you? That your mother should have handled things differently? Perhaps even that I should have intervened and changed her plans?"

Amalia nodded and, looking down at her lap, twisted Eberhard's ring, which she had not yet removed.

"Look at me, my dear, and tell me. What difference does it really make? Lorenz wouldn't have minded, you know. He was amazingly tolerant of Gretel's machinations."

"But what gave Mama the right to manage the thing at all?"

"She likes to think she's very clever at managing. It was something she could do for her brother. You must realize, though he never intended it, that she saw his way of life as a reproach to her and the things she valued. Lorenz had a way of making Gretel feel unimportant, you see, because his interests were always so very cosmic in nature."

"It's different for you, I think," Amalia said. "You see them as your children. But I suppose I have seen them as people who have power over me, power to shape my life. And, in the case of Mama, I sometimes resent what she's done with it."

"Yes, you have a lot of Lorenz in you. Perhaps, though, it's just your youth. In many ways, he never really grew up, you know."

"What do you mean?" Amalia's voice was suddenly defensive.

"Only this. When we are young, as you are, we tend to embrace grand ideals. We have such wonderful notions about what we will do with our life, how we will set the world straight." She smiled gently at her granddaughter and continued. "But as people become more mature, it is a regrettable fact that they tend to find such ideals cumbersome baggage. It's in little ways at first that they betray themselves. Perhaps they are forced to entertain some person of questionable morals in order to further an interest of theirs. Or maybe they find they prefer drinking schnapps to fighting thankless crusades. By the time most men are thirty, they are contented to call themselves realists."

Amalia perched on the arm of her grandmother's chair. "So, because Uncle lived up to his ideals and didn't compromise, you think he never grew up?"

"Perhaps I said it badly. What I meant was, he retained his youth, his enthusiasm for life. That is why you are so alike."

"I haven't so many ideals."

"Ah, but you have very strict notions about what is important and what is not. I imagine Toni and Wolf find you every bit as uncomfortable to live with as Gretel did Lorenz."

Amalia told her grandmother about her work with the baron over breakfast.

"This baron," her grandmother interrupted, "Lorenz used to speak of him. Von Schoenenburg, you say?"

"Yes. Rudolf is his Christian name. You know his people, I suppose?"

"I did. They're dead now. But I believe I remember something about that family. It happened a year or two ago, just after Charlotte and her husband were killed on that ocean liner." She examined her manicured nails. Then her face cleared. "Ah, yes. A sad story. Rudolf was not the original heir. He had an older brother, Georg or Wilhelm, I forget. But, you see, he shot himself. No one ever knew the reason. He didn't even leave a note. What is this new baron like?"

Amalia shrugged. "He looks forbidding, and he's a bit deep, but he seems kind. Tell me, Grandmama, truly. How are you managing?"

"I miss him very much, my dear, very much. But then, I am accustomed to loneliness." She poured out another cup of chocolate for herself. Then she stared into it as though she were seeing a time that had existed years before.

"Your grandfather was my best friend, my closest companion. There has never been any one else like him in my life. One must be so careful not to burden one's children." She smiled sadly. "I don't suppose you remember him at all, you were so young. But I felt his loss cruelly. I was even angry at God for taking him."

"But you're not that way now. How did you deal with it?"

"Not very well, at first. I looked around enviously at all my friends' marriages, angry because they took them so much for granted and would treat each other in the most abominable ways. It was only after many months that I realized that what I had had with your grandfather was very different from what I saw around me. Bereft as I was, I came to see that I was very fortunate. Mine was not the typical society marriage."

Amalia listened intently, her breakfast forgotten.

"It's difficult for me to explain, but the companionship I had with your grandfather made me quite a different person from who I was before I married him. More whole, or something. And the wholeness was still there, even though his actual physical presence was gone. He is with me now, in who I am." She shook herself a little and gave her light little laugh. "I expect that all sounds like mystical nonsense to you."

"No, Grandmama, it makes perfect sense. I feel very much the same about Uncle." Getting up she went over to her grandmother and kissed her velvety cheek. "Now," Amalia changed the subject, "how would you like to go with me to Clothilde to order some new dresses to suit my serious station in life?"

"First you must tell me what you have done to our young Pole to make him so agitated."

"Agitated? That sounds quite unlikely."

"He called on me the other day. You had been in high mourning, it seems, and not receiving visitors. Then he called at your house several times after that and was told you were out. I think he believes he's not being received. He was so frustrated, he didn't know whether he was coming or going."

Amalia stirred the sachet. "I didn't realize he'd called. He never left a card. Our butler doesn't like him for some reason and can be very snooty. There were a couple of days I kept to my room, and of course I've been out with the baron quite a lot, learning my new duties."

"Have you told Andrzej the truth about Eberhard, yet?"

"I almost did at the dinner party for Uncle. But it didn't seem like the right time. There may have been a misunderstanding."

"You'll probably be quite unhappy with me, but I found myself telling him that Eberhard was a handsome Prussian with a huge estate who adores you. It was like waving a red flag at a bull. I'm afraid that man likes a challenge."

"And what happens when I'm no longer a challenge?"

"I think the feeling runs very deep there, Amalia. You have quite a disarming quality, my love. I'll wager he is quite bowled over by it. For all your background, you're quite unworldly."

"That can hardly be a recommendation to a man of the world, Grandmama."

"You would be surprised. From now on, I would be very careful about how you handle things. Remember Maria. She'll have to be kept in the dark until everything is secure between the two of you."

"You seem very sure, Grandmama."

Her still-clear blue eyes sparkled. "I'm seldom wrong about these things."

Chapter Eleven

The first board meeting was very different from what Amalia expected. Having arrived with the baron in his motor car, Amalia faced with much misgiving the industrialists on the board of the charity that provided hot lunch for laborers. They stood up as she entered the dark paneled board room of the woolen manufacturer, Herr Otto Kunzler. The baron was the only gentleman in the room, by her grandmother's standards. All these men had fuzzy sideburns down their cheeks and wore clothes of heavy wool that her eye discerned were not quite of the best cut. They viewed her with cunning in their gazes. She was extremely glad to have the baron with her. Obviously these were middle class manufacturers, less prominent than her father but of his stamp.

"What is this?" A man with red hair and sideburns as bushy as the emperor's inquired. "What are you doing here with your lady love, von Schoenenburg?"

"Looks too well dressed to be the odd starving factory worker to stir our consciences!" said another man with oily black hair and a sneer.

Amalia didn't wait to be introduced. Straightening her back, she looked them boldly in the eye. "My name is Fräulein Amalia Faulhaber. I am Lorenz Reichart's niece and legally represent his concerns."

She seated herself at the table, composed outwardly but stiffening herself inwardly. With no intention of letting her uncle down, she didn't flinch as they grumbled about her age and unsuitability among them.

"Now, men, perhaps you could turn to the business at hand?" the baron said.

"Just what gives you the right to be here, Baron?" one of the men protested roughly.

"The Fräulein has engaged me as an advisor."

The man looked rueful. The baron had told Amalia that Lorenz provided more than half the funds for this charity. That gave her rights no one could dispute.

"What project do you have in hand at the moment?" she asked.

"We need to engage a new cook. One who can stretch the budget a bit. These workers are eating better than we are," said the red-haired man.

"And what would you do with the money saved?" Amalia asked.

The men looked down and shifted their feet under the table, lit cigarettes, and stared daggers at the baron.

"You would perhaps pocket my uncle's generous contributions to your cause? I've examined the records, and each of you puts in only a token amount to this charity. I won't have you pocketing my uncle's money. Give me an idea of what the workers are eating."

"They have meat three times a week," said the oily man sourly. "The rest of the time it's lentils or vegetable soups. They have fresh hot bread every day."

Amalia thought this an excellent diet for a factory worker. Probably the only good food he had all day. "I propose that we put it to a vote. I should like to vote that we keep the present cook and the present diet. I imagine that better fed workers work better, have less absenteeism, and are more inclined to keep their jobs."

A man who was almost totally bald with hard eyes spoke. "You need a second, and you're not going to find one among us."

Amalia rose, her heart quailing a bit at the opposition. "I can see my uncle's money is wasted here. I will withdraw it from this charity and place it where the people have hearts. My uncle loved these workers you seem to despise." She and the baron had talked politics, too. "Don't you realize that there are more of them than there are of you? If you don't keep them satisfied with their places, they will leave for better employment elsewhere or perhaps even vote to strike. Where would you be then?"

A wizened little man with white hair muttered, "She's Lorenz Reichart all over again."

Amalia's heart bounded at this ill-meant praise. The baron rose beside her.

"You're one of them, aren't you, Fräulein? A socialist!" the red-haired man challenged.

"No. I just like to see the workers fed. I will have a pamphlet commissioned that will say just why this misfortune has befallen the workers and whom they have to blame. I predict a strike within the month."

"I'll second your motion," the oily-haired man grumbled. "We'll not get a share of the old dreamer's money. Can't you see she's just like him?"

"Such a little slip of a thing to have control of all that money," complained the red-headed man who was smoking a pipe in furious puffs.

Amalia couldn't help a little laugh. "Maybe I'm saving your lives, gentlemen! When the revolution my Uncle Lorenz always predicted takes place, you will be known as good masters."

Her motion was reluctantly carried in the end, and the board agreed to go on as before.

As she assumed her muff and cape, the baron squeezed her shoulder. When they were finally out in the open air, he gave a chuckle. "You've got your uncle's blood all right, Fräulein Amalia."

"As Uncle always said, money talks," Amalia said. "I have even less hope for the brotherhood of man, I'm afraid, than I did before. Thank you for the preparation you gave me and for accompanying me today. Obviously I needed an ally."

"You did splendidly, my dear, and I think you will continue to do so. But I am at your service any time. Shall you turn the orphanage upside down?"

"No. That's one charity that seems to be run benevolently, thanks to your patronage. Are you certain you won't come in for tea, Baron?" she asked.

"I've an appointment, or I'd enjoy it," he apologized, as he helped her out of the motorcar.

"Thank you so much then. For everything."

"I haven't done a thing. Lorenz's blood obviously flows in your veins."

He took her gloved hand in his and, surprisingly, kissed it. After escorting her up the walk, he tipped his hat and left.

* * *

Andrzej was a block away from the Faulhaber mansion when he spotted Amalia standing in the street, allowing her hand to be kissed by a fellow with brown hair and buff-colored trousers. Before he could get a better look at him, the man had climbed into his motorcar and been driven off by a chauffeur.

Instead of going in, Amalia stood on the step and watched as the car pulled off, threading its way amidst the slower carriages, backfiring as it went. She still wore her severe black, even though the streets were vivid with the pastel silks of spring. Her hair was dressed oddly, he noted. Not the usual elegant coiffure but an arrangement low on her head that accommodated her black, large-brimmed hat. Not a bonnet but a matron's hat. Just what was she up to? As she was about to turn into the house, his cab drew up, and he stepped out, paid the driver, and faced her. Her glance was level and straight, not the least flirtatious. "Was that the elusive fiancé I saw driving off?"

"Good heavens, no!" she replied with spirit. "Have you come to call, then? I haven't seen you in a long time."

"Either the butler denies me or you're not at home. Where in the world have you been in that atrocious hat?"

She smiled broadly, and he detected a happy secret. Not quite the woman of the world, then.

"Come in, and I'll tell you." Once they had divested themselves of their outer garments and settled in the morning room, she faced him. "I've become a businesswoman. That was one of my fellow board members at the St. Stephen's orphanage."

Nothing she could have said would have astonished him more. Involuntarily, his eyebrows rose. He was speechless.

"I inherited all Uncle's trusts, and I've been learning to administer them. There are about five major ones, including a large bequest to the Socialist Party that I haven't a clue what to do with."

Andrzej burst into laughter. "Yes. I can see that might be a problem."

Board meetings? Amalia? Would she never stop surprising him?

"Do you know any socialists at the university?"

"Of course. Dozens probably. Some of them are rather dangerous. Full of plots to assassinate the emperor and that sort of thing."

"Oh." A frown appeared between her brows. "Uncle wouldn't have liked that at all. I'm completely at a loss."

"Just what are the qualifications you're looking for?" he asked, endeavoring to keep a straight face.

"Someone who believes intensely in the brotherhood of man."

She looked so serious and worried that he couldn't resist going to her chair, leaning over her, and putting a hand on her shoulder. "I'll have a try at finding someone. Go to a meeting or something. Would that help?"

Looking up at him, she smiled, and it was the smile that had first entranced him in the coffeehouse. "Very much, thank you, Andrzej. The baron could hardly do that for me."

He drew back, scowling. "Baron? What baron?"

"The man you saw getting into his motorcar. The Baron von Schoenenburg. The man who's been helping me with this business. He was a friend of Uncle's and knows all about how to administer trusts. I don't have any idea what I would have done without him."

"Oh? He's an old fellow then?" Though he'd missed her devilishly, he still hadn't decided what place Amalia could possibly take in his life. The thought of yet another rival unsettled him.

She dimpled. "No, Andrzej, not old. I would say he's about your age. But he's far more responsible and serious about life, so I suppose that makes him seem older."

"Sounds a dull fellow," he said, wondering if she was teasing him.

"No, not at all. There's a lot more to him than meets the eye. I find him unfathomable, and that intrigues me."

"Unfathomable?" he probed. He didn't like the sound of that at all.

"Yes. Unplumbed depths. Cobwebby rooms."

He forced a smile. "Are you certain it's not just your imagination?"

"No. He's tortured by something. Uncle would say he's a typical Viennese—one charming room for company and the dark back room where he lives."

Andrzej studied her frankly, aware of how shallow he must seem to her. Her eyes looked back at him, innocent of the dampening effect her words were having on him. "I don't think that's a particularly Viennese quality," he said finally. "I suppose the same could be said about most men."

"Well!" she said with a little laugh. "I certainly wouldn't know."

Remembering the waltz that was never far from his mind, he said almost without thinking, "You know much more than you let on."

She was quiet, her smile fading. He had long since retired to his chair, but he could feel the invisible pull between them, the chemistry that stirred his blood and made this little thing of nineteen so hard to put out of his mind. Possibly it was more than chemistry. He didn't know. He'd never felt so completely out of his depth, and he didn't like it.

"So!" he said, slapping his knees with his hands. "How are your orphans?"

"Delightful. I've just had the story room cleaned and painted. I'm going to have a parish book drive to get them more books."

"I'd give anything to be a fly on the wall when you're spinning fairy tales," he said, grinning.

"There's absolutely nothing to prevent your coming except your own laziness," she teased.

Suddenly, the idea of sitting at Amalia's feet and hearing her tell of dragons, knights, and enchanted forests was far preferable to a late night tryst with Maria. It was absurd, but there it was.

"I believe I'll do that," he said. "Just tell me when."

"Next Tuesday at three o'clock."

* * *

He stayed for tea, and when he left, Amalia reflected that all at once, life had become very good again.

Life continued to be good. By May she felt comfortable in her new roles, particularly the one of volunteer schoolmistress. With loving care she and Andrzej had transformed the small, drab schoolroom.

He surprised her with how much he entered into the spirit of the new venture. Together they had combed second-hand bookstores for broken-down books of fairy tales with wonderful illustrations. Andrzej had taken the books to a framer to remove the pictures and frame them for the story room. Now the walls were bedecked with nearly twenty small prints. He had spied a casualty of Antonia's redecorating, the old dining room carpet, remarking that it would be perfect for the orphanage floor. Most helpful of all, Andrzej had gone to his aristocratic friends, asking for books for their little library.

* * *

Rudolf entered the schoolroom, watching as the young doctor and Amalia shelved books, their heads close together. In his arms was an enormous tropical plant—his contribution to Amalia's effort. He observed their playfulness ruefully. Making inquiries, he had discovered without much trouble Zaleski's liaison with Maria von Beckhaus. But he had also observed the doctor sitting among the children as Amalia wove her stories. Something inside him had hardened at the sight. What kind of game was the doctor playing? Should he warn Amalia?

She might not thank him for interfering in her affairs. But Lorenz would have done something . . .

"How perfect!" she exclaimed, catching sight of him. "That's just what we needed."

"Well, it's the least I can do. Especially since you and the doctor have provided all the slave labor."

Zaleski looked up at him, his eyes narrowed in calculation. Rudolf decided in that instant that he neither liked nor trusted him. The doctor was insinuating himself into the innocent Amalia's life. And if Maria were to find out, he couldn't even begin to imagine the consequences. And what of the Baron von Waldburg?

"Fräulein Faulhaber, we have some orphanage business we must discuss. May I call at your home tomorrow, at say eleven o'clock?"

Zaleski scowled.

"Yes, of course. And you must stay to luncheon. Mama will insist." He gave her a short bow and left.

* * *

Andrzej knew the baron didn't trust him. The baron would use his self-appointed role as Amalia's advisor to warn Amalia against him. He knew it as certainly as if von Schoenenburg had issued him a challenge.

"Amalia," he said, as soon as the baron was out of sight, "Therese's playwright is having his opening tonight at the *Burgtheater.* Steller, you know. Baron von Altwald has taken a box. Why don't you have Wolf bring you? I'm certain he's coming. He's been seeing a lot of Therese."

Amalia grimaced. "I do wish he'd be a little more subtle. He makes himself so ridiculous."

Laughing, Andrzej replied, "The danger of the subtle approach is that it might so easily be missed. Don't worry. Therese takes it in stride. I think it amuses her. The Burgtheater then? Tonight at eight. I'll fix it with Therese."

She pulled out one of the new books, examining its binding. "I haven't been out socially since Uncle died."

"I realize that. But this isn't the least bit frivolous. Think of it as helping to launch an artist. Therese is gathering support wherever she can. She's fearfully worried no one will come."

"I'll think it over," she said.

He had no idea what he was doing. He only knew he had to see her that night. Before the baron got to her.

"How's Maria?" she asked.

He cursed silently. "Decidedly wearing. She's dropped out of university to concentrate on her social life."

"And when do you have time to be a doctor?"

"Fortunately, I'm doing pathology at the moment." He consulted his pocket watch. "The dead are much more patient than the living, but I do have a lab in twenty minutes." He stood. "I hope I'll see you tonight."

*   *   *

Walking home, the beauty of the Vienna spring smote Amalia afresh. The red and gold tulips in the park were particularly brilliant when a shaft of sunlight, slanting through an opening in the high, billowing clouds, struck them with direct intensity. A fresh breeze shimmered through the new green of the chestnut trees, and she quickened her step. She *would* go to the theater tonight.

Chapter Twelve

As she dressed with unusual care in her new, light sand-colored silk dress with the beaded bodice, Amalia studied her reflection. It had been so long since she'd worn anything but black. She submitted to Kristina's deft hands that dressed her hair in a high, elaborate evening coiffure.

A sharp knock preceded Antonia's entrance into her room, a rare event in recent months. "So you are going out, Amalia! I couldn't believe it when Wolf told me. What tempted you after all this time?"

"Therese's playwright, Steller," she answered. "He's supposedly quite a genius."

"Thank heavens. I do hope you'll exert yourself a bit, Amalia. I know Eberhard has given you a rotten time, but you musn't let that put you off men."

Startled, Amalia met her sister's eyes in the mirror. "What makes you say that?"

"Amalia! Why else have you been hiding yourself in that wretched orphanage? Don't worry, the gossip's gone the rounds and died a natural death. I do wish you'd take off the ring, though."

Looking blindly at the sapphire, Amalia heard her sister continue. "Word is that Baron von Schoenenburg, for one, is quite gone on you."

Amalia laughed. "Toni, you're as full of plots as Grandmama."

The older girl, arrayed in her dressing gown, sat on the bed and surveyed her sister critically. "I hope you aren't counting in any way upon Zaleski. According to Maria, they're getting ready to name the day."

Sitting up suddenly, Antonia addressed Kristina. "Don't you think we should persuade Amalia to wear Grandmama's diamond tiara?"

Amalia watched, quite detached, as they found the tiara wrapped in flannels in the jewel case.

Could it be true about Andrzej? Her hands trembled slightly in her lap as the little maid settled the von Hohenburg heirloom on her head. Even Amalia had to admit the effect was startling.

"It really would be quite wonderful," her sister said, "if you could catch the baron. Eberhard's nothing compared to him."

Bustling with that special frenzy of first-night fervor, the crescent-shaped theater perched directly on the Ringstrasse was alight and teeming with Viennese. Chandeliers reflected tiny rainbows of light upon the guests who were aglow in ancient jewelry and modern silks. Amalia ascended the staircase on the arm of her brother, who was completely turned out in full evening regalia.

Once inside the box, greetings assailed them from the assembled guests. Therese moved forward to claim Wolf, leaving Amalia to her father, the rather alarming Baron von Altwald.

"You're in magnificent looks tonight, Fräulein."

"Thank you, Baron. It was kind of you to include me."

"Well, it's Therese's night tonight, isn't it? Steller's her protégé, you know. We'll see if he has what it takes."

At that moment the box door opened once again, and Andrzej entered with Maria on his arm. She was attired rather grandly in Russian sables and midnight blue velvet. She proceeded at once in a high state of coquetry to pay her respects to the baron. Andrzej took the opportunity to edge Amalia away and whisper into her hair, "My wish has been granted, I see. The tiara is splendid."

"Amalia!" Maria joined them. "So you've shed the black at last. One quite despaired of ever seeing you again." She smiled up at Andrzej and took his arm. "Where shall we sit, darling? I do want to be able to see this wretched play."

It was a very odd experience to see Andrzej with Maria. Amalia realized she had grown to believe there was a special bond between them during their refurbishing of the orphanage. But this was his all-important nightlife. It seemed to be happening in another world.

She blindly took the only chair left, which was next to the baron. The curtain went up, but after the first few scenes Amalia gave up concentrating on the play, which was riddled tortuously with symbolism she cared too little about to decipher. Under cover of relative darkness, she studied Andrzej's profile as he sat next to the baron, in line with her view of the stage. Resting on the back of Maria's chair, his hand was balled into a fist. Amalia found it impossible to believe he was about to marry her.

He appeared completely intent upon the play, ignoring Maria's frequent attempts to claim his attention. The air of tension, absent at the orphanage, was evident in his tightly coiled languor. For the first time in months, she thought of the green-eyed cat of her dream. Hadn't he been stalking a bird?

At the interval, Baron Von Altwald excused himself to mingle with his own set, and Therese asked, "So what did you think of the play?"

Before she could form a charitable response, Maria interposed, "I think perhaps Amalia must have found it rather depressing."

Therese looked annoyed, and Wolf chimed in, "It wasn't exactly meant to be jolly, was it?"

But Amalia replied with outward calm, "I gather that Steller sees himself as the Homer of the bourgeoisie."

"I find his insights quite extraordinary," Therese replied.

But Andrzej differed. "I'm afraid he's rather pompous, Therese, darling. I mean, he's constructing the whole thing around some uniquely bourgeois crisis of conscience. Dull stuff."

"What is Steller's background?" Amalia asked her hostess.

"He's definitely middle class, and I should say he knows what he's talking about." Andrzej's criticism had apparently left her opinions intact.

Maria laughed, and Andrzej turned to Amalia. "Tell us, my dear. From your point of view, do you think this fellow has got it right?"

"Oh, yes, Amalia," Maria urged. "Do give us the true burgher's viewpoint."

The words were thrown like an unexpected spear. Amalia looked from Andrzej to Maria and said quietly, "I'm not ashamed of my birth."

Andrzej smiled broadly at her, but Maria continued. "Therese, the man must have learned all he knows of passion from you. Confess it! It has a quality quite beyond his station. I mean, a passionate burgher! The ideas are patently contradictory."

"Ah! But that is the point, darling," Andrzej said. "That's where the tension comes in. This unfortunate man has a secret, almost violent desire burning away inside him. It's threatening to get out of control, and his poor middle class soul isn't tempered to stand it."

Maria laughed her deep, throaty laugh. "I'm afraid the ending is dismally obvious. Either he gives in to desires that play havoc with his life and values, or he commits suicide."

Wolf, who was by this time very red in the face, turned abruptly and left the box. Amalia stood her ground, addressing her hostess in level tones. "Well, Therese, at least the play has the virtue of having aroused a spirited discussion. Perhaps it will be a resounding success."

Maria leaned forward impulsively and kissed her hostess on the cheek. "Yes, I wish him well, dear, for your sake. But, really, he should have left the flames of passion alone."

Andrzej put his arm around Maria's honey-skinned shoulders. "*Vive les aristos!* Eh, darling?" As he shepherded her out of the box, he looked back over his shoulder at Amalia, and his eyes were merry with mischief.

She stood looking after him, her lips tight, her heart bruised. Conspicuous and miserable, she felt as though she had come to a ball in a state of great anticipation to find herself the only one in fancy dress.

"Poor, dear Wolf," Therese sighed, studying the teeming crowd below. "I've never known Maria to be quite so rude. And she's turned

91

Zaleski into a hideous bore. I used to find him very pleasant. Shall we go find your brother?"

"I expect he's gone. And he'll have forgotten he's my chaperon tonight, so I'm afraid I must go, too. Thank you for asking me."

"But that was Zaleski's doing. I must say, I find the whole thing very strange. After inviting you here, he was quite unforgivable." Therese's hairless brows were raised in speculation over her caramel-colored eyes.

"Well, good night then, Therese."

Amalia arrived home twenty minutes later, weary with the effort of holding onto her dignity. She bade Georg pay her driver. He informed her that Wolf had not come home.

Going into the morning room, she stripped off her gloves, tossed them onto the occasional table, and sat ungracefully upon the divan. She plucked weary jonquils from the vase beside her, and purposefully stripped them to shreds. There was nothing quite as wounding as ridicule, especially from someone whom she had come to see as warm and caring. Andrzej had reached through to the essence of her soul again, to who she was in the deepest sense. This time he had used everything he knew of her to intentionally insult her.

She found her mind was in rebellion against the experience, hardly able to take it in. What had happened to her cohort of the orphanage, the doctor to her dying uncle, the companion of their extraordinary dance together? Who of all the Andrzejs she had seen was the real one? How could he have chosen just the words to specifically injure her? *The middle class incapable of passion. Their souls not tempered to withstand it. 'Vive les aristos.'* And all the while his arm was around Maria, who was unleashing her venomous spite.

All at once shredding jonquils wasn't sufficient outlet for her feelings. She took the glass vase and hurled it into the fireplace, hot tears stinging her eyes.

The muted rapping of the knocker sounded. Most likely Wolf had forgotten his latchkey. Dully her mind recorded the murmur of voices, but she had no desire to talk with her brother. It surprised her very much, therefore, when Georg opened the door.

"You have a caller, Fräulein."

"Who is it, Georg?"

"Herr Doktor Zaleski. He is quite insistent."

"Tell the doctor it is too late for callers. I've retired."

"Very good, Fräulein." She marked an ill-concealed smile on the butler's round face before he closed the door.

A moment later, however, he returned with a piece of paper. "The Herr Doktor wishes you to read this, Fräulein. He is still waiting."

Annoyed, she took the paper and dismissed the butler. It was only a short note: "Though you may not think it, you are equally at fault for what happened tonight."

She stood and, treading on pieces of decimated jonquil, pulled the door open to find Georg lingering close by. Behind him, pacing the black and white marble floor of the foyer, was Andrzej. His hair rippled in riotous waves, as though his hands had passed through it repeatedly. He walked over to her instantly, and ignoring Georg, said, "I thought that would bring you out."

"You may go, Georg." Amalia waited until the butler had retired to his pantry. Then, raising her chin, she looked Andrzej in the eye, "Say what you've come to say then, if you have the nerve."

Aware that he was skating on very thin ice, he said gently, "Do you intend for us to stand out here? What I have to say may take some time."

"We can speak here."

He turned his back and began his agitated pacing again, one hand in his pocket, the other running through his hair. He had been through agonies since he'd made such an idiot of himself at the theater. What had made him do it? Suddenly, he knew, and the answer surprised him. He must be honest, no matter where it led. "Very well. Have you ever thought what hell would be like?"

She snapped in annoyance. "Spare me any more of your philosophical absurdities tonight!"

"No, I promise you, this is entirely relevant. I've given it quite a bit of thought, one way and another, and I've come to the conclusion that hell is clearly seeing what you want but having it eternally out of reach. I owe the nature of this remarkable discovery to you, my dear. You've provided me with an excellent simulation of hell."

"Thank you very much. Make your point."

Abruptly ceasing his pacing, he put his hands on her shoulders. "I know that my behavior tonight was shocking, but what I'm trying to say is that you drove me to it, standing there so maddeningly untouchable in that chaste white dress."

"So now you ridicule my virtue as well. To you, I am like the poor man in the play. Couldn't you be content with belittling my birth?" Coldly, angrily, she took him by the wrists and firmly dislodged his hands.

But he looked steadily into her eyes. He knew he had no options left. He had to say it. "Amalia, how could you possibly *not* know how I feel about you? How I've felt about you since that very first waltz?"

She laughed, and the sound came out harsh and unfamiliar. "Tell me, do you always court your women so abrasively?"

"Look, we simply can't discuss this out here in the hall." Jerking open the door, he walked into the morning room. She followed him, shut the door and stood with her back to it.

"You laugh at my inexperience, my chastity. But I've never had any pretensions about being a femme fatale. And I did think that you had some respect for me, that you valued me as a person, if not as a woman of your set. It hurts abominably to find out how wrong I was."

"Amalia, that wasn't *me* tonight! How can I explain it? There was Maria hanging so everlastingly on my arm, and there you stood so cool and remote, disdain written all over your face." He sat down and stared at shattered glass in the empty grate. Had Amalia smashed something?

"It was as though I were completely taken over by this horrible desire to make you feel something, anything, even if it was only anger."

She walked through the room and stood by the mantle. "And you enjoyed it, didn't you?"

"I admit, I carried things too far. And Maria did enter quite enthusiastically into the spirit of the thing. I do ask your forgiveness, but the fact is, I'm not really sorry." His mood changed suddenly, and he grinned up at her. "It seems that at last I've blasted through your defenses. Did you throw a vase or something?"

She did not respond either to the grin or to the provocative statement. He found himself continuing, "You're a hard case, Amalia Faulhaber. I've quite given up on the subtle approach. You know as well as I do what we experienced during that dance. It was more than just an incredible magnetism. Didn't it move you? Didn't it change you? Why have you remained so remote? How can you continue in this mysterious engagement of yours? And what about this baron fellow?"

"Just what was it you expected me to do?"

She must be made to see, even if it meant a confession that took him by surprise. "Don't be a dunce, darling. I'm infernally in love with you, and you know it very well."

She stared at him in some form of shock. He had to admit his behavior that night had certainly not been lover-like. More like a last-ditch attempt to hang onto his public persona. But it had seared his soul to think of losing her. She had become vital to him as the only real person in a world where flirtation was a high art form.

He crossed to her. "Won't you forget von Schoenenburg and that wretched ghost of a fiancé?" Putting his arms around her, he pulled her to him quite firmly. "Say you forgive me, and for heaven's sake, marry me, Amalia."

Pulling back warily, she studied his face. His impetuous words had startled even him. What business had he with a wife? But now, at least he could kiss her with full propriety, delicately at first and then more intensely. It was the deep soul-probing sensation of the waltz again, and for a minute or two he surrendered to it, losing all contact with the outside world. Her mouth on his was soft and tender, in answer to his hungry possessiveness, drawing them into their own private reality. Finally, she began to struggle and pushed him away. He read panic in her eyes.

"For heaven's sake, Andrzej, ten minutes ago I hated you like poison. Give me a chance to think!"

He took her hands and kissed the palms. "Good sense isn't my ally, Amalia." He laughed a bit uncertainly. "There isn't any good reason for you to marry me. I have no title, no great expectations, beyond qualifying as a surgeon. My only recommendation is that I love you beyond reason. I never expected this to happen, believe me, but I think it must have been brewing for some time."

She regained her hands and put them on her hips. "What about Maria?"

He was silent for a moment, as he stooped to recover a jonquil stem from the carpet. He examined it thoroughly, hearing the shrewish voice of his mistress. "I find it quite difficult to worry about her at the moment."

"But you must, you know. Maria is quite sure of you. How do you explain that?"

"I don't. I've never mentioned marriage to her."

Amalia walked away from him and sat in a chair. "You really are quite ruthlessly self-centered, you know. Maria has had every attention from you for the last six months, and you think she hasn't a right to hope for marriage?"

"And what of your fiancé, for that matter? How long have you been engaged to him? You can't tell me that you haven't ceased to care for him long ago."

"You're like a tidal wave coming down on me, Andrzej. I can't think properly at all."

He stood across the room, arm stretched out along the mantle, one hand in his pocket. "Come, Amalia. We've come this far. Aren't you going to tell me that you love me?"

"Something tells me that you're much safer to have as a friend than as a lover."

"But, you see, I'm offering myself as both."

"You never said how you managed to get away from Maria tonight."

"Gross deception, but I think she saw through me. There'll be the devil to pay." He didn't want to think of it. Why had he become entangled with such a snake?

"And then some," Amalia agreed. "But it's your fault."

He grinned. "You do so like putting me in the wrong. Shall you always be that way, I wonder?"

"Possibly. My family tells me I'm quite contrary."

"Never mind." He pulled her out of her chair, and holding her by the shoulders, looked into her face. "Will you marry me?"

"I don't know, Andrzej. At the moment, I'm still quite angry with you."

"Then I'll take that kiss as a hopeful sign. It was, you know." If she had accepted him outright, things might have been awkward. At least he had time now to make adjustments in his bachelor existence.

Chapter Thirteen

Amalia spent a tortured night. Andrzej's kiss burned on like fire. Even his taunts and the vision of Maria in his arms couldn't extinguish it.

Could she truly believe he loved her? She knew very well that he had made the confession most unwillingly and that his spontaneous offer of marriage had surprised him as much as it had surprised her. She had learned much about society since Eberhard's departure. Rarely was anyone straightforward. And then there was the fact that Maria knew the truth about Eberhard. If Andrzej were to jilt the woman, Amalia had no doubt that Maria would tell all of Viennese society about her lie. Would Andrzej's love stand the test? Not at the moment. She had the instinctive feeling that he was skittish as a horse around explosives.

Did she want to marry such a man?

Then the memory of the kiss would overtake her, and she would toss again in her bed and go through the whole conundrum again. Love was certainly not the comfortable thing she had thought it would be.

The following day, Amalia received the Baron von Schoenenburg with curiosity. What could he have to tell her?

He settled himself in the very chair Andrzej had occupied the night before, retaining his gloves, which he slapped idly against his thighs. "I'm sure you'll think I'm playing maiden aunt," he said finally. "But think of me as standing in the place of your Uncle Lorenz."

"What is it?" she inquired. The baron's eyes seemed more hooded than ever and held an expression she could not read at all. His face was more forbidding than usual. "Have I done something wrong with the trusts?"

He cleared his throat. "No. You have far exceeded my expectations. I can see that Lorenz knew what he was doing with his legacy. You're rather an extraordinary person, you know."

He looked away, into the fire, and she couldn't read his eyes. From this angle, his hawk nose protruded almost alarmingly. She found herself glad she wasn't in his regiment.

"I find I must tell you a rather personal story. It's not generally known, and I would appreciate it if you would keep it to yourself."

Surprised, Amalia said, "Of course, I will."

"I had an older brother. Hans. Johann, actually. He should have inherited the title. He was born to it." He sighed but still kept his eyes fixed on the flames. "However, three years ago, he fell in love with a woman, a socialite. She was young and beautiful and musical and completely stole his heart. She would have been an ideal baroness."

Here he looked up, his eyes bitter. "But she had a flaw. She was inconstant. Once certain of my brother, she began to bestow her favors elsewhere. It turns out she has little moral sense. My brother took it to heart. He shot himself. He left a note for the woman, but I suppressed it. I didn't want more scandal added upon the suicide." He ruminated for a few moments. "I needn't have taken the trouble. She had moved on to another lover, and my brother's death seemed to have no effect upon her whatsoever."

"I'm very sorry," Amalia hastened to say. She was glad Grandmama had prepared her about the suicide, but all the same she was shocked nearly speechless by the unnamed woman's behavior. "It sounds truly dreadful. But why are you telling me this?"

"My brother's lover was Maria von Beckhaus, who is now enjoying an extended liaison with your doctor. I don't know what terms you are on with him, but I thought you had better be warned. You are such an innocent, I thought you might not be aware."

Amalia shrank into her chair as though someone had just shot her. Something black entered her soul. She knew exactly what the baron was telling her. Maria was an aristocratic demimondaine. A loose woman.

But Andrzej? Every meeting with him was at once cheapened, suspect. All her tossing and turning, trying to figure how she could accept Andrzej without harming Maria! Now she saw that his declarations of love were nothing but a trap. He had no intention of marrying Amalia. What in the world could she mean to him? A challenge? A little fling with the bourgeoisie? She had no believable reason to think that he wasn't treating her exactly as he had treated Maria.

Finally, she responded. "Thank you, Baron. I didn't know. He actually proposed marriage to me last night. I thought he was serious."

"Marriage?" The baron's eyebrows climbed, and then his eyes narrowed with anger. "I was willing to give him the benefit of the doubt, but this is beyond reason. Doesn't he know you're engaged?"

She squirmed a bit. "Things are uncertain with Eberhard at this point, Baron. I think Andrzej expects me to throw him over."

"A fortuneless doctor? A Pole? A philanderer?"

Seeing Andrzej through the Baron's eyes was not a pretty picture. His voice was harsh, unbelieving. It reduced her on-again, off-again romance to the status of a flirtation. She flushed and felt suddenly awkward. "You do sound a bit like a maiden aunt."

His eyes softened. "I care a good deal about what becomes of you, my dear. You are not an ordinary young lady. I don't want you to throw yourself away on someone who is bound to make you unhappy. I don't think such a sort could ever be faithful."

Amalia had never been more aware of her naïveté. Was there really a special bond between her and Andrzej, or was that purely imagination? Was he capable of constancy, chivalry, even heroics, as she had seen in that moment during their dance together? Or had she just been a romantic little fool?

"I will take what you have said to heart, Baron. I'm sure this was painful for you to tell me, and I appreciate it. Thank you for coming."

Going up to her room, she spent a long time in her rose-colored chair. At length, she decided that Andrzej's own surprise at his proposal was genuine. But could he be faithful? Was she no more than a novelty to him? She writhed at the baron's disclosure. She knew she was naïve. Her mother had never thought it necessary to talk to her about the intimacies between men and women. But her grandmother had. Grandmama would know how seriously to take this proposal. She would also be frank with her about the gravity of Andrzej's behavior. Did every man in society have a woman like Maria tucked away?

Amalia decided that if that were the case, she could not tolerate such a marriage. How could she ever trust Andrzej with her love, her future, her children? The blackness that had come upon her soul at the baron's disclosure darkened her world with a despair she had never felt before. She loved the man she had seen a glimpse of from time to time. There was indeed more than the ordinary magnetism between them. But was that enough? She wanted to be loved as Uncle had loved, as Grandmama had loved. Was that sort of happiness possible in the Vienna of 1914?

Until she had discussed the matter thoroughly with her grandmother and candidly with Andrzej, she didn't think she could take the risk. She would cling to the fictitious engagement with Eberhard.

In her head she drew a line from Eberhard to his cousin Lilli to Maria von Beckhaus. She was walking in dangerous territory. If Maria had any idea that Amalia was responsible for ending Andrzej's relationship with her, the results would be disastrous.

*   *   *

Eugenia was somewhat amused at her granddaughter's naïveté. "I do like Andrzej. I think you bring out his better side. You have lived a very sheltered life, but among the aristocracy such liaisons are far more common than you can imagine. Still, how can you be sure the baron's allegations are true? I am willing to believe that he has your honor at heart, but loyalty to his poor dead brother may bias his view of the relationship." Eugenia von Hohenburg Reichart stared into the past. How lucky she had been to have a husband of solid worth, who would never have thought of philandering! But what advice had she for Amalia? Was the Pole really right for her? Ought she not to be encouraging her to take up with von Schoenenburg?

"Amalia, just what do you think of this baron of yours?"

"He's not mine, Grandmama."

"There are rumors, you know. He is the complete misogynist. No one has ever seen him pay the attention to any woman that he pays to you."

"We are like business partners, Grandmama. He feels a little protective of me because of Uncle, that's all."

"I wonder if there is more self-interest in this warning . . ." She let the sentence trail off. "I think, Amalia, that it might be best if you let me handle this. We will pretend that you know nothing." She tapped her fingernail thoughtfully on the chair arm. "I will ask Herr Doktor to call on me, tell him what I have heard and that I will advise you not to marry him unless he breaks thoroughly with Maria and proves himself worthy of you." She smiled at her granddaughter, whose eyes were shadowed with fatigue. "I'm sure he will see things the right way."

"But even if he breaks off with Maria, how do I know Andrzej will be faithful to me?"

"What made you fall in love with him, Amalia?" Eugenia asked.

"I didn't intend to. But you remember the dance I told you about? The things I sensed about him? I believe in those things. I believe that for some reason he has put up a false front. I think with me, he doesn't have to."

"Many men are like that, dear. I think he must want to be the person you believe in, or he never would have come out with this surprising proposal. But we must be sure."

"Thank you, Grandmama. I trust your judgment. And what about Eberhard?"

"It won't hurt to keep Andrzej in suspense for a month. We don't want the termination of Andrzej's fling with Maria to coincide with your breakup with Eberhard. The coincidence would produce exactly the effect we wish to avoid. Let four weeks go by, and then announce that you have broken the engagement. I think Antonia's wedding— June 28th, isn't it?—I think that would be a suitable time."

Amalia took a deep breath. Her grandmother had only her best interest at heart. She would trust in that.

She denied herself all visitors and stayed in her room for three days, sitting in her rose chair and writing furiously in her journal, waiting for her grandmother to act. Spring was growing warm outside, and she watched the robins in the chestnut tree outside her window. Occasionally the black cat climbed the tree and chased them away. Lucky robins. They seemed to have more sense than she did.

She didn't want to see Andrzej until he had broken with Maria. Despite Grandmama's cautions to suspend judgment, she couldn't bear to think of Andrzej and Maria in that way. Had he kissed Maria with that same passion that had merged the souls of the waltz in some almost metaphysical way? Amalia had felt that she truly belonged to Andrzej—that he was her missing half. But she was dreadfully inexperienced. Perhaps the relationship she dreamed of was only the product of reading too many romances. Where was the young woman her uncle had taught?

Perhaps Andrzej was some kind of master of seduction—a Don Giovanni. She didn't believe he loved Maria. That he could involve himself in that way with one woman and propose to another was a dissonance she could scarcely accept. That was life in Vienna, Grandmama said. But it would take a long time for her to forget. Was what she felt for Andrzej sufficient to withstand this stain on his character? If he were ever unfaithful to her, she knew she would leave him, for he would have proven himself not to be the man she hoped he was. Could she risk that?

Grandmama had thought her very naïve. Perhaps she was, but she didn't know if she could ever really look at him the same way again.

So it was with mixed feelings that she wrote to her former fiancé, another man she knew would never practice such deceit.

Dear Eberhard,

   I am writing to tell you that I finally understand what it means to love as you told me I would someday. It is not very comfortable, and I pray that this will not cause you pain. You will always remain in my heart as a fond memory. I will never be able to picture you as a soldier, however. I will always see and hear you playing Bach and thrilling me with your performance. I hope the baroness is well. I devoutly hope you are wrong about the war.

> Auf Wiedersehen,
> Amalia

In spite of everything, she longed to see Andrzej again. She wanted to see if he looked any different to her now, if her feelings had changed. But she was also afraid of her own passion. At night, she lay under her Federdecke remembering his kiss, his declaration. Would her feelings outstrip her reason?

At breakfast, three days after she had talked to her grandmother, her sister was bursting with news. "Amalia! You'll never guess! Andrzej and Maria had a public quarrel last night at the opera! She told him she never wanted to see him again! It was too too delicious. He was very cast down, poor fellow. You should have been there."

Amalia trembled as she buttered her Semmel. "What exactly happened?"

"Well, you know Maria has never been able to abide the fact that he is Polish. He began carrying on about Chopin, saying he was the greatest composer of the nineteenth century—and that no one could match his skill or passion. Maria, of course, being a violinist, not a pianist, told him Chopin was an unlearned boor and Beethoven was far superior. It started out playfully, apparently. But then Andrzej got carried away. He said no one could equal the 'exquisite passion' of a Pole and that Beethoven was heavy-handed and obvious. He didn't understand subtlety."

"Antonia, it sounds as though you were right there!"

"I was. Andrzej sent a note yesterday to Erich, inviting us to go with them to the opera. But you haven't heard the best part!" Her eyes glittered with merriment. "He moved from that to Austrian society— he said we were all too rococo for words, stuck in a past that was miring us like horses in mud." Antonia giggled. "Maria didn't like being compared to a horse. I didn't blame her. He really is unsupportable, but I dislike Maria so much I couldn't help enjoying her fury. She told him coldly that he needn't think he had her reins and that Chopin was nothing but a neurotic dreamer, just like him. Imagine!"

"Maria has a temper," Amalia commented, holding her hands together to keep them still. "What then?"

"He had the nerve to criticize Mozart as another bore."

"Oh, dear."

"Yes, I know. Mozart is her idol. I think she even has his Küchel listings memorized. That put Andrzej beyond the pale. She accused him of coming out of the Polish gutter. I don't think she knew what she was saying at that point."

"What did Andzrej do?"

"He turned stone cold, made her a stiff bow, and said, 'Well, I don't suppose you'll want to be seen with a mere gutter rat. Adieu.' And he walked out!"

Toni seemed to be waiting for some response, but Amalia was lost in contemplation of Andrzej's manipulations. He had known exactly how to play Maria, as if pressing just the right keys on a piano. It was a little daunting. Was he playing her that way?

"You and I have always known Maria is a shrew. Remember how she treated me over Eberhard?"

Her sister nodded and laughed. "Two men in a row, throwing her over. She's probably flinging china and tearing her clothes to ribbons. She was so sure of Andrzej. Personally, I didn't think him much of a prize. I mean, he's well-born enough, but he hasn't any money or title." She simpered a little. "He is very good-looking, of course, and almost too charming, but I prefer my Erich."

Later that morning, Georg announced Herr Doktor Zaleski.

Chapter Fourteen

Amalia had dressed carefully in the sapphire blue gown that emphasized her eyes and splashed herself with gardenia scent. She felt far too grave, but maybe that was for the best.

"At last!" he greeted her, kissing her forehead. "What is wrong, Amalia? Why have you been having Georg turn me away?"

"I've been doing some heavy thinking, Andrzej, about your proposal. I didn't think I ought to be distracted by kisses."

*   *   *

Andrzej was more troubled than he was willing to admit. After that extraordinary kiss, he had been certain she was his. And he *had* proposed. He had never done that before. Now she looked apprehensive.

"What is it, darling?" he strove to keep his tone light. It had never once occurred to him that she might refuse him.

"I am finding this all very difficult," she said, looking down so he couldn't read her eyes. Alarm flashed through him.

"You don't want to marry me?"

"It's just that I feel manipulated, Andrzej. You've never courted me properly. And then, as you seem to forget, there is Eberhard."

It was true. He had forgotten the Prussian. But surely Amalia wouldn't have kissed him like that if she were truly in love with someone else?

"When does he return?" he asked curtly.

Walking to the window she looked out at the windy day. A storm was blowing in. "I have no idea," she said finally. "He thinks there will be a war shortly."

Andrzej looked at the sapphire on her finger. "And he expects you to wait for him?"

"I had always planned on it. I need time to think this through, Andrzej. It's a very serious step. And, of course, there's not just Eberhard. There's also Maria."

In some part of his heart, jealousy burned, but intellectually he respected her for her caution. He knew what she felt for him. It must be costing her private agonies. Going to her, he put his hands on her shoulders and smelled her fragrance. He kissed the back of her neck. "Maria is no longer an issue. She has thrown me over."

"You knew Toni would report the whole thing. That's why you invited her last night." She didn't turn around. "And it was only a silly quarrel. Maria wouldn't let herself be vanquished that easily." He could see her reflection in the darkening glass. It was troubled.

"Well, perhaps you don't know her as well as you think, Amalia. She came to my rooms last night, and our quarrel escalated until the breach was complete."

"What did she say?"

"It was as though she were seeing my surroundings for the first time. My flat is a very humble one. She told me she hoped I had never thought we had a future together when I was only a poor doctor from some obscure town in Poland. 'You are exceedingly amusing,' she told me. 'But clearly not husband material. You've overreached yourself.'"

Amalia was looking at him as though trying to read the truth in his eyes. She said nothing.

"Believe me, Amalia, Maria doesn't want anything more to do with me." Scowling, he dropped his hands. What did she want from him? "I suppose you want me to prove that I am a more worthy character than this Prussian of yours. Well, I'm afraid that's out of the question. I'm sure he's eminently suitable and would please your mother perfectly. But you're not in love with him. We have a bond, Amalia. You see things in me I have never shown to anyone else. This is no idle flirtation. I have never asked anyone but you to marry me."

Now she turned to face him. She looked as though someone were performing slow torture on her. Unable to bear it one more second, he drew her into his arms and kissed her with all the feeling he had kept buried since that first dance. She was born to be his true mate. He longed to bind her to him forever. It was she who ended the kiss.

"You can't kiss me like that, Amalia—with your whole soul—and then marry someone else." Andrzej was shaken.

Amalia put her hand to his cheek, her eyes questioning. "Give me a month, Andrzej. 'Til Toni's wedding on the twenty-eighth. If you remain faithful to me, and if I continue to feel this way, I will formally break my engagement."

A month! He broke from her and paced the room. Never had he felt such need. She was more than just a woman. He wanted her for his wife. He would have a family again. He had had none since he was young and petted and cosseted by his cheerful, loving parents and three sisters. Amalia would change that.

As he paced, the horror of the scene he had come upon as a ten-year-old revisited him. In one unforgettable night, he had lost his entire family. The sounds and smells of that time were part of the man he had become and certainly responsible for his unremitting hatred of the Prussians.

Carefully schooling his tenderest emotions since the trauma that ended his carefree youth, he had kept his heart out of sight. But Amalia held his future in her hands, and he must wait a whole month to see what she would do with it. "What do you expect me to prove in a month?" he demanded, anger in his voice. It seemed perfectly fitting that his rival should be Prussian. He was prepared to get his prize by fair means or foul.

Her face was calm. "That you can be constant."

Picking up his gloves from the table, he slapped them against his palm. "Very well. Be prepared to see me every day when my studies permit.

But," a little devil prompted him, "no more kisses. There's such a thing as playing with fire."

She looked at him levelly. "This isn't a chess game, Andrzej."

"I know," he said, forcing himself to be calm. "It's only my life."

"And mine," she responded. Seizing his hand suddenly, she gave his knuckles a fervent kiss and then fled the room.

*   *   *

Amalia threw herself into her work in order not to think of the conundrum she had involved herself in. Andrzej was devoted—at times playful, at times frustrated, but always there whenever he could be. Amalia just hoped that when she announced her broken engagement Maria would have moved on to other interests.

*   *   *

Rudolf was anxious to know the status of Amalia's relationship with the doctor, but he dared not ask outright. "Your sister is getting married, I see?" he remarked lightly one Thursday morning after her story hour.

"Yes, but surely you've had an invitation."

"I get so many. Whom is she marrying, may I ask?"

"Erich von Trauenburg. He's from Salzburg"

He looked at her mutely.

Amalia laughed. "You'd better dig out the invitation. I expect to see you there."

"Yes, and I'm looking forward to a waltz. By the way, I hear the doctor's lady love has quarreled with him and left for the country."

She reddened but didn't reply. "You may have a waltz, baron. I'm glad you will be there."

*   *   *

Rudolf knew it was a sunny June day, but until that moment, it had felt cold and dark. What was it about this girl that gave her so much power over him? He was past the age of schoolboy infatuation. But she only had to appear, and the dirty gray scrim that usually fell between him and the world seemed to lift, allowing him a glimpse of an alternate universe. It was a place where people were good all the way through, possessing no underhanded motives. A place where violence could not leap at you out of the darkness. He knew very well such a place did not exist.

Chapter Fifteen

The wedding was quite grand. At the reception ball given at Grandmama's palais, Mama received her guests with the broadest smile Amalia had ever seen her wear. It was evident that she viewed each titled guest as a personal triumph.

Amalia received next to her sister, who was a feverishly excited and blushing bride. Amalia felt awkward and silly in her role as maid of honor. Nearly a head taller than her sister, she was condemned to wear an unsuitable ruffled pink creation that had made her shudder when she looked in the mirror. It engulfed what subtle charm she had, and the color went poorly with her hair. Antonia, by contrast, looked decidedly rococo, her wide-skirted gown with its yards of ruffles giving the impression of a sweet, quivering confection. Her high-pitched laugh vibrated continually as she reached up to receive a kiss from each new well-wisher. Erich stood nervously by his new bride, impeccable as always, coloring either from pride or embarrassment.

Grandmama received on Amalia's other side and noted the precise moment of Andrzej's arrival. "He's here!" she whispered. Amalia looked toward the entrance. Over the past month they hadn't seen each other in society, and so the sight of his sleek, fashionable figure in evening dress nearly took her breath away.

Tonight she would tell him that her engagement to Eberhard was at an end because he had decided to join the army. Then she would be free to let their official engagement begin.

Grandmama whispered, following Amalia's glance, "How did you ever let Antonia talk you into that ghastly dress?"

"Don't try to provoke me, Grandmama."

"I believe our Andrzej could have made quite a career on the stage. Look at him bow and scrape to your parents, as though they were royalty."

"You've got the same devious kink he has, I think."

"But I do know the ins and outs of a flirtation, you must admit. Tonight all will be settled."

Eventually, the line progressed to the point where Andrzej was wishing the highest degree of happiness upon the bride and groom. Amalia's toes curled inside her shoes with anticipation.

Then Andrzej joined them. Could she really consider marrying this worldly, handsome creature of society? Tongue-tied, she left the greeting to Grandmama.

"This orchestra you have," he addressed Grandmama. "It plays waltzes?"

"But of course, Herr Doktor," Grandmama answered. "Shall you dance with me?"

"I would consider it a rare pleasure. Perhaps your granddaughter might consent to stand up with me, as well." He winked and passed on without her having said a word.

But it was the Baron von Schoenenburg with whom Amalia danced the first waltz. He arrived after the receiving line was dispersed and searched her out immediately. "Fräulein Amalia. You see, I have made it. Sorry to be so late, but what a wonderful relief it is to see you out of your schoolroom garb!"

Amalia wrinkled her nose and laughed as he kissed her hand. "You're only being gallant. The dress is horrible."

He stood back and surveyed her, his head on one side. "No, perhaps not your usual style."

Amalia was determined to enjoy their dance together. She was interested to discover the baron's mode of dancing.

After they had circled the ballroom one time, she was ready to judge. Unlike Eberhard, he appeared to enjoy dancing, but he did not have the flair of Andrzej. Though surprisingly energetic and adept, the baron was definitely masculine in his approach. Andrzej bestowed an individual grace to the activity that made it almost supernatural.

They passed her almost-fiancé, who stood watching them, an eyebrow lifted. He gave them a brief bow as they circled close to him. Amalia saw him frown when he thought they were no longer looking.

"It's rather a pity Lorenz had no children," the baron remarked, noting the magnificent mirrored ballroom with its frescoed baroque ceiling. "Your grandmother's palais is exquisite."

"I suppose it will go to Wolf, but it is difficult to picture him living here, isn't it?"

"Quite," the baron smiled. "Wolf's spiritual home would seem to be something solid and indestructible."

"Biedermeier, in fact," Amalia laughed, thinking of her uncle's hatred of the functional, middle class school of art.

The dance ended, and they made their way off the floor to where Andrzej stood. "Baron von Schoenenburg, what a pleasure!"

"Zaleski," the baron murmured, making a short bow.

Amalia watched the men survey one another. It was the only time Amalia could recall that the baron's manner had lived up to the hauteur of his features.

"Well," said Andrzej, in forced good cheer, "it was a grand wedding, Amalia. Your mother can feel very proud of herself. Rather makes one want to do the deed oneself, doesn't it, Baron?"

"I'm afraid I missed the wedding mass," he replied shortly.

"My dance, I think?" Andrzej offered his arm to Amalia.

She looked up at the baron and smiled. "Don't go yet."

Then she allowed herself to be led onto the floor, where she tried to prepare herself for the unguarded attraction she knew would overtake her.

But to her surprise Andrzej moved only a short distance from the baron. "There must be a place where we can be alone for a few moments."

Slightly off balance, Amalia answered, "Grandmama's sitting room. It's just off the main hall."

Once they had arrived in the apricot colored room with the scent of Grandmama's sachet, he placed his hands on her shoulders. "Well, then, what of the cursed Eberhard?"

"That's over," she replied simply.

"Is it truly? You have ended it then?"

"Yes. You see, he's actually enlisted in the German army. My parents don't approve."

His eyes lit, and without any more questions, he swept her into his arms and twirled her around while he kissed her with a passion born of triumph. For Amalia, it was as though she were watching the scene from above. A tight knot released inside her as she gave herself to his kiss, suddenly letting go of all her former doubts and fears. After months of denial, her emotions expanded, delicious and exhilarating, and she allowed Andrzej's kiss to launch through the artificial ceiling she had put on her feelings. Looking into his green eyes, she was surprised to see a suspicion of tears. What was this?

"Andrzej, Andrzej? Are you all right?"

"I haven't felt this happy since before my family died. Oh, how I wish they could meet you. My parents were always in despair that I would grow up to be a worthless rascal."

"All your family is dead?"

"Yes, darling, but it's a tragic story. Let's not go into it right now."

His eyes were shadowed with memory. Wanting to chase it away, she gave in to a long-held impulse. She stood on her toes and ran her hands through Andrzej's silky hair and then down the sides of his face where she felt the stubble of his beard. She bent his head to her and kissed each of the eyes that had been the carrier of so many messages. He opened them and looked at her gravely. She knew he could be in no doubt of what he meant to her. He kissed her deeply, as though he were discovering her for the first time.

When he at last let her go, Amalia put her index finger on his chin and spoke as severely as she could. "We must get back to the others. It's Toni's night. We can tell my parents tomorrow."

The first person Amalia saw upon returning to the ballroom was Maria von Beckhaus dressed in a chartreuse gown with a plunging neckline and a dazzling choker. Looking at Amalia and Andrzej arm in arm, she resembled a lioness.

For Amalia, June 29, 1914, dawned an ordinary summer's day with nothing appearing to distinguish it from any other day, except for her own happiness. She had been a little worried about Maria, but Andrzej had fortunately been very civil to her, ladling out compliments until the steel in her eyes softened.

Her betrothal to Eberhard had certainly never felt like this. She remembered Uncle's words. "Love is something most people only feel once. You don't really have any choice in the matter. You *want* to offer everything you have. Irrevocably."

She smiled, remembering Andrzej's actions of the night before. She had no doubt that Uncle's words applied as much to him, no matter how many women he had courted.

The proper routine of the orphanage seemed bothersome today. How much more fun it would be to pay an extravagant visit to the dressmaker! Or perhaps, dine alfresco in the park with Andrzej on garlicky, deep-fried *langos* pastries bought from a street vendor and apricots from the open air market.

She got out of bed and threw open the heavy drapes, the lacy sheers, and the window, leaning her elbows on the sill. Below her, the summer roses had begun to creep up the wall of the house, and she could smell their fragrance in the moist morning air.

Amalia dressed without Kristina's aid in a new summer costume of cream-colored linen with a high waist and a light jacket cut short under her breast. The chiffon blouse of periwinkle blue rose in a high pleated ruffle at the neck and deepened the color of her eyes.

Obliged to call Kristina to do her hair, she listened to the little maid's lecture. "I don't know what you think you're doing, wearing this dress to that dirty old orphanage. It'll be ruined."

"Perhaps I won't go to the orphanage today, Kristina."

"Not go? Why surely you owe it to the baron. He's been most kind to you. Do you think that just because you're engaged the world will stop in its tracks?" Kristina had been waiting up for her the night before and was, as yet, Amalia's only confidante. "I'm certain they need you just as much today as any other, Fräulein Amalia." She inspected her charge warily in the mirror. "You weren't this way the last time."

"I know." Amalia watched herself grin in the mirror.

After a brisk morning walk through the park, she eventually arrived at the orphanage. But her good humor robbed her of her dignity and infected the children, resulting in a boisterous morning. Hugging each one of them, she said, "You're going to be a hero someday!"

She was shelving books, paying no attention to what she was doing, when the baron joined her. Expecting Andrzej, she looked up quickly at his arrival.

"You're certainly bright-eyed today, Fräulein Amalia, for having enjoyed yourself so much last night."

"I didn't expect to see *you* here today!"

"I confess, I just arrived. Thought I'd look in on you to see how you were doing and if you needed some help. No cavalier today?"

"I think the late night was too much for him. He did rather indulge himself, you remember."

After she had agreed to marry him, Andrzej returned to the ball and became the life of the party, dancing with every female, young and old, toasting the bride and groom far more than was necessary, and partaking freely of food and drink.

"Yes, he was a bit frenetic," the baron conceded.

Amalia became suddenly self-conscious.

He laughed and added, "I don't suppose you'd like to come out with me for a stroll? Perhaps we could lunch at Redl's. I saw them putting the tables out on the promenade this morning. It's a fine day."

Though he was not her fiancé, she agreed. She always enjoyed his company. He was a very restful person to be with.

*   *   *

Redl's was filling up with other Viennese, likewise taking advantage of the fine weather to sit out under mint-and-white striped awnings and watch the world go by. Rudolf ordered chicken Kiev for two. There could only be one reason for the glow about Amalia. She was in love and felt that love to be returned. Though it was a glorious day, shadows were creeping in around the corners of his mind.

She declined anything stronger than mineral water, and so the baron ordered a small bottle.

"I must confess to a lively curiosity, Fräulein. What has made you so happy?" He pleated his napkin in uncharacteristic embarrassment. "I shouldn't ask such a maiden-auntish question, I know."

Amalia laughed. "My parents don't even know, but I'm certain you'll be discreet. I have decided to marry Andrzej."

He looked down at his silver and concentrated on moving it into military alignment. "I hope she hasn't done too much damage, then."

"Who? Maria? He broke things off with her some time ago. It was just a casual relationship."

Obviously, she knew nothing. Should he tell her? No, he couldn't. Maybe she need never find out.

Forcing a smile, he said. "It's nothing. Ah, here's our soup. Leek. They don't do it anywhere as well as they do it at Redl's."

*   *   *

When Andrzej still did not show up for afternoon story hour, she began to worry. But perhaps she would find him visiting with her family. It would be like him to turn up and get himself invited to luncheon.

He had not called. She pulled off her veiled hat and stuffed it on the shelf of the cloakroom. She went to the morning room where she sat in a large chair, her knees under her chin, watching the front walk.

Fifteen minutes later, she grew still more impatient and climbed the stairs to her room.

Moments later Kristina entered. "Herr Doktor Zaleski has arrived, Fräulein Amalia. Georg put him in the small drawing room."

Relieved, she leapt up at once, splashed herself with gardenia scent, repinned a lock of hair, and then hastened downstairs to scold her fiancé for sleeping so late.

But when she entered the drawing room, his posture warned her that all was not well. He stood in the middle of the room, his lips set in a hard line. His eyes were focused on her. They were hot with anger.

"What is it?" she went to him and took his arm, but he was unresponsive.

"Oh, only a trifle," he said, his voice tight with sarcasm. "But then it is rather a new experience for me to look a fool."

"A fool? You don't look a fool."

"Oh, no? Then why do you still appear such an innocent thing to me, even when I know better? It should be quite amusing that the one woman I thought above such wiles was capable of the worst deceit."

She withdrew a step as though he had struck her. "What *are* you talking about?"

"But surely you can't have forgotten already? Your very convenient engagement to . . . who was it? Oh, yes, the paragon, Eberhard. Some Prussian idiot who nevertheless had the good sense to see through you and decide, however misguidedly, that he preferred the military life."

She stood motionless. "What about Eberhard?"

"Still the innocent, guileless creature, aren't you? Is it so difficult to break character? Or is it just that you've played it so long that you believe it yourself?" He laughed without humor. "What I don't understand is why you thought it necessary. Did you think my devotion would be fanned into hotter flames if I thought I had a rival? And what made you decide I was sufficiently aflame that you could dispense with him? Tell me," he concluded cynically. "I'm fascinated."

Amalia's incredulity had turned bitter. "You've been talking to Maria?"

"Does it matter how I found you out? It seems I could have learned it from any number of people these past few months if they'd known I was interested. You weren't quite clever enough, Amalia. You fooled me, but apparently everyone else knew what was going on."

Unlike his, her anger was glacial. "How clever of Maria to appeal to your pride. The very idea that you might be thought a fool is quite enough to make you one." She turned to leave the room, but he caught her arm.

"You don't deny it then?"

"Would it do any good if I did?" As she stood looking into his fierce, hot stare, the fear that had followed her for so long came into focus. "I *was* the unattainable, wasn't I? You didn't love me; you loved the idea of winning some sort of prize. I'm not completely blameless, but that's not why you're angry. You're angry because you feel you've been deceived. But I loved you, Andrzej Zaleski. I loved you with everything I had."

She left him, but not before she saw bewilderment dawn in his eyes.

Chapter Sixteen

Once Amalia closed the door to the drawing room, her dignity collapsed, and she fled up the stairs like a child. The pain from this fresh wound was instantaneous, deep, and physical. When she reached her room, the happiness she had felt there mocked her, and shutting the door, she turned and walked to the end of the hall. There she ascended the stairs to the dark attic.

When she had received a severe scolding as a child, she had taken refuge in this dusty haven. The indifference of old trunks, ancient ceiling beams, and cobwebs living separately from all that went on in the house below them was comforting to her. Heedless of her new white linen, she sat down on the floor cross-legged and began to cry. Soon she was sobbing. It felt as though someone had sawn her heart in half and left it there, exposed and bleeding.

A certain amount of anger would have been understandable. What she had done was wrong and inexcusable. But the real damage had been done by his pride. The fear that he'd been made to look a fool was enough to change all his promises of undying love. She'd been tried, judged, and hanged without being able to say a word.

He had thought her perfect, but she was human. She knew very well he wasn't perfect when she fell in love with him. But now it was finished, and she remembered the rest of Uncle's treatise on love: You can't give it again. It isn't yours to give.

This part of her life was over. She must accept it. It was completely false. All her memories of him would now be tinged with the burnt edge of reality.

Had she always known he was so vulnerable to the censure and whims of his peers? Otherwise why had he kept up the façade of his courtship of Maria? Amalia must have known on some level that social approval was important to him. Why else did he make such a production of masking his true emotions?

Soon she could not reason, only sob as fragments of happy days flew into her mind. Particularly poignant were the tears he had shed last night. He *had* loved her, she was sure of it. But he could turn it off. Just like that. Even Eberhard hadn't been able to mask his pain. But Andrzej was a master. How many hearts had he broken?

Clutching herself in an effort to hold the hurt inside, she wondered how she could continue to live life in this house, in this city, knowing that Andrzej was here. Her heart couldn't stand the pain. Though he had proven false, the knowledge that she still loved him was inescapable. How could she ever go into society again, knowing she would see his back turn on her? How could she bear to see him with Maria or anyone else and have him treat her as a stranger?

She was drowning in a morass of emotion when she finally felt a longing for her bed. Going down to her room, she didn't even bother to undress but crept under the Federdecke and fell into an exhausted sleep. Oddly enough, she dreamed of Eberhard. Staunch, stoical Eberhard. She woke from the dream and saw that it was close to midnight.

In her dream, her former fiancé was wearing a pith helmet and had sprouted a mustache, but he was still Eberhard. Since childhood, she had had a recurring nightmare of being stuck at the top of the giant wheel at the amusement park near the river. This version of her dream featured an electric storm that necessitated Eberhard's riding a black stallion at the head of the German army to rescue her. As she woke she realized there was a storm blowing outside. She tried to hold very hard to the feeling of being rescued. She went up to the attic and dragged down the biggest trunk she could manage.

By nine o'clock the next morning, a large selection of Amalia's belongings was packed in the trunk, and an incurious Hans had taken it to the railway station. Kristina found her fully dressed and composing a letter.

"Where are you off to, then?"

"Oh. Kristina." Amalia handed her maid an envelope. "Could you see that this is delivered immediately? It's urgent."

For once, Kristina didn't quibble but took the note.

Amalia was struggling with her hair when the maid returned an hour later.

"The baron is here now," she announced. "And that won't do at all," she added referring to Amalia's inexpert coiffure. She watched as Kristina took the comb from her and with a few deft moves improved Amalia's looks greatly.

"You're very good to me, Kristina. Tell me, where is Mama this morning?"

"It's her morning with Clothilde."

"Good." Amalia rose and went to greet the baron.

He looked up in concern as Amalia entered the sitting room. "You're all in one piece, I see. I didn't know quite what to expect."

She apologized. "I fear my note was a bit dramatic."

Asking him to be seated, she found she could not meet his eyes and looked down at her hands instead. Her fingernails were torn from her struggles with the trunk. She hid them in fists and prayed that her nerve would not fail her.

"What is it, then, Amalia?"

His use of her first name did not escape her. She looked at him and saw nothing but gentleness there. "You once mentioned that I . . ." she paused, not knowing how to phrase the next part, "that I had some money coming to me for my work."

Von Schoenenburg's brows drew together, but his eyes remained sympathetic. "Yes."

"Do you think I could have it?" She looked at him directly now.

He met her eyes steadily, and when she dropped hers, he said, "Tell me, Amalia. What is this trouble you're in?"

She tried a laugh. "No. It's really just a silly thing, and I won't have you worrying about me. I'm not worth it, you know." She bit her lip hard. "I'm afraid I'm going to have to leave the orphanage, though, after all your kindness."

"If the money will help, it's yours." He removed a small leather portfolio from an inside breast pocket. "But there must be something else I can do. You can't mean to go off somewhere on your own . . ." He handed her a note of large denomination that she was sure she had not earned.

"Just the amount due me, Baron." She smiled. "This is a business arrangement, not a personal loan."

"I honestly haven't the head to total it at the moment, Amalia. And we never did agree on a wage. Let's just say this is what you're worth. The children would say it wasn't enough. We'll all miss you."

"You're too good to be real, you know," she murmured. Then, she reached across and placed her hand on the baron's sleeve. "I'm going away, but I haven't the courage to tell you about it. You'll think too poorly of me. But you mustn't worry. I'll be well looked after."

His hooded brown eyes suddenly seemed as deep and inscrutable as a well. Placing his square hand over hers, he said, "I could never think poorly of you. You have brought the sun into my life."

She withdrew her hand, uncomfortable under his steady regard. "I'll write you a line, giving you my new address. If it isn't too much trouble, I'd like to hear how the children are getting along. I'll do my best to manage the trusts by mail."

"Of course." He looked about to say something more, but at that moment, Georg opened the door.

"Excuse me, Fräulein. I thought you would like to know that there is another caller in the small drawing room."

Exasperated, she asked, "Who, Georg?"

The butler's smoothness had temporarily deserted him. At last he said hesitantly, "Herr Doktor, Fräulein."

Von Schoenenburg rose. "Auf Wiedersehen, then, my dear." He took her hand as she rose and kissed it gently, murmuring, "I'll always be ready to help in any way I can."

She looked at him, but her thoughts were in the drawing room. "I can't thank you enough, Baron. Auf Wiedersehen."

He hesitated a moment, still holding her hand. When she said nothing more, he turned and left.

"Bring Herr Doktor in, please, Georg."

She walked to the window and tried for composure. When Andrzej entered the room, he was beside her in two strides. His hair was wild, but his eyes were soft and repentant. "Amalia is there any chance that you can forgive me?"

She said nothing because she had lost the power.

He took her hand. "I am very, very sorry."

"No. I'm afraid this was the final quarrel, Andrzej," she managed finally. "Please go." Taking her hand away, she held it behind her back, clenched firmly in her other hand.

"I deserve for you to be angry at me. But surely you realize what happened. Maria twisted everything, and you were right. She did play on my pride. I never knew how devilish it was."

Amalia backed away from him and stood behind a chair, gripping it. "I realize very well what happened. And I'm asking you to leave, Andrzej."

"You are determined to punish me a little."

"I really don't care what you feel anymore. I would never be able to believe anything you said, and you wouldn't believe me, so as far as I can see, that is the end of it."

"Amalia! We've had a misunderstanding, and I was terribly angry. But these things happen! I expect it won't be the last time. And I'm repentant. Don't you think you were the slightest bit at fault?" He placed a hand gently on her shoulder, but she drew away.

"I freely admit it," she replied. "But you were ready to condemn me, to throw away every promise, every moment of happiness, our entire future, all because of your pride. We can never re-create what we had, Andrzej."

She walked to the door and held the doorknob. "I'm leaving for Berlin in half an hour. I'm asking you again to go."

"You *are* mad! Amalia, Amalia, apart from everything else, don't you realize we're on the brink of war?"

When she made no answer, he went to her and tried to lead her back into the room. "Nothing's beneath you, is it?" she said. "Since when has war become imminent?"

"Since yesterday!" At her raised eyebrow, he continued, "I'm perfectly serious. Is it possible you don't know that the Archduke Ferdinand was assassinated in Sarajevo the day of Toni's wedding?"

He was serious. She walked slowly to the mantle and turned her back on him to hide her trembling. Gripping the mantelpiece with both hands, she challenged, "So?"

"It's the little spark everyone's been waiting for. Eberhard's probably celebrating. He may even have been mobilized by the time you arrive. This is crazy, Amalia! I can't make myself believe you're doing this!"

He walked up behind her and put his hands gently on her shoulders, "Don't leave me, Amalia. How can you think of marrying someone else? Maria has done us both a great deal of harm, but let's not ruin our lives over it. I'll admit it's all my fault if you like, even though something tells me it's setting a dangerous precedent." He held a hand to her cheek. "The point is, darling, we've got to put it behind us. Let's look to the future. We could be so happy." He kissed her behind the ear as he spoke, and the tension began to ease out of her shoulders under his hands. "I know you love me. You mustn't throw everything away, just because your pride is hurt."

She went rigid and turned to face him. "But that's just what you did, isn't it? How could I ever believe you again when you say you love me one day and then turn on me so easily the next, cursing everything you loved the day before? And all because of *your* pride! You didn't scruple to hit me with everything you had. You didn't just break my heart, Andrzej. You tore it open." She walked to the door again. "I don't care how romantic you try to make it. I can't go through that again. Eberhard may be unimaginative, he may be devoted to things you scorn, but he loves me. That I know. And in the end, devotion is more important than passion."

"A very fine speech, Amalia," Andrzej said. His eyes were bleak, but he didn't try to approach her again. "I'll just leave you with one question before you ruin all three of our lives. Do you love *him?*"

In the end it was Amalia who walked out of the room and shut the door.

Part Two

BERLIN

JULY 1914 TO MARCH 1916

Chapter One

Amalia's compartment on the Munich-Berlin Express was stuffy in the June night. The tearing compulsion that had driven her to flee Vienna had subsided, leaving her exhausted. Any bravado she felt at the beginning of the journey had dwindled to a steady pounding in her head that syncopated with the boom-clack of the train's wheels. Although she had escaped in heroic style, her intentions had little to do with the reality of things. The only thing of which she was certain was that she had succeeded in putting a barrier of distance between herself and Andrzej. She had no idea what awaited her at the end of this journey.

What if Eberhard had been mobilized?

She sat alone in her private compartment, its berth already made up. Reluctant to change into her nightgown, she gazed at her reflection in the darkened window. Amalia put up her hand to hide the white ghost she saw there. Did Eberhard still love her? This short time was all that divided her from tomorrow's uncertain reception.

Sitting there in the dark was irrational. Still, she sat.

It ought to have been easy to picture Eberhard in his uniform, for he had never seemed to belong in civilian clothes, but all she could see was his face as he accused, "Sometimes, Amalia, you're too Viennese for words."

The other face with the green eyes still intruded. Hot, passionate, and full of fury, those eyes still made her tremble and she wondered if the memory always would. Until now she had been so caught up in the details of her journey, she had remained numb. But now those thoughts were seeping through to the present moment, and her heart was raw. *What am I doing?*

The green eyes demanded: *Before you ruin three lives, do you love him?*

No. She busied herself by taking her hair down. But she was very fond of Eberhard. Somehow she would learn to endure those whiskery, harsh kisses. It was a small price to pay for the steadiness of his character. Eberhard was a rock. He had never paid the least attention to Maria's spite. As for Andrzej, well, she must treat him as one of the dandelions in her little walled garden and pull him out of her life by the root. She would have to dig deep, down to the source, down to the very beginning—the waltz. That poisonous waltz that had ruined her peace of mind.

She had chosen. Pulling the brush firmly through her hair, she reminded herself again that she was going to a new life. She was going to have a new husband. Once that root was out of her soul, Andrzej would be nothing to her.

The only light now was from the stars in the summer sky. Though the little hamlets that they passed through might have been Austrian, she reminded herself she was in Germany, Germany, Germany.

A high, wailing screech woke her. The train whistle. How long had she been dozing? Where was she? Staring out the window she saw only night. Was pulling up the root really enough? Hadn't the dandelion's seeds scattered so far and wide inside of her, touching every emotion, every part of her life, that she could never get them all?

Climbing into her berth and pulling the starched white sheets up under her chin, she was reminded that she still had her virtue. That would be the gift she could give Eberhard, the part of her no other man had touched. And in giving that gift, she would displace Andrzej once and for all. She began to shiver and curled herself into a ball, as though protecting herself from a blow. Tensed in that position a long time, listening to the boom-clack of the train, she finally relaxed from pure exhaustion into a troubled sleep.

In the dining car the following morning, Amalia felt tension in her neck and across her shoulder blades. Her act was about to begin. She would play the role until this new life was real. Sipping her chocolate, she perused the *Berliner Tageblatt*.

The paper was full of reports about the assassination, alleging plots by Russia to deliberately insult the German and Austrian people. Serbia and Russia needed a lesson! Russian pretensions were to be decimated once and for all! The assassin had been identified as Gabriel Princips, a member of the anarchist organization "The Black Hand." How could such a small act incite a war? The man was obviously unbalanced. She doubted he had anything to do with the Serbian government and certainly not with Russia. It seemed to her that reason must prevail.

Wearying of the rhetoric, Amalia returned to her compartment to assemble her toilet things and spray herself with a last mist of cologne. Her arrival was imminent. Glad she had chosen to wear the cartwheel hat that hid the night's dishevelment, she thought she was all right until they approached the station. Then she experienced a moment of panic.

For some reason, the station looked grim and foreboding. The platform was alive with Germans, who seemed a race apart. There were no parasols or bright Parisian fashions. Instead there were men in impeccable uniforms who seemed to dwarf their women into insignificance.

Amalia closed her eyes tightly and deliberately summoned a memory of Eberhard on the day he had proposed to her. He had loved her because she made things bright. She had exercised a power over him that had made him discard his stiff, correct outer shell, at least for a few moments now and then. She was Viennese. She was the great-granddaughter of a count. She mattered. She wouldn't let these Prussians destroy her identity.

Thinking of how her grandmother would act, Amalia asked the conductor to summon a porter for her. When her trunk and small case were secure in a grim but spotless black cab, she was on the way to the von Waldburg townhouse.

As the horse pulled her along the streets, her spirits revived. A feeling of restless vitality pulsated from Berlin's long avenues, its shops, its people. It was stately and imposing and there wasn't a speck of litter anywhere. Unlike the Viennese, who strolled with fluid grace disclaiming all urgency, these Berliners walked smartly, quickly. It was only nine o'clock in the morning! Newsboys did a brisk business as everyone wished the latest word on the crisis. Amalia was amused at how many people stood and opened their newspapers on the spot, oblivious to the jostling of their fellow pedestrians.

Her cab drew up in front of a gray stone townhouse, which in spite of the white petunias in the window boxes, looked solid and forbidding. Instructing the driver to wait while she made certain she would be received, Amalia climbed down, walked to the glossy black front door, and rang.

A wizened little man with skin the color of a tobacco stain opened the door in answer to her summons. Yes, Baroness von Waldburg was at home. Who was calling? Would she please wait? The gnome indicated a formal parlor off the white marble hallway.

This room did nothing to alleviate the atmosphere, being stark and without color. The walls and ceiling were white, and a pewter gray carpet lay on the floor. The furniture appeared to be black ebony upholstered in gray. Even the flowers in the room were white—peonies in a silver vase.

"Fräulein Faulhaber? How extraordinary."

Amalia turned, startled by the woman's quiet entry. After the affectations of her house, the Baroness von Waldburg was not a surprise. Her face was small with aristocratic, expressionless features and waxy white skin. Even her hair had no color. Amalia supposed it had once been blonde, like her son's, but now it was completely white. The only thing alive in her face was a pair of intense, blue-black eyes that studied her visitor with blank shock.

* * *

Gertrude von Waldburg couldn't say another word. She had received a blow so sharp, she swayed. The young woman looked exactly like Lorenz. Was she his daughter? No. Of course not. Her name was Faulhaber. Trudi felt herself tremble as the blood left her head.

The eyes that were so much like Lorenz's widened, and suddenly the girl extended her hand to grip Trudi's upper arm. "Baroness! Forgive me. I didn't mean to give you such a shock. Can I call someone? Here, let me help you to a chair. *Himmel!* I think you're about to swoon!"

Together they made their way to her chair by the window. The young Fräulein began chafing her hands. "Baroness von Waldburg, I have wished to know you for a long time. I'm sorry my coming has given you such a shock."

Trudi attempted to gather her wits. Eberhard loved this girl. How could he not? She was as bright and alive as Lorenz. Wetting her dry lips, Eberhard's mother remembered who she was—a baroness, the mother of a twenty-five year-old son. But it was no good. The years seemed to collapse like a telescope to a time when she was this young woman's age, vacationing at Lake Como with an aunt who had taken her there to meet a famous pianist. Looking up from the intensity of Chopin's Revolutionary Etude, her eyes had met the bright blue eyes of a stunning, tall young man with heavy auburn hair falling over his brow. He was looking at her with concentration. Vitality emanated from him in waves that hit her with force.

"You are remarkable," he had said, his voice soft with wonder. "How does a woman so young possess such enormous fervor?"

Closing her eyes, Trudi took a deep breath. She must bring herself back to the present. Straightening herself in the chair and clearing her throat, she said, "Eberhard isn't here at the moment."

The girl smiled tentatively. She had Lorenz's dimple, too. "I don't blame you for being surprised. But I must ask you to excuse my extraordinary behavior, if you can. I understand there may be a war."

Trudi blinked. Yes. The war. Her thoughts flew to her cherished son, and she almost succeeded in banishing Lorenz from her mind.

"I've come all the way from Vienna to see him, Baroness."

This person, whatever her relationship to Lorenz, certainly had his impetuosity. She had apparently traveled alone. Trudi's sense of propriety stirred. "But your family, girl! What can they have been thinking of?"

"I left without their knowing. I won't let them force me into marrying someone I detest. Especially when I still love Eberhard."

The young woman had cast her eyes down and was pleating the skirt of her brilliant sapphire dress with shaking fingers. Admiration displaced Trudi's vague outrage. If only she had been so courageous! How different her life would have been. "You brought luggage?"

"It's in the cab. I didn't know if you would have me."

"My son would never forgive me if I didn't." She rang, and her butler appeared. After instructing him to bring in the Fräulein's luggage, pay the cab, and tell Ludmilla to bring tea, she bade her guest be seated. It was as though sunshine had entered her life. Until now, she had been so full of anxiety for her son, she had been strung tighter than his violin strings. The violin he wouldn't touch.

"You are quite different from what I imagined," she told her visitor.

"You must tell me. Has he been mobilized?"

"Not yet." Standing abruptly, she rearranged the peonies in their vase on her grand piano. "We expect to hear something at any time. He's on leave, actually, pending his orders." She turned around and faced Fräulein Faulhaber. "Tell me about this man your parents wanted you to marry."

"He's a Pole."

Trudi noted color rush into the girl's milk-white face. "A Pole!"

"Of course I couldn't marry him."

"I should think not!"

"Well, there it is then."

Tea arrived, and Trudi busied herself with pouring out. Something didn't feel right. The girl wasn't being truthful with her, and that stirred her anger. She doubted Lorenz had ever lied in his life. "Eberhard's head is full of war at the moment. You really mustn't expect him to be much impressed by this romantic escapade."

Fräulein Faulhaber drank the tea and didn't reply.

What was she to do with the girl? In spite of what she said, she knew her son would be overjoyed to see her. It was inevitable now that they would be married, unexpectedly connecting Trudi with her own lost love in a small way. She had thought the war would be the beginning of an endless vigil. She hadn't known how she could possibly bear it. But with this vital being who had Lorenz's eyes and devil-may-care spontaneity, perhaps she could just about endure it. At any rate, Trudi decided she would give the girl the benefit of the doubt for Lorenz's sake. "You'd better have the front bedroom. If you'll let me have your address, I'll cable your parents. They are undoubtedly anxious." She summoned Theodore once again. "Show Fräulein to the guest room."

*　　*　　*

Amalia looked around her at the glacial primrose and white bedroom that was to be her haven. Did the baroness want her here or not? She had seemed to blow both hot and cold. What a difficult woman! It had never occurred to her in those long hours on the train that if there were a war, she would be alone with Eberhard's mother. As she set about unpacking, she realized she missed Grandmama dreadfully. Without her or her uncle, she was in danger of losing her sense of self in this arctic mansion.

As she ran water into the tub in the bathroom down the hall, she reflected that it was not hard to imagine Eberhard in such a home. She began to understand his fatal fascination and alternating repugnance with the mixed bouquet of passion that was Vienna.

But to think of living in such a place did not actually chill her now. Having so recently been singed, she thought the icy purity of her surroundings would be healing. It would freeze away her feelings.

As she chose what to wear, her instinct told her to capitalize on her own vitality without appearing too loud. She blessed her grandmother for the choice of the mustard and white striped dress with the double-tiered skirt.

Studying her reflection, she hoped Eberhard would find her appealing but not vulgar. She splashed herself with scent and then went to await her fate alone in the cold parlor.

Eberhard's mother did not strike her as the sort that would swoon. What had caused her to experience such a shock? Studying her surroundings, she wondered if the petite woman played the enormous grand piano. She couldn't imagine it at all. Eberhard's mother had seemed to possess a peculiar stillness that would shun strong emotions of any kind. How long was she to sit here alone?

It was half past twelve when she heard Eberhard enter and greet his mother, who had obviously been awaiting his arrival, though not with her uninvited guest in the parlor. Amalia heard the life in her voice. "There you are, Son. Any news?"

"No. Nothing yet. There's some talk of an ultimatum to Serbia, but that must come from Austria, of course. I wish they'd get on with it." She heard the familiar note of impatience in his voice and smiled.

Their voices lowered then, and suddenly Eberhard strode into the room, a giant in splendid uniform, his face flushed with incredulity.

*　*　*

Was she a mirage, standing there brilliant in his mother's gray and white parlor? He didn't feel quite steady. "How can you be *here?*"

"Trains are marvelous, aren't they?" She rose from her chair. "You must have known I could stand only so much of your nobility."

"But you told me . . . Amalia, in your last letter, you said . . ." He found he couldn't repeat the words that had wounded him so deeply. Not in front of his mother.

She extended her hand to be kissed. It was the one with his sapphire on it. Flashing back to the day he had placed it upon her finger, he remembered the joy of possession he had felt. It engulfed him now, and for once careless of his mother's feelings, he took the offered hand

and pulled the woman who consumed him into his arms, held her tightly, and kissed her soundly. When he released her, she hid her head in his tunic, and he could feel her softly weeping. Instinct told him she had been unsure of her welcome, and he kissed her hair.

"Have you really come to me, then?"

"If you still want me." Looking up at him, tears fell as she smiled.

He grasped her hands and looked into her face, examining it feature by feature.

"Have you a handkerchief?" she sniffled slightly, and Eberhard released her hands to search his pockets.

Handing her the starched white square, he asked, "But what of your parents?"

"I left them a letter."

His mother made a little sound in her throat. "Luncheon is waiting."

Over the excellent *Sauerbraten* he could scarcely eat, he marveled at his good fortune. He was being rewarded by the gods for having chosen rightly. And what a prize! "Isn't she courageous, Mother?" he asked with pride.

"That, certainly," the baroness agreed.

"We'll be married as soon as possible, of course," he said.

Amalia smiled the smile that had bewitched him with its warmth. "How long will you have, Eberhard, before you have to go?"

"It depends upon a lot of things." He paused in the act of buttering his bread and looked at her again. Continuing, he said, "I'm on leave just now, as you can see. The unofficial word is that it will continue, pending orders to mobilize. It's anybody's guess when those orders will come. Up to Austria, as a matter of fact. I take your coming as a good omen."

He felt his mother's eyes on his face. "You do seem to be uncommonly blessed," she said with gentle sarcasm.

Eberhard's enthusiasm was threatening to break out. He never recalled feeling so completely alive. Now he had everything. "A crisis does bring everything to a boil. Makes one feel thoroughly alive. One suddenly faces what is important in life. One acts. Look what Amalia has done! If only the rest of her country would take their heads out of the sand."

"I hardly think Amalia's motives can be taken to be representative," his mother remarked.

Eberhard grinned. "But she's here, isn't she? And we're going to be married."

Chapter Two

I suppose you will need something to be married in," Eberhard remarked the following morning at the breakfast table.

"It doesn't really matter." Amalia forced herself to sound off-hand. Her wedding gown had been the subject of many dress-up fantasies when she was growing up. It was to have been out of fairy gauze with drooping sleeves and a long train. She smiled. "It doesn't matter in the least."

After a night of tossing and turning with the guilt of her lies, the last thing she should be concerned about was her wedding gown. Was she threatening her immortal soul by marrying under such false pretenses? Had her pride put her in danger of purgatory? She must seek out a priest for confession before her wedding. There were the lies she had told Andrzej as well. She hadn't been to confession for a long time.

"Not to me, it doesn't," Eberhard said.

But the baroness made an unexpected stand. "Every girl needs a proper wedding gown. It's something to remember." She rose from the table and left them.

Eberhard stared after his mother in amazement but said nothing.

"I wonder how well you know your mother, Eberhard," Amalia murmured.

"Just now, I'm wondering the same. I wouldn't have thought she had a sentimental spot in her whole makeup."

"She loves you very much."

He laughed shortly. "Well, I am her only child." He rose and, kissing her cheek, departed for the officers' club.

*   *   *

Trudi chastised herself for her fantasies. All night she had lain awake with her memories.

Lorenz brushing her long, blonde hair, Lorenz reading Goethe aloud in his lovely voice, Lorenz bending over her, turning the pages of her music, his fingers trembling with the emotion her playing aroused.

"Trudi, you must come away with me," he had pleaded. "Otherwise you will regret it all your life. Can you imagine feeling this with another man? We are two halves of a whole. If you go back to your parents, they will make you marry that man."

"I shall go with you, Lorenz. Gustav would drain me dry, I think."

And he had. But last night, there was only Lorenz. She longed to ask this girl if he still lived, if there was a chance . . .

But now she indulged her fantasy of the wedding gown she would have had, had her stern and proper mother not taken her in charge when Trudi was numb with the grief that she knew would never end. She hadn't even expressed an opinion. Because she was not marrying Lorenz, the wedding gown hadn't mattered.

*   *   *

In the end, Amalia could find nothing but an evening gown whose negligible bodice was studded with silver rocailles, sequins, and seed pearls. The skirt was of ivory chiffon, full and graceful with no crinoline to swell it.

"We are not in France, Frau Colbert," the baroness informed the bogus Frenchwoman who owned the shop. "That is quite inappropriate!"

Amalia put a soothing hand on the baroness's arm. "Wait a moment. Madame Colbert, would you have time to make a matching chiffon tunic to wear over that?"

"The very thing, Mademoiselle! It is what I would suggest. With a little high ruffled collar, so, and the cumberbund of silk. It will be exquisite! And Mademoiselle will tell all her friends about Madam Colbert, *non?*"

Amalia turned to the baroness. "Can you imagine it? It will be lovely, don't you think?"

Her future mother-in-law gave what was for her a gracious smile. "I can see you have quite made up your mind. You don't need my advice."

"Nevertheless, I should like to have it."

"Very well, then. I think it will do nicely. With the tunic, of course."

After having her measurements taken and settling some other small details, Amalia left the salon with Eberhard's mother, feeling happy with her choice. It made the wedding seem more real.

Just before unlatching the door, Eberhard's mother said, "You have very firm ideas for one so young, Fräulein."

Amalia felt herself color. "I suppose I do. I've had to be that way in my family, you see, or I should have been overrun. And I had a rather extraordinary uncle and grandmother."

The baroness surveyed her critically. "I'd say there was very little chance of your being overrun."

They entered the townhouse, and Amalia followed her into the parlor. Consulting the watch that was pinned to her bodice, the little woman remarked, "We have a few moments before my son is due." She pierced Amalia with her blue-black eyes. "I must say, I don't think you've been entirely frank with me, Fräulein. You must remember, Eberhard is all I have."

Amalia forced herself not to look away. This was her chance to makes things better. "I do understand that, Baroness von Waldburg. Believe me, he is all I have, too."

"I won't have him used."

"Why is it you don't like me?"

The older woman knotted her hands in her lap. "I do like you, Amalia, very much, as a matter of fact. But what I really can't understand is why you want to marry my son. You and he are very different."

"But you see, Baroness, that is why. He is strong and honest. I have not met with those qualities very often. I think they are of the utmost importance in one's husband. Surely, you agree?"

The baroness's waxy face remained expressionless as she picked up her workbasket. "It is a fact, however, that girls of nineteen are usually more interested in a grand romance than in these qualities you describe. And however much you admire him, I don't think you love my son."

"You can't know!"

The baroness put her work down in her lap and once again looked into Amalia's eyes. "I am not mistaken about this. I know what it is to love. I rather think you are not telling the truth about that Pole. But if you are determined to marry Eberhard for some reason of your own, I must tell you that neither of us will tolerate any indiscretions on your part. There will be no *affaires de coeur* or grand Viennese passions. I am not blind. I can see that for Eberhard you are like the sun. I won't have him hurt. Do you understand?"

"How could you think me capable of such a thing?"

"As much as I like you, and as much as Eberhard loves you, I can't help thinking this marriage is a mistake."

"What must I do to convince you that my eyes are open? I think it better not to be deceived by one's passions. They can so easily blind one to the more important things."

The woman did not even look up. "That sounds grand, but it hasn't been my personal experience. Have you really left this Pole behind you? In every sense of the word?" Her tone was not accusing, just pathetic and sad.

All at once, the front door opened, and Eberhard himself strode into the room, large, smiling, and alive with news.

The unofficial word was that Austria had prepared an ultimatum in terms exceedingly humiliating to Serbia. They had decided not to deliver it immediately, because Serbia's ally, Russia, was conferring in Paris with Britain and France. Eberhard patiently explained the existing pattern of entangling alliances. "Russia and Serbia are together in this. If Russia attacks us, we must not give France the chance to attack our rear. No, we will attack first, which will no doubt bring in the English against us, too. But our two great empires are a match for them," he said confidently. "No sense in giving that group a chance to discuss the ultimatum. Austria will wait until the Russians have gone home."

Then with a smile exuding well-being, he remarked. "So, we have time not only for a wedding but for a honeymoon as well."

He had also received word from his uncle, who was to accompany his commanding officer, General von Kluck, on a visit to the military commander, Falkenhayn, in Berlin on the sixteenth.

"He can be with us on the seventeenth, if we want to have the wedding then, Amalia. I'd like him there. Sort of a stand-in for Father. How does that sound?"

"Perfect, darling. Now all we have to do is settle about the flowers and see the priest at the church. I'm certain the banns are still good. He'll probably have to cable Bishop Benedict about them, though."

The baroness's head jerked up sharply from her needlework, and Eberhard said quickly, "That should be easy enough. Now that things are settled for the immediate future, I needn't haunt the club for news. We'll go to the florist on Unter den Linden tomorrow and then have lunch at the Kroll in the Tiergarten. I haven't done that in years. Perhaps we could even row on the river in the afternoon."

Amalia smiled at her fiancé. A day alone with him would be welcome. Especially after the disconcerting discussion with his mother. Would she discuss her suspicions with Eberhard? Amalia's conscience was not easy.

"Perhaps you could take me to the priest first. I should like to meet him."

"We'll go, first thing," her fiancé promised and gave her hand a squeeze.

That night as she lay in bed, she replayed the conversation with the baroness in her mind, along with other haunting phrases. *Before you ruin three lives, do you love him? This marriage is a mistake. There will be no grand passion. Most people can only give love once. Then it isn't yours to give.*

The baroness needn't have worried. Heady passion had brought Amalia nothing but unhappiness. Eberhard was big, bold, real. His love was not an illusion. He would never fail her. *Devotion is better than passion.*

So why did she still shrink at his embrace?

The matter of the church presented a small problem. Though Eberhard had converted to Catholicism for her sake in Vienna, his family was Protestant. At an opportune moment during breakfast, Amalia said, "If I'm not married by a Catholic priest, I won't feel married at all."

Baroness von Waldburg sighed. "I don't suppose it really matters. I haven't been religious for a long time."

"It's all the same to me, Protestant or Catholic," Eberhard said. "We'll be married at St. Maria's."

St. Maria's was a small, very old church that predated Martin Luther. It was in the back streets and had a smell of damp. Standing by the River Spree, it possessed two dirty rose windows and one gothic spire. Inside it was dark. Amalia saw from the notice on the door that confessions were heard every morning. She was in luck.

"Wait here, Eberhard," she told her fiancé in the nave of the church. "The priest is hearing confessions. I will go talk to him."

"Bless me, Father, for I have sinned," she said once she entered the gloomy confessional. "It has been six months since my last confession."

"I am here, my child," the priest said, his voice low and gentle.

"I have lied," Amalia said, tears starting to her eyes, "to the man I loved and meant to marry. And now to the man I will marry and his mother."

"This is rather a complicated business, my daughter. You can be forgiven if you say the rosary, but will that make things right in your heart?"

What an unusual priest, Amalia thought. She hesitated.

"I sense there is a story here that you had better tell me. My name is Father Ignatius. Proceed when you are ready."

It was a great relief, after all, to tell someone the truth. She related the entire charade over Eberhard that she had played with Andrzej, his reaction, her consequent flight to Berlin, and the lies she had told since her arrival. When she had finished, Father Ignatius said, "You have misrepresented yourself to the man you will marry. This is not an auspicious beginning. He sounds a worthy man. Is he of the Church?"

"He is now."

"And shall I marry you?"

"Yes, if you please. We should like to be married at the end of the week. Bishop Benedict at St. Stephens in Vienna has pronounced the banns of marriage. You may cable him for confirmation."

There was a long pause. "Marriage in the Church is a sacred sacrament. It is for life. It is not to be undertaken on a foundation of lies, my daughter."

Her heart fell into her middle. "I vow in the name of the Holy Virgin that I will make Eberhard a good wife. He is very deserving. He is good to me. Passions of the flesh are quite deceiving, I think."

"Passions of the flesh are at the root of adultery, a mortal sin. You cannot know what temptations will come to you. You are young."

"I will never see Andrzej in my life again. He detests Germany, and this will be my home, Father. When I left Vienna, I left my passions behind. I will be a good wife."

"Then there is the business of the banns of marriage. This is quite irregular, my daughter. You are to be married in my parish."

"Yes, but there is the threat of war, you see, and we can't afford to wait three weeks."

She heard a heavy sigh. "Say your rosary before the Virgin, and I will see what I can do. Come back and see me tomorrow."

For the first time in her life, Amalia did not feel as though a burden had been lifted when she left the confessional. Even after she had said her rosary.

Eberhard was insistent that her bridal bouquet be lilies of the valley with a matching circlet to crown the veil of chiffon she was making herself. Small nosegays of yellow roses and gardenias were ordered for

Eberhard's mother and his cousin Lilli, whom, it was hoped, would accompany her father and stand in as Amalia's bridesmaid. The men would be in uniform, so there was no need for boutonnieres. Clearly, her wedding was to be straightforward and free of all Schmäh. That, for some reason, made her feel less of a hypocrite.

Stepping out onto the boulevard once more, they headed towards the Brandenburg Gate and the Tiergarten beyond.

"I never imagined Berlin was so lovely," Amalia said, endeavoring to please her fiancé and assuage the guilt that wouldn't leave.

"Different from Vienna, though," Eberhard answered. "Vienna is like some huge volatile mass, a sort of imperial mongrel. You've everything in your shops from Bosnian folk dress to Parisian evening gowns." He patted the hand that rested on his arm. "But in Prussia we are simply Prussians. Very set in our ways and proud of it, I suppose."

"And being Protestant is part of the code. Did you mind very much having been baptized?"

"It mattered to you. That's the main thing. Shall you miss your cosmopolitan Vienna?"

She looked at the massive Brandenburg Gate with its green copper chariot and four horses. "Oh, perhaps someday I will want to go back for a long visit. After this war of yours. But right now I am content to be here with you. It is only my grandmother I miss."

He was silent for a while and then said, "Last night I decided I was perfectly mad to be marrying you just when war seems inevitable. You know, I can't really picture you in that house alone with Mother. You are used to such a different life."

She forced a smile and squeezed his arm. Everyone seemed to be conspiring to give her second thoughts. "What else do I have to do to show you I'm serious about this?"

Chapter Three

They enjoyed a light luncheon at the outdoor Kroll Garden to the music of a German band. The air was clear and just pleasantly warm. A breeze barely stirred their canopy of chestnut trees.

"It's hard to believe there will be a war," Amalia said.

Eberhard studied his fiancée in the sunlight. As beautiful as ever, she seemed, if anything, overly bright. He had sensed that something was troubling her since her visit with the priest, and he had been endeavoring to put out of his mind the man she had written about. The one she loved with all her soul. Suddenly assaulted by the idea that perhaps his beloved had lost her virtue, he wondered if she would ever be truly his.

Listening to the martial band, he knew very well it wasn't to her taste. All at once, it struck him that she was making a show of devotion. The only explanation he could think of was that the man had deserted her.

"Amalia . . . I think there is something we should discuss."

She looked at him in mild surprise.

"What happened after I left Vienna? Who was the man who finally won your love?"

Her cheeks flushed, and her eyes showed the panic of a trapped animal. "Isn't it enough to know it is over between us, Eberhard? He taught me to appreciate your devotion. He was inconstant. He had a liaison with Maria von Beckhaus."

Eberhard was momentarily stunned. He himself had found Maria quite accommodating. He shifted his gaze, looking steadfastly at the band. Was he anyone to judge her?

"Eberhard," she said solemnly, looking up from under her lashes. "I was hurt deeply. I came running to you because I believed in your love for me. In time, I will learn to forget him, I promise you."

She had come running to him. Didn't that argue great feeling on her part? An urge to protect that was new to him rose in his breast, dissolving his doubts. He would salve her wounded heart. He would earn her love. "My poor darling," he said, taking her hand and kissing it. "I will try to be worthy of your trust."

Then he changed the subject. "Our High Command plans on about six weeks. I expect I'll be home before the first frost. We can go to the estate for Christmas."

"It would be heaven to have Christmas in the country," Amalia said with a smile. She was blinking back tears but squeezed his hand. "Tell me about the estate."

"It's fairly medieval still. I don't suppose the hall has been changed since it was built in the thirteenth century. You will rattle around in it, I'm afraid. I'm far more at home here where things are always happening."

"Were you very bored, then, growing up?"

Should he tell her about his father? Not the whippings with his crop. He could never tell her about those. It would only show him as a coward. As would his hiding under the bed when his father had bullied and beaten his mother. "Actually, it wasn't a very happy time, Amalia. I don't like to think of it much."

Her brightness dimmed a little, and she peered into his face, as though trying to read his meaning. "Is that when you took up the violin?"

"Only when Father was off campaigning, which he was much of the time. I did it to please my mother. She's an excellent pianist. I think it was a great solace to her." Now that he was in love himself, he thought about his mother's life in a different way. How cold and barren it had been! "We used to perform together."

"I would love to hear you again sometime," she said. "Those are some of my happiest memories. You really have a talent, Eberhard."

He felt threatened and impatient at this talk. Shaking his head, he replied, "I've given up the violin."

* * *

When they returned that evening and the baroness had retired, Amalia went to sit on the arm of her fiancé's chair and kiss him on the cheek. She really must try to love him.

"Tell me something, Eberhard. Why did you ever allow yourself to fall in love with me?"

He laughed and playfully pinched her hand. "Heaven knows. Since I met you, I've never known a moment's peace."

"I'm perfectly serious. I want to know."

After a few moments his expression sobered. "We're very different, you and I. One might say we view the world from different poles. But have you ever noticed how human nature seems to long for a balance?" He took her hand in his. "It's hard to describe the effect you have had on me. It hurt at first. Like too much light."

Amalia's playfulness deserted her to be replaced by a dart of guilt. She could see in that moment how much he loved her and that his love was like a rough plow harrowing up his stoic roots. Her feelings for him caused no like stirring. Is that what the baroness had detected?

Seeking some neutral topic, she said, "I've often wondered why you ever came to Vienna to study. Why not Heidelberg or some other German university?"

"Mother."

Amalia raised her eyebrows.

"I see you don't believe me, but the fact is, Mother never wanted me to become a soldier." He stroked her hand absently. "When Father died, she made me promise to try Vienna for two years to see what it made of me."

"I find that unbelievable! That doesn't seem at all like your mother."

"She's got another side to her, Amalia. My father was difficult. She cultivated a hard shell, but inside she is warm and loving. I hope you will come to know that side." He paused, stroking her cheek with reverence. "I expect she thought if she got me out of Germany for a bit, I should broaden my horizons." He was silent for a moment. Looking beyond her, he mused, "It was hard to go against her wishes, but I was raised by my father from the time I could walk to be a soldier."

"Her scheme didn't work, obviously."

He grinned. "I don't know. She half succeeded. It seems I'm to have a Viennese wife."

The next day, they walked through the Avenue of Victory, where Eberhard pointed out to her the grand and heroic monuments to the men of might who had made Prussia great. She thought of her uncle and his assessment of the Prussian character.

How sad that Eberhard seemed to be ashamed of his talent! It occurred to her, not for the first time, that the person he was when he performed was the the only man she knew. This soldier was a stranger. It was the violinist who truly loved her. Even he was aware of the inconsistency in his character. Would he be ashamed of his love for her one day? Would he try to cut her out as well? She shivered, as though it had already happened.

"Cold, Amalia? It must be the warmest day of the summer!"

"Do you think of me as a weakness, Eberhard?"

Her fiancé frowned and seemed to struggle with the question. "I did once, in Vienna. But no longer. I know it sounds fanciful, but I feel as though the gods have given you to me. You complete me, Amalia." He took her hand and pulled her arm through his. "I hope, in time, that my love for you will heal you as well."

Amalia ruminated on these words and found that she didn't have much faith in them. The soldier could never possess her soul as Andrzej had done. Their relationship was like a poorly constructed puzzle. She didn't fit naturally into the life Eberhard had chosen. He just didn't realize it yet. But when he commenced fighting? There would be nothing to link her to that Eberhard. What would she do then?

Uncle Wilhelm, a colonel in the Kaiser's army, arrived as promised on the night of the sixteenth. He was a very large man with a grand red mustache and hair to match.

He let his eye run over Amalia. "I'm not disappointed, Eberhard," he boomed, clapping him on the shoulder. "The Catholic business doesn't really matter, you know." The two men disappeared into the library, where they discussed those things that, even at this moment, were dearest to their hearts.

She was left to entertain Wilhelm's daughter and Maria von Beckhaus's intimate friend, Lilli von Waldburg. A redhead with the unusual combination of brown eyes and olive skin, Lilli greeted her with an ironic twist to her smile. "So, Amalia. You've just about done it. Are you sure you won't think again? We can be off to Vienna in the dead of night. After a day, I've certainly had my share of Berlin for a while."

So Lilli knew. Anxious to get her away from Eberhard's mother, who was eyeing Lilli curiously, Amalia fashioned a bright grin. Taking the young woman's arm, she said, "Come! I'll show you my gown!"

Once upstairs, Eberhard's cousin ran a hand over the creamy chiffon. "But it looks just like you! However did you find it in this dreary place?"

Amalia related the tale of Madame Colbert.

"Yours has to have been the artistic eye behind it. She has no imagination."

"And is no Frenchwoman, either."

Lilli's eyes sparked with mischief as she seated herself at Amalia's spartan oak vanity. "I've just come from Vienna, you know. You checked Maria brilliantly. Andrzej won't have a thing to do with her.

He even claims she made up the whole thing to spite you. But hadn't you better go home to collect your winnings?" Lilli smiled her entrancing smile. "I can't see much point in your going through with this farce."

Before Amalia could reply, Lilli added, "It's rather a shame no one believes Maria's story, since it was basically the truth." Leaning over to inspect her flawless coiffure in the mirror, she went on. "Andrzej looks quite hollow and has announced himself to be thoroughly fed up with Vienna. I suppose he spends every waking hour at the hospital these days."

Turning to face Amalia, she continued, "The honors lie with you. Why throw it all to the winds?"

"You are a devil, Lilli," Amalia said as pain sliced through her. This was the last thing she needed to hear the night before her wedding. Was it right that she should proceed with her course when she had failed so totally to dismiss Andrzej from her mind? Late at night, he still visited her, alternately teasing or enraged. Or reading her worthless soul, ticking off the lies on his fingers. "Please don't speak of it."

"Seriously, what can you possibly see in my cousin? He's such a stick!"

Amalia hung the gown in the wardrobe. "More like a rock, I would say. I'm going to marry him, Lilli. He's good to me." She repeated the incantation she always used in the night.

Eberhard's cousin stood with her hands on her hips. "There's nothing duller than a rock. It'll be a disaster, Amalia! Imagine a whole lifetime with nothing but marble. This house feels like a monument or something."

"One can count on a monument. It's always there."

Lilli rolled her eyes. "Where is your spirit of adventure? Maybe he's what you deserve after all."

"Shall we join your aunt?"

As Amalia lay alone in her bed the night before her wedding, Lilli's words and her own concerns wove in and out of her thoughts.

It was an enormous step she was taking, and she was well aware she was only going in this direction because hurt and pride dictated it. *How could God possibly bless such a union?* she asked herself often but never received an answer. Now she suspected God had forsaken her because of her wickedness, despite Father Ignatius and the rosary. She had visited the little priest again, and he had probed but finally agreed to marry her to Eberhard when she remained obdurate. He reminded her once again that adultery was a mortal sin.

To her surprise, she had heard nothing in reply to Trudi's telegram to her parents. Her grandmother had written, however.

> You are quite mad, Amalia. Come home before it is too late. You have known love, real love. This union will never do. Andrzej has been here every day, hoping to hear that you have called it off. I never thought to see him so devastated.

Amalia burned the letter. She had found new purpose. Eberhard needed her to feed the part of his soul he couldn't acknowledge to anyone else. She would make him happy; that should do for her penance. But a lifetime's penance for a few lies and her pride? How disappointed her uncle would be in her.

A collage of memories, entirely of Vienna, took hold of her subconscious as she dozed. When she finally slept, she dreamed she was twirling through the Prater amusement park with a green-eyed panther on a Sunday afternoon. The German army invaded, this time led by the mustachioed Uncle Wilhelm, who pointed at her with his riding crop and bellowed, "The waltz! We do not permit it here!"

The church where Amalia Eugenia Faulhaber married Eberhard Nicholas von Waldburg on July 17, 1914, might have been small compared to St. Stephen's Cathedral in Vienna, but it was adequate. The couple made their vows in one of the small chapels, with only Uncle Wilhelm, Lilli, and Gertrude von Waldburg, erect in their Protestant disdain, as witnesses.

Amalia's mind would not focus on the nuptial mass. She felt foreign among all these Berliners. Maybe it was their uniforms or maybe the sad-eyed priest. Looking down at the bouquet in her hands, she felt near panic as though Amalia Faulhaber were being obliterated. She was now the young Baroness von Waldburg. But who was *that?*

Eberhard slid a slim gold band next to her sapphire, his own hands like ice. His mouth trembled slightly as he kissed her, and she felt an unexpected revulsion. *Oh, Andrzej, Andrzej, what have I done?*

The following half hour was a blur as a carriage conveyed them to the station. An hour's train journey would take them to the Spreewald, where they were to have a week's honeymoon. They spoke hardly at all. Her life had changed forever.

Their destination was a welcome surprise. Spiritually, if not actually, it was miles from Berlin. A small rowboat served as their taxi. A friendly fellow with large black eyes and the high cheekbones of a Slav manned it. Waterways formed the byways of the little town, which spread itself over the land amidst some two hundred branches of the River Spree. The unexpected novelty diminished Amalia's apprehensions.

"Can we still be in Germany?" she asked. "This seems to be a rural version of Venice."

The approach to the honeymoon cottage reminded Amalia of one of her orphans' favorite fairy tales. The river bank was mossy and thick with vegetation out of which a gnome might creep at any time. Willows drooped over the water, and there, amidst a small wood, was a thatched cottage, whitewashed and with a blooming rose garden.

While the boatman was busy with their luggage, Eberhard said, "Ever since we became engaged, I have pictured bringing you here for our honeymoon."

"I never would have accused you of so much imagination."

His arm went around her waist. "You have an unsettling effect on me. Do you think I'm fanciful?"

At that moment, a large young woman, undoubtedly a Spreewalderin, emerged from the cottage wearing the most extraordinary headdress Amalia had ever seen. An enormous, shoulder-width bow was mounted mysteriously on the back of her head, draped with an embroidered, fringed kerchief that complemented the brilliant red and blue of the shawl she clasped to her bosom.

"*Herr Oberleutnant* von Waldburg? *Wilkommen!*" the woman cried.

As she led them into the dwelling, Eberhard leaned down and whispered, "It's called a *Tucher*, that thing on her head."

Scrupulously kept, the cottage smelled of pine. Her new husband nodded at their hostess. "This will do very well, gnädige Frau."

Amalia pulled off her gloves and walked to the window. It was like something from a fantasy, and coming on top of her disconcerting wedding ceremony, it was doubly disorienting.

"However did you hear about this cottage?"

Eberhard walked about on the oak floors, poking his head into rooms. "Gliedt. Man in my regiment. Seems he married a Spreewalderin. She was nursemaid to a family in Berlin when he met her."

"He was smitten by her headdress, I imagine," Amalia giggled, trying to stifle her uneasiness at being left alone with her husband.

"He comes up here on leave and stays in this place. No one lives here. They just let it out. It seemed providential."

Amalia forced a smile as she turned to face her husband. "Well, if our hostess is in any way typical, I am sure Herr Gliedt must have a very devoted wife."

"I dare any man to produce a finer wife than mine," Eberhard said softly.

Despite the fairytale cottage and the tranquillity of the countryside, Amalia knew little peace or happiness in the days that followed. During that time, her body became a stranger to her. The shell she lived in had married a man, a good man, but no matter how she willed it, her inner spirit could not unite with Eberhard's.

She *had* made an unforgivable mistake. The priest had tried to warn her. Trudi had tried to warn her. Her uncle and grandmother had tried to warn her. And, of course, Andrzej. She had even had her doubts, but how could she have understood before marriage the true nature of intimacy? Now she had polluted a sacred thing with her deceit. Her act was unforgivable because one could offer oneself wholly only once, and she had done so without love.

Even if Eberhard did not perceive it, it was impossible to blind herself on this point. A hard core grew inside her, protecting her deepest awareness—her soul—from her husband's possession. Steeling herself not to shrink when he approached her, she could only pray that he would not notice. Willing herself not to feel anything, she became an actress.

Eberhard seemed to be unaware that he did not possess her wholly. As the peaceful days passed, his tenderness grew more open, until on the last evening his face and demeanor were so softened that they were painful for Amalia to observe.

*　*　*

They sat before the small fire that took the chill out of the night air, Eberhard at his bride's feet, his head against her knee. Never had he felt such content. He hadn't had a lot of experience with women, but their wedding night had confirmed that she was all his. Amalia was a gently bred, fastidious girl with no previous experience. In time, he was certain things would become more satisfactory.

"God bless you for this, my dear," he whispered. He sat upright and reached for her hand. "Do you know what your gift to me is?"

She raised her eyebrows in query.

"An awakening." He stared into the fire once more. "It sounds absurd, but there is a part of me that's just now coming alive. Like a barren tree that is finally giving fruit, if that doesn't sound too fanciful. Perhaps we will have a son." For a moment he was pensive, considering it. "Ever since I was a boy I've seen glimpses of the home I want. But I thought they were illusions."

"Why?"

He thought of the beatings, his mother's tears, his father's bellowing, the continual threat of the crop. "Because my home was grim, and I had no reason to suppose that anyone's home was otherwise."

Amalia was still. He wondered if his admission shocked her. But, finally, she said, "I think I can understand that." He wondered if she did.

Rising, he pulled her to her feet. "Now, do you know how I feel?"

"How?"

"As though I, a mere mortal, have tricked the gods and contrived to have everything." Pulling her to him, he whispered into her hair, "Now if only the war would just come."

Chapter Four

When they returned to Berlin, the news was that Austria had at last delivered its humiliating ultimatum to Serbia. The Kaiser was due back from a vacation in Norway in two days.

After hearing this, Eberhard left for his club in a state approaching jubilation. Amalia lunched with her mother-in-law.

"It appears the honeymoon was a great success," she said as she helped herself to the dainty *Schinkenrolle*. "I've never seen Eberhard so whole. It is what I had hoped Vienna would teach him, and you have done it in a week."

Amalia nearly choked at the praise. "You could tell?"

"It was obvious. I only hope the marriage will be as good for you as it has been for him. You seem quite unchanged."

"I am glad to have made him so happy."

Her mother-in-law's eyes were so soul penetrating that Amalia dared not risk a lie.

The cozy privacy of the honeymoon retreat seemed idyllic compared to the formality of the cold dining room. Amalia focused on a Dutch still-life that hung over the sideboard. The painted mound of citrus provided the only visual warmth in the room.

Lilli's description of the house as a monument distilled in her mind. This was her home now. Would her own personality ever be allowed to make its imprint here?

"Eberhard was telling me about the estate. It sounds magnificent. We hope to be able to visit there soon."

"It's doubtful now, Amalia. You must realize that war is a virtual certainty." The baroness's eyes hardened at the words.

"Yes, but Eberhard says the High Command feels it will last only six weeks."

"It all depends on Belgium."

"Belgium? What has Belgium got to do with it?"

"The tactics for this war have been perfected over decades. As a matter of fact, Eberhard's father used to talk to me about this Schlieffen Plan when it was late and he'd had too much to drink." Trudi rose from the table. "We shall await events, my dear. All should be decided in the first weeks. In Belgium, in fact. Then we'll know whether this war is to be a short one or whether it is to be a long, drawn-out test of wills."

The words chilled Amalia. She had never counted on a long war. But the "my dear" from her mother-in-law was not lost on her.

*   *   *

Eberhard returned home that night in excellent humor, bounding up the stairs several at a time like a child on holiday. As he dressed, he pictured himself marching through Belgium, their army making its way to Paris like a knife through butter—the goal of decades of Prussians. As a victor, he would be able to take Amalia to a France that would be part of the German Empire and she could have all the clothes her heart desired.

But he was beginning to feel that there was more to his wife than had met his hungry eyes and soul. Though he was certain he possessed her physically, on the train home she seemed aloof, drawing further away the closer they got to Berlin. He knew she did not relish the idea of war as he did. Perhaps that was it. Perhaps she was worried for him. Worried that he might be killed.

Shaking off the thought along with his uniform, he dressed in evening clothes and wondered how he could reassure her. Pausing, he looked at himself in the mirror. How he could reassure *himself*? He was aware that he was nothing like his father. But in the army, he had the feeling that he was part of something noble, something grander than himself. Amalia had once accused him of being a Romantic. He knew deep in his heart that she was right.

* * *

Several days later, when they were all worn to threads with the strain, Trudi and Amalia, who had been doing a linen inventory, were surprised to hear themselves hailed from downstairs. Trudi's heart clenched at the exultant cry.

They hastened down to find a joyful Eberhard. "It's started!" he crowed, sweeping Amalia into his arms and swinging her around.

Then seeing his mother on the stairs, he went to her and took both her hands. "Mother! It's going to go after all!"

Trudi stood looking dumbly into her son's radiant face. A memory flashed into her mind, almost blinding her: Eberhard standing with just such a triumphant face when he had placed first in the Mendelssohn violin competition. She had been certain that her beloved boy who was now in his twenties was all hers to love. That he would take the road she would have taken, had she been a man. He would become world renowned. His love for his art would purge his soul, cleansing him of the Prussian taint. He would become a man who could love with his whole heart. Like Lorenz Reichart.

Now she examined each of his dear features—the sky blue eyes, sparkling with idealism, the stubborn mouth that belonged solely to his father, and the aristocratic nose he had inherited from her. That mouth bothered her. Her husband's had screamed cruelties and obscenities. How could her gentle Eberhard *not* be changed by the war?

* * *

Amalia watched. *Can't he see the anxiety in his mother's face?*

"I predict we'll be at war within the week," he sang out.

Amalia left her mother-in-law to her private grieving and trailed out into the garden. The bees buzzed around Trudi's prize roses. It was so strange that she felt nothing but Trudi's reflected grief. But then, she had never lived through a war.

In the end, she was actually anxious for Eberhard to go. He wasn't the gentle Eberhard of Spreewald, as painful as that had been for her, but a stranger obsessed by a code of ideals she couldn't understand. He spent very little time at home. And when he was there, he spared no thought for her in their intimacies but was urgent and careless.

When she saw him off at the station, he called over his shoulder, "Be waiting for me to come home in six weeks!"

With Eberhard's departure, Amalia recommenced her journal writing, prompted by the vague idea that her uncle would have wanted her to document this war from her own viewpoint. She wrote now with a perspective different from that of the girl she had been in Vienna.

Journal
4 August 1914

Three days ago, Germany declared war on France and Russia. I'm not really certain how France became involved in all of this. It's like Europe is a gigantic mob, waiting for one man to slip and fall. The slip, I assume, was the assassination at Sarajevo. But now everyone has piled on top of one another and the initial incident seems forgotten. The tension has been broken and there is a feeling, "At last! We are at war."

Trudi says that Eberhard's army (the First) was one of those that invaded Belgium yesterday. As a result, England has declared war against Germany as well. Austria is busy fighting Serbs.

I feel nothing but numbness. So much has happened in my life so fast, after so many years when it seemed that everything was so everlastingly the same. It is only five weeks since I fled Vienna, thinking myself so brave and adventurous. Now I am not only removed completely from my family but living in a country more foreign to me than I could have imagined. It is ironic that I find myself more cloistered now than ever. But I chose this, and I will see it through. For poor Trudi's sake, I cannot help but be glad I am here.

*   *   *

The days crawled by with a kind of high-strung tedium, punctuated by newspaper reports of German victories as its armies swept through Belgium. Trudi had set up a map on the wall of her husband's study, with pins representing the position of the victories reported in the news. The Schlieffen Plan had been drilled into her so completely that she knew it as well as any of the generals and probably better than the common soldier. And she was worried, despite the successes reported. "They should have taken Liège by now," she kept telling Amalia. She could only be grateful for the girl's company. Often they would sit together in the parlor, Amalia working on monogramming linens and Trudi knitting socks for her son in case winter came before he made it home. For a few weeks, she had struggled to call her Mutter, but unexpectedly, Trudi had suggested Amalia call her by her first name.

One evening she said, "Oh, Trudi, I do miss my uncle. But I'm glad he's been spared this war."

Trudi's heart bounded in her breast and then sank. "He is dead, then?"

"Yes. Just after Christmas."

"You were close?"

"I was closer to Uncle than anyone in the world. You probably wouldn't have approved of him. He was a socialist and lived very simply, giving away all his fortune to charity. I have been quite busy lately trying to take care of his business by post. The board meetings were held before I left, but there are always the day-to-day things. Baron von Schoenenburg has been a great help, but of course, he is off to war now, too." She paused abruptly. "Do you know, I think I must return to Vienna for my board meetings at the beginning of September. There are only five charities, so it won't take long. I will plan so that I'll only be gone a week."

Trudi sat very still, hoping Amalia wouldn't notice her silence. *So he had gone through with it! He had given away his inheritance. Would he*

*have done so if her father hadn't caught her leaving the house that night
and prevented their elopement?*

"Yes, you must follow Lorenz's wishes," she said definitely.

There was a silence. "How did you know his name was Lorenz?"
Amalia asked.

Trudi froze. "You must have mentioned his name," she said finally.
"I can't think how else I would know it. Tell me about him, Amalia. He
sounds a most unusual man. Did he ever marry?"

Amalia stitched for a while in silence. "No. He was forever devoted
to a lost love. He said he hadn't love to give to anyone else." Her voice
faded away almost to a whisper.

But the words were an instant shot of pure happiness to Trudi.
Unable to sit still, she rose exuberantly and went to her piano. From
memory, she played the Revolutionary Etude, by Chopin, with a gusto
that she hadn't felt since that summer on Lake Como.

She didn't even notice that her daughter-in-law was weeping, until
Amalia got up and rushed from the room. Too late, she remembered
Chopin was Polish.

In mid-August, Amalia received her second letter from Grandmama.

Dearest Amalia:

I don't know what to say. Andrzej still comes to see me, of course,
but I can't think that he has told me everything.

Your parents, as you can imagine, are having a dreadful time, losing all their children at once. And, at the risk of making you feel
more horrid still, I must confess that I, too, miss you terribly.

This war is not going to be exciting. It will be a dreary affair, I
think. Serbs! They are not even gentlemen.

After Andrzej, I fear that Eberhard will not be exciting, either.
Did he hurt you? Andrzej, I mean. I think he must have. You are so
very earnest and proud, my dear. He should have known this.
Although I blame him for your going away, I cannot help but be
sorry for him. He is with me often, and there is such tension in him!

He looks dreadful and acts not the least bit charming. But I must suffer it. I imagine it is not a happy thing to know that you have lost something of value forever. Poor fellow! Apparently Lilli von Waldburg has given him a detailed account of your wedding, right down to a description of your wedding gown. I know it is the hardest thing in the world for him to know that you belong to someone else.

And you, dear! How I wish you had come to me with your troubles. We could certainly have found a less drastic solution! Nevertheless, I wish you well. I can't think that you will like Berlin.

Perhaps it is only because I am old that I feel this, but I fear things will never be the same. The ancient are sometimes fanciful, however.

Mit liebende grüsse,
Grandmama Eugenia

Amalia's response to the news this letter carried was to plunge it deep into her secret core before she could even feel it. This letter she also burned, should she weaken and want to read it again.

How was she ever to go back to Vienna, even for a short while? But she owed it to her uncle. She set about writing letters to her charities, arranging dates and times for her meetings there. Staying with her parents would be the right thing, though she would much rather have stayed with her grandmother.

She had finally received an uncomfortable letter from her mother.

Dear Amalia,

There have been many sad changes here since you left us. Your departure was but the first blow. We were entirely unaware of your intentions, and that hurt us very much. We had come to think that you would be married to that Polish doctor. Though he is not what I would have wished for, at least you would have been here in Vienna. Your grandmother, I believe, still sees him in spite of it all.

That Maria von Beckhaus tried to start some scandal, and I am afraid that must have been what drove you to Berlin. But you have always shown yourself to be so brave and heedless of convention, so it all seemed very odd to me.

This war, of course, is also very upsetting. I was not in favor of it, and Wolf thinks it an unwise course pressed on us by Germany, although he was ready enough to go and fight. And so, we have lost him as well. We pray daily for his safety, as well as for that of our two sons-in-law.

We expected dear Antonia to move to Salzburg upon her marriage to Erich, of course, but under the circumstances it has been especially difficult.

I have been unwell. I wonder if I might, like Lorenz, have a weak heart. I certainly can't seem to bear this strain. Don't you think it would be better for you to come home to Vienna for the duration of the war? I may not be alive when it is over. While I abhor what you have done, I am still your mother and you are still my daughter.

Please come home. As a baroness, all doors would be open to you, and it would be such a comfort for me to get out in what little society there is.

Mama

Somehow she would have to convince Mama that she couldn't go about in society while Eberhard was at the front. She dared not risk running into Andrzej. Were it not for the trust her uncle had placed in her, she wouldn't consider going back home at all.

On August 21, the newspapers trumpeted the word that von Kluck's army had taken Brussels. A small paragraph also informed them that the British Expeditionary Force was landing in France.

Several days later they read of the Battle of Mons, where those same British met von Kluck. This general of Eberhard's seemed to be always in the thickest of the fighting. When the battle ended in a British retreat, there was an ominous mention of valiant fighting and casualties.

"They don't say how many, Amalia," Trudi informed her with a tight face as she scanned the newspaper, "but we'll get a telegram if one of them was Eberhard." She pulled dying white roses from her silver vase. "One gets to dread the sound of the door knocker."

Although they received no bad news, the suspense continued, stretching their nerves taut, for it was becoming obvious that von Kluck

165

was the most daring and belligerent of the generals and one who did not spare his men.

As the days passed, Trudi became morose. "Something isn't right, Amalia. They must have abandoned the plan."

"But they keep winning!" Amalia protested.

"So far. But the advantage of momentum and surprise diminishes as the days go by. They should have taken Paris by now."

Despite Trudi's prophecies, Amalia and the rest of Germany lived in daily anticipation of a French surrender. She could not understand her mother-in-law's pessimism in the face of one spectacular victory after another.

Still, there was no news from Eberhard. He was presumably fighting or marching somewhere near the river Marne from what they could decipher from the newspaper accounts.

The excitement of the war kept Amalia fueled with nervous energy. Needlework was impossible, but she turned out her husband's room, relining drawers and packing away clothes. He had left her some money to refurbish her own wardrobe, and this she did, in the face of Trudi's disapproval, at Madame Colbert's salon. She was amused to find that prudence had forced the lady to drop her French accent, and she had become plain Frau Colburg. Trudi snorted at this information.

Amalia cajoled her into walking in the Tiergarten whenever she could, but Trudi always longed to be home, in case they should miss a telegram. It haunted her to think of Eberhard lying dead on a field somewhere in France, and them not knowing.

"The weather won't last much longer," her mother-in-law announced on their return from the park one day. "Summer is short in Berlin."

Journal
12 September 1914

It is now almost six weeks since this war began, and we received news today that Trudi feels means the first victory for the French. They are calling it the Battle of the Marne. She is very despondent and keeps muttering that von Moltke (the supreme commander) must go. According to her, he has departed from some almost sacred plan. Like a medieval soothsayer, she goes around the house, from room to room, prophesying doom and gloom. Even though the government is still confident, she says we're in for a bloody time. It's getting increasingly difficult to humor her. I really don't know how much longer she can stand the strain.

As for me, my emotions are a mystery to me. I feel no connection whatsoever to Eberhard. All I can say is that I feel as though I am swimming in waters that I don't understand. I don't know the depth or the distance to the shore. How I wish Uncle were here to put all these things in perspective for me. There is nothing familiar to me now—neither place, person, nor event. I live from day to day in anticipation of I know not what.

I have to travel to Vienna at the end of the month for board meetings. Though I am homesick and miss Grandmama, I have a presentiment that I should not go. It is difficult to contemplate leaving Trudi while she is in such a nervous state. But to be honest, I dread seeing Andrzej. I cannot even fathom what my emotions would be should I run into him.

Andrzej talked to me some of Sigmund Freud and his work, and while much of it seemed outré to me, I did grasp the concept of the restrained hysteric that the doctor saw so much of among Viennese society. I believe now that Trudi is suffering from that complaint. I urge her to play the piano for me, as that seems her only outlet. She plays one piece, Chopin, over and over. Chopin was Andrzej's favorite, of course. The piece is very disturbing, yet oddly triumphant. It seems to give her some kind of inner joy; she becomes lost in another world when she is playing it. For me, there is only pain.

Nevertheless, after she plays this particular piece, the glow soon wears off and she becomes fretful. But I can always calm her by talking about my family. She never grows tired of hearing about Uncle and his philosophy, which is quite strange, for she can't have much sympathy with the socialists. I know there is a side to her, the part of her that sent Eberhard to Austria, that I do not know yet. I am going to ask her to play some Mozart.

Chapter Five

On the thirtieth of September, Trudi said good-bye to her at the train station, as Amalia began the journey back to Vienna. Because of the demands of the military, there was now only one train a day to Munich, and it was crowded to capacity.

To keep her mind off Andrzej, she studied the reports her accountant had sent of her various charities. Everything seemed in order except the wool manufacturer's charity. There were too many miscellaneous expenditures, which she suspected were claims made by board members that ended up in their pockets. Was she going to have to clean house? What would the baron do? What would her uncle have done? The thought occupied her mind as she lay in her bed, listening to the train taking her back, taking her back, taking her back . . .

When she awoke, the train had arrived in Munich, and Amalia truly began to panic. Not only did a crucial business decision await her but she was aware that the distance between herself and Andrzej was closing. She was the Baroness von Waldburg, she told herself sternly. But she knew that her soul didn't belong to Eberhard.

The train journey from Munich to Vienna was far too short. Before she knew it, she had arrived and was met by her parents, gaily waving at her from the platform. Her mother was dressed in crimson, which did not become her, and was rather strange to Amalia after Trudi's unrelieved blacks. Papa looked as he always did, stolid and complaisant. Toni had been his favorite, but perhaps Amalia would get more affection from him now that her sister was gone.

"Amalia, dear!" her mother said. "How wonderful you look! Quite elegant. That blueberry color suits you. I hope you have brought your ball gown. The von Altwalds are having a soiree tonight."

The von Altwalds. Scene of her nightmare waltz. No! She couldn't possibly go. "I'm afraid I left my finery in Berlin, Mama. As I explained in my letter, this is a business trip. I wouldn't feel right going out in society while Eberhard's life is danger every moment."

"But, my dear, this soiree is specifically for you! Therese arranged the whole thing as soon as Grandmama told her you were coming home. It is an excuse to forget the war for a while. Society is becoming quite dull with most of the young men at the Front."

Amalia felt suddenly trapped, and her panic returned. She couldn't go to the von Altwalds.' She simply couldn't. How could Grandmama have betrayed her in this way?

She took a deep breath, closed her eyes, and gave her head a shake. A married woman now, she was not the silly, infatuated girl she had been the year before. She had burned to the ground all her bridges and now had only the bitter ashes of pride.

And she was here for business reasons. "Papa," she said, as they drew up before their townhouse, "I must speak with you about Uncle's trusts. I have a problem."

"Certainly, Amalia," he said, looking flattered. She realized she had never in her life applied to her father for advice.

Everything in the house was exactly the same, except that the furniture in the large drawing room was under Holland covers and the room was shut up. She turned to her father, who was standing eagerly by. "Let me bathe, Papa, and then perhaps we can have our consultation."

Georg brought tea and pastries to them in her father's study after Amalia had refreshed herself.

"Papa," she said, "I believe I'm being cheated." She pulled out the sheaf of papers she had received from her accountant. "Look here at the Woolen Workers Charity. All those withdrawals for 'miscellaneous.'"

Her father put on his little reading glasses and went over the accounts, going back to the time before her uncle had died. "Yes," he said finally, "I believe you are. Food has become more dear, not less, since the war began. And their expenditures are less."

She told him about her last confrontation with the group. "What can I do?"

"You're the majority trustee. As far as I can tell, they only contribute a few hundred schillings a year. "You can easily do without them. Instead of seeing your uncle's money get siphoned off by these fellows, I would simply go to the bank and withdraw Lorenz's money. Set up another trust account with you as the sole signatory. Do you trust the people who run this luncheon cafeteria for the workers?"

"I don't know. They could be pocketing money and feeding the workers gruel."

"Well, I think we should pay them a surprise visit tomorrow and see. When is your board meeting?"

Amalia consulted her appointment calendar. "Not until the day after tomorrow. Tomorrow is St. Stephen's Orphanage."

"Good. We will visit this woolen factory tomorrow at lunchtime. Then we will discuss what is to be done at the board meeting. I think we had better go down to the bank before it closes to set up your new account before the other trustees realize you are already in Vienna."

Her father by her side, she transacted this business. When they had concluded their transactions, Herr Schiblitz, her uncle's banker, said, "Rumors have been coming across our teletype for weeks. It seems quite certain now that the Germans suffered a major defeat on the Marne. They haven't admitted it, but it appears they've lost their momentum. Over a quarter of a million French dead, but apparently our side lost even more. The longer the war continues, the higher the cost of food will be."

Amalia thought of her mother-in-law's dire predictions. What a time to have left her!

"Uncle would rather see the money buying food, especially when it's short, than have his money sitting unused in the bank. If we have to spend principal, do so," she instructed.

"Knowing Lorenz, I agree with you, though that wouldn't have been my advice to another client."

"I'd like to make my father co-signer on all five trust accounts. I live in Berlin now. I am uncertain how often I will get to Vienna."

The banker looked through the files on his desk. "Very well, Baroness."

Their business finished, Amalia remarked to her father on the way home, "My mother-in-law thinks things are not going well at the Front, Papa."

"But the Germans have won almost every battle!"

Amalia shrugged. "We will see. War is going to be particularly hard on orphans, workers, and old people who depend on charity."

Even when involved in business, Amalia could not for a moment forget the von Altwald soiree. When she reached home, Kristina had laid out some of her old ball gowns on the bed. They looked terribly girlish to her. "What about my wedding dress, Kristina? I brought it to show Mama and Grandmama."

"Is that the one with all the beads and things on that skimpy little bodice?"

"Yes, but it has a tunic that makes it quite modest. And it doesn't look like a wedding dress. I think I would be more comfortable in that."

It was like déjà vu, entering the von Altwalds' townhouse. No quarter had been given to the war here.

"Ah, Baroness Amalia!" Therese greeted her, her own black satin gown slit up the side like a nightdress. "*Grüss Gott!*" She kissed Amalia on both cheeks. "I'm afraid we have mostly elderly men as courtiers tonight. All the younger ones, except a succulent few, have gone off to Serbia. But I did want to have a party for you. Sort of a homecoming reception. How is Eberhard holding up?"

"We actually hear from him very little," she said. "He's with von Kluck, so he's always in the thick of the fighting."

"Will you stay in Vienna with your parents for the duration?" her hostess inquired, mischief in her caramel eyes and her three-cornered smile.

"I'm afraid not," Amalia said firmly. "Eberhard's mother is a widow, and he is her only child. She's living on nerves, and my place is with her. I just came home to take care of some business."

"Oh, well," said Therese airily, "this war can't last forever! Come see some of your old friends. You know Lilli, of course, Eberhard's cousin, and Andrzej. They're becoming a twosome. It's quite enchanting."

Amalia was unprepared for the blow that fell upon her at this news. She had been expecting to find an importunate Andrzej, not to find him with another woman. Her grandmother was obviously not up to date.

She could see the back of his head as they approached, the casual set of his shoulders, so different from Eberhard. Suddenly assaulted by unwanted scenes from her honeymoon, she shut her eyes tight.

"What is the matter, Amalia? You're white as a sheet," Lilli said by way of greeting.

Andrzej spun around and looked at her intently. She stood helpless, staring at him like a child in a nightmare. His eyes were hard, and his mouth had new lines bracketing it.

Her mouth went dry, and she could only stare. "Hello, Lilli, Andrzej," she finally managed. "I must get some air."

Mastering her instinct to flee, she wandered gracefully into the garden, through the French doors. The moon was bright, and it was too cold for her thin dress without her evening cape. Her teeth chattering, she took shelter in the topiary garden behind a swan. This was all wrong. She should never have come back to Vienna. She simply could not bear it. With Trudi, she had thought only of the present, but now she realized Eberhard was bound to come home on leave. Then what?

Andrzej would have been gentle. The *verboten* memory of his kiss overcame her, and she began to shake, rubbing her sleeves with her hands.

Then, in a moment, Andrzej himself was beside her, taking her in his arms. It was just as it always was in her dreams. The tears came, and she wept her heart out on Andrzej's breast. She belonged here. How could she ever leave this tender fastness? He rocked her gently from side to side, as one would rock a child.

*　　*　　*

Andrzej had no idea at all what was going through Amalia's mind. He only knew he could not bear the sight of her frightened face. Had *he* frightened her with his anger when they last met? She seemed so vulnerable now, and he longed to kiss her. As this thought tempted him, she straightened and turned her face away so he wouldn't see the tears falling.

"Has it been bad, Amalia?" he asked gently.

She didn't answer but bowed her head.

"As long as I thought you were as happy as Lilli said you were, I could almost bear it. But now . . ." He wouldn't let her go this time. "You must stay here, Amalia. Stay in Vienna with your parents. We will be very discreet. No one will know."

It was the wrong thing to say. Her spine stiffened, and she said in a low voice, "I've taken sacred vows, Andrzej. What you suggest would destroy my soul, but God help me, I think I will love you all my life."

His heart wrenched inside him as he watched her walk away, this time into the house, to her parents, away from him forever. He stood in the garden for a long time.

Chapter Six

In the days that followed, Amalia kept to her room, endeavoring with little success to put Andrzej out of her mind. She kept seeing his face, full of devout adoration. It seemed impossible that there was nothing to be done about the feelings inside her. She must return to Berlin and Trudi and try to forget. She owed it to Eberhard. He had married her in good faith. She had thought he was rescuing her, but now it was hard not to think of herself as a prisoner.

It was a relief when she had a board meeting to attend. She grew close to her father for the first time in her life, treasuring his common sense and his gentle goodness. Her mother had given up on her and was going into society by herself.

Afraid of running into Andrzej at her grandmother's, she sent Grandmama a short note, asking her to call at the Faulhaber home.

"My darling!" Eugenia declared, embracing her once they were alone in the morning room. "I'm so sorry about the scene at the von Altwalds'. Andrzej has been by. He is at a total loss. You were crying, he said. I've never seen him so agonized, even after you left last June."

Amalia looked down and pleated the skirt of her sage green dress with anxious fingers. "How serious is it with Lilli?" she asked, ignoring her grandmother's unasked question.

"Oh, it's just a little light fun. He says she's made it her mission to console him. She is quite lively. Good for him right now, I think. He can't carry the torch for you forever, Amalia. Were you jealous? Is that why you were crying?"

Looking up sharply, she was annoyed for the first time in her life with her grandmother. "How can you think that?" Amalia demanded.

"Well, what am I to think?"

Amalia took a deep breath. "Grandmama, there are things married women do not discuss with others. Now, let's talk of something else. Would you like to see my wedding gown? It's quite original."

Eugenia lifted her chin, acknowledging the rebuke. "Of course, my dear."

The remainder of her visit was spent discussing the sad demise of Viennese society and the likelihood that nothing would ever be the same again. When her grandmother left, Amalia stood by the morning room window, watching her walk down the path to her carriage. Grandmama was bent over as she walked into the wind, and for the first time it occurred to Amalia that the woman who was so precious to her was old and very likely not to live much longer. "Please let her live until I can see her again," she whispered to God.

Little by little news trickled in about the battle on the Marne River in France. The French continued to claim victory. Germany refused to number their casualties and merely announced that they had made a strategic retreat.

The news only compounded her misery. How her mother-in-law must be suffering alone in that cold townhouse. She should never have left her. Only one more day before she could be on the train back to her duty.

Leaving her room that morning to find her mother, she located her in the breakfast room, sorting through a wooden box. The dreary morning made even the normally cheerful room seem grim.

"I thought, as your father is going to take over the trusts for you, that I ought to go through Lorenz's things, in case he wrote anything down we needed to know."

"Mama, I didn't realize you had them! What are those in your hand?"

"Oddly enough, Amalia, it appears Lorenz had a great love affair none of us knew about. These are letters from someone called Trudi."

She stood stunned. *Trudi?* Amalia's mind immediatly went to Eberhard's mother. No. Surely this must be a different Trudi.

"May I see them, please?" she asked, her voice trembling.

As her mother handed them to her, she recognized her mother-in-law's writing at once. Telling herself it was only to verify her suspicions, Amalia opened the one on top.

My darling Lorenz,

I am fully aware of how wrong it is to write, but I must or I will lose my mind. It feels like I am drowning. You are my source of air, light, and life. Without you, I am shriveling to nothing, and some-day they will find my lifeless body on the shore of Lake Como, my spiritual home. I live there in my mind. I feel your arms around me, your hands caressing me, your lips kissing the hollow in my throat . . .

Amalia's hands shook as she wrenched her eyes from the blue stationery and crammed the letter back into its envelope. It almost burned with its passionate heat. Amalia turned over the envelope and found no return address. Trudi must have been married to Eberhard's father at the time she wrote. Had she kept her married identity secret from Uncle Lorenz? It would have been just like him to have stormed the townhouse and carried Trudi off if he had known.

Amalia blinked back tears. The pathos of the letter was almost too much to bear. What had kept them apart? How had she ever existed without Uncle Lorenz all those years, living with that Prussian soldier?

Now her uncle's hatred of the Prussians had some flesh on it. But what if he had known that Eberhard was the son he should have had? What if Eberhard had known Uncle should have been his father? How many lives it would have changed! Eberhard might not be, at this very moment, on a battlefield risking his life. How could Trudi possibly live with such knowledge?

Her heart felt crushed by Trudi's despair. She needed to return to Berlin.

"We weren't meant to read these," she said to her mother. "But I know who wrote them. I will take care of it, Mama."

Her mother shrugged, obviously aware that she had been caught doing something a proper lady never would have done.

"I am leaving tomorrow, Mama. I've managed to get a place on the train. The news from the Western Front is very bad, and I must go back to the baroness in case there is a telegram. May I take Kristina with me?"

Suddenly alarmed, Gretel Faulhaber looked up. "You think that Eberhard . . . ?"

"He was in the thick of the fighting. The French lost a quarter of a million men, and they were the victors. Heaven only knows how many the Germans lost. They're not saying. It is beyond any sane person's imagination to think of that many people being killed."

"Oh, my dear!" Gretel said. "You must stay here! It is quite likely Eberhard is dead, and then you will just have to come home again!"

Turning her back on her mother, Amalia said with only a slight quiver in her voice, "I'm a baroness, Mother. I'm heiress to an estate. Even if Eberhard is killed, I must stay with his mother. It was his wish. May I have Kristina?"

Her mother nodded her head mechanically. Clutching the letters, Amalia ran up the stairs to order her maid to commence packing.

She arrived back in Berlin on a rainy day. Trudi, drenched and looking hopeless, greeted Amalia and her maid on the platform.

"Eberhard?" Amalia asked at once.

Trudi shook her head. "No word."

"No news is good news, Trudi," she said, taking her mother-in-law into an embrace. She was as thin and delicate as a small bird. Then she couldn't resist trying to cheer her up. "Let's go back home. I have a surprise I think will make you very happy."

*   *   *

Lorenz's letters from her! Trudi held them to her breast and looked into Amalia's smiling eyes. "Where were they? Where did you find them?"

"He kept them all these years. Mother found them in his things."

"You didn't tell her?"

"No," Amalia assured her. Then she sank into the divan. Supposing she had written Andrzej and years later someone found her letters? She had no room to judge Trudi or Uncle in the least.

"Oh, Amalia, it was wrong, but I loved him so! And he loved me. My father separated us because Lorenz was a socialist. We tried to elope, but we were caught." Tears streamed down the little woman's face. "I've loved him all my life. I've tried to raise Eberhard the way Lorenz would have raised him, but my husband was too heavy handed. He beat Eberhard into a soldier with his crop. We hid the violin from him. My poor child." She collapsed, weeping. "I've raised him to be so conflicted and such a stranger to himself. I'm so afraid what war will do to him."

"I think God must have brought us together, Trudi," Amalia said softly. "I loved my uncle like no one else. I think perhaps you and I loved him most in the world."

The woman sighed. "It brings me solace to know that Eberhard had that time in Vienna with you. It was the closest to Lorenz he could be."

"He actually met him once," Amalia told her.

Trudi looked up, hopeful.

"They didn't get on, unfortunately. I think Eberhard was put off by the smell of drains in my uncle's neighborhood."

Embracing Trudi, Amalia held her while they alternately laughed and cried.

* * *

Amalia, nerves stretched to the screaming point, stayed with her mother-in-law as days became weeks and weeks slowly crawled into months. Homesickness overtook her like a disease, though she did everything she could to ward it off. By sheer willpower, she left her grandmother's letters unopened, knowing they would only make her homesickness worse. She wrote determinedly cheerful letters, manufacturing a nurturing, fun-loving mother-in-law so no one would know the grimness of her life and feel sorry for her—pity she could not have borne.

"It looks as though it's a stalemate, Amalia," Trudi informed her one morning in mid-November. "The longer the lines remain fixed this way," she indicated two roughly parallel and jagged lines across the map of France, "the better fortified they'll be. No one's going to advance successfully against mortars and machine guns."

She proved to be right again. Amalia watched the pins on the map as the Front stabilized into two opposing trenches that ran from the English Channel to the Swiss border. Eberhard wrote of his life there:

> We live with our eyes at ground level, ankle deep in mud. Rain is incessant, as are the rats. During the day, all is fairly quiet. But at night we must stay alert for that is when the damage is done.

Amalia had formed the habit of attending early morning mass at St. Maria's. It was a reason to get up in the mornings, a reason to dress well, a breath of freedom, a link with the past.

The church was within walking distance, and no matter how bitter the weather, Amalia relished the walk. She was surprised when Trudi insisted on accompanying her, but she knew it salved her soul to light that candle each day.

Amalia savored the signs of life outside the townhouse—the motorcars, the horse-drawn carts and carriages, the little bundled children running in the tiny riverside park, and as she neared the river, the sight of the barges carrying their heavy cargo of scrap metal.

Inside the still church the morning light filtered through the east rose window. After mass, she sometimes spoke with kindly Father Ignatius, who had married her.

"How is your husband keeping, Baroness? He is still well, I hope."

"As far as we know. We haven't received a telegram."

Then she would buy a candle and light it for Eberhard.

One morning later in November when the cold had kept Trudi at home, the priest made a point of addressing her. "I hope you will not think me presumptuous, Baroness, but I am concerned for you. You are idle, and it is wearing you out."

She nodded at his perception. "You're right, but I don't see any solution for it. Waiting seems to be woman's work. I can't join my husband at the Front."

"Have you thought of becoming a nurse's aide? We have a very good hospital here. St. Catherine's. They need devout young women like you. Those of the wounded whose homes are near here are transported from the makeshift hospitals at the Front. Their increasing numbers are starting to become a burden to the present staff."

The thought of becoming a nurse had never entered her mind. Her first instinct was to reject the idea, but instead she merely replied, "I will think on it."

"A nurse's aide!" Trudi scorned when she mentioned it that evening at dinner. "You are forgetting yourself, Amalia. You are a baroness now."

"I think Eberhard would approve. It's my way of fighting this war."

"His approval is beside the point, Amalia. It's you I'm thinking of. You're much too frail for that sort of thing. Believe me, it won't be the least bit romantic. Scrubbing floors, sterilizing instruments, changing bedpans and bandages."

"I'm not as fragile as I look, Trudi. I think I shall try it, at least. If I have to endure many more days waiting here for a telegram, I shall lose my mind."

The next morning, following mass, Father Ignatius accompanied her to St. Catherine's. They had decided to introduce her as simply Frau Waldburg to avoid any awkwardness concerning her social status. The hospital was in an old building near the river. The wind whipped around her, and she gripped her hands together inside her muff. Winter was here. She must knit a woolen scarf for Eberhard. And one for Wolf, too. She was sure Trudi would teach her how to knit.

After one look at Amalia, the large spare woman in charge evidently arrived at Baroness von Waldburg's opinion.

"This isn't going to be any sort of romantic adventure, my girl. You don't look as though you could last a day."

The little priest drew himself up to defend his protégée. "She has a husband at the Front, Sister Therese. Frau Waldburg feels that serving in this way would offer Herr Oberleutnant her most wholehearted support."

The sister looked at Amalia suspiciously. "But, Father, the Waldburgs are surely a Protestant family?"

Amalia spoke. "My husband is now of our faith, Sister. I was born a Catholic."

Assessing Amalia once more, Sister Therese sighed. "Well, we can use you. But green volunteers can be more of a hindrance than a help. If I find you are not working out, you will have to go."

Sister Therese issued her a blue cambric uniform, a starched white apron, a wimple, and orders to report the next morning at seven o'clock.

Even with this dubious welcome, Amalia felt that any drudgery would be preferable to the enervating tension of the cold gray house. To postpone her return there, she went along to purchase wool for scarves. Gray for Eberhard. Scarlet for Wolf. Then on a whim she purchased some navy blue to make another for the Baron von Schoenenburg.

When she returned to the house, it was to find a letter from her mother, begging her once more to return home.

> Business is slow of course with all commerce to Moravia (our primary lace source) terribly hampered by the war. Your father expects it to get worse.
> Somehow I feel that we are all losing our grip, Amalia. The emperor rarely leaves the palace, and our social life is severely

curtailed by the lack of men. I am not at all well, and I continue to believe your place should be here.

The pathos of Mama's pleading sneaked under her guard before she could stop it, disturbing the old Amalia. Realizing she was still capable of tears, she excused herself from luncheon and went to her room to weep freely, while Kristina cosseted her by brushing her hair.

For the first time she was conscious of rage against this war that had invaded people's lives so indiscriminately. She confided her feelings to her journal.

Journal
December 15, 1914

Work in the hospital is grim. However, there is a wonderful woman called Louisa—a Brunhilde. She is a statuesque blonde with braids in rolls around her ears. She is unbelievably kind and has covered for me countless times when I have been ill at the sight of an amputation, the stench of gangrene, or the horror of prolonged dysentery. But I am learning to be a good aide.

It is Eberhard and his kind who started this war. We are entirely mismatched. He had a gentle side, I thought, but there is nothing gentle about war. I don't know how I can bear to see him again. The Germans are responsible for so many, many deaths. It is past my ability to comprehend how they could imagine this could be glorious.

And so the days passed, Trudi brooding over her map, knitting socks, and reading the newspaper, and Amalia disciplining her body and hands to the unusual vocation she stubbornly pursued.

Christmas came and went without much sign. Her friend Louisa gave her a scented candle. Amalia returned the gift with a small toilet kit full of spray scents, brushes, and soaps. She went to Christmas mass, and Trudi served goose. Presenting her mother-in-law with a suitably garbed gray and white Dresden shepherdess, she was moved nearly to tears by the gift she received in return—a gossamer-like Shetland shawl in champagne. The baroness had worked on it by day while her daughter-in-law toiled at the hospital. Amalia kissed Trudi's cheek. Her mother-in-law smiled her tight little smile, and then Christmas was gone.

Amalia submerged all thoughts of home. She had not heard anything from Vienna.

Several weeks later, they received an unusually long letter from Eberhard. It was addressed, as all his letters were, to both of them.

> Christmas in the trenches was a very eerie thing. I don't know if I can even properly describe it to you, it was so extraordinary.
>
> An unofficial cease-fire was called, in itself enough to set the day apart from the rest. It was so quiet and strange, being isolated in these muddy ditches, under the clear, cold sky, with acres of shell-holes, barbed wire, and desolation stretching out in front of us. No Man's Land, we call it. It looks completely unearthly anyway, and the silence made it stranger still.
>
> Then, little by little, we saw helmets appear across those acres. The Scots (for that is whom we face in this little stretch of hell) were climbing out of the trenches! No one fired a shot.
>
> Then some of our men began to emerge out of the ground. I thought it insanely foolhardy and ordered my men to stay where they were. It was very odd to see our spiked helmets congregating with those inverted soup plates the enemy wears. The men actually shook hands and spoke to one another. I heard reports several days later that there had even been a friendly soccer game played somewhere down the line. And singing. Christmas carols, if you can imagine it. Simultaneously, in German and English.
>
> The next day we went back to killing each other. I'm afraid the entire episode had a disastrous effect on morale. I'm glad I made my men stay down. It's easier to kill an anonymous, faceless enemy.
>
> My love to both of you.
>
> Devotedly,
> E.

Chapter Seven

As Amalia came to know her patients, she found many of them had been in the battle of Ypres, and one had even known her husband.

"He was my commanding officer, gnädige Frau," a blinded young man told her.

Amalia was interested in the corporal's account of the battle. "The Brits were spectacular. We outnumbered them three to one. I still don't know how they did it, but they just stopped us dead. They wouldn't retreat; they just stood and died." After a moment, he continued. "The Kaiser didn't think much of the English army. I'll wager he's changed his mind now."

She smoothed the young man's bedsheets. "You don't seem to be bitter about their blinding you."

"It's a soldier's lot to shoot or be shot. They didn't start the war." The patient relapsed into silence, his animation exhausted.

Interested to hear something of Eberhard, however, she persisted. "Did you know my husband well?"

The corporal's mouth twitched. "A proper *Junker*, your husband," was all he said.

The wounded who were now pouring in from the Front were in far worse condition than those from the earlier battles. Their wounds were always gangrenous. Weakened by disease and exposure, the patients Amalia tended seldom survived.

This picture of unalleviated gore was so disturbing that Amalia began to have trouble sleeping. It seemed to her that she must always be needed at the hospital. Many times she remembered her uncle's prophecy, "We're talking about men's *lives*," he had said. "It's not just tax money or noble tribute. It's *blood*."

Through the months of January, February, and March she saw the flow of that blood, as the wounded continued to arrive faster than the old patients died or could be discharged.

During all this time, a grim friendship flourished between Amalia and Louisa. There were few carefree moments and always an overbearing sense of responsibility, but Amalia sensed that the other girl was managing to keep a sense of proportion.

"What's a Junker?" she asked Louisa one day over canteen soup. "I never heard that term in Austria."

"It's basically Prussian. It refers to a nobleman of the old school."

"Meaning all that blood and glory talk," Amalia spoke bitterly. "A patient of mine called Eberhard that. I don't think he was being complimentary."

"But is Eberhard a nobleman?"

Amalia realized she had slipped. Lowering her voice, she said, "You must promise not to tell anyone. I didn't want to be treated any differently."

"Then you're . . ."

"Yes."

"And all this time I've been calling you . . ."

"It's what I wanted. It's what I still want. Do you think after what we've seen upstairs that I could possibly want to be known as a Junker's wife?"

Louisa smiled gently and put a roughened hand over Amalia's. "You mustn't judge him harshly. No one could have imagined it would be like this."

"But he *wanted* war. He was like a child waiting for Christmas."

"I don't think he was the only one, if it seems any comfort."

Amalia's own healthy body seemed a reproach as she looked at the suffering around her. She began to work later and later into the next shift. When she returned home, she often sought her bed with no desire for food. Trudi's scoldings were frequent. "Amalia, you've become a shadow! Eberhard will be stern with me for not taking better care of you. Certainly it's enough to work your regular shift without working half the next one, too!"

Amalia would just look at her sadly. "If you could see them, Trudi, you wouldn't begrudge them anything."

One day, Louisa took Amalia aside after their normal lunch routine. "Let's get a bit of air," she said.

Once they were outside, she remarked, "You have me worried, Amalia. Are you purposely trying to ruin your own health?"

"What does my health matter?" she demanded. "Those men upstairs have given everything. I'm just one drop in a great sea of misery."

"But Eberhard? Would he want you to work yourself so hard?"

"I told you about Eberhard. He's loving all this. It's all glorious!"

Her friend put a hand gently on Amalia's arm. "I'm afraid you're blaming him for the men upstairs. That isn't right, Amalia. It's not rational."

Amalia stared dully at a drainpipe emptying into the sewer.

Louisa continued, "You're working yourself to death as some kind of penance, aren't you?"

Amalia looked away. "I think it's time we got back. We'll be missed."

That day when she returned home, there was a telegram. Unable to bear the suspense, Trudi had opened it. It read: *Home 22 Mar on leave stop All well stop E stop*

Feeling only weariness, Amalia walked up the stairs like a sleepwalker. He would be home in just two days.

Journal
March 20, 1915

Today Horst, one of my patients, received a visitor, his mother. Her son is one of my favorite charges because of his ability to cheer those around him. Using his own nicknames for those on the ward, he bullies them into feeling better with his wit and smile. His leg had turned gangrenous from a wound received in the trenches and was amputated at the knee in an improvised hospital at the Front. Gangrene set in again after this first dismemberment. To save his life, he was facing an operation to remove the rest of his leg. His mother, a middle class widow from Dresden, had traveled to be with her son.

She looked straight into my face and said, "I'm here to help care for him."

I asked her if she'd like to bathe him. I went to fetch the towels and bath basin.

When I returned, I was dismayed but not surprised to see Horst turned to the wall and his mother sitting with tears rolling down her face. No doubt it had been the pain in her face that he could not bear.

I put on my best nurse's voice and showed her what to do. Frau Winkler dried her tears and soon had taken over. Later, as I was going down to the canteen, I remembered Horst would be in surgery. Deciding to forgo lunch, I walked back to the operating room.

Frau Winkler was sitting outside, her face gray with worry, staring at the hands that were intertwined tightly in her lap. At my approach, she looked up wildly, fear clouding her gray eyes.

I asked if she minded my sitting with her for a moment. Frau Winkler began to speak her thoughts aloud. "I know I shouldn't have let him see. But you must understand. It was the shock. Bathing him was almost more than I could bear. It was impossible not to remember when he was a baby. His precious, dear little feet." She was nearly hysterical. I could hardly bear it. "He used to kick and splash water all over me." Then she put her hands up to her face, ashamed of her emotion. "He was such a happy boy, gnädige Frau. I never thought to see him suffer so . . ."

Then she brought her hands back down to her lap and stared at nothing.

I told her I had observed that the war is hardest for mothers. She tried to tell me it is hard on wives, too.

I told her the truth: that I have only known my husband as a man who wished for war.

It was really no surprise but still a tremendous grief to me when the surgeon told me that afternoon that Horst had not survived the operation. The loss of blood had been too much for his infection-weakened body. I stood and stared at Horst's empty bed for a moment, and then, as if I could avenge him somehow, I turned my thoughts to Eberhard.

He is due home on leave. How am I to bear it? I do not want him to touch me. I don't even want to be in the same room with him. The thought makes me shrivel up inside.

How I wish I had never come to this awful country. What a willful, blind, idiot I was! I should have seen it in Vienna. When the mood was upon him, Eberhard was cold, stern, and unyielding. But, like many women, I thought I could change all that. What folly!

The next day Louisa asked her, "Amalia, have you given any thought to how much you've changed? Eberhard won't know you. And you have no way of knowing what he's experienced, who he is now. You're going to have to find each other again. I say, give it a chance."

Amalia answered her with silence.

Not knowing which train Eberhard would arrive on, Amalia and Trudi waited at home the next day for his arrival. Unable to settle to anything and black with resentment about her forced absence from the hospital, Amalia could stand it no longer. She threw down her knitting and left the room. Minutes later, she appeared in her uniform.

"You can send for me at the hospital when Eberhard arrives."

Trudi continued knitting. "You need a rest, Amalia. Your nerves are badly frayed."

"I'm sorry. I just keep thinking of Herbert. He's to have the shrapnel removed from his head today."

She looked up at Amalia, a frown between her brows, "Is this Herbert more important to you than your own husband, then?"

Amalia did not answer and could not stay after that.

It was a relief to mount the stairs to her ward and allow herself to be absorbed in the familiar drama of her work. She consciously blocked out everything but the present.

Sometime in the late afternoon, while she was waiting for news of Herbert, her sanctuary was invaded. Her husband strode energetically onto the ward, six feet tall and in full uniform. Without a glance at the wounded, he looked tight and unfamiliar.

Amalia stopped in mid-sentence, and there was silence as everyone listened to the soldier's boots thump across the floor. Standing, she handed the letter to her patient. "I see I must go now, Friedrich." With no acknowledgement of her husband she fled to the dispensary.

As she stood in the little room, the acrid smell of medications enveloping her, she clenched her fists, waiting for Eberhard to find her. She had been embarrassed by his presence out there on the ward. She didn't wish to be seen with him in front of her patients.

Eberhard entered hesitantly, and she saw immediately that he was changed. At first she thought it was the pallor, so similar to that of her patients. Then she saw the grim twist of his mouth and his still eyes, which seemed almost blind.

Standing straight and defiant, she waited for him to make his way to her.

"Amalia," he said simply, taking her hand and bringing it to his rough lips.

"You shouldn't have come here."

He looked around him dully.

She took his arm and moved him toward the door. "We need to get you home. You're exhausted."

* * *

He slept until the following morning, alone in the room next to his wife's. As he dropped into slumber, the clean white sheets and the goosedown mattress made him feel as though he were in heaven. But he couldn't leave the noise behind. Whistling mortars and crackling explosions woke him continually, causing him to bolt upright in bed. And the blood. He could smell the blood mixed with mud, even in his mother's sanitized house.

When he awoke in the morning, he was confused. Where was he? Where were his men? Where was his uniform? Slowly, it came back to him that he was on leave. Getting up, he looked through his civilian wardrobe like a stranger in a clothing store. Numbly, he put his muddy uniform back on. When he stared in the mirror, he didn't recognize himself. His eyes were great hollows. He had two days' growth of beard, and his cheekbones stuck out. Shaving in warm water was another luxury he wasn't used to. Too late, he realized he should have bathed. But he was hollow with hunger. Just now, all he could think of was food.

"The crocuses are up, Eberhard," his mother said, her eyes fixed on each move he made. "I think you should take Amalia to the estate. It's time she saw her home."

He turned from the sideboard, his plate piled high with ham, rolls, quince jam, and butter. Looking at Amalia in surprise, he realized that something about her had changed. She wasn't as anxious as he remembered. "That's an idea, Mother. But you'll come with us, won't you?"

"Yes," Amalia added. "We insist."

"No," Trudi replied, looking from one of their faces to the other. "I think it would be better if you went alone. You both need a good rest. You'll be ready to come back in a week."

"Perhaps that would be best," he agreed. Now that he was filling his empty stomach, he could think about his wife. She was cold and distant, not the warm, vibrant woman he had left behind. "I'm afraid you've let Amalia work too hard, Mother."

Trudi shrugged. "I have no control over Amalia. She is not a child."

He stared at the woman he had dreamt of these past months.

Buttering a roll, she was completely self-possessed, as though she were not even in the same room with him. "She's much too thin."

Rising from the table abruptly, his wife said, "There are many things to see to if we are to leave. I'm sure you'll excuse me." He swore to himself. Why was she looking at him with such loathing? Where was his bright, devoted bride?

*   *   *

Passing through the hall, Amalia saw that the morning post had brought her a letter. It was the first from her mother in a long time. To begin with, it was merely general news emerging in a plaintive whine. Then she said:

> But the main reason for this letter is to tell you some sad news. Your grandmother has died. She contracted pneumonia and didn't have the will to fight it. Your young man attended her and did what bullying he could, but it was no good. It was almost annoying the way she refused to get better. She kept telling me not to grieve, that her day was done, and her only wish was to join Father and Lorenz. All the same, it has been very hard to lose her just now.
>
> The doctor has changed, as I dare say we all have, with this war. He's quite serious now and dedicated to his work. He wasn't the least bit surprised to hear you were nursing, but he never talks to me of you. He and Mama were very close. He took her death very hard.
>
> I don't know what else could happen unless Wolf were to be killed. I'm quite certain I couldn't bear that.

The last door to Amalia's childhood closed. She sat looking at the foreign hands, roughened to dry scales, that held the letter. They were the most obvious manifestation of the outward shell she inhabited now. Grandmama's death touched the real Amalia but only distantly. Grieved by this numbness, she took Grandmama's unopened letters from the place she had concealed them. Reading them one by one, she could document her grandmother's decline. Why had she been so silly, so afraid of hearing about Andrzej, that she had not learned what was happening to Grandmama? But could she really have offered any consolation? Her own life had become a bitter, bloody battle. Life in her grandmother's Vienna was another world. Perhaps that was why she had died. In her last letter, Grandmama had warned that she had had to restrain Andrzej, in the harshest manner possible, from going to Berlin to carry her off.

Automatically, she folded the letters, slid them into her journal, and told Kristina they must sort out the clothes she would need for the country. She decided she must leave the little maid behind. Kristina saw too much.

*   *   *

The countryside was at last showing signs that the brutal winter was coming to an end. A green cast was barely perceptible in the muddy brown fields, and some cocky daffodils had joined the spiky crocus, nodding their heads in dormant gardens. It was eons away from the trenches. Was this the same world?

Eberhard sat smoking, silently pondering this, his legs stretched out in front of him. Through the slits of his eyelids he studied his wife. The mortar shells were less deafening now, and her behavior more puzzling. "Another thirty minutes, and we'll be there," he said.

"Good," she replied, keeping her gaze on the countryside.

Where had his Viennese sweetheart gone? Was all the world changed? Had she grown hard like the men at the Front? He thought of her occupation. She hadn't spared herself the gore of war. Remembering his jubilation at his mobilization, he ruminated on how much both of them had changed. Maybe the trenches were here, after all.

A gaunt old man met them at the train station for the fifteen-mile ride to Waldburg. The spring air was even colder here than in Berlin, and Amalia shivered uncontrollably in the open vehicle.

Eberhard pulled the rug up around her and then encircled her protectively with his arm. She stiffened. Mortified, he took his arm away.

Could the past not be reclaimed? It seemed like years that he had been fighting. While they were winning, he'd been exultant. But ever since the stalemate in the trenches had begun, the only thing that had kept him sane was the memory of his lovely wife. What had happened to make her treat him with such cold disdain?

* * *

Amalia tried to contain her distaste for her husband. How were they going to spend a week together?

The Waldburg manor house looked much as she had expected it would. Of plain gray stone, it was symmetrical with matching turrets and surrounded by a dense wood on three sides. In front was a spacious lawn with fountains.

Amalia better understood Trudi's passion for white when she viewed the interior. It was dark and gloomy with a lingering medieval air that the furnishings only enhanced. A tall, grim housekeeper greeted them correctly, as though they were royalty, and then preceded them to a large, dark-paneled room that appeared to be some sort of great hall. Amalia doubted whether the house possessed anything as simple as a drawing room.

Standing before the roaring fire that burned in a fireplace of heroic proportions, she observed the large heads of moose, elk, and deer peering down at her. Heavy iron chandeliers hung from the exposed beams. Dark velvet draperies all but shut out the sun.

"Well?" her husband demanded. "Does it pass muster? Or does it, like me, fail to meet with your approval?"

Turning to the fire, she warmed her hands, choosing to ignore the last part of his question. "It's just as I thought it would be," she responded. "In every detail."

They dined in a long room on cream of asparagus soup, spring lamb, parslied new potatoes, hot house peas, and a chocolate torte. At least, Eberhard did. Amalia had no appetite. To keep from thinking of what was to come when they were alone, she thought about her patients in the hospital. How was Herbert? Had he come through his surgery?

After dinner, her husband formally guided her though the rest of the house as though she were a guest. The dwelling seemed to have been built to house giants. As she peered out through a slit in the turret, Eberhard said in an offhand tone, "It's all yours, you know. You are its chatelaine."

"I suppose I'm rather awed by it all," she replied.

In the gallery that existed along the walls of the main staircase, her husband pointed to his father's portrait. The face in the painting had the look of Eberhard, but the lines were more deeply etched between the brows, the eyes colder. Only the stern mouth was the same.

"Old Moltke was his god, you know," her husband remarked with bitterness. "Father would have been in a purple rage over Young Moltke's shilly-shallying. I suppose he would have considered it treason."

Startled at the tone in his voice, Amalia turned towards her husband. "Wasn't Moltke the Younger your Field Marshal?"

"Was. Yes. It would have been interesting to see what Father would have done in von Kluck's shoes."

"Your general? What do you mean?"

"I suppose you've gathered that my general, as you call him, has a rather bloodthirsty reputation."

Amalia looked back at the portrait, teeth clenched.

"The fact is, von Moltke lost his nerve back in August and left von Kluck to struggle on by himself."

"He's a butcher!" Amalia declared fiercely. "He doesn't think of his men! He just sends them into the thick of things and lets them die."

Eberhard faced her, his eyes smoldering. "He has no choice if we are to win the war. This slaughter you deplore so much is not his fault but is a result of our Field Marshall's cowardly failure to back us up and carry out the plan." He left the portrait abruptly, and strode up the stairs. "His hesitation was fatal. He's been relieved, but it may have cost us years of war."

Caught off guard by these bitter reflections, Amalia followed her husband. "Surely there's more to see?"

"You despise me, don't you? You think I'm responsible somehow for all those men in your hospital."

Amalia looked down, away from his tortured face. "You were so anxious for the war Eberhard. And every day I see the misery it's brought upon the world. I can't understand you."

*   *   *

Something in his soul was crushed by her earnest words. He had seen himself as her hero, and she obviously saw him as an enemy. The ideals that had carried him since boyhood could not withstand her scorn. The Front had been hell itself, but even that hadn't smashed his self-consequence as she did. The gods must be disappointed in him to have played him such a trick.

Turning on his heel smartly, he left her standing in the picture gallery and headed off to the comfort of the one place in the vast baronial hall that was his—the room in the garrets that his mother had painted white and where he lived his private life away from his father.

Amalia called after him, following his long strides as best she could, but he did not stop for her. He needed sanctuary or the schism in his character was going to rend him in two.

*   *   *

After a good deal of searching, Amalia discovered her husband in his room in the attics. She recognized Trudi's hand in the white room. A vase of dried marigolds stood on a low table. Eberhard was lighting the fire in the small grate. It was very cold.

"What is this place?" she asked gently, hoping to soothe her husband's agitation.

"My place," he said simply.

Going to a large armoire, Amalia opened it and saw row upon row of albums, carefully arranged. Pulling one out, she began to turn over the pages.

It was a chronicle, probably assembled by Trudi, of Eberhard's childhood.

He laughed bitterly. "You think I was born in uniform, I expect. Perhaps you'll be surprised."

Amalia was intrigued in spite of herself. A picture emerged from the albums of a lonely boy bent on achievement to win his father's love. They contained photographs of his serious little face above a sailor collar, awards and official recognitions for scholarship, marksmanship, horsemanship, and atheletic prowess. There were ribbons, certificates, and medals.

"I'd forgotten this one!" he said, dropping his sour manner in a moment of enthusiasm. "A first for my experiments in cross-breeding sheep. Poor Mother. I wouldn't let her have them butchered, and she had to give them away so Father wouldn't find out. And this! Father was relieved when I finally entered the jumping competition. He was very keen on riding, of course."

It was no real surprise that he also possessed prizes for his exceptional skill as a violinist.

"What has become of your instrument?"

"It's here somewhere." He began looking through the armoire again. "You may find this difficult to believe of your soldier-husband, but once I took first in a Mendelssohn competition." Pulling a black leather case from its place of hiding, he opened it on the floor between them. "I'm probably as out of tune as it is, but I might be able to manage some Bach for you. I remember how you liked him."

She looked at her husband across the beautiful instrument she remembered from Vienna. His eyes had regained their life, and against what she now guessed of his boyhood he looked different sitting there.

"I would like that very much."

They descended to the vast, brocaded music room. While her

husband tuned his violin to the grand piano, she relinquished thoughts of war and hospital, telling herself it was only for this one evening.

After several warm-up scales, Eberhard managed a tentative version of a Bach minuet. When she applauded heartily, he proceeded with more flourish and confidence to play another.

Once again she marveled at the change that overcame the normally martial figure of her husband as he bent and swayed and gave himself to the instrument. With his eyelids half-closed and his face reflecting total absorption in his gentle task, he was transformed. In a flash of insight, she saw that Eberhard, too, had an outer shell. Inside it lived the lonely boy who had only his ideals for company and his absent father for a god. At his core dwelt the violinist. And the man who loved her.

Gustav von Waldburg had been a martinet of the worst Prussian tradition. It was easy to see, even with this unpracticed performance, the seeds of musical genius in his son. The waste of it all moved her from anger to pity to a new kind of caring. A desire emerged, perhaps an extension of her obsession with healing, to nurture the gentleness and light that burned so deep inside the man she had married.

In this merciful frame of mind, away from the sight and smell of war, Amalia submitted herself as a wife to her husband. Because desire for passionate romance had been burned out of her by grueling, relentless horror, she expected little, and so she wasn't disappointed.

The old Amalia capable of dizzying exhilaration, who had willfully loved and abandoned Andrzej, still existed far back in time. But she now belonged to this paradox of a man. She had come down to earth. The kind of love she had imagined as a girl was immaterial. This was real life.

Chapter Eight

The week passed more quickly than she had imagined it would. Amalia and Eberhard rode all over the estate on horseback, marking the daily growth of new green. They visited the tiny village of Waldburg where her husband, the baron, was greeted as the local hero and given the homage of bouquets and beer due such a person. Inspecting the wealth of memorabilia in the attic proved interesting when they uncovered an ancient harp, proving that some other von Waldburg had possessed musical talent.

In the evenings, Amalia attempted to read a history of the von Waldburgs that Eberhard's grandfather had written and published at his own expense, while Eberhard exercised his fingers playing scales.

"Why did you give it up?" she asked on their last evening.

"I don't know. Because I was trying to put you and Vienna behind me, I suppose."

"Will you take it when we go back this time?"

"If you like, but it will have to stay with you. I can hardly carry it off to the Front." He put his bow to the strings and produced the minuet he had been practicing all week.

*　　*　　*

After receiving spirited applause from his wife, Eberhard put the instrument on the piano and dropped down on the floor next to her chair. His face felt the warm glow of accomplishment. Looking into the fire, he rested his head against her knees. This had become a favorite posture of his.

"One needn't submit," he said, managing to think just then that the Front was a nightmare and this moment reality.

She put her hand forward on his shoulder and he smoothed its roughness. They had not spoken of the hospital or the war since the discussion of von Moltke.

"To what, Eberhard?"

He gripped the fingers that rested on his shoulder. He needed the essence of her fused to him somehow. It was the only way he could possibly go back.

"Brutality."

His wife didn't answer him but rose and playfully pulled him to his feet. They made their way up the broad, shallow stairway that led to their room. Later, lying in her arms, he suddenly jerked awake, wrenching himself into a sitting position. In the dark he fancied he saw barbed wire and heard shells screaming through the night. He yelled, "No! Go back, you fool! The other way!" He awoke fully, confused.

Amalia brought his head down onto her breast and stroked his hair. He was cracking. He could feel it. He must pull himself together! But soon he drowsed under his wife's tender hand.

*　　*　　*

Amalia lay awake, reflecting that it was only she who carried food, armament, and life to the person of Eberhard Nicholas, who dwelt inside the splintering fastness of Herr Oberleutnant von Waldburg.

They returned to Berlin in a far different spirit. Amalia felt softened, more at peace with herself than at any time since her marriage. Eberhard's face resembled the man she knew but with differences that made him more dear to her. Instead of the unyielding strength of his jaw, she saw the fragile pulse beating in his temple and the new hollowness in his cheeks. They held hands.

Upon reaching the train station in the capital, Eberhard's first action was to buy a newspaper. As he read it in the cab, she could feel him withdraw.

"What is it?"

He affected not to hear her.

Once they reached the townhouse, he was out of the cab, leaving the driver to assist her and bring in the luggage. By the time she had paid the man and entered the house, Eberhard had vanished up the stairs. Trudi stood on the bottom step looking up after him.

Amalia made to go up, but Trudi put a hand on her arm. "Leave him, Amalia. He's just had a rather wicked blow."

"The newspaper . . ."

"It appears that his company was nearly decimated in the spring offensive. I read it this morning. It must have been a defeat, because no victories have been reported, only casualties. As near as I could tell, it happened the day after he left."

Until that moment, Amalia had never felt Eberhard could actually be vulnerable to death. The war happened to *other* men. Her patients. Fear invaded her, and she sat down on the stairs.

A few moments later, dinner was announced. They were already seated at the table when Eberhard joined them, dressed in full uniform. "I'm off, Mother. Dinner at the club." Kissing Trudi's cheek absently, he completely ignored Amalia.

More puzzled than hurt, Amalia gazed after him. Her mother-in-law appeared not to notice. "Lilli's in town, Amalia. Her father has leave also, so she's come up from Vienna to keep house for him until he goes back. She was here today."

Determined to be diverted, Amalia began eating the excellent dinner Trudi had ordered for her son. "It would be lovely to see her."

"I thought we might have them in tomorrow night."

"Must we? We haven't had an evening yet, just the three of us."

"The next night, then."

When they had finished eating and the gnome had cleared away, Amalia said, "You were right. It was heavenly in the country. Eberhard even played his violin."

Tears formed in her mother-in-law's eyes. "He played for you?"

"Every night. And we brought the instrument back with us."

After a long bath, Amalia unpacked, waiting with increasing uneasiness for Eberhard's return. As the hours dragged on, fear began to grow in her that the fragile influence she held on her husband had already waned. She went to bed alone at midnight.

Many hours later a sound from her husband's dressing room awakened her. Peering in the predawn light at her little clock, she saw that it was five A.M. She slid out of bed and put her woolen dressing gown over her shoulders.

"Is that you, Eberhard?" she whispered, opening the door to his dressing room.

He veered around to face her, his face a drunken mask. Amalia felt a shock run clear through her. Laughing, he lurched toward her as she instinctively backed into her own quarters. "Ah, my little wife!"

She backed further into safety and gripped the doorframe. This couldn't be Eberhard! His eyes frightened her with their feverish brightness.

"I'll see you in the morning, Eberhard," she breathed, starting to pull the door shut.

All at once he was beside her, gripping her arms so that his fingers dug into her. "Afraid?" he asked.

Amalia shrank from the smell of liquor. Overcome with disgust she pulled herself up and tried to loosen his grasp. With clenched teeth, Eberhard tightened his hold.

"Am I hurting you?" he asked, laughing again.

"Stop acting like a fool, and go sleep it off!"

The scene in the soft gray dawn disintegrated into a nightmare as Amalia tried to escape from hands that held her arms in a vise. Eberhard's countenance turned angry, and, in an instant, she saw his expression turn to hatred. He loosed one arm to slap her viciously across the face.

"Get away from me," he roared hoarsely. "Keep out of my sight."

Even as she recoiled, he left her, slamming his bedroom door.

Nursing her sharply throbbing cheek, she withdrew quickly into her own room and locked the door from the inside. After she had done the same to the door opening onto the hall, she began to tremble violently and only climbed back into her bed with difficulty. She lay there, frightened, tearless, and impotently angry. She had lost. The bulwark was smashed. The insanity in their world had conquered.

Loud knocking on her door pitched her back into a waking nightmare.

"Who is there?"

"It is Trudi, Amalia," the woman called. "Are you unwell? Will you unlock this door, please?"

Amalia complied with reluctance. She watched her mother-in-law's waxlike face contort vainly against tears. Going to her dressing table, Amalia looked in the mirror.

A bruise blackened the entire left side of her stark white face. Trudi stepped behind her and gripped Amalia's arms, causing her to wince. "Oh, my dear," the older woman cried, hastily withdrawing her hands. "It's the war. It's this hideous war."

"He was certainly hideously drunk."

The little woman's black eyes implored her. "But you understand, don't you?"

Amalia sat slumped at the dressing table, staring past her reflection. "He hates the sight of me, Trudi."

"No, I think he's afraid, Amalia. That's why he's drinking. That's why he can't bear the feelings he has for you."

Amalia stood and wandered to the window. Parting the blinds, she looked out at the heartlessly bright day.

Trudi continued, "All those men dying. And he was here with you. Now he doesn't want to go back."

Amalia turned. "We've lost him, just the same. The Eberhard we know is dying from the inside out."

She took care not to encounter her husband for the remainder of his leave. This was not too difficult, as he spent nearly all of his waking hours elsewhere. Had it not been for the bruise, she would have returned to the hospital. As it was, she could do nothing but prowl restlessly in her room while waiting for it to fade, trying to reconstruct her life. Because she still cared for the man she had come to know in Waldburg, she found that her feelings could not be easily cut off. With her new understanding, she had also been robbed of the anger and bitterness that had been brick and mortar of her nurse's identity. Now she knew that because she cared, nothing could protect her but his absence.

When the bruise had passed from black to blue to yellow-green, she couldn't stand her own company any longer and went downstairs, secure in the certainty that Trudi's indifference to society would not burden them with callers.

Her mother-in-law had aged pathetically throughout the ordeal, and seeing her reduced Amalia's own feelings to smaller proportions. Alternating between condemning and excusing her son, the woman's appeals to her daughter-in-law were agonizing. "We must be patient. He still loves you, I know. Though how he could do such a thing . . . my Eberhard . . ."

Today Trudi's mood was one of condemnation, and she pronounced, "His father was just the same. I thought I had raised him to be different."

Amalia returned, "Eberhard's father has much to answer for."

"No, it's my fault. I tried and I failed." Trudi sat up very straight.

"Someone taught Eberhard to despise the gentleness in himself, and I refuse to believe it was you. I don't know how the two of you ever survived that man."

Her mother-in-law's eyes were glazed with tears. "How forthright you are, Amalia." Her figure sagged. "Perhaps we haven't."

At that moment the tobacco-colored butler announced Lilli. Amalia's hand went to her face, but she had no time to escape, for the girl entered on his heels. "Aunt Trudi! Amalia! I gave up waiting for an invitation."

Trudi stood and went to her niece. "You must forgive us, Lilli. Amalia hasn't been well. She was thrown from her horse at Waldburg."

The young woman stood like a goddess, her looks vivid in the colorless room. Amalia thought she herself must have appeared similarly to Trudi all those months ago when she had arrived fresh from the capital of splendor.

"But if she had fallen on her face, surely her neck would be broken?"

"Of course. You're right, Lilli." Amalia sat erect, her eyes challenging. "It wasn't a horse. But you won't mention it, I hope?"

"Father is really quite concerned about Eberhard." Lilli seated herself.

"He needn't be," Trudi answered coldly. At the appearance of an outsider she had become, almost magically, her former self.

"You're telling me then that it's perfectly normal for him to become horribly drunk every night and knock Amalia about?"

At this, Amalia stood, annoyed to find she trembled. "He's drowning in his own humanity, Lilli." She added bitterly, "Apparently your father hasn't any."

Eberhard showed no desire for his wife, departing at dawn when his leave was up without saying farewell. Amalia's bruise had also faded enough for her to conceal its last vestiges with face powder. As she resumed her work at the hospital, she was physically rested, but her emotions were more than ever coiled like a watchspring. She dreaded her first conversation with Louisa.

The girl approached her tentatively after lunch her first day back.

"You look like a different person!" she said. "The time away must have agreed with you."

Unable to meet her friend's eyes, Amalia concentrated on the bandage she was rolling. "I'm sorry, Louisa, but would you mind terribly if we didn't talk about it?"

Her friend pulled back slightly as though she'd been struck. "I'm sorry. I didn't mean to intrude in any way. We won't speak about it again."

Amalia looked up in gratitude and saw the concern in her friend's eyes. She felt guilty for shutting her out. In the days that followed, she sought her friend's company less and less. Louisa seemed to sense her need for solitude and didn't approach her in the canteen or on the ward, except for infrequent, trivial chats.

Spring became summer and passed inexorably. Her world-weariness hardened into bitter resentment, her sadness into despair. They heard nothing from Eberhard. The war news was the same. The wounded kept coming, and the suffering continued without ceasing.

One night as she was leaving the hospital, she was surprised to see Louisa standing, waiting for her. She had worked almost two full shifts and was near collapse.

"You need a friend, Amalia, and you've been avoiding me. Let me walk you home."

Too tired to protest, Amalia allowed her friend to accompany her. She kept her eyes straight ahead and thought that if she were rude enough, Louisa would leave her to herself.

"Do you think I can't see you're in pain?" her friend began.

"The whole world is in pain!"

Louisa said nothing for a while. Then she ventured, "And you hold God to blame, don't you?"

Tears burned in her eyes. Her voice was flat and dead. "God doesn't care, Louisa."

Louisa stopped, and Amalia stopped beside her. Now that they were out, she felt her words lay like a challenge between them. But her friend's eyes disarmed her. They were wet and hurt, supplicating her. Louisa looked as though Amalia had just run her through with a bayonet.

"You don't know, you *can't* know, what you say. You've forgotten that because of our Savior, death is not the ultimate tragedy."

Amalia clenched her fists at her sides and spat out the words, "Yes. I agree with you there. The ultimate tragedy is life!"

Louisa resumed walking. "You're wrong, Amalia," she said quietly.

"I don't deny that we're all suffering. Some of us terribly. But after all that life can *do* to us, it is we alone who decide what it will *make* of us. We still have that power, at least. Believe me when I tell you that every one of us has the seeds of his own greatness inside his own sorrow."

"And what is the ultimate tragedy, then?"

"To become less than we were born to be."

Amalia took a moment to absorb this surprising statement. "That's not doctrine."

"It's truth."

Amalia stopped and looked at her friend. "You're a funny kind of Catholic. You remind me of my uncle. Are you a heretic?"

Louisa shrugged. "Probably. I read a lot of philosophy. Don't tell sister. Look, here's your house. We'll talk about all this some other time. But think about what I've said." Louisa leaned over to kiss her friend on the cheek. "I hope we can be friends again."

"I'm sorry . . ." Amalia began, but Louisa stopped her with a finger on her lips.

"We've all been going through a rough time. Good night."

Amalia watched her friend walk away into the night, Louisa's words distilling in the turmoil that was her consciousness.

September brought an unexpected letter from Lilli:

Dear Amalia,

Hope you are surviving your dreary grind. What drives you to it, I cannot imagine unless it is sheer boredom. But, of course, Berlin is always grim, I think. Vienna, I am happy to report, is infinitely better, in spite of the fact that even your good countrymen are becoming a bit wearied. Imagine! They still haven't beaten the Serbs! The High Command is giving all sorts of excuses, and victory is always 'imminent,' of course.

But enough of the war. I thought you might be interested to know that Andrzej is doing well, although sadly lacking in his customary charm these days. He is caught up in the same morbid life as you are and will be fully qualified next year. We have seen a little of each other, although his time away from the hospital is very scarce. He was exceedingly interested in your fall from the horse.

But I hope to make him forget you in time! Wish me luck, won't you?

> Your devoted cousin,
> Lilli

Amalia crumpled the letter and threw it in the waste bin. Lilli's Vienna was as distant in time and place as the Holy Roman Empire. Scoffing at the new little ache in her heart, she left for another day at the hospital.

Although the war news from the Western Front remained the same, a new German offensive in East Prussia had pushed the Russians three hundred miles back behind their own lines. The Austrian victory over the Serbs did not come until October, fourteen months after the outbreak of the war. Word came from home that Wolf had been granted an extended leave after fighting himself to exhaustion. She heard nothing about her friend the Baron von Schoenenburg and wondered whether he had survived the protracted battle. In a letter to Wolf she inquired about him.

November brought his reply:

> I might tell you that any reports you have heard about your Austrian allies have been filtered through the German propaganda mill. I think that is such a wonderful word: *Propaganda*. We are doing our best to fight the war that the Kaiser foisted on us, but the fact is we are just being used. It's not an inspiring feeling, to be used. And I must confess I'm feeling rather black at the moment. This is definitely Germany's war. But you're a proper little German now, so I won't burden you with the Austrian viewpoint.
>
> Your baron is fine—it is one of the only good parts of this war, to be able to serve under him. With the world going mad, it's comforting to fight under someone who still represents the old values.
>
> That reminds me, as a matter of fact. He heard a ridiculous story about you and came to me in a fury the other day. Someone with nothing better to do has put it about that Eberhard has turned swine

and begun beating you. I told him that the first part was entirely possible; the second, most doubtful. I informed him that you were an expert at taking care of yourself, though you don't look it, but he wanted convincing. I don't think I really satisfied him in the end. I can't imagine what he thinks he can do about it, but as I say, he represents the old values.

The rest of the letter contained an account of several of Wolf's heroic exploits. On the whole, Amalia thought it a sad letter, pulling her emotions back to her former home. The baron's anger touched her, and Wolf's dismissal of the matter made her smile. She found a nostalgia in her brother's self-centeredness, and it was nice to know that some things had not changed. This letter she kept, along with the few others she had saved from home.

Chapter Nine

Following her walk with Louisa, Amalia resumed their friendship, although they didn't talk of God or Eberhard again. Louisa shared with her friend the great joy she felt when her brother got leave. He was also whole but discouraged and in need of all Louisa's nurturing qualities.

"He doesn't want to go back," she confided to Amalia. "It's taking all my faith to let him go."

"What choice do they have?" Amalia asked with a sigh. "Just send him off with lots of love and good memories of home. Your faith is strong enough for both of you. It will be a great comfort to him. You have a source of inner strength, tranquillity," Amalia elaborated. "Where does it come from?"

"I spend a lot of time in meditation and prayer when I'm not at the hospital. The way I see it is that God isn't going to come down here Himself to do His work. That's what we're supposed to do. Every day I begin with a prayer that I can be His hands."

Amalia stared at her friend. "That's exactly what my uncle said on his deathbed. No wonder we're friends. You have his tranquillity."

In mid-December came the tidings that she had half dreaded and half hoped for. Eberhard was to have leave at Christmas.

Amalia had received only one letter from her husband that even obliquely referred to the disastrous March leave. It came in early December.

There seems to be nothing in the future but a continued stalemate. That, and another winter. I have become a man whom I scarcely know, operating from day to day like one of those nursery toys that you wind up and then watch wander stiffly around the floor. Events take place but only at some emotional distance from me. The only thing that is real is the life I live with you in my imagination. If you can't forgive me, there is nothing left.

Because of that letter, she half-desired to see him. She kept those hopeful feelings submerged, and it was not until she saw Eberhard in the flesh that she knew she could forgive him anything.

He stood before her on a cold December evening, unrecognizably thin with sunken eyes. Gray and lined, his face looked old, and the hands that reached out for her shook. Pity undermined any remaining caution, and she went to him and allowed him to embrace her. He had no words of greeting but just held her fiercely. She knew she was crying.

The first night he slept fourteen hours. When he awakened in the morning, she heard him calling down the staircase, "Amalia? Amalia!"

She came out of the library and looked up at her husband. "I'm here, Eberhard. What would you like to eat?"

He dogged her footsteps the rest of the day. His hand would find its way to her shoulder, squeezing her gently. At night he wanted only to hold her. As she lay there she felt his mental wounds bleed confusion, horror, and despair.

Trudi went ahead to prepare things at the estate where they were to spend Christmas. The day before they were to leave, Amalia spent the morning wrapping gifts. Eberhard was at her elbow. "And did you think I deserved a Christmas present this year, my love?"

She turned into his arms and kissed him lightly. "Wait and see!" she teased.

"I must go off after lunch to find your gift. The merchandise at the Front was hardly suitable."

In her brisk nurse's voice, she replied, "It'll be good for you to get out, even if there's a bit of snow."

She felt him shudder next to her, and looking up at his gray closed face, she regretted her words. After winter in the trenches, snow would always mean a different thing to Eberhard than it did to her.

"Never mind," she amended quickly. "You needn't go out. My dearest Christmas wish is for you to have a good leave." She put her hand up to his cheek. He took it and kissed the palm.

"No, I'll go. It won't take long. I know just what I'm going to buy for you."

* * *

Eberhard set off for Unter den Linden in an unusually introspective mood. Amalia was all that was good in his world. She was not quite the girl she had been when she had arrived, fresh and vibrant from Vienna. But she was a woman now. He never could have imagined she would shoulder the horror of this war and be *his* bulwark. Impatiently, he put that thought from his mind and concentrated on finding the jewelers.

When he left the shop half an hour later, his purchase wrapped and ready, he found himself in the midst of a white-out. The snow was blowing so hard down the avenue that he could not see across to the other side. For a moment, he stood there, blinded. Then the present dissolved.

He was freezing cold, up to his thighs in frigid mud. A mortar was sailing towards him, whistling straight for his head. He threw himself face down in the trench, choking on the mud. The mortar exploded, and the deafening sound went on and on, finally convincing him he was not dead. Through the nearly solid curtain of swirling snow, he saw red. Blood. Crawling on his belly, he reached Friedrich. His head was blown open. Weeping from weakness, grief, and the death-noise that would never end, he buried his face in his friend's muddy, blood-spattered tunic. The gods had forsaken him. Where had they gone—those winged heroes from the Avenue of Victory? Where had victory gone? Where was glory? The only answer was the never-ending fire of mortar shells discharging death all around him.

* * *

Amalia was not alarmed when her husband had not returned after an hour. When he had not returned by four o'clock, she began to wonder, and when he was still not in for dinner, she did begin to worry.

While eating her solitary meal, she tried to shake her foreboding. Eberhard was a grown man and a soldier, and it was absurd to think that he should need her protection for a short excursion to Unter den Linden. But where was he, then?

At nine o'clock, she was pacing in the parlor when the door knocker sounded. She ran to answer it, forestalling Trudi's butler, who retreated with disapproval to his pantry.

A strange soldier stood there, an officer, from the look of him. Amalia said, "My husband isn't home, just now."

"I'm aware of that, baroness. At this moment, he's asleep in the back of my automobile, actually." He gestured behind him, to where the long, expensive vehicle stood parked in the street. "I'm Herr Hauptmann von Schonerer. I'd like to speak with you before I bring in your husband. He's quite safe with my chauffeur for the moment."

Amalia led the captain, a big, stocky man with golden hair, into the parlor. His mild blue eyes had a compassionate look as he studied her before beginning to speak.

"I expect you've been worried, baroness. I'm sorry it took me so long to get him home, but he wouldn't say where he lived. Finally, someone who knew him came along and gave me the address."

"Was he very drunk?"

"Very, Baroness. But before you become angry, I think there is something you need to know."

She sat, her back straight, on the edge of the chair. "He was going out to buy me a present."

"Ah!" von Schonerer pulled a battered little parcel out of his pocket. "This must be it. I impounded it for safe keeping. In his state, he was bound to lose it in one way or another."

Amalia took it and laid it beside her without interest. "I am very grateful to you for bringing my husband home, Herr Hauptmann, but now I think I should be getting him to bed."

Her guest sat down on a chair without invitation and, leaning forward, studied her face for a moment. When he spoke, his voice was supplicating. "Be kind to your husband, Baroness. He can't help himself. Can you guess where I found him?"

"In a beer hall?" she asked, her voice arch.

"No. I found him huddled, almost frozen, under the elevated tracks along the Spree."

"What?"

"Have you no idea why?"

"Dead drunk, I suppose."

"No. Not then. I don't think your husband is really a drinking man, is he, Baroness?"

"Not until the war. On his last leave he was never sober."

"It's called shell shock."

"Shell shock?" Amalia repeated. "Eberhard?"

"You know something about it then?"

"Yes. I work as a nurse's aide. I should have guessed." A dozen clues came forth to explain his behavior. It had never occurred to her that someone like Eberhard could become shell shocked. How could she have been so blind to what had happened to her own husband?

"This is how I've reconstructed it, Baroness. When the blizzard started this afternoon, he probably headed for home. It was rather thick around three o'clock. Probably reminded him of the trenches. Has he been home long?"

"Three days. But today was the first time he would go out."

"All right, then. He panicked and became totally disoriented. Who knows? He may even have imagined he was back at the Front. At any rate, he became lost over there by the river, and then the train came along those tracks over his head."

"And the noise set him off!" Amalia finished.

"About finished him off, I'd say. He was huddled down there

213

between the wall and the fence, 'taking cover' for long enough to be close to freezing. I recognized the uniform as I was passing. Tried to get him to come out, but he was totally dazed. Couldn't even understand what I was saying."

She was professionally absorbed by this time. "You were reassuring?"

"Not at first. I really didn't understand, you see. One doesn't expect to see shell shock on the streets of Berlin. I thought he was drunk. Gave him a dressing down for conduct unbecoming an officer."

"And that just made him worse, I expect."

"Yes. It was when another train came and the poor fellow put his hands to his ears that I guessed. And he had that horrible, blank expression one comes to recognize."

"What happened then?"

"I managed to urge him out in a more friendly manner and took him to the Officers' Club. He drank several schnapps rather quickly. Too late I realized he had no head for drink. He was mortified, of course, and wanted to obliterate any memory of his actions."

Pity jabbed at her conscience. This then was the reason for his behavior. Self-disgust. A feeling he had failed.

"And the more drunk he got, the less he wanted to come home. Afraid of what you'd say, I expect."

"He felt he'd let me down, Herr Hauptmann. He was determined that things would be different this time." She stood. "But things will be better now that I know what's wrong. Let's bring him inside."

Together they managed to get him up the stairs. Barely cognizant of what was happening to him, Eberhard seemed to have no idea where he was or who his benefactors were. As they laid him, fully clothed, upon the bed, he suddenly sat up and searched his tunic pockets.

"'Malia's ring . . . 'Malia's ring . . ."

"It's all right, Oberleutnant. I have it for you," the captain reassured him.

"I can manage now, Herr Hauptmann," Amalia whispered. They walked together out of the room and down the stairs.

"Which army is your husband with?"

"The first."

"Ah. Von Kluck," he nodded to himself in some private understanding.

"I can't even tell you how grateful I am," Amalia said. "For what you did for Eberhard, and for explaining things to me. It's going to be better for us both now, but I should have known."

*   *   *

The next morning, Eberhard woke to find Amalia supervising the packing of his clothes in his dressing room.

"We're not going, Amalia," he said, asserting the words in sudden panic. He wasn't emerging from this townhouse for the rest of his leave.

She looked up at him. "It will be better for you there. Remember last time?"

"I'm not going. You can if you like." He rolled over so his back was to her, not wanting her to read his face.

"But your mother! She has everything ready . . ."

"I tell you, I'm not going. If Mother wishes to see me, she can come home," his voice was rising, and he sensed Amalia beginning to shrink away from him.

Then she said, her voice soft, "It's the train, isn't it?"

The panic leapt to his throat. How did she know? "What do you mean?"

She put her hand on his arm. "You don't like the noise, do you? It reminds you of the trenches . . ."

He shook off her hand. "What is this? What are you talking about?" Cold sweat beaded on his forehead. Could she *feel* his fear?

Amalia tried again to put a hand on his arm, but he brushed her off and said, "Leave me now. It would be better. I want to be by

215

myself." As she went, he was conscious that for his pride's sake, he had rid himself of the one comfort remaining in his life.

Getting up, he turned the key in the lock and then returned to his bed, where he shuddered uncontrollably, curled in the fetal position. He was an infant. Yellow. A coward.

* * *

Amalia had sensed his terror. She sent her mother-in-law a telegram: *E shell shocked stop Train too loud stop Christmas here query Amalia stop*

By the time Trudi returned home, Eberhard had regressed to his former behavior. Seemingly unable to bear the sight of Amalia, he spent all of his time either drinking himself into a stupor or sleeping it off. She unwrapped the little box the captain had given her. It held a ring of closely set small sapphires that completely encircled the band. The gift, from the man inside her tormented Oberleutnant, fed the compassion that grew in her. She wore it on the same hand as her wedding band. Eberhard, locked in his own private hell, never noticed.

Not until Christmas Day was she able to speak to him alone. He had turned on his heel and was leaving the dining room when his long-suffering mother reproached him for his appearance. Amalia had followed him up the stairs.

"Eberhard!" She reached the door just in time to prevent his shutting her out. "Let me in for a moment."

She looked at him, his disheveled uniform, his defeated posture, and his bloodshot eyes. Her heart hurt. Closing the door behind her, she watched him sit on the bed and sink his head in his hands.

He said nothing, and she went over and sat beside him. He did not respond when she put her hand on his knee. Overcome with tenderness, Amalia attempted to embrace him. "Oh, Eberhard, I do love you so . . . don't hurt yourself like this!"

He pushed her away. "Love me? You pity me! No one could love this . . ." he indicated his body as though he would dissociate himself from it.

"Would you love me less if I were sick?" she asked softly.

"Sick? I'm not sick, just a weak-kneed old woman, frightened to death of her own shadow."

He got up and walked away from her.

"Eberhard, you are sick. You have a bona fide illness—shell shock. I've seen it in the hospital. I know."

"It's nothing that fancy, Amalia. It's just plain cowardice."

She went to him and clutched his iron-hard arms. "Listen to me. *You are not a coward.* Your nerves are sick. They've had too much noise, too little rest, too much strain . . ."

"But a real soldier can take it . . ."

"Eberhard, there's never been a war like this before. Day after day. Night after night, shelling and screaming. I know. My patients never stop talking about it, even in their sleep."

"You can't possibly know, Amalia," he whispered. Then, collapsing in a chair, he stared at the wall. She sat on the chair arm and put her own arm around his shoulders. They sat quietly for several minutes.

"You must get your leave extended, you know, until you can get well. The doctor at the hospital can take care of it."

But her husband pulled himself up wearily. "No. I have to go back, Amalia. It wouldn't be right for me to leave my men out there. There's no excuse for me."

He continued to stare sightlessly in front of him, and Amalia knew he was hearing shell fire and screaming.

She was cheered to see her husband at the breakfast table the next morning. Though his hand still shook as he moved fork to mouth, his eyes had a decisive look about them. He greeted her with the news that he was going to see the family attorney. "I should like you to come with me, Amalia."

She filled her plate. It seemed like a long time since she had felt like eating. "If you like, Eberhard."

Trudi looked at her son sharply but said nothing beyond "Good morning."

Soon they had taken leave of her and gone out into the dismal morning, which threatened yet another blizzard. A memory assailed Amalia as she walked, hands in her muff, trying to match her stride to her husband's.

"This weather reminds me of the day you said good-bye in Vienna."

Eberhard did not smile at the reminiscence. "It would have been better for you if you had taken that as final."

Determined to lighten his mood, she laughed. "However deceived you were about my character then, you ought to know now that I always get my man."

His lips tightened. "I was going to be such a hero."

They walked along for a while without speaking, and then she said, "Eberhard, I know you never had much time for my Uncle Lorenz or his views, but he predicted that this war would be different. It's not the kind of war your father fought in or dreamed of. The heroes in this war will be the men who simply endure, just as you have done."

They had arrived at the old stone building where Eberhard's attorney practiced. As they ascended the steep stairway, Amalia wondered for the first time about the reason for their visit.

A bony clerk of middle age showed them into the office of Herr Doktor Grau. Amalia's precarious spirits slid into gloom as they entered the crowded little cubicle.

"Herr Doktor Grau has handled the Waldburg estates since he was a young man in my Grandfather's time," Eberhard told her as he made introductions. The shrunken little man made a curt bow.

He peered at the young soldier through rheumy eyes. "So you followed your father, after all," he said, his voice hollow sounding.

Reaching for his pipe among the clutter on his desk, he said, "You'll want to update your will now that you're married, then."

These words came as her husband was seating her, and she was glad of the chair. She should have anticipated this, but it came as a shock. Her husband was answering, "A provisional will only, just for the duration of the war. If I survive, we will change it."

Amalia shuddered and wanted to weep. Even with all the death she had seen, it was hard to imagine herself as a widow. The gloomy room certainly engendered thoughts of that nature.

"The usual procedure is to leave the income to your wife until your eldest son reaches majority, at which time the estates pass to him, with the provision that your wife is to receive a dower portion of the income."

Eberhard shifted in his chair. "I would like to depart from the usual procedure, if I may. I don't wish to tie my wife to my property, should I be killed. She is young, as you can see, and all her family is in Vienna."

The little lawyer opened his mouth to object, but Eberhard raised a palm. "Please. I have thought this out very carefully. In the event of my death, I think it would be best if you and my Uncle Wilhelm were to act as joint trustees of the estate until it could be sold. I would like my mother to continue in possession of the townhouse and for her to continue to receive her present dower portion of the estate income. Amalia will receive the rest of the income, and eventually my mother and wife can divide the proceeds of the estate sale. Thirty-seventy, I should think. The largest percentage to my wife, of course."

As he slipped from the subjunctive into the future tense, Amalia panicked. *He was certain he was going to die.*

"And if you should have issue?" the lawyer asked.

"That won't arise," her husband replied coldly. He stood. "Can you have that ready for me by this afternoon?"

"Certainly, if there is a good reason for such haste. Tomorrow afternoon would be more convenient."

"I leave for the Front tonight."

Amalia felt as though she had been punched in the stomach.

"Then it shall be ready for you by, shall we say, four o'clock?"

Eberhard nodded crisply, thanked the old man, and ushered his wife out of the door, through the secretary's chamber, down the stairs, and out into the street, where at last she exploded. "Tonight! But, Eberhard, there is still a week of your leave left!"

He took her arm, and led her briskly along. "I'll not discuss it with you in the street, Amalia."

It was not until they had lunched with Trudi and retired to Eberhard's room where he commenced packing his kit that he allowed her an opportunity to question him. Avoiding her eyes, he took the offensive. "You and I both know that I'm worthless to you, Amalia. I'm not what you bargained for." As she stood indignantly, he held up a palm, much as he had to the old lawyer. "I'm not what I thought I was, either. It seems that nothing I have placed my faith in, including myself, has come up to expectations." He paused and passed his hand through his hair. "You may not believe it from my actions, but you're the only thing I care about anymore, and you would be wrong not to despise me . . . don't interrupt! You think you love me, Amalia, but it's only pity. Perhaps you don't realize it yourself, but last night was the first time you have ever been able to bring yourself to tell me that you loved me."

Guilt washed over Amalia in a scalding wave, and she looked down at her hands. Now that he had paused, she found it impossible to speak.

He continued, "I thought about that all night, you know. I want to ask you something." He walked over to her and tilted her chin up so that she could not avoid looking at him. "Why did you marry me?"

She saw his tormented face, eyes bloodshot and burning, brow contracted, mouth taut, and she dared not hurt him. But she realized also that he would know instinctively if she lied.

"I fled to you, Eberhard," she said quietly. "You were my rock, the one thing I knew I could always depend upon. I told you Andrzej was not constant."

His features relaxed, and he sagged onto the bed, covering his face with his hands. "A rock!" he moaned.

Presently she saw that he was shaking with sobs, and heart and conscience smiting her, she got up and crossed to him, kneeling on the floor in front of him, her hands on his knees. "I came to you, Eberhard, because I knew that you loved me. I was right. You do. Whatever else has happened, it hasn't been because you haven't loved me. I'm certain the war has turned everyone's marriage inside out." She went on before she could stop herself, "And if anyone is at fault, I am. It is I who have let you down by not loving you enough . . ."

"But you *have* loved me, Amalia." Eberhard put his hands under her elbows and drew her up next to him. "Perhaps not as a woman should love a man, but as one human being who is good and kind loves another who is less fortunate. There are many women who could not have borne what you have taken from me." She started to protest again, and again he interrupted her, "But it is only the weakness in me which arouses that love." He stood suddenly and recommenced his packing. "I *hate* my weakness."

Nothing was said for several minutes. Amalia searched her mind for something bracing to say, but everything she could think of merely reinforced his theory.

He stopped for a moment and looked her full in the face. "That's why I'm going back tonight. I'm going to face this squarely and overcome it, or die trying. I can't stay here and be smothered by your sympathy or continually drown myself in drink. It's better to be dead than to be an object of pity."

Amalia watched silently as her husband packed.

She accompanied him to the station that night. The good-bye to Trudi had been painfully brief. His mother had, for once, not been able to contain her unhappiness, and in an uncharacteristic manner had chided him, "You don't care about us, Eberhard. You've become unfeeling . . . just like your father."

Her husband's mouth gave its new taut smile, and he answered, "Would that I had." He had kissed his mother, and then they left.

Amalia's own emotions were a confusion of guilt and tenderness. There was also fear. After the cab had disgorged them at the station, she walked with him to the train, trying to think of what she could say to ease his self-loathing. Finally, she stopped him.

"Eberhard, you must listen to me." Multitudes of women and soldiers eddied around them, and she fixed him with her eyes. "You are mistaken about me. I never could really love Eberhard the soldier. That is true. But I have come to love Eberhard the human being. And it is a far deeper and greater feeling than you imagine." She put her hands on the lapels of his greatcoat. "At the same time, I have come to hate and despise war for what it has done to you. If you, whom I love, should sacrifice yourself to that which I hate, just because you think it is some sort of redeeming gesture, I would see it only as an utterly futile act. I could *never* forgive you that. I want only you, my loving husband." Her eyes pleaded with him. "I want to have your sons, Eberhard."

He looked down at her gently in the old way, touching her cheek. "We will see, my dear."

She thought then of Louisa's words: *After all that life can do to us, it is we alone who decide what it will make of us.* Eberhard had made his decision. The peace in his face disturbed her far more in that moment than all the pain she had seen in it before. It was the peace painted on the faces of the martyrs in the great gray churches of Vienna.

They walked the rest of the way to the train.

Chapter Ten

Word of Eberhard's death reached them on March 27, 1916. It was said that he had died a hero's death at Verdun along with 336,000 other Germans.

Though Amalia had suspected the day would come ever since she had seen into her husband's heart at the train station, his death did not register fully in her mind. The appalling numbers of those who died along with him made his particular death seem meaningless, as though he had just been some matériel carelessly squandered. It was impossible to mourn him as an individual when he was only one among so many.

Nor was there a body to mourn. Even dead, he would never come home from the Front. To her, it seemed that he would always be out there, somewhere in France, fighting the enemy and, most terribly, himself.

Everyone was very kind. Louisa took several days off from the hospital to stay at the townhouse with Amalia and Trudi. Amalia noted her presence and the fact that she was running the household, but she was in a world of her own, sleeping in Eberhard's bed, plucking the strings of his violin, packing away what remained of his clothes. Trying to feel the terrible thing that had befallen her.

Trudi was a ghost, going from room to room, barely speaking. When Louisa left, she showed no interest in taking over the running of the house, so Amalia stripped everything down to essentials: three meals a day, laundry, and a presentable house. She put Ludmilla and Kristina in charge.

Her family wrote, urging her to return to Vienna. "Now that Wolf has gone back to the Front, we are so sadly alone . . ." her mother penned.

Amalia was unable to take any actions or make any decisions. For one thing, she could never leave Trudi in this precarious mental state. She felt guilty even going to the hospital, but she knew she had to have something to engage her physically, if not mentally. Waiting for that sense of loss, waiting to know that she was a widow, was an eerie feeling, as though she were suspended between two lives. Underneath it all, she knew she still hoped for news that it was a great mistake and that Eberhard was merely wounded or held prisoner. It had been known to happen.

Six weeks after the news of her husband's death she was awakened by the scream. Struggling out of a nightmare in which she had been at the Front, looking at body after body strewn across the earth, trying to find her husband, she identified the screamer. It was Ludmilla. Not even pausing to put on her dressing gown, she ran straight to her mother-in-law's suite.

She found Trudi lying there on her bed, her face eternally composed, and now irreversibly wax-like in its final sleep.

A note lay on her bed stand addressed in a tight hand to "My dear daughter." Saying nothing at all to Ludmilla or the other servants who were gathering, Amalia took up the note, and leaning down, mechanically kissed Trudi's white forehead. Then as though this were a continuation of her brutal nightmare, she drifted out of the room, her mind seeing bodies everywhere. As a sleepwalker, she entered her own room, bolted the doors, and crawled back into bed. Opening the note, she read it without bothering to turn on the lamp.

> I know well the curious respite of shock and unbelief that somehow initially softens the sudden death of someone close. Until now, both you and I have been sustained by it, but tonight, Amalia, I realized he will never come back. As you know, I have never been deeply religious—I do not know where he is or if I shall be permitted to join

him, but my reason for living is gone. If there is such a thing as an afterlife and if I am not damned, I go to join Lorenz.

I have given a son to satisfy the dreams and power lust of a father and a whole class just like him. I realized, but only too late, that Eberhard was not like them—he was a gentle man, a man who was made for peace and not war. He should never have been born a Prussian. No, that is not right. I cannot dodge my own responsibility. I should have had the moral courage to raise him differently. I was too hesitant about my own beliefs.

His love for you tore at the basic fabric of his lifelong teachings. I do not regret that he married you, although I did not think it was wise at the time. At least if he was to be cheated on life, he was not cheated on love. His feelings for you caused him much perplexity, for he had little experience of tenderness, but those feelings were based upon a higher truth than the manic idealism of a few Prussian war gods.

Do not think you failed either of us, my dear. I know your motives in coming to us were not entirely pure, but you have given us all the light and beauty of your warm and generous nature. We were too far advanced in our drama before you came upon the scene. You could not have changed us with any amount of love or devotion. We were bent on our destinies, and you traveled with us for a brief while—just long enough to make us doubt the wisdom of our journey.

I take my life because there is no altering of that destiny now—my son is gone, my life is gone. The night has come. I have failed.

Germany will lose this war, Amalia. I knew that in my heart in August, 1914. It may take years, but we will lose. Do not feel bound to the von Waldburgs. You, mercifully perhaps, have no son. Go back to Vienna, my dear. Sell the estate, and marry an Austrian—a good, happy man who will be contented with life. One day, this war will end for you.

For me it ends now.

> Auf Wiedersehen, dearest daughter,
> Gertrude Anna Sophia von Waldburg

At the end of her reading, all reality withdrew. Amalia's unrestrained double grief dwarfed any need to eat or sleep and made even the simplest communication impossible.

As despair took possession of her, she would not allow the servants into her quarters. Drinking only water from the pitcher by her bed until it was gone, she lay, watching scenes play across the ceiling: Eberhard absorbed in Bach, bending and swaying with the grace that so undermined his stoicism; Trudi, watching her son with anxious eyes as he swung his new wife in joy at the outbreak of the war; and worst of all, the hollow face that shone with peace, reflecting Eberhard's inner decision to sacrifice and obliterate himself. And Trudi! She had known in the end that her sacrifice of her only son was a fraud, an irreversible, horrible mistake.

The pain within Amalia was so sharp that she waited to die of it. She existed in this void, between life and death for two days, indifferent to either course. To live might be bad, but what was it to die? Merely another sea of pain?

On the morning of the third day, there was a tremendous crash and the door fell inward, landing beside her bed in a great cloud of plaster. In the ruined doorway silhouetted against the light from the hall, stood Louisa, Kristina, and Ludmilla. Striding into the room without invitation, Louisa trod on the door and stood beside her, at once putting a cool hand on her forehead. Kristina marched after her.

The dramatic entrance was not enough to rouse her from her lassitude, and Amalia only stared up at the face of her friend. She realized vaguely that Louisa and the servants had broken the door down themselves.

"She needs water," Louisa told the hovering maid.

Sometime later, she was propped up against a mound of pillows, submitting to the bathing of her face. It did not seem at all odd that Louisa should be here performing this duty. She had already drunk what seemed to have been gallons of beef broth and water.

"The servants would like to know what is to be done with the remains of the baroness."

Amalia turned her face away. "You must know what Protestants do with suicides."

"I'll find out," Louisa promised. "They must have had a pastor. Who was he, do you know?"

"No. They weren't religious."

Louisa ceased her labors with the face cloth and carried the bowl to the sink. "I'll find out what would be best."

"One church, another church, what does it matter? My so-called faith hasn't given me a bit of comfort, Louisa. I'm not sure I even believe in God anymore."

Returning to Amalia's side, Louisa looked down at her. Amalia felt herself close her heart against her friend. She didn't want to be preached to.

"You must not, you cannot, carry this alone, Amalia," she said very gently.

Anger surged up from some pocket of strength within her, but before she could speak, Louisa had laid a hand on her arm. "There is only One who ever had the strength or the goodness to bear the consequence of such evil as we see in this war. He has already done so. Long ago, in Gethsemane. He knows everything there is to know about suffering. Give it to him."

Amalia looked at the woman who stood above her. Her carriage was erect, and her face shown with a luminescence that transformed her homely features. There flowed a transfusion of warmth through her hand into Amalia's arm. "You must not lose faith, Amalia."

She was able to cry out her sorrow then, in great angry sobs. Louisa did not leave her or try to stop her but merely sat by, bathing her face from time to time and fetching fresh handkerchiefs.

"Part of faith is not giving up hope for a better world," she said finally.

"But life is such a bitter gift!"

"At the moment, it seems like it. This is a very dark passage you are in. But it would be a mistake to see that passage as your whole life. There is nothing in this world more deceptive than darkness. You think you live in a void, but actually there are colors and textures and beauty all around you."

"I don't want to see them . . ."

"Because you think that it will hurt."

"Yes!"

"That is the lie of the darkness." She smiled and took Amalia's hand. "The price we pay for immortality is to know both this darkness and the light and to choose between them." She leaned toward her and offered a drink from the cup she held. "You are a particularly radiant person. You must not let the darkness win, Amalia."

Part Three

VIENNA
1916 TO 1917

Chapter One

I t seemed all wrong that Vienna should still appear the same. It was as if Amalia had only traveled back in time. Although her childhood surroundings seemed untouched by war, she had been irrevocably changed and saw everything through a stranger's eyes.

The midsummer landscape was covered with the alpine glory of wildflowers, the air was warm and balmy, and the women who crowded onto the platform to meet the train were dressed in vivid colors with impossible hats and little dogs on jeweled leads. Moving with the languor she remembered, the Viennese allowed themselves to be kissed passionlessly on the cheek by new arrivals and then moved off, their laughs tinkling grotesquely in the bombastic clamor of the station. After Berlin, the atmosphere appeared wholly artificial and exotic.

Her parents were on the platform, too, looking solid and dull but with something different about them—an air of dilapidation. They might have been two wounded sparrows standing beside one another at the edge of a tropical bird bath. In spite of superficial appearances, had the war wrought its dark changes here as well?

She had left Berlin the day before, three months after her mother-in-law's death. It had been a wrenching leave-taking, seeing Louisa's bright but teary face as she waved at her from the platform.

She had not been sure she wanted to return to Vienna, to try to fit into a life that she saw as irrelevant. In her gentle way, Louisa had encouraged her.

"There's nothing in Berlin as important as your family," she had said. "I know you don't think you've got any to spare, but it's obvious they need your strength."

Suspecting that Louisa was just trying to infuse her life with purpose, Amalia had at first refused to consider what she said. But time had brought changes in her attitude. Anger replaced her lethargy. She moved through the stages of grief, lashing out at life, at Louisa, at God, but most of all at the futility of the war. In her mind it was inextricably linked to the Prussian values that had destroyed her husband's peace and life.

Eventually, her rage spent, she awakened, exhausted, to the fact that she did have a desire to survive and even to prevail. If she had to live this life, she somehow had to make a difference in the world. That was when she realized the cold marble townhouse was too much like a tomb.

It was the thought of leaving Louisa that kept her tied to her husband's home. Throughout the ordeal, her words of sober truth had carried Amalia. Her friend's goodness had deflected her bitterness, and her warmth was the only kindling she knew in her frigid world.

When she attempted to express this one day, Louisa's response was, "Then it's time you left, Amalia. I am bound to disappoint you one day and I couldn't bear for that to happen. You can't build any kind of foundation on me."

"But you're my dearest friend!"

"But I'm not your God. It's time you came to know Him. I think sometimes I'm standing in the way."

With reluctance, Amalia had begun making plans to return home.

Now, she stepped off the train, dressed in a black suit with a white blouse that she knew was unflattering. How she hated black! Kristina, who had commenced an almost bubbling, cheerful conversation as soon as they had crossed the Austrian border, followed her.

Smiling, Amalia went to meet the parents who appeared so suddenly shrunken and old. Her battered heart softened, and she stretched her arms out to them impulsively for the first time since she was a child.

Mama's mouth trembled, and tears coursed down her face as she returned the embrace. "I wouldn't have known you, my dear. How like Mother you have become!"

Amalia's father stood silent, nodding his head and smiling, his eyes glazed.

"I'm very glad to be back," she announced, setting out to please them. "And I don't intend to leave again."

As they still seemed to wait for something, she took their arms and, walking between them, signaled the porter to follow. The next surprise was the hired Fiaker. Her mother had always been intensely carriage-proud but offered no explanation. Her luggage followed them in another taxicab.

"How much the same everything is!" Amalia remarked lightly. Her mother smiled and patted her daughter's knee. Her father still said nothing.

"Wolf is all right, isn't he?" Amalia demanded, wondering if some problem with her brother could be at the bottom of their behavior.

"We haven't heard anything to the contrary," Mama answered. "But he doesn't write much."

Increasingly dismayed by her parent's lack of response, Amalia kept up a steady patter of questions. When the Fiaker pulled into the familiar neighborhood of her childhood, she ceased to worry about anything for the moment. Drawn once more into the familiarity of her first memories—window boxes planted in primroses, hunter green shutters, mellow gold plaster, and the well-remembered eccentricities of the bricks in the walkway, she knew she was home.

Georg, the butler, was not there to greet her. She left her cases on the front stoop, and as her father seemed to have forgotten, paid off the taxis herself. She entered the house and went at once to the morning room. Kristina, noting the absence of a butler, went back to the stoop and began carrying the luggage upstairs.

Amalia's mother stood in the morning room, looking at her

helplessly as she noted the worn chintzes on the furniture, the dust, and the air of shabbiness.

"I remember how you loved this room, Amalia," she said. "We almost live in it now. I've shut up the drawing rooms."

Standing there for a moment, Amalia was saddened by what she saw. The house she had once railed against, with its stolid unimaginative routine, now seemed forlorn, like a diseased giant. Her mother looked like an elderly housekeeper, overborne by her task. Pity emerged from Amalia's personal sorrow. Pulling off her hat, she asked, "Is money a problem, Mama?"

Her pity grew as Mama sank onto the small ottoman, covering her face in her hands. Amalia acted instinctively, almost professionally. Casting off her gloves, she knelt beside her unhappy mother and gave her a handkerchief.

Mama was not able to speak until sometime later. "That Pfeiffer disappeared. You know I never trusted him."

"You wrote me about Pfeiffer, I recall. But I'm afraid I didn't realize . . . it was shortly after Eberhard was killed, wasn't it?"

Her mother blew her nose. "I don't remember just when it was anymore. So much has happened. But, you see, your father hasn't been well for some time, and Pfeiffer had been managing things for him. After the man left, your father still kept going down to the warehouse every day, but he was very vague, and I realized after a while that he had lost himself somewhere." Mama paused and stood. She walked to the mantle and automatically adjusted the picture frame that held a photograph of her son in uniform. "He has gone into the past, and he won't come back."

Having observed her father, Amalia was not surprised to hear this, but it saddened her still more. Nodding encouragement to her mother to continue, she found it more difficult to accept her demeanor. Whatever her shortcomings, Margareta Faulhaber had always radiated control and determination.

"I felt I should consult Radl. He's our family attorney, you know.

He administers my trust, along with your father. It's the money I inherited from your grandfather. I asked him to look into the business, and do you know what he found?"

Amalia raised her eyebrows in query.

"There is no business!"

Already prepared for this blow, Amalia waited for her mother to explain further.

"Herr Doktor Radl told me that your father had been drawing rather heavily upon my capital lately, but he had assumed I knew. The capital is only half what it had been. When he looked into the situation at Faulhaber and Son, he found that Pfeiffer had embezzled everything."

"Everything? How is that possible?"

Her mother rallied somewhat in support of her husband. "You mustn't blame your father, Amalia. I don't think you realize his age. He's nearly sixty-eight. He was looking forward to retiring and letting Wolf take over, but Wolf preferred to have someone to manage for them. Your brother isn't really cut out for business, you know, Amalia." Pride in her son's lack of middle class responsibility cut through her sorrow for a moment. She considered him more von Hohenburg than Reichart or Faulhaber.

Amalia prodded her mother to continue, "So, Pfeiffer was the manager of choice, I presume? Or of desperation, at least, with the war on?"

"Yes. Your father trusted him completely."

"And he proved unworthy."

Her mother's tears were dried now, and she continued in a flat tone. "Over the last two years, he was slowly embezzling the company's profits and turning the assets into cash and putting the cash into his pocket. We're just a trading company these days, you know, so there was nothing to speak of but inventory. We were getting less and less money out of the business, but he explained it all to your father by saying that both our suppliers in Moravia and our markets here and abroad were drying up because of the war." She stopped to blow her nose.

"It sounded reasonable, but in the end he disappeared with every schilling. There is nothing of our business left but some moldy old ledgers."

"And when Papa discovered that Pfeiffer had disappeared with the cash, he never told you?"

"He couldn't face me with it, I suppose." Here Mama hung her head. "He just went on pretending, drawing on my capital, and thinking that when the war was over, Wolf would somehow put it right."

"And Wolf, does he know of this?"

For a moment Mama's face resumed its old sternness. "No, and he's not to be told. You've no idea what he's contending with in this war, Amalia."

Amalia found it surprisingly easy to let this injustice pass and walked to her mother's side. "Never mind, Mama," she said, leading her to the divan. "Eberhard has left me well provided for. I shall help you, of course."

Her mother's eyes filled with fresh tears. "I knew you would, dear." She smiled at her daughter and blew her nose again.

Amalia did have to quell a twinge of annoyance at this easy assumption. Later, as she sat in the old black and rose chair in her room, she chided herself. Where else had her parents to turn but to her?

Louisa had been right. It appeared that in two years Amalia had gone from being the sheltered daughter to the family provider. She sat up long into the night, absorbing and dismembering feelings. She realized that she belonged here now, more than she ever had as a child. She had purpose.

The income from the von Waldburg estate was enough to fully staff the house once more. Amalia also purchased an automobile and hired a chauffeur, informing her parents that it was time they made some concessions to the twentieth century.

Nothing made the shift of the household balance of power more plain than when her parents objected to her plan to return to nursing.

She smiled and said gently, "I'm sorry, but this is something I'm determined to do."

In November, with the war still at a stalemate, Amalia volunteered her services as Frau Waldburg at the local Catholic hospital. She received an unexpected reception. They told her she was far more needed at the University Hospital where the war-wounded were being taken.

University Hospital was linked in her mind with Andrzej. Sitting in her black and rose chair, with the bleak autumn twilight imparting melancholy, she wondered what she ought to do. In her mind, she was still Eberhard's wife, and every memory of the foolish creature she had been before her marriage filled her with self-loathing. She had played so carelessly with serious things.

Acknowledging finally that she was afraid, she wondered if there hadn't been enough turmoil in her life. Shouldn't she make certain that those see-saw emotions of the distant past stayed buried beneath the tragedies of the last two years? Even the memory of Andrzej was enough to unsettle her, and she despised herself for it.

Walking to the dressing table, she turned up the gas lamp and looked into the mirror. It seemed many years since she had been inclined to study her face. She observed that the bones were more pronounced in her cheeks and jaw. Her eyes appeared larger and more emphatic in a countenance stripped down to its essence. The woman she was looked back at her. There were no longer any dreams there, but there was purpose. She realized she had taken up Louisa's challenge. In her small sphere, she would see that the darkness would not win.

Her decision was made. She was a nurse. A good one. She was also needed. So, regardless of what it cost her personally, she would go where she was needed. Whatever happened, she would manage. She was no longer a girl of nineteen.

Chapter Two

Y ou can't imagine how much we need you," the plain-faced young woman with the stark black hair was telling her. "They've sent almost all of our able bodies to the Front. And of course, all the strong, young women want to go there." She sighed. "And so will you, I expect." Her direct gray eyes looked straight into Amalia's own.

"No, I don't want to go to the Front."

"Children?" The name plaque said her questioner was Fräulein Gruen.

"No. I'm a widow. But my parents aren't well, you see. I can't leave them."

"Ah! Well, that's fortunate for us, isn't it? When can you begin?"

"Whenever you need me."

"Tomorrow, then? The three P.M. to eleven shift?"

Amalia rose. "I'll be there."

It was hard that night to avoid thinking about Andrzej. It was almost impossible not to wonder when she would see him for the first time and how he would react. Would she be able to demonstrate at once that she was entirely indifferent to him? Without realizing what she was doing, Amalia constructed scenarios in her mind, planning possible reactions. She could not sleep.

Finally at 2:00 A.M., she arose, angry with herself for her juvenile behavior. Among the things in her mother-in-law's sewing room she had found the most recent album of Eberhard's personal history. She dug it out now from the deep drawer in the bottom of her wardrobe. A picture in the back showed Eberhard with some of his fellow officers, taken on the day he was commissioned. The photographer had caught him at a moment when he was exulting in pride and happiness, his head thrown back, the sun glinting on his forehead—the Olympian god she remembered from before the war. The picture hurt. It represented the lies that had entrapped him. That alone made it sobering enough for her purpose.

She found her manicure scissors and, there by the light of the lamp, cut out the head and shoulders of her lost husband, placing the circle in a locket of Trudi's she had kept. The current picture in the locket was of him as a child, making the token doubly significant. Fastening this talisman of identity about her neck, Amalia retired again. This time, she slept.

She arrived at three P.M. the following day to take up her duties at the hospital, her hair pinned back severely to accommodate the prim cap. The locket was around her neck.

After a welcome from the earnest Fräulein Gruen, she was taken to the recovery room next to the operating amphitheater on the second floor.

"Nurse Klein, this is Frau Waldburg, come to join us. She's nursed as an aide for two years in Berlin."

The young Jewish girl grinned, showing beautiful teeth. "We welcome you with open arms." She offered her hand in a mannish fashion. As it seemed to be expected of her, Amalia took the small, strong hand and shook it.

"I'll leave you, then." Fräulein Gruen smiled tentatively and exited.

Amalia was introduced to several doctors who were in and out of the recovery room, none of whom was Andrzej. As she was engaged in learning procedures, she soon forgot to expect him. Nurse Klein, obviously anxious to determine her level of expertise, tested her skill continually. When eleven P.M. came, Amalia found that she had given little thought to her own concerns since early in the shift. That was as it should be.

As they parted at the hospital entrance, Nurse Klein said, "You'll do very well, Waldburg." She pulled on her gloves with an impatient gesture. "Do consider the qualifying exam. You could pass, I think. Gruen has the details. No reason why you shouldn't be paid a nurse's wages. They're little enough."

"Qualifying exam?"

"It's something they've devised to accommodate those, like you, who've learned to nurse on the job. They test you, and if you already know everything they could teach you in nursing school, you qualify as a full-fledged nurse. How are you getting home? Tram?"

"No. My chauffeur will be along. Can we drop you anywhere?"

The nurse gave her a one-sided smile. "No. Thank you." She hurried off down the walkway to the tram stop.

The routine was agreeable to Amalia. While the work was demanding, it was not as punishing physically as it had been at St. Catherine's. She knew exactly what was expected of her and when, and laborers did the floor scrubbing, meal delivery, and more arduous tasks. Especially fascinating was the work in the recovery room, for she was quick to see that the quality of surgical care her patients received was of an entirely different caliber than that given her German patients. Andrzej had told her, she remembered, that the University of Vienna was foremost in the world in the field of surgery.

After three days, she had almost forgotten to expect him. On her fourth day, she arrived on her shift to find that there was a patient whose blood pressure was falling rapidly following surgery. Nurse Klein alerted her, "Keep taking his pressure every couple of minutes. I've got to wait for the doctor to get out of surgery, but I think it may be an internal hemorrhage.'"

Amalia looked at the young man's gray color and the reason for the nurse's alarm became obvious.

"What can be done?"

"I don't know. They've been experimenting with blood transfusions, but they're not always successful. Perhaps they'll have to open him up again. They've got to stop the bleeding."

Amalia took his pressure and consulted the chart. "It's still falling. Perhaps you'd better find another doctor."

"I'll try. Maybe someone is available in the other theater."

A few moments later Andrzej entered the room with eyes only for the patient. After one look, he tersely ordered that they prepare for a transfusion. Amalia remained with the patient while Nurse Klein departed to get the necessary apparatus.

Andrzej continued to examine the patient and his chart. Looking at him covertly, Amalia saw that in addition to his obviously grim expression, his mobile face was now grooved with lines on the forehead and between the eyes. His movements were no longer lazy but deft. The green eyes were sharp and might never have held a trace of laughter.

"Nurse, get a pillow for that arm," he ordered Amalia without looking at her. "And we've got to get these legs up." She began cranking the foot of the bed. It gave her something to do with her trembling hands.

He muttered to himself, "I just wish I knew . . ." She felt his eyes light upon her absently as she turned the crank.

Nurse Klein returned. "I think I managed to locate everything we'll need . . ." She broke off, and Amalia looked up to see both nurse and doctor staring at her. Gone was the sharp, intense expression on Andrzej's face. Instead he looked dazed and disoriented, as if he'd been awakened in a strange place. The nurse was openly curious.

As Amalia's eyes met his, he looked away swiftly and recovered himself. "I'm not going to bother with transfusion now. We must find the source of the hemorrhage. It's something major. A rupture or . . ."

He stopped suddenly and then said, "Klein, help me wheel him into the other theater. We've got to move."

Unasked, Amalia assisted. Andrzej's base of operations was on the floor below and it was an awkward business to get the gurney into the lift, but they managed. Once in the operating theater, the surgical

241

nurses took over. Amalia and Nurse Klein walked out of the room. Andrzej, busy scrubbing, did not even look up.

They took the stairs to their station. "Tell me, Waldburg, are you by any chance Zaleski's past?" the little nurse teased her. "I've been trying to distract him for years without any success, and you did it first time out. He's never given any indication before that he considers nurses to be part of the human species."

Amalia made her voice light. "We knew each other before the war. He was surprised to see me, I expect."

"I'd say that was in the nature of an understatement!"

As a result of this encounter, Amalia could no longer work with single-mindedness. She strove to concentrate on her tasks, lectured herself continually, and spent her hours out of the hospital as busily occupied as possible.

There were her neglected trusts to see to. Since her father's mental collapse, things had been let go. With the devaluation of the schilling, she found she actually had few resources remaining. Her principal had been seriously depleted in the effort to keep up the former standard of care for widows, orphans, and workers. She decided to cease donations to the Socialist Party and concentrate all her resources on her four other charities.

Using her off hours to visit the orphanage, widows' home, soup kitchen, and woolen factory, she found that they were all now staffed almost completely with women, most of the men having gone off to war.

"Baroness, your contributions are a godsend," Sister Wilhelmina said when she visited the orphanage. "You are the only remaining patron, except the Baron von Schoenenburg. We can barely manage to feed the youngsters."

Amalia found that in spite of her efforts she began to feel more fragmented rather than less, for Andrzej was part of her Vienna, and she couldn't seem to get through a day without thinking of him.

She grew increasingly self-conscious in the hospital. Twice she looked up to find that Andrzej had come into the recovery room while she worked there with Nurse Klein. Neither time did he acknowledge her, but she knew he had been watching her. His face never changed from its grim, tenacious expression.

After a week of this kind of tension, Amalia determined that she must clear the air. When her shift was over, she went downstairs and entered Herr Doktor Zaleski's recovery room. Only a tall, angular nurse with a slight mustache labored there still.

"Pardon me," Amalia said with professional firmness, "I must know where I can find Herr Doktor Zaleski."

"Downstairs. He's trying to eat his dinner. He's been in surgery since seven o'clock this morning."

"It's only a question I have for him, Nurse. Thank you."

The bowels of the hospital were dark and nearly deserted. As she heard her heels tap hollowly in the dim corridors, Amalia almost lost her nerve. Soon she had entered the canteen. There were groups of white-coated doctors sitting amidst newspapers and clouds of smoke as she stood somewhat confused in the doorway.

At length, she felt a pair of eyes on her, and turning to her left, found that Andrzej was studying her. He was sitting with his legs stretched out in front of him, ankles crossed, sipping something from a large mug.

* * *

There she was. For two years this war had been stripping him of every vanity, but her words on their last meeting had never left him. *God help me, I think I will love you all my life.*

However, with all the death and dying around him, their former relationship existed in another sphere. He had come into his own as a doctor, and he fought against his attraction for her, not wanting her to distract him and play havoc with his life as she once had. But, heaven help him, she was no longer a girl but a beautiful, sophisticated young woman with high, aristocratic cheekbones.

Amalia made her way over to him, pulled out a chair, and sat opposite him. "I only want to ask you one thing, and then I'll go," she said, her color heightening. "Would you prefer that I quit here and go to work at the parish hospital nursing appendix cases and women in confinement?"

He set his mug down and looked at her with all the indifference he could muster. "That's a very leading sort of question. What's it supposed to mean?"

"I don't want to interfere with your work, Doctor. I can see that it's important."

He was suddenly amused in a dark way by her formality. "You think I might be reduced to quaking jelly in your presence?"

She stood, obviously angry. "Not at all. But it's not difficult to see that my being here is displeasing to you. I merely wished you to know that I came here only after weighing the matter carefully. I am a good nurse, and I wanted to go where I was needed."

"Sit down, for heaven's sake, and stop acting like a scorned demimondaine." He could feel the knot inside him that had been growing more secure over the last two years start to unravel, and it made him angry. But he was like a moth to the flame of her countenance. He could see her grandmother in her, but there was something else. He didn't quite know what it was, yet. Would he never be over her?

For a moment she appeared to debate, but he held her with his eyes. She sat.

"I understand your husband was killed," he said baldly.

"Yes." She looked away. "At Verdun."

He continued to speculate. Was it widowhood that had changed her, refined her down to this steeliness? But her husband had been a beast! "I don't know what to say," he remarked, keeping his tone lazy. "Are sympathies in order?"

Amalia bent her head. "You are abominable."

He didn't reply for a few moments. She was right, of course. But he had been tormented by the worst kind of jealousy for two years. He managed to gentle his tone, saying, "I'm sorry, then."

She raised her eyes to his. "This is all very silly."

"Probably. But human beings are silly sometimes. Why else do they go to war?"

"I intend to continue nursing here."

"That is quite noble of you. I am certain that we could never get on without you."

"Why have you become such a beast?"

He leaned back in his chair and studied her through narrowed eyes. "Cynicism isn't so much a weapon, you know, as a defense."

She looked away, confused, letting her eyes travel the room. "Nothing in the world will ever be the same, Andrzej. Do you realize that?"

Her appeal was dangerous. The world-weariness that was almost automatic in him was no proof against her artlessness, and he knew it. "Your world has very narrow definitions."

"But Poland has been a battleground! Surely this war will leave scars."

"True. But Poland has been nothing but a mass of scar tissue for centuries." He tried to be offhand, but her words had touched another nerve.

She stood. "Won't you please forgive me, Andrzej?"

The knot was almost completely undone. He forced a laugh that came out sounding as hollow as he felt. "How very melodramatic you have become, my dear. I have nothing to forgive you for. It is only myself that I can blame, after all." He rose, too. "I'll see you home."

"Thank you, but my chauffeur will be waiting." With one more hesitant look at him she turned and left the room.

He looked after her, aware that personal havoc could not be restrained, no matter how firm his intentions. Clenching his mug, he vowed that he would be strong enough to continue on his present course and let the emotions of his younger, more callow self rage in a domain that he would override with work and Lilli.

Chapter Three

The effect of the conversation was questionable. She didn't know Andrzej's feelings, but Amalia felt on no safer ground emotionally than she had before. He gave her an absent smile when he met her in the halls and requested that she assist him once or twice when he relieved the surgeon on her floor. Amalia berated herself. The work of the hospital was serious business. It had no room for the emotions of a nineteen-year-old girl who had allowed herself to be too carried away by a dance.

Meanwhile, the war seemed a permanent fixture in their lives, for there was no hint that it would ever end. Amalia wondered if it would just go on until everyone was dead. There was not a family she knew who had not somehow been touched by the war, economically, physically, or by death itself.

But the sense of urgency they all lived with was forming a new culture as the old one was dying. Women no longer existed primarily for ornamentation. They found themselves forced to center themselves in other interests, as Amalia had done.

Mama's refusal to admit to the changes around her and the reality of the war caused Amalia abiding frustration. Only when she was out of the house could she tolerate her mother's fretting. At the head of her mother's list, of course, were Amalia's "lower class" tendencies, meaning her nurse's occupation.

"They don't even realize you're a baroness!" she expostulated.

Perhaps it was her desire to stay away from home that led Amalia to agree to go to the coffeehouse with Nurse Klein, or Rosa, as she preferred to be called off duty. They arrived there at the end of their shift, Amalia having sent a message home to her mother with her chauffeur. She felt a small thrill of adventure to be mingling with the crowds of students, doctors, and nurses as they walked the short distance to the coffeehouse. She remembered the first and only other time she had been in a coffeehouse—the day she had been caught in a blizzard and met Andrzej.

She realized now that the occasion had marked the first time she stepped out of the carefully prescribed mode of an upper middle class Fräulein. She had been stepping out of it ever since, until she no longer fit at all.

Amid the smoke and chatter, she spotted Andrzej again, alone in the corner, a newspaper propped up against an empty mug, sipping from a fresh one. She and Rosa found a table where some students were preparing to depart, stood by as they collected their belongings, and then took over the table.

At last they were settled, waiting for their orders to come. Rosa lit a cigarette, a habit Amalia found annoying, and after blowing smoke into the air above her head said, "Your husband was a German."

"Yes."

"How long were you married, then?"

"Not quite two years, but we were together only a few weeks in all that time." She waited while the stocky waiter deposited mugs on their table. "He was killed at Verdun in March."

The little nurse deposited ash thoughtlessly on the floor. "Zaleski's seen us," she said.

Amalia drank from her mug. "Is that why you brought me here?"

"Partly. I can't help meddling. It's a Jewish trait."

"I really wish you wouldn't, Rosa."

She grinned, showing her perfect teeth, and stubbed out her cigarette. "You're so very predictable, you know, you society types. It's rather poor sport, actually, to meddle in your affairs. Perhaps I'll reform."

"Andrzej is anything but predictable. Still, I believe all this scorn and drivel is only because you're wary of affairs yourself. You'd rather watch other people complicate their lives."

"You're wrong, actually. I do it out of sheer boredom."

Andrzej approached their table. "The little Nightingales!"

"Grüss Gott, Herr Doktor," Rosa said heartily, offering a hand to shake.

Amalia smiled her greeting.

"May I join you, or are you plotting something private?" he asked.

The little nurse indicated a chair. "No, we were waiting for you, actually. Or rather, I was."

Andrzej raised an eyebrow, and Amalia felt her face flame.

"Please invent something to satisfy her craving for excitement, Herr Doktor." Amalia said lightly. "She's bored and threatening to meddle."

Andrzej frowned. "You can't have enough to do, Klein. We must put you on double shifts."

Rosa lit another cigarette. "I doubt if that would do it, you know. Meddling is a necessary part of my makeup. You Gentiles tend to make such a mess of everything."

His eyes sparked in the old way. "I assume I am the Gentile you refer to. I assure you, I feel singularly clear-minded at the moment. I was just about to ask if I could accompany Frau Waldburg home. You, I believe, live quite close."

Nurse Klein beamed. "Quite close." She stood. "I'll be off then." Slapping some coins onto the table, she went cheerfully out into the night.

Amalia and Andrzej took the streetcar home. It was noisy and not conducive to conversation.

Andrzej turned away to look out of the dirty windows. "Are you still keeping up with your orphans?"

"Trying," she said. "Uncle's money doesn't stretch as far these days."

"I believe your uncle would be on a soapbox in the Hofburgplatz decrying this war with everything in him."

"And I'd be right next to him," Amalia said.

The doctor gave a flash of the smile she remembered.

After this exchange, she sat in the tram and swayed, looking out at the grim wartime streets, trying to hide her embarrassment. *Does he think I've confided in Rosa?*

When they stood on her front step, she said, "I haven't told Rosa anything. I don't know where she's gotten her ideas. You didn't need to see me home."

"But now that I have, shouldn't you ask me in?"

She unlocked the door and led him into the morning room, which her money had restored once more to its cheerful frame. Golden chrysanthemums adorned the side table. Stripping off her gloves, Amalia touched a match to the fire that was laid in the grate. Then she turned to look at her visitor.

Considering the last scene that had taken place in this room, he was looking at ease, even cheerful. "It might have been only a few months since I was here last," he mused.

She sat. "Yes, I had that feeling too, at first. But it's strange how deceiving things like houses can be. You grow up thinking that their walls are some kind of protective shell for you and your life—almost an extension of you. Then everything else changes, and they stay the same. It's a kind of mockery."

He looked at her face closely. "You have had a rotten time, haven't you?"

"No more so than many others. Losing a husband in this war almost deprives one of the luxury of grief. There are so many others who suffer that grieving for one man seems almost self-indulgent."

"And yet you do grieve. I can tell. You are very changed."

"I was such an unendurable little fool, Andrzej," she murmured, stroking her gloves in her lap.

"A fool, perhaps. But certainly not an unendurable one. And you weren't by any means the only fool."

"Tell me about you."

"My life has settled down. As you can see, there isn't time for much else but medicine. You know I haven't any use for the war." He shifted in his chair. "What did you think of Germany?"

"It's not a topic I can discuss rationally. Why haven't you been sent to the Front?"

"I've only just qualified as a full-fledged medical doctor. No doubt they will catch up with me in time."

She shuddered. They were silent for a few moments, and then he leaned forward, examining each feature of her face almost professionally. "I've got to know, Amalia. It's kept me awake at night. Is it true he beat you?"

Unconsciously touching her face where the bruise had been, she answered quickly, "Lilli exaggerates."

A frown still marked his brow, and she went on, avoiding his eyes. "I don't want there to be any misunderstandings, so I'll tell you how it was. There was only one instance, Andrzej, and it was nothing compared to the violence he did to himself. He had shell shock and despised himself for it. He thought it was cowardice. I tried to explain it was an illness, but he wouldn't listen." Amalia looked down at her lap, unable to keep the tears from forming. "He knew there was someone else, and he didn't think I loved him. I couldn't do anything to help him. If only he had gotten some treatment, I know he'd still be alive. He died thinking he was unworthy of me and unworthy of Germany. The truth is, he was much too good for either of us."

"Poor wretch," Andrzej muttered. He stood and walked to the mantle. "This *is* a filthy war." He brooded in silence.

"I don't regret my marriage, Andrzej. I loved Eberhard, though perhaps not in the way a woman should love a man. Probably, if it hadn't been for the war, we wouldn't have had much of a marriage, but as difficult as it was, I think it brought Eberhard a happiness he'd never had. What I do very much regret is my foolish behavior where you were concerned."

"We were both young fools," he said roughly. "It sounds like your marriage was some version of hell, but if you don't regret it, I suppose it's all for the best. For my part, I still wish I had used any means I could to stop you."

He looked straight into her eyes and then ran his hand through his hair in an impatient gesture. "We'll both be dog-tired in the morning. We'd best save all this for another time." He moved for the door.

"Good night, Andrzej," she said quietly.

After this encounter, Amalia tried to minimize her contacts with him as much as possible, and she suspected he did the same. Tension seemed to radiate from her throughout the entire hospital.

Impatient with herself, Amalia sought out Nurse Gruen and obtained textbooks to study for the qualifying exam. Between studying, her hospital work, and spending time with her parents, she had little room for social life.

On November 21, Emperor Franz Joseph died, causing even Mama to reflect that perhaps time was not standing still. Symbol of the empire, he left a void that his nephew Karl I could not begin to fill. Something almost tangible had died with the old emperor. His day was disintegrating in this new age of total warfare. Almost simultaneously, the Allied blockade had attained a grip on the old empire, and what had once been a land of plenty was suffering acute shortages.

Amalia sensed that Vienna's gaiety now had a frenetic quality, like a man dying of poison. She observed her own mother's attempts to achieve the impossible standard of living they had enjoyed in prewar days. Her inability to do so caused her heart-breaking bewilderment. But then she conceived her grand gesture. Mama intended, despite the war and Franz Josef's demise, to prove that the empire was eternal.

"Amalia, I think we ought to have a small ball over the Christmas holidays."

"I'm in mourning, Mama," Amalia stated wearily.

"Are you? Well, it's a rather peculiar style of mourning, I must say, which allows you to wear a nurse's uniform and work away from home six days out of the week!"

"Please try to understand, Mama. Nursing is not a fling, and I'm certainly not the merry widow. I'm trying to get on with my life, to salvage something . . ."

"Oh, you're far too serious, my dear. You need a little fun. You're as thin as a shadow and almost transparent. Besides, it's not just for you that I want to have the ball. I've had word today. Wolf will be home for Christmas!"

"That's wonderful news, Mama!" Amalia exclaimed, embracing her mother. "Of course we must have a ball! That is . . . are you certain that's what he will want?"

"Perfectly. He particularly mentioned the need to kick up his heels. Poor boy. What a dreary time he's had. He needs to be reminded of what he's fighting for!"

How *had* the war affected her brother, who had always seemed so content with the old ways?

Several days later, Amalia was pondering an anatomy textbook during her lunch break in the canteen when she felt someone standing over her. Looking up, she was startled to see Andrzej there. He was clearly amused.

"Qualifying exam?"

"I certainly wouldn't be reading this for fun. What you already know seems so much more formidable when you read about it in technical language."

"I ought to introduce you to Fritz. You can even borrow him if you like. He got me through anatomy successfully."

"Who or what is Fritz?"

"My skeleton. Keeps me company in that dismal rooming house. But then, I'm hardly there."

"I've noticed you work double shifts most days."

"That, and then, of course, there's Lilli—your cousin by marriage, isn't she?"

Amalia felt a blow and grew sticky with embarrassment, but managed a little laugh. "Oh, yes. I remember now. She wrote to say she was taking upon herself the daunting task of diverting you from your work."

"I suppose it will be permissible for me to bring her to the soiree?"

"What soiree is that?"

"Surely you knew? I've received an invitation to your ball on the 19th."

"*My* ball?"

"Well, I presumed it was yours. At any rate, your mother is giving it."

Amalia realized the reason for the encounter. "And you thought I asked her to invite you, perhaps?"

"The thought crossed my mind."

"And so you thought it would be politic to let me know about Lilli?" Amalia persisted.

"Well, yes. I mean, I wouldn't want to offend you by bringing her."

"You can rest assured, Andrzej, you and Lilli have my blessing. The ball is for my brother, who is returning from the Front." She made a swift decision. "I'm not at all in favor of it and was not intending to appear because I'm in mourning. Your invitation is entirely my mother's idea. No doubt she still thinks I should have married you."

She signaled her dismissal of him by reopening her book. If he was rebuffed, he did not show it. "I'm sorry you won't be there. I was looking forward to a waltz."

Amalia kept her eyes glued to the print, and eventually he walked away.

Chapter Four

Wolf's arrival was a happy event. Although he looked pale and exhausted, he was clearly overjoyed to be home. He embraced Amalia warmly. "Himmel! It's marvelous to see you again!"

He looked over the house hungrily. "I'm so glad to see everything just the same. But where is Georg?"

Amalia said hastily, "He . . . he wanted to join up."

"At his age?" Wolf was incredulous. "They wouldn't take him."

"Well, he's gone anyway. Maybe he's valet to a general or something."

Wolf dismissed the explanation with a shrug and strode into the library. Until that time, Amalia had forgotten that Wolf had no idea of the turn in family fortunes, nor that it was her money that now ran their childhood home. Now was clearly not the time to tell him.

He said nothing about Eberhard, she noticed. It was odd, but as she was not anxious to discuss the subject, she didn't really mind.

Following him into the library, she found him sitting in his favorite chair. "How is Baron von Schoenenburg?" she inquired.

"Ah, you mean the Herr Oberst! Quite well. Exhausted by this beastly war, as we all are. He's got leave as well. Intends to call on you, I think."

Amalia was warmed by this idea.

"You know Mama has laid on a ball for you. In three day's time."

"Splendid!" Wolf beamed. "And where are the parents?"

"Out calling, I expect. They didn't know when your train would arrive."

At that moment, the door opened and pandemonium struck as the Faulhabers greeted their only son.

"Wolf, my darling boy, you look so terribly, terribly tired. And so thin! We must feed you up while you are home. Papa? It's Wolf!"

Fortunately, Papa managed a response. With tears running down his cheeks he embraced Wolf and patted him heartily on the back. *Wolf must be part of the good times he remembers.*

Amalia left them to their joy and went to her room to study.

The baron called the next morning. Amalia was already dressed for the day in her nurse's uniform. He was attired in proper morning dress, obviously enjoying the change from his uniform. His face was brown and slightly thinner, increasing his likeness to a hawk. The brown eyes were warm as ever as they sought hers.

*   *   *

Rudolf had never thought he would see her again. Only made blacker by the war, the darkness inside him lightened. But she had changed! The woman he saw now was not the innocent girl he had last seen. Life had given her a patina of sophistication he was not at all sure he welcomed. "Baroness von Waldburg, I was deeply saddened to hear of your loss."

"Thank you, Baron. Your condolences are appreciated. But last time we spoke, you were calling me Amalia, I think. It's been such a long time."

"Almost two and a half years," he murmured, annoyed at himself for remembering the last time he had been in this room. He had left in haste at the arrival of Zaleski, knowing his presence was no longer desired.

They seated themselves in the morning room, and Amalia shyly opened the subject of that last morning. "I have never thanked you properly for your kindness on that day—the day I left. I'm certain you thought very poorly of me when you found out what I had done."

He reflected on his savage emotions at the time. She must never know. "I couldn't understand it, it's true. But I doubt that I could ever think poorly of you."

"You are too fine, Baron. I'm afraid you have some exalted idea of my character. I've been very foolish and headstrong. In those days, I hadn't a clue what I was doing."

He looked directly into her eyes. "This man you married, von Waldburg . . ." he left the sentence hanging.

"He was a far finer man than I deserved." Amalia raised her chin as though she were being challenged. "I tried to make him happy. An impossible task, as it turned out."

Recognizing her defenses had risen, he pursued the subject no further. But he still remembered the red anger he had felt when some society matron had off-handedly dispensed the news that Amalia had married a man who abused her quite dreadfully. "And you're nursing now, I see. I might have guessed."

She smiled suddenly. "Yes, and I love it. It's my salvation, just as the orphanage was. I'm afraid I've been rather lax in my trustee duties, however. I left everything up to Papa, you see. And the depressed currency has made everything very dear. But I've tried to trim costs."

"Yes. Everyone has just about given up on St. Stephen's. I will see what I can do while I'm home, but it's wartime. Where are you nursing?" Was she seeing that Polish renegade Zaleski again?

"University Hospital. It's the best, you know. I'm a recovery room nurse's aid and am studying to become a fully qualified nurse by taking a special test. But how is your war going?"

"Badly," he answered broodily, "but don't say I said so. The men's hearts aren't in it." The last thing he wanted to discuss was the bloody farce with the Serbs. All his weariness returned. What was it to him if she was seeing Zaleski? She was a woman now. She didn't need his protection.

Amalia raised her eyebrows.

"Our unit was almost totally obliterated during the Serbian fighting last year. This year, that Russian general Brusilov took almost all that remained. Wolf is one of my few original men."

*   *   *

Amalia sat very still. She had never conceived that things had been that horrible for her brother and the baron. She had focused almost entirely on the Western Front.

"I hadn't any idea it was that bad." Impulsively, she put her hand over the baron's. He put his other on top of it, gripped hers briefly, and then let it go.

He smiled a tired smile. "No. I don't suppose you had. That German, Falkenhayn, isn't concerned with our troubles. On the whole I think the Germans are fairly disgusted with their allies."

"Yes, I had the impression the Austrians were the 'poor relations,' but I thought it was just the Teutonic exaggeration of their own importance—they don't think terribly well of anyone but themselves."

"True, but our army has become a chaotic mess, especially since most of the German-speaking Austrian troops and officers have been killed. In my regiment, for example, only about a tenth of the men speak German. The rest are predominantly Hungarian, a few Czechs, and some Croats and Slovenes. There were some Italians of course, but they've long since gone over to the other side. That's where we're off to next, by the way. Italy."

"How loyal are the non-German speaking troops?" Amalia wanted to know.

"Less and less. What do they care for the empire?"

Amalia sighed sadly. "Uncle was right about the war."

"I'm afraid so. I see little point to our continued fighting. I wouldn't be surprised if our new emperor feels the same way. He's made no secret that he's a peace-loving man. Serbia's been put down. Now we're just a not very useful pawn in the hands of Germany. We went to war with the idea of consolidating the empire, and we may well lose the whole thing."

"What's going to happen, do you think?"

"Someday it's got to end," the baron answered grimly. "Whether our old empire will survive, I don't know."

Amalia's determination to sit out the ball in her bedroom was undermined by both her mother and brother.

"Amalia, it would do me such good to see you in all your finery! Quite like old times," her brother insisted.

"It's wartime, Amalia. Half the women there will be in mourning—no one will think badly of you, my dear!" her mother urged.

"But I haven't anything suitable to wear," she maintained.

"Clothilde can have something ready. She's coming this afternoon to see you. These new drapey fashions are so simple. There's almost no fitting to be done."

It was true. The evening fashions of the day had only a casual illusion of shape. They consisted mainly of a long drape of material over the shoulders, crossed very low across the bosom, belted loosely at the waist and left to trail asymmetrically at the hemline.

After an afternoon's work, they finally decided upon a gown of this type in midnight blue silk. Neither the style nor the color was flattering to her delicate complexion and slender bones, but Amalia showed little interest. She would wear the sapphire earrings Eberhard had given her, and the locket, of course.

Both drawing rooms were opened to create a large space, almost the size of a small ballroom. Amalia greeted guests by the side of her mother and brother. That December evening, 1916, many came seeking diversion from sorrow and tedium. The women wore gowns that would have been scandalous before the war. Now anything that would "cheer up the troops" was permissible. Their brittle laughs competed with the rising tide of eager voices.

It was strange to be at a ball again. The old magic touched her peripherally, but she remained tense and preoccupied on the inside.

"Amalia, do try to look more as if you were enjoying yourself," her mother entreated between arrivals.

Her daughter smiled and obediently fanned herself, but at that moment the event occurred that Amalia had been dreading all evening. Lilli entered on Andrzej's arm, and Amalia was thrown mercilessly into déjà vu. It was as though she were back at the Burgtheater and the triumphant Maria had made her appearance on Andrzej's arm in her Russian sables. Eberhard's cousin wore a timeless satin gown of Christmas green with a vivid plaid cumberbund that enhanced her hourglass figure. Her olive skin was golden and her hair, redder than Amalia's, was like a crown. The whole effect was to make Amalia feel pale and insignificant in her unflattering gown, and she cursed herself for ever having come downstairs.

It was clear, even from a distance, that Lilli was in love. Andrzej, his face perhaps grayer than before, was still the gallant courtier, attentive and amusing.

This startling sense of past made present confronted Amalia suddenly with her dormant hopes. She had tried to banish them in the night when they came tip-toeing into her consciousness. Eberhard belonged to another life. The part of her that had been banished with her marriage, she realized now, had been coming slowly and secretly out of the place where it had survived deep within her. She felt once again as vulnerable as she had been at nineteen. Her heart was racing.

Closing her eyes briefly, she willed it to slow. It was too late for her to recapture what she had thrown away. Lilli was no Maria. She had won Andrzej's heart by fair means after Amalia had discarded him. He had been right to warn her, even if it had sounded arrogant. The surprise would have been a terrible jolt. Now at least she could greet them with a semblance of composure, though despair overcame her as they moved nearer, making the brilliant evening suddenly gray.

Lilli's eyes lit when she saw Amalia. "My dear! Andrzej said you wouldn't be here! I'm so glad you changed your mind!" She enveloped her cousin in a jasmine-scented embrace and whispered, "Thank the Lord you've been released from that nightmare!"

Startled, Amalia pulled away and looked in Lilli's face. Only then did she realize that Eberhard's cousin had been referring to her marriage. Before she turned to greet Andrzej, Amalia murmured to her cousin, "You're wrong about that, Lilli. I hope we can have some time to visit."

Lilli raised her magnificent brows. "We'll make a point of it," she said.

Amalia extended her hand to Andrzej without trembling. The exchange with Lilli had helped to steady her. She even smiled. He kissed her hand graciously and looked her steadily in the eyes but did not return her smile.

* * *

"I'm glad you haven't rigged yourself out in black bombazine at least," Andrzej said, endeavoring to pass off the meeting with a joke. She withdrew her hand and turned coolly to the next guest.

He cursed inwardly as Amalia turned away. Lilli's hair was too strident, her figure too fulsomely vulgar, and her head empty of anything but society gossip. Worst of all, she took him as she found him.

Even as a girl of nineteen, Amalia had comprehended things about him Lilli never would. What a fool he could be, for one thing. But now, as a woman who had swum in very deep waters, she possessed the wisdom to see the world as it really was. Again, she appealed to the person he knew he should be—the person that cynicism had warped with his effort to cope with his private reality. But he couldn't afford to be caught emotionally naked again. It was far too painful.

Much better to stick with Lilli. She thought he was something wonderful and was totally undemanding.

* * *

The baron arrived late, after the dancing was well under way. Wolf escorted him over to his sister. "Herr Oberst von Schoenenburg," he announced, clicking his heels. His commanding officer, dressed in full uniform, bent to kiss Amalia's hand. Amalia smiled the first genuine smile of the evening.

"Must I call you that?" she teased.

"I forbid it," the baron laughed. Wolf looked at them speculatively and, with unusual tact, wandered off.

"You'll always be 'Baron' to me," Amalia said firmly.

As was his way, her guest looked her directly in the eyes as though searching for something. "That will do for the time being." He invited her to dance, and they moved out onto the floor.

"I'm so glad you came," she said, not bothering to hide her enthusiasm. The baron invoked in her nothing more complicated than straightforward pleasure. "This is my first social occasion since, well, since before my marriage, I guess. I feel awkward."

"A less awkward creature doesn't exist," he said firmly.

At that moment, Andrzej and Lilli waltzed by. Andrzej smiled and must have followed them with his eyes, for the baron tightened his hold on her waist.

"Zaleski is here, I see."

"Yes. That is my husband's cousin he is dancing with. I expect they will be married shortly."

"Indeed?" He searched her face again.

"Don't worry. I'm all right," she told him.

He stiffened and then laughed. "Were my thoughts so obvious?"

"Yes, they were," she teased. "But you musn't worry so about me."

"I hope you don't take it as impertinence. It's not meant that way. I have a great regard for you and for your happiness. I happen to know that things have not been easy for you."

He looked suddenly serious, and Amalia sobered. "You musn't believe everything you hear, Baron. Eberhard was a good husband to me. Better than I deserved."

He merely raised an eyebrow, and they finished the dance. She was taking him to greet her parents when Andrzej intercepted them.

"Herr Oberst?" He bowed smartly and grinned. "Zaleski. We were acquainted before the war."

The baron took his hand. "Yes, I recall, Herr Doktor." He spoke icily, and Amalia saw him as the Herr Oberst, not her baron. His eyes were remote, his face impassive.

"I'd like to present Lilli von Waldburg, Amalia's cousin, by marriage, actually. Lilli, this is Wolf's commanding officer, Herr Oberst von Schoenenburg.

Lilli smiled her lively smile. "It's an honor, Herr Oberst."

The baron bowed formally over her hand and kissed it. "Did you see much of Baroness von Waldburg in Berlin?" he asked conversationally.

"Baroness . . . ? Oh, you mean Amalia. Yes, I was bridesmaid at her wedding, as a matter of fact. She was a lovely bride."

Amalia noticed that Lilli did not have the unfortunate habit of clinging to Andrzej's arm that Maria had.

She broke into the conversation. "Lilli's father secured my husband's commission. How is Uncle Wilhelm, Lilli?"

She rolled her brown eyes. "Up to his chin in mud and relishing it, I'm sure."

Andrzej had stood passively throughout this exchange and now remarked casually, "It's time I did the honors with my hostess. Amalia?"

She smiled at him, trying to appear offhand, and then turned to the baron, taking his arm. "Perhaps later. The baron and I were just going to speak to my parents."

The baron made a bow to the couple, and they walked on. Amalia had noted the thoughtful look in Andrzej's eye.

When he found her later in the evening, he would accept no excuse, so Amalia had no choice but to dance with him. As he led her out onto the floor, she steeled herself against the sensation she feared she would feel. She was a widow of only a few months. Her husband had died a tragic and useless death. Men were still dying, this very minute.

Her only defense was to refuse to look at his face. After all that had passed, nothing could be the way she had once known it.

"Amalia," he said softly. "You must look me in the eye. It's necessary."

"Necessary?"

"I must know if it's still there. I don't want to know, but in heaven's name, I must."

His voice was hesitant, and that lack of confidence touched her. This was the real Andrzej, stripped of his world-weariness. The one she had loved so wholeheartedly. She raised her glance at last. As she saw the gentle query in his eyes, it was as if all the madness and horror in the world fell away. Their gazes locked.

This is why love endures. It is the only thing stronger than hate. She knew she was once again as glass to his gaze, but she was no longer frightened at what he would see in her. In his look she found the odd touch of vulnerability, the sense of honor and chivalry that existed so far beneath his social persona. Impossible as it seemed, they moved in their own world once more. The war and her marriage simply did not exist for them.

Andrzej, normally so agile, bumped a fellow guest slightly, causing Amalia to tread on his toe. Reality. Not a dream then. Growing suddenly shy once he was distracted, she moved her eyes to focus on his tie knot. The spell was broken.

"You shouldn't wear that color," he said.

"I know."

"The baron doesn't approve of me," he remarked. "I wonder why?"

"I've an idea he thinks you treated me badly."

"Have you acquainted him with the particulars?"

"No. That's just his impression. We don't discuss you, believe it or not."

"Shall you tell him the true story, or shall I?"

"Is that a threat?"

"It depends on how highly you value his regard."

"I wish you happiness with Lilli. She's a lovely girl."

"Yes, she is." Andrzej remarked. "She seems to think you're some kind of saint."

"What?"

"To have lived with her cousin. She maintains he was dangerously unbalanced."

Amalia stiffened. "She's wrong. I explained all that to you. I thought you understood."

"My dear, you forget, I'm a doctor. I've seen what shell shock does to people. It causes them to withdraw, not to strike out. There was something else very wrong with your Eberhard."

Trembling, she answered, "There were other circumstances. Why are you so determined to think badly of him?"

She felt his gaze on her face and knew he was seeing the blow Lilli had reported.

"You're loyal, anyway," he remarked.

For the first time, Amalia left Andrzej's arms without reluctance. Moving swiftly through the guests, she clasped her locket in one hand and fled to her bedroom, closing and locking the door. How could he? When she had so carefully explained? He had seemed so sympathetic. For a few moments, everything had been as before. And now he was back to the hardened, cynical Andrzej.

Cynicism isn't a weapon but a defense, he had told her. A defense against what?

The prewar past was engulfing her like the blinding mist along the Danube. The look that had passed between them at the beginning of the dance had been too powerful to mistake for anything but love. Why had she looked away? That's when the trouble had started.

Maybe she simply couldn't bear the intensity, couldn't climb on the see-saw again. And he had become cynical because he knew it.

Clenching her hand about her locket, she tried to remember

Eberhard's face as it looked when he departed on the train for the last time. *I shouldn't have gone down tonight. It wasn't right.* Tears started in her eyes, and she drew her knees up under her chin as she sat in her rose and black chair.

Oh, Himmel! How I still love him! Her body was warm from his embrace.

There was a knock on the door.

"Amalia, it's Lilli. May I come in?"

Wiping her tears with the back of her hand, she tried to compose herself and moved to unlock the door.

"Yes?"

"May I come in for a moment? I have a message from Andrzej."

Amalia let her cousin in reluctantly. Lilli turned up the gas lamp. "You shouldn't sit here in the dark, Amalia." She sat on the bed. "Andrzej is afraid he might have upset you. About Eberhard, I mean. He's truly sorry. I've never seen him so distracted as when you left to go upstairs."

Amalia said nothing.

"Why were you sitting in the dark, Amalia? Surely, you can't be missing that old mausoleum in Berlin."

Amalia looked over at her guest. "I am, in a way."

"Amalia! This is where you belong. Enjoy life! You were a superb wife to that Prussian stick. Now find yourself some real flesh and blood."

Standing, Amalia flashed, "Don't you ever talk about my husband that way! You've no right! You didn't know him, and in your ignorance you've spread disgusting things about him to all my friends—"

Lilli interrupted calmly, "I am sorry. That was wrong of me. I'm incorrigible sometimes. But, Amalia, he did beat you. Don't tell me you're one of those women who like it, because I won't believe it. It's too sickening."

"No. I didn't like it one bit. He struck me once, but that was the only time it ever happened, and you had no right to draw all sorts of conclusions from it. Eberhard was very ill. He was shell-shocked, if you know what that means. He hated himself, and he hated me sometimes because he thought—oh, what does it matter? It doesn't matter to any-one but me and his mother, and now she's dead, too."

Amalia knew she was verging on hysteria, and Lilli, obviously alarmed, slipped off the bed and put her arm around her. "I'm terribly sorry, Amalia. You've had a rotten time."

After a moment, Lilli continued, "Now is probably not the time for this, but I must know. Do you mind terribly about Andrzej and me?"

Amalia was glad that her composure was already broken, for there could be no more loss of it for Lilli to detect. She spoke as truthfully as she could through her tears.

"Emotions are unpredictable things, Lilli. It's hard to know what I feel." She went to her bureau for a handkerchief. "After what I've been through with my marriage, I'm a different person. All I know is that right now he's making me pretty miserable. But then he always has brought out the worst in me."

Lilli smiled with a touch of sadness. "I sometimes wonder whether it will ever be over between the two of you."

"I wished him happiness tonight."

"One never really knows with Andrzej," Lilli said with a sigh and leapt off the bed lightly. "I had better get back before he's begun an intrigue with some countess twice his age."

Amalia managed a little laugh. "Yes, my worst rival, other than Maria, was Grandmama."

Lilli said, "Oh, yes. I've heard about her, too." She paused at the door. "Will you be all right now? Should I send for someone?"

"I'll be all right. Forgive me the hysterics, and please don't worry."

"Give the Herr Oberst a chance, Amalia. I think Eberhard would approve." With that, Eberhard's cousin closed the door, leaving Amalia with enough to think about that for the rest of the brief night she didn't close her eyes.

After all she had seen and experienced, after all the darkness she had come through in Berlin, how could she have let herself slide like that, back into the past that could only have been superficial?

But it wasn't superficial. They were connected, she and Andrzej. Hadn't she tried to kill this part of herself in order to bear her marriage? Now her soul stood unguarded, waiting still for him. Didn't she love him more than ever, now that she had seen him adept and serious in his role at the hospital? How could she possibly deny it? And how could she ever endure it if he married Lilli?

Chapter Five

The remainder of the Christmas holidays passed peacefully enough, though Amalia contrasted them continually with the two preceding Christmases she had spent in Berlin. The first had been cheerless and dismal, punctuated by her own homesickness, and the second full of painful love and jarring pathos. It had been the last time she had seen her husband alive.

For that reason, she found it difficult to enter into a Christmas celebration financed by her husband's money that gave no quarter to the war. She wrote to Louisa

> I didn't enjoy those Christmases in Berlin, but somehow I feel that to ignore the war is worse. Mama is spending exorbitant amounts on sugar and chocolate to keep us in Christmas treats. We have a tree, suitably decorated, and underneath a pile of presents. I think so often of Trudi and her gift to me of the shawl she had knitted. How much more that meant to me than all of this.
>
> And I can't help but miss Eberhard and go over and over his last leave, wondering if I could have done things differently, wondering if I could somehow have gotten him help.
>
> Now that I am back in my "normal" life, I realize that it was probably wrong of me to marry him. It caused him terrible stress to divide his loyalties between me and the battlefield. But I did give him a kind of love he'd never known, and surely that's better than nothing?
>
> Mit liebende grüsse,
> Amalia

Wolf's attitude was totally inexplicable to Amalia. Compared with the agonies her husband had suffered on leave, her brother seemed lighthearted and might never have been to battle at all.

"We need to redo the house again, Amalia. Lighter colors this time. Perhaps Antonia should come to supervise."

"Frau Schindler, is a marvel, isn't she? That Christmas *Dobostorte* was the best I remember."

"Whatever became of Maria von Beckhaus, Amalia? As I recall, she tried to cause you some trouble or another."

This last Amalia could answer. "I understand from Lilli that she's gone to live in Graz. She is apparently engaged to some titled man there."

"Graz? You couldn't pay me to live in Graz. For me, it's Vienna or nothing."

At first, Amalia admired this cheerfulness, but when he persisted in his refusals to acknowledge any changes in their household, such as her widowhood and their father's obvious incompetence, she began to wonder if he were altogether healthy himself.

She decided to approach the baron about her concerns the next time he called. He seemed his normal self, in spite of everything.

"Wolf is a good junior officer, Amalia. He keeps up the spirits of the other men tremendously," the baron asserted. "But still I get the feeling that it isn't quite real to him. I don't think he allows anything to touch him emotionally. There is one incident in particular I have in mind. It's the reason I haven't promoted him."

"Please tell me," Amalia urged. "I think it's important for me to understand. The war does such odd things to people."

"It's not a particularly nice story, but I know you haven't been sheltered in that job of yours." He hesitated and then stood to pace the morning room as he talked, his mind obviously back at the Front.

"It was in the Serbian fighting. He had a particularly close friend, Ludwig. They were very merry together, and we all thought they had tremendous dash and bravado to keep up their spirits in the face of all that ugliness. They even wrote some particularly naughty songs about the enemy and their women."

Amalia raised her eyebrows at this. "That doesn't sound much like Wolf. This friend must have had a bad influence on him."

"Perhaps," the baron ceded with a smile. "At any rate, we were losing a lot of men. The fighting was dirty. Those Serbs don't fight like gentlemen—they've spent too many years fighting the infernal Turks."

He looked out the window over the front walk. "One night, Ludwig and Wolf had patrol duty. They were ambushed by two Serbs. Wolf managed to get away, but we found Ludwig in the morning with his throat slit from ear to ear."

Amalia winced. A knife was such a personal way to kill a man. "And how did my brother take it?"

"It was very queer. He reported back from patrol as though nothing unusual had happened. When we asked about Ludwig's whereabouts, he merely replied that he had lost him. Since they had strict orders to remain together, we had difficulty understanding how this could happen."

Amalia turned to him, puzzled. "And?"

"Well, he said it had been dark and not to worry. Ludwig would turn up in one piece. He specifically used that phrase."

"Go on."

"Wolf's boot prints were there in the mud, right at the scene. When we brought Ludwig's body back to camp, Wolf was nowhere around. We found him later singing ditties to the boys on latrine duty. He never showed any interest in Ludwig or his fate. He didn't even attend the memorial service we had for him. I thought the whole thing quite odd."

"Yes," Amalia pondered. "Rather like the way my mother and father are handling things."

"Head in the sand?"

"Worse, really. Perhaps I shouldn't tell you this, but my father was ruined by a business manager who embezzled what little capital remained in our business after the war had taken its toll."

The baron's expression showed concern, but he said nothing, waiting for her to continue.

* * *

She was so incredibly valiant. Was any other woman ever so selfless? It was obvious she still loved Zaleski, and yet she was making no play for him. As she described the situation she had found upon her return from Berlin, his heart felt unusually heavy. If only he could relieve her worries somehow. He knew that Wolf would be of no help whatsoever.

"But, my dear, what are you living on?"

"My husband left me well provided for," Amalia soothed. "So there is no concern there. It's just their refusal to accept change. My father still goes down to that empty warehouse, day in and day out."

"But does Wolf know about this? That you are supporting your parents, that there is no business?" His desire to protect her seemed about to overmaster him.

"They won't have him told. They don't want to worry him."

His indignation would no longer stay contained. "But that's insane! It's his inheritance!"

"They expect that all will 'return in one piece' eventually. That's what I mean about their coping in the same way Wolf is. I think if he knew, it wouldn't make the least difference to him. He will expect to be made trustee of my money, I'm certain. Perhaps he can invest in a new concern and manage it for me. We can live very comfortably. Especially if the estate is sold. Then I should have quite a large sum."

"And if you remarry?" the baron asked, his voice roughened, his emotions still out of control.

Amalia looked at him in surprise. "Remarry? But I don't intend to remarry!"

This surprised a grim laugh out of him. "You will, Amalia. You're only what is it, twenty?"

"Twenty-two," she amended. "Just."

What a game little thing she was! And she looked so incredibly fragile in her nurse's uniform. Her neck was so long, so lovely, so white . . . He turned away and looked out the window to the dirty snow in the street. "I know you think you can handle life very well alone, but the time may come when you fall in love."

"Love?" she said behind him. "I think I've had all I really want of love, Baron. I'm staying clear in future." She switched to the offensive. "What about you? Why haven't you fallen in love?"

And open myself up to heaven knows what calamity? No. Never. "I'm a confirmed bachelor."

"But your title?" she asked gently. "Surely you must marry."

"Maybe," he said, turning around finally. "But that doesn't mean I need to fall in love."

"How very cynical you are!" she marveled. "I would never have guessed it."

She was so appealing. So desirable. Thrusting his hands behind him, he gripped them together. "I've seen what love can do. It's not anything I care to experience. Life is hard enough."

Her eyes softened. "I felt a form of love for Eberhard . . . it can make bitter things more bearable . . ."

"You can't tell me that's been your experience," he said bluntly. He felt himself flush. What ugly feelings he had! How could he say such a thing! "I'm sorry," he murmured, going to the door. "I had no right to say that. If you ever need anything, Baroness," he bowed formally, "I am at your service."

*   *   *

Amalia stood staring at the door through which the baron had gone. She had never seen him as anything but gentle. His manner baffled her completely.

Life at the hospital was more awkward than ever. From time to time, when she would see Andrzej bending over a patient or tersely requesting assistance from a nurse, she would experience a stab of longing. It hurt her to see him and not be able to talk to him in the old way. Would things ever be comfortable between them? She couldn't imagine it. Her jealousy, her fears, her attraction to him, her knowledge of the man underneath his outer layer that he would not shed—why wasn't life as simple as it was when she was nineteen? As life got more complex, it manufactured more layers.

She thought of her favorite novels. *Don Quixote*—the mad old man who had insisted on thinking the best of everyone until they became what he imagined. Of course, it was Uncle who had shared that with her. And then there were her hoarded translations of English Victorian novels, where heroines changed everyone around them by living true principles and extending pure, unselfish love. What would happen if she did such a thing? If she, in fact, became like Louisa?

She wasn't made the same, though. She was selfish, deceitful, resentful. Hadn't these qualities all but ruined her life? What made people good?

As she was pondering this mystery, absorbed in changing a dressing following surgery, she looked up to see that Andrzej had entered the room. He had been studying her silently, and when their eyes met, he did not smile but looked quizzical, as though he were trying to solve a puzzle. He nodded briefly and left her to finish the job. Her thoughts fled and she concentrated on trying to steady her hands.

Lilli did not report any change in the relationship. There was no engagement, but they kept seeing each other as frequently as his schedule would allow. With a jolt, Amalia realized that their relationship was, in all probability, intimate.

Amalia continued to study for her qualifying exam, now only weeks away. She had taken to holing herself up in a corner of the coffeehouse where the general noise blended enough to render it almost as good as a quiet room. She was studying the circulatory system when she was

approached by Andrzej one morning before her shift. She had thought
he would be safely at the hospital at this hour.

"What are you doing here?" she asked baldly.

"I wanted to talk to you. Doctor Kraus is covering for me for a bit.
I understand from Nurse Klein that this is your study spot. Why not
home?"

"The less time I spend there, the better," she told him. "What did
you want to say?"

"That I'm sorry about the ball. Lilli said you were nearly hysterical."

"I've told you before, Lilli exaggerates."

"She says you really loved Eberhard. I'm sorry. From something you
said, I didn't get that impression."

Blood rushed to her face.

"You said that perhaps you didn't love him as a woman should love
a man."

Embarrassment made her flash back, "Does that make how you
spoke to me any less despicable?"

"I see you are determined to quarrel."

Bowing her head, she said, "I was just so disappointed, Andrzej. I
thought I had made you understand, and then you spoke of him so
cruelly."

"I'm sorry, Amalia, but what he did was cruel. By anyone's standards. I suppose he was drunk?"

She nodded as tears formed. He watched her as they spilled over.

"You know I absolutely can't bear this," he said. Pushing back his
chair, he stood abruptly and walked away.

After this encounter, it became even more difficult to hold onto the
brief past that was her marriage. She wrote Louisa:

> How I long to spend some time with you at St. Catherine's.
> Somehow here the war seems less real, and I find myself thinking far
> too much of things that do not really matter. I am viewing my

patients more dispassionately. I don't get overwrought at a death or loss of limb. I feel that I am losing part of my humanity.

As this happens, my link with Eberhard lessens. The whole tangle of his emotions is less clear to me. Perhaps it is Vienna. It is an undermining place for anything so dire. I want to remember every detail, no matter how painful, because I feel that that is the only way I can fight it.

How are things with you? Is life at St. Catherine's still the same? Is your brother safe?

Mit liebende grüsse,
Amalia

Louisa wrote back by return post:

Amalia, dear,

You are beginning to heal. It is a natural process. Let it happen. You are not a frivolous girl. You are a professional, doing important work.

Life at St. Catherine's is exactly the same. I don't think the wounded will ever stop coming. I really feel from their increasing numbers that we must be losing the war. I think Verdun was some kind of turning point.

My brother was invalided out. He has lost several toes due to frostbite but feels very lucky to be home. I must confess, I feel it an answer to my prayers.

Mit liebende grüsse,
Louisa

The baron was also a frequent correspondent from his posting in Italy. She was very careful not to be too personal in her replies, for she feared she might somehow turn him against her. He often referred to their conversations at Christmastime about the war.

This war is increasingly strange. The countries of our empire are of course not anxious to fight for Hapsburg glory, which is perhaps understandable. But if they don't fight for us, that means they stand with the Russians, and that doesn't sit well with all of them, at least not the Poles and the Czechs. The Serbs like the Russians well enough. But the upshot of the whole thing is that there is a feeling, almost, that all these Eastern Europeans are sort of sitting on their hands, waiting to see which way the wind blows. Meanwhile, we fight the Italians, of all things. It's not a war one feels one can get one's teeth into. Especially considering that wretched stalemate on the Western Front, with which you are of course all too familiar.

I have thought more about our conversation regarding your marriage. I don't wish to cast aspersions on your brother, but do you really think it is wise to put all your money in his hands? If he learned to consider it his own, which of course he would do should you set him up in business, it could be awkward if you married and he had to answer to your husband. I don't think Wolf would like that much.

I know you feel you have little alternative, but perhaps something else could be worked out. Wolf is little enamored with the world of commerce and might prefer to support himself in some more 'gentlemanly' way, as he would put it. I have various connections in government and perhaps could find something to suit him. If you don't think me too impertinent, I would advise you to be your own trustee. Your judgment about such matters has proven to be sound.

Perhaps this has offended you, and that was not my intention. As you know, I take an inordinate and inexplicable interest in your welfare. Possibly it is something to do with Lorenz or maybe it springs from something less easily defined. Be that as it may, if you don't want me meddling and advising, please say so in your usual forthright manner.

Amalia considered his advice without offense and in the spirit in which she knew it had been written but decided to go ahead with her previous plans. She had little intention of marrying anyone, and therefore the argument had little force. A government appointment would be splendid for Wolf, and she wrote to thank the baron and tell him so, but there was no reason why Wolf could not hire a manager and act as her trustee. That would have been the plan had he inherited his father's estate as intended.

As for her determination not to remarry, she knew that sprang from two disastrous romances. She was not prepared to risk a third.

Amalia continued to see Andrzej and Lilli at the very few concerts the three of them managed to attend. It did not hurt any less. At the hospital benefit ball, he approached her to ask for a waltz. She said, "Under the circumstances, Andrzej, I don't think that would be wise."

He had stared down at her, the irony missing from his face, and replied, "I was being selfish. I'm sorry. Perhaps you are right."

Then she watched him return to Lilli. Amalia did not go to any more dances.

Chapter Six

Amalia passed her qualifying exam. When she received the results in mid-February, she had been on the morning shift. She planned some sort of mild celebration for herself when she returned home at three P.M. However, when she arrived she found her father awaiting her just inside the door. His expression was more vague than usual, as though he did not know where he was. He did recognize Amalia.

"Papa? What is it?"

Wordlessly he gestured towards the morning room. Amalia found her mother collapsed on the divan. Her face was bluish-gray, and Amalia was immediately reminded of her Uncle Lorenz. She took her pulse. It was weak and erratic. She could be suffering heart failure.

"Papa!" Her father entered the room gingerly. She noticed he was kneading a piece of paper in his hands. It looked like a telegram. "What is it, Papa? Wolf?"

Her father's eyes clouded over, but he still clutched the paper. Finally she managed gently to take it from him.

Sincerely regret to inform you your son reported missing stop Believed to have been captured by Italians stop When last seen still alive perhaps wounded stop My prayers with you stop Rudolf von Schoenenburg

Amalia sat abruptly. Wolf! And Mama! Well, there was nothing she could do for Wolf now, but her mother needed immediate attention. At least Wolf wasn't dead.

Her mother appeared to be sleeping. Finding a blanket, she covered her gently and then went to the pantry where she had recently had a telephone installed in case the hospital needed to call her.

"This is Nurse Waldburg," she told the switchboard operator. "It is a matter of life and death that I speak to Herr Doktor Zaleski immediately."

"We will try to locate him for you, Nurse, but it may take a few moments."

Eventually, he was traced to the emergency room. "Amalia?" he exclaimed. "What's wrong?"

"It's Mother. I think she's having heart failure like Uncle Lorenz. Would it be asking too much for you to come?"

"I'll be there directly with an ambulance," he told her crisply.

The sight of him walking into the house to care for her mother filled Amalia with warm assurance. She knew that whatever happened, Mama would receive the best possible treatment.

"Her pulse is only sixty, and it's very erratic," she informed him. "I think she must have had one attack already. I came home to find her like this."

"What about your father? Can't he tell you what happened?"

"Papa's not himself. He didn't know what to do."

"Well, let's get her on a stretcher and into the ambulance. We're trying oxygen in cases like these. Maybe that will help."

Amalia rode in the rear with her mother and Andrzej, assisting him as he connected the bulky oxygen paraphernalia.

"It was Wolf," she told him. "He's missing. They had a telegram."

"That makes sense. But I think this kind of heart disease must run in your family. I'm sorry to tell you, darling, but I really don't think she's going to make it."

*   *   *

He had let the "darling" slip, but he wasn't sorry. Andrzej became aware as soon as he saw her in distress that his passion for this woman was overmastering him. He knew all about grief. More than he could

279

ever tell anyone. But deep beside that grief lived a full-bodied love for this woman beside him. These submerged emotions were mixing together in a turmoil, creating an energy all their own.

Amalia became very quiet. Once they had her mother admitted and tucked up in the ward with other heart patients, Andrzej convinced her to go with him to the canteen for a few minutes. "They'll let us know if there's any change. They know where to find us."

They settled at a table in the corner. Trying to keep a professional rein on his inner turbulence, Andrzej ordered coffee for himself and chocolate for Amalia.

"I could bear it better, I think, if Grandmama were still alive. She was the head of the family," Amalia said. "I understand you treated her, but she refused to get better."

"Yes. She was just tired of living."

"I can't imagine Grandmama tired of living!"

"I think it was the war. Maybe she sensed that it was the end of an era. Most of her friends and her son had gone, and I think she just decided it was time."

Amalia looked down at her chocolate, her eyes filled with tears. "That makes me very sad. Maybe things would have been different if I had been here."

"I don't think so. She was ready. Not like these youngsters who are being shot to bits forty or fifty years before their time."

She looked up at that, her lips tightly compressed. "I'm sick of it all!" she cried suddenly, the tears spilling over. "There's got to be an end somewhere! Eberhard and his mother are dead, Wolf's missing, and Mama's dying because of it. Papa's business is gone, and he's more senile than ever! I've given my entire family to this war." Her voice had begun to rise in pitch. "Andrzej, I tell you, I can't stand much more!"

He pulled her to her feet and gripped her shoulders, shaking her slightly, feeling all at once that he had a perfect right to do so. Seeing her so close to the brink crashed through the last barrier inside him. "You *will* stand it, Amalia. You're a survivor. Maybe the only one in your family, but you're a survivor. You look like an angel, but you're strong as steel on the inside. Maybe that's one of the many reasons why whatever I do, I can't help but love you from the bottom of my soul."

* * *

Amalia stared as she felt the hard grip of his hands bite into her thin shoulders. Then he released her, and oblivious to the surroundings, she allowed him to pull her to him. A current of well-being flowed into her body like honey. He held her a long time. It was so natural that soon she was herself again. The whole self she had discarded two and half years before when she boarded the train for Berlin.

Later that night, Mama died after another heart attack. Amalia sat by her bed, numb with this new loss, while Andrzej went to find her father. She recalled the time after her uncle had died. That had only been the beginning. She was becoming far too used to death. Leaving her mother's bedside only to cable Toni, she was there when Andrzej brought Papa.

He stared with bewilderment. "Gretel? Gretel, where have you gone?" Then he began to cry.

They came to take her mother's body away. Andrzej and Amalia took Papa home and put him to bed.

Andrzej expressed his condolences at the door.

"She was having a great deal of trouble adjusting to this new world, Andrzej. It bewildered her. I really think she's better off now, though I will miss her. But I've kept you away far too long. Thank you so much for everything. I don't think I could have gotten through it without you."

Taking her face between his hands, he kissed her gently. "I meant what I said in the canteen, Amalia. Every word of it, God help me."

She looked into his worn face and when she could bear it no longer, she put her arms around his neck and kissed him hungrily with all the accumulated want of nearly three years. His lips were as passionate and possessive as she remembered. Everything inside her that had grown hard with war and death melted. This was where she belonged.

"How long has that been brewing?" he asked with a grin that restored his tired features to normal.

"I don't know," she confessed. "It came on suddenly."

He closed the door and led her into the morning room, where he lifted her into his arms as though she weighed nothing and then sat upon the divan with her in his lap.

"There is a way to get away from all this dying, you know," he said.

She put a hand up to his cheek and smoothed it. "By loving? Do you think we can really manage it, Andrzej? After all we have put each other through?"

"I don't think it's a matter of will, Amalia. Love happened to us almost at the first moment. I've given up trying to understand it. There's a tie between us that pulls so hard it hurts. Heaven knows I've fought it."

She nodded. "Oh, yes. You're here." She put her hand to her heart. "In a core I've kept safe from everyone else. But I don't see how we'd get past all these barriers we've built . . ."

"Let's not talk of them. Now that Eberhard is dead, they no longer have substance. Why did you turn your face away during our dance?"

"I was frightened. It was very bewildering." She looked down. "I didn't know I could still feel emotions as strong as those. I've just come through a very bad time, Andrzej. The part of me that loves you was so deep inside, I had thought it might be dead. I wasn't ready. And then there was Lilli."

"Those problems remain. Why have you decided to trust me again?" His eyes were gentle, vulnerable. She had only seen this side of him when they were dancing.

"Because I can't *not*. I haven't got it in me any longer. When I saw you with Mama tonight, the dam just broke, and it all came spilling out. Uncle told me most people can only give their love once, Andrzej. I gave you mine a long time ago."

He held her to him and kissed her forehead. "Oh, Amalia, if you only knew the hell I've been through. I can't believe you're in my arms again."

They kissed once more, and she felt as though decades of tension and unhappiness were being erased by the smooth, warm response of his mouth to hers. Shaken, she said, "And now you've got to go. I know better than anyone how much they need you."

Andrzej checked his watch. "But my shift's over."

"Well, you need your sleep, and however appealing it might be, you can't sleep here."

"I know you've had a rotten day, so I'll leave in a bit," he told her. "But first, indulge me. There's something I've longed to do since we first met."

Soberly, he unpinned her nurse's hat. Then, one by one, he took the pins out of her hair until it fell all around her shoulders, nearly to her waist. Burying his face in it, he stroked it with one hand.

"I think I'm beginning to believe it now. You're here," he said.

"Yes." Pushing him back onto the divan, she bent over him, allowing her hair to drape over his face as she kissed him once more. "I'm afraid I am."

Chapter Seven

A malia lay awake most of the night, unable to believe life had taken such a turn. Andrzej still loved her! Far more than she had ever imagined. His tenderness surpassed any previous actions on his part, and slowly her heart and mind adjusted to the fact that, in the midst of this horrible war, despite her mother's death and the telegram about Wolf, she might just have found happiness.

The following day, Amalia received a return cable from Toni: *Dreadful about poor Mother and Wolf stop Cannot leave Schloss now as Erich on way home from Russian Front stop Haven't seen him for a year stop Letter follows stop Love Antonia stop.*

The telegram was a relief, for now she needn't organize a formal funeral for her mother. With Wolf gone and her father in his present state, a simple funeral mass in the parish church was enough. Her mother's few friends, her father, and Andrzej attended. Then it was over.

Amalia cut her household staff to the bone. Friedrich, the butler, was the first to go. "I don't need to pretend any more," she told Andrzej. "We can live in this world and leave the old one behind."

Amalia and Andrzej were sitting in the hospital canteen. He covered her hand with his. "Yes, we're done pretending."

They had had little opportunity to be together since the night her mother died. Andrzej had been particularly busy, and Amalia had taken time off to see to her mother's arrangements.

Now he spoke. "I should be finished at eleven tonight. What about you?"

"Are you offering to escort me home?"

"If you're willing to massage some of the kinks out of my neck. I think I've worked the last three days straight."

"What *would* my mother say?"

Once they arrived home, Amalia made Andrzej some coffee herself. "I don't know how good this will be."

He sipped it. "A little on the weak side but not bad. Where did you learn to make coffee?"

"I had to do it once in a while at St. Catherine's. I did a bit of everything there."

"Did you like it?"

"You couldn't like an experience like that. I endured it. I knew it was necessary. I felt I was doing my part to make up for the horrible suffering those men had gone through."

Andrzej looked at her over the rim of his cup. "You really hate this war, don't you? I mean, with a personal sort of hatred."

"Yes. I hate it with all my heart. I consider it to be a wholly unnecessary slaughter."

"And you believe it killed your husband in more ways than one, don't you?"

She stiffened slightly.

"I'm sorry, Amalia," he said. "But we really do have to discuss this. My feelings and yours. Before we can get any further with us, we've got to lay Eberhard's ghost and all it means to rest."

Sighing, she walked over to the fire Andrzej had laid. With her back to him, she gripped the mantle, her knuckles white. "It's not going to be easy for me, Andrzej. I still don't understand so much of it myself."

"Maybe I can help you there."

"It's also going to be hard to tell you the truth instead of what I think you want to hear. I'm not so sure this is a good idea."

* * *

His desire to possess this woman was so great, he absolutely had to know everything. Why did she mourn this abuser so much? Had she ached the way he himself had ached at their separation? Remembering her face in the von Altwald garden when she had visited Vienna, he had thought she had. He had even hoped the day would come when she would leave Eberhard and come back to him.

"I want the truth, Amalia. It won't be easy, but I think it's the only way to go forward."

"Well," she began in a small voice, "first of all, you were right. I was wrong to go to him, to marry him when I didn't love him. But I was so intent on healing myself somehow, I didn't realize how selfish I was being."

"I assume you mean healing yourself from the hurt I inflicted on you," Andrzej shrank at the awful memory that had replayed itself so many times.

"Yes. You have no idea how deep that went, Andrzej. All I could think of was finding someone safe, someone to stop the bleeding."

"Yes. I had my own hell to endure, Amalia." Her image was apt. "I wasn't fueled by anger any longer like you were, so I was only left with the worst kind of desolation. Realizing I'd driven you away! And the most hideous part was knowing that you were going to be another man's wife!" Andrzej ran both hands through his hair in agitation. "You can't imagine how that tormented me! If I could have brought you back by force, I would have. But you can't force someone to trust you. That's what I've had to keep living with. Every day. Over and over. Until I saw you in the hospital that afternoon." Abruptly, he ceased and returned his attention to her. "I'm sorry. I've gone on too long about what I was feeling. Continue."

Amalia had turned from the mantle and seated herself on the ottoman at Andrzej's feet. "I'm so sorry, Andrzej."

"Come here."

She rose, and he took her in his arms, removed her cap, and cradled her like a child. "We'll make up for it now, my darling. Now tell me, why did you feel selfish?"

"Because as soon as I married Eberhard, I knew I'd made a dreadful mistake. I'd polluted something that was meant to be sacred." Here she paused and looked into his face. He closed his eyes. Had she seen his pain? The pain that had been almost past bearing?

"Go on," he said tightly. "I have to hear it."

"I didn't understand about the intimacy between husband and wife, Andrzej. I didn't realize how much I still loved you until I had to give myself to him. At least, I gave him part of me. My shell, I thought of it. But most of me was never his and never could be, and for that I feel ashamed. It was the worst kind of deception. He guessed it in the end. He knew I didn't love him with my whole heart. He always knew I loved someone else."

Andrzej opened his eyes and took a deep breath, as some of the tension went out of him. "I know it was bad luck for Eberhard, but you can't imagine how much better it makes me feel to hear you say that. The idea of someone else possessing you body and soul was like a demon in my mind. I couldn't sleep for months. It still hurts me. I'm afraid I'll be jealous of Eberhard forever."

"You needn't be, Andrzej. Believe me. But is that why you made those horrible comments about him?"

"Yes. Couldn't you guess? But there was more to it than that. Go on."

"Well, except for my unhappiness, which I think I successfully hid, everything was fine until the war broke out. You can't imagine how he wanted it, Andrzej. It's this mystical Prussian thing I'll never understand. Anyway, when he left, I took up nursing.

"You were living with his mother?"

"Yes, and she didn't approve of the nursing, but she knew I must do something. We were getting on each other's nerves waiting in that house for a telegram."

"So you became a first class nurse's aide." What hell she had been through.

She proceeded to tell him her story of disillusionment. He followed her deepest feelings as she described the resentment she had felt against her husband and how she had blamed him for the war. As she recounted his leaves and the way he had treated her, helpless anger swelled inside him. He had so much to make up for! "I know this can't be easy," she said at one point, stroking the stubble of his beard. "But I am trying to be honest. Would you rather I stopped?"

He would overcome these feelings. He had to. "No. Let's get it over with." He began unpinning her hair as though the action would calm him. "Did he ever do this?"

"Andrzej, please. I don't think it's right for you to ask such questions. They can only hurt us both, and that's behind us now."

"You're right, of course," he said. Chastened, he ceased his actions.

"So you understand now?" she pleaded. "His hitting me?"

Andrzej put his hand on her cheek and turned her face so she looked into his. "No. Not that. That was twisted and sick. That arose from some deep place in him I don't want to know about."

She was quiet, taking this in, and he knew she was remembering. "I think he *was* sick in some way. Remembering it now, I suppose I represented every loving emotion he felt. I think he saw that as weakness. This helps me to understand it better. You see, Andrzej, it was as though I were the enemy. In a way, he really hated me."

"Oh, Amalia!" He buried his face in her hair. "Can you imagine how I felt when Lilli described that bruise? Not only had I lost you, but you were being hurt, terribly hurt. I wanted to take the next train to Berlin. I came very close to doing so. It was only your grandmother Eugenia who made me see it would just make matters worse for you. Where was it?"

"The bruise?"

"Yes."

"Just here."

Andrzej took her face in his hands and kissed her tenderly upon the site of the former injury. "I love you so much," he said, his voice breaking, so grateful was he that she was finally his.

She put her forehead to his, and they were silent for a moment.

Then she began the tale of Eberhard's next leave and her lingering sense of guilt.

He could see she was tremendously wearied by these memories. "You'll be finished with this in a moment or two, darling. It's like having a tooth drawn. So he wasn't violent on his second leave?"

She continued more briskly. "No. As a matter of fact, he suddenly quit drinking and took me to the lawyer, made his will, and cut his leave short by a week. He said he was going to conquer his cowardice or die trying."

Tears dampened her cheeks. "He told me I had never loved him. That what I thought was love was only pity. He thought that if he proved himself on the battlefield that would change things. I wouldn't pity him anymore." Pausing, she used Andrzej's handkerchief to wipe her face. "He couldn't stand my pity," she went on. "The awful thing was, I couldn't convince him otherwise, because it was true. My love did spring from pity. That's why he left. I tried once more at the train station to make him stay, to let him know I loved the gentle parts of him, but he couldn't accept that." Now she turned her tragic eyes so they looked directly into Andrzej's. "I knew then I would never see him again. He knew it, too. He was killed three months later."

He continued to hold her close and stroke her hair. "So all you had was about two decent weeks together in all that time." He knew it was shameful of him, but he was tremendously relieved.

"But I meant a lot to him, when he wasn't hating me. He said I was the only good thing in his life. I have to believe our marriage did some good. Otherwise, I wind up thinking all I did was tear him apart, dividing his loyalties and emotions."

"If you did tear him apart, it was because the code he lived by was false, not because trying to love him was wrong." He sighed and wound her hair around his fist in a gesture of possession. "I do pity him, Amalia. Can you forgive me for making those beastly comments about him? Like I said, I was jealous and livid with him for hurting you."

"But why were you so rude to me? That first day in the canteen?"

"Like I said at the time, cynicism is a good defense. I didn't know how you felt about me, whether you could ever love me again. I was afraid to hope, and the sight of you was too much to bear."

"I was afraid to hope, too. I couldn't believe you'd still love me, and the sight of you made me practically useless at my work. And then there was Lilli. I was sure you were in love with her."

Andrzej sighed. "I suppose I would have married her in time. But as your uncle said, you truly love only once."

"You give all your love away. Irrevocably. Then you can't give it away again, because it isn't yours to give. That's the essence of what he said."

"A very wise man, Uncle Lorenz."

"So are you satisfied now about Eberhard?"

"As much as I am ever likely to be. It's a tragic tale, my love. It'll take some years for me to love all that pain away." He traced her mouth with a finger and then kissed it. "Shall we talk of us, now? When will you marry me?"

She grinned at him and took his face in her hands like a child's. "Haven't you missed a step, Herr Doktor?"

"You think I'm being presumptuous when I have you here on my lap with your hair all undone? I'd say that for propriety's sake, at least, you'd better marry me."

"All right. For propriety's sake."

"You little devil." He kissed her with pent-up ferocity. "When?"

"How about a month's time. Will that do?"

"What? No protestations about a big wedding or mourning your mother?"

"I shall be married in a tasteful suit with Rosa to stand up for me unless Toni chooses to come home. Mama was against mourning, as she told me many times. Will you publish the banns?"

"I shall, with pleasure, Baroness. How will you like losing your title?"

She punched him in the ribs.

"And you realize, of course, that we will live in Poland eventually. That is my home." He held his breath, awaiting her answer.

"We were meant to be together, darling, and if that means I must leave Austria, I shall. But there's Papa . . ."

"We can easily take him with us."

"And Wolf. There's a chance he's still alive, imprisoned somewhere."

"Well, if he does return after the war, I should think your father would be much more at home with him in Vienna."

"Probably." She was suddenly serious. "Andrzej, when we became engaged the last time, you told me you had lost your family. Will you tell me about it?"

He sobered instantly. "I suppose I must. It's one of those experiences that changes one forever, so you certainly have a right to know." Looking away, he began. "My father was a Polish patriot. We lived near Posen on a sizable estate he had inherited from his grandmother's family. He used to go into Posen for meetings. Perhaps he was just a dreamer, but he agitated against the Prussians. From what I understand, his group performed acts of sabotage against the army and the government."

He stopped and raked his hair with both hands. Hands that were trembling.

"One day, the army decided it had had enough. They sent a whole company of men to our house."

He felt Amalia shudder.

"They murdered my parents and then shot my sisters while they were asleep. The youngest was only two!"

"Andrzej!" she whispered.

"They set fire to our home after tearing everything inside to bits."

"Where were you?"

"I had been in the basement playing with my dog. When I saw what they were doing, I had the good sense to run out the back with the servants. We went to a neighbor's house, several kilometers away. When they were sure the Germans were gone, the neighbors took me to my uncle's. It was my Uncle Paul who raised me. He's the only family I have left. The Germans went to the university in Warsaw and executed my elder brother, even though he had done nothing."

*　　*　　*

Amalia was horrified. She couldn't imagine going through such a hideous thing at any age, much less the impressionable age of ten. "Oh, Andrzej, darling! I'm so sorry! We must have a big family with lots of children. And, of course, we'll live in Poland."

As the days passed, Amalia realized that there were only three obstacles to her complete happiness. The first, of course, was concern for Wolf. Worry over him and his situation was never far away, no matter what she was doing. Was he even alive? If he had been captured, were the Red Cross caring for him properly? Had his wounds grown gangrenous? Or was he just lying dead and unclaimed somewhere in a field?

Second was her father. She and Andrzej were to make a trip to Poland for their honeymoon to meet his uncle Paul and his family. Would Papa be all right in the care of his valet? Would he miss her too much for her to leave him?

She and Papa had begun spending their mornings together, going for walks when the weather permitted. He still went to the warehouse each afternoon, and in the evening he worked on his stamps. If only Toni would come! But she had cabled to say she couldn't leave the estate. Erich had left her a long list of things to do after his last leave.

The third and most pressing matter was Lilli. Amalia felt tremendous guilt and sorrow where Eberhard's cousin was concerned. Andrzej waited until a week after they became engaged to tell her, as his schedule had been unusually heavy. He wanted to take his time over it.

On the day Andrzej was to break the news, Amalia sat down to write her a letter

> Dearest Lilli:
>
> I am deeply sorry to be party to causing you such unhappiness. You have been a bright fixture in my gray life over the past two and a half years. I know what your feelings towards Andrzej have been, for you have not hidden them from me.
>
> All I can tell you is that Andrzej's regard for you was and continues to be deep and sincere. Neither of us intended for this to occur. We both fought it, partly for your sake.
>
> When my mother died, something happened to me. I couldn't keep my feelings in check anymore. I have loved him since I met him and probably always will. It all came tumbling out before I could stop it. He will have told you of his feelings. I think the last thing he wanted was to have me back on his hands when I had already caused so much pain in his life.
>
> I shall always cherish you as a dear cousin but will understand if you find it impossible to return that regard.
>
> Mit liebende grüsse,
> Amalia

Amalia received no reply to her letter, but when she asked Andrzej how Lilli had taken the news, he said, "Like a woman of spirit."

"Naturally," Amalia replied. "She's a von Waldburg."

Chapter Eight

Between her hospital duties and preparations to become Frau Zaleski, Amalia was busy. During the mornings she was fitted for the trousseau she would need if she were to meet Andrzej's family. For her bridal costume, she purchased a pearl-colored dress of silk gabardine with a matching jacket trimmed in beadwork around the neck and front placket.

She also supervised the turning out of Antonia's old room, which connected with hers. It would be her husband's dressing room. She recklessly ordered new chintz draperies for each room to replace the old velvet ones. During all of this, it occurred to her that she had never discussed the subject of money with Andrzej.

"My father's business was ruined when I came home," she told him one evening at the coffeehouse. Andrzej reacted only by raising one eyebrow. "You probably ought to know that the money I'm living on is from Eberhard's estate. I managed to sell the townhouse, so I have that money. But the estate is starting to worry me. My tenants aren't able to keep up their rent because the men are fighting and the prices for staples are going up, so they have to use their money just to eat. I can't turn them out. And right now, no one seems to be interested in buying an estate. So, I have the money from the townhouse invested and I'm living off the interest and what little money I'm getting from the estate. I thought you should know."

He put a hand over hers. "I wouldn't mind if we lived in a boarding house, Amalia, you know that. It's you I'm concerned about. You're used to the finer things of life. What of your parents' townhouse?"

"We own that outright. There's a little of Mama's capital left, but all that goes to Wolf. Unless he dies." She rolled over her hand and clenched his palm. "Oh, Andrzej, I'm so worried."

"I wish I could reassure you, Amalia, but I really don't know what to say."

"I wish Louisa were here," she said suddenly. "She would know what to say, and she would love to see me so happy. And meet you."

"Who's Louisa?"

"My dearest friend. She saved my life."

"Literally?"

"Literally. There's still a lot you don't know about Berlin."

"Then I think you had better tell me about this woman."

"Tonight," she promised.

Andrzej ended up having to stay most of the night in surgery, and the next night she insisted he go home to bed right after his shift. Three days passed before they talked again.

"First of all, let me say I hope this doesn't disappoint you. You say you love me because I'm a survivor. There was one time when things could have gone either way."

"What do you mean?"

"After Eberhard died, I was in shock for a long time. I didn't feel anything. So many men had died, I just couldn't feel like an individual widow, if you see what I mean. And there was no body—he was still in France, just as he always had been. But one morning I woke to find Trudi, his mother, had taken her life."

"What?" Andrzej interrupted. "I knew she was dead, but you never told me about this!"

Amalia recounted the letter that Trudi had left and then took a deep breath and bit her lip. Andrzej shielded his eyes with a hand. "What a sad epitaph. It sounds as though his poor mother thought she was guilty of Eberhard's death."

"She did. Never mind that there was a war on. But the effect of her death and that letter were devastating to me. I was pitched into a horrid double grief. I had made a mess of everything in my own life. Eberhard and Trudi were dead, and for what?" Amalia's voice began to rise with remembered pain and anger. "I saw absolutely no purpose to existence. Do you know how many Germans were killed at Verdun?"

"Not precisely."

"336,000. Then there were all my patients—their suffering. What was it for? I didn't even have the will to commit suicide. That was too assertive an act. Instead, I just locked the door and lay in my bed for days, going slowly out of my mind. I think I was dying by degrees."

During this speech, Andrzej's eyes had never left her face. Sitting across from her, he was growing increasingly agitated.

"But you *could* have died, Amalia! What were you thinking of?"

"I wasn't thinking. I didn't care. That's the point."

Grasping her shoulders, he pulled her close.

"Then, there was this tremendous crash!" Amalia looked up into his face. "Louisa had missed me at the hospital, called at the house, found out from the servants what the situation was, and marshaled them all to break my door down." She relaxed against him as though in relief. "By then I was nearly unconscious and didn't know what was happening. Louisa revived me, and then the hard work began. She had to pull me out of the darkness."

Continuing to search her eyes, deep lines scoring his brow, he demanded, "What if you had died? What if that wretched situation had killed you? You would have been gone, and what would I have done? I would never have recovered. Never have forgiven myself. Never."

Amalia couldn't bear the look of pain on his face, and so she looked away. "For a long time I didn't care whether I lived or died, but Louisa was very patient with me. She taught me something I'd never really realized before." Here Amalia detached herself from Andrzej, got up, and began pacing the room. "It gave me a new perspective on what I was enduring. It was all about darkness and light. She said darkness is really a lie, because all the goodness is still there. God is still there. Ultimately, everything is redeemed. But you can't see it because there is no light. Does that make sense?" She stopped her pacing and looked into his face. The frown had gone.

Continuing, she said, "The darkness is like this thick vapor that blinds your soul. You can choose to dwell in the darkness, or you can seek for and choose the light. Then she said that our immortality depends on choosing the light instead of the darkness."

Andrzej was thoughtful. "That makes a lot of sense. It's like choosing to go into medicine instead of watching people die. What a remarkable woman your Louisa must be."

"She told me I was a person who was meant for the light and not to let the darkness win. It was like setting me a challenge. It worked. Here I am. Fully in the light." She spread her arms, as though presenting herself. Then she dropped them at her side. "Except for my worry over Wolf."

"Thank heaven for Louisa. It sounds to me like she was sent by God. She is a a very unusual person."

"She always kept me balanced."

"Now we have a much happier item of business." Andrzej pulled a small box out of his coat pocket. "Your ring."

Gasping with pleasure, she unwrapped the little parcel. Inside lay a large pearl flanked by four diamonds.

"It's marvelous!" she exclaimed. "So different."

"I knew you'd expect something totally unconventional from me."

"Frankly, I didn't expect a ring at all," she laughed. Then she proceeded to rain kisses upon him mercilessly.

With her new status as full-fledged nurse, Amalia assumed new duties in the emergency room. She enjoyed it in spite of the demanding pace. Andrzej rotated in and out, which gave them a chance to work frequently together. They were together on a particular night in late February when they heard the familiar screech of the ambulance. The drivers came in bearing their stretcher. They were terse as they laid their burden down.

"Don't know who he is, or where he's from. All his papers are gone."

The body on the stretcher was clothed in a filthy gray uniform caked with mud.

"Where did you find him?"

"A lady in Wiener Neustadt called us. She lives near the tracks. He was lying in back of her barn, delirious. He's unconscious now. Leg's in bad shape."

Andrzej bent to examine the leg that stank of gangrene. "It started out as a flesh wound, apparently, but the bullet's still in there, I think. It's probably never been cleaned or bandaged. Poor beggar. We'll have to take it off, now." He signaled to Amalia to begin emergency surgical procedures, but she had felt the blood leave her head and knew she was going to vomit. She barely made it to the sink.

She heard Andrzej bark orders to the two remaining nurses to carry her to a gurney.

"No. No. It's all right," she told them, grasping the edge of the sink. "It's Wolf."

Chapter Nine

I'm afraid we're going to have to postpone the wedding, Andrzej," Amalia told him four days before their scheduled nuptials. Full of regret and disappointment, she added, "I can't possibly get married and go to Poland to meet your family, leaving Wolf in this condition. I'd have no peace. He needs constant care."

"I understand, darling. This is far too important to both of us. We need to make a new beginning. Wolf's not taking it well, is he?"

"He's angry at me for not letting him die. He really wishes he were dead."

"Well, he almost was. If it hadn't been for your nursing, he would be. He was in very critical condition. Maybe it's time someone told him that."

"It would only make him angrier at me," she said sadly. "He just stares at the wall."

After several weeks of Wolf's behavior, Amalia's nerves became frayed and she was so tired from her vigil at Wolf's bedside and her regular hospital work that she wondered if she would ever get enough sleep. Beneath it all, she was deeply disappointed, as the weeks went by and her wedding had to be continually postponed. She knew Wolf's recuperation was likely to take months, and there was no one else to care for him.

One day when Andrzej was visiting him to check his progress, Wolf lashed out bitterly, "Why couldn't you have had the decency to let me die?"

Amalia was bending over him at the time, smoothing the sheets.

"Faulhaber!"

Wolf looked at him, hate plain in his sunken eyes.

"I'm sorry about your leg, but you must pull yourself together. Have you any idea what your sister has been through?"

"My sister!" he exploded incredulously.

"Yes, your sister. First, her husband is killed and then her mother-in-law commits suicide. She returns here to find her father half-crazed, and then you go missing and your mother dies. After much worry and anxiety, you turn up, but it's not certain whether you will survive. We manage to save your life, but it's largely due to her constant care. Do you know she slept in that chair for two weeks and did her regular hospital work as well? And then you come round and start in on her for saving your life!"

"Mother's dead?" he said in bewilderment.

"You didn't know that? You haven't ever wondered why she hasn't been to see you?"

"No," Wolf answered. His turning to the wall signaled that the interview was over.

"What about your sister, Amalia?" Andrzej asked. "Surely it's time she did a little something to help out."

"Toni hasn't left Salzburg once during the entire war."

"But she should be informed of what's happening," Andrzej insisted "Don't you think she'll want to see Wolf? When he's well enough, maybe he could go to Salzburg to recuperate. The mountain air would do him good."

Amalia ran one hand through his hair and along his cheek. "We'll give it a try, but don't expect much. Toni never liked you, you know. You snubbed her at Uncle's viewing. She won't feel any obligation to make our path easier."

Antonia replied at once to say that she had just found she was expecting a baby and was too ill to make the trip to Vienna. As for Wolf recuperating with them, she could not inflict it on her mother-in-law's household. It would be too difficult for them. They were so worried about Erich that Wolf's injury would only upset them.

Amalia was too tired to be indignant. She allowed Andrzej to brush her hair, and she slept for eight hours that night. Then the following day, they began once again to plan.

"Perhaps he'd go to Poland. We could be married there and leave him with my people while we honeymoon."

Amalia was doubtful. "In his present frame of mind, he'll refuse to go."

"He'll be discharged Monday. We can ask him."

"Poland! I'd rather go to hell," Wolf responded in disgust. "Have you any idea how the Poles feel about us, Amalia?"

"What have politics got to do with it?" she asked wearily.

He looked at her venomously. "If you had the mistaken judgment to save my life, then I am afraid you're going to have to live to regret it. You're stuck with me. And while we're on the subject, I'm afraid I have to say that I don't approve of this marriage at all."

Andrzej stepped forward. "May I ask why?"

"It's time you did, Zaleski. Just who are you, anyway? Some scape-grace second son of a Polish farmer! I'll be controlling the purse strings in this family now, and you'd better look elsewhere if you think your marriage will bring you anything."

Andrzej's face turned dark with anger. "Faulhaber, if you weren't ill, I'd set you straight. As it is, I'll only say this. Your sister's generosity is what you're living on, and nothing else. I suggest you treat her a little better if you don't want to find yourself a pauper."

"Andrzej!" Amalia pulled his arm.

"What's this, Amalia?" Wolf demanded.

"We needn't discuss it until you're feeling better, Wolf."

He insisted very unpleasantly that it be cleared up that instant. Amalia related to him, as delicately as possible, the state of the family's affairs.

His reaction brought stinging tears to her eyes. "And knowing this you still thought it necessary to save my life?" he questioned fiercely. "What do I have to live for, if you don't mind telling me? My family is for all intents and purposes dead, except for my two loving sisters, one of whom might as well be dead for all the good she is to me. And then you want to marry this scoundrel. Do you think I want to live off your charity?"

As her tears spilled over, Amalia said, "You can't think how happy and relieved I was to find that you were still alive, Wolf. I've worked with all my strength to keep you that way because you're my brother and I love you. It hurts terribly when you say you wish you were dead."

Wolf busied himself by pouring a glass of water. He seemed to have no reply.

"You might try earning a living, Faulhaber," interjected Andrzej, encircling Amalia with his arm.

Wolf laughed. "What do you suggest?" He indicated his missing limb.

This action goaded Amalia into speech. "You're not the only one who's suffered, Wolf. I deal with multiple amputees and blind men every day. Some are even completely paralyzed. There's not a family I know that sorrow has not touched in some way. The loss of your leg is not an isolated phenomenon."

"To you, my leg may be merely a statistic, but to me, it's *gone*. I notice your lover has kept himself nicely intact. Why didn't he fight for his empire?"

"You know as well as I do there is no Polish empire." Though Andrzej spoke calmly, his jaw was tight.

Wolf laughed wildly, and they left him.

"We could always get married and just stay here in the townhouse," Amalia suggested.

"That would be like living with a venomous snake. I refuse to start our married life living with Wolf. I want you to hire a full-time nurse for him so he'll stop abusing you and start getting used to not having you around."

"But I still can't leave him altogether until he's recuperated," she sighed.

One day in mid-spring, Andrzej met Amalia as she came on duty. His manner struck her at once. It was as though he were the old Andrzej from before the war. There was renewed vitality in his posture, and she was reminded again of the panther ready to spring. His eyes, no longer tired and patient, were sparking with life.

"What is it, Andrzej?" she asked, catching some of his excitement.

"The Czar has abdicated!" he crowed.

"Really?" Amalia's mind raced. "In favor of whom?"

"A fellow called Kerensky. Aleksandr Kerensky. He's setting up a provisional government—a *democracy*. Think, Amalia!"

They were striding together briskly towards the emergency room where they were both on duty.

"But what will this mean? Will the Russians make a separate peace?"

"No one knows yet. The Allies are justifiably nervous."

"But that's wonderful," Amalia said, catching some enthusiasm. "Then we will only have to fight on the Western Front. There'll be a treaty or something with Russia, won't there?"

They had arrived at their destination, and Andrzej was busy clipping his fingernails, prior to scrubbing for his first case.

When he looked up he was grinning broadly as though he had a secret he could not wait to share.

"So why should that make you so happy?" Amalia demanded. "Assuming you have Poland's interests at heart, this will place her entirely under Germany's thumb. I fail to see the joy."

He tried to straighten out his grin without success. "Granted, there are far too many 'ifs.' But Amalia, for the first time in centuries, there's a glimmer of hope. Just think. *If* the Russians do make a separate peace, and *if* the terms of the treaty relinquish all claims to Poland, then what do you think would happen *if* by some heaven-sent chance Germany lost the war?"

"Oh!" Amalia saw the light that was dazzling her fiancé. "An autonomous Poland."

Then in a moment, she saw the rest of the picture. Whereas

Andrzej had remained neutral throughout the war, this new possibility would have him square in the Allied camp, fighting Germany.

"Would *you* fight the Germans?" She asked tersely, part of her mind registering the wail of the ambulance sirens.

He looked past her, his face still alive. "Of course. I'd kill if there were any possibility for a free Poland."

"It's the ambulance from the train station, Andrzej," Amalia said automatically.

They became immersed in the task of administering to the wounded who were arriving from the hospital train. It was, as always, a frantic time, and their hands and thoughts were totally absorbed. Amalia reflected bitterly that Andrzej's preoccupation with killing was arrested by his profession of saving lives.

That evening as she lay exhausted, but sleepless under the new chintz counterpane she had recently bought for her wedding bed, she remembered the conversation. How like Eberhard he had sounded! How like Eberhard he had looked! Was there any possibility she would lose yet another husband to the Western Front? Her body trembled, and she felt the darkness begin to creep back over her with its terrible power of doubt. Was she going to go back to that awful time, that terrible uncertainty and suffering? Andrzej meant everything to her. Was she going to be entirely swallowed by the darkness this time?

She couldn't allow that to happen. That must never happen again. She was going to have to search out the light. Getting out of bed onto the cold floor, Amalia turned on the lamp and wrote Louisa a letter telling her of her fears. But Louisa couldn't make Andrzej stay home. Louisa couldn't keep him alive. Only God could.

For the first time, she began to wonder about the source of Louisa's faith. It was a practical, almost tangible thing. She used it in her daily life. It was powerful and yet delicate when needed to deal with a bruised spirit.

Kneeling by the side of her bed, she prayed a new kind of prayer. It wasn't the rosary or a Hail Mary. She prayed simply in her own words. Not that Andrzej wouldn't go and fight, not that he wouldn't get killed, but simply that she could bear whatever happened.

Several days later, Kerensky promised the Allies that Russia would not desert them in the war effort. The news scarcely affected Andrzej and his new dreams. "Something might yet happen, Amalia. This is not a popular war in Russia, and if Kerensky means to have a democracy where the people rule, then I don't think they will fight much longer."

Wolf appeared totally unaffected by the news. Amalia suspected that he was drinking heavily during the night when everyone else slept and then spending his days in oblivion. Where he got the liquor she could not imagine, unless he was having Papa get it for him.

In April, Andrzej met her outside the hospital with more exciting news.

"America has entered the war. That can't help but boost the Allies' chances, even if the Russians don't pull out!"

Though she had become accustomed to thinking of herself as a neutral, Amalia was jolted. "But why did they do this? I thought they were determined to stay out of it!"

"Some business about an intercepted telegram. It seems they found out that Germany has been tempting Mexico to join the war on its side with the promised spoils to be some of the border states the Americans took from them years ago. Together with the submarine business, Wilson really had no choice but to declare war."

In the days that followed, Andrzej reminded her more and more of Eberhard before the war. One evening, Amalia was especially anxious to talk to him during their customary sojourn at the coffeehouse. When they entered the little hostelry, the smell of beer and cigarettes was pungent and a gramaphone blared a tinny tune. After making their way through the congestion to their spot, they both sighed luxuriously as they sat after a day spent mostly on their feet.

While they waited to place their order, they observed the antics of the crowd. Wilhelm, a mimic of some talent, was engaged in doing an imitation of the Kaiser, who was his namesake. It was not at all a reverent performance, and his public was convulsed with laughter.

"*Käse-Toast und Schokolade mit Schlag,*" Andrzej ordered in the midst of the uproar.

"Andrzej," Amalia began, as the waiter moved away and the barrier of patrons granted them a semblance of privacy. "I'm very concerned about Wolf. I don't know what to do."

Her fiancé's eyes had the faraway look she was becoming accustomed to.

"Ungrateful cur," Andrzej muttered. "He enjoys wallowing in his bitterness. It makes him think the world owes him something."

Amalia studied Andrzej. His mouth was twisted in a wry smile as his green gaze rested pensively on Wilhelm and his fingers tapped out the rhythm of the tune on the dark oak table.

"He's suicidal, Andrzej," she said firmly.

His gaze reverted slowly to her face. "What was that?" he asked absently.

She snapped, "I said he's suicidal. We're talking about my brother, who happens to be about my only living relative."

"He's manipulating you, Amalia. It's the classic ploy. You know he's against our marriage." Thus dismissing the topic, he returned to his own thoughts.

Amalia repressed a strong desire to shake him and cry out her frustration to get his total attention. But instead she sat, staring at his averted face.

Then their order came, and he savored it eagerly. "Starving," he explained. "Haven't had a decent meal today. Have you heard what's been happening in the *Reichsrat?*"

"No."

"A sort of revolution. The South Slavs and the Czechs are demanding autonomy. The old empire isn't in much shape to do anything about it at the moment."

"It doesn't surprise me," Amalia shrugged. "The baron writes that the Czechs and the Croats have become very unreliable. They keep deserting and there's not really much we can do about it."

"Ah, you're still in correspondence with the baron, are you?" Andrzej asked, eyebrows lifted.

"Yes, he's been quite concerned about Wolf."

Andrzej leaned forward, both elbows on the table, and looked directly into her face. "Has it ever occurred to you to wonder whether your brother deserted?" he asked.

"He was a prisoner. He escaped," she disputed, lifting her chin.

"Has he told you that?"

"No. The baron did."

"And how does your precious baron know?"

Amalia stood. "I'm going, Andrzej. Good night." She threw on her cape and walked out just as he was getting to his feet. She could hear him calling her, but she kept on going.

During the days that followed, Amalia tried in many feminine ways to communicate her irritation to Andrzej. His only response was an absent verbal pat. All he cared to talk about was the crumbling of the Hapsburg Empire. Amalia's content crumbled as well, and she began to have difficulty sleeping. Was she going to lose Andrzej forever the way she had lost Eberhard? The wound would go so much deeper this time; she couldn't bear it. It might not kill her, but her heart would certainly be past mending. She twisted and turned in her sheets, picturing the trenches on the Western Front and Andrzej turning gray and hollow eyed. She could almost hear the guns. Every injury she had treated at St. Catherine's rose up in her memory, and she imagined Andrzej blinded, a double amputee, a victim of rampant dysentery.

One such night, she determined to drug herself with Wolf's veronal. She had been without a good night's sleep for some time, and she was losing her grip on her emotions. She could scarcely keep her mind on her work. And she had lost patience altogether with Wolf, Papa, and Andrzej.

Climbing out of bed, she tiptoed down the draughty hall that was suddenly illuminated by a flash of lightning. Thunder rumbled, and rain instantly began to pour with crashing din upon the copper roof. She knocked gently on Wolf's door in case he was awake. Receiving no answer, she opened the door. As if in tableau she saw her brother sitting in the dark room, silhouetted against the window as it was lit by another blaze of lightning. He was hefting his service revolver in his hand, totally unaware of her entrance, which had been muffled by the storm. He stared at the bed where his leg should have been.

Horrified for a moment, Amalia stood rooted. Then flying across the room, before Wolf was fully aware of her presence or intention, she wrested the revolver from his hand.

He stared dumbly at her, and she saw by his eyes that he was either drunk or heavily drugged. Saying nothing, she left, carrying the gun away with her, the cache of veronal totally forgotten.

The next evening, Andrzej waylaid her on the way down to the hospital canteen. "Come out with me for a while, love. I've got something to say."

Seeing the now familiar excitement in his face, Amalia obeyed with dread. They left the hospital for the little park that surrounded it.

"Let's walk," he suggested firmly, taking her arm.

She still said nothing, and for a moment they walked in silence. It reminded her ominously of the walk she had taken with Eberhard so long ago in the Hofburgplatz.

"I want you to go to Poland with me, Amalia." He said finally, excitement evident in the timbre of his voice.

She stopped and stared at him. "Andrzej, we've discussed this. Wolf won't go. I can't leave him."

"He'd be better off without you, Amalia, he really would. He'd be forced to pull out of it."

But Amalia was haunted by her lightning-lit vision of the night before. "And if he kills himself? What then?"

Andrzej was clearly impatient. "I've told you. That's just a ploy."

"I don't believe it. You've been so wrapped up in whatever it is you're so wrapped up in that you haven't wanted to listen to me. But last night I couldn't sleep . . ." She told him heatedly of her experience the night before.

"If he wanted to kill himself, he'd just do it. No dramatics." Andrzej stated coolly. "Don't let yourself be bluffed, Amalia."

"Andrzej, he had no idea I was coming into his room. I never had before. I still don't think he even knows I was there, he was so heavily drugged."

They had reached a small alley behind the hospital. Andrzej turned into it, pulling a reluctant Amalia by the hand. He put his hands on her shoulders and looked directly down into her face.

"I want to go back to Poland," he breathed. Then he paused, reflecting. "No. It's more than that. I *have* to go back. There are all sorts of things happening. Pilsudski's trying to arrange some sort of independent legion, and I want to be part of it. But I won't leave you here, Amalia. I want you with me."

Anger seized her, and she jerked herself away from him. "So I can be a war widow again? Sitting, waiting, with whom? People I don't know! In a country as foreign to me as . . . as . . . Africa!"

He laughed at her anger. "No, we're not quite as primitive as that. And quite a bit more friendly than Germany." He sobered and took her two hands. "I need you, Amalia. You are as essential to me as breathing."

Looking at his excited green eyes, she was suddenly very tired.

"You don't need me anymore than Eberhard did." Her eyes wandered away vacantly, examining the scarred wall of the hospital building. "All I did was complicate his life, and so I would yours. There's no room for more than one loyalty inside you now." She kissed him with great tenderness. "Come back to me when it's over, Andrzej," she said softly.

He embraced her suddenly, and tears rolled onto her cheeks.

"My darling, dearest one," he said, his voice husky. "Please, please come."

"Write to me," she said hoarsely and then, slipping away from his grasp, ran toward her home, crying.

Chapter Ten

Amalia's life was narrowly circumscribed by her hospital duties and the extremely trying atmosphere of her home life. The happy days with Andrzej were increasingly difficult to keep in mind. Wolf continued to drift on his narcotic, alcoholic cloud, making only occasional descents into reality, during which time his scathing tongue did not spare anyone. Papa wandered in his private world, submitting like a child to Amalia's plans and schedules.

She corresponded with Andrzej, but letters were slow to arrive because Poland remained in the heart of the war zone.

She read anxiously in the July newspapers of the internment of the soldiers in the first and third brigades of the Polish Legion, who had refused to take an oath of allegiance to the German army. These were the Polish general Pilsudski's own special troops, and he himself had been imprisoned. She had no idea if Andrzej had joined the legion or not. It had been his desire, she knew. Thoughts of him interned in a German prison camp haunted her sleep. She could think of nothing else. She saw him in dirty clothing, malnourished, his hair and beard unkempt. But at least he wasn't at the Front.

Finally, in early August she received an uncensored letter from him, carried by a friend who was returning to Vienna.

Amalia, my love,

No doubt you have been anxious if you have heard the fate of the first and third legions. Rest assured that I was not among them, even though that had been my original intention. I do, however, greatly applaud their brave act in refusing to take the oath. It seems we Poles excel in futile heroism.

There is another general, Haller, who saw the situation more clearly than Pilsudski and is negotiating to join the Russians. The situation there (Russia) is extremely tenuous. A group known as the Bolsheviks are trying to gain control of the soviets (the individual districts of government). They are opposed to the war, and if they gain control, Russia will not continue to fight. Before that happens, Haller hopes to obtain transport for his second brigade from Russia to the Western Front to fight alongside France, England, and the U.S. I hope to be with him.

My family is well and anxious to meet the angel in my life. I continue to wish you had left Vienna with me. We are quite safe here. But knowing your nature, I suppose you made the only choice your conscience would allow.

How we have changed, Amalia! Remember the days when all you worried about was Maria's nasty tongue? But for all the tragedy and sorrow, there is a possibility that something grand may come of this war. I can honestly say that I feel more alive now than I have at any time in my life.

I pray that God will grant that we can be together again.

All my love,
Andrzej

Amalia went completely numb at the receipt of this letter. This time she wouldn't even get a telegram. No one would know if he had died, for he was on the side of the Allies. She would not know anything until the war's end. Once he was behind enemy lines, his letters would cease. She felt a hundred times worse than when Eberhard had been fighting. The only way out was to deny all feeling.

One morning, Wolf sent his nurse to summon Amalia to his room. Surprised, she went at once, leaving her interview with the cook until later.

"Yes, Wolf?" she inquired upon entering the darkened room. It reeked of an unclean body and stale, medicated air. Wolf would not let them open the drapes or windows and the close, dark atmosphere was stifling.

"Sit down, Amalia. I'd like to discuss our financial situation," he said in the tones of the older brother she remembered.

Surprised but glad that he seemed more his old self, she acquiesced, sitting on the chair by his bed.

"Just where is your income coming from at the moment?"

"Well, I sold the Berlin townhouse and invested the proceeds at Herr Doktor Radl's advice in consols—consolidated bonds. He's joint trustee of Mama's estate and I felt I could trust his judgment. The other income is from Eberhard's estate, which I'm trying to sell. I'm worried about that, though. No one is interested in buying an estate in East Prussia at the moment."

"No, too near the Front. It probably won't sell until the war's over," he mused.

"Between the two incomes, there is just enough money to live as we do with a small surplus which I reinvest. You still have some interest coming from Mama's capital, I believe. And of course you own this house. I've been waiting for you to start to get better. I thought you might want to start a business of some sort."

She laid her hand over his, but he dislodged it and grimaced. "No, business is not and never was my line." He changed the subject. "I was wondering about Grandmama's palais. I could move in there and leave this place to you and Herr Doktor, if he manages to survive the war."

Amalia hesitated. She had dreaded this conversation. "Wolf, the stipulation in Grandmama's will was that it was to be left to you only contingent upon a marriage that was acceptable to her. You didn't marry, and when she died her will remained unchanged."

"What!" he exploded, wrenching himself into a sitting position. "You mean to say that she left it to someone else?"

"Yes, as a matter of fact. In the event that you failed to marry before she died, she left it to her husband's brother's family."

"What? Those piano makers?" He contrived to make his great uncle's occupation seem obscene.

Amalia forebore mentioning the occupations of his own father and grandfather. Wolf's color was dangerously choleric, and his hands trembled.

"Wolf, when we sell Eberhard's estate, we'll buy one of our own, here in Austria," she soothed.

"That does *me* little good, Amalia. How can I offer your estate as a home to my future wife? And what happens when you marry your precious Andrzej?"

"If he survives the war, we are planning on living in Poland. As far as I'm concerned, you can live on the estate and manage it for me all your life," she said firmly.

He still looked unsettled.

"Zaleski. Does he know what you intend to do?"

"I imagine he has a fair idea. He's not marrying me for my money, Wolf, no matter what you think."

"Still, he'll have control of it. What if he takes exception to your plan?"

She lifted a corner of her mouth. "I don't think he will, but it wouldn't hurt you to be a bit more civil."

He grunted. They sat in silence for a few minutes, and then he remarked, "I've a friend who's cozy with moneylenders. He'll know where you can get the best return on your money. I'll send him a note today. Perhaps he can come by tonight."

"I'll be at the hospital, Wolf," she reminded him.

"That's all right," he assured her. "I can handle this by myself."

The money was reinvested in German securities that were paying high dividends, and Amalia felt pleased that Wolf had at last taken an interest in something. He had begun entertaining a few associates who, like him, had been invalided out of the war. Often when she returned late from the hospital, she smelled the masculine aroma of cigars coming from the library. This evidence of merriment lifted her oppressed spirits a bit.

She continued with an existence suspended between past and future. It was a strange life.

One evening in late November, she returned home through the first snow, eager for some hot chocolate and a warm, soothing bath. It had been an abnormally strenuous day. As she passed the door to the morning room, she noticed that it was open and that a lamp was burning. Walking in to turn it off, she stood still. There, sitting on the chintz divan, head drooping forward on his chest, was Andrzej.

She moved quietly to him, and leaning down, gently kissed his brow. "Amalia!" he was instantly awake, his face lit up, and all trace of his recent doze vanished. He rose and embraced her with fervor.

"I couldn't let you know I was coming. I hope it isn't too much of a shock," he said, laying a hand against her cheek.

"The most wonderful kind of shock," she sang. "Oh, Andrzej, I thought you might be dead! Have you come back to work in the hospital again?"

He grinned. "No, sorry, love. I'm on my way to France, but I couldn't go without seeing you. I wanted to see if you were still wearing this." He held her hand and indicated the engagement ring.

The momentary gaiety was gone. Amalia sank to the divan. The real war was just beginning for Andrzej. He sat beside her and pulled her head onto his shoulder. "I love you, Amalia," he said quietly. "I'm desperately sorry to put you through this, but you understand, don't you?"

She knew her private agony must be reflected in her face as she looked up at him. "I don't really understand, Andrzej. But then, you must remember, I'm not Polish," she responded in a flat voice. "It wouldn't do any good for me to try to keep you, though. I haven't that kind of power."

"No one does," he said gently. "Amalia, I love you more than anyone on this earth. I love you even for your fears. I know how you hate war. But surely this is different? Think of it." His eyes were lively, his face looking young again. "I'm not fighting for any grand and glorious empire or to prove how brave and masterful I am. I'm fighting because *I want to be free!* I want the right to be a Pole, not subject to anyone else. I want to speak my own language, to be able to educate our children as we see fit, to govern my own life in my own way . . ."

He was up and pacing the room, punctuating his sentiments with sharp turns. Amalia said nothing, and at last he stopped and looked at her. "You do understand don't you, my darling?"

She nodded sorrowfully. "Oh, yes. I understand." Eyes glistening, she asked him bitterly, "But where and when is it going to end? I imagine everyone in the world wants what you want. But you don't, even if you fight to the last man, have the power to achieve it. Why must you forever identify yourself with Poland? There's never even been a Poland in your lifetime. Why can't we live in Austria when we marry? Then you'd not be subject to anyone."

He sighed heavily and sank into a chair opposite her. "You're wrong, you know. We do have the power to achieve it, and it's an irresistible opportunity that may never come again! Russia's out of the war now. Ever since Lenin threw out Kerensky, the Russians have been so busy fighting one another that they haven't time for anyone else. A treaty with Germany is just a matter of time. Haller's managed to escape to France, where he's gathering what Polish nationals he can find. I missed him in Russia, but now, it's just as well. Practically the whole legion was killed by the Germans. It must have been your prayers that saved me."

Amalia trembled and put her head in her hands. He had been so close to death already! How many more times could he escape it?

"Remember what I told you about my family? My father would shout for joy at this opportunity to fight the Germans and secure a future for Poland. How can I do less?"

Uncovering her eyes, she looked at him. He was so earnest. Could

315

she really blame him? It was just the same as Eberhard. Her late husband had been raised to fight this war, and Andrzej had been raised to hate the Germans.

Amalia was silent. Had she had such a horrific experience, wouldn't she feel the same as Andrzej did? Instead of anger, she was overcome by a sense of futility. Was there no end to the hatreds that had bred these hostilities?

As though answering her, Andrzej said, "I'll kill or be killed to make Poland a state again."

She recognized the gleam in his eye. She had last seen it in Eberhard's the day war was declared.

It was several hours before he left her, sitting with the dead calm of apathy, her eyes dry, all feeling gone from her heart.

Part Four

VIENNA

JUNE 1919 TO NOVEMBER 1919

Chapter One

The day had been unseasonably warm, and Amalia was wilted as she let herself into the little flat that was now her home.

Wolf was sitting in the hallway. Looking up with his habitual scowl, he asked, "Where've you been? Papa's missed his luncheon, and you know I'm useless in the kitchen with those things." He indicated his wooden crutches resting against the wall.

Amalia ignored him, went to the kitchen and hung her battered headgear on a peg. Her brother followed her. "Amalia, now that summer's here, I've decided we should move back into the townhouse. This place is rat-ridden, foul-smelling, and they want to raise the rent again."

Amalia was wrapping a large butcher apron around her. It almost encircled her twice. She pushed a strand of hair back into her uninspired chignon, and rolled up the sleeves of her prewar blouse.

"We've already discussed it, Wolf. I can't keep it up on my own, and we haven't the money for servants. Winter is bound to come around again in a few months' time, and we'll be even less able to afford coal than we were this winter."

"Only *you* could manage to think of coal on a day like this," he muttered, seating himself clumsily in a kitchen chair and mopping his pasty brow. Amalia was slicing a large loaf of pumpernickel.

He continued, "Things are bound to improve before the winter, Amalia. Now that the war is ended, the von Waldburg estate shouldn't be long in selling."

"No right-minded German is going to buy a rapidly dilapidating estate with no tenants, situated right in the middle of Poland!" Amalia told him as she took her knife to a large round of headcheese.

"East Prussia is still German!" Wolf protested.

"Only technically. No one's going to *move* there, for heaven's sake, with Poland surrounding it on all sides."

"Well, maybe some wealthy Pole will buy it!"

"And land himself right in the middle of all those nasty Germans when he can buy an estate in Poland?"

Wolf mused, "It's a pity all the tenants left."

"They were murdered," Amalia corrected flatly, as she spread the mustard sparingly and finished constructing her sandwich.

"Oh, come, Amalia, it was war!"

"They were civilians."

Putting water on to boil, she seated herself. "I've been hired to begin at the University Hospital again tomorrow," she announced and then took a large bite of the sandwich, pretending not to notice Wolf's outrage.

"You can't," he said tersely.

"We haven't any money, Wolf. Do I need to remind you?" she asked with careful calm.

Her brother's skin glistened with perspiration. He doubled his fist and pounded on the table. "And Papa and me? We're just to rot here, I suppose?"

"Perhaps I can hire a servant soon." Amalia went to the whistling teakettle and poured the water into a teapot. Her hand trembled slightly.

Wolf took up his crutch and hurled it at his sister. Jerking to avoid it, Amalia spilled the scalding water all over her hand. Wincing in pain, tears stinging in her eyes, she whirled on her brother, "How dare you!"

Wolf looked at her, eyes bulging in unrepentant wrath. "Have you no human feeling?" he demanded. "Are you made of ice, Amalia Faulhaber?"

At that moment, their frail old father shuffled into the kitchen. "I'm hungry, Amalia," he complained in his thin, sad voice.

She indicated the remainder of her sandwich on her plate and left the kitchen without a word.

Climbing the narrow, dim stairway to her airless room, she sought the womblike sanctuary of her old rose and black chair, cradling her burning hand. It was so wrong to wish they were dead. She fought the feelings down, as she had come to do with increasing regularity. She tried instead to wish herself dead. But she couldn't. There was still hope. The war had been over for six months, but what if Andrzej had had problems returning home? The Poles were technically German allies.

He couldn't be dead, she kept telling herself. After months of waiting, she had finally received a letter mailed shortly before the armistice by a comrade in arms who had been captured and taken to a Red Cross hospital. He had sent the letter to "Frau Waldburg," at the University Hospital, Vienna. They had still been living in the townhouse, though she no longer worked at the hospital. The hospital had found her, and the months-old letter finally came into her hands. After a year of enforced silence, not knowing whether her fiancé was alive or dead, the letter made her so jubilant that the entire world was beautiful to her again. It was winter, but she found enchantment in the ages-old buildings of the fallen empire, steeped in snow. Wolf and Papa continued to be impossibly demanding, but now that she knew Andrzej was coming she could tolerate it. She could bear doing the work of all the servants she had had to dismiss when Wolf's investment of her money had proved disastrous. She could even bear it when they had had to move from their home into this horrible flat.

The letter had simply stated that her correspondent knew Andrzej would want her to know that he was alive and well. He had spoken of her much to this friend, and he knew she was a nurse. The comrade hoped the letter would eventually find her.

As the year's weight of tension and worry slid from her shoulders, she began to make plans. Perhaps they could get a nurse for Wolf and

Papa and move to Poland. She would meet Andrzej's family, and they would watch together as the Polish political scenario unfolded.

Amalia imagined her fiancé slowly unpinning and then burying his face in her hair. She remembered his rough stubble of beard as he kissed her after a long day at the hospital. It was even easy to feel the feather-light touch of his finger on her lips as he traced her mouth before kissing it.

Slowly, however, her weeks of waiting had turned to months. She began to fear that he had, in fact, been killed in that last week of fighting. Why else hadn't he come to her? When he found the townhouse unoccupied, surely he would have learned her forwarding address from the neighbors. When she finally fell exhausted into her narrow bed at night, she would remember again and again the last evening she had spent with him. He had dealt so tenderly with every fear, allowing her to cry out all her grief and frustration. He had disarmed her when she tried to fight him and let his passion flow over her like a wave. He had promised he would return and never leave again. There could be no doubt in the world that he loved her with every part of his being.

So what, aside from death, could be keeping him from her? Poland was independent now. Andrzej's dream had come true. But there had been no letter from him. Other mail, of which there was very little, had made its way to their new home. His would have been forwarded with the rest. Even if one letter had gone astray, he certainly would have written again. She had no idea of his address, or even where he was, so she could not write.

Tomorrow she would begin working again. She quit her job when the servants were dismissed, so she could take care of Wolf and Papa, but they had never needed money more. Prices were spiraling higher and higher because of the shortages, and the little money they had left was buying less and less. Wolf was just going to have to manage on his own.

If only Andrzej would come.

She nodded into a doze, sitting there in her old chair. Twenty minutes later her peace was interrupted by a hesitant knock on the door.

"Amalia?" queried a thin, feeble voice. "Someone's here." Her father shuffled back down the stairs before she had risen from the depths of sleep.

Someone here? Andrzej? It must be! Rising quickly, she glanced in her mirror. What a changed woman he would see, she thought fleetingly. She had ceased to dress her hair fashionably, and it was dull and lifeless. The purple smudges under her eyes seemed to have grown darker. The rust-colored silk blouse she wore was no longer in fashion and hung on her thin body. But there was nothing she could do. Pallor and thinness seemed to be a permanent part of her now. And she had no fashionable clothes to help her carry it off.

She tried to pinch some color into her cheeks and then smoothed her hair back with nervous fingers. The burn on her hand throbbed painfully, and she noticed that a large, puffy blister had formed.

Unable to endure the suspense, even to make herself more presentable, she threw open her bedroom door and ran lightly down the stairs. The little parlor was off the front hall, and Amalia stopped abruptly before she entered. She was trembling from head to foot. Taking a deep breath to steady herself, she opened the door.

There, investigating the bric-a-brac on the mantle, stood Rudolf von Schoenenburg. Disappointment threatened to flood her into a faint. The baron turned, and seeing Amalia, he beamed.

"Baroness! I am delighted to see you again! And what a time I have had finding you."

Amalia stood where she was, unable to answer him. She concentrated on remaining erect.

"You are not well?" von Schoenenburg asked, his brown eyes full of concern. Crossing to her side, he led her gently to the divan.

"Forgive me," she murmured, staring at his hands. "You gave me a shock."

She felt his eyes on her bowed head. She was unable to meet them.

* * *

Rudolf had gone to the townhouse that morning to report to her the status of the orphanage. When he found the house shut up, he had had a devil of a time tracing them here, not far from Lorenz's old flat. She looked almost like an old woman, she was so thin and pale. And right now, she looked as though she might be sick.

"You were expecting someone else?"

Looking up slowly, she turned her stricken eyes on him. They filled with tears, and he felt his heart soften unwillingly. Damnation! He never should have come.

She said nothing. He handed her his handkerchief, and sat by while she wept, motionless, except for his eyes that traversed her thin form. The old bitterness crept over him. Why did women always prefer rotters?

Finally he spoke her name. "Amalia, what is it?"

Blowing her nose with complete disregard for ladylike conventions, she managed to say, "How good it is to see you."

"I'm glad," he replied dryly. "But I have disappointed you by not being someone else. Zaleski, I suppose?"

She nodded, looking at the pearl ring that was now too big for her finger and slid around constantly to the underneath side of her hand. "He was fighting in France with the Allies. I haven't heard from him since the end of the war."

"You are engaged?" he asked abruptly. So Zaleski had turned traitor?

"Yes," she replied.

He stood and walked once again to the mantle, distancing himself from her as far as he could. "If you don't mind my asking, Amalia, how did you come to live here?"

At that she almost managed a smile. "It all comes from disregarding your good advice. I put my affairs into Wolf's hands, and he invested in some armaments company in the Saar. Now it looks like France is going to take over that part of Germany and shut down the armaments factories. Everyone is selling out. Our stock is worthless. My estate in East Prussia hasn't sold and isn't likely to. All its tenants were burned out of their homes, so there's no income there.

"The townhouse was too expensive to heat, and we couldn't afford servants to keep it up. This set of rooms is about all I can manage on my own. We're trying to sell the townhouse."

The baron nodded crisply. "And what of Lorenz's charities? Surely he wouldn't begrudge you using the money for yourself."

She shook her head. "All the money is gone. I instructed the banker to use the principal when the interest wasn't enough, and with prices the way they are, it didn't take long for it to disappear."

"And Wolf?"

"I suppose he should be getting a pension of some sort, but it hasn't come through. He sits and broods most of the time."

She doesn't know, then. Well, it certainly wouldn't come well from me. Let her find out some other way. "I saw him briefly a moment ago and couldn't believe the change in him. He's become rather nasty, hasn't he?"

Amalia expelled a small sigh. "I'm afraid so." He felt her studying his averted face.

"And you?" she asked. "Did President Wilson leave you your estate, or is it now in—what is it called? Yugoslavia? Or Czechoslovakia, perhaps?

He was glad to tell her that he had been spared. "President Wilson decided to leave me alone. My *Schloss* is in German-speaking Austria, thank the Lord. Near Graz. I've just come from there, as a matter of fact."

"And your tenants? Did they survive?"

"Some did. The widows and children are working the land of the ones that didn't. It's a new world, Amalia. I wouldn't feel too bad about your German investments. Their economy is even worse than ours. I don't think anything is safe anymore except gold and land."

Amalia looked down at her reddened, blistered hands. He felt such a wave of protectiveness rush over him that he couldn't keep himself from going back to her side. "See here. It hurts dreadfully to see you like this. Let me help in some way. At least until Zaleski turns up." As his eyes looked steadfastly into hers, he watched her become suddenly self-conscious. "For your uncle's sake," he added solemnly.

"I don't know what there is for anyone to do. Even when Andrzej comes back, it's going to be troublesome leaving Wolf and Papa. I'll have to find a full-time caretaker for them. Wolf refuses to go to Poland, and I can't leave him here alone."

The baron stood and said with the brusqueness of command. "That's the first order of business then. There's no reason why he shouldn't become independent. Other men in the same position with families to feed are doing it all the time."

"But Wolf won't," she said wearily, leaning her chin on a cupped hand. "He feels it's the world's duty to support him because he's been treated so unfairly."

"Then, by heavens, he's got some waking up to do!"

He strode to the door of the room, and bellowed in battlefield tones, "Faulhaber!"

Amalia heard the clump of her brother's crutches. When he reached the parlor, his face was a mask of insolent fury. "I'm no longer yours to command, Schoenenburg," he snapped.

"Not in the conventional sense, perhaps, but it would be to your advantage to hear what I have to say."

Wolf looked at him sharply.

"There were witnesses, Faulhaber. It took them a while to come forward, but they did. They didn't want you to get your pension, you see. Not when they'd stuck with it and you hadn't. I've kept it quiet. So far there's been no talk of a court martial. That would ruin you, of course."

Wolf's face was flushed and his lower lip pushed out belligerently, but he held his anger. "I'm listening," he said.

"I am going to see that you are fitted with an artificial limb, and you are going to rehabilitate yourself and support this family. Do I make myself understood?"

Wolf gave a raspy, mirthless laugh. "Support my family? Doing what, might I ask?"

"What you did before. Government service. You were shot in the leg, man, not in the head."

"You'll see that I get a job?" Amalia's brother taunted.

Exasperation broke through von Schoenenburg's hauteur. "Yes, confound you, yes!" Then he rounded on his victim again. "But in the meantime, Faulhaber, I'll have a wheelchair here tomorrow. There's no reason why you can't get your own meals and your father's too. I imagine Amalia needs to get back to work."

* * *

Her spirit had been freed! In a few words the baron had managed to emancipate her from the principal burdens that had been hobbling her for the past two years. He couldn't have done anything she needed more.

Smiling sunnily at him, it was all she could do to keep from embracing him in gratitude. The tears started again, and she let them brim onto her cheeks, unnoticed.

Wolf started sullenly out the door.

"One more thing, Faulhaber," his former colonel warned, "I'll be visiting here often. Remember the appearance of honor is the only thing you have left. Save it, if you can."

Chapter Two

Amalia's new hours at the hospital were somewhat unconventional, but she knew she was lucky even to have work considering the abundance of nurses in post-war Vienna. She worked two four-hour shifts—the first from eight A.M. to noon, and the second from eight P.M. to midnight. Although she experienced some difficulty getting used to the schedule, it was a tremendous relief to be back at work.

She and Rosa Klein celebrated by having lunch together in the canteen. They were working together in the emergency room.

"Is Zaleski back yet?" the little nurse inquired, sitting in her masculine posture with both elbows squarely on the table, smoking a cigarette.

"No," Amalia said shortly. "I'm quite certain he'll remain in Poland now."

"But weren't you engaged?" Klein persisted. "What are you doing here if he's there?"

"Rosa, it's none of your business, as you know very well."

"But how can I meddle if I don't have the picture?"

"As far as I know, we're still engaged. I just haven't heard from him. I suppose it's even possible that he's dead."

The nurse was instantly repentant. "I'm sorry, Amalia. What a bother I am. I should have used my brain. It was clear to everyone that he was deeply in love with you. I sincerely hope nothing terrible has happened." She stood. "It's good you're back at work. It'll help you to bear the waiting."

Still, she talked of Andrzej the next morning during a lull. "Zaleski was one of our most gifted surgeons. He seemed to have a sort of intuition, if you know what I mean. Not many of them have it. They approach surgery rather like a plumbing job—you go in, you find out what's wrong, and you try to fix it."

"But Andrzej wasn't like that?"

Klein tossed a curly wisp of black hair out of her eyes. "He knew how to take calculated risks, and they nearly always paid off. He was something of a miracle worker, surgically speaking."

Standing there in the room where she had spent so many hours working beside her fiancé, Amalia felt the ache of nostalgia and loneliness. By his side, they had literally revived the dead. Where was he?

She murmured, "You worked with him quite a bit more than I. I've never assisted in surgery, you know. And please, Rosa, don't speak of him in the past tense."

A flush darkened Nurse Klein's cheeks. "I didn't mean to imply that he was dead, Amalia. Just that he wouldn't be coming back to us in this hospital if he plans on practicing in Poland. Forgive me."

Amalia busied herself readying a cart of instruments for their next trauma victim.

"I don't mean to upset you, but whatever has happened to Zaleski, I want you to remember that you're an important person in your own right. Don't forget that. You can carry on."

Amalia tried to feel the spirit of these words, but how could she possibly tell this bright, young optimist that she *had* been carrying on? Day after day for eighteen long months, wracked with fear and then buoyed by hope, only to have that slowly draining away.

About a month after she had been back at work, she met the baron by arrangement after her morning shift, and they strolled to Amalia's favorite *Konditorei*, Demels, for a light lunch. It was unusually cool for July, with a gentle breeze. The streets in this fashionable quarter were lined with women in their brilliant postwar garb, idly strolling along Kartnerstrasse, both to see and be seen.

Amalia, in her sober gray uniform and white apron, felt self-conscious. Von Schoenenburg took her arm, and smiled at her.

"You're looking much better," he said.

"I feel a great deal better, thank you."

"And how are things on the home front?"

"Wolf curses me regularly, but I'm not there much to hear it. He's adapted much better than I thought he would to the chair."

"He'd better," the baron said grimly.

"You know, Andrzej hinted that he thought Wolf was a deserter. I wonder what made him suspect?"

Her companion did not reply, and they strolled along in silence for a few moments.

"Have you done any thinking about your future, Amalia?" he asked as they entered the sophisticated pink and gray of Demels. They were seated at a small table near the front, so they could view the street with its sunshine and passers by.

Amalia answered shortly, "I think of little else."

"And what have you decided?"

She perused the menu. "Käse-Toast, I think. And some Fruchttorte." She smiled at the baron. "You do worry about me, don't you?"

His countenance remained serious. "I suppose I always will, to some extent."

"And why is that?"

Looking embarrassed, he said shortly, "For Lorenz's sake, of course."

Amalia felt a presence loom over her and looked up. She was startled to see her cousin by marriage. "Lilli!" she cried. "What a surprise!"

"Yes! Isn't it? I saw you through the window. Baron von Schoenenburg, it's a pleasure to see you again." Bending over, she kissed Amalia's cheek.

It was the first time she had encountered Lilli since the engagement fiasco. It seemed impossible, but Lilli had maintained her prewar lifestyle, and so the two had had no opportunity to meet.

"Please join us," Amalia urged, indicating an empty chair.

Lilli smiled, and the baron rose to seat her. "I see you're still nursing, Amalia. I can't imagine why." Arranging herself in her chair, she folded her gloved hands in her lap. "I'll just have a lemonade," she said as the waiter approached.

As the baron ordered, Lilli put her head next to Amalia's and murmured, "Isn't it perfectly marvelous about Poland?" Her eyes sparked excitement.

Startled, Amalia laughed. "Lilli, one would never take you for a loyal German subject!"

"For heaven's sake, don't ever repeat that remark to my father, or he'll cut me off without a pfennig!" Her face registered mock horror.

The baron joined in the conversation. "So, your father came through all in one piece? I'm glad to hear it, Fräulein."

"Call me Lilli, please. Yes, he's in one piece but ready to explode after the treaty. He's one the French call 'unregenerate.' He was with those who threatened to go back to war rather than sign the treaty. Fortunately, he was in the minority."

Von Schoenenburg brooded. "That treaty's a mistake, I'm afraid. It's too humiliating."

Amalia flushed and sat up straighter. "I disagree. Everyone knows there wouldn't have been a war but for Germany! Let them suffer for it. There isn't a family in Europe who hasn't been victimized by their greed." She almost spat the words, entirely unconscious of any rudeness.

"You're entitled to your opinion, my dear, but I'd keep my voice down if I were you," the baron cautioned. Turning to Lilli, he asked, "And you, as an expatriate German, what are your thoughts?"

The waiter set their order before them. Lilli shrugged as she sipped her lemonade. "I'm glad for Poland's sake. But I do think, Amalia, that Germany is being treated too harshly. You see, no matter what you say about war guilt and all of that, the fact is Germans can't bear disgrace. There's nothing the least bit humble about us, and we don't handle losing well." Setting her drink down, she continued, "I'm afraid there will be a class of people, typified by my own father, who won't rest until they've erased this defeat. Even if it means another war, bloodier than this one."

Amalia felt the flush die on her cheeks. "But that musn't happen!" Her Käse-Toast sat untouched, forgotten. She felt the baron's eyes on her and looked up to see that he was frowning in concern.

"Do *you* think there will be another war?" she demanded.

"I pray not. We must do our best to prevent such a thing."

Lilli shrugged again. Then her face became suddenly animated. "Andrzej writes that he hopes to get a post in the new government. Isn't it splendid?"

"Splendid," Amalia echoed, her mind shocked into paralysis.

The baron hastened to inquire, "And you, Lilli, what exciting things have you been doing?"

"Parties, the theater, you know, the usual. It's so marvelous now that the war is over, of course. Everyone seems to want to make up for lost time." She consulted the tiny watch pinned to her blouse. "Speaking of time, I must run. I'm to meet Frederich and Julia at the museum in quarter of an hour. There's a new exhibit. A man called Mueller, or something equally bourgeois. He's quite the rage. Thank you for the lemonade, Baron. Amalia, it was wonderful to see you. It's been far too long."

She left silence behind her. Von Schoenenburg slid his hand over her trembling one. "Wasn't Zaleski engaged to her at one time?" he asked quietly.

"No," she answered fiercely, doubling her fists into knots. "Until a few moments ago, I thought he might be dead!"

"You look very pale. Do you need some air? Some tea?"

She shook her head mutely.

"Perhaps his letters to you have gone astray since the move. Maybe he has no idea where you are."

"That still doesn't explain why he should be corresponding with Lilli," she said tightly.

"I can see you have more reason to be hurt than I can ever fix," he said, his voice oddly abrupt. "But I do think some air would help. Drink a little water, and we'll go for a walk."

They left their meals untouched. The baron said little but pulled her hand through his arm. Several times she felt he was on the verge of speaking. She wished he would. Her mind was a montage of unwelcome images that threatened to break her down. But somehow she managed the walk with dignity.

After going through her night shift like a ghost, Amalia went home to her rose and black chair. There she sat, numb, unbelieving. *It was over.* For some reason she didn't begin to understand, Andrzej had chosen to live his life without her. What other conclusion could be drawn from the facts? He wasn't dead. He hadn't come for her, hadn't even written her, but he had written Lilli. Slowly, she removed the pearl from her finger, and then in a flash of rage, threw it against the wall, where it fell behind her bed.

She wasn't going to suffer anymore because of this man. She would not allow that pain she knew would tear her heart open again and fill her with blackness. Anger would hold her together and get her through this. It shouldn't be that hard. After all, she *was* ferociously angry. Angry that he had so skillfully manipulated her emotions for so many years. Angry for the toll the last eighteen months had taken on her as she had lived in dread of his death. Angry that he could dismiss her from his life with no attempt at an explanation. Angry for all those soft words, those gentle kisses, that had meant nothing. And most of all, angry with herself for letting him into her heart.

Removing her shoes, she threw them, one after another, at the wall with as much strength as she possessed.

She was going to start again. She would surgically remove Andrzej Zaleski from her heart and from her life. It was the only possible way.

Chapter Three

The following day, Amalia stifled the ache thrumming in her heart and scrutinized her life without Andrzej. There was surely something left! How could she turn this anger into a tool to eradicate Andrzej from her consciousness? How could she make it count? Rosa had said she must have a goal. Maybe that was where she should direct all this furious energy.

She didn't think a career in medicine was the way to turn. She needed a fresh start in something that had no connection with her former life. To her surprise, her brother seemed interested in the same issue. That afternoon, he invited her into the parlor after her morning shift.

"Amalia, have you thought much about your future?" he asked. "Excuse me if it's a painful subject, but it looks like Zaleski's out of the picture. Do you intend to go on working at your hospital until you're old and gray?"

"Since when have you become concerned about *my* future?" His question made her wary.

He smiled his old easy smile. "Now don't be too hard on me, Amalia. I know things have been difficult, but I'm going to be fitted with my leg next week, and beyond that I think I'm beginning to see a way out of our problems."

Before he could elaborate, she informed him, "As soon as you're settled in your new post, I'm enrolling at the university."

Wolf laughed. "Whatever in the world gave you that extraordinary idea? Who do you think is going to pay for it?"

"You are. I've supported you for two years. It's time you returned the favor."

Her brother's eyes bulged, but she was amazed to see that he kept his temper. "And why the university?"

"It's what I want to do. My reasons wouldn't interest you."

"And what does Herr Oberst have to say about all of this?"

"I haven't discussed it with him, but I am sure I will have his unqualified support."

"Oh, I'm sure you will. Which brings me to my idea. Why do you think the baron, as you insist on calling him, takes such an interest in you?"

He leered at her, and Amalia looked away uncomfortably. She fixed her gaze on the fraying shabbiness of the hearth rug. "He's very kind, and he feels a responsibility for us. It's his nature. He's been this way since I've known him."

Wolf raised his heavy eyebrows.

She reasserted herself. "It's true, Wolf. He feels some sort of debt to Uncle Lorenz, and of course he wants to see you fixed up. I think it's thoroughly decent of him."

"And what are your feelings for this decent fellow?"

Amalia's eyes narrowed. "What business is it of yours?"

Leaning forward in his chair, Wolf fixed her with his prominent eyes. "Has it ever occurred to you, dear sister, that the man is in love with you?"

Amalia answered swiftly, her eyes wavering from Wolf's. "He's told me he will never fall in love. He's quite a cynic, actually."

Wolf grinned. "I wonder about that. You know he has to have an heir."

"It's really none of your concern," Amalia said shortly.

"None of my concern if my sister marries one of the wealthiest men in Austria? Be realistic, Amalia!"

"And love?"

"Love! Amalia, you don't know what love is. You thought you loved that Prussian stick, and he made you miserable. I won't even deign to mention the white knight Zaleski. When are you going to outgrow these romantic, school-girl ideas?"

She stood up. "I won't discuss this with you anymore, Wolf."

At that moment, they heard the knocker on the front door. Moving quickly past her brother, Amalia went to answer it. The baron stood on the front stoop, pleasure at the sight of her softening his brown eyes.

She stood on the threshold for a moment, staring at von Schoenenburg as though she had never seen him before. His smile turned quizzical. She had never noticed, but his lips had a sensual quality at variance with the sharply prominent cheekbones.

Wolf wheeled up behind her. "Greetings, Baron. Come courting my sister?"

Amalia turned on him as though he were poisonous vermin. "Go away!"

Her brother laughed and wheeled away in the direction of the kitchen.

"May I come in?" von Schoenenburg asked hesitantly. "Or have I chosen a bad time?"

Amalia tried a welcoming smile but couldn't carry it off. "I'd like to talk to you, Baron, but could we walk, perhaps? The atmosphere in this house is a little explosive at the moment."

He acquiesced with good grace, as always, and offered her his arm. They walked quickly out of the alley into the main thoroughfare, where he dismissed his car, telling the driver to call back for him in an hour. As they walked in an easterly direction toward the Danube, they encountered an urchin here and there playing ball in the gutter or an elderly lady laden with string bags of purchases. Amalia, who had grown used to her surroundings, was reawakened to them with embarrassment.

"I'm sorry," she murmured. "I've become so used to this neighborhood, I didn't think. This is far from a pleasant stroll."

Rudolf patted the hand that rested on his arm. "It's the company that matters. I came to check on you, Amalia. I hope you won't mind my officiousness, but I left you in rather a perilous frame of mind yesterday." *And I was close to murdering that Polish traitor,* he added silently.

She stood up straighter and raised her chin. "I'm perfectly fine now. Determined to get on with my life. Let's not speak of Andrzej again."

He stopped and turned her to face him. If there was one thing he knew about, it was grief. She was so wasted away, it might just kill her. Why did this have to befall her after her miserable marriage? "I'm sorry. But it can't possibly be that easy. I, of all people, know how long and how deeply you have loved him."

She looked straight into his eyes. "I was deceived. And now I'm horribly angry, mostly with myself."

He resumed their walk. "I confess I don't understand his behavior. I sat up late into the night trying to make sense of it all, but it doesn't make any kind of sense. I still think we're missing an essential piece of the puzzle." This was true. In spite of his dislike of the man, he had seen Zaleski bewitched by Amalia. What would he think if he were to see her now? The root of his own feeling was not physical love, he told himself. He savored her company more than ever when he realized how bravely she had carried on.

"He doesn't love me. That's the piece. Now. Can we please talk of something else?"

"If you wish. But I just want to say one more thing. The day will inevitably come when this anger is going to give way to tears. I don't want you to hide them from me, Amalia. Wolf will be no comfort at all, and you have no one else." It showed his depth of feeling, he thought wryly, that he was willing to be a pillow for her to cry on. He deplored hysterics. But she had the pure soul of a child and brought out all his protective instincts.

"You don't understand. I've cut Andrzej out of my life. I don't love him at all anymore. I despise him."

The baron was silent. Then he said finally, "My offer still stands. And would you call me Rudolf?"

This last caught her off guard, and she laughed. He could hear the strain of hysteria in it. "I don't think I can."

"Why not?"

"You're a lofty figure in my life. The font of wisdom and security. I can't be on a first-name basis with a god."

Stopping again, he frowned down at her. "Is that truly the impression you have of me?"

"Truly."

He was unreasonably annoyed. "It's a damnable one. Do I need to act like a scoundrel for you to believe me to be a mortal?"

"No. Please, no. I promise to call you Rudolf."

On an afternoon the following week, Rudolf returned to the flat with Wolf, who was wearing his artificial limb for the first time. Amalia was waiting with lemonade and a special torte she had purchased on her way home from the hospital. She had even unearthed her mother's Delft china and laid an elegant tea in the shabby little parlor.

Wolf, in pain and irritability, had declined the celebration and shut himself in his room. Papa was down at the warehouse as usual, and so Amalia served her solitary guest, not unhappy to be left to entertain in peace.

"How did it go?" she asked.

"He's in some pain but should adjust quickly. I think it's just that things are going a bit fast for him," the baron replied, allowing himself to be served a generous portion of *Käse-Torte*. "He's grown too used to indolence. Now there's nothing to prevent his reentry into civilization. I informed him today that I've a post in mind for him."

Amalia surprised her guest by kissing his cheek. "I can't believe how much you're doing for him. *I* thank you from the bottom of my heart, and I'm only sorry that he never will."

"I'm not doing it for him. I wouldn't be inclined to do a thing for him if he weren't such an obstacle in your life."

She looked at him thoughtfully, her glass poised at her lips. Then she set the drink down, untasted. "You're a bit of a dragonslayer, you know. Like the Rudolf in the stories I used to tell in the orphanage." Her eyes remained fixed on his face, and he did not look away.

"You see this Rudolf in far too romantic a light, I'm afraid," he said at last. "And I don't think you're at all used to being treated well. Living with Wolf must be a nightmare."

"It has been pretty hellish. But other things have been worse." To her shame, tears started in her eyes.

"Let them come, Amalia," he advised gently.

"I can't," she said, brushing them away, "Or I'll never stop."

Busying herself by serving Rudolf more torte and lemonade, she said fractiously, "Why do you accuse me of being a romantic? I've always pictured myself as the practical sort."

He gave a chuckle. "If you wore all of that marvelous hair of yours streaming down your back, all you'd need would be a veil of gossamer and you'd be straight out of a fairy tale yourself. But I'm well aware that you're not as fragile as you look, Amalia."

The image he painted was so close to that of Andrzej's that she choked on a sob.

"I'm not that person! I'm not! I don't even believe in romantic love. It's all an illusion. It feels good. But it's not real. Not like death or blood or suffering."

* * *

Her voice had risen in hysteria, and the tears were starting to come. As though drawn by some metaphysical thread, Rudolf moved next to her and gathered her to his side in a fierce grip. He *would* make her quit hurting, he *would*. It was simply unbearable to see her like this.

"No one can really fill up what's missing in our lives. It's like a bottomless hole. All we're looking for is some way of making ourselves feel good," she said, obviously grasping for a way to minimize love.

He asked her softly, "Was the love you had for your husband like that?"

Her tears flowed more freely, making it difficult to speak. All she could see was Eberhard's face on the railway platform. "No. It wasn't, in the end. You're right. To begin with, he filled a need in me. He gave me security. But in the end, it was an illusion, because his strength wasn't real. It was a part he played. If I ever loved him, it was *after* I realized that. But it wasn't romantic love, Rudolf. It was something else."

He handed her his handkerchief. "And your love for Zaleski? Surely that was real."

"The ultimate illusion. Otherwise, it wouldn't have ended. It would have gone on forever. It must have been no more than an animal attraction."

He didn't believe her for a minute. She had loved Zaleski body and soul, he was sure. Rudolf was more determined than ever never to let himself in for such pain. It was the sort of pain that could drive one to murder or suicide. She began to cry wholeheartedly.

At that moment, Wolf wheeled cheerfully into the room, followed by a guest who had arrived unperceived by either Amalia or Rudolf.

Lilli said, "I'm sorry. It looks as though I've come at a bad time."

Amalia stayed where she was, in the circle of his arms. She couldn't even answer, she was crying so hard.

Her cousin persisted. "The hospital gave me your address. Amalia, what has happened to all of Eberhard's money?" She looked around her in disbelief. Wolf abruptly wheeled himself out of the room.

"Fräulein, as you see, perhaps now is not the time," Rudolf began.

"But does Andrzej know?" she demanded.

At this Amalia managed a reply. "I haven't the least idea, Lilli."

"You mean you haven't told him?"

"No."

The baron rose augustly. "As you see, Amalia isn't herself at the moment. Perhaps you could call another time?"

"But I'm just off to Warsaw to visit an old school friend. I wondered if Amalia wanted to send a message with me for Andrzej."

"No message, Lilli, thank you."

Wolf reappeared to show Eberhard's cousin to the door. Rudolf heard him say, "Wonderful fellow, von Schoenenburg. He's been a life-saver to us."

He resumed a seat a little way from her. "That must have been another blow. I'm so sorry. I should have bodily removed her. Your wretched brother!"

Amalia just wept.

"There are many more tears where those came from, I'm afraid, Amalia." What did he know of love? But some part of him seemed to have the required wisdom as he continued, "No matter how much you want to be through with Zaleski, your memories aren't going to make it that easy. Your life has been woven into his for too long. It's going to take some time."

She was like a broken doll. Simply unable to bear seeing her that way, he gathered her to him, and she put her head into his shoulder. Protectiveness surged through him. "You don't have to bear the load of this household on your back much longer. Give yourself that time. You don't have to be the good little soldier any longer, my darling."

The endearment had slipped out, but Amalia wasn't noticing anything to do with him.

However, it signaled to him that it was past time he left. Promising to stop by the hospital and tell them she wouldn't be able to take her evening shift, he left her at last.

*   *   *

Amalia went upstairs to the sanctuary of her room. This grief wasn't as cosmic as the soul-destroying grief of Eberhard's and Trudi's death. Nevertheless, this sorrow was mixed with terrible hurt. No one had the power to hurt her like Andrzej. She had never loved anyone as much, and so the space carved out inside of her by love was now completely filled with pain. And there was anger, too, of course, but mostly now there were just devastating questions, which she could only answer by cutting them off at the heart and suffering the bloody consequences. Hope drained out of her with this metaphorical blood. How could it have happened? How could this be real? She went back to the attempt to make herself believe that to Andrzej she was nothing. And so the hurt and pain began again. Surely if such a thing as love existed, they had known it. So there must not be such a thing as love.

Chapter Four

September 12, 1919

Dear Louisa,

Since I last wrote there have been some major changes in my life. I am emerging from another tunnel of darkness now and am determined to rebuild my life along different lines. This last trial was particularly harsh and has uprooted all my sense of what I can trust and believe in. Andrzej has gone from my life permanently. I won't give you the details, but trust me that it is so. I am now enrolled at the University of Vienna studying history. Wolf actually has a job, and he and what is left of our money are supporting me.

I feel the need of new ideas in this new world we are building. That is why I am at the university. People are already saying there may be another war. I feel very alone in my hope that this might not happen and am trying, futilely, perhaps, to arm myself with knowledge of how this European imbroglio ever began. I feel that unless we know that, unless it is bred into our bones and those of our children, we will not be able to avoid this happening again. It has become my crusade.

I miss you exceedingly but am trying to emulate everything I remember of you, dear friend.

I hope your life is going well. I shall miss you when you move to America. A continent and an ocean seem impossibly far away, whereas Berlin is a comparatively short train journey. But I understand your desire to start anew. Is your whole family going? How is your brother?

Mit liebende grüsse,
Amalia

September 20, 1919

Dearest Amalia,

I was so sorry to hear of your recent trials. But I am glad you didn't get lost in the dark tunnel, though I'm very sad you had to pass through it.

Yes, my entire family is to move. My brother is completely rehabilitated and doing well as a mail carrier. He rides a bicycle that isn't too hard on his feet.

I send you all my love and best wishes in your new life. We will leave for the States in the spring. Please write again before then.

Mit liebende grüsse,
Louisa

Wolf settled into his new job as a bureaucrat. He was clerk to the member of the *Bundesrat* from the district that bordered on Rudolf's estate. Much to Amalia and von Schoenenburg's surprise, he had, after initial complaints regarding the discomfort of his new limb, adapted remarkably well to the job.

His attitude improved as he realized that his artificial leg was well concealed and that a limp was a badge of heroism these days. He never acknowledged his debt to the baron, but both he and Amalia were so glad to see Wolf take a responsible position in the household that they overlooked his lack of gratitude.

The baron was now actively seeking a buyer for their old home. He had already been very helpful in discovering for them an excellent housekeeper who was willing to sleep in the small quarters behind the kitchen. She was efficient, looking after Papa, doing all the cooking and marketing, and supervising the housemaid who came in each day. The dreary flat became bearable.

Rudolf, though supportive, was amused by Amalia's determination to study history. "I can understand why you want to go to the university, Amalia, but why not go into medicine? Why must you study history, of all things?"

"Because I know all of medicine that I am interested in knowing but am very ignorant of history."

"And what makes it so urgent that you become an historian?"

"I want to know how we got into this mess!" she said vehemently. "It's the first step to avoiding another one, which might even be worse."

With an unusual cynicism, Rudolf replied, "Don't you think that if the university could teach men the answer to that, we would have the problem solved by now?"

"Don't laugh at me, Rudolf. Can't you see that I must do something? It may not make much difference in the course of world events whether I am educated or not, but I can't just sit by and watch while the world goes crazy again. Women have more influence now than they did before the war. Perhaps I will take up a teaching position. Have I ever told you about my friend Louisa in Berlin?"

The baron shook his head and sobered, seeing how much in earnest she was.

"She was a nurse with me in the hospital and a very remarkable person. She had a theory, and it sounded important to me. I think Uncle Lorenz must have believed in it, too."

She sat on the divan in the parlor, bemused for a moment, her mind carrying her back to those terrible days following her mother-in-law's suicide. Turning to face Rudolf, she came back to the present and continued. "She says that we are each responsible in our own way for the course history takes. We can nurture the good in man, or we can give up and let the selfish and the evil predominate."

Rudolf nodded thoughtfully. "It is what I've always wanted to believe, but I'm afraid the selfish and the evil do predominate. And you, how would you nurture the good?"

"I don't know yet. She says we must each find our own way, find the thing we care the most about, or the thing we do best. For Louisa, it was being a good nurse and nurturing others' spirits. For my uncle, it was promoting the brotherhood of man. Perhaps as a teacher, or maybe even a writer, I can record the horrors of this war, so that future generations won't make the same mistakes."

"So you are looking for a cause. You are good at medicine. I believe the medical school is open to female students now. You could become a doctor."

"Yes, but my interest is no longer there, Rudolf. During the war it was the only thing I could do to . . . to try to stop the evil. But even then I was politically motivated. Now I'm interested not in preventing disease but in preventing war."

"So you're telling me you want to go into politics?" A glint of interest appeared in his eye.

"I know it sounds perfectly absurd. Please don't laugh. It isn't possible for me to actually go into politics, as you put it. I need to be educated, so it sounds as though I know what I am talking about."

"Ah," the baron nodded thoughtfully. "I begin to see where your thoughts are leading."

"Education, political education, is very important. Look what it did to Eberhard! He was willing to martyr himself for Prussian glory at the age of seven! And Andrzej! All his life he's wanted a united Poland. He was taught to want it. He never knew it from his own experience."

"And what would you teach the children to want? How would you indoctrinate them?"

She grimaced. "Indoctrinate is a terrible word. It sounds so contrived."

"Well, you must have something to offer as a counterbalance to those philosophies, Amalia. The thinking of the Poles and Germans is the sort of thinking that leads to war. What belief or philosophy do you have to offer that is attractive enough to prevent war?"

"I don't know. That's why I want to study history and politics and even different religions. I probably sound terribly naïve, but aside from the conversations I had with Uncle, all I was taught was how to carry on a fliration."

He looked at her with his gentle smile. "I wish you luck on your crusade."

Chapter Five

To begin with, university life was exciting. Amalia strolled the academic halls, books under her arm, awed by the sheer novelty of it all. Young men in tweeds, pipes in hand, rushed in a never-ending stream to their various forums of learning. Here and there was an earnest young woman, garbed in woolen stockings and sensible shoes, endeavoring to look as though she belonged.

Amalia balked at the sensible shoes. She wore the shapeless, mannish fashions of the day, long blazer jackets and slim skirts hemmed just above the ankle, but discovering a new vanity about the slimness of her feet, she affected elegant Italian pumps. They were her one extravagance, and Wolf had given her no end of grief about them. Her hair was hidden under a masculine "pork pie" hat, and she tried in every other way to look as earnest as all her university sisters.

Her professors, almost without exception, were men who had come to the university to teach in the 1890s and were now in their midfifties. They sported long mustaches and sideburns, reminiscent of Emperor Franz Josef, and confined all discussions to the world as it was before 1914.

This was extremely frustrating to Amalia. In the *Ratskeller* between lectures, Amalia spied another student from her classes. Boldly asking if she could join the earnest little mousey-haired woman, she said, "I'm Amalia von Waldburg. I've noticed you in some of my classes."

The young woman held out her hand. "Gerda Winkler. You're new aren't you?"

"Yes. Tell me, do all the professors refuse to discuss the postwar situation?"

Her new acquaintance gave a toothy grin. "They're all monarchists. They don't know the first thing about any other kind of political system, nor do they want to. You see, the divine right of kings has been bred into their bones. Without it, their world is in chaos. They think America has imposed democracy on us and that it will never succeed. What were you expecting?"

"I don't know exactly. I suppose I just thought someone who knew more than I do about the situation would be anxious to discuss the war and its causes and what we've learned from it. But it seems to me, they are still teaching the philosophies that led to the war in the first place. Very likely they contributed greatly to its happening."

"I'm afraid they're rooted in the old system and likely to stay that way. It's the only thing they understand. They have no reference point for a government without a strong leader. As far as I can tell, they're just sitting around waiting for democracy to fail so we can go back to the monarchy."

"But that's absurd. We have this wonderful opportunity now to change things. People need to be educated about democracy!"

"I'd keep that attitude to yourself. In class at least." Gerda picked up her books. "Are you doing anything special tonight?"

"Only reading. I wanted to get that Freiburg piece finished by tomorrow."

Gerda hesitated and then put her books down again. She smiled at Amalia, her teeth thrusting over her bottom lip. "I'm going to give you some advice. Only part of what's involved with university life is studying. What you need to do is relax and absorb the atmosphere. Join some groups." She indicated the Ratskeller with its little conclaves of students discussing rather noisily and punctuating their words with laughter and an occasional fist on the table. "Come with me tonight— a group of us are getting together to hear a man called Grosch."

"Who's he?"

"Some fellow who's convinced he's solved Austria's problems. It should be interesting. He's been attracting quite an enthusiastic following."

"May I bring a friend?"

"Why not?" Gerda smiled overpoweringly once again. "Why don't we meet here at seven?"

Rudolf was happy to accompany her, amused at her desire to court the university atmosphere.

"You do nothing by halves, Amalia," he said with a chuckle.

Meeting Gerda at the Ratskellar, they proceeded to one of the larger lecture halls. At Rudolf's suggestion, they seated themselves close to the exit, should the speaker prove too long-winded. Others in the heterogeneous group drifted noisily forward to sit within heckling distance of the lectern.

Herr Grosch was a man of decidedly military bearing who looked to be in his forties. It became quite obvious, early in his speech, that he was not one of those Austrians who could live with the Treaty of Versailles. He referred to it as a "castrating document" conceived by "fools and cowards." President Wilson was an "ignorant meddler" whose interference with "matters under the jurisdiction of the Hapsburg Empire" would reap economic chaos and political disaster. Naming Bolshevik Russia as their most fearsome enemy, he dismayed Amalia by referring to Germany as their only friend.

On the topic of Germany, Grosch waxed eloquent. Amalia sat stiffly as she listened to him tell his audience, now totally enthralled by his rich rhetoric, that the only hope for economic survival and prosperity for their country was an *Anschluss,* or union with Germany. They had been most brutally deprived of their empire, which was now a multitude of hostile little states wanting nothing to do with their former protectress. It was time to band together with those of common heritage, language, and ideals to show the West and the East that they were still to be reckoned with. And one day, with God's blessing, they would rise again!

Amalia sat in horror as Herr Grosch smilingly acknowledged a thunderous applause and standing ovation. Sickened, she rose and exited quickly, Rudolf at her side.

"Haven't they learned anything? They want another war!" she exploded as they strode rapidly out into the street.

"It's a very popular viewpoint, I'm afraid, Amalia. People are frustrated beyond bearing. They feel like the roast that's been carved up for Sunday dinner. There's only about a seventh of it left. Who are they now? What is their place in the world?"

"Do you feel that way?" she demanded.

"I must confess that I feel somewhat lost, but I'm certain an Anschluss with Germany and another war is not the answer. But people have to get over their feelings of entitlement. Remember the empire existed for centuries. Vienna is used to being the center of the world. The upper classes feel they have been robbed. They don't know how to go forward in this new world."

"What is the answer?"

"I'm not certain. But it's imperative that we find out, or popular opinion is going to have us yoked with Germany for sure."

He left her that evening in a thoughtful mood.

Days later she was approached again by Gerda in the Ratskeller as she was trying to read a boring text written in the last century.

"How did you enjoy Grosch?"

Amalia looked the woman straight in the eye and pronounced, "He made me ill."

Gerda looked taken aback. "Surely that's a bit strong, isn't it?"

Amalia's chin went up. "I feel strongly about it. I lived in Germany during the war. My husband was raised in Prussia. I would do anything to keep my country from their grasp."

"Anything?" Gerda asked, amused.

Amalia faltered slightly. "Well, almost anything, I suppose."

The mousy woman surveyed her critically. "Is it true you're Lorenz Reichart's niece?"

Mystified, Amalia nodded.

"Come to another meeting, Amalia. A secret one this time. No friends. I'll notify you when and where."

Amalia raised her brows in silent query, but Gerda left without further explanation.

When she recounted the discussion to a half-interested Wolf that evening, he looked at her in sudden concern. "I knew no good would come of this university business, Amalia! I forbid you to go to that meeting. Absolutely. Do you know who this crony of yours is?"

"No, and I don't see how you could either," Amalia said defensively, "You've never met her in your life."

"I'll bet you anything you like she's a Bolshie."

"A Bolshevik?"

"Yes, and she's setting you up to become one, too. Going to university is bad enough, but I absolutely draw the line here." His countenance became menacing as his eyes bulged and his mouth drew back in a tight grimace. "Uncle Lorenz was all very well. Crazy as a loon and harmless. But these people are dangerous. They're talking revolution and 'death to the aristos' and all the rest of it. You stay away from them!"

Despite the pejorative reference to Uncle Lorenz, what he said alarmed her. What she knew of the Bolsheviks did not square at all with Uncle Lorenz's vision of utopia. Since Russia had made a separate peace, there had been nothing but bloodshed in that country as numerous factions vied for power.

Wolf snorted. "As far as I'm concerned, von Schoenenburg is responsible for this—getting you mixed up with questionable types, putting my job in peril. Do you know what would happen to me if you started consorting with Bolshies?"

Amalia calmed him. "I've no intention of doing so, Wolf. Now that you've warned me, obviously I'll stay away."

"You're not to see her again."

Her hackles rose at his tone. She would go. But she wouldn't tell anyone. Not even Rudolf.

Amalia judged it prudent to end the discussion there. She thought she had assuaged Wolf's worries regarding Gerda; however, the next evening when Rudolf came to escort her to the opera, Wolf was waiting for them.

"Want to talk to you, von Schoenenburg," he announced peremptorily. Ushering the taller man into the now spotless parlor, he said, "Come, Amalia, you need to hear this, too. Things have gone far enough."

Rudolf raised his eyebrows at Amalia and followed Wolf. He seated himself on the sofa next to the hearth. She joined him, frowning at Wolf as she smoothed her new Chinese red evening gown. She had thought it might be hard to get Wolf to part with money for her wardrobe, but to her surprise, he had insisted. "How can you catch another husband in those old things you wear?"

Now she said, "Wolf, if you've any idea of blaming the baron for what happened yesterday, forget it."

Wolf stood looking down at his commanding officer like a sly cat contemplating its prey. "Shall we tell your friend about it and see what he thinks? After all, you know he has your welfare very much at heart. Or seems to, at any rate."

Rudolf looked at Amalia, his smile gone. "What's this about?"

"Nothing important, believe me. It's just . . ."

But Wolf held up a palm and interrupted. "Allow me to give the baron the facts. As I said before, you're far too naïve to know what's involved."

He recounted the incident, giving it a dramatic and dangerous flavor that caused Amalia to laugh scornfully. "You've missed your profession, Wolf. You ought to be writing melodramas."

The baron was concerned, nevertheless. "I don't blame you for your concern, Faulhaber. It alarms me, too, to think of Amalia unwittingly associating with such types. But tell me. Why do you blame me? And why do you do your sister the injustice of thinking she would be taken in by such people?"

"I'll answer the last question first. You know as well as I do how devoted Amalia was to our uncle. Undoubtedly, these people would cleverly have persuaded her that she was carrying out his wishes . . ."

"But, Wolf," Amalia protested.

"Faulhaber, don't you think your sister has a mind of her own? She *thinks,* man! Believe it or not, like any rational human being."

"Yes, she thinks, all right. Do you realize she is actually questioning whether or not she should remain a Catholic, in addition to everything else?"

Rudolf gave Amalia a questioning glance and then renewed his defense of her. "Like I said, she's rational. No doubt she has a reason for what she's doing."

"The Catholic Church was given to her with her mother's milk. I consider this search for something else to be symptomatic that she is far from rational . . ."

Amalia could stand it no longer. "Wolf. People have free will. They can choose governments. They can choose religions. For a long time in Austria we haven't been able to do either. Now all that is changing. We're coming into a new age."

"What Amalia says is certainly true. We must embrace this new age if we're not to go stumbling back. But I still don't understand, Faulhaber. Just why do you hold me responsible?"

"Because you've come to exercise quite an unjustifiable hold over my sister. I don't know what your game is. Do you get some sort of pleasure out of molding young minds or something? Don't tell me this all arises out of some vague duty to Uncle Lorenz. I don't buy that anymore. No one on earth could be as disinterested as you're pretending to be."

The baron stood, excusing himself in an undertone to Amalia. He was flushed a deep red, and his fists were doubled at his sides. "Hold it, Faulhaber. I don't owe you any explanation. Your sister is of age, and she is a widow. She's proven she can stand alone and make her own decisions. If anyone's mind has been molded in the relationship, it's mine.

"You're indebted to her for your life, the roof over your head, and your well-being. Had she not been your sister, I would have had you court martialed long ago. I can still do it. I won't further insult you by reminding you who you have to thank for your employment." He paused, but Wolf broke in with undiminished hauteur.

"And who is to look out for her honor, if I don't do it? You've made a fine job of gaining her trust . . ."

Amalia stood and said icily, "Who are you to talk about honor, Wolfgang Faulhaber? If I were to entrust mine to you, it would be badly tarnished before the month was out. Quit pretending you care about my honor! I won't have the baron forced into marrying me at the point of your pitiful little sword!"

Rudolf looked at her appraisingly, and Wolf sneered, "You've spoiled it now, little sister."

He left the room, hauteur still intact, and Amalia sank shakily into her chair. To her surprise, Rudolf picked up the poker and, flexing his muscles as though he would bend it, exploded, "Blast the man."

Amalia barely restrained a chuckle at his outraged expression. "Why? Has he gone and discovered your subtle scheme to set me up as your mistress?"

Rudolf looked at her, eyes wide with horror. She laughed. "I'm joking! Poor Wolf! He thought he was being so clever."

He gazed at her, his frustration still obvious. "He was clever. What do you think of my motives, Amalia?"

Suddenly uncomfortable, she shrugged. "I suppose it's rather selfish of me, but I have always thought of you as just *there*. Rather like a rock. I can't imagine your not being part of my life." Then she managed a laugh. "And it's easy to see why you prefer my company—it's the intellectual stimulation I provide."

The baron's black mood passed, and he threw the poker aside with a hearty laugh. "That is surely one reason. I never know where you're going to turn next. What's all this about a new religion?"

"I've told you about Louisa."

"Yes. Is she a heretic?"

"I'm not sure. She definitely has a more personal relationship with God than the priests lead you to believe is possible. I'm tired of dealing with intermediaries. If God exists at all, I don't think He operates that way. Louisa has very powerful faith. Her understanding is large. She meditates, and she's actually read the Bible in German."

"Ah! A Lutheran!"

"No. I don't really think she's tied to any faith, though she's nominally a Catholic. But everything she ever said to me and the way she lives her life—I want to be like her. Her beliefs give her comfort and strength I don't have. I've about given up on God, as a matter of fact. But before I do, I feel I have to pursue a new direction. And maybe I will end up something other than a Catholic."

Rudolf studied the bric-a-brac on the mantle over the fireplace. "You realize of course that Catholicism is much more than a religion to Austrians. It is part of our culture and has been since the beginning."

"Yes, I know that. But I don't intend to cut myself off from anything, Rudolf. I just want to build on it. I need to find out if there really is a God and if He really is personal. If He really cares about me as a person."

"I can see you're serious about this."

"Yes. Louisa saved my life, you see. Now, I refuse to give in to despair. She convinced me that my life is a series of choices, not just blind acceptance and empty ritual."

The baron consulted his watch. "Well, where we're going right now is the opera, I think. I'll be surprised if we haven't missed the overture."

Chapter Six

The next evening, Amalia took the streetcar to a middle class neighborhood where she was received by a glass manufacturer and his wife. A small group was waiting, some obviously of the working class. Gerda, dressed in trousers, greeted her with a mannish handshake. Amalia was surprised to see Rosa Klein, her friend from the hospital.

"What're you doing here, Waldburg?" the girl asked, her sunny smile ominously absent.

"I'm not exactly sure. Gerda asked me to come. She told me not to tell anyone."

At that moment, a short, thickset man with an unshaven face and an olive drab cap pulled down over his brow called out, "Can this woman be trusted?"

"She's Lorenz Reichart's niece," Rosa said.

The man in the cap looked at Amalia sharply, his eyes burning into hers. Then he gave a swift nod. There were about a dozen people in the room, so Amalia lowered herself as gracefully as possible to the floor. She was joined by Rosa.

"Our ideals have been betrayed by Karl Renner," the man announced, his rough voice announcing his working class origins. "He has just made it known that he favors an Anschluss with Germany. You are to take this information back to your units. We are going to stage a public repudiation. Grober, you write the article for the newspaper. Klein, see what can be done about a demonstration at parliament."

Amalia felt a shiver go down her back. She knew that Renner, a nominal socialist, was the head of the provisional government.

"It is a betrayal of the communist ideal," the man went on. "We must follow the Russian model, not this cobbled together so-called socialism that still keeps the Old Guard in power. Germany wants another war. We are not ready. We must follow the Leninist code and settle things here on the home front. Comrade Lenin is having success in putting the Marxist ideal to work in a country that was more corrupt than Austria ever was. We must follow his example here if we want socialism to survive. Remember Reichart!"

Amalia was jolted at the name of her uncle. So these were his friends. She began to be intrigued. Could Uncle's friends be dangerous?

To her surprise, the man in the cap pointed to her. "Where is our money?"

"I was forced to divide the funds among his other charities—all causes I am sure you would approve of."

"She's all right," Rosa announced. "She nursed with me during the war, even though she had plenty of moncy."

"Ah," the ringleader said. "So it is not too latc."

"I'm afraid it is," Amalia said, trying hard not to sound defensive. "All my uncle's principal was eaten up by his charities during the war. There is none left. And my own fortune is lost, as well."

"So. Why are you here?"

"I don't want a union with Germany," she said definitely. "I hold them responsible for a pointless war that cost us far too many lives."

The man in the cap seemed to ponder. "Sounds as though you might be squeamish about bloodshed. I think perhaps it would be better for you to leave." Then he gave a half-grin that was almost a leer. "If we have anything to say about it, there will be no union with Germany, if that's a comfort to you."

She stood awkwardly. Her foot had gone to sleep. "I wish you luck, then," Amalia said.

"No tales," the man said. "You were never here, is that understood?"

Gerda showed her out. "Sorry. Franz must have something up his sleeve. We have to be frightfully careful. You won't betray us?"

"I don't even know who you are!" Amalia protested.

"That's all right, then. Go along home and forget you ever met us."

All the way home on the tram, she pondered the words, "squeamish about blood." What were they planning? Some kind of revolution, like the bloody one in Russia? With twelve people? But then she remembered, these were just unit heads. She had no idea how big the units were. Perhaps they had the whole Social Democratic Party organized.

Karl Renner was the socialist her uncle had always met with. If Uncle hadn't died, she realized, it was likely that he and not Renner would be head of the government. And he would never have had any pan-German ideas.

By the time she got home, she was weary and confused. If it weren't for Rosa Klein, she might consider breaking her word and telling Rudolf about the group. Whatever they were up to, it was dangerous, she was certain.

However, any questions about the meeting were immediately put out of her mind by the surprising letter she received the next day from her cousin by marriage.

November 20, 1919
Warsaw

Dearest Amalia,

It's a thrill to be here in this capital reborn. The vitality and sheer energy of these people is beyond anything—and I was used to thinking the Poles were so indolent!

The new state is tremendously big on pomp and ceremony, and Natasia has taken me to several balls given in honor of this and that landmark event.

At one of the first of these I encountered your fiancé. Or is he still? I must say it was all very strange. He said nothing of you—and when I mentioned I had seen you just before leaving, he changed the subject.

I know you think me an ill-mannered ghoul, but what is going on? If you have your eye on the baron, Amalia, don't you think it's only fair to let this poor man know? He looks quite hollow, by the way. Much as he did after you married my cousin. If I hear nothing from you to the contrary, I intend to launch a salvage mission. And this time I mean it to be a success!

> Mit liebende grüsse,
> Lilli

Amalia hadn't thought she could be hurt anymore by Andrzej, but this communication was an unexpected blow. He wouldn't even speak of her! What had she done to cause such disdain? And why should Lilli feel Amalia had something to do with whatever pain Andrzej was apparently feeling? Instead of eating with the family, Amalia locked herself in her room and gave way to the thoughts Lilli's letter caused. She now had an image of him in her mind—disdainful, sullen, proud. Where had her Andrzej gone? The one who had loved her so much he had come to Vienna to say good-bye on his way to France? The one who had held her as she cried and promised devotion to her until death and beyond? She had had no doubts whatsoever of his sincerity. And then the letter after the war from his comrade. *What had gone wrong?*

It simply made no sense unless she convinced herself that she didn't really know or understand Andrzej after all. He was there in Warsaw. Alive. Supposedly unhappy. But he wanted nothing to do with her, not even to hear her name. She had all the evidence. It was so. Once again the cataclysmic pain overtook her, and she sobbed in frustration and bewilderment. *Why?*

Little by little her pain turned outward and became anger. Picking up pen and paper, she composed a letter to Lilli.

Dear Lilli,

I must confess your letter puzzled me greatly. I do not know why you believe that I am to blame for the demise of my relationship with Andrzej. I must assume it has met its demise from what you have told me. He has lacked the courage or honor to inform me of that fact himself. Indeed, until you told me that you had received a letter from him, I thought that he might even be dead.

Cherish him, by all means, if you wish it. I cannot think that he is worthy of your devotion, but no doubt my opinions carry little weight with you in this matter.

As for my relationship with the baron, you have entirely misinterpreted the matter. He has stood as a great friend to me and has even found employment for Wolf. He has asked nothing in return. There is no grand passion there, Lilli, believe me.

I wish you luck on your salvage mission and hope that it will prove to be what you desire. Please do keep in touch with me, Lilli.

Mit liebende grüsse,
Amalia

That Lilli would succeed with Andrzej, she had no doubt. It was over now, for certain. She must anchor herself somehow before she fell into the void yawning at her feet. The existential void, Uncle had taught her. The one that existed when one ceased to believe in God. She wouldn't give Andrzej that power. She was very confused about love and God and the horror of man's inhumanity to man, but she was determined to sort it out. Frantically, she cast her eyes about her room. They lit upon her textbooks, but her mind revolted. She needed something solid to soothe her ravaged soul. To reconnect herself to humanity before she fell off the edge of the world. During the war, she had existed in a perpetual state of crisis—life and death were before her constantly. Now she had far too much time to think.

It was no use going to mass. She could no longer pray to statues of the impassive Virgin and receive peace. Thinking of what Louisa would do, she went to her tiny nightstand where she had put her copy of the German Bible. By chance, she opened to the book of Esther. She read the short account of the Jewish queen and her mission to save her people. At her cousin Mordecai's words, "And who knoweth whether thou art come to the kingdom for such a time as this?" she felt peace flow into her. She didn't know what she was going to do. But somewhere there must be a less dangerous faction of Austrians who didn't see unity with Germany as the answer to their problems. She must ask Rudolf. She had no illusions about being an Esther, but she remembered clearly Uncle's last words: "We are God's hands."

Her confusion did not cease with this memory, however, for just then her eye fell on Lilli's letter, and her doubts about God visited her again, whipping her into a turmoil.

Why did the universe seem to be run by hate? Even in Esther's time. The more she learned about Andrzej's defection, the more full of doubts she became. If there was love, that love must be a different thing altogether from what she had felt for Andrzej. Was it possible what she had felt was only lust? *Was* there another kind of love?

Remembering Louisa's strength and selflessness almost balanced the scales. Amalia had been a romantic, that was all. The interludes with Andrzej were totally unreal in the world as it existed today. They had been an illusion. Costume dramas in the old, glittery world where women's identity depended on flirtation, a soul-wrenching, heart-racing affair.

She felt reality slip away beneath her. What was this new world where everyone had such different ideas about what was important? The old standards had clearly gone. And twenty-five years of her existence with them. She felt more than ever that she must forge a new path.

Pressing her fingertips on her temples, she tried to arrest the whirling of her head. It was up to her to choose a course through this crazy life that would bring light to as many people as possible.

But what did she know of light? She must study. She had spent too long in the dark.

If there was a purpose for her existence, if there was a God, she needed to find out. Taking up her Bible again, she sat on her bed and began reading St. Matthew.

A letter arrived the next day that caused her mind to spin once more. Antonia was proposing after all this time to pay them a visit. She was to be accompanied by her son, now eighteen months old, who supposedly wanted to "make the acquaintance of his grandfather, uncle, and aunt."

It was clear that Antonia was besotted with the child and was certain he would be admired by his Faulhaber relations. Amalia wrote back hastily to say that they were welcome to come but they would have to share her room with her.

She busied herself in her hours away from the university obtaining a baby cot (from a relation of their new housekeeper) and helping Frau Schiller to make room in her own drawers and wardrobe for Antonia and little Matthaeus's things.

Her father, so vague now that one hardly bothered to inform him of what went on in the real world, seemed to grasp that he was going to see his dear Toni.

On the day of her sister's arrival, Rudolf was kind enough to take her to the station in his automobile. Amalia told him as he settled himself next to her in the comfortable rear seat, "I'm glad of your support. I suspect this reunion will be rather strained. We haven't seen each other since her wedding day, you know."

"A lot of water under the bridge since then," the baron remarked thoughtfully.

"It will be a dreadful shock for her to see where we live. I couldn't really prepare her . . . I mean, she wouldn't have believed it. She may even refuse to stay there."

The baron raised an eyebrow. "Then my car will be at her service to return her to the train station," he remarked dryly.

Amalia laughed and impulsively drew her arm through his. "I'm glad you'll be there, for my sake, when she catches her first glimpse. But perhaps she'll be on her best behavior with you. She's rather a snob."

Rudolf smiled thinly. They had arrived at the *Sudbahnhof.* Amalia, always thrilled by the air of expectancy and busyness of the railway station, alighted from the automobile almost eagerly, and the baron took her arm as they made their way to Platform 8, where Antonia's train was just pulling in.

Some five minutes later, she saw her sister descend from the train, carrying nothing but a small reticule. Wondering what had become of little Matthaeus, Amalia was horrified to see a small child descend the steps behind his mother, holding the hand of what obviously was his nurse-attendant in her pink starched uniform.

"Of course she *would* bring her nurse!" Amalia muttered. "Where on earth shall I put her?"

Antonia, smartly attired in a suit of cherry red with an ermine boa and matching hat, was looking about, unable to recognize her sister. Amalia had temporarily forgotten what time had done to her own appearance for Antonia looked much the same as always, if not better. And of course, von Schoenenburg stood at her side. Antonia would not expect that.

"There she is," breathed the baron, nodding in Antonia's direction.

"Yes," sighed Amalia. "She doesn't recognize me. I suppose we'd better press on."

They moved forward through the throng, Amalia clutching her mustard colored coat, feeling suddenly threadbare and unattractive. But she forced a smile. "Toni!" she called brightly. Her sister's neat little head turned toward the voice, and she stared in open puzzlement.

She quickly recovered herself, however. "Oh, Amalia, what a relief! I was beginning to think we hadn't been met, and dear Matthaeus does so need his nap!"

She pulled her fat-cheeked child forward. "Son, this is your Aunt Amalia!" But the little blue-eyed boy had eyes only for the august personage beside her. He gazed up in awe at Rudolf's imposing figure.

Amalia laughed at his expression. "Don't be frightened, Matthaeus. This is my friend. He is a baron. That's what you can call him."

Antonia recognized the baron for the first time and shot her sister a surprised look. Meanwhile, Rudolf bent down to shake the youngster's hand. "I'm very happy to meet you, little man," he said robustly.

The little fellow smiled suddenly, revealing a sunny, dimpled grin that quite unexpectedly touched Amalia. Her own smile of greeting grew warmer. Rudolf stooped to the child's height. "I expect you're rather tired, aren't you? Would you like a ride?"

At a tentative nod from the child, Rudolf suddenly swooped him up on one shoulder. Matthaeus gave a hoot of delight, and the group began its progress to the automobile, followed by a heavily laden porter.

"How nice of the baron!" Antonia exclaimed, beaming with a delight almost as great as that of her child as she watched man and boy stride down the platform ahead of them. "I didn't even get a chance to say hello!" Then she acknowledged her servant. "Amalia, this is Fräulein Koss, Matthaeus's nurse. Fräulein, this is my sister, the Baroness von Waldburg."

The two women exchanged nods, and Antonia continued, "I know you said space was a problem, but I didn't think you'd mind. I can't manage without Fräulein Koss. And Matthaeus would have been lost without her. In fact, I don't think I could have gotten him to come."

Amalia replied graciously to the nurse, rather than her sister, "That's a very high recommendation, Fräulein. I hope you won't be too uncomfortable. I'm afraid we'll have to put you in with our housekeeper."

The little woman in pink stammered in confusion, "But Matthaeus—I am used to sleeping with Matthaeus. Where will he be put?"

Her alarm and concern were so evident, that Amalia hastily reviewed things in her mind, and said, "Well, perhaps we could persuade my brother to move in with Papa, and then the two of you could have his room."

Antonia looked appalled but mercifully held her tongue.

The ride home was merrily accomplished. Fräulein Koss rode in the front beside Rudolf's driver with the two sisters in the commodious back seat. Matthaeus insisted on sitting on the jump seat with his new friend and busily explored Rudolf's many pockets.

Though apprehensive, Amalia enjoyed the sight of Rudolf with her nephew. Antonia still had the old habit of gushing.

"Really, Baron von Schoenenburg, this is such a happy surprise, your meeting us with the automobile."

"Glad to be of service," Rudolf replied, never taking his eye from the "calling card house" he was constructing on the unsound foundation of his knee.

Antonia's expression of rapture faded, however, as they neared Amalia's home. "But this neighborhood, Amalia! It's nearly as bad as Uncle Lorenz's. Surely, you don't live here!"

"Yes, I'm afraid so. But cheer up. It's really not a bad place. We've fixed it up quite decently. As a matter of fact, the baron has found a buyer for the townhouse, so we can move out soon into something a little nicer if we like."

Antonia's shock had not affected Amalia the way she had thought it would. She found it almost amusing rather than infuriating. She added, "But we may stay on. I must admit, I've grown quite fond of the place."

Rudolf twinkled at her, and Antonia looked quite horrified. "You're joking! You must be! Why, Erich never would have let me come if he'd known!"

"Well, I did try to warn you, my dear," Amalia said dryly. "You must get used to the fact that you have poor relations."

Antonia sat upright in her seat, steeling herself to look at the chauffeur's back rather than out the window. Her always expressive face mirrored revulsion, but she did not reply to Amalia's remark.

Chapter Seven

When they pulled up before the flat, Antonia allowed herself and her entourage to be assisted inside with the kind help of the baron and his chauffeur. Once they were inside, Antonia looked around and relaxed a bit as though she were relieved to find that she was not to stay in a rat-ridden hellhole. Impulsively, she turned, not to her sister but to the baron, whose ears were being persistently pulled by her son and heir.

"Honestly, Baron, I can't understand how you can want to be seen here!"

Amalia flushed angrily, but Rudolf set down little Matthaeus and took her hand protectively in his. He turned to Antonia and said gravely, "Madame, it is an honor to know your sister were she to reside in hell itself. She is a woman of great character and courage, and one day I hope to make her my wife. Now, if you'll excuse me, I must go home to dress. Amalia and I are invited to the American ambassador's for dinner."

Both women stood speechless as the man moved majestically out of the door, followed by his chauffeur. Amalia, mind reeling, recovered first and called for her brother. He came limping in from the parlor, grinning cheerfully, for he had obviously heard what had just passed.

Ignoring her brother completely, Antonia turned to her sister in wonder. "But, Amalia, you might have told me! I mean, was he serious? He's one of the wealthiest barons in Austria!"

Amalia felt mirth ascend above her churning emotions. She laughed heartily. "Antonia, you're such an unremitting snob. Don't you realize you've just been thoroughly put down?"

Antonia shrugged and looked around. "But it is perfectly ghastly, Amalia. I meant every word of it. How can *you* stand to live here?" she asked, acknowledging her brother's appearance for the first time.

Wolf's cheerful look faded, and he said peevishly, "Can't you let up now, Antonia? The nobility has departed. We're just family. And like it or not, we're the only family you've got."

Amalia looked at Wolf with approval and proceeded to tell him, "Antonia's brought her nurse, Wolf. Meet Fräulein Koss." Wolf nodded irritably, and she continued. "It seems she's used to sleeping with young Matthaeus . . ." Amalia looked around and not seeing her nephew, went on, "who seems to be exploring somewhere. At any rate, I don't know what to do, unless you go in with Papa and let them have your room."

Wolf shrugged, "Impossible. Can't manage the stairs with this leg, you know." He departed for his room, totally uninterested in their problem.

Amalia, who knew full well that Wolf could manage the stairs when he wanted to, said, "Oh, yes, I was forgetting the leg. Well, we'll just have to adhere to the original plan then."

Young Matthaeus was found in the kitchen after a short search, sitting on his grandfather's lap.

Old Matthaeus, nearly deaf, had not heard the arrival of his daughter and could not possibly know that this was his grandson and namesake, but nevertheless it was obvious that the two were *en rapport*. The chubby child's face shone with delight as he played with the old man's pocket watch and listened to the wheezy strains of a nursery tune his grandfather was endeavoring to sing.

Amalia halted in the doorway, unwilling to interrupt, but Antonia ran forward and embraced her father and son together.

"Papa!"

Her father looked up and his initial bewilderment cleared as he recognized his oldest daughter.

"Dear Toni," he whispered. Then looking at the youngster on his lap, he announced as though he were very pleased with himself, "You see, I have made a friend!"

"He's named for you, you know, Papa."

The old man looked confused, as though he could not see the connection.

Puzzled, Antonia said impatiently, "He's your grandson, Papa. My son, Matthaeus. We call him Matti."

The cloudy look Amalia knew so well came into her father's eyes, and he lifted the little one off his lap. Standing, he patted his watch pocket and, finding it empty, began to look anxiously about his person. "I must have mislaid my watch. I'm certain it's time for me to go back to the warehouse," he whined.

Amalia took the watch gently from her nephew and handed it to her father. "Here, Papa. The little boy had it."

"Ah!" Relief came into the old man's eyes as he snapped it open. "Yes, it's time to meet the afternoon shipment. I must be going." He bowed slightly in Antonia's direction.

"It was lovely to meet you, Fräulein. You remind me of someone. Can't think who." He ruffled the boy's hair and shuffled out of the room.

Antonia started after him, her fine brows drawn together in puzzled bewilderment, "Papa!"

Amalia restrained her sister. "Let him alone, Antonia. I wrote to you about it. He can't take it in. Anything that's happened since about 1915 is too traumatic or something. It's some kind of senility. His mind is closed to the present, and he lives totally in the past."

Antonia's eyes filled with tears. "But I was so sure he'd be pleased to see Matthaeus," she cried. "We even named him for Papa."

"I'm sorry, Toni. I know it must be a shock."

Her sister looked around the homely kitchen, all of her former distaste returning. "I should never have come. It was a mistake."

But Amalia had gathered little Matthaeus in her arms. "How would you like some bread and jam?"

After the child had feasted, she settled him on her lap and told him the story of Rudolf the dragon slayer. She knew he didn't understand a word, but it was so comforting to talk of "Rudolf" just then and to hold the warm little bundle of child. Antonia had been up in her room with the nurse, supervising the unpacking. When they came down, Amalia carried the little boy upstairs and tucked him in the baby cot. Then she descended again to try to placate her sister.

"What am I to do in this dreary old place while you're at this American dinner?" Antonia asked, her fingers drumming impatiently on the arm of the chair.

"Wolf will be here. You have a lot of time to catch up on. I'm sure Frau Schiller will have something special for dinner. She's an excellent cook. A treasure, in fact."

Antonia looked doubtful. "I don't understand why you had to go tonight of all nights, Amalia. After all, you've known for a week that I was coming."

"This is rather a rare occasion, you know, Toni. It's not every day one is invited to the American embassy," Amalia replied carefully. Bless Rudolf! Were they, in fact even going there? They had had no previous engagement for the evening, precisely because Antonia was coming, but perhaps he had always intended to go alone. She had no way of knowing. She smiled a little at his insistence that he was endeavoring to persuade her to be his wife. He *had* gotten a little carried away there. Antonia must have really gotten his dander up. It had been very comforting. She would wear her new Chinese silk.

Antonia, meanwhile had been talking. " . . . don't like his manner. I mean, at least he can be civil!"

Gathering that her sister was now talking about Wolf, Amalia tried once again to soothe. "You must understand, Antonia. The war changed our lives. Permanently. It doesn't seem to have changed yours, so it is difficult for you to fathom. Wolf has only recently accustomed himself to his artificial leg. It's quite painful and makes him grouchy. As a matter of fact, he's pretty hard to live with. But at least he's supporting the family now. He came home early today, just to greet you. That says something."

Antonia laughed bitterly. "And so you're just going to traipse off to the American embassy of all places and leave me here with a nasty brother and a crazy old man . . ."

Amalia stood abruptly. "Don't you ever speak that way about Papa!" Her eyes snapped, and Antonia lapsed into a sulk. Amalia started for the door. "I think you can tolerate it for one night. I seem to have managed for a number of years. Now, I must dress."

It was with some trepidation that she departed an hour later, however. Wolf had gone out, and Papa, having returned, was puttering around his room, immersed in his stamps. Antonia took a very cool leave of them, the baron's social status notwithstanding.

"Perhaps I shouldn't have gone," Amalia sighed once they were settled against the leather upholstery of the automobile.

Rudolf took her gloved hand in his. "Don't be absurd. She can stand it for one night. It'll be good for her. Perhaps she'll even decide to leave," he said hopefully.

Amalia laughed, and put her head on his shoulder. "Thank you for coming to my rescue again. Where are we going, incidentally?"

"Do I ever lie? To the American embassy, of course. I hadn't planned on attending, but they issued invitations to everyone in the Bundesrat. We might as well go, though it's likely to be a bit of a crush."

"What are your duties in the Bundesrat? You never talk about it very much."

"That's because we don't do much under the new constitution. We just have a sort of suspended veto power. All the real power is in the Nationalrat."

"And they're elected by universal suffrage, aren't they? The so-called lower house?"

"Yes."

"Why don't you try to get elected to the Nationalrat, then, Rudolf?"

"Because I'm not at all sure I want to be that active in politics, Amalia. I'm not sure I'm wise enough!"

Amalia began to protest, but he silenced her gently. "It takes a unique type of individual to be a politician, Amalia. Particularly in a democracy. One has to have ideas worth fighting for and then be willing to give one's life to the fight." He patted her hand. "I'm not sure I'm that single-minded."

"Oh," she protested, frustrated. If only she were a man! "But, Rudolf, you are such a good man. You could do so much good for the country!"

He laughed briefly. "I'm aware that you think so, my dear. But goodness isn't necessarily a requisite quality in a politician."

"Well, it should be!" she said firmly, as the car halted before the embassy.

Rudolf chuckled. "You'd change the world if you could, Amalia."

He handed her out of the car, and they ascended the broad shallow steps to the brilliantly lit embassy building.

Chapter Eight

Amalia found herself totally enchanted by the occasion, her vexation with Antonia instantly banished. How long it had been since she'd enjoyed an evening such as this! Women in long evening gowns, men in splendid evening dress, all mingling in a frenzy of sociability. It might almost be before the war.

And yet, there was something different here. Something a bit more frenetic. There was a strange undercurrent of energy that had been lacking at those old occasions.

Amalia knew she looked her best, if not quite as romantic and dreamy as in prewar times. She, too, was different, dressed in Chinese red, now a perfectly acceptable color for a respectable widow. Her hair, still dressed high on her head, made her look more sophisticated than she felt.

She progressed through the receiving line as one slightly dazed, her spartan senses overwhelmed by the unaccustomed gaiety.

Rudolf glanced down at her as they walked into the main salon. "I can see you are relishing this, Amalia. I find these things so dull, I've never thought to bring you before."

She looked up at him mischievously. "I daresay there are many things that are commonplace to you that wouldn't seem so to me. Perhaps that's why you enjoy slumming so much. It gives you a change."

"Amalia!" The baron looked shocked and uncomfortable. He drew her to one side of the crowded room.

"Can you really think that? I'd do anything to bring you and your family out of that slum, as you call it."

She was immediately repentant. "Forgive me, Rudolf. I was just teasing. You have made all the difference in our lives." Her chin went up, and she smiled. "It's amazing what losing everything will do for your perspective. There are so many things I appreciate now that I took for granted before." She looked musingly out over the throng of brisk men and effervescent women. "And then, there are so many things I can see now aren't important at all. This sort of thing used to be my world. I never thought beyond it. Now I have so many questions."

"Any answers so far?"

"I'm searching. Tell me, Rudolf, isn't there any party in Austria that doesn't want union with Germany?"

"My party. The Christian Socialists. But we're not in the majority just now. Renner and his Socialist Party are very pan-German."

"Yes. I realize that. But your party could make a difference, Rudolf."

He seemed to ignore her. "And what else have you found in your search?"

"I've begun reading the Bible. In German. It's very plain. It doesn't have rituals and grand men in satin robes. I think Uncle was right when he said the modern church has little to do with God. He would have been more like Peter—a simple fisherman. I can see why Uncle wouldn't attend high mass in the cathedral with incense and chanting in Latin. What good does that do anyone?"

"I know what you mean. Lorenz may not have thought himself a Christian, but he was a Christian in the most fundamental sense."

"So are you."

"I'm just a crusty old Catholic."

"I think not," she said playfully. "I've seen under that crust."

Her escort grumbled a bit and actually blushed.

A tubby little American with an eyeglass introduced himself, and their quiet exchange ended, but Amalia could sense Rudolf's eyes on her from time to time throughout the evening and wondered what was passing through his mind.

Her dinner partner was an anemic looking young man with a toothbrush mustache who turned out to be a very junior secretary in the embassy. Rudolf was partnered by the wife of the army attaché.

As they sipped something that seemed to be an American soup made of peas, her partner fidgeted awkwardly and asked, "Is your husband in the *Bundesrat?*"

Surprised, Amalia looked up at the young man. Then she smiled what she hoped was a kind smile. "He's not my husband. My husband was killed in the war."

The young man was now doubly embarrassed, she supposed. But really he should have been more attentive during the introductions.

He stammered through a conversation, making one gaffe after another.

Amalia found herself thinking, *How can he think the Austrian middle class is made up of German Nationalists? Heaven help the Americans if this is the best they can do!*

It only remained for her to listen to the after dinner speaker, who was the ambassador himself. She was relieved, for America's sake, to find that he was quite inoffensive and very diplomatic, wishing only for greater friendship between the two "great democratic nations of Austria and the United States of America."

She recounted her conversation with the silly young man to Rudolf on their way home. He laughed at her animated description. "He certainly doesn't seem to be an overbright specimen. His father is probably someone important, I should think. That's the most likely explanation for how he came by the post."

"Somehow, I thought America was above that sort of thing, I guess," Amalia mused.

"Nepotism or stupidity?"

Amalia laughed. "The former. But imagine! Saying that the whole

Austrian middle class is German Nationalist. What a sweeping statement!"

"Not far wrong, however," the baron said quietly.

Amalia turned on him. "No! It is wrong!" she protested.

"Just how many middle class people do you actually associate with
anymore, Amalia?"

"Well, there was Rosa at the hospital. She hated the Germans as
much as I did."

"She's a Jew, though. The Jews tend to favor internationalism or
communism. Who else?"

"Well, I don't have many friends at the university, just Gerda."

"Who's either a communist, according to Wolf, or an ardent
German Nationalist—remember the meeting she invited you to."

"But, Rudolf! Isn't there anyone who wants an *Austrian* democracy?"

"Yes, the Christian Socialists do, supposedly. But they're primarily
made up of the peasants and the old landowners like myself. The
Viennese are mostly Social Democrats. Most of them favor democracy,
but there's a feeling they've been infiltrated by the Reds."

"Hence the term Red Vienna. Yes, I've heard of it." Amalia was
silent for a few moments. She was tempted to tell him about the strange
meeting she had been to.

"What chance do you think democracy has of survival, Rudolf?"
she asked quietly after a few moments.

He gave her question some thought before replying. "I wonder,
Amalia. That's not an easy question to answer. It may be that people
will see democracy as an answer to their problems, but more likely
they'll make it some kind of scapegoat forced on them by the Western
powers. They'll blame it for all the economic problems we will continue
to have due to the demise of the empire. It's too easy for people to
dream. They're saying how much better things would be if only . . . but
everyone has their own 'if only.' If only we were part of Germany. If
only we had the monarchy back. If only we had the empire back. If

only we were a true socialist state, governed by the people, as in Russia. Everyone is dissatisfied."

"It's rather frightening." Amalia shuddered.

"Yes," the baron agreed. "It is." They were silent the rest of the journey home.

* * *

When they entered the parlor, Rudolf was relieved to find it unoccupied. He had been worried they would find a bored and petulant Antonia lying in wait. And there were things he wanted to say. The whole evening he had been marveling over the statement he had made to Antonia regarding his intention to marry Amalia. Such an idea must have been sleeping in his mind unawares. What he knew of close human relationships was bloody and lethal, laced with neuroses. And there was that dark room inside him where he kept the gruesome things he did not want to acknowledge. *Could he marry without revealing his inner self?*

He knew that he was not in love with Amalia in any romantic sense, of course. His feelings were avuncular—he had merely replaced Lorenz in her life. He would be safe enough from the insane jealousy that plagued the members of his family. She did not have the power to pry open his psyche, and he would not give it to her.

"Amalia," he said in a serious tone. "There's something I need to talk to you about."

"Of course, Rudolf. Would you like something to drink?"

"No, thank you," he answered absently. He had walked to the window that looked onto the dirty street and abstractedly pulled the cord on the new blinds. He started as they rattled open and hastily closed them again.

He turned to her. "I wanted to explain my little speech to Antonia this afternoon. That wasn't just spite or dramatics. I meant what I said about marrying you. I'm sorry it came out in that particular way. She'd goaded you so much, and then when she appealed to me as an equal in her condescension, it was just too much."

Amalia smiled gently and went to stand next to him. "You don't have to carry me off on your white charger, Rudolf. I feel quite rescued enough with all you've done for me."

Rudolf turned abruptly and hit the mantle with his hand. "Blast! I was afraid you'd take it that way, Amalia. This isn't an offer made out of pity!"

"What else can I think, Rudolf? I know you're not in love with me. You run the other way when the word is mentioned. And you know my feelings about the matter. I'm fed up with romance."

He looked at her steadily. "Have you ever considered a marriage of convenience? I know how you will always feel about Zaleski. But you are young, and you have these ideals about democracy and such. What if I *did* go in for politics? You could be my equal partner. In exchange, you could give me an heir. We get along very well and always have. No drama, no disagreements. I don't believe I have the power to hurt you. It would be a nice companionable marriage."

Amalia took a seat on the sofa, watching him. He could almost see her brain whirling.

He seated himself at her side, taking her hands in a strong grip. "Look, Amalia, I know you love Zaleski. I don't know what went on before the war between the two of you, but I know you loved him then, even when you left to marry von Waldburg. You made the best of a bad thing there, and no one, least of all me, knows what you went through. It must have been pure hell."

He rose and strode across the room, his voice becoming rough with anger. "I saw what you looked like after von Waldburg's death. You were changed beyond recognition, but you still had your dignity and your strength. Then I didn't see you again until after the war. I returned to find you in an even worse frame of mind. You said you were engaged.

"Again, I didn't know what had happened, except that you were obviously waiting for Zaleski, and he hadn't come. You were scarcely recognizable to me." He returned to her and searched her face. "It was as if a light inside you had gone out. I can't tell you how it wrenched my heart to see you like that!"

Amalia looked away. He felt once again the anguish he had experienced at her plight.

"You were a saint to me," she said, emotion making her voice tight.

"I did what I could, Amalia. But I know no one can really make up for what you have suffered in your heart. As a matter of fact, I still think there must be some explanation for Zaleski's behavior."

He put his fingers gently to her lips as she attempted to protest.

"No man would leave you willingly, my dear. I do know that. If you'd like me to, I'll go to Poland and see what I can find out."

Amalia's eyes filled, and she jumped up.

"You're too good! Why would you even consider doing such a thing for me? You just asked me to marry you, unless I'm mistaken!" Her glance held a particle of resentment.

He answered simply, "Because I don't think you'll be totally at peace until you know the truth. I want you to be happy, Amalia. That above all things."

She melted back onto the sofa, her head in her hands.

"My suffering and unhappiness are as much my own doing as anyone else's." She clenched one hand in a fist and pounded her knee. "You don't know what a hot-tempered, selfish, proud little beast I can be."

He walked to the mantle again, hands in his pockets. "Shall I go to Warsaw?"

"To prove what?" she replied. "No matter what you would find out, I don't think I could bear it, Rudolf. I've adjusted to things as they are. Please, let's leave it."

"And how exactly are things?" he asked gently. "I must know, Amalia."

"Over," she stated, her hand clenched in a fist.

"Unresolved," he corrected.

She flashed at him, "*Over!*"

He looked into her flushed face for a few moments and then sighed. "How can I compete with things you say you don't feel, Amalia?"

"Those things are part of the past. There is nothing Andrzej could say or do to change the way things are. I could never trust him again. I have put him behind me."

"Very well." He paced around the room for a few moments while she braided the fringe of her shawl. "Could you marry me, Amalia? Nowadays it needn't be a Catholic wedding. I should like you to be free to divorce, if . . . if something should happen."

"I don't know how you could even want me to marry you," she said shakily, "with all you know of my past. I'm definitely damaged goods, Rudolf. My ideas of love have been shattered. Who knows what I have left to offer you?"

"I will take it, whatever it is, Amalia. No matter what you think, no matter if you love Zaleski till you die, I think there is enough warmth and affection left over for me. I am damaged goods, as well. So damaged, in fact, I doubt I'll ever be able to open myself to you as a husband should. But, remember, this is to be a marriage of convenience. I will give you a comfortable life. I can give you companionship, if not romantic love."

"But how can I enter into a marriage where all the goodness and giving and forgiving are on your side? I owe you so much, but I won't do you the injustice of marrying you out of gratitude. You need a wife, Rudolf, not a burden, not a burnt-out shell of a human being."

"I don't see you as a burnt-out shell. You have passions still, Amalia, including passion for your country. Maybe between the two of us we can accomplish something there. Maybe I would feel less inept in the political arena with you by my side. And you have a passion for these new religious ideals of yours that I see may yet heal your heart. I want to help that healing."

"But you don't think you could ever love me?" she said in a small voice.

He asked softly, "Do you *want* to marry me, Amalia? That is all I need to know."

Searching his eyes, Amalia appeared to be looking for something. Whatever she was trying to find, evidently it was there, for she said, "Yes, Rudolf. I find that I do want to marry you." She smiled then. "In spite of all the arguments against it."

He took her hands in his and kissed the palm of each one. "As soon as possible, I think."

For so many months, she had held herself as rigid as a soldier. Now, he sensed her whole body relax. Tears streamed down her face, but she no longer sobbed. He took that as a favorable sign. Cupping her face in his hands, he wiped away the tears with his strong capable thumbs.

Part Five

VIENNA
1933 TO 1934

Chapter One

Amalia came running in out of the early spring rainstorm through the door her butler held open. She handed him her sodden cape. "Thank you, Max. Where is the baron?"

"He just telephoned, Baroness, to say he will be detained at the chancellery. But he will be home in time to escort you to the Polish embassy ball this evening."

She nodded and proceeded up the gracefully spiraling staircase. She had been mistress of the von Schoenenburg palais for thirteen years now, and yet she had never begun to take this lovely home for granted. Rudolf had had it redecorated precisely to her desire, and it was a constant delight to see her cream and gold furnishings against the ancient paneled and marbled von Schoenenburg walls. It was her home, as no place she had ever lived had been hers.

After hurrying up the second, steeper flight of stairs to the top of the house, Amalia stealthily opened the playroom door and peeked through a crack for an unobserved preview of her children.

Rudi, her eldest son, aged twelve, sat cross-legged on the floor shooting marbles. He was, as usual, discoursing to his younger brother, Christian.

"He's nothing but a big bully, you idiot! You musn't believe everything Walter tells you. I think Father knows more than your silly friends."

He glanced up as his mother entered. "Mother, do tell this foolish brother of mine that Hitler is a louse. He seems to think he's some kind of hero!"

Amalia, only a little amused, raised an eyebrow. "Who've you been listening to, Christian? Walter Kohl?"

"Yes, *Mutti*," the ten-year-old said, looking down at his still-chubby fingers.

"Now, there," she said brightly, going over to the boy and giving his golden head a pat. "It's all right. Rudi is just telling you that you mustn't believe everything you hear. He's right, you know. You have to make up your own mind."

The little boy's lower lip was prominent as he muttered, "But Walter is my best friend. He likes me. He wouldn't tell me a lie." Amalia cast her eyes heavenward and looked at her eldest over Christian's head.

"It's not a matter of lying, Chris," said his brother, controlling his exasperation admirably. "What were you talking about Hitler for, anyway?"

"Walter's father is going to Germany to listen to him. He wants to take Walter, too, but Frau Kohl won't let him miss school. Walter says Herr Hitler's the new chancellor of Germany and that soon we'll be part of Germany and he'll be our leader, too. He says then we can be part of the Hitler Youth and go to summer camp and wear armbands and learn to march."

Amalia saw her own consternation reflected in Rudi's face as Christian concluded, "I think it sounds like fun."

Her mind racing for a rejoinder appropriate for a ten-year old, she quelled Rudi's retort with a look and ruffled her younger son's hair once more. "I dare say it would be, but then you couldn't go to the Schloss in the summer, could you?"

Christian's sulky look vanished. "I couldn't?" he asked.

"No. And anyway, despite what Walter says, Hitler's not going to be our leader. You like Herr Dolfuss, don't you?"

Christian nodded his head enthusiastically. The Austrian chancellor was a frequent guest both at the palais in Vienna and at their Schloss near Graz, where they spent the summer months.

"Well, if Herr Hitler became our leader, what would poor Herr Dolfuss do?

The little boy's face cleared suddenly. "Walter is a little confused, I think. I'll have to tell him."

"I think it's better if you don't talk about such things, Christian. His father thinks one way, and yours thinks another. You should just agree to differ."

"What does that mean?" he asked, puzzled.

"Like when I want to play marbles, and you want to have a pillow fight," Rudi shouted, assailing his younger brother with a down-stuffed missile.

All dialogue was quickly reduced to muffled shouts, and Amalia left the playroom to bathe and dress for the embassy ball.

The conversation had disturbed her more than she had shown, however, and she brooded upon it while trying to relax in a warm bath. Then, suddenly impatient, she climbed out and began toweling herself vigorously.

"It's absurd the way I let that man haunt me!" she exclaimed aloud as though to banish a presence. "Surely the Germans can see what he is! A common thug with an uncommonly good sense of theater!"

Those forebodings that had gripped her repeatedly since the last war had hold of her again. It was clear that thug or not, Hitler had breathed new life into Germany. He had emerged to fill the vacuum created by economic chaos, ruined lives, and trampled national pride. He was bigger than life, stronger than reason, a product of a country in search of a hero. Images of Hitler Youth wearing Eberhard's beaming countenance visited her. Like an Old Testament prophet, she wanted to cry a warning to the world before it was too late. But she was just one person. One solitary woman, though Rudolf did voice her concerns as his own in cabinet meetings. But it wasn't enough.

Amalia gave her head a little shake to clear it and rang insistently for her maid. With great mental effort she switched her thoughts to the evening before her. The Polish embassy ball was certain to be a lavish affair. The Poles seemed to spare no expense in proving to the world that they knew how to be a nation. Thoughts of Andrzej teased at the edge of her mind. What was he doing these days? Did he have a position in the government? Did he and Lilli have children? The last thought caused her an involuntary stab of pain as Kristina entered the room and walked briskly to the wardrobe.

It had been a great comfort to Amalia when Rudolf had found Kristina once they were married. She had had to dismiss her after Wolf had lost their money. Rudolf teased his wife frequently about her submission to her maid. "Herr Dolfuss would never believe it if he could see you cowering through one of Kristina's scoldings."

"Kristina hasn't the illusions about me that you seem to have," Amalia replied frankly.

Now she agreed to wear her long pearl-colored satin gown, which was sculpted to her still slender body. The Schiaparelli original flared gracefully at the knee and plunged to the middle of her back from its cowl-necked drapery in the front.

With some reluctance, she had finally cut her hair the year before. Rudolf was dismayed by her action, but she had merely sighed and said, "I can't go around looking like a relic of the lost empire! You want your wife to have a modern, democratic look."

Her mahogany red mane was now waved all over and worn close to her head, a few wispy tendrils escaping the general regimen at the nape of her neck. Rudolf had been forced to admit that the new style suited her completely.

Once dressed, Amalia allowed herself the luxury of pirouetting slowly before the mirror, watching the line of her dress as her body moved. Kristina interrupted her satisfied reverie. "The baron gives you all this jewelry, and you never remember to wear any of it."

She pulled out Amalia's pearl and diamond bracelet, a gift from Rudolf on their tenth anniversary.

"Quit scolding me, Kristina. I fully intended to wear just that bracelet," Amalia replied as she splashed herself with her gardenia scent.

At that moment, her husband arrived. Kristina made an unobtrusive exit.

Striding at once to her side, Rudolf kissed her neck. "You look and smell divine, Amalia." He stepped back and surveyed her appreciatively. "I'll only be a moment. How're the boys?"

Amalia made a face of distaste. "Arguing over Herr Hitler, of all things."

"How on earth did that come up?" Rudolf asked from his dressing room.

"Walter Kohl's father is a believer, it seems. He's going to Germany on a pilgrimage. Young Walter has filled Christian's head with all sorts of nonsense about the Hitler *Jugend*."

She heard her husband grunt disapprovingly.

Rudolf strode out of his next-door dressing room, his broad chest bare. "Where are the gold studs for my shirt front, Amalia? I can't seem to find them."

"In my jewelry chest, Rudolf."

Her husband sat wearily on her dressing table bench, and Amalia could see that the Hitler discussion was troubling him. "Remember when we used to talk about educating the youth with some kind of an ideal that would stand up to nonsense like this?"

Amalia, coming up with the last of his studs, turned to him. "Yes. How long ago that seems. It was one of the principal reasons we became involved in politics in the first place. I don't know how well we've done. Although, I must say, Rudi seems to see through Hitler well enough."

"You've raised him well. He doesn't automatically go along with the crowd. He seems to think things through."

"You can be proud of him, Rudolf," Amalia said, glad of his kind words.

"Rudi is rather an extraordinary child. He takes after his mother, you see." He pulled his elegantly clad wife down onto his knee.

She looked at his tired face and kissed him gently. He held her to his still-naked chest. "If only we could stay at home once in a while," he said wistfully. Then he kissed her with hearty thoroughness followed by a gentle push. "Off to work," he said as he arose and took the handful of studs with a little sigh.

The ball proved to be every bit as glamorous and full of ceremony as Amalia had anticipated. Entering on her husband's arm, she prepared for the endless receiving line of Polish notables.

Heads were inclined, hands were kissed, and as usual they were received with all of the graciousness due to an Austrian cabinet minister and his wife. Amalia felt gazes linger on her, some masculine ones for an embarrassingly long interval. Rudolf was firm in his determined movement along the line. When at last they were through, he whispered to Amalia, "Sometimes I think I'm asked to these things just so they can look at you."

"Rudolf, I'm thirty-nine years old."

"You're timeless," he replied.

She tapped him on the cheek with her fan. "You were asked to these things long before you had me in tow! There's something about you, Baron." She grinned at him. "People think they can trust you."

He laughed and took her arm, and they strode into the throng. The orchestra was very fine, and Amalia was immediately invited to dance by one of Rudolf's fellow ministers, the Baron von Aggstein.

He launched at once into a diatribe against their hosts. "These blasted Poles. Can you believe what this must have cost?"

"Well, it's quite evident they know how to throw a party," Amalia said. "I haven't seen such splendor since before the war."

The portly minister's shiny face lit with malice, "The poor fools. They're going to wake up in Hitler's pocket one morning and pouf! No more Poland! And nobody will be surprised but them."

"One can only pity them, Baron," Amalia said coolly. "It's not a choice I'd relish, Hitler or Stalin. They've got to be allies with one or the other."

Von Aggstein merely looked sage. "They should have been aware of the perils of statecraft before they launched their ship, my dear."

An imp prompted Amalia to quiz him, "Which would you choose, Baron? Hitler or Stalin?"

"I thank all my stars that that is not a choice I have to make, Baroness. One can only hope the German people will see through that charlatan before it's too late. It's already too late in Russia."

"One wonders if it's not already too late in Germany," Amalia said sadly. "President Hindenburg hasn't been much more than a figurehead since the Reichstag fire. Hitler's like a pawn run amok—the queens and kings are all dead. There's no one left to check him."

Her rotund partner nodded somberly. "Of course, he set that fire himself and then blamed the communists. Everyone's so frightened of the Reds that when he declared martial law, no one lifted a finger to stop him. He's got the devil's own brilliance, that man."

The dance ended, and Amalia was relieved to be returned to her husband. Von Aggstein, it was rumored, could depress even a maiden on her wedding day.

Rudolf was deep in discussion with an envoy from the Hungarian embassy. "Oh, Amalia," he beamed, "Come and meet Count Gyorgy."

The evening passed in this unremarkable and predictable way until eleven o'clock when the orchestra struck up the first waltz of the evening. This was rather unusual in these days of the fox trot and rumba. Rudolf looked at his wife across the small group of people that separated them, and they nodded simultaneously their decision to dance.

As they stepped out onto the floor, it was as though they were carried back to the days before the war. The glitter of the setting added to Amalia's sense of déjà vu, and she found herself remembering the sensation of dancing with Andrzej. A memory of him had lingered just below the surface of her mind all evening as she mingled with his countrymen. But only now as she and her husband performed this relic of her past did she actually feel Andrzej's presence. The waltz and Andrzej would always be inextricably connected, no matter how many years intervened. Did he ever remember her when he waltzed with Lilli?

It was an idle thought and no more. She chased it out of her mind as soon as the dance ended and put her arm contentedly through her husband's as they walked off the floor.

Then she saw him.

The subject of her reverie stood directly in front of her, his eyes looking straight into hers. Shock halted her, and she trembled. Where had he come from?

At that same moment, Rudolf, looking in the other direction, said, "Oh, I see Dolfuss has finally arrived, my dear. I must speak to him. Excuse me, will you?"

He was gone, leaving her with legs she was unsure would support her. Aware that she was staring rather stupidly at her former fiancé, she dropped her gaze and turned to follow her husband. Andrzej was beside her in a moment, holding both her arms, his green eyes searching hers.

"What have you done to your hair?"

Amalia gave no thought to the absurdity of the question. She felt as though his hands were the only things that were holding her up.

"I cut it."

For a long moment they stared at one another. The hunger in Andrzej's deep green eyes transfixed Amalia. His face was permanently marred by parallel frown lines between his brows, his ironic grin nowhere in sight.

Finally she managed, "I didn't see Lilli. Is she here?"

"No. Lilli's not here. I'd like to talk to you, Amalia."

She inhaled and willed herself to stop trembling. It didn't work. He still held her by the arms as though he realized she needed the support.

"I should join my husband, actually." She could make no move to leave and was aware that her voice was high and artificial. "We'd be happy to see you at home, if you'd like to call on us. I'm anxious to hear about Lilli. She hasn't written in years."

But Andrzej might not have been listening. He held her away from him and looked her over from the crown of her head to her toes. Then finally he smiled, the old lazy smile. The desperation was gone from his eyes. "The baron seems to take adequate care of you, I see."

His return to type had the effect of steadying her at last. She stepped back and, crossing her arms, put her hands where his had been. "Perhaps you ought not to visit after all, Andrzej. Now, if you'll excuse me, I must go."

Panic took over as she practically ran from his side. She finally found Rudolf in the vast foyer, deep in conversation with the chancellor. The latter's eyes lit up as he saw her. "Baroness, I thought I wasn't going to have the pleasure of seeing you tonight!"

She gave Dolfuss her gloved hand and received a kiss in the air over her knuckles. He continued, "You're in extraordinary looks tonight, my lady. How are the boys?"

"Well, thank you, Herr Chancellor," she smiled a trifle wanly. "You must pay us a visit."

"Thank you, I shall. I look forward to another little retreat at your Schloss this summer. It's the highlight of my year, you realize."

With that, the dapper gentleman, who had so little to recommend him as a great leader in either form or figure, made his adieux and left Amalia standing with her husband.

"I'd like to leave now, Rudolf, if you don't mind," she said quietly.

His eyes rested upon hers for a moment. Their glance wasn't the warm one she was used to seeing. It was distant and chilly. "All right, Amalia."

During the drive home, Rudolf made no attempt to engage her in conversation. She sat staring absently out of the window at her beloved city that was lit in its usual mellow evening glow. So Rudolf had seen Andrzej. And now he suspected the worst.

* * *

Rudolf knew the time of reckoning had come. As the years passed, Amalia had found a way to carry her light into the darkest parts of him.

He had allowed her passage, and before he knew where he was, he was fathoms deep in love with her. Perhaps he always had been. Now he sat, mute, stunned. *Zaleski.*

What he had almost forgotten to fear had come to pass. Amalia would surely leave him. In fact, she must leave him for her own safety. With his family history, there was no telling how he would react to this situation. He could already feel the tentacles of despair. He deeply regretted that he had been so careful to leave her the loophole of divorce.

Finally, in the privacy of her boudoir, Amalia asked him, "Did you know that Andrzej was in Vienna?"

"Not until tonight," he replied, studying her. What was going through her mind? What was she feeling?

"I was shocked to see him. Did you see him when you left to go to Dolfuss? Why did you leave us alone?"

Rudolf stood and went to the window. "I knew at once I was *de trops.* You should have let me go to Warsaw, Amalia."

She came up behind him, encircled him with her arms, and nestled her cheek against his shoulder. She said softly, "Don't think what you're thinking, Rudolf. All is as it should be."

"He's just arrived, Amalia," he replied stiffly. "There is no denying this is going to be awkward. I'll try not to interfere."

Dropping her arms, she walked quietly out of the room. He knew she was deeply disappointed in his reaction.

When she had gone to her bed, he sat in the dark, willing himself not to give in to his longing. He must leave her alone tonight. Putting his head in his hands, he tried to cope with the black thoughts that descended upon him.

She would go now. She would take the boys. And leave him struggling with the beast inside, which always threatened to tear him away from sanity. The love and light provided by his little family had been the only things that kept it in check. It was only rarely now that he would struggle for days to see the dawn.

He had never told Amalia about his melancholia. He had never told her that she was his sun, that he loved her. Afraid of disturbing the balance of their marriage of convenience, he had stayed away from her when he needed her most. Now he felt himself carried along through the fog that normally concealed his blackest fears.

He was twelve again, hiding behind the long drapes in his mother's bedroom, while the work of death was going on. Peeking through the drapes, he could see his mother, who had succored him all his life, repeatedly stabbing his father until all that remained was a bloody pulp. Rudolf couldn't understand what was happening. She was screaming at his father about someone called Constanza. Then she stabbed him again and again, each time crying some other woman's name. Rudolf knew he should stop her, but he froze, afraid of the knife, frightened of this woman he had never seen.

Then his older brother came into the room, and though he was only sixteen, he had lunged for the knife, wresting it from his mother's grasp. She broke down like the madwoman she had become. He led her away. Rudolf came out to find blood everywhere and his father dead. The shock of the gore made him physically ill all over the floor.

His brother came back, briskly commanding him to get hold of himself. Together they had rolled their father's body in a bedsheet and dragged it downstairs to bury it in the garden. The servants were unbelievably loyal. To this day, everyone thought the Baron von Schoenenburg had run off with one of his mistresses.

Their mother had grieved herself into an early grave. But neither of her sons had ever been the same. There was his brother's liaison with Maria von Beckhaus and his subsequent suicide. And Rudolf's young mind and heart had been permanently scarred. No, he had told himself then, he would never love. It was too risky for the passionate nature he had inherited.

But he did love with everything his wounded heart had to give. And now the sun, which had shone so unexpectedly in Lorenz's dark rooms that day long ago, would go out.

Chapter Two

The next day it rained again. Unable to settle to any task after a troubled night's sleep, Amalia sat in the window seat, clad in her modish emerald silk trouser suit, gazing steadfastly at the weather. Rudolf had not come to bed last night. He'd had one of those increasingly rare nights when he locked himself in his study. She never knew what caused them and didn't feel intimate enough with him to ask.

Max soundlessly entered her sitting room near half past eleven with a card on his silver salver. Andrzej was below, and her heart was pounding. Though longing to see him, she was afraid. Who would have thought he could have this effect on her after all these years? *Especially after the way he treated me.* This last thought rescued her, and she was able to tell Max, "Kindly inform Herr Doktor Zaleski that I will be happy to receive him this afternoon when the baron will be able to join us."

The inscrutable Max bowed and went to deliver her message. Sighing, she got up from her seat. Andrzej was unsettling her far too much. It had been fifteen years since she'd seen him. Last night that time dissolved to nothing. The fact that she was married with two sons wasn't sufficient armor against him. Though she had thought that her feelings for him had been buried long ago, they sprang to life, surging to the fore. Pain flooded her. How could Andrzej stroll up to her calmly as though nothing had happened? As though he had the right?

She castigated herself. Her feelings were only a girlish longing for that all-encompassing passion she had known when she was young.

Over thirteen years, she had become devoted to Rudolf. The problem was, she believed her feelings were not returned. While Rudolf was outwardly warm and affectionate, the core of her husband remained sternly separate, as he held himself away from true intimacy. Part of her still remained hollow and lonely.

Sitting at her desk to answer her morning correspondence, Amalia knew she needed solid, dependable Rudolf at her side this afternoon.

Unfortunately, he telephoned just before lunch. "I'm sorry, Amalia, I won't be home for luncheon or the afternoon. Something unexpected is breaking, and I can't get away." She felt the tension in his voice and decided to say nothing of Andrzej. It was certainly a minor matter compared to affairs of state.

After a morning wasted imagining various uncomfortable scenarios, Amalia decided that her nerves could not take the suspense of postponing the inevitable meeting. She wanted it, and she wanted it behind her. She would just have to handle it alone.

Changing purposefully into a plain afternoon suit of light fawn-colored wool, she contrived to look as matronly as possible, her single adornment a modest strand of pearls. When Max announced the Herr Doktor's return, she descended to the morning room, praying for outward calm at least.

As she entered, she saw that he stood looking at the family photographs prominently displayed on the mantle. She forced a smile and approached him. "I see you are admiring our sons! Aren't they marvelous?"

He turned, and she saw that he was not smiling. "They look like wonderful children," he agreed.

Saddened by the pathos in his once merry eyes, she asked quietly, "Have you and Lilli any children?"

"No," he answered shortly.

She seated herself quickly and bade him do the same. He remained standing, pacing the room.

Twisting her hands together, she apologized. "I'm sorry my husband isn't in. He's been held up at the chancellery. There's been some crisis, or he would have been here."

Andrzej looked at her from across the room, his eyes burning into hers, but he did not speak.

"Tell me about what you are doing in Vienna. Why didn't Lilli make the trip with you?"

"We're separated. Our divorce will be final at the end of the year."

Amalia felt suddenly winded. She stared at Andrzej, who never took his eyes off her, and searched for words. Finally she managed, "I had no idea. I'm so sorry. I'm certain it's a painful subject, but how can you divorce?"

Andrzej smiled, one-sidedly. "It was a Protestant ceremony, not Catholic, fortunately. But spare me your sympathy. Our marriage has been over for years, Amalia. At best, it was an illusion. I doubt whether you or I knew Lilli very well in the old days."

"What do you mean?"

"Suppose you tell me what you remember of your cousin by marriage?" he suggested, seating himself and crossing his long legs easily.

Nettled, Amalia responded, "She was rather fond of society, though no more than most of us, I think. She liked her own way, but she wasn't entirely without scruples. She was no Maria von Beckhaus, certainly. I had to be careful what I told her, because she was a bit of a gossip. But I suppose I chiefly remember how vibrant she was. She seemed to brim over with life."

Andrzej looked at her sadly for a moment. "I would have painted a like portrait. She was always lively company. Diverting. Ravishing in a rather unrestrained way. But we were dead wrong about her, Amalia. Lilli has a nasty kink in her character.

"Tell me about the von Waldburgs. Is there any history of . . ." he hesitated, appearing to search for a phrase, "mental instability?"

Amalia's brows drew together. "What kind of kink are we talking about? According to you, Eberhard had a drinking problem and some capacity for violence. Don't tell me Lilli is violent!"

"Only to herself. But she is prone to addictions. I'm sorry to discuss this with you, but I'm not really an outsider, you know. One could say we're cousins-in-law. I've been married for twelve years, and after about six, I belatedly admitted I didn't know Lilli at all."

Amalia lowered her chin and her eyes. "Was this why you wanted to see me?"

"In part. It's something I've wondered about for a long time. Was there any other instability you knew about?"

"I'm sorry, no. I didn't know Lilli's father well. Except that he was a typical Prussian officer. I always understood that her mother died when she was young."

"I suppose I should have written and asked. But I didn't like to risk Lilli's finding out. Part of her problem has always been a morbid sort of jealousy."

Amalia was not surprised. Andrzej was an incorrigible flirt. "Did you give her cause?" she asked without sympathy.

His eyes narrowed and glinted at her. "She knew our history. That was enough."

Swallowing, she tried to remain calm. "As far as I can see, Andrzej, this is really nothing to do with me at all."

He stood suddenly and walked again to the mantle, facing away from her. "Just why did you give me up, Amalia?"

Incredulous, she sputtered, "I don't know what you mean! Give *you* up?"

Andrzej turned to look at her then, his eyes warm with the love she remembered so well.

The door opened and Rudolf came into the room.

"Zaleski!" he said formally, holding out his hand. "Max said you were here."

Amalia welcomed her husband with wholehearted relief. "Rudolf, I'm so glad you got away. We've been waiting for you." She held up her cheek to be kissed.

Then, ringing for Max, Amalia said, "Andrzej and I have been discussing Lilli. Apparently she's been having some problems."

Rudolf studied his wife and then looked at their guest. Max entered the room.

"Yes, Baroness?"

"Coffee for the Herr Doktor and the baron, please, Max."

As the door shut behind the butler, Andrzej spoke. "I was just telling your wife that Lilli and I are divorcing." He looked at the baron unwaveringly.

Rudolf cleared his throat. "I'm terribly sorry to hear that, Zaleski. Divorce is a sad thing. Children?"

"Fortunately, no," Andrzej answered, turning to face the portraits of the von Schoenenburg children. "Lilli never wanted to be bothered with them."

"You have business in Vienna?" Rudolf asked.

Andrzej said, "Yes, I've a connection in the Foreign Office and managed to get attached to the ambassador's entourage here in Vienna. It's sort of a goodwill mission. I'm to arrange a kind of scientific conclave, an exchange of ideas, etcetera, between the Poles and the Austrians. It's my own idea. I'd like to see the ties between our countries strengthened."

"Is your feeling representative of anyone except yourself?"

Andrzej laughed shortly. "It's not terribly popular, no. Most Poles are all for Hitler at the moment. He's appearing to give us some assurances against Stalin, you see."

"But you? You don't believe in these assurances?"

"I don't like fascists," Andrzej said decisively. Amalia smiled at his vehemence and was obscurely grateful for it. At least they were on the same side politically. "I would rather see us throw in our lot with Austria," he added.

Max entered with the coffee, and Amalia poured. "I'm glad to hear it," she said. "We are definitely anti-fascist. Rudolf has influence in the cabinet, but it's a battle. This ministry is determined to make Austria survive as a democracy."

All were silent, having run out of polite conversation. The men sipped their coffee.

"One has to take a stand, don't you agree?" Amalia demanded. "There are too many people who need to see how necessary it is to think for themselves." She laughed. "I sound like Uncle, don't I?"

Rudolf asked, his manner still stiff, "Did you know Lorenz Reichart, Zaleski?"

"I only saw him the night he died. I've always thought I missed knowing someone important."

"You did," Rudolf said. He finished his coffee and stood. "I just ducked in to see you for a moment, Amalia, to tell you I won't make it home to dinner. I must be getting back to the chancellery."

Amalia flashed her husband a look of panic. "Don't go yet, Rudolf. You scarcely got here!" She stood and took his arm to detain him, but he pulled out his pocket watch and shook his head. "I really must be on my way. Nice to have seen you, Zaleski."

To Andrzej, Amalia said, "Excuse me a moment while I see Rudolf out."

When they were in the foyer, she stopped her husband and whispered, "What is it? What's wrong?"

He searched her face for a moment, his own worried and tired. "Nothing definite. It will wait until tonight." He looked significantly at the closed door of the morning room.

She read his glance. "I don't know what to do with him. This is most uncomfortable. I thought you would be home this afternoon, or I never would have asked him. He called first thing this morning, but I put him off."

Rudolf stood apart from her and looked into her eyes. "I can't help you with this one, Amalia. I know how you love him." His face took on a gray, grim aspect, and Amalia was almost frightened.

"But he treated me abominably! Do you think I would leave you and the boys?"

He left without answering. She stood for a moment, her fists doubled at her sides, and then, taking a deep breath, she reentered the morning room.

Her guest had just set down his coffee cup and was preparing to go.

"I can see you're worried about what your husband's thinking about us, Amalia. I'll go for now. But we will continue our discussion again. There are some things I've waited a long time to know."

She looked at him gravely, her hand on the doorknob. "Sometimes it's better to let things lie, Andrzej. I'm sorry you aren't happy, but perhaps it would be best if you left now."

He paused on his way out the door and looked at her with a solemn gaze she had never seen before. Then, abruptly, he left. Amalia went to her room, distressed and shaken.

It was as though an earthquake were starting deep underground and she could see the cracks in the pavement beginning to form. She sensed that her history was being rewritten, and she didn't want that at all. To her surprise, she was still susceptible to Andrzej. And Rudolf knew it. Not only that, he seemed resigned to it.

It was late that night when she finally heard her husband in his dressing room. She rose from the divan where she had been attempting to read and opened the adjoining door.

When she observed her husband's unusually harried appearance, she was alerted once again to the possibility of a government crisis. The mists of her selfish preoccupation vanished, and she was once more the Amalia von Schoenenburg of 1933.

"Bad day?" she asked gently.

"That blasted Otto Bauer!" he exploded, referring to the leader of the Social Democrats. "He's got some plot afoot. I can feel it. It's been worrying me for days," he continued querulously, pitching his shoe unceremoniously into the cupboard. He had always preferred to be his own valet and normally prided himself on the neatness of his cupboards.

Amalia unthinkingly rescued it, put on the appropriate shoe tree, and asked, "This railway debate?"

"No, it's more than that. He wants Dolfuss out. I think he believes he can do it over this issue."

"But you still have the majority, haven't you?" Amalia asked soothingly.

"If you can call one seat a majority! Any attempt at policy-making deteriorates into a nightmare! We can't get anything done as long as those socialists are breathing down our necks, making political hay out of every jot and tittle."

His ill humor was rare, and Amalia tried to mask her own concern for his benefit. She approached him hesitantly. "This is a democracy, remember? Right will prevail."

He tried to smile. "Even in a democracy there can be mistakes if the ignorant gain the majority."

"They won't," she said confidently. Then, as she hung up his necktie, she commented, "I discovered why Andrzej was so anxious to see me. He wanted to find out about Lilli's family background. I gather he thinks she's suffering from some kind of mental disturbance."

"It's a little late for him to be checking into that, I would think. How long have they been married?"

"Twelve years, he says."

"Presumably their problems are of some years' standing. Why wait until you're divorcing to seek the cause of the problem?"

"Perhaps he wants to help her in some way. He says she's not the woman we knew."

"What does he think you can do?"

"I don't know. We didn't really discuss it in detail. I made it clear that I didn't want to be involved." Her husband studied her, and she tried to appear unconcerned. "I don't expect he'll bother us any more."

Rudolf sighed. "Don't deceive yourself, Amalia. You'll have to reckon with him sooner or later. I saw the way he was looking at you. The poor man's starved." He gave her a severe look. "There is more on his mind than a disturbed wife."

Amalia couldn't keep the dismay from her voice. "Oh, Rudolf, I hope you're wrong."

"If I'm not, Amalia, and I don't think I am, I would rather have you divorce me and go with him than stay with me out of a misguided sense of loyalty."

She felt as though she had been stabbed. He would dismiss her so easily? She walked back into her own room and sank to the floor. As her husband shut the door between them, she tried to tell herself that he must know she would never leave him. It was the political crisis that had pitched him once again into the despair she had never been able to penetrate. Or was it simply one of his black moods? She dared not approach him tonight. He would undoubtedly visit his own private hell that she was never allowed to share and emerge from his study tomorrow or the next day looking as though he had wrestled with the devil.

Chapter Three

Amalia heard it on the news the next afternoon. Renner had resigned as speaker of the house. Realizing immediately that Renner was now free to vote with his party, the Social Democrats, and against the government, she knew that this was the Bauer power play that her husband had feared. This act of Renner's could cause Dolfuss's party, the Christian Socialists, to lose its slim majority and the current government could fall. That would signal the end of Austria's democracy. Stalin was probably watching closely with his beady black eyes.

She spent the afternoon in a state of nervous anxiety, personal considerations wholly forgotten as she was caught up in the crisis that would determine the future of her country. Pacing the room, she could not settle to anything, was sharp with the children, and dismissive of Kristina. The suspense was almost unendurable. In her mind, the evil represented by the communist leanings of Otto Bauer's Social Democrats was nearly equal to the threat posed by the fascists, who were represented in parliament by the German Nationalist Party. Rudolf's centrist party had had an increasingly difficult course to steer between the two extremes, a course not made any easier by the obvious greed of Austria's fascist and communist neighbors. So much pressure had been brought to bear on this neophyte democracy! Rudolf and his compatriots had worked so hard and fought so diligently to maintain the present government. Would they now fail?

She heard her husband arrive shortly before the evening news was to air, and she ran to meet him in the foyer.

"I heard about Renner. Has the government fallen?" she asked breathlessly.

Rudolf gave her a surprisingly cheerful look and, after Max had taken his raincoat, motioned for her to precede him into the morning room. He waited until Amalia was seated, and then, looking extremely pleased with himself, announced, "We've outfoxed Bauer."

"How, for heaven's sake?" she demanded. "Don't just sit there looking like the cat that swallowed the cream! Don't you realize what I've been through this afternoon?"

He laughed. "It's all right, Amalia, really it is. We were prepared for Renner's resignation and had already talked the German Nationalists into playing along with us. Remember, there are two deputy speakers—one from our party and one from theirs. Both received their instructions to resign shortly after Renner did."

"And?" Amalia prompted, still not understanding his jubilation.

"Dolfuss then declared Parliament incapable of functioning, and we adjourned."

Amalia was stunned.

"Are you telling me that Dolfuss dissolved Parliament?" Amalia demanded.

Rudolf nodded, still pleased.

"But, Rudolf, that's a fascist trick! No one can oppose him now. In fact, no one except those actually in the cabinet have any power to govern. It gives him absolute control!" She paused, an incredible suspicion growing. "Is that what you're so pleased about? You can't mean you actually support this action!"

"Amalia, calm yourself and think. What is the greatest danger we face at this moment?" He paused, but his wife refused the bait. "You and I both know it is Germany. We have a choice: we can either face Hitler from a position of consolidated strength or from a position of fragmented weakness. How can we stand against anyone as strong as Hitler, when our government is only hanging on by its fingernails? We must present a unified front!"

"You know as well as I do that true unity can't be forced, Rudolf. People must be persuaded to unify; they must do it because they want to," Amalia argued heatedly. "You yourself have always said that anything but a representative government has to resort to oppression to keep it in power. Soon there'll be nothing to choose between you and the fascist bullies!" Her voice rose dangerously close to hysteria. "You'll have your own pet army, and decent people who have every right to their own opinions will be afraid to speak. It's the end of everything we've always fought for and believed in!"

"Amalia, I appreciate your concerns, but believe me, there's no time for persuasion," he responded heatedly. "Don't you realize what we narrowly avoided today? A leftist revolution! We have enough on our hands with Mussolini and Hitler breathing down our necks. Shall we invite Stalin, too?"

When his wife made no reply, he added, "Not only that, but socialist economic policies would be a death knell right now. We must consolidate our resources and economic strength for whatever lies ahead. Face it, Amalia, we're sitting between two maniacs, and we're a very tempting bite for either one. Our only hope is to play one off against the other. We'll need all our wits. We can't afford to be weakened by contention among ourselves."

"Do you really believe your high-handed coup is going to do away with contention? Instead of fighting in parliament, you'll be fighting in the streets!"

Her husband made no reply but got up and began to pace the room vigorously.

She cried out, "I can't believe this is *you* talking, Rudolf. How many times have I heard you tell Rudi and Chris that if one's ideals mean nothing in a crisis, they mean nothing at all?"

"Amalia, don't you see there is no other way?"

She raised her chin, tears of anger making her eyes bright. "I only know it would have hurt me less if I'd discovered you'd taken a mistress."

She saw that the brutality of her words hit him with all the shock of a physical blow. Turning, Amalia ran from the room, unable to bear any longer the violence of feeling that was plowing up the roots of her marriage—a marriage that had been founded on political goals and nurtured by mutual respect. What a time for Andrzej to make an appearance!

The following morning, her anger having grown overnight as she had thrashed about in the humidity and linen bedsheets, Amalia break-fasted in bed in order to avoid meeting her husband at the table. Rudolf's air of self-satisfaction would be unbearable this morning.

While toying with her food, she perused the newspaper, a normally irritating activity because of what she insisted was its leftist slant. Today, however, it mirrored her own horror at Dolfuss's actions. It even gave her some details that her husband had not divulged. Armed guards, presumably of the *Heimwehr,* Austria's "home army," had barred access to the parliament building and would continue to do so. Amalia threw the paper and bedclothes from her in a gesture of angry disgust, realizing that the scenario she had described to Rudolf was already unfolding. It would be only a matter of time before the very newspaper she was reading was either forced underground, or made to comply with the politics of the Dolfuss regime.

If that incident fired her anger, however, another that took place on the same day gave her pause. Elections were held in the German parliament, and Hitler won enough seats to consolidate his absolute power. The threat from German Nazism was greater than ever.

Amalia belonged to a set that met frequently at the home of a Professor Horstmann, an informal salon to discuss politics and promote a healthy democracy. It was a circle of some fifteen or sixteen people from different walks of life, all of them influential within their own spheres. She knew that her friends would collect themselves tonight at the Herr Professor's home, and she was more than usually eager to attend, as she wished to define her position as being separate from that of her husband.

Accordingly, she set out at eight that evening for the professor's home, shortly after hearing the news about Hitler's triumph broadcast over the Munich radio. Her scholarly friend reminded her on occasion of Uncle Lorenz and had often caused her to wonder whether her uncle would have moderated his politics if he had lived to see the disaster that had befallen Russia. She comforted herself with the supposition that he would have and that he would have applauded her own efforts in support of a democracy, the tenets of which tallied so well with his faith in humanity.

The Horstmann residence was in a district near the university. Frau Horstmann opened the door and welcomed her solemnly. "We have been expecting you, Baroness. Herbert and Hilde are already with the professor. They have brought along a friend of Herbert's from the hospital." Her long melancholy face wore its habitual expression of worry and despair that so contrasted with Professor Horstmann's round, cherubic countenance, now beaming with pleasure at her arrival.

"My dear Baroness! I was certain you'd come. This is a wretched business, isn't it? Your husband must be dreadfully upset." Before she could reply, however, he stepped aside and bade her enter the drawing room. "Allow me to introduce you to Herr Doktor Zaleski, a Polish colleague of Herbert's from the university hospital. Herr Doktor, the Baroness von Schoenenburg."

Amalia willed herself to be calm, though without perfect success. She inclined her head. "I've been acquainted with the doctor for some years, Herr Professor." What was Andrzej doing here?

"Ah!" her host beamed. "Splendid!" He waited while his guest seated herself in the straight-backed chair near the fire, and then implored, "My dear, you must know more about this horrible thing than any of us. What can you tell us?"

* * *

Andrzej could see immediately that his presence had thrown Amalia into confusion. He was heartened. Had she felt nothing, he didn't think he could have borne it. But now he knew there was hope.

Though he regretted her cutting the hair he had thought about over the past fifteen years, she had never been more beautiful. She wasn't the naïve nineteen-year-old he had fallen in love with, nor the alluring yet steel-strong nurse he had planned to marry, but a gracious, self-confident baroness, *soignée* and passionate with political fervor. *Would she, could she, ever be his?*

She looked at the fire, her hands working unconsciously in her lap. "Rudolf believes Dolfuss's move was the only way to avoid a revolution from the left. The government was on the point of falling over this railway business. Personally, I don't agree with Dolfuss's actions. I think they're bound to lead to disaster."

Andrzej watched her keenly. According to what he had heard from his new friends, she was Rudolf von Schoenenburg's conscience and advisor. A completely different woman from the one he had known. And at this moment, clearly on the defensive. He kept his face carefully expressionless, as his mind worked. There had to be some way to win her back. She belonged to him, not to the stodgy baron she had married. The room was silent.

Finally, Herbert spoke, "It's a ticklish situation. There aren't many alternatives," he said, stroking his short black beard. Tall and stork-like, with large hands and feet, Herbert contrasted rather humorously with his young wife, Hilde, a tiny blond with protuberant gray eyes. He was a warm and level-headed man who had, in their conversations, always shown a marked respect for Rudolf. His gathered brow and sharp black eyes were evidence that he was alive to the serious and yet ironic nature of Amalia's statement. Perhaps only he could guess at her feelings.

Andrzej spoke, "Have you heard the news from Germany, Baroness?"

"Yes," Amalia answered shortly. "Things look very grim, I'm afraid." Then in a livelier tone she addressed the party in general. "But surely Britain and France are watching, too. Do you suppose they will stand by and let Germany rearm? Don't you think it would be in their best interests to protect us?"

"Not now," Andrzej answered. "They have little sympathy for anyone but themselves at the moment. And none at all to spare for countries who appear to scorn democratic procedures."

Herbert interjected, "You sound as if you speak from personal knowledge, Zaleski."

"Unfortunately, I do." Andrzej stood and moved to stand nearer the fire. He was within touching distance of Amalia, who sat rigidly still. "The Western Allies created Poland and then promptly lost interest. The only power that appears willing to protect us from Russian aggression is Germany. It's really not too surprising that many in my country think Germany is our only friend."

Hilde lit one of her little cigars, an affectation that reminded Andrzej of Lilli. Then the woman asked in her high childish voice, "But, you Herr Doktor, you hate fascists, as we know. So you leave Poland to come here." She laughed her tinkling little laugh. "What do you think of us now?"

Amalia clenched her fists in her lap. Andrzej knew she was torn between her own beliefs and the need to defend Rudolf. The woman he loved had never been short on loyalty. Looking closely at Hilde's expression of wide-eyed innocence, he could detect signs of enjoyment, and anger stirred within him. What was going on here? Was this wife of his friend really so petty?

"What would you have the government do, Hilde, just out of curiosity?" he inquired.

The woman laughed again, and turning her bulging eyes on Amalia, took a puff of her cigar and exhaled slowly, watching the smoke as it wreathed between her and the other woman. "I'd have let the Social Democrats have their day," she replied incisively. "They are our greatest insurance against the fascists ever gaining power. They balance each other nicely, and we need that balance for democracy to work properly. To destroy one faction gives unwonted ascendancy to the opposing one."

"I'm certain that the baroness is aware how democracy works,

Hilde," her husband drawled in annoyance. "She was championing it when you were still a girl."

Amalia managed a laugh. "I appreciate your support, Herr Doktor, but you make me sound like a very senior stateswoman indeed!"

Presently the room filled with other concerned citizens, and Amalia ceased to be the uncomfortable focal point of everyone's attention. Andrzej was now free to speak to her.

Looking down from his position by the fire, he observed quietly, "I fancy you didn't expect to find yourself defending the government tonight, Amalia."

She admitted, "No, I came ready to condemn." Looking up at him, she seemed to have regained her composure. "And how do you happen to be here?"

"One has only to be acquainted with Herbert a comparatively short time before one hears the lovely baroness's praises sung. Could that be why the good Hilde was sneering so obviously?" The last he imparted in a confidential tone, leaning close to where she sat. "When I discovered the connection, I determined to be here tonight." He paused and grinned. "I thought it would be quite a harmless way to see more of you."

Unfortunately, he was finding that just looking at her was in no way satisfactory.

*   *   *

His frankness assailed her, and Amalia felt herself begin to tremble again. She cursed her disloyal nervous system. Suddenly, the governmental crisis seemed very distant. She felt at a disadvantage seated, so she stood.

"Just what are you after, Andrzej?" she asked, glancing down at her hands. Her knuckles were white. She couldn't bring herself to look into the intensity of his eyes.

"It should be fairly obvious," he said shortly.

Her color rose, and her eyes sparked, but she took care to keep her back to the rest of the room. "You think you can waltz into my life after what you've done? And that in spite of a husband and two children, I'll welcome you with open arms? I didn't realize you had quite so much gall, Andrzej, or so little respect for my morals."

His grin twisted. "I still bring out the best in you, I see."

Then every trace of amusement vanished from his face. When he spoke again, it was in earnest. "The fact is, Amalia, I've only recently realized from something Lilli let slip while in her cups that neither of us really knows the truth about what happened all those years ago. I want to get to the bottom of it. That's the real reason I've come to Vienna."

She could feel the blood leave her face. She sat as her knees buckled. It was worse than she had feared. "Let it alone, please, Andrzej. We've each of us built a new life over all of that . . ."

He raised her again by taking a hand and pulling her gently from her chair so he could look directly into her eyes. His own were earnest and pleading. "My 'new' life has crumbled, Amalia. Entirely, I suspect, because it was built on faulty foundations. I can't help but wonder how your marriage fares. If I'm not wrong, this little storm has proven it wasn't built upon a rock." He indicated the inhabitants of the room, managing to imply that the storm was the current political situation.

Her anger resurfaced. "Your marriage is your own business. Mine is certainly no concern of yours. You gave up all rights to any part of my life fifteen years ago. You can't come back to me just because things have gone wrong with the choices you made then. I've gone on with my life. I've put you behind me, Andrzej." But instead of moving away as she should have done after administering this reproach, she stayed rooted to the spot, her hand still in his. He brought it to his lips and kissed the inside of her wrist. She looked into his fervent eyes, her wrist burning.

"Did the baron know of our engagement?" Andrzej inquired softly.

Her eyes traversed the finely etched lines of care on his face, and she saw a tiny muscle flex in his jaw as he clenched his teeth. No matter

411

how it hurt both of them, she had to put a stop to this. She took her hand back. Inhaling deeply, she said, "Really, Andrzej. I think it would be best to discontinue this discussion." Searching for her gloves in the envelope bag she carried, she continued, "But for your information, yes. He did know of it. And to show you how rare a man he is, he insisted that he visit Warsaw to see you before he and I became engaged."

Andrzej's eyebrows rose. "And you refused to let him, I suppose. Why?"

She could hold it in no longer. "Because I had had enough of pain!"

Turning from him while she was energized by anger enough to move, she quickly found the Horstmanns and made her farewells.

On her way home in the taxi, she gripped her hands tightly together in her lap in an effort to control their shaking. The earthquake had intensified and was breaking up the surface now. She must not see him again. But her undisciplined mind kept rerunning the scene just past as though it were a cinema newsreel. What had Lilli let fall while "in her cups?" What new information had brought Andrzej to Vienna as though he had a prior claim to her? Clenching her fists to still her hands, she shut her eyes tightly as she tried to banish the questions. This was now. This was 1933, not 1918. She couldn't go back. It was impossible. But what was she to do with these treacherous feelings?

The taxi had been stationary some time before the driver said gruffly, "This is the address, gnädige Frau."

Rudolf was standing in the foyer when she entered, making an encounter unavoidable.

"How were things at the Horstmanns'?" he inquired.

"How did you know I'd come from there?"

"I surmised it. We're inclined to flock there at every crisis. I suppose you were very hard on us?" he asked, his face intent.

She shook her head in obvious disgust. "No, as a matter of fact I left all that to Hilde."

Fleeing up the stairs, she sought her room. Dismissing Kristina, she undressed herself and then fell to her knees before her bed in prayer.

What was she to do? Her heart was pounding. She needed these feelings to be gone, to disappear. Surely they were wicked.

As her heart calmed, she realized that there wasn't going to be any quick relief. Andrzej was not going to disappear. She was going to have to rely on the person she had become. It was rather like the virgins with the oil in their lamps. You never knew when you were going to need it. Had she accumulated enough oil in the past fifteen years? Was she strong enough?

Chapter Four

Amalia awoke determined to put as much distance between herself and potential sources of conflict as possible. She would go to the Schloss to supervise the remodeling of the kitchen that was to commence in a few days' time. The more she reviewed the idea, the more rational it seemed. She simply had to get away from Andrzej. Immediately. And perhaps if she were away from Rudolf for a time, the anger within her would die down, and she could use the solitude to sort out her conflicting emotions. The deep hurt she felt at his political betrayal must heal. Surely there was more to her marriage than shared political views!

That was her rational self arguing. Her other, less tractable self simply sought an escape from the storm of emotion that was fast destroying her peace. The combination of the cleft in her marriage and the appearance of Andrzej couldn't be more dangerous. She must not deceive herself about that. The only reasonable course was flight.

How much Kristina knew of events, Amalia was not certain. Nevertheless, her maid wasted no time in preparing for the departure. The rustle of tissue paper and the heady smell of Amalia's gardenia sachet filled the room as she threw garment after garment onto the bed to be packed.

* * *

Into this scene Rudolf walked, intending to bid his morning farewell to his wife. He stopped in the doorway, his face hardening at the unexpected sight. "So you are leaving me?" His thudding heart was betraying him, and he felt suddenly ill. What a fool he had been to marry!

Amalia, who hadn't noticed his entrance, turned in surprise. "Oh, Rudolf. I decided it would be a good idea if one of us went down to the Schloss to oversee the remodeling. I know you can't leave now."

"Oh," he said, relief exploding in the single syllable. He sat heavily on the bed, his destination forgotten.

In that moment, Amalia seemed to comprehend his misapprehension. "I thought it would be best to put some distance between us at the moment, that's all."

Her words further desolated his already depressed spirits. "I'm sorry you feel you have to run off." Was it him or Zaleski she was running from?

"I think it's best," she repeated. "I need time to get some perspective on things, Rudolf."

"By things, I suppose you mean my decision and our marriage."

"Yes. Unfortunately, they are rather bound up together. You must understand that I need to sort out my feelings."

His face must have betrayed his misery, for Amalia said, "You'll have the boys to keep you company."

He turned to her, his weary eyes searching hers. "You're certain you intend to come back?" he asked, his voice husky.

She nodded gravely. "I just need some time alone, Rudolf."

Suddenly restless, she rose and went to the bureau where she sorted impatiently through multicolored silk undergarments.

"Has Zaleski anything to do with all of this?"

Her back went rigid, and she answered without turning, "Rudolf, you know how I feel about what you're doing. All of our marriage, we have worked together. How can you merely write if off as feminine pique? You haven't let yourself love me, but at least you've always respected my opinions. I don't know where this leaves us."

He stood abruptly and said with some heat, "What would you have me do? Withdraw from the political scene altogether?" Then he added more quietly, "I will if you wish it."

She turned to face him, tears in her eyes, her fingers pressing on her temples. "I don't know, Rudolf. Just give me some time to think."

He went to her then and standing behind her put his hands on her shoulders. They looked at their image in the mirror above the bureau. "I know you think I've sold out, but if I refuse Dolfuss my loyalty now, all I'll do is weaken the cause of independent Austria. At least in my present position, I can try to put some restraints on him."

Amalia bent her head, and locating a linen handkerchief in the drawer, used it to dry her eyes. Then, looking at her husband's face in the mirror, she said flatly, "Austria under a dictator can hardly be called independent. We have been yoked together in a common cause. Now we are on opposite sides."

He stepped back stiffly. Amalia resumed her packing. After several minutes, Rudolf withdrew without another word. She was more distant than she had ever been. It was he himself who was pushing her into Zaleski's arms.

* * *

The boys were less easy for Amalia to part with. Chris clung to her and reproached her for going without them. Though she knew she needed to leave, she realized the cost of it when he said, "Mutti, with Father gone so much, we'll be awfully miserable."

But Rudi, with customary insight, came to her aid. "Mother, I think you look tired. The Schloss is always good for you when you're tired." He gave her a brief but violent hug, and tried to look happy. She kissed him tenderly and told herself that she was doing what she could to preserve this little family. In the end it would be for the best. But she sent them off to school with tears in her eyes.

The car was ordered after lunch to take her to the family estate. But when she arose from the luncheon table, Max apologetically approached her with a calling card on his salver. Her eyebrows rose, but he merely said, "She's come a long way, Baroness, and she doesn't seem well. I took the liberty of admitting her, because she said she's your cousin."

"You did the right thing, Max. Thank you." Curiosity as well as dread accompanied her to the morning room where she found Lilli von Waldburg Zaleski.

It was well that Andrzej had warned her of the changes in Lilli, for Amalia would not have known her otherwise. Her cousin's vibrant hair was cut so close to her head that it was indistinguishable from a man's. The lovely olive complexion that had glowed with radiant health in days gone by was now sallow and told of illness. A gash of scarlet marked her lips, and her once candid eyes were deadened with too much makeup and something else Amalia could not define. It was as though something were missing in them, they were so strangely vacant. Her cousin held a long, jade cigarette holder in her elegant hands, the fingernails of which were painted a matching green. But most surprising of all was her attire. It appeared that she was draped in nothing but lavender and purple scarves, tied at the waist with a sort of green leather girdle. Around her person dangled strands of ivory, jade, and jet, causing her to resemble a mad gypsy in fancy dress.

"Lilli?" Amalia ventured.

The apparition approached her and enfolded her enthusiastically. "Amalia, darling!"

Amalia pulled away as gracefully as she could when she found Lilli's embrace engulfed her in an unfamiliar and highly unpleasant odor. The sight of Andrzej's wife, thus garbed, deprived her of speech.

Lilli appeared undaunted by her stunned reception. Seating herself easily on the divan, she said, "I understand my husband is in town." She took a puff of her cigarette and then held it at arm's length so she could study the glowing tip.

"Yes, I believe he is," Amalia managed, seating herself across from her guest. "We saw him at the Polish embassy ball the other night."

With the appearance of casual ease, Lilli studied her surroundings and then suddenly bit her lip. Amalia watched, appalled, as her guest's face crumpled.

Lilli whined, "He won't see me, Amalia. You've got to get him to see me. Tell him I'll give it up, if that will make him take me back."

Amalia moved forward on her chair. "I'm afraid I don't understand you. I'm not in your husband's confidence—I don't know what you're talking about."

Lilli's face, now full of sullen hatred, looked up at her. "Don't play the innocent with me, Amalia. I know he came straight to you. I always knew he would, once he knew the truth."

Straightening in her chair, Amalia replied, "I haven't any idea what you're talking about, Lilli. But if you are implying that I am somehow the cause of any problems between you and Andrzej . . ."

Her guest threw back her head and laughed wildly and harshly. "If you could only see how ridiculously prim and self-righteous you look! *If I am implying!* I don't need to imply. I know you are." Her face returned to its hard implacability. "Have you any idea what it's been like all these years?"

Amalia's eyes narrowed. "What are you accusing me of, Lilli?"

But Lilli had walked to the mantle and was studying the pictures of Amalia's sons. Suddenly her claw-like fingers seized on the one of Rudi at aged two and a half. Taking it up, she hurled it into the empty fireplace so violently that the glass smashed.

Amalia jumped up in horror, but her anger was immediately staunched when her cousin collapsed in a heap on the hearth, dry sobs wracking the body under its gaudy swathing.

Kneeling by Lilli, Amalia asked quietly, "Tell me where to find Andrzej, and I'll have him here as soon as I can."

"He's at the hospital today. At least that's what they told me at his rooms," she muttered, not raising her head.

Amalia rang for Max and then met him at the door to the room. "Please get on the telephone to the University Hospital at once. Tell them there is an emergency here, and we require Herr Doktor Zaleski to come immediately."

She stayed beside Lilli, who had given herself over completely to uncontrolled sobbing, until Andrzej arrived twenty minutes later. He strode into the room, eyes wild with anxiety until he saw the purple heap. Amalia, who was watching him closely, saw the mask of disgust descend over his face.

"When did she get here?" he asked, anger stirring in his voice.

At the sound of her husband's voice, Lilli became still. Amalia stayed by her side.

"Just after luncheon. She's extremely upset. She says you won't see her, and for some reason she insists that it's all my doing. Please tell her how mistaken she is, Andrzej." Her voice was low and steady. Her eyes commanded him to be kind.

But Lilli sat up then and, her eye makeup hideously streaked, threw her head back for another of her terrifying laughs. "Yes, reassure me, my darling. Tell me that you don't love Amalia, by all means!"

Andrzej ignored his wife, but he had seen the smashed picture in the grate and now he retrieved it. Looking at it, he snapped, "Don't try to blame your misfortunes on her, Lilli. You alone are responsible for what's become of you and me." Turning to Amalia, he indicated the picture and apologized. "I'll have this repaired." Tucking it into the pocket of his jacket, he pulled his wife roughly to her feet.

"Perhaps, if it wouldn't inconvenience the baroness any further, you could use her washroom to mop up this muck," he suggested, attempting to clean Lilli's face with his handkerchief.

Amalia rang again. When Max entered, she said, "Send Kristina."

In the interim, Lilli mercifully was silent, clinging pathetically to Andrzej's sleeve, her head bowed in evident mortification. Andrzej, ignoring her entirely, stared, jaw set, into the fireplace.

All were relieved when the door opened at last to admit the little maid. Amalia instructed her, "Kristina, would you be so kind as to take my cousin up to my boudoir? She's not well. Perhaps you can help her clean up a little."

Lilli followed Kristina meekly, and as the door closed, Amalia sank with relief onto the divan.

Andrzej seated himself across from her. "Please forgive me for this, Amalia. I ought to have known she would come straight here."

"But what's happened to her, Andrzej? And why does she blame me? If you hadn't prepared me, I never would have recognized her."

He sighed. "It's a long story, none of it pleasant. And I'm certain I'm at least partly to blame. However, I suspect now that it started long before we were even married."

She raised her eyebrows for him to continue.

"Let me ask you a question, Amalia. You won't understand at once, but it has a direct bearing on all of this." He stood and, as was his habit, went to lean against the mantle. "What was the last letter you received from me?"

"I never received any letters from you. The last communication I had concerning you was from a comrade of yours in the Red Cross hospital. It was written a week before the armistice to tell me that you were alive." Amalia's voice was almost a whisper as she remembered those awful days.

"Did you move or make any changes around the end of the war?"

She furrowed her brow. "Yes, that's when Wolf's investments went bad and we had to let the servants go. Our money was gone."

Andrzej studied her. "Continue, Amalia, if it's not too painful."

"Didn't Lilli tell you? We moved into a little flat so I could keep it up without any servants and so we wouldn't have the expense of heating the townhouse. It was in another district altogether. Not too far from where Uncle used to live. No one knew us there."

"When was the mail delivered, and who was generally the first to get hold of it?"

Amalia stared at him. "Wolf," she said slowly. As she said her brother's name, she instantly realized what must have happened. Her heart began pounding. "Wolf, who didn't want me to marry you!"

"Exactly," Andrzej sighed. "And Lilli. She knew, didn't she, that you hadn't been receiving my letters?"

"I don't think I said anything specific about it, but she must have known. She knew we weren't in communication at any rate."

Andrzej suddenly looked very tired. "As soon as Uncle Paul and his family were settled after the Germans withdrew, I was coming to Vienna for you. But I should have come here first. I had no idea of your situation." He paced angrily across her Aubusson carpet. "Can you ever forgive me? Uncle had been imprisoned. And I wrote you on my way back to Poland, from every major city where I stopped. I was certain when I returned home there would be letters from you waiting. I kept writing, but when time went by and there was nothing, I knew something was wrong. I wrote to Lilli about you, but she said she hadn't seen you. I suspect she made it her business to look you up, because I finally received a letter informing me that you had taken up with the baron. I didn't want to believe it, Amalia." He turned and pounded the mantle with his fist. "But it was my monstrous pride. I should have gone to Vienna myself. How long did you wait for me before you gave up?"

"I waited for you all through the war and then for eight months afterwards. I couldn't imagine what had gone wrong. At first I thought you were dead," Amalia's voice shook. "But then Lilli told me she had had a letter from you, so I supposed that for some reason you didn't love me any longer. I was tremendously angry that I had to find out from Lilli that you were even alive. Not knowing had been the worst agony possible." Amalia was too angry to weep. "Then Lilli went to Warsaw."

"And eventually informed me of your engagement." Here his features took on an unwonted ferocity.

"And informed me that you weren't speaking my name and wanted nothing to do with me. That was the real end, I suppose." Amalia clenched her fists.

"She'd guessed what the truth of the matter was," Andrzej said bitterly. "She didn't know why you weren't hearing from me, but she knew you thought I'd given you up. She knew how angry and upset I was because *I* thought *you'd* given *me* up. She admits it now, when she's had too much liquor or cocaine . . ."

"Cocaine!"

"Yes, Amalia, that's the tragedy of poor Lilli. She's just honorable enough not to be able to live with a dishonorable act. She knew how much you were to me, knew you were my whole world, my whole future, yet she kept her knowledge—knowledge which would have changed everything—to herself and let me believe a lie. She watched me suffer for more than a year. She watched me try to hate you. And then she offered herself as consolation." He shook his head sadly. "I'd be more bitter if the consequences to herself hadn't been so tragic."

Now Amalia went to the vase of roses on the table by the window. Removing a coral flower, she began systematically tearing the petals and throwing them on the floor. The hurt and anger of those long ago years were with her once more. The light cream and gold room took on a different aspect, losing its familiarity. She was back in the chintz morning room of her parents' townhouse, and Andrzej was lost in her hair, telling her he would come to her as soon as the war ended. The intervening fifteen years might never have happened.

"If the circumstances had been what they seemed, it's possible that Lilli and I could have had some sort of happiness. As you know, she used to be a delightful, if not inspiring, companion." Here he paused. "But soon she started to act very strangely. She began, almost at once, to test my regard for her. She taunted me continually with you. I have never been able to tell her that I love her. She took me knowing that, hoping to change it in time, but soon she was unable to forgive me for it."

Amalia threw the naked stem on the carpet and picked another rose. She stole a look at her former fiancé and wished she hadn't. The tortured eyes and bitter mouth reflected his deep unhappiness. She looked at the flower she was dismembering. In spite of the former satisfaction she had felt with her life, it suddenly seemed arid. Only a thorny branch. She and Rudolf had never spoken of love either. She had been fond of him for years but hadn't told him because of their agreement. Now her marriage seemed a lopsided thing, not the full, beautifully unfolding flower her relationship with Andrzej had been.

"How you must have hated me!" she said. "In spite of my marriage and my boys, I've never forgotten that time. It made me very hard and bitter. I don't think people recover from things like that." She looked at him. His face was drawn in pain.

"In fact, I decided that if what we had wasn't love, then there was no such thing as love. And if there wasn't any love, then there couldn't be any such thing as God. I married Rudolf, knowing I could never really love him. But I am fond of him. Over time, he has assuaged my bitterness with his kindness. But the irony is that for some reason he can't seem to love me." She paused, unconsciously dismembering the second rose she held. "Ours is a marriage of convenience. I truly think, Andrzej, that romantic love is a delusion."

He crossed to her and took her hands in a tight grip. "We have been robbed, Amalia. Robbed of the future that was meant to be ours. Left to marry elsewhere when our hearts were still intent on each other. We have suffered cruelly because of the malignant machinations of two people. Romantic love is not a delusion."

She let his words sink in. Her indignation was as great as his. To her dismay, she couldn't believe her own words. Every particle in her wanted what she had never had. She looked down at his hands. Surgeon's hands. She had always loved them. The fingers were long and tapered. Once they had caressed her with whispers of gentleness. Was there truly no remedy for this longing?

She turned her head away, and her eyes fell on the portrait of Rudi and Chris playing leapfrog at the Schloss.

"Rudolf was right, then," she said, forcing the words out. "It all could have been avoided if I had just let him go to Warsaw. I know he suspected something like this. But I was too bitter. I too had my pride. And I couldn't bear to be hurt anymore."

"And by then, I imagine you were afraid of hurting him. I know he always loved you."

"No. I told you, ours is a marriage of convenience." She dropped his hands, swept by a feeling of futility. "For some terrible reason I do not know, Rudolf doesn't believe himself capable of love. I think it must be related to these terrible black periods he has. He shuts himself in his study, sometimes for a couple of days." Her body was rebelling against her mind. She wanted to go to Andrzej's arms, where she now knew she was loved completely. In these moments, she realized that her love for him was wholly different from what she felt for Rudolf. It wasn't calm or nurturing; rather, it was exciting and enabling.

Physically weak from emotions she hadn't thought to feel again, she dropped her head and stared at the crumpled roses.

Andrzej said softly, "What now, Amalia? Are we going to let this ruin the rest of our lives as well?"

She couldn't answer. Rudi and Chris's faces smiled at her from the mantle. Would she make them innocent victims? "I'm off to the country today, Andrzej."

"You are running away."

"What else can I do? There's not just Rudolf to consider. There are the children. No matter what my feelings are, I must think of my family first." She turned to him desperately. "You must understand. It would be best for everyone if you were gone when I come back."

"No, Amalia," he replied firmly. "I'm not going."

She did not turn. "All of this is so confusing, Andrzej. I can't take it in. But we can't allow our feelings to overmaster us. What have my children done? They are innocent. They love me. They love their father." Her sore heart protested her words. "They're wonderful, Andrzej. Being a mother has taught me there is love and there is God. It would be a sin to desert them or take them from their father." Her eyes filled with tears of deep frustration. "I was convinced I was happy enough with things until you came back and told me all of this."

Lilli reentered the room then, and her world-weary eyes darted from one of them to the other. What she saw appeared to give her satisfaction of a sort. She sat with ungraceful suddenness on the divan. "Is Amalia coming with us? Wouldn't we have a delightful time?" she tittered.

"You're going back to Warsaw, Lilli," Andrzej said firmly as he hauled her to her feet.

"Oh, no, Andrzej, darling, I'm not," she simpered. "I have some unfinished business with Amalia's dear friends in the cabinet."

Chapter Five

Amalia felt as though she were pursued by furies as she rode toward the Schloss. Her emotions flew through anger, futility, self-disgust, and finally settled on despair. Tears that she refused to cry made her head ache. She tried to imagine what things would have been like had Andrzej come for her in 1918. Would she have become immersed in Polish politics or would she have continued nursing to be near Andrzej? Would they have had little green-eyed children? Could she possibly have loved them more than she loved Christian and Rudi? One thing she knew for certain: the longing she had repressed to be truly loved, to have a mutually satisfying marriage, would have been fulfilled.

She missed entirely the majestic sight of Alpine slopes and valleys, still burdened with winter snows. As the car climbed higher into the mountains, instead of craning her head to see the view out of the back window as she customarily did, she pondered steadily every detail of the conversation just past, trying to visualize what it must have been like for Andrzej all those years ago when she thought he had put her out of his life so cruelly.

He had nothing but memories. She had those, too, but she also had Rudolf, she told herself belatedly. Whatever his shortcomings, Rudolf had been steadfast and true, though unable to admit her into his heart of hearts where she knew the blackness dwelt. And she, though giving up on romantic love, had made a life with him. A good life. She felt cherished and protected, as she had when he rescued her from her life of drudgery after the war.

As the car began its descent into Graz, she sat up straighter and endeavored to take an interest in her surroundings. She had done the right thing. But she would probably hurt for a long time. She didn't know if she could bear to return to Vienna. And then there was Lilli's threat.

Andrzej had never been to the Schloss, so memories of him would not haunt it. It would remind her of all the best of her present life— her boys, her station, her husband's generosity, and all of the good fortune that had been hers since Rudolf had walked into her life.

As they approached the von Schoenenburg country estate, she was relieved to feel her customary pride swell within her. It was such a beautiful old place. She remembered when Rudolf had brought her here as a bride. The biscuit-colored exterior of the fine old mansion had won her immediately with its white baroque trimmings, so much like the "whipped cream" that had adorned her grandmother's palais in Vienna. The estate with its gently rolling terrain, its clear, cold lake, the sweet meadows of edelweiss and mustard, and its thick and magical forest of ancient trees was like a dream of childhood. This was where the princess would come to live happily ever after.

Perhaps, she pondered, if they had lived here instead of making their home in Vienna, if she had encouraged Rudolf to manage his estate in person instead of embarking on a hopeless crusade, perhaps their marriage would be happier and stronger at this moment.

Amalia dismissed the car to go back to Vienna, greeted the housekeeper, and saw her baggage safely stowed in her spacious suite. Then she put on walking shoes and ventured out in the dying light for a welcome home circuit of the lake. Its tranquillity and everlasting sameness was a balm to her turbulent spirits. She filled her lungs with the sweet, sharp country air. Rudolf might have done things much differently had he not married her. He was an able, hardworking statesman. But politics was not an obsession with him as it had become with her.

Sometimes, especially when she had seen him come in after hunting with the boys, or when they had enjoyed an afternoon on horseback scaling the highest hill on the estate and viewing the enchantment of it all, she had wondered whether she was really cheating Rudolf of the life for which he had been created.

Did she want him to give up politics? Would that mend the rift? It was hard to say, because politics had been the cement of their marriage. Without politics, could she be content to live as a happily-ever-after princess here at the Schloss? What would her life be like? And how could she stand being away from the center of things? Could she still make a difference if they remained in Vienna? Or was it more important to give up the life that was tearing her marriage apart and concentrate on mending her fences? Andrzej would never come here. She would be safe. The matter deserved her serious consideration.

As she oversaw the changes that needed to be made during the remodeling, Amalia felt herself distancing herself from Vienna with each day. She decided to have the boys' rooms repainted, their floors refinished, and new draperies and coverlets made. She did not suppose they would notice or care, but it gave her something to do for them.

The activity towards which Amalia's entire day built was her late afternoon ride. She hurried into her riding habit after her chores were completed and hastened to the stables where her mare, Elisabeth, was saddled and awaiting her. As soon as they were out of view of the Schloss, she spurred her mare into an unrestrained gallop, as satisfying to Elisabeth as to herself, and she would allow her thoughts to tumble out. It was then that she allowed herself to mourn for Andrzej and what they had lost.

She often rode with tears streaming down her face. It had been years since she had indulged herself this way. She was nearly forty. She knew that compared to most people she knew, she had a satisfactory marriage. Her regard for Rudolf strengthened the longer she spent at the Schloss, as she settled into her accustomed role.

But those old, treacherously sweet memories remained and it seemed there was nothing she could do to censor them. It had been so long since she had felt any passion in a life that had become so prosaic.

The emotional intimacy she had shared in Vienna with Andrzej had never been part of her life with Rudolf. They kept to their own rooms for the most part, and he had always kept his ardor restrained, as though vaguely embarrassed by it. Always after a period of particular sweetness between them, he hid in the "cobwebby rooms" in his mind for days at a time. Sometimes a whole week. Once she had tried to penetrate his gloom, and he had frozen her out with harsh words, locking himself in his study. She had never made the attempt again. And so she had never spoken of her fondness for him, fearing it would trigger one of these episodes. And now, just as Rudolf had always feared, Andrzej had returned for her.

And so she prayed as she rode. She prayed that she would learn to live without passion, or at least without passion for Andrzej. She prayed that her feelings for Rudolf would deepen and that she would be able to fill her aching sorrow with his kindness and gentleness. She prayed that he would admit her to his deepest self. That she could be more understanding of the problems facing her husband in the government and that he could still be a force for good. As the days passed, she could feel herself grow in spiritual substance. Wild emotions quieted and a peaceful feeling grew in her breast as she thought of her little family and all they meant to her. She endeavored to sink the grief deep inside where it had lived for so many years unacknowledged.

Inevitably, the day came when she knew it was time to return to Vienna. She had reconciled herself to the fact that her grieving process might take some time—years, even—and that she couldn't put off real life until it was resolved. She would just have to hope that her new serenity regarding her family would provide the shield she needed against Andrzej. She had decided this during a ride that had ended in an unexpected cloudburst. Drenched, she returned to the house to find Rudolf awaiting her with hot chocolate. Pleasure flooded her at the sight of him here in his accustomed setting. "Rudolf!" she cried. "When did you arrive? What a lovely surprise!"

He arose and seemed to be waiting to see if she would come to him. "I find I do very poorly without you, Amalia," he said simply.

She approached him with sweet feelings of wifely tenderness and kissed his cheek. Heedless of her damp attire, she pulled him down beside her on the divan. "I'm so glad you've come, Rudolf. It's begun to seem very strange without the family."

He looked at her closely for a moment, and then said lightly, "I see you've begun several projects, my dear. The kitchen looks as though it's well on its way to total annihilation, so I assume you are pleased. I also smelled paint and followed my nose to the boys' room. Green?" His eyebrows were raised in a proprietary tease.

"Green," she echoed firmly. "Restful, Rudolf. I'm hoping it will filter into their subconscious during the night and make them less of a handful while they're here. Once they leave the city, I think they're more like Turks than civilized sons of nobility." She knew her laugh sounded a bit wistful.

"I left them well, Amalia, so don't fret, my dear. I can tell this time away has been good for you. Despite your rather unusual appearance," he smoothed a damp curl that had plastered itself onto her forehead, "it's easy to see you've got your serenity back again."

She laughed, realizing at the same time how long it had been since she had done so. Rudolf dispatched her to change into dry clothes, promising to save a few of the pastries.

Upon her return they settled to the business of eating and drinking and over their Fruchttorte discussed affairs at the chancellery. Amalia was determined to maintain her peace of mind. Her husband's deeply scored brow and tired, bloodshot eyes told of his need for a confidante.

"The chess game with Hitler continues, my dear," he remarked wearily. "Just between you and me, it seems that every power play our government attempts turns to our disadvantage in the end. I'm sure I'm not the first to say it, but it's true, nevertheless—the man has an evil genius."

"I've been here nearly six weeks, Rudolf, and have purposely ignored the news. Tell me what's happened, if you think you can bear it."

A curtain of caution seemed to settle over her husband's features. "I thought your welcome was a bit too forgiving," he said. "I don't think you *can* bear it, Amalia."

Alarm sparked in her eyes, and he extended a palm. "I might as well tell you the worst, or you'll accuse me of keeping it from you." He braced himself, a hand on each chair arm. "Immediately after you left, Dolfuss disarmed the *Schutzbund*. We seized their weapons, and from henceforth the army of the Social Democrats is illegal."

A sigh escaped her, but then surprisingly she gave a little smile. "It's no worse than I feared. I never thought private armies were desirable in a democracy, anyway. The only problem is that now he's left us at the mercy of the Nazis. The Schutzbund could have neutralized them for us, you know."

A look of surprise animated Rudolf's solemn face. "Amalia, we're trying to prevent civil war, not encourage it!"

She smiled and replied, "Let's not differ, especially when you've just arrived. Tell me about Hitler's newest abominations—at least we agree about him."

He relaxed. "Actually, you're right about the Nazis. Together with their sympathizers they've become horribly violent since you left. Now that he's certain of his own power base in Germany, Hitler's using his terror tactics abroad. I've no doubt that we're his first target. He refuses to recognize that we're not one with his blighted Fatherland."

Amalia shuddered at this and felt the old gloom wrap itself around her. For a moment she was imprisoned by her memories of wartime Berlin. She saw Eberhard's face as he celebrated the beginning of the war. Then visions of St. Catherine's Hospital assailed her. And finally, Eberhard's face on the train platform the last time she had seen him.

They were silent for a while, their personal differences swallowed in more universal problems. Finally, Amalia replied, "I suppose all this has had the effect of driving Dolfuss closer to Mussolini."

"Yes. After all, he's rather desperate for a savior. He's planning a trip to London this summer but doesn't expect much to come of it."

Remembering Andrzej's comment regarding Western sympathies, she had to agree. Soon they dropped the matter entirely and discussed estate affairs. Then Rudolf changed his clothes, and they walked around the lake before dinner, a tradition they had begun soon after they were married.

He put his arm about her shoulders as they walked and studied her profile from time to time. She felt his scrutiny but continued in her light, seemingly effortless recital of the events that had made up her days.

"Have you been in touch with Zaleski?" he asked finally, halting so he could examine her entire face.

She looked at him squarely. "No, Rudolf, I haven't. That was one reason I came away."

"Kristina told me of Lilli's visit."

"I suppose she's worried about me?"

"Of course. I'm glad she's on my side, my dear. Have you any idea how profoundly she distrusts Zaleski?"

"She hasn't any facts."

"What are the facts?" he asked flatly, his eyes now carefully trained on the swans that were picturesquely outlined against the dark green woods.

She hesitated only briefly before telling him of Lilli and Wolf's deception.

The baron scowled. "I might have figured that out for myself if I hadn't been such an interested party." He picked up a stone and hurled it savagely into the lake.

"It's all in the past, Rudolf. You did what only an honorable man would have done in offering to go to Warsaw. Any blame is mine for refusing to let you go."

She put her hands on his shoulders and looked up into the gentle brown eyes that now mirrored her pain. "I wanted safety then, Rudolf. Not more violent emotion. I'd had too much."

They stood for a moment, silhouetted against the dusk. "It's Lilli who's suffered most, Rudolf. She's a cocaine addict, among other things. It's hideous."

But he murmured, "My pity is all for Zaleski."

Her eyes stung.

Chapter Six

The following morning began cheerfully enough, though they had slept in their separate suites. It was a clear spring day, and they had fresh strawberries for breakfast. When the mail arrived, her husband received a fat communication she surmised came from the chancellery. Then she noticed that she, too, had a letter. The return direction was printed boldly in block letters that her husband could not have missed: Doktor Andrzej Zaleski, 19 Lindenstrasse, Wien. She slipped it into her pocket with the full intention of later throwing it away. Then she lingered, interested to see what her husband's news would be.

He folded his letter at last and gave a gusty sigh. "I didn't tell Dolfuss of my plan to come here—I knew he'd try to keep me. But I did leave a message for him. Now he's written, an express letter as a matter of fact, demanding my return."

His wife grimaced. "It's a shame you're so valuable. More trouble, I presume?"

"He's nervous. He knows your views, incidentally. He asked for them when he didn't see you at any of our recent official functions. I imagine that at this moment he's probably horribly afraid you'll convert me."

Amalia's eyebrows rose and she smiled faintly. "He should know there are limits to my influence."

"Don't, Amalia."

"What will you do?"

He turned to face her, his torn emotions evident in the tight jaw and furrowed brow. "What can I do? He needs all his supporters now. It's critical."

"Why now, in particular?"

Her husband moved uneasily to the window and stared out at the well-kept flower garden full of blooming irises. She sensed there was something that he did not want to tell her.

"He's about to launch a new program. It's to be called the 'Fatherland Front.'"

"That sounds sinister. Too much like Hitler."

Rudolf turned abruptly to face her. "I suppose you'd think so. It's his bid to consolidate his power. He's going to try to put an end to both the Nazi and the Social Democratic parties under the guise of this blindingly patriotic program."

There was silence. Amalia's lips narrowed and her nostrils flared in suppressed indignation.

"Have you given any more thought to the idea of my just quitting politics?" he asked, his weariness evident.

Amalia left the table and joined her husband at the window. "I have. And I think perhaps you'd be a lot happier."

"But what about you, Amalia?"

"I don't know. I don't know if I could stand to live here and leave the world to the bullies. Hitler will win for sure if someone doesn't stop him."

"I don't have that kind of power, Amalia."

"No. But you are a good man. And I'm sure you do your best to give Dolfuss good advice, whether he listens or not."

"Whatever the case, Dolfuss is my chief, and I feel at this point that I must be loyal. You know I don't agree with everything he's done, but the fact remains that democracy or no democracy, we need a strong leader to negotiate for our protection. He's the only one we've got."

"And so you'd rather stick by him than quit?"

"I guess so. I really would feel as though I'd be letting everyone down by quitting. Even you."

Amalia sighed. There were no easy answers. "Very well. I guess things will have to go on as they have. But please promise you'll at least listen to me, Rudolf."

"I always do, Amalia." He left the dining room, slowly and deliberately. She did not try to stop him but shut the door behind him and sank limply in her chair. Things were not going to be easy. She was not going to be able to support Rudolf's chief, no matter how much he might wish it. And that meant they were going to be forever at odds. Nothing had really changed.

Somewhat defiantly she took Andrzej's letter from her pocket and opened it. She paused before unfolding the stiff pages, then she deliberately began to read.

My dear Amalia,

I wonder how you are faring. That is, of course, an understatement, for I have thought of little else since you left. My principal purpose in writing, however, is to tell you that I packed Lilli off to my aunt in Warsaw before she could do any undeserved damage to your reputation. She will stay there until the divorce or receive no settlement. I am truly sorry for the scene you witnessed, but perhaps it is just as well, for you were at last able to learn the truth of what happened so long ago.

Maybe you would also be interested to know that I have seen your brother. He was only too happy to admit his guilt, giving as his rationale the fact that Rudolf was and is the far better man. You may not know that he is now an officer in the Heimwehr.

I have thought of our last conversation endlessly, and I apologize for what must have seemed to be an overbearing selfishness. Love is such a terribly personal sort of thing that sometimes we don't see the entire picture as we should. I do want you to know that I understand what you tried to tell me about your family.

From where you stood and what you knew of me, you made the best possible choice after the war. You would not be the woman I love so enduringly if you weren't willing to stand by that choice. At the risk of sounding patronizing, I am proud of what you have elected to do with your life. Seeing the woman you have become makes it all the more difficult for me, but undoubtedly you are right—our love does belong to another chapter. The only problem is, I'm stuck at that point in the story and can't seem to move forward.

If you like, I'll cut my mission short and depart at once for Warsaw. However much it may have seemed to the contrary, I want only your happiness. It is all that is left to me.

Andrzej

Coming on top of her discussion with Rudolf, Amalia found that the fresh pain caused by the letter more than repaid her for the folly of opening it. But her peace was spoiled. There was no longer any point to remaining at the Schloss. She went in search of her husband, forgetting the letter still clutched in her hand.

She found him stuffing the last of his shirts into his traveling bag. He looked up as she entered the room.

"Rudolf," she said, "I'm coming with you. I had already decided to return to Vienna before you came."

Hope softened his expression for a moment, but then he caught sight of the letter in her hand. "Very well, but who will complete what you've started here?"

"Frau Schratt will manage. The worst of it is done." She left to go in search of the housekeeper and see to her own packing.

Rudolf had driven himself to the Schloss, so they traveled back unaccompanied by the restraining presence of a chauffeur. Nevertheless, the drive was very tense. Amalia did not want to discuss the government, and she knew that Rudolf was curious about Andrzej's letter. Yet she couldn't bring herself to tell him about it. She didn't know how she felt about it herself. She ought to encourage Andrzej to go. That was the only right thing to do. But she wanted to see him one more time. Just to tell him that it wasn't easy for her, either, but that there was no future for them.

*   *   *

For a brief hour or two that morning, the darkness had lifted. But Rudolf was now sunk in gloom once more. In Amalia's mind there seemed to be no separation between him as a person and the political agenda he was bound to uphold. And now, here was Zaleski, offering his heart.

Had it been unwise of him not to tell her of his feelings for her long ago? Did she still see theirs as only a marriage of convenience? If so, what was there to keep her with him? Especially now that he had deviated from her ideals?

Most men these days could take it in stride if they were estranged from their wives. They tolerated their wives' infidelities and retaliated by being unfaithful themselves. But Rudolf knew that his wife was not ruled by physical attraction alone. She wouldn't ever be able to separate that part of her from the rest. If she gave herself to Zaleski, she would give him all of herself. And what would he do without her? Like a case of the mumps coming late in life, love was a lot more virulent for him than for the average man of his age. And his boys. If she left the boys, they would suffer for it all their lives. And if she took them, it would be almost impossible to keep the blackness from overpowering him.

It seemed to him that they were all pitched on the edge of disaster.

Not able to stand it any longer, he asked, "You will be seeing Zaleski?"

"He says he'll leave if I want him to," she replied shortly. "But I want to see him one more time."

He did not answer but accelerated in a burst of speed.

*   *   *

Her sons greeted her with unbridled enthusiasm. "Mutti!" Chris yelped ecstatically, hurling himself at her like a young cub. While he embraced her ferociously, Rudi looked on, grinning from ear to ear. At the first break in his young brother's ardor he kissed her cheek. "Welcome home, Mutti."

Amalia's heart lightened, and she bade them tell her all their adventures. First, however, she had to answer their inquiries about their horses and pets at the Schloss, the state of the strawberry patch, and the temper of the cook. Midway through Christian's recital of his capture of an unfortunate garden snake, they were interrupted by the dinner bell. Bidding her sons to run down while she changed, she hastened off to her boudoir for a wash and a fresh frock.

Kristina, whom she had not yet seen, was waiting for her. "It's time you were back," she greeted her mistress. Looking at her as though she were a potentially troublesome child, she commented further, "I hope you'll behave yourself."

Amalia flashed, "I'll wear my cream-colored silk, Kristina."

The baron did not join them for dinner. Amalia's reaction was equally divided between relief and sorrow. The family seemed sadly incomplete, and yet she was glad of a relief from the tension.

That night she slept poorly. Self-digust, disappointment, and grief vied for supremacy in her tired mind, and just when her thoughts had run down enough for the illogical leap that presaged sleep, another wave of emotion would seize her and she would be wide awake again. She sought the solace of prayer, but she was aware that her frame of mind was far from humble, and so her demands brought no peace, only feelings of unworthiness. By morning, her nerves were prickly with fatigue and her body heavy with exhaustion.

Kristina brought her morning tray and the newspaper. One look at her mistress and she pursed her lips. "A hot bath and back to bed," she prescribed definitely. "You haven't slept a wink."

"No, and staying in bed all day isn't going to help," Amalia declared rebelliously. "Has the baron gone out already?"

Her maid nodded sharply. "He didn't look his best," she remarked. "Max said he spent the night in his office with a bottle of schnapps."

Amalia threw back the covers impatiently, leaving her tray untouched. "I'm going out. To the dressmaker."

That morning she ordered her entire summer wardrobe and felt considerably better for it. At least it was something constructive and positive.

The state of affairs between her and Rudolf had still gone unmended when Andrzej called upon her the next afternoon in response to the note she had sent him. Steeling herself to put an end to her dangerous romantic fantasy, she asked Max to show him into the boys' playroom where she had been going through their books.

Andrzej entered to find her seated on the floor of the long, low room, surrounded by piles of books. "Shades of the orphanage," she said, looking up. "I'm not nearly as good a mother as I was a teacher."

He was inspecting the walls. "Aren't these our old prints?" he asked.

"Yes," she answered self-consciously. "I asked Rudolf for them after the boys were born. I'm afraid we leave the orphanage to others these days."

They were both quiet for a moment. Andrzej knelt down and began to look through the books. "Ah, how well I remember these stories," he murmured, turning through the color plates of *Die Brüder Grimm*.

The door flew open, and Rudi and Chris entered boisterously. They stopped dead at the sight of a stranger in their room.

"Herr Doktor Zaleski, I'd like you to meet my sons, Rudolf and Christian," Amalia announced, glad of their appearance. "Rudi and Chris, this is an old friend of your father's and mine from before the war."

The boys smiled sunnily at the stranger and then turned to their mother. "Can we go to the bakery, please, Mutti?" Rudi importuned, "I've just won a bet with Jan and have money of my own to spend."

"Enough to buy something for Christian, as well?" she asked.

"Oh, I'm rich!" her son assured her. "I may even buy something for you and Father."

She laughed. "All right, then, but be careful."

They were gone before she finished her sentence. She turned to Andrzej with a sigh. "It's so hard to keep them cooped up here, even for their own safety. Our footman usually goes with them, but I hate to ask him to run out every time the boys take it into their heads to dash off somewhere. It'll be a relief to take them to the Schloss when school has ended."

Her guest did not reply at once but stood and walked slowly around the room, looking closely at the prints they had found together all those years ago. "They're lovely boys, Amalia. I confess it hard to believe you're their mother."

"It's sometimes hard for me to believe, too." She laughed. "I don't really feel any older until I look at them and realize that they're the last twelve years of my life made flesh!"

"I shall always wonder what our children would have been like," he said, turning and watching her as she continued to sort through the books, putting some in a stack at her side and some back on the shelves. She felt a heat flush her entire body but continued her task with enforced calmness.

Without drawing closer, Andrzej remarked, "I need to know what you're about, Amalia. Once, long ago I made the mistake of misinterpreting your actions. You went to Berlin. We've suffered for it ever since, or at least I have. I don't want to do it again."

"What do you want to know?" she asked, not looking up from her sorting.

"What do you intend to do about us? Or don't you intend to do anything? Do you think I'll be a tame admirer who follows you around with misty eyes, reminiscing about the romantic good old days and respectfully keeping my distance?"

"I suppose you have some sort of affair in mind?" she asked, heart thumping.

"Amalia, don't cheapen my feelings. I want more than just an affair. I've tried to respect your wishes with regard to your family, but your feelings seem so ambivalent."

Her hands stilled on the books. Rudolf was so distant, the schism in her marriage so deep. She longed for a whole relationship, for someone who was all hers, who didn't disappear into blackness she couldn't understand.

What am I made of, anyway? the stronger part of her mind queried. Were she to go with Andrzej, she knew suddenly, she would trade selfish desires for lifelong regret. Even if Rudolf didn't need her, her boys needed him, and he needed them. Rudi was the next Baron von

Schoenenburg. She couldn't take them to live in Poland. Her path, though difficult, was clear.

Drawing a breath that pierced her through, she said, "Sometimes feelings run contrary to duty." She made a show of wiping her dusty hands on her handkerchief. "I apologize for giving you any reason to hope, for there is none. I can't leave Rudolf. He's too good a man, and he's entrusted me with his sons. He deserves my loyalty. I could never reconcile myself to an affair. I'm not cut out for adultery, Andrzej. It goes against everything I believe in. Everything that makes me me. And a divorce would scar my boys forever."

She stood and looked out the window, her back to him. "Our life is not perfect, but I am very fond of my husband. I owe him so much. You have no idea what things were like when he rescued me after the war. And I'm devoted to my sons. I wouldn't ever consider leaving them, either." She turned to face him, her head silhouetted against the dying afternoon light. Despite her brave words, she felt her tenderness for Andrzej rush to the surface. "But you're right, Andrzej. It isn't easy at all."

He moved to her and tilted her chin up, as he had done so often in the past. She instantly pulled away from him. "How can you be so heartless?" he demanded.

"Let's not sully our memories with any actions that would only be dishonorable now. I want to leave the past safely and innocently locked inside me." He pulled her roughly to him, but she struggled loose. His eyes were imploring. "Amalia, I have nothing but memories. I have no present to console me. It won't be easy for me to give up hoping."

Before she could reply, they heard a shout on the stairs, and suddenly Rudi burst in upon them. His hair was wildly disheveled and his face red with tears and small streaks of blood.

"Mutti, Mutti! It's Chris—they've hurt him . . . I don't know if he's . . . oh, please come. At the bakers . . ."

Chapter Seven

Andrzej was already running down the stairs, but Amalia stood rooted, feeling as though the sun had just been blotted out. She swayed as Rudi pulled at her, his earnest face screwed up in urgency. "Mutti, Mutti, please come. We must go now!"

At last she responded, instinct taking charge, and she followed Rudi quickly down the stairs, out of the house, and around the block to the baker's small shop. The plate glass window had been shattered, and Amalia smelled fire. She bolted through the entrance, heedless of the shards of broken glass that seemed to be everywhere. Andrzej was already there, bent over Chris, who was lying in the midst of the debris, white and still.

She could only manage to gasp.

"Concussed, I think, but alive," Andrzej reassured her. "I'll move him out as soon as I'm certain no bones are broken. You'd better check the kitchen—the baker may be unconscious, too, and there's a fire."

But Amalia could only stare at Christian, unable to take in what had happened. Rudi moved swiftly to obey Andrzej's order and was back in an instant, coughing.

"Fire!" he sputtered as smoke followed him through the now open door. "Herr Steiner—he's lying on the floor. I think he's dead."

At his words, Amalia finally roused herself. "Go to him, Andrzej. Rudi and I will manage." She moved swiftly to her younger son and cradled his head in her arms. He was so unnaturally, pathetically still. Even in sleep, he had never looked so quiet.

Her nursing skills took over, and she completed the cursory

examination of his bones. "I don't think anything is broken. Let's try to move him, Rudi," she said, suddenly aware of the increasing density of the smoke.

Rudi took his brother's feet and Amalia his shoulders, and they moved him out to the sidewalk and laid him gently down. In a moment Andrzej staggered out. He looked at Amalia, his eyes red with rage, and gave a silent shake of his head.

"Let's get out of here," he said, and stooping, he gathered Christian in his arms and led the way back to the palais.

They put him on the couch in Rudolf's study. Andrzej rang the chancellery, while Amalia knelt by Christian and rocked a badly frightened Rudi back and forth.

"Von Schoenenburg? Andrzej Zaleski here. I think you'd better come home. There's been some trouble."

"No, everyone's alive. Just."

He hung up and then bent to take Chris's pulse. "He's on his way. I didn't think it wise to say much on the phone." He turned to Rudi. "Now, my young hero, suppose you tell us what happened."

Rudi gulped and looked at the doctor with large brown eyes, so like his father's. "We were buying some pastries, when suddenly," he covered his eyes, "there was a terrible crash." Amalia held her son to her and stared into Andrzej's grim face. "Then the room was full of men, big men in black shirts, swinging clubs. I scrambled behind the counter, but Chris . . . they must have hit Chris right away. Then they disappeared into the kitchen. They were yelling all the time. Screaming *'Juden! Juden! Juden!'*"

The boy shuddered. "As soon as they went into the kitchen, I went to Chris. He wouldn't move. I got scared and ran here for Mother." He looked up shyly at the doctor. "Thank heaven for you, Herr Doktor. I don't think Mother and I could have managed."

"Oh, I wouldn't say that," Andrzej said with a friendly grin. "I think that together, you and your mother could manage just about anything."

Amalia started to rise, for she heard Rudolf in the hall. But Andrzej gestured for her to stay and hastened out to meet the baron himself. She heard them murmuring outside the door for a few moments, and then her husband strode in.

His anxious eyes went first to Chris's unconscious form where they rested only briefly before seeking those of his wife. She rose and clung to him, suddenly giving in to angry weeping. Rudi wrapped himself around both of them, and they stood thus for a moment, with Andrzej looking on from the doorway.

Rudolf finally said in a soothing voice, "Zaleski says he'll recover, Amalia." And then he spoke to his son. "You acted bravely, my boy. The doctor told me. I'm proud of you."

"Rudolf!" Amalia cried, "You must do something!"

But her husband only moved nervously over to the window and peered out behind the closed drapery.

She continued, her voice rising in hysteria, "How can you stay so calm? Those murderers could have killed your son, just as they did Herr Steiner!"

He looked at her helplessly, his eyes full of pain, and then turned to the other man. "Perhaps you can explain. She might listen to you."

Andrzej said, "First, I think I'll phone for my kit, if you don't mind. Amalia needs a sedative badly. And can we have some more chairs in here? It's a bit awkward for us to continue standing about."

All instinctively acknowledged his authority. When they were settled after his telephone call, Andrzej spoke in soothing, professional tones to Amalia and Rudi. "What happened to Chris today was a terrible thing. Up until now, I think I'm correct in saying that the only known victims of the Nazis in this country have been Jewish . . ."

Amalia blazed, "Does that make their crimes less terrible?"

Andrzej raised his hand. "Wait until I'm finished, please."

She stifled her tirade. Rudolf looked at her with sad eyes and then back at the doctor.

"The thugs didn't know who Chris was, Amalia," Andrzej explained. "This wasn't an intentional situation—they thought your son was some random Jew, if they thought at all. They certainly had no idea he was the son of the Baron von Schoenenburg. But the Heimwehr wouldn't see it that way. They're looking for just such an excuse to launch an all-out attack on the Nazis. The result would be tantamount to civil war and just the excuse Hitler is looking for to send in his troops to make the most of the situation. Voila! Anschluss by tomorrow evening at the latest."

"I don't see what difference it would make!" she argued, knowing she was irrational but unable to stop herself in her blistering anger. "If we keep giving in to terrorist attacks, standing by and doing nothing, then Hitler won't need to invade us . . ."

"Amalia, we're playing for time," her husband interrupted. "We've got to get Mussolini in our corner; we've got to have some protection before we can afford to provoke Hitler. What Zaleski says is right. The Heimwehr is becoming increasingly difficult to restrain."

She stood and glared at both men, fury narrowing her eyes. "I think you're both cowards. Those horrible men were nothing more than an illiterate bunch of thugs, and you're going to let them get away with this and with murdering Herr Steiner. If the Nazis finally do take over this country, it's going to be because people like you stood by and did nothing." She started for the doorway.

"Amalia . . ." Rudolf pleaded wearily. She did not stop.

Andrzej's voice was hard. "If you have any ideas about going to Wolf and the Heimwehr with this little story, you should forget them."

She whirled around. "How did you guess? It's rather comical, isn't it—that I should have to turn to Wolf for once, instead of one of you. My shining heroes!"

Rudolf bowed his head under the weight of her contempt, but Andrzej returned her glare with the added hauteur of a raised eyebrow. Then Christian moaned feebly, and Amalia's outraged figure relaxed into lines of maternal softness and concern. All else receded as she was drawn to her son's bedside by the pathetic but welcome sounds.

After receiving the sedative, Amalia slept a full eighteen hours, waking at ten o'clock the following morning. At first, she was conscious only of a terrible lethargy she could not understand, until she remembered she had been drugged. With this memory came an overwhelming urgency that succeeded at last in fully awakening her. She must see Christian. As she raised her heavy head from the pillow, however, she saw that she was not alone in the room.

Rudolf rose quickly from the window seat. "Awake, my dear? How are you feeling? Zaleski said you might be a bit muzzy-headed."

Sitting up, she asked, "How is Christian?"

"Much more fit. He ate a hearty breakfast, as a matter of fact. That's a good sign, don't you think?"

She swung her legs over the side of the bed and then sat fighting the invisible weights that pulled her back into downy comfort.

Rudolf approached her hesitantly. "You don't look very well, Amalia. Chris is sleeping quite peacefully at the moment. Suppose you just lie down for a while longer. I'm supposed to keep you in bed as long as I can."

"I just want to see him, Rudolf." She dragged herself up and shuffled to the washstand where she turned on the cold water and watched it run into the basin. "I do feel rather hideous. Did Chris say anything to you today about . . . about yesterday?"

"No. Zaleski says that with a head injury it's quite common to lose memory of the trauma altogether."

"That's true. Let's hope he never remembers, Rudolf." She gritted her teeth and then put her entire head under the faucet. After a moment, she came up and reached blindly for a towel. Drying her head vigorously, she walked to the window seat and sat next to her husband.

"Unfortunately, I'll never forget it as long as I live." She sat limply with her hair wildly askew, and looked absently out the window. What she saw was not the street below bathed in spring sunshine but a little boy lying amidst pieces of a shattered window, his face deathly white and still.

Rudolf gathered her to him as though she were a small child in the midst of a bad dream. "You'll catch a chill, my dear."

He carried her over to the bed and put her back under the goose down Federdecke. "Shall I ring for Kristina?"

"Rudolf, what did you tell Dolfuss? Does he know you're home today?"

He sat tentatively on the edge of her bed. "I told him the truth," he said heavily.

"And what did he say?"

"What you would expect? He likes Christian, you know. He was aghast."

"What is he going to do?"

He turned to face her, and she noted how terribly tired he looked. "Nothing, Amalia. As we tried to explain to you, there's nothing we can do now that would be responsible."

She averted her face.

"How did Zaleski come to be on the scene so opportunely? I never asked him."

"He was calling on me at the time."

Rudolf walked back to the window. "I thought you said he was leaving Vienna."

"Rudolf, don't drag Andrzej into the conversation. He isn't the issue."

"Isn't he?" her husband asked.

"No! How can you even think he has anything to do with it at all? We're talking about our son, our son who was almost killed yesterday."

"Not really, Amalia," he disagreed wearily. "That's the immediate crisis, but your irritation with me doesn't really spring from that. Is it just a coincidence that ever since Zaleski has returned we've been at odds? Do you want to have an affair with him? Are you fighting your feelings?"

"I've told Andrzej that I will neither have an affair nor leave you. How can you think me capable of those things? I'm trying desperately to save our marriage. Rudolf, you know how I feel about what you're doing in the government!"

"And Zaleski agrees with you, doesn't he?"

"I certainly thought so, until last night."

"Amalia," he asked abruptly, "what makes you so sure you're right?"

She went to the vanity, where she began to pull the comb brutally through her tangled wet locks. "What makes you so sure *you* are?" she countered.

"I'm not at all sure that I am," he answered. "But I'm wondering whether our government could have succeeded under any circumstances."

"What do you mean? Democracy has been proven—it's not some hypothetical utopia. It works in America and in Britain, too."

"Do you remember the Bible cautionary tale about putting new wine in old bottles?"

"What are you trying to say?"

"The Pharisees were the Jewish aristocracy, if you will. The old bottles. The new wine was the new law . . . love one another, not an eye for an eye, a tooth for a tooth."

Her anger cooled as she thought over the implications of his analogy. "And you think that applies? The Austrian aristocrats are the old bottles?"

He spoke heavily in the voice she dreaded. "I'm afraid we're proving to be. We're too used to the old ways, Amalia. We don't have the faith in the people that you seem to have. Perhaps your vision is some sort of legacy from Lorenz."

"Oh, Rudolf! Don't say that! You're breaking my heart." She put her head in her hands.

Resting his hand on her shoulder, he murmured, "And I'm breaking mine, Amalia. You don't know what it's costing me to disappoint you. Perhaps you'd be better off with Zaleski, after all. I'll leave that up to you. I've already told you I'll give you a divorce."

His eyes were distant and full of pain. She knew that look and it frightened her. Rising hastily, he left her alone.

Chapter Eight

Tears welled, and Amalia wept steadily, her whole body jerking, her head on her arms. Rudolf had withdrawn from her. She had forced him back into that place inside where he suffered things she could not comprehend. He really thought she would leave him and go with Andrzej. He was almost driving her to it.

Vaguely aware that Kristina had come and discreetly gone out, Amalia tried to collect herself, but the emotional strain of the past twenty-four hours was too great. Her son had nearly been killed. Rudolf had refused to take action. And now she had lost him to his private darkness. What caused his behavior? Would she ever know? His separation from her at this particular time drained her of all safety and security. Since the days following the war, he had been her dragonslayer. Now he had put down his sword and acknowledged defeat.

Then, with devastating clarity she saw that even Andrzej could never take Rudolf's place in her life. Her baron was and always had been her rescuer, the father of her wonderful sons, her protector, and her willing partner in everything that was important to her. He was only in the government because that had been his part of the agreement when they married.

She knew he fought demons, but now she realized they might be the same ones his brother had fought before he took his own life. Horror paralyzed her. Was her relationship with Andrzej driving her husband to suicide?

No. That wasn't possible. She took a deep breath. Rudolf didn't love her. For some reason she would never understand, he wouldn't allow himself love. He might be her knight, but he was securely ensconced behind his armor. For their entire life together she had accepted this truth, but now that their marriage was threatened, she wondered at it. Why wouldn't Rudolf allow himself to love?

It was not until Rudi timidly entered sometime later that she was successful in controlling herself.

"Mutti," he said tenderly, "don't cry. Chris is all right. I came to tell you he's asking for you."

She dried her eyes hastily and embraced her son. "You're such a fine boy, Rudi. I do love you."

"Do you still love Father, too?" he asked anxiously. The scene in the study the night before had obviously troubled him.

"I do, Rudi. You mustn't let what I said last night disturb you. I was upset, and when people are upset, sometimes they say things they don't mean."

"But does Father know you didn't mean it? He seems so sad today. He's locked himself in his study again."

"Your father has a lot of worries just now. These are worrying times. I hope you and Chris won't go out alone again, now that you see how dangerous it can be." She drew on her dressing gown as she pulled herself together.

Christian querulously demanded to get up. "I'm not the least bit sick, Mutti. Ask Rudi. I ate a bigger breakfast than he did."

"Wait until Herr Doktor Zaleski sees you. He should be here sometime soon. If he says you can get up, then I'll let you."

* * *

Andrzej called after luncheon and was pleased to find his young patient eating a good meal in the company of his mother and brother. "Well, young Christian, how's the head?"

"Why does everyone ask about my head? It hurts a little, but I'm all right. I want to get up."

Andrzej examined Christian's pupils and took his pulse. "No reason why you shouldn't," he agreed. "But don't challenge Rudi to any fist fights for a while. In other words, mind your head for a few days."

The child joyfully bounded out of bed in a single leap, and Amalia sent him off to get dressed. She accompanied Andrzej down to the morning room.

"How is my other patient doing?" he asked, surveying her with a doctor's eye.

"Better. I'm sorry I screamed at you yesterday. I'm surprised you didn't drug me into next week. I must have been hysterical."

He caressed her pale cheek. "Amalia," he murmured fondly.

She moved away from him and sat unsteadily. "Thank you, Andrzej. I'm very glad you were here."

"You've decided not to take your grievances to Wolf, I hope?"

"I won't go to Wolf. But still, something must be done."

He went to the mantle. How could he say this without disappointing her? "I'm afraid things have progressed too far for that now. There's no parliament, only armies. The Socialists' Schutzbund is still active, you know. They've just gone underground. So now you've got what amounts to three private armies. That's a lot of explosives."

"What do you think is going to happen?"

"It's inevitable that something is going to blow up. Just what and just when are anybody's guess."

"Rudolf talked to me this morning."

"So I would imagine."

"He says you can't put new wine in old bottles. Do you agree?"

Andrzej abandoned the mantle to sit next to her. "Yes, I'm afraid I do. We've got the same problem in Poland. Now that we've got our ancient borders, the nobility feel we should have ancient rule as well. But where do you find new bottles?"

"If the aristocrats are eliminated, that leaves the working class, who are socialists, and the middle class, who are pro-German."

"All except you."

"I must be a cross-breed or something."

452

"A very enchanting one. Perhaps that's the mystery of your charm," he teased, trying to lighten her mood.

"Andrzej! I'm serious."

"I am too, in a way. You're an interesting study. You have none of the cynicism of my world-weary class, you know. I think that is, in part, what classifies you as a new bottle."

"I suppose you find me naïve."

"Not at all, Amalia. That's what's so peculiarly fascinating about you. You're such a unique combination of the idealist and the realist. Take your marriage, for example." He rose and walked to the mantle again. "If you were playing by my rules, you'd feel perfectly free to leave your husband."

"Rules, as you call them, have nothing to do with it, Andrzej." She turned her back to him. "I believe Rudolf's are the same as yours. He actually told me this morning that I would be better off with you. It was only then that I realized that no one could ever take his place in my life. Not even you."

*   *   *

Andrzej stared at this woman who had been his obsession for so long. He knew she couldn't possibly mean what she was saying. Angered, he lashed out, "Then why, when he asked you not to go to Wolf last night, did you ignore him? When I told you not to go, you obeyed. It would seem to me that if you truly loved him, you would show him more respect—you would obey his wishes."

She replied with glacial vehemence, "I stayed because of Christian. You had nothing to do with it." She stood and walked to the door. "And Rudolf doesn't command me. He doesn't confuse women with dogs, as you seem to. There is a mutual respect between us that allows free choice. And I've never been unworthy of his trust."

Andrzej looked at her speculatively. Things were obviously a lot more complicated than he had realized. "Perhaps he's wiser than I give him credit for."

"He's not arrogant enough to think he has all the answers, at least. If anything, his fault is that he's overly modest."

"He sounds a paragon . . ."

"Why do you always speak of him with such disdain? It's not worthy of you, Andrzej, to despise a person for his virtues."

He raised an eyebrow, his face a polite mask concealing the sinking feeling within. Andrzej had never believed she wouldn't eventually be his. Her marriage seemed so obviously a misfit. And he knew she loved him. "I can see I'm losing ground. Perhaps I had better leave."

She opened the door wordlessly. As he left, she found that for the first time since their reacquaintance she was free from any lingering trace of regret.

*　*　*

Rudolf remained in his study in his private darkness, probably thinking his presence unwelcome. Resolving to disabuse him of these thoughts should he come out, she sat up late, writing in her journal, listening to the radio, and reading. But the sedative of the night before still drugged her system, and without meaning to, she dozed off, propped up in bed with the light still burning.

She dreamed vividly as her subconscious attempted to deal with the vicious batterings her spirit had been dealt in recent hours. In a twisted nightmare she relived the events of the murderous attack upon her Christian, only this time when she bent to look, she did not see the pitifully battered body of her son. Instead, it was his father who lay there amidst the shattered glass, his hawkish features still and prominent in a chilling mask of death, the once tender and soulful eyes now staring vacantly into her own.

The subconscious scream she struggled to voice awakened her, and for a long moment she lay wildly disoriented in her lamplit bedroom. Even when she realized she had only been dreaming, Amalia could not rid herself of the horror that still gripped her. She struggled out of bed, now fully awake, and ran bare-footed through her husband's dressing room.

But his bedroom was empty, his turned-back bed untouched. Trying to stifle her growing alarm, she looked at the mantle clock. It was two A.M.

Detouring through her bedroom for a dressing gown to cover her nightdress, she crept down the stairs to the pantry and seized Max's keys. Then she went to the study and unlocked the heavy oaken door. Rudolf was there, lying fully dressed upon the couch where his son Christian had so recently lain ill. As Amalia stood, holding fast to the door handle, warm relief melted the icy fear that had gripped her. She trembled weakly and then knelt quietly next to her husband and gently loosened his collar, studying his deeply exhausted face, so vitally different from the specter of her dream. The lines in his forehead were etched heavily even in this state of complete relaxation, contrasting with the full mouth, which was vulnerable as a child's in slumber.

He said he was incapable of love, but at that moment she knew it wasn't true. He felt love, but was for some reason afraid of it. A full consciousness of the pain she had caused this tender and trusting man pierced her, and she bent her head in remorse.

Remembering their conversation of that morning, she saw again the defeat in his face as he confessed his inability to be what she wanted him to be. "St. Paul was once a Pharisee," she murmured, laying her hand gently over Rudolf's.

He stirred in his sleep, seeking comfort from the cold, unyielding leather of the couch, and she had to restrain herself from embracing and waking him. He badly needed his rest. She had deprived him of far too much as it was.

As she made her way slowly back up the dark staircase, she remembered something that caused her a shiver of recall, and the vision of Rudolf's lifeless face revisited her. Amalia had forgotten the rest of the story. St. Paul had died a martyr for his new beliefs.

Chapter Nine

It was obvious to Amalia that she would feel secure only if she took her sons to the Schloss early for their summer holiday. But, even after Christian's ordeal, the peace of the estate became stifling. The days were long and sunny and quiet. Too quiet. She began to be very lonely.

Rudolf wrote of the big ceremony at the Schoenbrun Palace during which Dolfuss had unveiled his new Austrian ideology, the foundation for the fascist Fatherland Front that Rudolf had prepared her for. He sent a newspaper clipping that recounted a portion of the chancellor's stirring speech: "Austria has a European mission. Lying at the heart of the continent, Austria is the predestined intermediary between the all-German culture, of which for centuries the Austrian people were the oldest and most distinguished bearers. . . . Austria, this small but honorable German Danubian and Alpine land in the heart of Europe, has for centuries taken a creative part in world events. . . . Vienna was for more than half a thousand years the symbolic city of the Germans, of the all-German emperor. . . . We will be true to the inheritance of our forefathers."

Amalia crumpled the paper and threw it across the room in frustration. "The fool! Does he think he's some kind of Austrian answer to Hitler? He's only going to make the man more incensed."

Her feeling of isolation grew, only partially alleviated by the obvious enjoyment her sons were taking in their country holiday. Their pale winter faces filled out and tanned with the aid of thick country cream and warm sunshine. They all rode horseback together in the afternoons and kept early hours at night out of sheer exhaustion. But Amalia was not surprised to observe that the soothing green of their new rooms had not the slightest effect upon her sons' temperamant. They were as unrestrained as ever.

June brought the news of Dolfuss's trip to London, as unproductive as she and Rudolf had feared. Increasingly bored and impatient, Amalia found little to keep her interested on the estate but remained there because of the hideous fear that had been born among the glass in the little Jewish bakery.

Eventually, however, her boredom overrode even that memory. A letter from Rudolf kept her from the precipitate return to Vienna she had been beginning to contemplate.

Amalia,

How glad I am that you are safe in the country. The growing violence is being fanned into a blaze by Nazi propaganda broadcasts from Munich, as well as by a flood of leaflets. They actually asked for two seats in the government! Of course we refused them.

Mussolini keeps up the pressure for us to root out the "Marxists"—saying that as soon as we do, he will be willing to discuss guarantees. I'm afraid he's not the man to stand up to Hitler. I'm beginning to wonder whether anyone is. He seems to have Western Europeans hypnotized.

With all this talk and worry about politics, I fear I haven't taken the time to tell you how very dear you are to me. I know you think I haven't any respect for your opinions. But you're wrong. I respect them far more than you realize. Perhaps it's just that I'm not the policymaker you think I am. Since parliament's been dissolved, my position is really only an unofficial one, and Dolfuss no longer wishes to be advised, only supported. Were I to decline that support, I would be out. I still cling to the hope that this is the best place to be should a crisis come. Perhaps I may be able to do some good, to have some influence.

But there I go, digressing again into politics. What I really meant to do was to tell you that the only reason any of this has meaning for me at all is because I want my family to be safe, to live in an independent Austria. You and the boys are my life, not politics. This becomes increasingly evident the longer you are away. I never realized the city could seem so hopelessly empty. Ever since I first saw you at your uncle's you have filled it for me. Even during the war, when you were in Germany and I was at the Front, I still could not think of Vienna without thinking of you. You and you alone are my home, Amalia.

I am not a great romantic hero, like Zaleski will always be, but you are my world.

> Your devoted
> Rudolf

So she had been right. He did care for her. Warmth spread through her, even into that empty place she had so longed to fill. Amalia walked out to the lake where the boys were having a regatta with boats they had been busy assembling for the past week. The missive was the closest her husband had ever come to saying he loved her. She had indeed seen the truth that night in his study. But would she ever understand him? Seeing their sons squat by the edge of the lake, their hair ruffled by a gentle breeze, and hearing their boisterous shouts, she felt her eyes sting with sudden emotion. She touched the letter in the pocket of her dress. No, Rudolf was not a great romantic hero, but he was *her* hero. It was only for her sake he was fighting this battle that could some day cost him his life. Would he do that if he didn't love her?

Lest the boys should see her and have their tranquillity disturbed by the sudden strength of her emotions, she turned her steps toward the stable, where she spent an industrious hour currying Elisabeth, who did not seem to mind her irrational tears.

By the end of August, she could bear no more. She was uneasy about Rudolf and his moods, determined, finally, to get to the bottom of the problem. The boys had begun, after an entire summer at the Schloss, to complain of missing their father and their friends. Amalia thought if she had to endure another night's solitude she would go mad. They would just have to be very careful. School was about to resume. If it seemed they were in any danger, they could certainly return, but meanwhile Amalia badly needed to reacquaint herself with both civilization and her husband.

It surprised her how deeply she had missed him. He had been a presence in her life for so long that she had taken for granted his strength and goodness. She just wanted to place her head against his chest and be cherished. His letter stayed under her pillow.

When she finally decided to go, she was in such a hurry that she did not bother to telegraph for the car to be sent. Instead, she and the boys took the train. They arrived in Vienna at dusk, totally unanticipated by the baron. Amalia had half-expected the train station to be taken over by a mob of stone-throwing Nazis, but she found things to be quite peaceful. After hiring a cab, they proceeded to the Shoenenburg palais. Other than the streets were being patrolled by soldiers in the uniform of the Heimwehr, all seemed quiet. Nevertheless, she was considerably relieved when they reached their destination, paid the cab driver and were finally admitted by an imperturbable Max.

"Welcome home, Baroness," he said with his customary frozen dignity.

"Is the baron at the chancellery?"

"No, Baroness, he is in his library."

Amalia and the boys flew to the door of the old oaken paneled room. When they threw it open without so much as a knock, Rudolf looked up sharply, and for a split second Amalia saw a flash of fear exposed in his eyes. As the boys flung themselves at him, he managed a breathless laugh. "Good heavens, I couldn't imagine who was so anxious to see me! Why didn't you tell me you were coming?"

Amalia stood watching her husband with their sons and pondered that fleeting look of fear. Had she merely imagined it, or with all the racket they had made, had he thought they might be the Nazis? She apologized, "It was silly of us, but we so wanted to surprise you."

She did not acknowledge the other reason she had wished to arrive unannounced—she had been afraid he would tell them not to come.

Rudi was speaking. "Father, it wasn't nearly as much fun without you. Mother was hideously bored, weren't you?" He turned to his mother for corroboration, but Christian had already claimed his father's attention with a tale of yet another garden snake.

"Boys, I'm happy to see you, but I desperately need to kiss your mother," Rudolf said, pushing them off his lap. They tittered at this and then clambered away, anxious to see all their familiar possessions that awaited them in the playroom.

Rudolf approached his wife, and after holding her face between his hands for a moment, kissed her soundly. She laid her head on his broad chest and sighed contentedly. "If not hideously bored, I was at least hideously lonely," she whispered.

"You couldn't have been worse off than I was," her husband countered. "I've taken to sleeping with your pillow—it has just a trace of your scent clinging to it."

Amalia laughed. "Safety is very boring, after all. I'd much rather be here with you and face things."

Rudolf's face settled back into lines of concern. "You'd be much better off at the Schloss."

"That's why I didn't tell you we were coming!" she said teasingly and led him up the stairs.

After her self-imposed exile, Amalia was hungry for all the current news. She went to visit Hilde.

"Dolfuss is a pompous little dictator. He doesn't have Hitler's sense of theater, so his pageantry is ridiculous! How your husband can remain in the government, I can't understand."

"He's trying to be a moderating influence. But if it's any comfort to you, he hates every minute of it."

"Everyone will be at Horstmanns' tonight," Hilde said.

Rudolf had told her he would be dining with Dolfuss and an emissary from Mussolini, so she felt free to go out. Anticipating her plans, Rudolf had taken a cab and left her the car and the chauffeur, a new man of suspiciously bulky build.

Once she had seen the boys settled in bed, Amalia dressed swiftly in her electric blue summer frock with the tiny black dots. Kristina watched her mistress as she critically examined the arch of her eyebrow and gently tweezed an errant hair. She said nothing, but Amalia felt her disapproval. Finishing her toilette swiftly, she said, "Don't wait up, Kristina. These evenings always run on."

"I promised the baron I'd wait up if he isn't home yet. It's your safety he's worried about."

Amalia flushed in annoyance at Kristina's tone. "All right, it's up to you. But I assure you I'm planning a perfectly virtuous evening."

"Then why, with all your careful primping, have you not noticed you're missing an earring?" the little woman asked sourly, fishing in her mistress's jewelry case.

Thoroughly exasperated, Amalia took the earring her maid held out to her. Fastening it as she walked, she hurried out of the room.

A short time later, her ever-charming host greeted her with obvious delight, "Amalia! We were just talking about you. Zaleski was saying he was sure you were still in the country."

"I missed the city dreadfully, and all of you." She allowed her eyes to travel the room but not to rest on anyone in particular. "The country is safe but boring as prison after three and a half months."

Professor Horstmann nodded with enthusiasm, and then his eyes brightened still more as a new arrival entered behind her. Amalia moved inside the room, and soon the other guests had pressed about her. When she had received the cider she requested and was ensconced in a comfortable chair, Andrzej approached.

"You look lovelier than ever. Boredom certainly agrees with you," he said, his eyes dancing.

"Let's stick to politics, Andrzej."

He threw back his head and laughed. "Do you remember our first conversation in the coffeehouse? You were bound and determined to pin me down about the war. It was enchanting."

"I really wanted to know. I felt so ignorant. And you were very obliging." She laughed. "Now look how vain I've become—expecting to have my views eagerly solicited and then actually taken seriously!"

"You certainly do have a reputation for good sense," he admitted. "Perhaps it all started in that coffeehouse."

"Why don't you ask me my opinion of the chancellor?"

He bowed mockingly. "And pray, what is your opinion of the much maligned Dolfuss, Madame La Baroness?"

She answered seriously, determined to change the tone of the discussion. "He's lost my mandate, I'm afraid. It's obvious his paranoia can't coexist with democracy."

Andrzej nodded, his face assuming a bemused look. "Yes, paranoia does seem to be the order of the day, doesn't it? Apparently it's contagious. Madman A has irrational fears that lead him to extremist actions, which in turn cause fear in his perfectly rational neighbor. The neighbor must respond either by ignoring the threat and risk being deemed a dangerous fool by posterity or by becoming an extremist himself."

"So you think that because of one madman, all of Europe will be driven to extremes?"

"I submit that there are at least two, if not three, madmen. Hitler, Stalin, and perhaps Mussolini. In the face of such a triple threat, a strong dictatorship appears very attractive, I admit. Democracy may have failed to provide a feeling of real security, but I'm afraid I can't see fascism as a responsible alternative."

"The Americans seem secure."

"America was created out of whole cloth, however, and modern Europe out of imperial remnants."

She mused, "Perhaps what we need is forty years in the wilderness to drum out all the glory that was Egypt."

"Or another war," Andrzej suggested.

She glanced up at him sharply. "I pray not."

His look turned suddenly mischievous, and he took her hand. She pulled it back and responded, "Andrzej, please, let's not lower ourselves to the level of a drawing room flirtation. You know my feelings."

The sparkle went out of his eyes, and he became serious.

"You must know Rudolf is in danger, should the Nazis ever gain power. I want you to know that I'm ready to take care of you and the boys. I'll see you safely to Switzerland if I must."

Amalia stared, frightened by his grim vision of the future. Sadly gathering her dignity around her, she moved away to bid adieu to her host and hostess. Then, as quickly as she could, she left.

Chapter Ten

The chauffeur escorted her safely to the door and let her in. Max emerged from his pantry, and she questioned him anxiously, "Is my husband back yet?"

"No, Baroness," he replied inscrutably. "And he hasn't telephoned."

Sagging with disappointment, Amalia climbed up the stairs, feeling a miserable emptiness in the large, lonely house. She needed Rudolf badly.

Going to the boys' bedroom, she cracked open the door and stole in to look at her sleeping sons. Kneeling by Rudi's bed, she put her head down next to his and calmed herself by listening to his slow, steady breathing. She stroked the crisp, chestnut hair that was moist with the effort of dreaming. He stirred, and she kissed his forehead lightly and left before she should awaken him.

Falling at last into an uneasy sleep, Amalia did not wake until late the next morning. She went immediately to her husband's room but found that he was already up and gone. Returning to her own room, she rang for Kristina.

"Has the baron left already?" she asked when her maid appeared.

"He's just gone but asked me to tell you he'd be in to lunch."

"And the boys?"

"They've gone on some expedition with the footman."

Amalia nodded. She asked Kristina to draw her bath.

When the water had been turned off, she lay in the tub with no desire to begin her day. Through the bathroom window she heard a marching band of Black Shirts—Austrian Nazis. Were they aware that this was Rudolf's house? Was her husband's life, even now, in danger? She stood in the tub as panic suddenly seized her. When she heard him arrive home at noon, she flew to greet him, dressed in a filmy afternoon dress of ivory organdy. In a moment of whimsy, she had even tucked a late coral rose into her belt. She twined her arms around his neck and kissed him with unwonted fervor.

Surprised, he looked at her with a question in his worried brown eyes. "Have I forgotten our anniversary or something?"

Amalia squeezed his arm. "No, I'm just glad to see you." She put her arm through his, and they walked to the dining room. "I missed you last night."

A frown deepened between his eyes. "Sorry." Then he put on a fresh smile. "And how did everything go at the Horstmanns'?"

"Fine," she said lightly. "I didn't stay long."

They dined companionably on a luncheon of soup, fish, a cold vegetable plate, and gooseberry tart. Over the tart, Amalia said, "Rudolf, do you think you're in danger? I mean right now?"

He laughed grimly. "Not with the Heimwehr breathing down my neck. No one would dare touch me."

Amalia breathed a small sigh of relief. Of course. The Heimwehr would make sure nothing happened to members of the government. "Do you mean you have a bodyguard?"

"Yes, in a manner of speaking. My chauffeur. He's one of Starhemberg's."

Amalia had not realized that Rudolf had his own chauffeur. Klaus must be solely for her, then.

Somewhat reassured, she went back to her other concern, the one she had come home to tackle. His melancholia. "We need to talk, Rudolf. When would be a good time?"

"Won't right now do?"

"I'd rather we were somewhere more private. Could we take a drive? We haven't been to Grinsig this summer."

He looked apologetic. "That's an excellent idea. I wish I could. Unfortunately, Dolfuss has asked me to take care of the final security arrangements for his speech in the Trabremplatz on the eleventh. He's planning a ride around the Ringstrasse on horseback in full uniform." Rudolf sighed. "Accompanied by a military band, no less."

Amalia frowned in annoyance. "He only makes himself ridiculous with all these nationalistic spectaculars. He must realize he can't compete with Hitler when it comes to showmanship. Why doesn't he put his effort into something besides all this phony patriotic drivel?"

"How about this evening? I should be free then. We can drive all the way to Semmering and dine at the Pan Walter if you like."

"That would be lovely, if you can manage it."

As it happened, however, Rudolf was held up in an emergency cabinet meeting, and Amalia dined alone with the boys. She retired early and though she meant to stay awake, she drifted off before her husband returned.

The following day, he was up and gone before she rose. All morning Amalia planned her approach to the problem of Rudolf's moods. Then he telephoned and left a message that he wouldn't be in for luncheon. *At this rate, we'll have to take up letter writing.* She wondered if she could ever get beyond his shell to the place where she knew he loved her. If she could, their marriage would be whole.

Pondering increasingly upon his periods of darkness, she wondered again if they were caused by some deep-seated fear that he perhaps shared with his brother.

Then she had an idea. Surely, Rudolf would have sought answers himself. Going to his library, Amalia perused the books on his shelf. As she suspected, there was an entire section devoted to melancholia. Selecting a stack, she sat down to read. Maybe she could learn enough to coax him somehow to share the reality of those dark places he retreated to. She determined to try.

She was glad when Max announced at eleven o'clock that she had a visitor, Rosa Klein. Perhaps Rosa knew something about melancholia.

"Oh, Rosa, you can't imagine how glad I am to see you," she told the little woman with the concerned face. "You must have been inspired to call."

"I just today heard from Zaleski what happened to Chris in the spring," the other woman said. "I can't believe Rudolf didn't retaliate somehow."

"No, he felt any action might trigger a civil war and that Hitler would step in to halt it. Things are rather tense. Tell me, how are things going for you?"

She led her guest to the divan.

Rosa sighed. "I may lose my job at the hospital, Amalia."

"No! Because you're Jewish?"

"Patients are refusing to allow me to treat them," she said, pulling out a cigarette and lighting it with a shaking hand. "It's been the same for centuries, Amalia. The Jews are the scapegoats. Everything that is wrong in Austria is blamed on us."

"Oh, Rosa. Surely you ought to be thinking of your safety. Aren't you afraid to walk the streets alone?"

The woman scoffed and tossed back her curls. "Just let them touch me!" she said. "I know jujitsu. They'll be laid out on the pavement."

Amalia pondered this. "I've been thinking that we need to be considering such things, as well."

"I would, if I were you. The Dolfuss government isn't popular with the right or the left. I'm worried for your husband."

"There are more worries, as well, which is why I'm more than usually glad to see you. Look, Rosa, I've never told anyone this before, but Rudolf has these black periods. His brother was a suicide. Is there any chance these things run in families?"

"As a matter of fact, there is. The University Hospital is one of the foremost in the world in the study of melancholia. They have done studies tracing it back generations."

"I think sometimes I'm the only thing that stands between Rudolf and suicide. He spends days alone in the dark in his study with the door locked. When he comes out it looks like he's been to hell and back. And now, things are especially grim." She paused. "Oh, Rosa, I've been so blind about my feelings for him. Ours was supposed to be a marriage of convenience, but now, even though Andrzej is back, I am determined not to leave Rudolf."

"I thought Zaleski deserted you," Rosa said with a frown.

Amalia related the story of Wolf, Lilli, and the letters. "At first Rudolf was pushing me to leave him. You see, he's never told me he loved me. But I've been discovering things I didn't know were there. Now, I think that in spite of himself Rudolf does love me. He's always been so good to me. And now his life is in danger because I wanted him to go into politics."

"He's always known you loved Zaleski."

"Yes, and I think that's one of the things that brings on the blackness. It would be like murder for me to leave him to his despair. Besides, I don't know if anyone could really take his place in my life. Andrezj is passionate and exciting, but I'm no longer a girl."

The little nurse stood. "Well, you're far more noble than I would ever be. Poor Zaleski."

"We've loved each other since I was nineteen. That's twenty years, Rosa. But the feelings I have for Rudolf are woven into the woman I've become."

"Does Rudolf know that?"

"I don't think he'd believe me if I told him. But, Rosa! Is there anything I can do about these black spells?"

"There might be triggers. Try to get him to tell you what they are. Freud says everything comes back to your relationship with your mother, but who knows? Do you know anything about his mother?"

"Nothing. I'll try talking to him, if I can ever get him to stay home long enough."

"I imagine you've been fighting frightfully deep in your soul," Rosa said solemnly.

"I didn't think communists believed in souls."

"Jews do. Which brings me back to what I came for. You and Rudolf need an escape plan. I just wanted you to know that my friends and I have one all arranged if the worst happens." She handed Amalia a scrap of paper. "Keep this somewhere safe. It's the name and telephone number of a man who can get you to Switzerland."

Amalia surprised her friend by putting her arms around her. "Thank you so much, Rosa. I've always known what I must do, really, but it seems Rudolf and I have been at daggers drawn over so many issues lately that it's been hard for me to be who I need to be." She paused, letting Rosa go. "You know, my uncle once told me you could only really love once in your life. But there are different kinds of love, I think. Grand passions are one, and domestic felicity is another."

Rosa stepped back and looked into the face of her friend. "So the great writers and musicians have been telling us for centuries. But I wouldn't be in your shoes for the world."

Amalia's heart felt much lighter until that evening when Rudolf delivered unwelcome news.

"Well, my dear," said Rudolf. "It looks like you may be lonely for a while. I'm off to Italy tomorrow."

"Oh, no!" she said. "Must you go, Rudolf? There's so much we need to discuss."

He smiled sadly but didn't come nearer. "Shall you really mind?"

She put down her embroidery and approached him. "I'll miss you terribly. How long will you be gone?"

"I don't know. A couple of weeks, perhaps a month. Negotiations. Nothing you would approve of, I'm afraid."

He looked down into her eyes, his own a careful blank. "Why does a Polish patriot come to Vienna to practice medicine?"

The tenderness swelling within her subsided into flatness. "You think I know the answer?"

"I think you *are* the answer, no matter what either of you says," he replied. Leaving her there, he went upstairs to pack, undoubtedly believing she would take advantage of his absence to see her former fiancé.

Chapter Eleven

I t was snowing for the fourth day in a row. Amalia paced restlessly in her sons' playroom, glancing briefly out the window now and again only to see a mounting pile of white. The room was dim and dreary without its inhabitants. Overcome with loneliness and uneasiness, she had been drawn there while she waited this mid-afternoon in January.

Where was Rudolf? Dolfuss's threatened protest against Hitler to the League of Nations had been read over the radio at noon. It was a bold move, and she knew well that her husband was in large measure responsible. At first when she heard the strong denunciation of Nazi agitation, she had been exhilarated that her government was standing up to Hitler. Now with her husband's failure to appear at luncheon, she had begun to grow worried. There were the ugly realities of what happened to Germans who stood up to Hitler. Would Austrian Nazis take things into their own hands?

Since his return from Italy, Rudolf had increased his efforts to safeguard his country. The distance grew between husband and wife, as he worked day and night. She had never had the opportunity even to touch on his melancholia. But today he had promised to be home at noon so that they could listen to the broadcast together.

The boys arrived. "Mutti, look! I bought three slices of Dobostorte, and I'm going to eat them all by myself." Christian sent his brother a triumphant look.

Rudi, assuming a mask of boredom, declared, "I hate those things. Nothing but chocolate!" But then boredom fled, and he was suddenly an eager child again. "Can we go to the Kino Saturday, Mother? There's a matinee—a pirate picture. Heinrich saw it last week—he said it was tremendously exciting!"

Amalia looked fondly at her sons and wiped a smear of chocolate off the younger one's cheek. "We'll see. Perhaps your father has something planned already."

Rudi grimaced. "I doubt it. He'll probably be conspiring again. It would save a lot of time, don't you think, if someone would just assassinate Hitler?"

Grinning wryly, his mother answered, "I'm sure it's been tried already, Son."

After the boys were in bed for the night, Amalia awaited her husband. She sat by the radio in the drawing room, nervously trying to concentrate on a word puzzle. When Rudolf arrived at last, she jumped up, anxiously searching his expression. She read only exhaustion.

As usual these days, he greeted her with an apology. "Forgive me, my dear, it's been a dreadful day! Suvich arrived, and he's kept us in conference until now. I only just escaped dinner. Dolfuss took pity on me and let me leave through the back door."

"Suvich is something in Mussolini's cabinet, isn't he?" Amalia asked as her husband kissed her absently on the cheek.

"Foreign Undersecretary."

"After you again about the Social Democrats, I suppose?"

"Right. He's rather pushing this time. Any chance of something to eat?"

They moved into the dining room, where Amalia saw that he was served with a full meal, kept back in case he should arrive unfed. As he sipped his soup, she asked, "What else can you do to the poor creatures, outside of imprisoning them all? You've banned their army, their newspaper, seized their weapons . . ."

"As you once prophesied, we've only made them desperate. They still publish, and they still have an army. They're just underground."

Amalia studied her husband's face. He had aged rapidly over the last few months. The grooves in his forehead were permanent now, even when his face was in repose. The cheekbones were more sharply defined, and his high-bridged nose seemed to peak more austerely. Seldom did he look at her directly, and Amalia no longer felt the warmth in his gentle brown eyes. They were tired, worried, and restless.

"Rudolf, let's go away," she said quietly. "Let's leave all of this and bury ourselves in the country. Matters have gone too far. I'm frightened for you."

He did not even look up. "If I'd left the government last year, we'd be living under Hitler by now, Amalia."

"Rudolf!"

"It's true. Two weeks ago, Dolfuss was on the verge of negotiating with one of Hitler's henchmen."

She stared at him. "I can't believe it."

"It's true," he repeated wearily.

Thin perspiration broke out on her brow, and Amalia felt the blood leave her face.

After a moment of silence, Rudolf looked up at his wife. "My dear!" He stood abruptly and came around to her side of the table, where he pulled her gently to her feet.

"I hadn't any idea things were so desperate," she murmured.

He had his arm around her waist and was moving her gently towards the door. "Don't let it make you ill. The danger's passed, for the time being . . ."

"For the time being," she said drearily. "But if he came that close once, it's only a matter of time before he'll give way. He's not really committed, Rudolf, he couldn't be." She stopped and looked up at him, color returning all at once to her face, "Thank God for you, Rudolf!"

He brought her protectively to his chest, and she clung like a child. "Thank God," she repeated.

The days that followed were confusing ones. Her husband was gone more than ever, and when he returned he was tense and withdrawn. She knew something was brewing regarding a final suppression of the Social

Democrats, and though months before she would have been vocal in her opposition to such action, she was now resigned. The Western democratic powers had washed their hands of them and their "fascist" ways, leaving them to the dubious protection of Mussolini, who, Rudolf claimed, had warned Britain and France not to intervene in Austria's affairs. Amalia felt like a blind woman waiting for a blow to fall from some unknown direction, from some unseen hand. Eating was impossible, as was sleep. She rarely left the house for fear that trouble would erupt and Rudolf would need to reach her.

That was why when Hilde telephoned one Saturday in early February, Amalia persuaded her to come for luncheon at her home, rather than at Demels, as her friend suggested.

"Of course, darling," Hilde replied, "although I rang you particularly to get you out of the palais. You didn't look at all well the other night at the Gruenwald reception, Amalia. Much too thin and deathly pale."

Hilde arrived at noon, laden with gray fox furs and bearing a sheaf of hot house white gladioli. "From Andrzej, actually," she said casually, after Max had disappeared to find a vase. "But as far as anyone in this house is concerned, they're from Herbert and me. Here's the card."

"I don't want it," Amalia replied shortly. "But I suppose I'll have to keep the flowers. Max would certainly think it strange if I sent them home with you."

They walked to the sitting room to await the luncheon bell. "Working hard at being virtuous?" Hilde inquired as she lit one of her small cigars.

"I don't know why I put up with you, Hilde," Amalia parried. "I hate your blasted cigars, and your tongue is worse."

Her guest laughed her girlish laugh, as Amalia had known she would. "But I'm so stimulating, darling."

"How is Andrzej?" Amalia finally asked, grudgingly.

"Better, I suppose, now that his wretched divorce is final. Poor as a churchmouse for the time being, however, and about as much fun. He works day and night and looks about as gray in the face as you do. Are your ailments related?"

"Not unless his is due to the political situation."

"Ah, politics, always your first love."

Amalia shrugged. "It hasn't always been that way, as a matter of fact. But Rudolf is so completely tied up with the situation that it puts all my concerns in one basket. If he fails, he will undoubtedly be imprisoned or shot out of hand, Hilde. Do you realize that?"

"By Hitler, you mean?"

"Yes." Amalia stood, no longer able to sit still. She began to strip leaves from her indoor lemon tree that lived on the window seat.

"The tension's unbearable," she continued. "I never realized how much I've taken him for granted, Hilde." Amalia suddenly stopped her destruction of the hapless plant and turned to face her guest, brow earnest, and hands doubled. "I don't know what I'd do without him. I'd be lost. Completely lost."

Her guest considered her, head cocked to one side. "Are you telling me that you love your husband, Amalia?" she asked. "How novel!"

Amalia stamped her foot. "Yes! But no one will believe me. Least of all, Rudolf! We don't discuss such things. But what if he were to die, still not knowing?"

Hilde sat up straight. "You're really worried, aren't you? I've never seen you like this."

The bell rang for luncheon then, and so they went to dine, of necessity limiting their talk to general things while the servants waited table. But as she was leaving, Hilde turned to Amalia in the hall and said impulsively, "Can't you just *tell* him, darling? I don't understand the difficulty."

Amalia bowed her head. "It goes back too far and is too entirely complicated to unravel, Hilde. And he's so desperately tired."

Her friend kissed her on both cheeks, a thing she never did. Amalia did not return to the sitting room that day, and it was never used or even entered by the maids on Sundays. Therefore, it was with an acute stab of horror that she saw Andrzej's little envelope there Monday morning, carelessly opened and discarded on the floor. Remembering that Rudolf had entertained a visitor in that room Saturday evening while she read to the boys, she hastily picked up the note. The envelope bore no one's name, which explained why Rudolf might have opened it. Nor had it been sealed, it seemed, as the flap was not even gummed. Rudolf had probably seen it lying where Hilde had dropped it and, interested in the sender of the flowers (which were clearly visible on the mantle), had opened it.

She drew out the note with agitated fingers.

My dearest love, these brave and beautiful flowers begged to be sent, they are so very like you. I found I couldn't resist the impulse. I will love you always. A.

Collapsing on the divan, Amalia crumpled the offending note in her hand. The worst of it was that among all his other cares, Rudolf had taken this blow silently and privately, not even bothering to ask her about it. He had spent all night in his study and hadn't even emerged Sunday. She had assumed he had left for the chancellery, but what if he was still in there?

Going to the study door, she tried the knob. It was locked. Finding Max in his pantry, she asked for his keys. She didn't know how she was going to go about this, but she had to try.

Taking a deep breath, she unlocked the door. Rudolf was sprawled across the top of the desk. He appeared to be asleep. In his hand was a revolver. Amalia stifled a scream. Then, taking several deep breaths, she removed it from his limp hand. He was breathing. There appeared to be no gunshot wound.

Closing the door, she held the revolver in her hands, unsure what to do with it. When she had regained a measure of control, she realized she must confront him with it. She put a hand on his arm and whispered gently into his ear, "Rudolf, wake up, darling. It's Monday morning."

Her husband jerked awake, his eyes wild and bloodshot. For the first time she saw the schnapps decanter and became aware of its odor. Rudolf never drank to excess!

Cradling the revolver in her lap, she sat on the couch, her hands perspiring and her mouth dry. "Is this what you do when you lock yourself in here? Drink yourself insensible and resolve to shoot yourself? Why, in heaven's name?"

He focused on her face, and she was startled to see something resembling Eberhard's drunken countenance. Hate?

"I'm the type of man who should never have allowed himself to fall in love," he said, making certain every word was distinct.

"Are you in love with me, then, Rudolf?"

"For years. Ever since the first day in the orphanage. So determined, so *good*. Light around you."

"But, Rudolf, why didn't you tell me? Why haven't you *ever* told me? What's the gun for?"

He shook his head to clear it. "May I have some water?"

Amalia left him briefly to get it herself, not wanting Max to see him in this state.

"It's the darkness, Amalia," he answered after he had emptied the tumbler. "The pain of living with things that are too sharp, too bloody, too awful ever to share with a woman like you. I thought that if I didn't bind you to me too tightly, perhaps I wouldn't feel betrayed when you eventually left with Zaleski. I knew you could never love me . . . But your light. I couldn't live without your light."

Amalia's soul bled, and she wept. "Dearest, dearest Rudolf, what a horrible world you are locked inside! I have loved you. I do love you. But so many times you practically shrink from my touch. You act as though you *want* me to go with Andrzej! He hasn't a tenth of your nobility, believe me."

"But you love him. You always have."

"In the way one always loves one's first love. But my love for you is seasoned, tried, and tested. We have sons together. If you had ended your life, it would have been the end of me. Besides Uncle, you are the kindest, gentlest man I know. I want *all of you*, Rudolf. I don't want half a marriage. I want to fight this blackness with you."

Rudolf went to the wooden cabinet that housed his small wash-basin. Putting his head under the faucet, he wet his hair and face, straightened, and then shook his head like a dog, sending drops flying through the study.

"You don't want to go there, Amalia, believe me."

"Do you know what triggers it, at least?"

"It's in my blood. Morbid, bloody jealousy. It's actually quite surprising my line has survived at all with all the havoc it has brought. I only hope our boys escape it."

Getting up, Amalia walked to her husband and embraced him wholeheartedly. "I'm so sorry for all this beastliness with Andrzej. I'm not going to leave with him. I promise you that. I haven't spoken to him in months. I was surprised by the gladioli. He's just quixotic that way. I'm not having, nor have I ever had, an affair with him. There."

* * *

He *must* believe her. He knew Amalia couldn't lie. Had it been his good fortune to fall in love with the most honest, forebearing woman in Vienna? His eyes grew wet, and he leaned down to kiss her with his whole heart.

"Take the revolver, Amalia. Hide it somewhere and then toss it in the lake at the Schloss. It has a long and bloody history."

Chapter Twelve

A malia's days assumed a much belated honeymoon quality they had never had. She could scarcely bear to be separated from her husband. Some days after their reconciliation, she was unable to restrain herself from doing something she had rarely done before: She called the chancellery. No one answered at the switchboard. That was odd. She tried again five minutes later. Still no one answered. After attempting to get through repeatedly for half an hour, she became alarmed. She left the pantry and went into the drawing room, where she turned on the radio.

She sat, waiting for it to warm up with her mind in a turmoil, trying to tell herself she was an alarmist. After several minutes, she checked the instrument impatiently. There was no dull red glow behind the backboard. It was not on. She checked the knob again. It was still turned to the "on" position. She checked the connection. The cord was plugged securely into the socket.

Curious, she gave the radio a sharp slap. When it still did not respond, she tried the lamp. It did not light. As understanding dawned, she walked briskly to find Max.

But she could not find him. Exasperated now, she inquired of the cook, "Have you seen Max? The electricity's gone off."

The plump woman grumbled, "He went at noon. Took his hat and coat. I asked where he thought he was going right before luncheon on Monday afternoon, but he just told me I'd know soon enough."

Exasperation turning to puzzlement, Amalia went again to the pantry to telephone the electricity company. No one answered that switchboard, either. After half a dozen tries, she finally deduced that the problem must be widespread. She gave up temporarily and went to eat her luncheon.

After lunch she still could not get through to the electricity company, and so she tried the chancellery again. Still no one answered.

As the afternoon wore on, her feeling of uneasiness grew into something more alarming. Then her boys ran in the door.

"Have you heard, Mutti?" Rudi called.

She met him in the hall. "Heard what?"

"Strike," he said succinctly. "The Social Democrats have called a general strike. For once I was glad to have a chauffeur pick me up. The fellows who take the tram will have a long walk home."

"The trams aren't running?"

"No, the electricity workers were the first ones to strike. They said at school they struck around noon. I guess it was the signal for all the other workers to strike."

Amalia's eyes widened, and she gripped her son's shoulders. "Max!" she breathed, horrified.

Rudi was clearly startled. "What?"

But Amalia went into the nearest room to find a chair. Her legs were like noodles. Rudi followed.

"What about Max?" he demanded.

"He must be a socialist, Rudi. He walked off at noon, no explanation."

Rudi whistled. "A spy, probably. Just think."

Amalia had begun to shake. She rubbed her arms. "I'd rather not."

He said with sudden cheerfulness, "Better a Social Democrat than a Nazi, Mutti."

She shook her head vaguely. "He probably listened at doors, Rudi. It makes me feel . . ." she stopped, aware that she could not speak her uncensored thoughts to a twelve-year-old boy. She had meant to say *naked*, or perhaps even *violated*.

"Sick," he finished for her. "But don't worry, Mutti. You've always stood up bravely for the Social Democrats. I've heard you, clear in the playroom, as a matter of fact. Max'll put in a good word for you."

"It's not myself I'm worried about," she said before she could stop herself.

Rudi's face hardened then, and he looked older than his twelve years. "They won't do anything to Father." He sat on the arm of her chair and took her hand. Obscurely comforted, she smiled at him.

Soon Amalia heard the first explosion. It was immediately followed by what seemed to be a small earthquake.

Rudi ran out into the street before his shocked and stupefied mother could restrain him. With part of her mind she heard Christian clattering down the stairs from the playroom, but she remained frozen in her chair, eyes staring in terror. Was it the Nazis? Could they be using the strike as an excuse for a coup?

And then suddenly she too was on her feet, running out to join the boys on the front walk. Another violent explosion sent a sharp pain through her ears. Intending to herd the children back into the comparative safety of the house, she stood transfixed by the black smoke coming from the direction of the Karl-Marx Hof, the great blocks of workers' flats that had been erected by the Vienna city government. In a moment there was another explosion. The home army was shelling the Socialists!

Her initial relief was almost immediately replaced by disgust. "Let's go in, boys. We shouldn't be standing about. It's not the Nazis. It's our own Heimwehr."

Her sons went reluctantly indoors. "What are they doing, Mutti?" Christian asked, thrilled with the unusual excitement.

"Trying to end the strike."

Rudi observed her quietly. "You don't think much of this, do you, Mutti?"

"The Heimwehr are nearly as bad as the Nazis," she said shortly and went into the drawing room to wait for the restoration of electricity to bring her radio to life. Her sudden alarm had been followed by an overwhelming sickness of spirit.

But the radio remained dead, and by dinner Amalia's anxiety had grown to debilitating proportions, for Rudolf had neither returned nor sent word. Neither had Max. It was an unnerving, terrifying feeling to reside a few kilometers from what amounted to a civil war and to have no idea what was happening. Were the Social Democrats able to fight back? Was this more than a one-sided slaughter? The boys were watching the smoke from the third-floor windows of the playroom, and she passed the time by pacing in the vast drawing room that was lit with old oil lamps unearthed that afternoon in the garret.

At seven o'clock she heard the knocker and remembered after a moment that there was no Max. Both curious and alarmed, she answered the door. Feeling completely disoriented, she found it was Andrzej who stood on the stoop.

"I'm just on my way back to the hospital," he began hesitantly. "I thought perhaps you were all alone here and might be frightened . . ."

"Come in."

They went to the drawing room to sit by the dead radio whose knob was still waiting in the "on" position.

"What can you tell me?" Amalia asked, anxiety making her voice taut.

"Have you heard nothing from Rudolf?"

"Nothing. I've begun to worry . . . it's the Heimwehr, isn't it? Shelling in the Karl-Marx Hof?"

"Yes. And they've had more opposition than they bargained for. The Social Democrats are standing their ground. They must have had an arsenal in there."

"And the government? Have they made a statement?"

"No one knows. No radio. I bought an evening paper."

He handed it to her. "The shelling must have begun after they went to press, but there's a rundown on the strike. No statement from the government, though."

"I wonder where Rudolf is."

"I imagine there's an emergency cabinet session. Have you telephoned?"

"No answer at the switchboard. Our butler is a spy, by the way."

"Max?" he demanded, green eyes on hers.

"Yes. He walked out when the electricity failed. I suppose that was the signal he was waiting for. I've checked his room. He's definitely cleared out. He must have been planning this for days, because the cook says he took only his hat and coat when he left."

"Remarkable."

Tension ruled the ensuing silence. Amalia paced.

"Perhaps the telephone workers are on strike," Andrzej suggested at last.

She looked up sharply. "Yes. You may be right. Perhaps that's why I haven't heard from him."

"Would you like me to go to the chancellery? I could carry a message or something."

"Oh! Would you?" She halted her pacing and stood before him. "It would mean so much to me just to know he's all right!"

He looked at her suddenly animated face for a moment and then answered. "Of course."

She ran from the room to get pen and paper. In the study she scribbled a brief note:

The boys and I are fine but worried to death about you. Send word if you can. Andrzej stopped in on his way to the hospital and offered to go to the chancellery for me, as I've been sick with anxiety. The telephones are out. May God protect you, my love. Amalia.

When she finished her task, Andrzej was standing in the doorway of the study. "Bless you for doing this, Andrzej," she murmured, handing him the little note, which she had hastily folded over.

"I'll return as soon as I possibly can," he said. "Try not to worry.

The streets are jammed over by the chancellery. I can get through with my doctor's pass and an ambulance, but it may take some time." She nodded briefly, concern surfacing again in her face. Somehow she had thought the fighting was limited to the Karl-Marx Hof. But of course there would be fighting outside the chancellery. Perhaps Rudolf could not get home at all until it was over. He might be a prisoner, trapped inside the building. What were they doing to him?

Andrzej put a hand to her cheek. "Don't worry. I'll find him. I won't stop until I do. Are the boys all right?"

"Not a fear in their minds. They're loving it. It's the excitement, I suppose. Why didn't I have daughters?" she smiled feebly.

"Try not to worry, Amalia," his eyes traveled over her face, but he did not touch her again.

"Thank you, Andrzej."

He inclined his head slightly, and with an unnaturally solemn face, he left her. She listened as his feet traversed the flagstone walk.

It was impossible to envision what was taking place only a few districts away. She sat by the radio again, and resting her head on the back of the chair, she closed her eyes and tried to envision the violence. It was dark now. The shelling had ceased some time ago, but there would be sporadic gunfire, she imagined, and the foolhardiness men would call bravery. She shuddered.

The Karl-Marx Hof was built on the ground where Uncle Lorenz's flat had once been. One of the major achievements of the socialist Viennese city government had been to demolish the old, unsanitary flats and build a modern new complex for the workers. How dreadful for them to see it destroyed by mortar shells. No wonder they had fought so valiantly.

She thought then of her Uncle Lorenz, and the memories calmed her. What would he have done today? If he were alive, she thought suddenly, Rudolf never would have gone along with the government's persecution of the workers' party. Her husband knew Lorenz was not some troublemaker. But then, if Rudolf had abandoned the cabinet, perhaps

Dolfuss would have been even more extreme. That unbelievable business about negotiating with Hitler, for instance.

Suddenly brisk, she got to her feet and looked at her wristwatch. Eight-thirty. Time the boys were in bed. She had to pretend things were as normal as possible.

When at last Rudi and Christian had been settled down with their teeth brushed and their stories read, it was after nine o'clock. Andrzej still had not returned. She tried to telephone Hilde but still couldn't get through. Further evidence of problems with the telephones, she supposed. In despair, she tried the chancellery again. No luck.

Though she willed it not to, panic began to rise within her. Without radio or telephone and with the fighting in the streets, she was totally cut off from the outside world. She sat in the tiny butler's pantry, a candle at her side, and fought down the frightening surge. She kept asking herself, "What would Rudolf want me to do?" But she could not think of the answer. Her mind could only repeat the question, over and over, as she stared at the drab walls that had been Max's domain. Was it possible she might never see Rudolf again? Her hands and feet became icy with fear. She breathed deeply and tried to rid herself of her panic, but it persisted. He might never come home. She sank her head in her hands. This was all her fault. If not for her, he would never have become involved in all of this.

And then, at last, she heard the sound she had been straining to hear for hours. The knocker. Seizing the candle, she hastened to the door and threw it wide. It was not Andrzej who stood there, however, but Rudolf.

"I didn't want to startle you," he apologized as he entered the dark hall. "So I thought I'd better knock."

At first she could only stare at him as though he were a stranger. Then she set her candle precariously on the hall table and wrapped her arms around him fiercely, sobbing great, noisy, heaving sobs. All the fears she had pushed firmly down fled in the release of her tears, and he held her silently. Finally, he scooped her up in his arms like a fragile child, and managing the candle in one hand, he carried her up the stairs.

After settling her against the pillows of her bed, he sat beside her on the edge. "Zaleski got me out. I don't know how he managed it, but he did. He was able to rescue one or two others as well. In a hospital ambulance."

"Have many been killed?" she managed.

"It's difficult to tell. No radio, no telephone, streets jammed. Zaleski says the wounded can't even get to the hospitals."

She looked at the wretchedness in his face. "Why did they do this, Rudolf? I know it wasn't your plan, but what did they hope to gain from a civil war?"

He sighed and stood wearily, pulling off his tie and jacket as he did so. "Heaven knows. You know Starhemberg is leading the Heimwehr now. He hates the socialists, and he especially hates the Jews. He's convinced there's some sort of conspiracy between them, that they're mortally dangerous. His support is vital to Dolfuss because he's the head of the only army we have that can fight effectively against a Nazi uprising. The strike was just the spark that set the whole thing off. We were planning to arrest their leaders on Wednesday. Somehow they got wind of it."

"Max is a spy, Rudolf."

"So Zaleski told me. That must have been a frightening discovery to make."

"Maybe that's how they knew about Wednesday."

"I never discussed it here, Amalia. Don't worry. His espionage was quite unfruitful, I can assure you."

She shook off a shudder. "What will happen now?"

Shirtless, Rudolf sat beside her again. "They'll be crushed, I'm afraid. Eventually. And the country, or at least Vienna, will be in a turmoil."

She sat up and put her head against his chest. "Rudolf, I don't care about the country anymore. I don't care about anything or anyone but you. And the boys, of course. Do you know that tonight I thought I might never see you again? I felt like I was being sucked into some terrible void . . . it was all I could do to hang on to my wits. And then suddenly there you were. Safe. It was like a gift. A gift I don't deserve. I've been so foolish."

He held her and kissed her hair.

She continued, her words bitter, "My silly little dreams have been a lost cause since the beginning. You knew it, but you wouldn't discourage me. You knew I couldn't bear it, and so you kept on. But now it's dangerous, Rudolf. We're going to fail eventually. I feel it. My love, you mustn't go down with the ship."

"Don't you fail me now, Amalia," he whispered. "I'm still hoping for a miracle."

He held her to him, speechless for a time. "You're my life, Amalia," he said finally. "Everything I do, I do for you."

Chapter Thirteen

B y Friday, it was over. The army of the Social Democratic Party,
the Schutzbund, was completely routed and all its leaders
arrested, with the exception of Bauer and Deutsch, who
escaped, it was thought, to Czechoslovakia. Bitterness, as Rudolf had
accurately predicted, was deep on both sides. The government had lost
more than a hundred men at last count, but the hospitals were crowded
with nearly a thousand wounded from both sides of the conflict. The
death toll among the Schutzbund was higher, but no one knew yet the
exact number. Amalia wondered how the hospitals could possibly deal
with antagonists who were in all probability lying shoulder to shoulder.

Amalia felt a deep sorrow for the events that had turned her countrymen against one another. But her greatest sadness, shared by her husband, was that the rest of the Viennese did not seem to feel this sorrow
but only an intense hatred for their opponents. It certainly did not bode
well for internal Austrian unity, and Amalia's dream of a united, strong
and independent Austria seemed further from reality than ever.

After a statement issued from Bauer in exile, claiming that their
actions had "restored the self-respect and courage of the socialists of the
world," the furor seemed to die down a bit, and Dolfuss turned his
energies toward the forming of a new "corporative" constitution,
designed, Rudolf said, to heal old wounds and consolidate the strong
authoritarian government.

The new constitution was unveiled on the first of May to blot out
any memories of the Social Democrats. Although there were no provisions for a parliament, seven groups of business interests were to be

represented in a federal council that had power to make recommendations to the government. These recommendations were not binding, however, and the council had no power to debate government policies. There was also, of course, no provision for the trade unionists.

Rudolf continued his weary but dedicated service, and Amalia put away her immediate anxieties. She and the boys prepared for their annual retreat to the Schloss in mid-June.

Andrzej kept his distance following the harrowing events of that first night of fighting. Both Amalia and Rudolf had invited him to join them for dinner to thank him for his service to them, but he had declined firmly and politely.

One early June evening, after an unusually restful meal, Rudolf leaned back in his chair and announced, "I believe I'll come with you to the Schloss, my dear."

Rudi, who together with Chris had joined them, exclaimed, "Truly, Father? You can leave off conspiring for a bit?"

Christian showed his elation more crudely, as might be expected of a boy his age. He whooped.

Amalia grinned delightedly and felt a relaxation of the ever-present tension in her tightly held body. Maybe she could finally help her husband exorcise his demons.

"That would be wonderful, Rudolf."

"I need a holiday," her husband stated simply.

And so it was that on the fifteenth of June, the family set out together for the peaceful countryside of Upper Austria, leaving behind them a year of turmoil and tragedy but taking with them an internal feeling of peace and unity that was all the stronger for having been threatened.

They passed an idyllic month, riding, hiking, walking, enjoying the tranquillity and clean air. But in the evenings, sometimes Amalia would catch her husband staring into space, his mind clearly absent from them, his brow creased and his eyes troubled.

489

One such time, he looked up, surprised at her scrutiny. "I'm sorry, my dear. I just can't help wondering how long Austria can hold on."

"You're not in one of your black moods?"

"No, Amalia. Not with you beside me."

Fortunately, Rudi and Christian teased him into taking a climb that involved several days' hiking and camping in the Alps, and Amalia encouraged them to go, determined to give father and sons this special opportunity together. All their associations seemed laced with that peculiar sweetness of stolen time, of moments made precious by their rarity. There was also a sense of impending change, of future uncertainties.

The mail arrived the last day of her solitude, containing the dreaded thick express letter from Vienna that she knew would eventually arrive to call Rudolf away. She made a decision then.

"We're going with you," she said before her husband could do more than eye the letter with obvious foreboding.

He looked up quickly, as he slit the envelope. "The boys won't want to return so soon."

"Yes, they will, I think. They want to be with you. And so do I, Rudolf. I know you dread returning. If we all go, it won't be so bad."

Her husband sat down heavily, still attired in his Lederhosen with four days' growth of heavy chestnut beard bristling on his chin. He had looked so young, almost boyish, when he had arrived, singing, albeit a bit off key, with his two tired offspring in tow. Now the lines deepened in his forehead again, as he studied the letter from the chancellery.

This time Amalia knew there was no sense avoiding the issue. "Bad news?"

"No, at least, I hope not. It's all rather ironic, though. Would you believe it if I told you that Hitler is now agitating for free elections in Austria?"

Amalia sat stiffly. "The devil."

"You never thought you'd get him on the side of democracy, did you?"

"I suppose with no parliament, the Nazis can't have any influence at all in the government."

"That was Dolfuss's idea. The only way they can gain control now is with a direct takeover. A coup of some sort. Anschluss."

"Hitler would rather not resort to that, I suppose. It doesn't look nearly as good as if he could come to power 'legitimately.'"

"This letter says he's now pressuring Mussolini to use his influence with us. Rather humorous, actually. Mussolini was the engineer behind our present government."

"Neither of them is known for his logic. That's what is so insidious about them. You expect them to play according to the rules, but they just keep making up new rules as they go along."

"Power politics, it's called." Rudolf sighed. "I must go back in the morning. Can you be ready by then?"

Vienna was hot and sultry after the comparative cool of the country. But no one complained. Instead they wore their cheer like Sunday clothes, carefully and dutifully. There was strain beneath all their actions, communicated to them sympathetically from Rudolf.

At first it seemed Vienna was deserted. Most all of their friends had gone to the country or were busy preparing to do so. Amalia had much opportunity to bless the existence of the local cinema for the entertainment it gave her boys, who were trying so valiantly not to be restless. Amalia allowed them out of the house only with a footman in attendance, and she made sure their excursions were few and specific.

One evening, Rudolf returned home with an intriguing looking package for Rudi and Chris.

"But," Rudi stammered in surprise, "it's not one of our birthdays or anything . . ."

"It's to make up to you, at least in some measure. I know how much you wish you were at the Schloss," his father answered. "I just wanted you to know how much I appreciate having you here and your allowing your mother to be here, too. It means a lot to us, Son."

Rudi and Chris hastily unwrapped the parcel and found it to be a microscope. Rudi's eyes grew large in obvious delight, and he whistled. "Father! This is tremendous!"

Amalia looked fondly at her husband and sons. "You'll have to let Christian look through it sometimes, dear," she admonished quietly.

"Oh, we'll have a marvelous time!" her eldest cried exuberantly. "*Danke vielmals,* Father."

From that time forward, the playroom became a laboratory for botanical and biological research, and Amalia had no more concerns about bored children.

But she herself was not so easily diverted. She worried too much, she knew. She tried everything she could to cast off her gloomy thoughts, but they pressed down on her with unrelenting weight. Even her posture began to reflect her state of mind, for instead of being regal and upright, she walked with a certain hesitancy and even lassitude, as though she were not quite sure of the ground she walked on.

One evening, she sat embroidering beside the radio, listening to a Brahms symphony of which she was not particularly fond and reflecting on how ironic it was that she occupied herself so much with a task such as embroidery, which she liked so little. She was even thinking of Antonia, now the mother of four, and her very superior needlework. Rudolf was, as usual, out conferring with the cabinet over some recent rumor concerning the Austrian Nazis in Bavaria.

She heard Fritz, whom they had now promoted to butler rather than risk another spy in their household, open the door and admit someone. Without much interest she listened to the measured tread that made its way to the drawing room where she sat. When she looked up, however, she was considerably surprised to see Andrzej. He wore a hurried, urgent air, and her surprised greeting stopped in her throat.

"What is it?" she cried, rising abruptly, her embroidery clutched in her nervous fingers.

*   *   *

"Amalia, is Rudolf here?" Andrzej asked the woman who still ruled his life as the darkened moon pulled the tides.

"No, but if it's urgent I think I can reach him. Why?"

He darted an appraising look at her. Her concern was all for Rudolf. He must be crazy, trying to save the man's life again. But he remembered the horribly quenched look on her face that had spurred him to his heroic act the evening of the strike. It had surprised him that his love had evolved into something so uncharacteristic. Amalia obviously loved the taciturn Rudolf. He couldn't bear for her to suffer a loss then, and it was the same now. "Remember I told you I had a connection in the Foreign Office?"

"In Warsaw, you mean?"

"Normally, yes. Only he's here at the moment, trying to get me back to Poland, in fact. A thoroughly interfering relative, if you want to know the truth."

"Yes?" she prompted.

"He's, well, call him pro-Hitler, if you like. Anyway, he's had wind of some of my activities here, in the civil war and so forth, and he's trying to get me home before I 'find myself in serious difficulty.'"

Amalia raised her eyebrows. "He made a trip here to bring you back? He *does* sound officious! Doesn't he realize you're out of short pants?"

Andrzej frowned. "He didn't trust his news to the mails, Amalia. You see, according to his sources, Hitler is getting ready to move against Dolfuss."

Amalia sank into her chair. "A coup?"

"That's what he thinks."

"When?"

"He doesn't know, but soon. Does your husband know about the Austrian Nazis massing themselves in Bavaria?"

"A rumor has reached them, actually." She looked at his anxious face keenly. "What would your 'connection' think of your coming to us with this?"

Andrzej gave a harsh bark of would-be laughter. "Need you ask? I only got away by saying I had a 'debt of honor' to repay this evening. He's amazingly feudal, you see."

"And yet, I believe you were telling him the truth, Andrzej." Her voice was soft, her look peculiar. He couldn't read it.

"Yes, I believe I was."

They remained quiet for a moment, each studying the other sadly. Finally, Amalia said, "We owe you so much already. We can never repay you for what you did for Christian and for all of us during the fighting . . ."

He stopped her. "It's all I *can* do for you, Amalia. And it's little enough."

"I'll telephone Rudolf. He's not far. Can you wait?"

"Oh, yes. I'll wait."

*   *   *

Like Amalia, Rudolf did not show much surprise, only great sadness. He and Andrzej sat together long after Amalia left them. As she tiredly climbed the stairs, she reflected that she had never thought the day would come that those two particular men would be so engaged.

But there had been a change in Andrzej. A change that frightened her, for she had recognized the look in his eyes tonight. It was the gallant, chivalrous look of their first waltz together. Her former fiancé had shed his worldly disguise, and what remained was the man she had always known he was capable of becoming. To that man, selfless and noble, she feared she was not invulnerable.

The air was sultry and hot even before breakfast the next day. Rudolf rose tiredly from her bed where he had joined her in the early hours of the morning.

"What's today?" she asked groggily, feeling swollen and irritable, smothering in the steamy blanket of humidity.

"The twenty-fifth of July."

"What time is it, for heaven's sake?"

"Six. I phoned Dolfuss last night, and he called a seven A.M. cabinet meeting. I'm to report in full."

"Andrzej helped?"

"Whatever my feelings have been for that fellow in the last twenty years . . ."

"Oh, don't say that. You make us seem so old."

"I apologize. He may have saved Dolfuss's life."

"He did it to save yours, Rudolf."

"Fool. For years he's wanted me out of the way."

She studied the ceiling absently. "I think perhaps he's stopped thinking only of what *he* wants, Rudolf."

Her husband looked down at her speculatively. "That only makes him more dangerous, my dear." He kissed her gently. "It proves he truly loves you."

She looked at him, surprised at his perspicacity, but he was smiling gently. "There's nothing I can do about it, especially if he's determined to be my life insurance."

She looked solemn. "You need it. Be careful today, Rudolf. You know my friend Rosa has a plan to smuggle you out of the country, should you need it."

He sighed. "If I ever leave the country, I'm going with you and the boys. I'll not bolt like some scared rabbit." He ran his hand over his hair. "But it was nice of her to think of me. I'll keep you informed. I know you worry about me."

He went to his dressing room, and she tried to summon the will to rise. Presently, Rudolf stuck his head through the doorway. "Why don't you telephone Hilde?

"Hilde?"

"Yes, it would do you good to have some company."

And so it was that Amalia was sitting with Hilde in the drawing room before lunch, listening to the midday news on Vienna Radio, when an unfamiliar voice rasped, "This radio station is now under the control of the National Socialist Party of Austria. We announce that as of this morning, Herr Doktor Engelbert Dolfuss has resigned as chancellor of Austria. He will be replaced by our own Anton Rintelen, a man of exceptional ability and foresight."

Hilde was just in time to prevent Amalia from striking her head as she collapsed in a dead faint.

Chapter Fourteen

When Amalia revived, it was to see Hilde bending over her, frowning, with a cold cloth in her hand.

"You must pull yourself together, my dear. Where are the boys?"

Amalia got to her feet but then sank into a chair almost instantly. "They're at the Kino. Would you mind sending Fritz after them? I'm going to be ill, I'm afraid."

Her friend rang for the butler and dispatched him to the Kino without ceremony. Trying desperately to keep the room in focus, Amalia got to her feet again and made her way unsteadily to the washroom where she was indeed ill. Gripping the washstand, she tried to collect her wits.

"The Schloss!" she said suddenly. With this clear focus for her actions, she seemed instantly to recover her equilibrium. As she left the washroom, she encountered Hilde coming from the telephone in the butler's pantry.

"My husband says to stay here. He's going to try to find out what's happening. I think that's a good idea."

"I'm taking the boys and going to the Schloss," Amalia announced. "That's what Rudolf would expect me to do."

"You musn't panic, Amalia. You can't just dash out of here like that. It mightn't be safe. And this is where Rudolf expects you to be."

"Rudolf may be dead," Amalia said flatly. "Don't you realize that, Hilde? My husband may be dead!"

"And he may be trying to get home to you. His first thoughts would be of you and the boys."

At that moment, the boys came scrambling into the hall, all agog. It seemed so heartlessly normal to see them run to her, their eager faces alight with childish curiosity. Amalia squared her shoulders, and a calm entered her heart from somewhere.

"Rudi and Chris, we just heard over the radio that there's been a Nazi takeover. We're waiting to have it confirmed, but meanwhile, I want you to go upstairs and pack some clothes. We may have to go to the Schloss."

She had reckoned without the fact that Rudi was thirteen and no longer considered himself a child. "What about Father?" he asked calmly.

"We don't know about Father," she answered, trying to keep her voice steady.

"You think he's been taken prisoner?"

Hilde intervened briskly, "We don't even know for certain there's been a coup. Perhaps the Nazis just seized the radio station and made that announcement to start a panic. And whatever else happens, we mustn't panic." She put her hand lightly on Rudi's shoulder.

"I'm glad you're here," Rudi responded in his most grownup way. "Come along, Mother, you must show us what to pack."

Moments later, Amalia was standing in the boys' bedroom, dazed but competently supervising her children, who gave her their total cooperation. Fritz had been instructed to bring down the trunk that held their winter clothes.

When he entered with it, Andrzej followed on his heels, "Amalia!" his greeting was excited, almost gay.

She turned a blank look on him.

"Hilde sent me up," he said quickly. "There's news. Rudolf just called. He had only a moment, but he wanted you to know he was safe."

Amalia stared, eyes huge, as she tried to take in what he was telling her.

"He's not at the chancellery! He's at the defense ministry with the rest of the cabinet."

Amalia stared, incredulous. Rudi interjected anxiously, "He's safe? Father's safe?"

"Yes. The Nazis stormed the chancellery, thinking to catch the cabinet in session. But they had met earlier and were already adjourned. Only Dolfuss was there."

Sinking down on a chair, Amalia put her head in her hands. "Thank heaven."

Hilde joined them. "So the Nazis haven't seized control, then?"

"They have Dolfuss. That's all we know. Karl von Schuschnigg is heading up the remaining ministers over at the defense ministry. Rudolf couldn't go into details. Things were extremely chaotic, as you can imagine."

The group finally decided to descend to the drawing room to listen for further news. The radio may have been under Nazi control, but that news was better than nothing.

By this time, however, the Heimwehr had regained possession of the radio station and was broadcasting more optimistic news. "The Austrian Government has not, we repeat, *has not* fallen to the National Socialists. We remain in complete control. The cabinet, under the leadership of Karl von Schuschnigg, is at this moment negotiating for Chancellor Dolfuss's release from the chancellery where he is held prisoner. The chancellery is surrounded by the Heimwehr, and we have every confidence that the perpetrators of this miserable act will shortly be in custody."

Amalia sighed and sat white-faced, staring at the deceptively neutral countenance of the radio. Rudi came to sit next to her. "Mutti, it's all right. Everything is going to be all right."

Andrzej stood at the mantle, his face naked in his concern for her. "Amalia, I think you need to lie down."

But she resisted. "No, I'm fine, now. It was just the shock. I've been dreading this for so long. I had begun to think it was inevitable, that at any moment the government would fall. The thought would never leave me; it was always there. Every time I've said good-bye to Rudolf, I fought the feeling that it would be the last I'd see of him."

"Well, he's coming home to you today," Hilde said comfortingly. "I'm certain he'll be here as soon as the Heimwehr has things under control."

Andrzej took one of her hands and chafed it. "She's been so full of fear, she can't believe it, still."

"I feel such a fool. I honestly thought they had the devil's own power. I never doubted that they'd succeed," Amalia admitted.

Andrzej murmured, "It certainly seems they've failed this time."

The boys soon grew bored and asked to be permitted to go work with the microscope. Hilde's husband arrived shortly thereafter to collect his wife.

"Take care of her, Zaleski. I never thought I'd see the day when the Baroness von Schoenenburg would faint at anything," Hilde said.

After they left there was another broadcast. "We have just learned that Chancellor Dolfuss has been wounded. His captors claim that he was shot while trying to escape. They are refusing to allow him to see either a doctor or a priest. Meanwhile, negotiations continue.

"Mussolini is said to be standing by with troops at the Brenner Pass, ready in case of a German invasion."

Amalia darted a look at Andrzej. "Those Nazis in Bavaria! They were waiting for this, weren't they?"

"So your husband concluded. That is undoubtedly why the early cabinet meeting. I imagine they went from there over to the defense ministry to plan their strategy. Did you really faint, Amalia?"

She flushed. "Yes. Hilde got me on my feet, though. I am rather embarrassed at my behavior. When you came, I was setting out to flee to the Schloss."

"I'm glad your instincts for self-preservation are in working order. I don't want anything to happen to you."

She smiled at the concern in his green eyes. "How can it? You take good care that we are preserved from all manner of evil—SDP mobs, Nazi invasions . . ."

He drew closer to her, still solemn. "You give me too much credit, Amalia. My motives, as always, are purely selfish ones."

She returned his serious look. "I think not, or you wouldn't take such care of Rudolf."

"I find I can't wish harm on those whom you choose to love, Amalia."

As he looked at her, his eyes spoke of a depth of pain beyond these words, and she could no longer meet them. Staring at her knotted hands, she whispered, "Your goodness is too hard to bear, Andrzej. It would make it easier by far if you could hate me."

"I've become somewhat of a philosopher, Amalia." Andrzej strolled to the mantle, a wry grin lightening his features. "I like to think that loving you has made me into some sort of decent human being. I really wasn't good enough for you all those years ago. A better man wouldn't have let his pride stand in the way. Do you read the Greeks?"

She flashed her dimple. "Constantly."

"No, I'm serious. You see, I've become rather enamored of the idea of the tragic flaw. It explains so much."

She actually laughed. "Andrzej, I refuse to see you as a character in Euripides. You're much too complex, for one thing. No one is ruled by only one emotion or idea."

"I wouldn't be too certain, Amalia. Look at Hitler and Stalin."

"To say they are ruled takes away all concept of choice, Andrzej. People choose to be who they are."

"I see I can't convince you I'm a tragic figure, Amalia."

"No, Andrzej. No one with your finely developed sense of irony could ever be called tragic."

"I suppose not."

"Tragedies are so one-dimensional."

He cocked his head in a musing posture. "I suppose to a man or woman of faith nothing is ever wholly a tragedy."

She looked at him in surprise. "Exactly, Andrzej."

"But I still love you like the devil, Amalia," he replied bitterly.

Her dimple disappeared, and she looked down again. Mozart's Symphony No. 39 in E-flat major was interrupted by a somber announcer.

"We have just learned that Chancellor Engelbert Dolfuss lies dead in the chancellery. His assassin, one Otto Planetta, has been captured along with seven other members of the Austrian National Socialist Party. Their bid for power has failed. Nevertheless, they have stilled the life of a great hero and statesman, who gave that life for his country. We mourn him with a deep reverence, at the same time praising his government for saving and preserving the freedom in our beloved land. We have shown our neighbor to the north that we will not be intimidated into an Anschluss. We are and shall remain an independent Austrian nation, governed by Austrian leaders who are not deceived by the bullying tenets and practices of National Socialism."

"It's over," she breathed. At that moment the front door opened, and she sprang up to meet Rudolf.

They embraced tightly in the hall. Amalia almost couldn't believe he was real. Her heart flooded with gratitude. She kissed his lips, his eyes, his cheeks, his nose. "We did it!" she exulted. "We stopped them! They've failed!"

Rudolf held her more tightly and buried his face in her neck. "Yes, my dear. We captured them all."

She stood back and looked at him, pride shining in her eyes. "You saved us."

"At a price," he said wearily. "Dolfuss is dead."

"But think of him as a martyr to freedom, Rudolf. His assassination will speak to the world. They'll know what kind of hoodlums they're dealing with now."

Her husband summoned a slow smile. "You're right, as usual, Amalia."

She kissed him enthusiastically once more and then called to the boys, "Rudi! Chris! Your father's home!"

"We couldn't have done it without Zaleski's warning, you know," the baron said.

"Oh, he's here. You'll have to tell him." Amalia looked around the hall, expecting to see her guest. She walked back into the drawing room. "How odd," she said. "He's gone."

Part Six

VIENNA
1938

Chapter One

I t was nearly four years later that Amalia spotted Max on the Mariahilferstrasse. Detecting signs of the wear of poverty in his winter coat, on impulse she followed him into the *Drogerie*.

At first he did not see her, and she further observed his worn heels and impeccably creased but shiny gabardine trousers as he requested a cough elixer. When he turned and saw her, his face remained as inscrutable as always, and he merely raised his hat.

"Baroness," he mumbled, as though disposing of a slight acquaintance. He moved quickly out the door. She followed with rapid steps and stopped him before his long stride outdistanced her on the street.

"Max, may I speak to you?"

He stopped, and turning, silently waited for her to state her business. His countenance reminded her forcefully of sculptured granite.

"I wanted to thank you for your service to our family, Max, and for not taking advantage of the situation."

He still said nothing but continued to regard her steadily, the thin line of his lips the only betrayal of emotion. She continued boldly, "I realize, of course, that any of us would have made a rather valuable hostage."

"I'm a socialist, not a blackguard," he responded coolly.

"What's more to the point now, are you employed?"

He startled her by emitting a powerful, gusty laugh which she had never heard before. "I'm not actually a butler by profession, you know."

"No, I had worked that out. No self-respecting socialist would be. But I think I've spotted your true line of work."

He looked amused.

"You're an actor, aren't you?"

He swept off his bowler and gave the dramatic bow of a Hapsburg courtier. "'Resting' at the moment, as we say."

"I suspect that even your name was just part of the act."

The man grinned, and she declared bluntly, "We need a butler, Max."

"You need a bodyguard, Baroness."

Amalia smiled ruefully. "Yes, we live more on the edge than ever."

"And the edge is being honed away," he remarked, looking past her with narrowed eyes.

"I always thought you were rather muscular for a butler."

"What has become of my footman? Surely he was promoted to fill my place."

"Fritz? He's very ill. He won't be returning to work, I'm afraid." She did not add that Fritz was, in fact, dying of kidney failure in the hospital.

"I'm not really the faithful old retainer type, you know."

"But you don't actually despise us too much, do you?"

He studied her upturned face for a moment. "You look very like your uncle, incidentally."

"So my husband tells me."

"He knew Reichart?" the actor replied, betraying some astonishment.

"Very well. It's through him that we met, actually."

There was a few moments' pause while he considered his answer. "I'll come."

"We'll try not to expect too much subservience."

"I'll do it for Lorenz. He was not only a great socialist but a great man, Baroness. If it hadn't been for his death, he would be heading the party, not Bauer. Going into exile solved his problem, but it hasn't done much for the party."

"I've thought that myself. But Uncle wouldn't have approved of Dolfuss or Chancellor von Schuschnigg, either."

"Perhaps he would have worked with them, though, instead of threatening them. The thing about your uncle was that he really loved the working man. I think he was above politics."

"You're a funny sort of socialist."

"You're a funny sort of baroness."

They laughed together, there on the Mariahilferstrasse, and it was agreed that Max would come back to work the next day.

Without exception, the entire family welcomed him. Rudi, seventeen years old and with his sharp blue eyes the image of his great-uncle Lorenz, asked pointedly, "Do we continue to call you Max? Mother says that's just your character's name."

Max's butler character remained unruffled. "Max is the name of the character I am playing at present. My stage name is, in fact, Kaspar Prachner. It is for you to decide how you will address me."

They continued to call him Max.

Fortunately, despite their plots, Max could not be made to break character, and soon the boys gave up baiting him. The only significant difference in the present relationship with their butler was that they now accorded him a measure of affection they had not felt for the old Max, of whom they had both been slightly in awe.

Amalia, finding herself in the pantry while he polished silver his first week back, asked him, "Do you find us much changed?"

"The young masters, though bigger, seem much as they ever were. Perhaps Christian has outgrown his perpetual high spirits to some extent, although it's hard to tell."

"I'm afraid he's still rather prone to them at times, but he's discovered a fascination with science and has really become a model student. I never would have dreamed it of Christian," she chuckled.

"And Master Rudolf? What is he fascinated with?"

"Oh, he's much like his father. A good, brave boy, as always. He hates school and Nazis, in that order, I think."

Max nodded and continued polishing. It was very restful to have such an intelligent, receptive ear in the household. The tenuous alliance that existed at present between their political factions as they united against the Nazis had put butler and mistress at least temporarily in sympathy with each other.

"It's the baron whom I find the most changed, of course. I suppose I shouldn't be surprised, but he's almost completely gray."

Amalia nodded with sadness. "He hardly sleeps."

"That business last weekend in Berlin was rather ominous. What does he think of it?"

Realizing that he referred to Hitler's "housecleaning," in which several top generals, diplomats, and the minister of economics had been sacked, she replied, "He hasn't commented on it, but I could tell he was chewing on something. What's so ominous about it? I mean, no one has done more to appease Hitler than von Papen. So why should he be replaced?"

Amalia referred to Hitler's ambassador to Austria, who had been a victim of the bureaucratic purge.

"What's undoubtedly worrying Schuschnigg and your husband is that the men removed were either weak and ineffective, like von Papen, or too conservative to support a really aggressive policy." Max absently examined an ancient von Schoenenburg tray for nonexistent scratches. "Polishing silver is a very calming occupation, you know." Under his hand the tray took on a lustrous gleam. "But to continue: Von Ribbentrop, von Neurath's replacement, is a puppet. He doesn't have independent opinions on foreign policy, as von Neurath did. And of course by firing Field Marshal von Blomberg, Hitler's now in a position to take over as commander-in-chief of Germany. That's not just ominous but downright frightening. I mean, the man was only a corporal in the last war. Suddenly he's in command of the biggest war machine in Europe."

Amalia absorbed all of this. "What you're saying, then, is there's no longer anyone in his government to stop him, no matter what he decides to do?"

The butler nodded. "It looks like he's got everything his own way. And yet, I really think that with the possible exception of Schuschnigg, the full significance of that is lost on the rest of Europe. Everyone wants to look the other way."

A few moments of gloomy silence ensued, while each thought privately on these facts. Then Max offered another gambit. "Our socialist brethren across the channel tell us that Chamberlain will do almost anything to appease Hitler. Of course, Britain's totally unprepared for war, both militarily and psychologically."

"We do seem to be without any friends." Amalia squared her shoulders and lifted her chin. "But I must say, you're a very refreshing butler, Max. It's a comfort to have you here."

He preserved his demeanor admirably while continuing his task. "It pays better than being an out-of-work actor."

"I for one can't see why you should be out of work. Your talents must be greatly underestimated."

"Politics."

"Oh."

Amalia, while glad to have Max to talk to, was far from lighthearted. The situation grew more serious by the day. But through the long string of crises since the brief civil war, she had become almost numb. She had also learned that panic and worry were destructive to her effectiveness. She preached to herself the doctrine of fatalism: What will be, will be. Deal with it when it happens, not before.

Danger taught one to see more clearly, she had found. It had a way of stripping the nonessentials from one's everyday thoughts. A day did not pass that Amalia did not consciously hold her husband close with a clear knowledge of what he meant to her. They shared a bedroom now. When he was home.

Sunday morning they were awakened early by the shrilling of the telephone. They had recently had an extension put in Rudolf's dressing room to avoid midnight forays down to the butler's pantry where the main line was. As her husband left her bed, she felt the alarm that came so easily these days with every telephone call, every knock at the door. She knew deep down that their days were numbered. Straining to hear Rudolf's end of the conversation, all she heard were "Ja's," short and clipped. Then, "I'll be ready in half an hour."

He returned to the bedroom, his face as gray as his hair, shoulders stooped in defeat.

"I'm afraid the time may have come, Amalia. Hitler's summoned von Schuschnigg to Berchtesgaden."

Amalia sat up, her heart slamming inside her chest. "And you? You are going too?"

"The chancellor asked me to go. I'm certain I won't be present in any meeting, but I'm to be a witness that he went in good faith. Frankly, I don't think he has the courage to go alone, and I don't know that I blame him."

"Why should he go at all?" Amalia demanded. "Who is Hitler to summon the head of an independent state?"

Rudolf dropped onto the bench by her dressing table and put his head in his hands, raking his fingers through his hair. "It was made very clear that this meeting is for negotiating the terms of our existence. It's either this little conference with Hitler or immediate invasion."

Jumping out of bed, Amalia knelt next to Rudolf's hunched and defeated figure. "Let him invade! We have an army. Let's show England and France that *we* at least are willing to fight for our independence."

He looked at her with such deep sadness that her anger left her, and she felt breathless. He had never looked this way before. She knew instinctively that he was showing her the interior of his darkest room.

"You and I are willing to fight, Amalia, but the army isn't. You don't know how deep the passion for that maniac goes in this country. Things have changed in the last four years. The real weakness of our situation lies not across the border, not in the lack of support from

France and England, but in the number of Austrians who see Hitler as a savior."

Her husband's red-rimmed, bloodshot eyes looked through her as he continued, "They think he will resurrect Austria as he seems to have resurrected Germany. They don't see our country as anything to be proud of. All they see is a castrated, truncated remnant of a once glorious past. They want Hitler, Amalia. And, as God is my witness, they will live to regret it, but they will get him."

Amalia felt the depth of his pain, for it was hers too. There was nothing she could say or do to make him feel better. The sight of him, so hopeless, so resigned, drove all other concerns from her mind. She wanted so desperately to heal him. *I've brought him this pain,* she thought. *He's given everything, and now he feels he's failed me, failed Austria.*

"Rudolf," she whispered, "this country will get what it deserves. Even God himself is helpless to alter people's choices. You have done all you can."

His eyes focused on hers, and his face softened. Standing, she held him to her fiercely, as though sheltering him from the insanity that was coming down upon them. "You must go," she murmured finally.

"You're right," he said at last, his voice flat. He stood, and his shoulders were once again squared.

He was ready when the limousine pulled up in front of the palais. Amalia watched from her upstairs window as he climbed in next to von Schuschnigg. "God go with you," she whispered. Her breath clouded the windowpane, and the limousine was gone.

Anschluss. To her it meant only one thing now. Rudolf's life. She must get in touch with Rosa Klein. There was a pipeline out of the country for those who were in danger. Rosa must take it herself. Amalia knew that Michael Webern, Rosa's contact, would see Rudolf safely out of the country. He had a car and contacts in Innsbruck who would help Rudolf over the mountains into Switzerland. Perhaps it was time to put the plan into action.

Amalia trembled. This was the day she had dreaded for years. Was she finally going to come face to face with the reality of losing her husband?

Her eyes were dry, for she had long ago wept all her tears.

Chapter Two

As the early morning progressed, it looked different to Amalia. Perceptually, the edges of her surroundings seemed sharper, as though they were no longer blurred by long familiarity, but now stood out, each detail separate and distinct. The morning light was silvery bright as Kristina pulled the curtains, her rheumatism making the maid's motions even more abrupt than they had been in Amalia's youth. How many years had Kristina performed this service for her?

"The loden green today?" Kristina asked as she held Amalia's recently purchased suit up to the window to check for spots, lint, or other irregularities.

"Yes, but right now I must telephone Rosa."

After arranging to meet her friend, who shared her concerns about the gravity of the situation, Amalia proceeded to get ready. Kristina hung the suit and drew her bath. Afterwards, she sat at the vanity while Kristina did her hair. Perhaps as a counter to all the uncertainty, she had recently redecorated her boudoir, trying to invest her life with a sense of permanence. But the pearl gray and white room, with piquant accents of shrimp and navy blue, was no guarantee of peace. Evidences of the senses were illusory. Even as her eyes traveled through the reflected light of her mirror over the pleasures of her habitat, and even as the gardenia scent she was applying evoked its strong memories, another part of her forced these sensual perceptions back and cold fact overlaid them.

It must have been the resilience of youth that had given her the ability to fashion a new life on top of her old one in this beautiful palais. But she did not deceive herself. She had not the arrogant ignorance of her mother and grandmother. Houses, conventions, food, and clothing had no real power over life. They gave no guarantees against change, loss, or disaster. No amount of money or status could buy such security.

After her toilette was completed, Amalia left the boys in Max's strict charge and went to Rosa's flat.

She was welcomed with a kiss on the cheek. She described Rudolf's situation and said, "All of us may have to leave at any moment. The boys and I can travel by train—I don't think anyone will be after us— but Rudolf must go underground. And so must you, Rosa. It is foolhardy for you to stay any longer."

The little nurse answered with a dangerous glitter in her black eyes. "I know Michael Webern seems like an average sort of person. Medium everything. But believe me, he has many modes of travel in his repertoire and a few unexpected connections. He's led an interesting life," Rosa told her reasssuringly. "He will find the best way to get Rudolf to Innsbruck. Then Horst Dohlmann will take over. He's the mountain guide. Rudolf will meet you in Switzerland."

"And you're sure it works?"

"We've used it twice. Once for Jacob Handel, who came to the attention of the S.S. when he aided a Jew. The other time was for Fräulein Gruen. Remember her? The head nurse at the hospital? She was being spied on, and the S.S. was on their way to pick her up. Both of them made it to Switzerland safely and are now living in Zurich."

"How do we get in touch with this Michael Webern when we need him?"

"I will alert him that you are in need, and he will stay by his telephone or have someone reliable who can reach him immediately. I will give you his address, if Rudolf simply needs to bolt somewhere. It's a very unobtrusive flat near where Gruen used to live. No one would expect Rudolf to go there."

Rosa wrote down the information and gave Amalia a hug. "I think

I will put my own preparations in order. I hope it doesn't come to this, but I must admit things don't look good."

Amalia stared at the information she was holding. Would Rudolf use it? She could only pray that he would.

That afternoon, Amalia had an unexpected visit from Hilde. Without prologue, her friend launched into her message as soon as she was seated in the morning room. "Amalia, you've got to get out. Herbert has heard from Andrzej. You remember his connection in the Polish foreign office?"

The reference was startling. At Amalia's request, Hilde had not mentioned Andrzej in four years.

Her friend continued, "It seems his uncle has been quite thick for some time with von Ribbentrop. You know, Hitler's new foreign minister. He reminds me of a fat spider spinning a huge web."

Amalia grimaced. "Go on."

"It's true, he's a dreadful man. The very last person I'd trust."

"How do you know so much about him?" Amalia asked impatiently. "It sounds as though he's your personal enemy."

"I still do my background work on Hitler's henchmen. They're all thugs, but von Ribbentrop has a veneer of respectability. I think it makes him worse."

"Get on with it, Hilde, please."

"Well, von Ribbentrop has hinted to Andrzej's uncle that the Anschluss will be soon. Very soon."

Amalia sat thinking that perhaps it was even taking place as they spoke, but she said nothing.

Fixing her hostess with a curious eye, Hilde asked, "Are you ever going to tell me about him?"

Amalia raised an eyebrow.

"Andrzej. Herr Doktor Zaleski. Self-proclaimed knight errant of the Baroness von Schoenenburg. He told Herbert he's coming. He's worried about you, and he's worried about Rudolf."

"All this is a very private matter, Hilde. I'm afraid I don't feel comfortable discussing it. But thank you so much for passing on the warning."

"Andrzej never remarried, you know. Lilli bleeds him white, I hear."

"You know more about him than I do, Hilde."

It wasn't until late that afternoon that she heard from her husband. He telephoned from Salzburg, the distant connection making his voice sound forlorn and small. "It'll be on the radio tonight, Amalia. It's bad news, but it could be worse."

"It's not an Anschluss, then?" Amalia broke in.

"Not quite. We've got Nazis in the government, though, and Dolfuss's murderers will be freed. Their party's legal now, so stay off the streets tonight. You know how the Nazis celebrate. A few heads will be bashed, I expect."

"When will you be home?"

"Schuschnigg's in a state of shock, but I'm doing my best."

"When will you arrive?"

"Probably very late."

"I love you, Rudolf," she said, but the connection had been broken.

Listlessly she wandered into the drawing room to wait for the news. It wasn't long before an announcer broke in and made public all that she had just heard. Rudolf had not told her, however, which posts the Nazis were to have. When she heard, she understood better why von Schuschnigg was in a state of shock. The newly legalized party was to have control of the army, the police, and the economy. In fact, the announcer intimated, the Austrian economy was to become part of the economy of the Third Reich.

"And this isn't Anschluss?" she said to the empty room bitterly.

Her sons arrived home from their friend's house where they had been spending the afternoon. "There's an enormous mob forming in the Kartnerstrasse," Rudi related. "They've got swastika armbands on and they're shouting that imbecile slogan of theirs, and nobody's doing anything to stop them!"

Christian goose-stepped with his hand in the Nazi salute, proclaiming hoarsely, "*Ein Volk, Ein Reich, Ein Führer!*"

Too dispirited to protest, Amalia put her head in her hands. Christian stopped in midstride and both boys knelt by her chair trying to see her covered face.

"What is it, Mutti?" they asked with sudden anxiety.

She told them the news, and about their father's mission that day. They sat stunned, and Amalia knew that the hardest thing for them to grasp was that their father's cause had failed. With a mother's special insight, she knew that their faith in him, in spite of all that had happened, had been still essentially a child's faith in his father. Until this moment, he had been invincible. Nazi mobs had held no terrors for them. They had looked upon such demonstrations and seen the face of blind fanaticism which surely must be doomed in a sensible world. To them such beings were objects of ridicule, and that such could have the power to triumph in a world partially governed by their own father was not only bewildering but inconceivable. They insisted on waiting up with Amalia to greet their father when he arrived home.

At midnight when the limousine pulled up, the boys ran to intercept him before he even made it into the house. In the hall, Amalia could scarcely see her husband as he was completely enveloped in a double embrace by his sons who were now taller than he.

When he was released, Amalia went to him for her own clinging embrace and then they adjourned to the sitting room. It was then that she noticed the look of hopeless despair he had worn that morning was gone. He held his head as he used to, and his eyes, in spite of fatigue were bright and purposeful.

"It's time to pack," he announced.

Chapter Three

I'll telephone Antonia tomorrow," he said seating himself on the divan. "As soon as it can be arranged. I'm putting the three of you on the train for Salzburg."

"What's the good of that?" Amalia sank heavily into a chair. "The last place I want to be in case of invasion is with Toni. She and Erich have far too much tolerance for Hitler."

"That's why you'll be safest there. Also, it's close to Switzerland. I want you three to be able to get out, Amalia, if the worst happens. Go to the Hotel Metropole in Zurich."

"And you?" she asked faintly. "Have you given any thought as to what you will do?"

He looked away from her. "I'll face it when the time comes."

"No. You're going to face it now." She took the name of Michael Webern and his address and telephone number out of her dressing gown pocket. She had known she must face Rudolf immediately about this. "I already have an escape route planned for you."

She explained the plan. Rudolf merely looked at her. Then he took the piece of paper and studied it. "These people are willing to do this for me?"

"Yes. They're not only willing to, they're expecting to. Please memorize the address and telephone number. We won't leave without you, unless you promise to use Michael Webern to get yourself out."

"I suppose it's a good plan. This way we travel separately. I'd just bring danger to you if we were together."

Amalia shuddered, and Rudolf went to her, pulling her to her feet and into the protection of his arms. "I'll arrange for most of our cash assets to be wired to Zurich in the morning. You'll need some money to travel with, too."

The boys looked on somberly. "Don't worry, Father. We'll take good care of her."

"Why are you finally deciding to take this seriously?" Amalia wanted to know.

"We never had Seyss-Inquart and his Gestapo before."

Amalia did not sleep well that night. She was too conscious of the precious, steady breathing of the man who yet lay beside her. She wanted to gather his muscular body tightly in her arms, but dared not, for he needed as undisturbed a sleep as events could give him. Even without physical contact, however, she could still feel his vitality, and a tenderness approaching pain grew in her.

During the next few days, Max stealthily conveyed a number of large trunks to the train stations after dark. Dressed in a variety of different disguises, he took them at different times, to different stations. But their destination was always the same: The Hotel Metropole in Zurich, Switzerland.

As the contents of the upstairs rooms disappeared into the trunks, the downstairs remained untouched, thus avoiding the impression of imminent flight should they have any interested callers.

The boys, glad to be doing something which required action, entered promptly into the spirit of things. Rudi called on Michael Webern to set up a communication line which he thought might be useful once they were separated.

One afternoon, Rudolf passed their train luggage which was assembled, two days before the planned departure for Salzburg, at the top of the stairs. Amalia was busy with her own suitcase, trying to decide what minimum of things would be serviceable both for the intervening "visit" with Antonia, as well as for an Alpine escape should they need to make one.

"I feel uneasy about Toni. If we should need to escape from her for some reason, we'll rendezvous with you in Innsbruck," she said.

"I'm perfectly certain that won't be necessary, but plan for it, if you must." Rudolf said. "I'm beginning to feel like someone out of a Saturday matinee."

"Perhaps I'll just try to convince Antonia we want to make a daytrip to Innsbruck."

"You really won't like mountain climbing."

"I'll like being trapped at Toni's even less. She's very concerned about this visit, you know. I have the idea she thinks she's going to be harboring dangerous hostages."

"Don't let Antonia get to you now. For once in your life you need her. Just don't trust her. I think she'd do anything to save her skin if she thought her family was in danger."

"I don't feel good about it, Rudolf. She knows too many Austrian Nazis. Her father-in-law has some sort of official position."

"It can work *for* you, if you let it. No one is going to think anything of a visit to the pro-Nazi von Trauenburgs. But I wish to heaven I were going with you."

She kissed him lightly. "Don't listen to my complaints. This is the best plan. I just don't see Toni calmly letting us board a train for Switzerland while there's a manhunt on for you, that's all. I think a reunion in Innsbruck is a far safer plan."

"Just get word to the Innsbruck contact, then. I won't leave from there unless I know you're safely away." Rudolf wandered closer to observe her progress. "Your lilac neligee?"

"That's an act of confidence. It's your favorite, isn't it?"

He chuckled. "Yes, but it won't keep you warm on the Alpine slopes."

"Some things have value which exceeds the practical."

Preparations were nearly complete for their visit to Salzburg when von Schuschnigg suddenly decided to take a stand. Amalia and the boys listened to his radio address in which he warned Hitler that Austria had gone to the limit of her concessions in the Berchtesgaden agreement. "This far and no farther!" he said. He proclaimed that Austria would never voluntarily give up the independence symbolized by its red and white national flag and ended in patriotic fervor with the words: "Red white red, until we are dead!"

A thrill went through Amalia at the words. Perhaps she was wrong to flee.

She waited impatiently for her husband to return to see what effect the speech had had on him.

The evening news carried a story about rioting in Graz against von Schuschnigg's speech. The news correspondent said there must have been at least twenty-thousand people waving swastika banners and screaming, "Hang Schuschnigg, Heil Hitler!"

"Sometimes I think those reports are exaggerated," Amalia told her sons.

They ate dinner without Rudolf and then went back into the sitting room, where they heard more reports of the riots broadcast on the radio. Why didn't the police have them under control by that time?

"You've forgotten, Mutti. Seyss-Inquart controls the police now. The Nazis aren't going to arrest their own," Rudi reminded her.

"How can all the policemen have become Nazis overnight?" The boys shrugged, and they continued to listen to the appalling reports. Rudolf didn't return home until much later.

"Weren't you pleased with Schuschnigg's speech?" she demanded as he sat down to his warmed-up dinner.

"I'm surprised at you, my dear."

"Why? It was splendid. It made me feel proud to be an Austrian!"

"And how do you suppose it made Hitler feel?"

"He's got to realize that we're not going to stand for an Anschluss, Rudolf. This is the first really positive thing Schuschnigg's ever done. We've got to stand firm!"

"Words are all very well, but what about what happened in Graz this afternoon?"

"Surely that was grossly exaggerated by the press, Rudolf. After all, they're controlled by the Nazis."

He looked at her sadly. "Our information wasn't from the press."

"But surely there couldn't be twenty thousand Nazis in Graz!"

"They're not German Nazis, Amalia. They're Austrian, and they love Hitler. I swear they think he's some kind of god."

"But there must be more loyal Austrians. They just aren't vocal."

"You may be right, but the fact is, Schuschnigg hasn't got a weapon to his name. Seyss-Inquart controls the army and the police.'

"What about the Heimwehr? Starhemberg has always been virulently anti-Nazi!"

"Not any longer. He's seen which way the wind's been blowing for some time. He's gone 'pan-German' on us. In the past few months he's been saying it would be fratricide to kill our German brothers."

Amalia felt a sense of wild desperation. "But the Socialist Party! You've known for sometime the Schutzbund has existed underground. Wouldn't they fight with you?"

He sighed and shook his head. "No. You were right there, Amalia. In '33 you said the Socialist Party would be a counterbalance to the Nazis, but we didn't listen." He brooded silently while Amalia watched him with a sense of growing sense of futility. "The fact is, we've been talking to them tonight. We've succeeded in weakening them to the point that any resistance they could put up against Hitler's army would be pitiful. It's too late, Amalia. In spite of von Schuschnigg's brave words, it's too late."

She stood and paced the room, frustration and grief building in her.

Her husband squeezed the bridge of his nose between his thumb and forefinger and screwed up his eyes as though he were in great pain. "We thought we chose the right thing at the time. But if it's any consolation to you, a socialist Austria wouldn't have been any less tempting to Hitler. More so, if anything."

Amalia could think of many flaws in her husband's reasoning. As she paced her frustration grew. But who was to say she was right? What if they had ended up in Stalin's lap? Would they be any better off?

Seeing her pacing had slowed, Rudolf said, "Von Schuschnigg's decided to hold a plebiscite, a popular vote to determine whether the Austrian people want to remain independent. Of course, he's going to couch the thing very diplomatically, but that's the gist of it."

Puzzled, she looked at him. "Then why are you so pessimistic? Surely the Social Democrats and the Christian Socialists together will give us a majority!"

"Yes, and I'm sure Hitler has that figured out. It isn't to be announced for several days, but when it is, Hitler will fly into one of his rages. He's not about to let us tell the world we don't want to be part of Germany! He's got them all fooled—England, France, the Soviet Union, even America. They think we want an Anschluss. That is what they want to think. They don't want war over Austria."

"Self-delusion. Hitler won't stop with Austria. Haven't they read *Mein Kampf*?"

"I don't know. It should certainly be required reading for all of Europe, I would think."

"Well, I suppose I can sympathize with their view. No one wants another war, including me."

"The plebiscite will incense Hitler. He won't allow it."

"You think he'll stop it?"

"Yes. I don't want to seem defeatist, Amalia, but the fact is we have no options—military, political, or diplomatic. There's nothing to stop him now from taking over Austria completely. He's just looking for the right opportunity. Von Schuschnigg is about to hand it to him with this plebiscite."

She sank limply back into her chair. "How can we just let him get away with it?"

Rudolf knelt by her chair, lifting her chin gently with his hand. "I know this seems like the end of the world, Amalia, but it's not. I want to make certain we live to fight another day. Resistance from within Austria is senseless at this point. If the record is clear on anything, it's that Hitler deals ruthlessly with dissenters. But perhaps, if we get out, we can make our voice heard in the rest of Europe. There's one statesman left who hasn't yet been fooled by Hitler. Winston Churchill, in England."

"But, Rudolf, I'm an Austrian! What does it matter what happens to the rest of Europe, if there's no Austria? How in the world can Churchill help us? If what you say is true, and I'm afraid it is, the time for help is past."

"England and France have got to have their eyes opened. If we don't help them see through Hitler's propaganda, there will surely be another war. Do you want your sons fighting for the Germans?"

She was very still.

"No," she replied.

They arose and embraced with great tenderness. In the last four years, Rudolf's reserve had been broken brick by brick until he had let her into the innermost places inside his heart. She couldn't lose this man who had finally entrusted her with his love.

Chapter Four

The escape is on, then, Mutti?" Rudi verified the next morning. "As soon as everything is ready," she replied, saddened by his obvious eagerness and yet understanding it. Rudi was scarcely younger than she had been when, full of an excitement heightened by other surging emotions, she had embarked on the great Berlin debacle. Now, as she sat savoring her flowery morning room, she knew the true cost of what she was giving up.

She found herself wondering aloud to Rudolf what they would remember about this critical time in their lives. He did not answer, and she thought that perhaps he had not understood.

"I mean," she elaborated, "I think what I'll really remember are the poignant things. How your face looked in the firelight, how worried I was the nights you didn't come home, and then how wonderfully relieved I was when you did."

She sat on the arm of his chair and traced the outline of his ear with her finger, adding, "It's as though all this tension and fear have welded me to you."

Some of the grimness passed from his expression, and he looked up at her.

"What will you remember?" she persisted.

"I'm not as philosophical, Amalia. My memory will always be that I failed . . ."

"You didn't fail, Rudolf . . ."

" . . . and that, in spite of it all, you stood by me."

She sighed. "After my performance a few years ago, I suppose you could have expected me to leave you."

"It's a great burden to disappoint someone who thinks you have it in your power to be all wise, my dear."

Amalia put her head on his shoulder. "Can you forgive me?"

He stroked her cheek, his eyes full of tenderness. "If it makes you feel any better, yes. Perhaps, in retrospect, you might see that your love for me seemed to grow after you realized I was mortal."

"It's true," she sighed. "It's very difficult, after all, to love a god. One can feel gratitude and reverence, perhaps, but for a flesh-and-blood sort of love, there must be something a bit more mortal. Maybe a feeling that the loved one is just the tiniest bit vulnerable?"

"So," he replied, "after all, perhaps we do owe Hitler something. He lit the fire that forged our true union."

She passed her hand over his broad chest. "And we'll go on, my love, long after Hitler's forgotten."

Rudolf sat quietly as she spoke and then mused gently, "I believe you're right, Amalia. Whatever the mold that shapes our lives, it scarcely matters, does it? It's the product, our character, that's important. The mold is, after all, only finite. Temporal." His eyes took on a serenity she had never seen there. "But the *person* exists beyond that, doesn't he? He, himself, along with what life has made him, is infinite."

"Anything else wouldn't make sense. And you claim you're not religious. This very thing is what I've been telling you for years. We're here to choose our path, to make our life the best we can, despite the obstacles. To become, not necessarily to arrive."

He got up and pulled her to her feet, encircling her in his arms with great deliberation.

The plebiscite was to be announced on the ninth of March. On the morning of the eighth, the final arrangements were in progress for Amalia and the boys' departure that afternoon. Fortunately, the number of mundane details to be seen to gave her little time to reflect further on the possible permanence of her farewell to the palais, Vienna, and her husband.

As she was boxing the last of her hats, which were to be sent on to the Metropole, Max entered the boudoir to announce that her brother had called.

Breaking character, he warned her, "Brother or not, I wouldn't let him know of your intentions, Baroness. He's got dangerous connections."

Amalia looked up in surprise. "Don't take Wolf too seriously, Max. He's nothing more than a poseur."

But Max was stubborn. "He may not intend to betray you, but the Gestapo is persuasive, trust me."

Chilled, Amalia granted the truth of this and descended to meet her brother. He was in high spirits, crowing over his various new accomplishments and connections. Amalia listened with an appearance of interest, mentally reviewing her list of things to do, until he stated suddenly, "Toni wrote that you're coming to her. Seems to think you're running from thc Nazis."

Amalia laughed. "Trust Toni to add intrigue. Rudolf just thought we might be happier in Salzburg for a while. There's so much tension here. Toni claims things are quite peaceful there."

"Why not the Schloss? Too far from Switzerland?" he asked with a heavy attempt at casualness.

"Do you seriously think I'd leave Rudolf and go to Switzerland alone?" she asked with a scornful laugh.

He studied her. "It's the only thing that makes sense. It's no secret that you haven't any love for Toni."

She turned on him. "Why do you hate me, Wolf?"

His mask of insolence dropped, and for a moment he looked startled. Amalia did not relieve the tension of the silence but deliberately waited for his answer.

Finally he managed a laugh. "Don't go all dramatic, Amalia. Hate's a strong word, don't you think? And I always thought we were such a loving family!"

He fussed about for a few seconds, gathering his gloves and newspaper from the divan. "Rudolf won't get out of the country alive, you know," he said in a peculiar voice that was neither wholly ominous nor wholly cheerful. "For what it's worth."

After he left, she pondered on his words, heart thudding, unable to decide whether they were a threat or a warning. It was rather stunning to think that Wolf could be her enemy.

Rudolf dismissed the episode. "Throwing his weight around. He acts more dangerous than he is. You must have antagonized his touchy ego."

Not wishing to cloud their last moments together, Amalia was willing to agree. Max entered the boudoir for the luggage, and she summoned every effort to act as though this were just another visit away from the palais to the Schloss.

She knew that her husband was anxious for her to be brave. For his sake she smiled.

"You and Webern will leave as soon as there's a hint of danger?"

"I promise," he told her, gathering to him her figure which was unusually plump in its winter traveling clothes.

The drive to the station was prevented from melancholy by the spirits of the boys. Their father warned them once again. "Rudi and Chris, it's most important that you keep all word of your plans private. Don't discuss them at all in your aunt's house, even if you think you are alone. The servants may be Nazis themselves. Salzburg is riddled with them, I hear. You are responsible for your mother, and I will hold you accountable should any harm come to her."

His stern voice subdued them and sent a chill through Amalia, overheated though she was under all her layers of clothing.

Good-byes at the station were necessarily brief, however Amalia couldn't help but remember that it had been at a train station where she last saw Eberhard. She looked into her husband's face. "Oh, Rudolf, don't do anything foolish." She hugged him. "You're my world. I can't get on without you."

He looked at her solemnly. "I'll take the best care possible, but you must be brave Amalia. You are a resourceful, independent woman."

They kissed as the crowd eddied around them.

"It looks as though we were lucky to book our seats," Amalia commented as she stepped aboard.

"These Jews are the wise ones, I think," her husband remarked. "I wish more of their friends would follow their example. In a few days, I fear it will be too late for them."

The jostling and shoving became intense, and the air of panic increased the longer they drew out their good-byes. Finally, Amalia, trying not to look closely at the concern in her husband's eyes, squared her shoulders, and rising on tip toe, whispered lightly in his ear. "Until Innsbruck, my love. Let Webern take care of you. And God be with you." Afraid of the tears that were starting in her eyes, she turned away to enter her compartment.

As the train pulled slowly away at last, her sons stood at the window and waved until their father was out of sight. But Amalia sat, gloved hands limp in her lap, staring at the empty seat across from her. She allowed the tears to fall. Her heart was thumping madly as it registered her anxiety. They were on their way now. Would they make it?

Would Rudolf?

Chapter Five

As the train neared the bucolic normality of Salzburg, Amalia began to think that perhaps they had panicked. Not only was Salzburg manifestly calm but the city still looked as it had when she had visited it as a girl, long before the Great War. Men strolled in loden capes and Tyrolean hats, and the picturesque town teeming with provincial activity looked like a swollen village in comparison to the tumultuous and cosmopolitan Vienna.

Feeling a bit silly and melodramatic, she was relieved when Antonia did not meet them in person. It gave her time to absorb the peace and normalcy around her and make a transition from the mentality of flight. After all, this was not to be a visit born of panic, was it? She had little faith in her ability as an actress and dreaded the first encounter with her sharp-eyed sister.

She told the boys to take off their extra winter clothes, leaving only their topcoats. She checked the bulkiest things, which they would not need until their escape over the mountains, at the left luggage counter and pocketed the claim check. A porter followed them with the rest of their luggage, and presently they were met by the von Trauenburg chauffeur, a cadaverous man with brown teeth.

Antonia's home, which Amalia had visited only once, seven years previously, was on the outskirts of the town, surrounded by a high, tree-lined wall. A gatekeeper opened up for them, and they entered the fastidiously maintained grounds just as dusk was falling. Tall plane trees bordered the gravel drive, and even in the drabness of a March twilight, Amalia was able to appreciate once again the loveliness of the von

Trauenburg home. The house itself was golden yellow, trimmed in white plaster, large, but not imposing. That fact probably grated on Antonia, she thought with a smile. All its lovely proportions aside, it would not be big enough in Antonia's eyes to weigh against the Schoenenburg palais or the Schloss. Poor Antonia! How miserable she made herself.

The butler informed them that neither Antonia nor Erich was at home. They were at an important charitable function that evening. A cold supper awaited the guests, and their rooms were ready, of course. Amalia tried to be amused rather than offended. The boys saw nothing strange about this reception, merely inquiring after their cousins.

"Young Gustav is asleep in the nursery. Margreta is with her governess. Masters Matthaeus and Wolfgang are away at school, of course."

Uninterested in the baby or their female cousin, the boys followed their mother up to their rooms. Amalia had the turquoise suite. It reminded her very much of her sister's personality as a young girl, and softened her somewhat with those happier memories. Everything around her was lace and flounce. Even the ceiling was papered with the same turquoise and white forget-me-not paper as the rest of the room. Amalia remembered that the view from the window had been lovely on her last visit, made in summer, when the flower gardens had been at their showiest. Now of course, all was in winter darkness, waiting for the spring that seemed so long in coming. She was suddenly glad Antonia and Erich were from home, rude though their intentions may have been. She was too tired and too overwrought to play any charades tonight.

In a sort of forced solemnity, the boys ate their dinner in the dining room, eyeing the servants with caution as they remembered their father's warnings about Nazi ears. Amalia could see that it was necessary for her to brief them again. Surely Antonia would sense something if her nephews were continually looking over their shoulders and refusing to speak in front of the servants.

She followed them into their bedroom, which actually belonged to their elder cousins. It was a very formal room, with dark walls and navy blue velvet drapes. The boys sat on their beds, and Amalia leaned against the bedpost.

"Relax," she instructed them. "Try not to act like you're matinee heros. Just be yourselves, or Aunt Antonia will suspect something, believe me."

"It doesn't really matter about Aunt Antonia, does it, Mutti? Just the servants," Rudi objected.

She sighed. "I wish I could say it doesn't matter. But I don't think we should take any chances. It's difficult to explain, but sometimes . . . well, sometimes your aunt and I don't see eye to eye."

"You mean she's a Nazi?" breathed Chris.

"I don't know," their mother answered heavily. "It's possible, you see. Uncle Erich's father definitely is. I've told you that."

Rudi squared his shoulders and looked suddenly serious. "We won't let you down, Mutti."

"Your father's life may depend upon it," Amalia said solemnly.

Saddened that she had to place such a burden and anxiety on her sons, she returned to her own room, where she spent a lengthy time on her knees, praying for her husband's protection.

Amalia was awakened from her slumbers the next morning by a sound she associated with the Schloss. Early robins were twittering on the large, still leafless chestnut tree outside her window. Morning sunshine filtered through white organdy, lightening the cheerful room. It took some seconds for her to orient herself as she lay there. It was impossible to feel dismal in the cheer and comfort of her surroundings. All would surely be well!

She rose and washed in the bedroom sink, for she had already had a lovely long bath the night before. Choosing her clothes with care, Amalia reflected that she could not afford to outshine Antonia, who would be doing her best to impress her. A plain brown wool skirt and cream silk blouse with an ascot tie were her final choice. She dressed quickly.

Erich was in the breakfast room, sipping coffee and buttering a Semmel, when she made her entrance. He rose briefly.

"Amalia!"

"Good morning, Erich. It's wonderful of you to have us on such short notice."

"It's time you came to visit us. Help yourself," he gestured to the buffet. "Sorry we weren't here to greet you last night. One of Toni's charity fêtes. She had overseen the whole thing, and I didn't want to have her miss seeing the fruits of her labors." Erich lolled back in his chair and studied her with a self-satisfied air, adding before she could reply, "I wish you could have seen her, as a matter of fact. She looked absolutely splendid. A new gown she bought in Paris last month."

"So Antonia has gone Parisian?" Amalia remarked, marveling at a world where charity fêtes were still important. "I'm certainly glad you didn't stay home on our account. We were very tired after our journey and wouldn't have been much company."

"And Rudolf? How did you leave him?"

"Harried. But grateful to you. It's such a relief to him not to have to worry about us. Vienna is so unsettled at the moment."

Erich arrested the movement of placing the last bit of Semmel in his mouth, as though he were going to comment. But apparently thinking better of it, he finished the roll in a leisurely fashion and took his leave.

"Toni will be down in a moment, I expect. Sorry I can't wait to see the boys, but I need to go into town this morning. I'll see you all at luncheon, I imagine."

"Thank you, Erich," Amalia murmured.

He left, and Amalia felt relief that that, at least, was over. He had seemed friendly enough, though supercilious as ever. The boys came down next, and as always when they were present, the room seemed very full.

"What fabulous Semmeln, Mutti. Do look how big they are!" Christian was, of course, primarily interested in food.

"Sleep well, Mutti?" Rudi asked, looking very tall and suddenly much older than seventeen. Except for the strong cleft chin, which he had clearly inherited from his father, he looked more like his great uncle Lorenz than ever today. He had begun to carry himself like a man, she noticed, and a sudden respect for her son rose in her.

"Marvelously, thank you, Rudi."

Then Antonia bustled in. She was dressed like a young girl's fantasy in a flounced and ruffled organza tea gown in a deep rose shade trimmed with black. However, her hair had the tell-tale greenish tinge of dye, and her face was heavily rouged. The thought went irrelevantly through Amalia's mind that her sister resembled a demimondaine.

"Well, I see you arrived in one piece," Antonia announced archly.

Amalia went to her sister, intending to embrace her, but Antonia held her at a distance and fixed her with bird-bright turquoise eyes. "You've aged," she pronounced.

Startled, Amalia said involuntarily, "Have I?"

"And the boys have sprung up. Let's see. Rudi, you're three years younger than Matthaeus, right?"

"If Matthaeus is twenty, then I am," Rudi replied cheerfully. "How do you do, Aunt Antonia? It's kind of you to have us."

Christian, moving with Rudolf's compact grace, showed his wide grin, so like his father's until the dimple showed. Shyly he ask, "And Wolf is my age, isn't he? Fifteen?"

"Yes, but he's much taller."

Christian's eager smile diminished, and Amalia strove to keep her sister's pettiness in perspective. "Matthaeus is enjoying university life?" she asked as she sat once again.

"Very much. Heidelberg is such a stimulating place right now."

Finding her appetite had suddenly vanished, Amalia pushed her plate away. So Germany was stimulating, was it? *If that was not a calculated statement of position, then I'm the demimondaine,* she thought.

As soon as the boys left, Antonia proceeded, without preamble, to make her position even more clear.

"I hope Rudolf realizes what a dangerous position he has put our family in."

"If our being here is a danger to you, we'll leave, Antonia," Amalia said, trying hard to keep her voice even.

Antonia's eyes widened, and she smiled a mocking little smile. "For Switzerland?" she asked. "No. I'm afraid not, Amalia." Then she left the room.

For a moment, Amalia could not entirely absorb what it was she had just heard. Then, feeling as threatened as she was undoubtedly meant to, she stared through the French doors at the sunlight on the still-frozen garden. It was a suddenly bitter scene, deceiving its onlooker with what she knew was only an illusion of beauty.

Antonia had implied that they were being watched. Why, if it was so dangerous, had her sister agreed to their coming? It was hardly in character. The only way Toni would have contemplated doing such a thing would be if it were in her own interest. Was she involved with the Austrian Nazis? Why shouldn't she be? She was a von Trauenburg. How blind they had been to think they might be safe here! She knew Antonia had Nazi sympathies but never would have believed she would connive at their being watched. Were she and the boys trapped in this house?

But, Amalia reflected, Rudolf had said no one would think they were contemplating flight if they stopped with Antonia. She squared her shoulders. She must not allow herself to be intimidated or placed on the defensive. They would be three innocents.

A deep breath steadied her. She went to find the boys, reflecting that today the plebiscite was to be announced.

The proclamation was made over the radio that afternoon. She and the boys listened in Amalia's suite over the portable radio they had brought in the luggage. When she heard that the plebiscite was not to take place until the following Sunday, five days away, Amalia jumped to her feet in frustration. "Can't they do anything right? Why not just ask Hitler if that gives him enough time to get his invasion force in order while they're about it?"

Rudi stood suddenly. "I'm going to town, Mother."

"But how will you get there?"

"Autobus. I went this morning before breakfast. It stops not far from here. Runs on the hour. I'll be back for dinner."

Not questioning him further, she allowed him to go and Chris along with him. It was safer for them out of the house in the present mood.

Taking out her embroidery, she worked it mechanically, her mind in Vienna. Luncheon had been an ordeal. Antonia and Erich had badgered the boys relentlessly about their father. They had replied only monosyllabically, trying desperately not to be rude. It was easy to see that her two sons had been targeted as sources of information.

Antonia had gone out for the afternoon and had not offered her sister the opportunity to accompany her. As the winter sun slanted low in the sky, Amalia was forced to turn on the lamp. She began to worry about the boys then and was therefore greatly relieved when Rudi burst upon her, coming through the door like a gust of wind, Christian at his heels. Her fears receded a little, and she smiled.

"You look terribly dashing—right out of the matinee."

Her oldest son handed her a piece of paper that looked much like a telegram. It was. A telegram from Michael Webern, apparently in reply to one Rudi had sent that morning. "All serene," it said. Tears started in Amalia's eyes, and wordlessly she stood and hugged her sons to her.

When they had left to dress for dinner, she reflected with some degree of comfort on this odd turn of events. With Rudi's birth, seventeen years ago, there had been born within her a mother's instinct to protect her young. But, this day, instinct had risen in that same boy, to sustain his mother, who was in need of strength. Rudi was definitely his father's son, and for the moment that was joy enough.

As it transpired, it was just as well she was possessed of such comparative peace of mind when she descended for dinner, for Antonia and Erich had a guest. It quickly became apparent to Amalia that the whole household were in awe of this man with the distinctly military bearing and harsh Hamburg accent, for he was not only a German but quite obviously a Nazi as well.

Chapter Six

A smile stayed upon Amalia's lips as though it were alien to the rest of her. As Herr Dietrich, the Nazi guest, studied her with unconcealed interest, her disdain caused her to hold her chin a bit higher. He reminded Amalia of a hungry wolf, with his sleek black hair, his small head, and little darting black eyes.

"Baroness, I understand your husband is the close associate of von Schuschnigg. One sees the Baron von Schoenenburg mentioned from time to time in the press."

"Yes, Rudolf is affiliated with the government."

"But he is your second husband, is he not?"

"Yes," she answered shortly. Her sons were watching her keenly.

"And your first husband? Am I wrong or was he a German?"

"You *have* been well informed." She felt anger building.

Obviously, she had been discussed by Herr Dietrich and the von Trauenburgs. Now Antonia and Erich sat serenely by, appearing only idly interested in the conversation.

Rudi broke the silence. "My mother's first husband was Eberhard von Waldburg. He died in the Great War. You must understand, Herr Dietrich, that the subject is quite painful."

Dietrich turned sharply and faced the boy, whose tone had been just short of rude. "And you? Whose son are you?"

Amalia watched Rudi's face as it colored, and summoning all the hauteur of her husband's station, said coldly, "You must have missed the introduction. Rudi will be the next Baron von Schoenenburg."

Antonia interjected sweetly. "Amalia, you mustn't mind Hans. He is as curious as a child. He means nothing by it, do you, Hans?"

Dietrich gave a little bow and smiled, showing white teeth. He spoke with a trace of apology in his voice. "I did not mean to revive painful memories, Baroness. It is just that I fancy I knew von Waldburg once."

Amalia raised an eyebrow.

He continued, "At Verdun."

Even more than twenty years after Eberhard's death, Amalia still felt the sense of loss and chill that always accompanied the name of that futile battle in which he had lost his life. She averted her face from Dietrich and sat down on the couch. "My first husband had a great talent, Herr Dietrich, which perhaps you were unaware of. He loved to play the violin. I have a theory, you see." She fixed him with her eyes, and he watched, a grin of patronizing amusement twitching at the corners of his mouth.

"And pray tell us, what is your theory, Baroness?"

Antonia's laugh tinkled. "Yes, tell us, by all means, Amalia!"

"Eberhard was happy when he played his violin. To him it was a form of beauty, you see. Of reverence for life." She glanced away from Herr Dietrich and her eyes settled on Christian, who was impatiently looking in the direction of the dining room, undoubtedly wondering when dinner would be announced. She continued, "But his father was a Prussian," she mocked the old colonel with an ostentatious boom in her voice. "His son had to be a soldier, of course, to carry on the great Prussian tradition. The violin was put away and forgotten, and Eberhard was sold Lucifer's version of beauty. Glorious victory or glorious death. In other words, reverence for slaughter."

Herr Dietrich continued to look amused. "All Germans are not Prussians, my dear Baroness," he shrugged. "But is this your theory, then? Do you see the violin as the ultimate deterrent to war?" In his insolence he invited the others to laugh. Antonia did so.

Amalia's look was burning now, as she challenged her opponent.

"My sons will not be victims of German greed, Herr Dietrich. You can't sell them the grand illusion."

Dietrich's look changed briefly to one of speculation, and then all at once he laughed a sharp, stacatto laugh. "Baroness, are you warning me, by chance?"

"Really, Amalia!" Antonia laughed again. Erich continued to watch the scene, apparently bored.

Herr Dietrich looked at Amalia, the amusement gone and only curiosity remaining. "You're a very determined woman, aren't you, Baroness?"

"I've learned I must be," Amalia replied softly.

At that moment, dinner was announced.

The next morning, Antonia descended upon her at breakfast with every evidence of pique. "I must ask you, Amalia, while you are staying here, to attempt to behave civilly to my guests, whatever their political persuasions."

"Will you then ask them to behave civilly to me, or am I to be interrogated with all the grace of Herr Dietrich. What is he? Gestapo?"

"Amalia! This is *my* house."

"Antonia, why did you allow us to come? It's obvious you don't want us."

"Rudolf arranged it all with Erich," Antonia said, and like a sullen child turned her back and began filling her breakfast plate at the buffet.

"Erich would never have accepted without consulting you. Or was it Herr Dietrich he consulted?"

Antonia turned towards her, her pretty face contorted with spite. "You've always thought yourself so morally superior to the rest of the family, Amalia. I'm surprised you don't leave, as a matter of principle."

Amalia gazed at her sister steadily. "Perhaps I should," she murmured.

At that moment Erich entered. "Perhaps you should . . . what, Amalia?"

"Leave. It's awkward for you and Toni to have me here. I can see that. I shouldn't have come in the first place."

"What?" Erich looked at his wife, and Amalia detected, for the first time in her memory, that he was displeased with her. "Rudolf would never forgive us, Amalia! Wherever would you go? Surely you realize that the plebiscite has been announced . . ."

"Yes?" Amalia prompted.

"You realize, of course, that there is likely to be some trouble."

"Trouble for Rudolf?"

"I sincerely hope not."

But Antonia was looking at her so smugly that Amalia wondered just how sincere her husband was.

Erich asked irritably, "What've you done with the newspaper, Toni?"

"It hasn't come."

"Hasn't come?" his face took on a look of excitement. He was suddenly impatient to be gone and left without eating his breakfast or taking leave of his wife. Antonia stared after him for a moment and then turned to Amalia with a sweet smile. "Another Semmel? My cook does such a good job on them, don't you think?"

Amalia declined in what she hoped was a sufficiently unconcerned manner and went in search of the boys. At length, she gave up trying to locate them, and realized they must have gone on their morning trip to the telegraph office. Feeling helpless and anxious, she could not settle to her embroidery. It was as though she were standing, blind, in the path of a runaway horse and had nowhere to seek shelter. She could hear it getting closer, she could smell and taste the dust it was raising, but she could not see. She could barely keep down the panic that was gripping her.

Finally, she heard Rudi and Chris's spirited tread on the stairs and intercepted them in the hallway. Motioning them to her room, she followed inside and shut the door firmly. "Something is about to happen," she told them.

"Everything was quiet enough this morning," Rudi countered.

"Too quiet, perhaps. There was no newspaper delivered this morning, and your Uncle Erich seemed to be quite excited by the fact."

"Just because there was no newspaper?"

"Think, Rudi. Who normally controls the press?"

"The government?"

"Unfortunately, yes. Why would the government not want to print the newspaper today? It's just two days away from the plebiscite. Surely they want all the publicity they can get, don't they?"

Christian was thoughtful. "But the Nazis couldn't stop the presses, Mutti."

"Couldn't they?" she asked. "I think that's just what they did. Hitler doesn't want the plebiscite, remember, and the Austrian army and the police are his to command. Stopping the presses would be only a minor chore for them, as far as I can see."

Outraged, Christian replied, "But that's not right. How can they get away with it?"

"They're going to invade, aren't they, Mutti?" Rudi asked, his jaw hardening.

"Yes, and we've got to get out of here. I don't think your aunt will let us go willingly. She thinks she's got us trapped here. I don't know what she's planning, but we're not going to wait to find out. Go back into town and get our warm things from the train station. Here's the claim ticket." She passed over the pale green paper stub and looked at her sons with anxious eyes. "Try to find a safe place somewhere nearby for the coats, but don't bring them back here. Also, try to find something we can use to climb out the window. We're going to try to get out about four o'clock tomorrow morning."

"Where will we go? The trains won't be running that early!"

"We'll have to hide somewhere. Check the train schedule, Rudi, and buy three tickets, westbound, on the earliest train tomorrow. To Innsbruck." She pulled some currency out of the crown of her Tyrolean traveling hat and handed them to her older son. "Buy food, too, and hide it with the coats." She smiled. "And try to remember we can't live on candy and pastries. A little bread and cheese would be nice."

Eyes shining with excitement, the boys left quickly, and Amalia pretended to settle once more to her embroidery. Her heart was thudding and her hands shaking so terribly that she pricked herself badly with the needle. Tears started in her eyes, and throwing her embroidery hoop across the room, she strode over to the window, where she watched her sons weave through the orchard and then scale the garden wall. Today they were unhindered, but tomorrow after they had vanished from here in the night, the hunt for them would be on. And what of Rudolf? Would he get away in time? She had never felt so completely alone.

That the boys were not back for luncheon caused comment. "I didn't know Rudi and Chris were so enchanted with Salzburg. Where can they be?" Antonia queried.

Amalia watched her fat, four-year-old nephew spoon mashed potatoes into his greedy little mouth. "I think they wanted to visit the Hohensalzburg today."

"The castle? Good heavens, Erich would have taken them, if he'd known."

"Oh, they're very adventurous. I'm sure they'll be fine on their own."

Antonia looked at her sister sharply and then said casually, "Herr Dietrich is coming for tea. I hope they'll be back by then."

"Oh, I'm certain they will be."

In fact, it was a near thing. They had just arrived in their mother's room when the tea bell rang. "I haven't time to hear anything now. Run and get changed. That horrible man is coming to tea."

Then Amalia descended, mentally ordering herself to control her tongue.

"Baroness!" Herr Dietrich rose as she made her entrance. He went quickly to her and taking her hand, raised it to his lips and kissed it. She was just able to keep herself from snatching her hand away, but when he continued to hold it, she gently disengaged herself.

"And where are your brave boys? I understand they have been combing Salzburg this afternoon."

"They'll be down in a moment, Herr Dietrich," Amalia assured him. She seated herself, and Antonia poured her a cup of tea.

"Why is it, Antonia, that in all that you've told me about your sister, you never mentioned that she was a beauty?"

Antonia handed her sister the cup. "Yes, men have always found Amalia attractive," she said airily.

Amalia interrupted her. "Where is Erich?"

Toni held her head proudly. "He'll be in presently."

Dietrich studied the baroness. "I'm amazed your husband can bear to be parted from you, my dear."

Amalia looked at him levelly. "He has other concerns at the moment."

Rudi and Christian made their entrance then, and their aunt asked cheerfully, "And how was the Hohensalzburg, then?"

Their expressions became blank, and Amalia cued them gently, "The castle, she means. That's its proper name, you know. The Hohensalzburg."

Rudi's face cleared, and he smiled. "We decided not to go, after all, Aunt Antonia. I wanted to visit Mozart's house."

"Ah! Yes. And how did you enjoy it?" Herr Dietrich inquired smoothly.

"It was lovely once we found it," Rudi temporized.

Mercifully, Erich entered at that moment, and the subtle interrogation was cut short. Erich strode silently to the radio and turned it on. Amalia was surprised to hear the Chancellor's voice: " . . . ordering him to nominate as chancellor a person designated by the German government. Otherwise German troops would invade Austria.

"I declare before the world that the reports launched in Germany concerning disorders by the workers, the shedding of streams of blood, and the creation of a situation beyond the control of the Austrian government are lies from A to Z. President Miklas has asked me to tell the people of Austria that we have yielded to force because we are not pre-pared even in this terrible situation to shed blood. We have decided to order the troops to offer no resistance.

"So I take leave of the Austrian people with a German word of farewell uttered from the depth of my heart: God protect Austria!"

An old and scratchy version of "Deutschland uber Alles" played to the reverent silence of the von Trauenburg drawing room. Amalia wept silent tears, and the boys flanked her protectively. Finally, they managed to get her to her feet and out of the room. She made no farewells but left her sister, brother-in-law, and their guest to their obvious triumph as the new chancellor, Dr. Arthur Seyss-Inquart, began his address.

Chapter Seven

A malia lay on her bed and stared at the ceiling while the boys listened to the low murmur of the radio in her room. It was as though her brain were frozen. She kept hearing the strains of the scratchy German anthem and seeing visions of Eberhard and his tortured face as he boarded the train for the last time, the waxlike face of his mother as she lay in her final sleep, and finally, the beloved anxious face of her husband as he bade them farewell just two days before.

She thought she had been prepared for this, but now when all hope was finally gone, she realized she had never really envisioned it happening. As of now, Rudolf's life was in danger. He was a fugitive from the new Nazi government. Did he get away? Would he make it to Innsbruck, where she could see him again?

All was in readiness for their escape that night, and she tried to focus her thoughts on that. Warm outer clothing and food were hidden nearby and tickets procured for the seven A.M. train to Innsbruck. The boys had even been able to purchase a climbing rope from a shop that catered to mountain climbers. They were now busy knotting it for their escape through Amalia's window.

It was very late when they finally covered her with the Federdecke and left her, fully dressed, but sleeping, with the alarm clock set for three A.M.

She was at the Schloss, and the edelweiss was blooming. Elisabeth was very swift that day, and the air had the heavy sweetness of late spring before a thunderstorm. Rudolf rode beside her, his sturdy body straight in the saddle with pride for what he was giving her—his estate, his heart, and his fidelity. She felt warm with the sense of being cared for, and whatever it was that had frightened her dropped away . . .

Someone was shaking her. At first, in the dim light, she thought it was Rudolf. "What is it, dear?"

"Mutti! Someone's here!" It was Christian.

She struggled awake to see both of her sons, fully dressed standing by her bed.

"We were too excited to sleep, and so we finally got up and dressed. It's just one o'clock," Chris continued.

"We heard something crunching on the gravel in the drive and looked out. It's that Herr Dietrich's car, I think."

The name brought Amalia back to reality. "He's come about your father, I think. You had better go on without me."

They heard loud rapping at the front door.

"No!" Rudi insisted. "Father said we were to take care of you."

Amalia's thoughts stumbled over one another. One thing was clear. The boys must be gotten away safely. "Look," she said carefully. "This may mean your father got away and they think we know where he is. We'll be followed now. You must get to Innsbruck and meet Herr Webern and your father at the mountain guide's house." She jumped out of bed and took her Tyrolean hat from the top wardrobe shelf where she had hidden it behind discarded tissue paper. She heard footsteps crossing the marble hall below.

Handing them a wad of banknotes and a piece of paper, she whispered. "Here. I've memorized it all. It's the directions to the house. If I don't show up where you've hidden the coats by 5:30, go on without me and tell the mountain guide what's happened. He'll be in touch with Herr Webern and your father. Tell them I'm probably being watched. Now, go! Use the dressing room window!"

She must have convinced them this was their best chance of helping her, for they walked through to the next room and shut the door just as Amalia heard someone begin to ascend the staircase. Hugging them quickly, she kissed each of them and watched as they secured the rope and prepared to climb through the window. Then she went back to her room, climbed into her bed, and tried to feign sleep, listening as the boys made their escape from the next room.

A sharp knock sounded on her door. "Amalia!" Erich called.

She allowed herself to continue to play at sleeping, giving the boys a few more precious seconds.

"Amalia!"

She called sleepily, "Come in, Erich, if you must. What on earth is the matter?"

He burst in, looking harried and unusually rumpled. "Amalia, I'm very sorry to wake you, but Herr Dietrich is downstairs. Actually, it seems, he's Colonel Dietrich. S.S."

He looked so terrified as he said this that Amalia concluded he had not actually known the man's true identity until moments before. "For our sake, Amalia, could you please answer his questions?"

She sat up indignantly, pulling the bedclothes with her to hide the fact that she was dressed. "Why on earth has he come to question me at this hideous hour?"

"I gather it's something to do with Rudolf."

She looked at him steadily, and he could no longer meet her eyes. "Then you had better leave," she said. "I'll need to get dressed."

"You're to come as you are, he said," Erich informed her, hastily walking to the wardrobe. "Surely you must have a dressing gown or something!"

"If he wishes to see me, he can wait until I'm dressed, Erich. Now, go."

"Amalia, I know you won't believe this, but we didn't know he was S.S. . . ."

"Will you please get out?"

Shoulders slumped, her brother-in-law finally left her alone.

Throwing back the eiderdown, she leapt out of bed. Going into the dressing room, she looked out into the blackness and prayed the boys would make it. She drew in the rope and closed the window.

Hastily hiding the rope under her mattress, she forced herself to take deep breaths. She must put away her panic and appear to be calm but irritated by this intrusion. Everything depended upon it. She changed out of her rumpled clothes, putting on a tweed suit that she hoped would serve her well for whatever awaited her. As she pulled the comb through her hair, she tried to order her thoughts for the ordeal ahead, but her stomach was clenched with tension.

Erich apparently waited just outside her door, for at intervals he requested her to hurry. Buttoning the jacket to her suit, she finally joined him, and they descended wordlessly to the sitting room.

Herr Dietrich was attired in the gray uniform of the Nazi S.S. His back was to her when she entered the room, and he turned slowly to face her as she stood in the doorway. He smiled his wolfish grin at her upraised chin. "No need for theatrics, my dear Baroness. A simple matter, really. The fact is, I've just had a call from Vienna. It seems your husband, the good baron, can't be located. He's wanted rather urgently. Surely you must know where he is?"

A whole scenario instantly planted itself in her mind as she stood there praying what to say. It might just work if she could pull it off. Boldly, she stepped into the room and seated herself in what she hoped was a careless manner. "So all his fascist posings did him no good in the end? I told him how it would be."

The colonel's brow contorted, and Erich looked stupefied. "Fascist?" her brother-in-law echoed. "Rudolf a fascist?"

"Of course! Oh, not the Nazi variety, unfortunately for him."

"Where is he, Baroness? That's all you need to tell us," Dietrich demanded in a harder voice.

"Even if I knew, do you think I'd tell you? We're separated, but I still care enough about the poor devil not to make things easy for *you.*"

"Separated!" Erich said nervously. "Of course you're separated."

"Ah, but the baroness means something more than you do by that term, von Trauenburg, don't you Baroness?"

Amalia dismissed Erich with a sniff. "He's such an anachronism, I knew he'd never have an about-to-be divorced woman in his house, so I didn't tell him. But the fact is, I'm the last person Rudolf would tell where he was going. He suspects I'm only too happy to see him stew in his own juice."

"But you can't get divorced, Amalia," Erich cried.

"If you recall, my wedding was civil, not Catholic, Erich, so I am perfectly free to divorce."

Dietrich advanced, the grin back in place. "Baroness, I'm warning you, it's best not to waste my time. You're an excellent actress, but remember I was here earlier tonight. You weren't acting when von Schuschnigg resigned. I saw your tears, witnessed your collapse. It was far more convincing than this performance."

She turned on him with surprising venom. "You think a woman can only grieve for a man, then? I was grieving for my country! The country which my husband betrayed and which you will surely destroy! Is it beyond your cretinous mentality to understand that I love Austria? Love her more than my traitorous husband?"

"What about your sons?" Dietrich inquired softly. "Do you love it more than your sons?"

Amalia heard Erich take his breath in sharply and heard someone else enter the room, but she kept her eyes defiantly on the eyes of the S.S. officer. "Leave them alone," she said tersely.

The colonel turned then and greeted Antonia with a delighted smile. "Ah! Frau von Trauenburg! Perhaps you would be good enough to summon your nephews for me. I'd like to take them with me for a little questioning."

Antonia stood looking in patent horror at the man she had thought was her friend. "Rudi and Chris? What do you mean?"

"Your sister claims that she cares nothing for her husband, whom she describes as a traitor, and that she cannot help us, for he would never tell her where he has gone. I would be very much surprised, however, if his son and heir were entirely out of contact with his father."

Antonia looked at her sister, agony contorting her brow. It seemed to Amalia that Antonia had shrunk noticeably in stature since entering the room.

"It's all right, Toni," Amalia said flatly. "They've already gone."

Dietrich turned sharply. "What's this?"

Amalia held up her chin. "Do you really think we are so ignorant of your tactics, Dietrich? We knew what you would try to do. They left right after the broadcast this evening. They're undoubtedly in Switzerland by now."

"You ask me to believe this? That you would let them go without you?"

"Oh, they will be well looked after, I can assure you. And they are resourceful. Herr Churchill is most anxious to hear their story. You know of Churchill, don't you?"

"You bluff well, Baroness. But I think I'll have a look just the same. Von Trauenburg, search the house!"

Amalia sat while this was accomplished, outwardly serene, but inwardly praying that they would believe her taunt. If they chose to search the woods or check the railway stations, Rudi and Chris were as good as caught. Her stomach cramped agonizingly. She prayed never to see Rudi and Chris in the hands of the S.S.

Antonia reentered the room, incredulous, "They really have gone!"

Dietrich followed her. "You knew nothing of this?" he challenged.

Before the terrified woman could answer, Amalia intervened. "No, my sister and brother-in-law have been all that you could wish in this matter. We haven't trusted them an inch."

Dietrich's eyes narrowed. "There's only one reason you would let those boys go on ahead. You are waiting for your husband."

Amalia laughed, and her laughter was shrill. "Here? You really think I would wait for him here?"

"What are your plans then, Amalia?" Erich asked.

"I won't trouble you much longer, Erich."

"No. She won't, as a matter of fact. Because she's coming with me!" Dietrich announced, wrenching Amalia from her seat and marching her from the room. As she left the house, Amalia had one brief glimpse of her sister's terrified face.

The S.S. headquarters were set up temporarily across from the train station, a situation that caused Amalia a great deal of worry. The search of the von Trauenburg house for the boys had taken some time, and it was now approaching three A.M. Amalia hoped she could keep Dietrich's attention fixed anywhere but across the street.

Apparently, however, the colonel had decided that a little time to herself would be beneficial in bringing her to her senses, and so he locked her in an empty room. It was a cold little cubicle, not really designed as a cell but serviceable enough.

What was going to happen now? Amalia could not worry about herself. All her thoughts were centered on Rudi, Christian, and Rudolf. She prayed as she paced that they would make it safely to the rendezvous in Innsbruck. She heard through the moderately thick walls an occasional barked order, the ringing of telephones, and from time to time the scream of tires in the otherwise quiet street. Heavy boots echoed down the wooden corridor and other doors were slammed and locked. She felt terror grow within her and stifled it by redoubling her prayers for her sons' and husband's safety. Forcing all other thoughts out of her mind, she paced and prayed, repeating the words in accompaniment with her steps until they quelled her rising fears. She found that her fury was enough to keep her warm.

At last the sun began to rise, and Amalia felt obscurely comforted. She allowed herself to sit, with her legs curled under her for warmth, and soon she had nodded into an uneasy sleep.

She was awakened by shouting. At first she could not distinguish it, but it moved nearer and nearer to her door. It was a familiar voice, but the words were still unclear. Then she heard her name, and she knew without a doubt who it was.

"Amalia!" Andrzcj shouted.

Dietrich intervened. "You can't go back there, Herr Doktor!"

It did not seem at all strange that he was there. She went to the door, pounding on it with her fists. "Andrzej! Andrzej! I'm here!"

Standing outside with Dietrich apparently behind him, Andrzej demanded, "Where is the key, Colonel Dietrich? I must insist that you give it to me immediately, or I shall inform my government of your terror tactics. My uncle is highly placed in the foreign office. He wouldn't like to hear of this little incident. And in case you're thinking of incarcerating me as well, he knows exactly where I am. I am in this country on official business for the Polish government."

"Yes, I quite understand that. But what, pray, is your connection with the baroness?"

"We are to be married."

Amalia heard the key scrape in the lock as Dietrich opened the door. She pushed past him and threw herself into Andrzej's arms.

"Darling!" he breathed. She did not speak but merely clung to him, tears of relief running down her face.

"Ach! So here is the reason you left the good baron!" Dietrich boomed, eyeing them speculatively. "All this talk of fascists and traitors was just for your sister's benefit, wasn't it?" His face was ironic. "You were a bit too heroic to be true, you know."

Andrzej interjected, "We don't have to stand here for your insults. All that concerns you is that the baroness is not a traitor to the Reich; in fact, she has very little interest in it. She is about to become a good Polish citizen, aren't you, darling?"

Amalia nodded docilely. The colonel was apparently struck favorably by her transformation, for he let them pass.

"Proceeding directly to Poland?" he inquired, following them to the front of the building.

"There's a little matter of a divorce," Andrzej explained.

"Oh, that shouldn't be too difficult," Dietrich smiled. "The good baroness should be a widow before much longer."

Amalia looked away.

"I must just trouble you for the address where you'll be staying, Herr Doktor."

"We're going to be relaxing in Innsbruck for a few days. I have no idea where we'll be staying."

Moments later, they left the headquarters of the S.S. and, climbing into Andrzej's automobile, drove off towards Innsbruck.

They were not allowed the luxury of many moments rest from anxiety, however. It became evident immediately that Dietrich was having them followed.

Chapter Eight

"They didn't believe us then," Amalia sighed.

"Not entirely. You're too good a lead, my dear. But if we put up a good front, they'll give up after a while." Reaching across the back of the seat, he put his arm around her shoulders and drew her closer. She was trembling so that her teeth chattered, but still she stiffened at his touch.

He smiled grimly. "All part of the act. I left your husband," he consulted his watch, "three hours ago, dressed in filthy clothes heading up the Inn on a barge."

"You've seen him? He's alive?"

"Yes, Amalia. He's alive. However do you think I found you?"

But the news that Rudolf was alive had released her tenuous control, and she could not answer. She wept silently.

"When can I see him?" she finally asked. Andrzej handed her a handkerchief, and she blew her nose gustily.

"I know you're anxious, but we have to keep our heads, my dear."

Amalia looked involuntarily over her shoulder and saw that the black Mercedes sedan was several bends behind them but following them still.

"Can't we lose them somehow?"

"Not just yet. We can't afford to make them suspicious. If we do, then they'll know we're up to something. Are the boys really in Switzerland?"

"God willing, they're on the train for Innsbruck . . ."

"Splendid. So Antonia and Erich couldn't be made to tell if they wanted to."

"There are so many things I need to know, but I'm so cold. Isn't there any kind of a heater?"

"Here." Andrzej pulled a tartan rug from the backseat, and she spread it over her. Unconsciously she welcomed his arm holding her at his side and speeding the return of warmth into her shock-chilled body.

"We'll be there soon," Andrzej assured her. "How long since you've eaten?"

"I don't remember. But tell me, how did you come to join Rudolf? Does Toni know you were with him? And how did you account for your visit to her?

"It's a very long story, Amalia."

As they wound their way through the mountains to Innsbruck, Andrzej told her of the past twenty-four hours. He had arrived in Vienna by train the morning before, equipped with the knowledge that Hitler planned to invade that weekend. His uncle in the foreign office was indeed a crony of the blustering von Ribbentrop and had just returned from Berlin. Wasting no time, Andrzej boarded a train for Vienna and went straight to the chancellery, where he had Rudolf called out of a meeting, saying it was a matter of life or death.

"Rudolf, of course, came thundering out. I didn't know you'd already gone and that he'd immediately assumed something had happened to you."

"Did they know about the invasion?"

"By that time they suspected. Seyss-Inquart was pressuring von Schuschnigg to resign to 'avoid bloodshed,' so my news was no surprise. When I got there, von Schuschnigg was already urging everyone to flee as it was just a matter of time before Seyss-Inquart's thugs arrived. He knew he would be forced to resign."

He paused to negotiate a hairpin turn. Amalia allowed herself for the first time to study his face. She had not laid eyes on him in nearly four years, but he had not changed greatly. A few more strands of silver laced his hair, but he did not have that bitter, unhappy look she remembered from their last meeting. She reflected that he looked now, as he tore down the road toward their Innsbruck rendezvous, rather as he had before departing for France—full of energy, an alert glint in his clear green eyes, every muscle taut, preparing in one panther-like spring to finesse the enemy.

"It was a near thing," he continued. "I was just urging Rudolf to think of you and the boys and not to go down with the ship when we heard a lot of commotion out in front. Von Schuschnigg hadn't a hope of escape, but I managed to get your husband out the back."

"My greatest fear has always been that he wouldn't even try to get away," Amalia said flatly. "He feels he's failed. Thank you, Andrzej. Thank you so very much for being there."

He dived back into his narrative. "He knew the address of a place we could go. A Michael Webern. Apparently you had set the whole thing up beforehand. Webern had this car standing by. It isn't much, but it isn't traceable to von Schoenenburg and it has wheels. It was wonderful to see this car. It gives us so much flexibility. We never could have reached Salzburg as fast by train. The next one out was at three, and by then the S.S. would surely have been watching the station."

"But what did you do when you got to Salzburg?"

"Webern had given us the morning cable from the boys. They mentioned someone who must have been Dietrich."

"What did they say, for heaven's sake? That was dangerous!"

"It would have been more dangerous if they hadn't. Because of that telegram, I was able to convince Rudolf to follow Webern's plan and go to Innsbruck by barge, on the condition that I stop in Salzburg and check on things myself. If the boys hadn't alerted us, you would still be sitting at S.S. headquarters. Who is he, a friend of Toni and Erich's?"

"They thought so. I wonder what they think now."

"Their eyes are open, I'd say. They were quite willing to help, as long as they weren't involved—as usual. At least Erich was. Toni still hates me, it seems."

"I did warn you," she remarked. "But continue."

"They told me of your ruse, how you claimed to have left Rudolf. I must say you had them quite confused. They half-believed you themselves. It must have been a brilliant performance."

"You know what I'm like when I get angry."

He turned briefly to study her profile as she sat. "To my eternal detriment, yes. Poor Colonel Dietrich. He doesn't know what to think. Especially with me turning up to give credence to your tale. It worked out rather brilliantly."

"He didn't believe me until you showed up. And it looks like he's still not certain."

"Erich and Toni seemed to take my appearance rather in stride, as though they expected it. So did you, come to think of it."

She looked at him then and smiled slowly. "You always have had the most uncanny way of turning up, you know."

He took his eyes from the road, and they rested on hers briefly. "I told you if things came down to this, I'd be here." Then he turned back to concentrate on the task at hand. "But I didn't tell Toni and Erich what I intended to do. I left them before they even had a chance to do more than tell me what had happened. When Dietrich tells them you left with me, they won't know what to think."

Amalia managed a little laugh. "And now?"

"We play the guilty, absconding pair for a while. Rudolf and Webern will go to the mountain guide's home in Innsbruck. Quite an enterprising fellow, your Michael Webern. That is where the boys are headed?"

"Hopefully." Amalia was silent for a few moments. "I almost forgot them for a minute. How could I?"

"Amalia, you've got to relax. If you don't, you'll be ill. I've never known a boy as resourceful as Rudi. Remember the day Chris was hurt?"

"I'll never forget it. That's another time when you just happened to be there."

"Don't make me a hero, Amalia," he said sadly. "After the war, when you had every right to expect me, when you needed me most, I wasn't there."

"This is the time I needed you most, Andrzej. We all need you." And then in a faint voice, "Thank heaven you came."

It was mid-morning when they drove into the narrow streets of Innsbruck. The snow had not yet begun to thaw here, and Amalia thought with dismay of her winter coat back at Antonia's. At least the boys should have her loden cape. If they had made it.

"How long before we can risk contacting the boys?"

"What time did their train leave?"

"Seven."

"They should be pulling in soon. This Horst Dohlmann, the mountain guide, isn't on the telephone, but perhaps later this afternoon we can send a message with someone who wouldn't be connected with us."

He pulled in to a tiny *Gasthof* situated discreetly against the mountainside and well out of the center of town. "This looks as good as anything. Respectable but not showy. Just the kind of place they'd expect us to hole up in."

Amalia watched casually as he registered them as Herr Doktor and Frau Zaleski and, her mind elsewhere, did not even notice the peculiar look the innkeeper's wife gave them when Andrzej answered that they had no luggage to be carried upstairs.

The room they were given was a spare chamber, with scrubbed wooden floors, white walls, and pine furniture. There was one bed, covered with a vast Federdecke in its clean white cover, and only one small chair.

Frau Zeller stood back as they inspected the room. "Will it do?" she asked, eyebrows raised.

Andrzej laid on his most charming manner. "I'm terribly sorry to be a bother, but have you anything with two beds, perhaps? We were just making a short trip this morning when my wife fell ill. You can see perhaps that she isn't well? I shouldn't like to disturb her sleep, and this room has no place where I can comfortably sit."

At once the woman's manner thawed. "Ach, of course. You may have the front room. It will cost you a little more, but I think gnädige Frau will be much more comfortable."

Across the hallway she threw open the door to another room, twice the size of the first, decorated far more cheerfully, and with two full-sized beds. "We keep this for families who come here for the skiing," she explained.

Amalia was suddenly too tired to appreciate Andrzej's cunning, and she merely sank onto the bed. She fell asleep as he was finishing with Frau Zeller.

When she woke it was growing dark, and she was alone in the room. The other bed was rumpled, and a newspaper had been carelessly strewn across it, but Andrzej was gone.

Getting up slowly, she realized she was stiff and very hungry. She walked to the corner washstand and inspected herself listlessly in the little mirror that hung above it. Her hair was sticking up in a ridiculous manner, her eyes were swollen from tears and sleep, and her lips dry and chapped. Removing her jacket, she rolled up the sleeves of her silk blouse and proceeded to wash in the warm water. As she was drying her face on the white hand towel provided, the door opened and Andrzej walked in.

"Ah, the beauty awakes at last!" He presented her with a set of tortoise shell brushes and a comb, a small lipstick, and a bottle of gardenia scent.

"You are a dear, Andrzej," she said, barely restraining herself from giving him a hug of gratitude. He stood and watched in his lazy way as she did her hair, applied her lipstick, and dabbed on cologne.

"All ready to eat now?"

"Any word yet?"

"I sent a village lad off on his motor bike about an hour ago. Met him when I was buying your gear. He should have a message for us soon. I told him to meet us in the local Ratskeller."

"Is the Mercedes still around?"

"No. But I'm certain the watch has been locally delegated. It could even be the good Frau Zeller, for all we know."

"This young boy? Can you trust him?"

"I had to trust someone. He's one of the locals who likes to make a schilling off the tourists. No reason for him to think anything about it. I told him they weren't on the telephone."

They were ready to leave. "I haven't a coat, Andrzej. Dietrich hauled me off without it. I haven't got my hat either, and it has all my money in it."

"What else did you leave behind?" he asked sharply.

"Nothing incriminating, if that's what you mean. Rudi's got Herr Dohlmann's address."

He relaxed. Then, with the air of a magician, he opened the door and reached behind it, producing a large box tied with a silver string.

"Oh!" she cried. Inside was a short fox jacket. "Andrzej, this must have cost a fortune. You can't throw your money about like that!"

"It's Rudolf's money. Relax. Put it on. You must be starved."

The Ratskeller was crowded, smoky, and warm. Amalia wanted nothing more than a hot lemonade and sat sipping it, waiting anxiously for the appearance of Andrzej's youth.

"What kind of food are you interested in, my dear?" he asked, in an effort to divert her. "Try to look as though you're enjoying yourself," he added wryly.

She smiled brightly. "Not German."

He patted her hand and then looked up sharply. "He's at the bar. I'll just go happen to meet him, shall I?" He took his empty glass and approached the bar through the noisy crowd.

Moments later Andrzej returned, looking nonchalant, his glass once more brimming with the local beer. "Let me finish this, and then we'll go find a very un-German dinner."

She read the message in the car, by the feeble light of the street lamps.

> Glad you've arrived. We'll have Webern telephone you at the Gasthof when he arrives with your things. I'm sure he took good care of them, so don't worry. See you soon.

The message was in her oldest son's handwriting. Amalia laughed shortly. "Whatever you thought of your local lad, it's clear Rudi didn't trust him much. Oh, what a relief to know they arrived safely!"

She was actually able to enjoy her dinner. They ate at a Swiss establishment that specialized in fondue. A central fireplace conveyed both warmth and subtle light. The clientele seemed happily unaware that their country was in the midst of a crisis of any sort, and for a moment she allowed herself to be lulled by food and atmosphere.

"I can see I needn't feel the least guilty for endangering your life, Andrzej. You're actually enjoying this, aren't you?"

"Being Polish, I thrive on intrigue. Life's so much more meaningful when you're in imminent danger of losing it."

She looked into the flames of the enormous fireplace. "So is love," she murmured after a moment.

He studied her face quietly in the firelight.

Chapter Nine

They spent the following day endeavoring to lay to rest the suspicions of their unknown watchers. Walking the streets of Innsbruck, arm in arm, they inspected the shops. Under the auspices of their supposed relationship, Andrzej took the opportunity to outfit Amalia in a warm pair of insulated trousers, a fur-lined parka, and a heavy ski sweater. He wanted to buy her some skis, but Amalia stood firm.

"I'd be certain to break a leg," she maintained. "And then what good would I be?"

Andrzej affected a sigh. "What a pity. You'd be so decorative on skis. "I've always had a secret longing to see you glide down a mountainside."

As soon as Amalia arrayed herself in her new purchases, they took luncheon at the fashionable Café Wagner midway up the mountain, patronized by the idle rich who came for the skiing. While waiting to be served, Andrzej advised her, "We haven't got a lot of time to throw them off the scent, my dear. Every day Rudolf remains in Austria gives the Nazis another day to tighten their grip. We've got to give them a first class performance." He smiled at her gently across the square little table. "Think of it as a play, if you must. And try hard not to resist when I touch you, all right?"

She looked at him levelly, tilted her head to one side, and said, "To do this really well, I should have a cigarette in my hand. Women always look so terribly romantic holding a cigarette while they are being wooed. But I don't smoke.'

Andrzej scowled. "It's an abominable habit. Not the least romantic, I assure you from personal experience."

"Don't scowl, Andrzej," she admonished. "You're supposed to be enjoying yourself, remember? Who do you think our watcher is today?"

Andrzej shrugged a bit, and then leaned across the table to cover her hand with his. She felt her lips twitch, but kept the smile pinned to them.

"I put my money on the fellow in the serviceable tweeds over by the window. He doesn't fit in with the general ambience somehow."

Leaning toward him, Amalia lowered her chin and looked at him from under her lashes, whispering in what she hoped was a provocative manner. "How's this?"

He raised an eyebrow. "Careful. They'll snatch you away and put you in films." He stirred uneasily in his chair, and she laughed lightly.

"Shouldn't you chuck me under the chin, or something revolting like that?"

The scowl was back. "I'm hanged if I will. I believe you're enjoying this." He leaned back and sighed. "Ah, well. I suppose it wouldn't seem real if it were all sweetness and light. Lovers do quarrel, after all." Averting his eyes, he added, "And we more than most."

Their luncheon was served at that moment, to Amalia's relief. In spite of his earlier admonition to appear lover-like, Andrzej said little during the rest of the meal. She speculated to herself on the perversity of the situation and wondered what their watcher made of it all.

When they returned to their hotel room, they were disappointed to find there had been no messages. Insisting that she rest, Andrzej, still in uncertain humor, left her.

Amalia watched the door sadly for a few moments after he left. Perhaps it had been a mistake to be playful, but it was the only way she could bring herself to carry it off. Their charade could not help but arouse dangerous feelings, long buried, and she sensed that it was becoming as difficult for him as it was for herself. Being with Andrzej was distracting, to say the least. They must find Rudolf soon, for all their sakes.

Only a short time later, it seemed, she was awakened by a knock on the door.

"Gnädige Frau," Frau Zeller summoned, "the telephone is for you." Her heart jumped into high gear, and she made her way down to the little booth in the lobby. Leaving its doors open, lest a wish for privacy make the woman suspicious, Amalia picked up the receiver. She kept Frau Zeller in view, in case she were to take up an extension. The hefty woman made no move, however.

"Frau Zaleski *hier*," she remembered to say.

"Michael Webern *hier*," her friend answered. "We have arrived. Are you well?"

"Splendid, thank you! It's wonderful to hear your voice."

"Do you know the climber's shrine near the Café Wagner?"

"I'm certain my husband does."

Webern paused a moment. He phrased his next sentence carefully. "A midnight rendezvous would be nice. Can you arrange it?"

Amalia thought quickly. "Sounds lovely, but could we make it a bit later?"

Frau Zeller was standing very still, as though not to miss a word. Dangerous or just curious?

"Two, then?"

"Perfect. I'll speak to Andrzej. Thanks so much for calling." She put the receiver in place and looked up to see that "her husband" had just come in. Going to him, she kissed his cheek lightly. "Darling, that was crazy Michael," she announced ingenuously.

"Oh? And what did the old flirt have to say for himself?" he asked playfully, leading her up the staircase. His irritation with her had apparently vanished.

She waited until they were shut in their room to answer him. "Two A.M. at the shrine up the mountain from the Café Wagner. He wanted it to be midnight, but I thought we'd have a better chance later. I hope Zeller hasn't got an extension in his office."

"There is no Herr Zeller. I've been making inquiries. Frau Zeller runs this place herself. Her sympathies are rather fascist, however."

"Nothing more?"

"Not for certain. Did she overhear you?"

"All she could tell from my end was that he was an old friend who wanted to meet with us."

"We'll chance it, then. Let's hope that your openness disarmed any possible suspicions. We can go to the café for a late aperitif and take it from there."

Amalia was so relieved to know that Rudolf was safe, she sank her forehead onto Andrzej's chest. "He's alive, and I will see him tonight, God willing. Oh, Andrzej, thank you so much for everything you've done!"

He put her from him gently. "I think it's time for you to prepare for dinner."

They enjoyed dinner at a French bistro, danced and laughed at the local *Weinstube*, and then went back to the Gasthof where they changed into their après ski ensembles (Andrzej had purchased one for himself that afternoon). Then they made the drive up to the little café where they had lunched. It was alive, even at this late hour, with a very fashionable set, who were making merry in groups, or pairing off into the darkened corners, while a great fire blazed in the central fireplace.

"Have you noticed if we are being followed, tonight?" Amalia asked, her false gaiety deserting her now that they were so close to their object. Would she really see Rudolf again?

"Just a little longer," he encompassed her with his arm as they found a seat near the hearth. "You're doing splendidly." Then he turned to face her. "Behind me, over by that window. The same fellow as at noon."

Amalia's heart plunged within her, disappointment bringing tears close to the surface. "We can't risk it then," she said heavily.

"Don't, darling," he whispered. His eyes were soft with a look she knew to be quite genuine, and he took her chin in his hand and then kissed her gently on each cheek as though she were a small child. "Courage, ma petite! Believe me, I am as anxious to meet up with them as you are, and we will do it. But right now we're going to drink this up and then return to the Gasthof where we'll appear to settle for the night. If all is well, perhaps we'll risk a foray later, but I must tell you I never expected this to work. Michael will think of something better once he realizes how closely we're being watched. He's a clever fellow."

Amalia allowed herself to be shepherded back to the little room she had hoped she'd left forever. "Frau Zeller must know I'm feeling better with all this racketing around we're doing. How will you explain our continued stay?"

"I told her today that we like it so well we decided to stay a few days. Thin, but what else could I do? I flattered her shamelessly about her hospitality and the glory of Innsbruck, and she lapped it up."

Later, as she lay fully dressed under her Federdecke, Amalia remarked idly to Andrzej who stood stationed by the window. "All of this is so strange to me."

"I hope so. It would alarm me very much if I thought you'd lived your life on the run."

"No. What I mean is, I don't feel like me. I'm so different without the boys and Rudolf. It's rather like I've lost my appendages, and I'm moving about randomly in space with no anchor." She paused and then said irritably, "I've mixed my metaphors."

"Your family's out there somewhere, Amalia."

"You've been splendid, Andrzej," she said with sudden energy. "I'm sorry if I've acted silly. But that's what I'm trying to explain. I'm not myself—everything is so disorienting—being here in Innsbruck, away from my home in Vienna, perhaps forever, running like a criminal. Being here with you . . ." Her voice tightened, and she stopped.

"Yes." Andrzej ran his hand through his hair. "I know what you're feeling. It's a wretched circumstance. The sooner we restore you to your proper husband, the better. But I'm afraid it won't be tonight. Our pet Nazi is still on guard. He must be frozen."

"It's hard to believe they want Rudolf as badly as all that."

"A matter of principle. They can't have anybody left who could rally resistance. They've got to make an example of him." Andrzej's voice was grim and hard, and without warning Amalia began to cry.

"He should be living quietly at his Schloss, totally unaffected by all of this! They're going to kill him, and it's all because of me and my ridiculously futile ideals!" Her sobbing became wild, but Andrzej, jaw clenched, stood at his post by the window.

"Don't imagine that, my dear," he said coolly. "I know your Rudolf well enough to know he couldn't have stood idly by while the Nazis had their way with Austria. No more will I stand for it, for they won't be contented now. It will be Czechoslovakia next and then Poland."

"Don't! Don't talk that way! I can't bear it!"

He went to her, and his voice was as brisk as a slap. "Whether you can bear it or not is beside the point, Amalia. That maniac has tasted power. Nothing is going to stop him."

"Someone must stop him!" Amalia's tears were suddenly quenched, and she sat up straight, eyes blazing.

Andrzej sat beside her and took her hands. "That's more like it, my love. We can't give up now. The real fight is just beginning." His face was softened to such gentleness, and his eyes looked into hers with such fervor, that she felt an unwilling tenderness steal over her. Tearing her hands away from his fierce grip and trembling all over, she climbed unsteadily out of her bed. She stood looking at him uncertainly.

He returned her gaze, his own unsteady also. Then, rising abruptly, he said, "I'd better go out for a while. Good night, Amalia."

He left, but she stood in the same spot, trembling, for some time. Finally, feeling as though every vestige of strength had left her, Amalia got back into her bed and pulled the Federdecke over her. She slept, hearing only dimly Andrzej's return hours later.

The next morning after breakfast, Andrzej took a call from Webern.

The new scheme he proposed sounded much more promising. An anti-fascist actress acquaintance of his from Vienna, named Marta, was holidaying in Innsbruck and throwing a masked ball that night at her rather enormous chalet. They were cordially invited.

"It's perfect," Andrzej crowed when they were alone together in their room. "But you'll have to be very discreet, Amalia. Our Nazi friends will guess something's up. When you spot Rudolf, you'll have to sit on your hands."

She laughed suddenly with pure happiness. "Oh, don't worry, I'll carry it off! It will be quite enough for me to be in the same room with him, to know he's alive! I'm going to be a good actress when all of this is through. But what will we wear?"

"I see signs that you're returning to normal," he grinned.

The rest of the day was spent rounding up everything necessary for their costumes. Innsbruck being far too tiny and provincial to run to a costumier, they had been forced to take Frau Zeller into their confidence, much to that woman's delight.

"A friend of ours from Vienna, Frau Zeller," Amalia explained with enthusiasm. "Do you know the actress Marta Morgen? All of her guests will have brought elegant things, and we can't be shamed! What shall we do?"

Frau Zeller, to her great satisfaction, knew a local thespian who was, in fact, director of Innsbruck's amateur theatrics in the summer. She introduced her guests to this hairless little man, and they spent the afternoon piecing together costumes of an eighteenth century Italian count and his lady love.

Later, in their room, an enormous powdered wig upon her head, Amalia applied the exaggerated makeup of the age. She observed, as she placed a beauty patch, "I have my doubts about climbing to freedom in this! She stood and exhibiting her absurdly broad skirt of red silk brocade, twirled about the room.

"Actually, it's perfect for your needs, my dear. Wear your trousers underneath, and we'll tie your sweater to that wire cage thing that holds your dress out!"

Her spirits were high, and her cheeks, which had been far too pale were flushed as she made these arrangements behind the screen. "I wonder what sort of things women used to hide under these things?" she remarked.

"Fat thighs and enormous hips, I imagine," Andrzej answered as he tied his cravat in an elaborate arrangement which would have done justice to a count of the period.

She was sad to leave behind her new fur-lined ski jacket, but Andrzej convinced her it had no place in the toilette of an eighteenth-century contessa. "Your fox fur will do much better. Rudolf will have your loden cape."

She turned and looked at him, suddenly contrite. "You will come with us, won't you? You can't stay here. It won't be at all safe."

"Never fear, my dear. There's nothing to keep me in Austria now. I'll see you safely into Switzerland. Eventually, I'll probably go back to Poland to try putting some sense into my compatriots. Perhaps the uncensored details of this Anschluss will awaken something in them."

"I hope you succeed," she murmured, her gay spirits deserting her quite suddenly. It occurred to her that she might never see Andrzej again. Andrzej, who had been part of her entire adult life. As she looked into his eyes now, she saw honor, chivalry, and gentleness. He had, indeed, become the man she had seen inside him so many years before.

How could she even think these things when her dear husband was in such peril? She pulled her eyes away from those of her former fiancé and became outwardly engrossed in her dressing.

"What will Rudolf do, now that he has suddenly become a man of leisure?" Andrzej asked.

"Go to England, I expect. He thinks it may do some good to talk to Churchill."

"And you, will you go with him?"

"Oh, yes!"

They stood looking at one another across the small room, garbed in their theatrical gear, a silence stretching between them. Suddenly Andrzej laughed wryly.

"This is the positive height of absurdity! I've become so terribly noble, I don't even know myself. Redemption of the soul seems to be possible, after all. What else could account for it? Let's be off to this soiree and get it over with, or I'll say something we'll both regret!"

He escorted her down the stairs, where they modeled before Frau Zeller, who was favorably impressed.

"You are as lovely a couple as I've ever seen!" she exclaimed in delight. They left the warmth of the Gasthof then and swept out into the cold evening air. A light snow was beginning to fall.

Chapter Ten

Marta's chalet was perched on the mountainside with a splendid view of the town. As Webern's car climbed laboriously up the mountain, they could see the lights below twinkling through the snow.

Amalia looked out the window. "It's so wonderfully picturesque here. Who would ever believe all that's going on behind the façade?" she commented as they arrived finally at the sprawling chalet, built solidly into the mountainside.

"One might say the same about your face, my dear," Andrzej returned lightly, as he helped her out of the car. "Mind you don't slide. And take care no one sees those boots underneath that thing. Remember that Italian countesses had to appear very chaste and never showed as much as an ankle in public."

It was ten o'clock, and the party was well under way. Andrzej and Amalia picked up their sequined masks at the door and joined the throng. Leaning sedately on his arm, she tried not to be too anxious to identify her husband and sons.

She was immediately taken aback by the incredible brilliance of their hostess. "Ah, you must be Michael's friends. Herr Doktor!" She inclined her cheek for a kiss, and Andrzej obliged. "And Frau Zaleski, I hope you will let me call you Amalia! You must call me Marta, of course! Both of you."

Her costume was that of an exotic bird. As far as Amalia could tell, apart from the mesh tights that encased her splendid legs, every other part of her costume was made of vivid feathers, culminating in a splendid, towering headdress of ostrich plumes. Her face a mask of glitter and cosmetics. Only her eyes betrayed her shrewdness. She was a very strange associate for the nondescript Michael Webern to have.

"The rest of Michael's friends have yet to arrive. Why don't you just make yourself comfortable?"

Amalia relaxed her vigilance after this information, assuming that Marta meant Rudolf was not yet there. She tried to amuse herself by studying the other costumes, some magnificent, and some entirely strange.

"My dear, look!" she said to Andrzej, and pointed out a man who had come as a bowl of fruit, with actual apples, oranges, bananas, and other miscellany somehow holding together around his person as he moved about in what looked to be an inverted wooden skirt.

He countered by showing her a woman who was clad in a grape-purple body stocking, wearing half a cello. "I think she must be something by Chagall," he remarked. "I'm afraid we're shockingly conventional."

She laughed. "We couldn't have done more to call attention to ourselves, could we?"

At the moment, she desired nothing more than to drink something hot and observe her fellow guests, a blessed distraction that dispelled some of the tension building inside her. Soon, the five-piece orchestra, which had apparently been taking a break, struck up a fox trot, and every available scrap of floor was used for dancing. Amalia was asked to dance by a short, dark man in a black cutaway coat and knee breeches. She handed over her cup to Andrzej and rather recklessly left him to dance with this mysterious partner.

He was a very precise but uninspired dancer, and not once did he smile or speak from behind his mask. She began to think this quite curious in such a light-hearted, merry group. As he returned her to her "husband," he bowed over her hand after the manner of the courtly gentleman he was impersonating, and then straightening, he smiled. There was no mistaking him then.

Amalia's heart thudded sickeningly in her breast. "Why, Colonel

Dietrich! What a surprise!" she managed. "I can't say, in all honesty that it's a pleasant one. I had devoutly hoped never to see you again. Have you deserted my poor sister, then?"

"Duty calls, Baroness."

"Please!" she pleaded. "Don't give me away! I'm known as Frau Zaleski among these people."

He raised his eyebrows and, clicking his heels, pronounced, "You can, of course, rely on my discretion, Madame."

He walked away, and Amalia began to tremble. "What's he doing here?"

"I doubt he was invited, but there's nothing we can do about it. Frau Zeller must have been a spy, after all," Andrzej answered. "Cheer up. You carried that off marvelously. We had better dance."

It was inevitable, perhaps, that at that particular moment the little orchestra was overtaken by nostalgia and chose to play a waltz. It was very queer to see a bowl of fruit, birds, a cello, pierrots, pierrettes, and harlequins intermingling upon the floor, swaying and whirling to the music of a dead empire. But Amalia did not notice, and even Dietrich was forgotten for the moment.

"How is it, Andrzej," she asked, "that music, more than anything else, can so eloquently call up the past?"

His eyes, vividly green behind the mask that hid so little, locked with hers as the room turned around them. "Perhaps it's because music speaks to the heart, Amalia, not the mind. The heart is damnably unaware of the passage of time."

When the music was over, its magic was slow to recede, and Amalia was left with a heart pounding as though she had run a race. Would this be the last time she waltzed with Andrzej?

It was several moments before she became aware that she was an object of someone's scrutiny. Finally, looking around, she saw that Dietrich, standing nearby, was gazing at her with unabashed steadiness. Her color rose as she realized that she and Andrzej had just staged a performance that lent great verisimilitude to their charade.

"Oh, where's Rudolf?" she thought in sudden desperation.

Not many minutes later she first noticed him. He was arrayed somewhat unimaginatively as a harlequin with a black silk cape. His muscular shoulders and the shape of his head gave him away to her at once, but she dared not let the observant Dietrich realize any change in her. Turning to her partner, with cheeks flushed she said rather loudly, "I'm so glad we came, darling. Marta is so clever to throw a party just now when everything is so dismal."

"Don't overdo it, Amalia," Andrzej cautioned with his back to Dietrich. "I know that Rudolf has arrived, but you must calm yourself."

She demanded that they dance again, a rather spirited polka that knocked her wig askew. Her hiking boots also made her clumsier than she would have liked. The next dance was a Charleston. Although it had never been a favorite of hers, it would have been a wonderful outlet for her nerves had she been able to do it in a hoop skirt. As it was, she was condemned to sit and watch as Rudolf partnered the exquisite Marta. He looked slightly comic in his strange costume doing the idiotic dance, and her feelings of fondness overwhelmed her.

A man that Andrzej told her was Michael Webern appeared, dressed as a jester. Surprisingly, he swept her onto the dance floor, and she enjoyed as much as she could enjoy anything the novel sensation of dancing with this extraordinary man. She noticed, halfway through, that Dietrich still watched her closely. Could he think that Michael was Rudolf? She laughed recklessly and felt her cheeks burn.

"Danger puts a sparkle in your eye, Frau Zaleski."

"That's hysteria, as Andrzej will tell you. I'm as nervous as a cat, Michael. I couldn't live this night again for anything. Any more surprises?"

"The boys are helping in the kitchen, discreetly out of sight."

"They had better be. Antonia's Nazi is here. That ghastly little man in the black coat and breeches." She smiled meaninglessly in case the man in question was watching them.

"The thing to do is to be very gay, . . . ah, Amalia. I'll pass you around the room. Perhaps you'll even get a dance with the harlequin. Then leave everything to Marta. She's a marvel. Quite ingenious."

The next hours were a blur as she danced minuets, polkas, tangos, fox trots, and even another waltz. Her feet felt large and clumsy in the hiking boots, but as her skirt dragged on the floor, cascading down from its hoops, nothing was visible underneath. Andrzej and Rudolf both remained somewhere on the fringes until finally, near one o'clock when her nervous energy had begun to flag and she was growing desperate, Rudolf appeared, and spirited her out onto the floor. The music was a tango, which neither of them did well, but at least it gave them an excuse to hold one another. They did not speak, but she could feel his body rigid with tension as they went through their act.

It was the most disorienting experience of the entire bizarre evening, to dance with her husband and yet not show in any way that they had ever enjoyed a moment of intimacy. She thought she might scream from the tension. He spoke only once. "Thank heaven Zaleski got you away."

She answered with what she hoped was a flirtatious smile. "That S.S. man is here. Please be very careful."

Not long after that, Andrzej claimed her, and while she was fanning herself limply with her costume fan, Marta appeared at her elbow.

"My dears, I have the most fabulous idea! It's a storybook night, and you *must* see the view from the top of the mountain. Right now! Come, come, come!"

She led them back, Michael Webern at her elbow, through a baize door and swiftly through the brightly lit kitchens. Suddenly they were through the back door in the frigid night air. A chauffeured limousine stood idling there, and inside a minute, they were off, climbing the snowy mountain road, the ghastly gaiety behind them.

As soon as they were away from the house, the three black shapes that had been huddled on the floor materialized into Rudolf, Chris, and Rudi.

Amalia could not speak as she tearfully embraced first one son, then the other, and finally Rudolf. She held him to her, smelling his unique scent of leather and soap, feeling the tension in his hard compact body, the pulse beating under her cheek in his neck. She savored his closeness which she had thought more than once never to feel again. Andrzej looked on, his face unusually solemn and worried. Michael and Marta sat in front behind the glass next to the chauffeur.

Amalia found a shaky voice at last. "You seem to be in one piece. Thank God for Michael Webern."

Rudolf looked at her, the harsh lines of his hawk-like face relaxing until his countenance shone with tenderness. Stroking her cheek, he added, "And thank God for Zaleski. I should never have sent you away."

"But everything has turned out for the best, Rudolf, so don't let's think of it now," she answered briskly. She turned to the boys. "Aren't they wonderful, Rudolf?"

"Of course," he said. "They come of excellent stock. Give your mother her loden cape, Christian. She can hear about your adventures later."

"But, Mutti, you can't hike to Switzerland in that!" They had been pulling heavy wool sweaters over their shirts.

She pulled up the edge of her skirt demurely to exhibit trousers and hiking boots. "I've got a heavy Innsbrucker sweater somewhere tied to my hoops," she said with pride.

The car halted, and Marta's chauffeur lowered the glass. "I'll lead you to the hiker's shelter where Horst Dohlmann will be awaiting you to guide you over the mountain," Michael Webern told them.

He slid out of the front seat and opened the door for them. He had pulled on warm clothing over his costume during their drive up the mountain. Amalia hastily discarded her skirt, and Andrzej pulled off his outer clothing to reveal warm, sleek ski clothing underneath.

As they removed the backpacks that had been stored in the trunk, hasty but warm farewells were exchanged with Marta, who would return alone to the party below, sending the car back later for Michael.

The shelter was not far from the road. It was nothing more than an old goatherders hut, previously stocked with provisions for their journey. Horst Dohlmann turned out to be a giant of a man, practically invisible underneath his winter clothing. He shook Rudolf by the hand. "I'm glad you made it, Baron."

"Dohlmann, you are an exceptional man to do this for us."

"It's not such a wonderful evening for hiking," Webern said, indicating the snow that was falling.

"It's perfect for our purposes," Dohlman replied grimly. His quick eyes darted from one of his charges to the other.

With their mother safely restored to them, the boys were anxious to be on their way. The men in the hiking party shouldered the backpacks that had already been filled with the most basic provisions.

"What's Marta to say when she arrives back without us?" Andrzej wanted to know. "Colonel Dietrich's no fool.'

Michael patted his shoulder. "Leave it to Marta. She can manage.'

"Thank you so much, Michael. God bless you," Amalia said fervently.

The baron shook his hand as did each of the boys and Andrzej.

"Godspeed, then," Michael Webern said.

"I don't think we ought to linger," Andrzej said shortly.

Amalia assented. "I just want to get away from here." Rudolf squeezed her hand, and she looked at him with all the assurance she could muster. "I'll be fine. This is good-bye then, Michael."

The medium-sized man leaned forward and kissed her cheek.

A great deal of snow had fallen since the evening began, but Horst Dohlmann apparently knew the terrain well, for he had no difficulty finding the trail that wound across the white breast of the mountainside.

They had all reached the narrow path and begun to make slow progress through the knee-deep snow, when suddenly a sound reached them, muffled but unmistakably foreign to their woodland surroundings. It came from the direction of the road, and they had no difficulty in identifying it at once. A car door slammed, and men were being ordered in sharp, guttural German to take to the trail.

Chapter Eleven

N o one moved for a moment. Amalia's heart slammed into her chest. Were they not going to make it, then? Would they get Rudolf?

Dohlmann whispered urgently, "Our only hope is to lay a trap. We'll never outdistance them in this weather. Here's my rifle, Zaleski." The guide tossed his weapon and then pulled a revolver out of his knapsack.

Andrzej nodded grimly and said, "You take Amalia and go down. I'll go up. Rudolf had better stay with me. Rudi and Chris, hide! There are some snowdrifts over there."

Taking him at his word, the boys darted down the path and were quickly lost in the rapidly falling snow. Amalia tried to follow them, stumbling down the slippery trail, vainly searching through the blizzard. Rudolf had been behind with Andrzej, and now she had lost sight of them as well. She suddenly felt herself pulled off the path, and she scrambled, half sliding, down the mountain. A strong hand pushed her behind a large rock. It was Horst Dohlmann. He remained next to her, eyes level with the top of the boulder, scanning back the way they had come.

"Where are Rudi and Chris?" she gasped, breathing hard, only a step away from flat out panic.

"I can't see anyone," replied Dohlmann, "friend or foe. That's good at this point."

Terror for Rudolf swelled inside her. She choked it back. The wind-whipped snowflakes curled around the rock. Somewhere in the whispering, white landscape among the jagged gray boulders and drifting snow were hidden those she loved most in the world. She faced this terror with an unknown man at her side.

As though sensing her thoughts, her protector smiled fleetingly at her as he checked his revolver. Then they heard the door to the hut creak, and he half-stood, squinting to see through the darkness and thick snowfall. A moment later the door slammed shut and a shot was fired.

"Schoenenburg! Zaleski!" Dietrich shouted from the vicinity of the goatherder's shelter. "I have your little bird and her friend here. She's a brave little bird, but you should know I'm holding a gun to her temple. My associate is doing likewise to your very accommodating friend."

Beside her Dohlmann tensed and she saw his face turn ugly with rage. He and Michael were close friends. Amalia put her hand on his arm but dared not make a sound.

"Unless you come forward, before I count to ten, we are going to have to kill this charming bird and her friend. I should hate to do that, you know."

Dohlmann tried to struggle to his feet, but Amalia, motivated only by some blind instinct held firmly onto his coat. Her heart was racing. What would Rudolf do?

"*Eins!*" they heard ringing out over the mountainside. Dohlmann crept silently below the boulder back toward the hut, leaning into the side of the mountain.

Out of the corner of her eye, she detected another stealthy movement against the whiteness of the mountain above the path. Where was her husband?

"*Zwei!*"

Andrzej's voice. "How do we know you've got her, Dietrich?"

"*Drei!*"

Then she heard Rudolf. "This is von Schoenenburg. Show us the prisoners, and I'll show myself."

Amalia struggled to her feet. "No! Rudolf!"

The door to the hut swung slowly open. Marta, her headdress gone, could be vaguely seen outlined in the doorway. Michael was pulled up next to her and dropped in the snow, unconscious or dead. An S.S. trooper's arm was clamped around Marta's throat and a large gun was pointed at her head.

Marta screamed, "Don't, Baron! It was my chauffeur! I'm not afraid—" Her sentence was cut brutally short as her captor tightened his hold around her neck.

"*Vier!*"

A dark shape that Amalia took to be Rudolf minus his backpack was moving boldly down the mountain. A shot suddenly rang out from the slope below the hut. Dietrich threw himself to the ground and Marta broke loose, running towards Dohlmann's shot.

"Now, now!" Dietrich shouted.

Three more S.S. men jumped from behind the hut, their machine guns ready. "Fire, you fools! They've got guns!" screamed Dietrich.

One of the S.S. began to spray bullets blindly, covering the advance of the other two up the mountain path. Amalia ducked behind the boulder as bullets cut across its face.

"Stop your fire!" It was Rudolf. "I'll come quietly, if you'll leave the others alone."

"It's only you we're after, Baron, I assure you," called Dietrich, who was now hidden behind the hut.

Amalia screamed out to her husband, "No! Rudolf, don't!"

She saw the dark shape continue to climb down the slope.

"No, Father!" Rudi screamed somewhere to her left. But the man continued his silent descent. Amalia could stay behind her rock no longer. She had to get to her husband.

"No, Amalia! Stay where you are!" As the man turned towards her, she saw suddenly that it was not her husband but Andrzej.

"So, you would try to trick me," said Dietrich. "Fire! Kill them all!" All four of the machine guns raked the mountainside. Andrzej threw himself to the ground. Amalia dived back behind her shelter and sobbed. She heard her husband's voice ring out in the tones of a battlefield command. "Stay down, Zaleski! It won't work. I'll go. Stop your firing."

"Cease fire," shouted Dietrich. "No more tricks, Baron. Come slowly with your hands over your head."

She struggled to her feet. The firing had stopped, and Rudolf was now making his way down the slope to the path. His hands held no weapon. Amalia could see Andrzej holding his rifle as he crouched behind a tree.

She stood, hands clenched, waiting for a miracle, while Rudolf walked toward Dietrich. Two of the S.S. men stood immediately above him on the hillside, carefully following his progress with their gun barrels. Two more were stationed below near the hut, their weapons likewise trained on the defenseless man.

"Well, Baron!" the little man dressed in black mocked. "It's very gratifying to meet you at last."

Rudolf was silent.

"I congratulate you on the resourcefulness of the baroness. I was nearly convinced by her behavior. She seemed to be the soul of the unfaithful wife! But I'm not often tricked, as you see."

Her husband still made no comment. Amalia couldn't believe this was happening. Why didn't Andrzej or Dohlmann shoot? Were they just going to allow Rudolf to be captured?

Then she saw Dohlmann slowly move around the corner of the hut, his revolver reversed in his hand. As the S.S. guard in front of him watched the conversation between the baron and Colonel Dietrich, the mountain man brought the butt of the gun smashing down on the guard's neck. Dietrich whirled at the sound of the guard's groan, and the baron leaped forward, knocking him to the ground. The colonel's black gun flew out of his hands as he fell and buried itself in a nearby snowdrift. The two men tumbled, rolling down the mountain in the snow.

The S.S. men ran to help the colonel, one of them stumbling and falling as Andrzej, somewhere above, shot him cleanly through the chest. Behind the hut, another shot rang out as Horst Dohlmann hit the third guard. The fourth hid himself somewhere behind the dense curtain of snow.

Dietrich and Rudolf struggled, locked together, sliding down the bank toward Amalia. She stood horrified and unable to move. She could see that Dietrich had his hands around Rudolf's neck. She screamed and saw the boys come running up the path.

"Down, Amalia!" Andrzej bellowed. "Rudi! Chris! Stay out of there!"

Rudolf brought his fists up between Dietrich's wrists and in one burst of strength hit them simultaneously, breaking the Colonel's grip on his neck. Seizing the advantage, he rolled over on top of him, striking the Nazi's face with his fists. Dietrich was younger, however, and in spite of his small stature, stronger. He managed to throw Rudolf off, and the two men rolled closer to her. When their roll was stopped by a protruding rock, Rudolf was on top. He seized the other man's neck and smashed Dietrich's head on the rock.

The last remaining Nazi guard was creeping towards them now, hidden from the others above the path. Only Amalia could see him, as he crept closer, machine gun trained on the struggling men, waiting for the moment they separated.

"Andrzej, Horst, hurry!" Amalia cried. Dohlmann appeared a few yards above her on the path peering down onto the mountainside.

"Down there, he's behind me!" she screamed. The mountain man began to run down the slope but lost his footing and fell heavily in the snow.

Amalia looked back to where her husband fought. Dietrich lay motionless, his face staring blankly upwards. Rudolf stumbled toward her.

Struggling to his feet, Dohlmann did not yet have a firm grip on his gun. Instinctively, Amalia left the shelter of her rock and ran towards her husband.

"Rudolf! Get down!" she shouted.

At that moment, the S.S. guard broke cover and fired, pumping bullets into Rudolf, who still struggled towards her.

She screamed again and again and could not stop.

"Amalia," her husband cried.

Dohlmann fired, and the uniformed man fell and rolled down the slope, disappearing far below.

She ran the few remaining meters to where her husband lay, blood pulsing from his neck in great spurts. But she saw only his face, turned towards her expectantly. Kneeling in the snow next to him, she put his head gently in her lap, her eyes never leaving his.

"Quickly," she called to Horst. "Something to stop the bleeding!"

Rudolf looked at her and weakly smiled. His eyes looked as gentle as they ever had, and he seemed possessed of a curious calm.

"Oh, my love," she whispered. There were so many things she needed to tell him, but his eyes shut then, and his mind closed to her as he lost consciousness.

She tried desperately to wake him, and failing, a fury took hold of her. Throwing herself upon his body, willing the warmth to stay, she tried to stop with her hands the blood that still pumped out of his wound.

She begged, "Don't go, Rudolf, don't go. We've made it this far. Don't go!" She felt hysteria rising within her as someone tried to pull her off.

"Let me go," she fought, savagely kicking, clawing at the person who held her. "He'll get cold! Let me go!"

"Let her go, Dohlmann," Andrzej's tired voice commanded.

Horst released her, and she crawled once more to cover her husband with her body. But the blood was not spurting anymore, and his face matched the white of the snow. She cried with total abandon, her head buried in his blood-soaked sweater, her arms holding the heavy, still body.

Andrzej knelt beside her and felt Rudolf's pulse. Amalia looked up at him, her eyes wild.

His eyes were wet and full of pain. "Amalia, I would have given my life for this not to have happened."

"He's not dead!"

He extended his hand as though to touch her and then dropped it. He could only nod.

Amalia's eyes were blinded. She was completely unaware of anyone who stood in the circle around them, even her sons. Unconsciously she brought her hand up to her cheek, which was covered in Rudolf's blood. Her gaze pricked to life then, and she looked uncomprehendingly at her fingers. A moment later she collapsed in a dead faint.

Chapter Twelve

When she regained consciousness, Amalia was on the floor of the goatherder's hut. Rudi and Chris were kneeling beside her, peering anxiously down at her face, each of them holding one of her hands. She lay there for a moment as the fog cleared from her mind, and bit by bit the memory of what she had just witnessed returned. Sounds of activity outside the shed dimly penetrated through to her awareness. Andrzej was shouting to Webern, who seemed to have regained consciousness. Something was being dragged through the snow outside the hut.

A figure stood silhouetted against the snow in the doorway. It was Marta, wearing what appeared to be the greatcoat belonging to one of the S.S. guards. Amalia shuddered and closed her eyes.

"She's awake now, Fräulein Morgen," Chris said tentatively. "Her eyes were open."

"Baroness!" Marta called to her. "I'm sorry, Baroness, but you must rouse yourself. Every moment we stay here we are in danger!"

Opening her eyes once more, Amalia struggled up on her elbows to look at the actress.

"We are taking the car over the road to the Brenner Pass," Marta continued briskly. "We're hoping that there won't be a roadblock at the Italian border and that we can get into Switzerland from there. That should give you time to recover a bit. Boys, you'll need to help your mother get up!"

Apparently glad of someone to tell them what to do, Rudi and Chris helped their dazed mother to her feet.

"What is to happen to my husband?" she asked through numbed lips.

"He goes with us, Baroness, don't worry. Andrzej and Michael have moved him to the car."

Shuffling almost blindly then, every movement an effort, Amalia found her way to the car. The snow had finally stopped falling, and the landscape was still, as though observing a reverent quiet, thus to obliterate all signs of violence. Amalia's body felt heavy and clumsy, and more than once she tripped and would have fallen were it not for the strong support of her sons, who each held one of her arms.

When they reached the vehicle, which had so short a time ago witnessed their happy reunion, it was only with tremendous effort that she could get herself inside. Michael was there. There was no sign of Rudolf's body.

"He's wrapped in a blanket, Amalia," Andrzej stated as though reading her mind, "back in the trunk. I'm sorry, but it was either that or leave him here."

Amalia said nothing but felt suddenly sick. Horst Dohlmann appeared, panting with exertion. "Done," he said cryptically.

"Rudi, Chris, wrap your mother in blankets from your knapsacks. She's in shock. Where's Marta?" Andrzej demanded.

"Coming," Michael said. "She's getting rid of whatever's been left in the hut.

Marta was making her way slowly up the slope to the car, walking stiffly as though her legs would not bend at the knee. Michael went to her and, picking her up in his arms, carried her the rest of the way.

"Andrzej, get more blankets. Marta hasn't got anything but sandals on her feet. She's frozen through."

The sky was just beginning to lighten as the heavily laden limousine pulled away and nosed slowly down the mountain road, leaving behind, though Amalia knew not where, the freezing remains of those it had carried not a half hour before.

"What did you do with *them?*" Amalia asked, her voice flat.

"They won't be found until the snow melts considerably, Amalia, you can be sure of that," Andrzej stated with a harsh firmness. He sat across from her. Rudi and Chris were on either side of her, holding her hands. Dohlmann, Webern, and Marta were in the front. Webern drove. Amalia looked at her sons. Rudi, his face no longer that of a boy, stared grimly out the window. Christian sat huddled beside her limp, cold figure as though for warmth. Without being aware of her action, she put an arm around his shoulders and pulled him closer, bringing her cheek to rest against his head as it lay on her shoulder.

While the climb through the dawn-lit mountains progressed, Amalia became more lethargic as all caring and hope drained slowly out of her. Her entire being, mind, body, and heart, seemed suspended somewhere in a state of frozen lead. Though she looked straight ahead, she saw nothing. Where had her life gone? With the Anschluss and Rudolf's death, the purpose that had driven her since the last war had collapsed. And Rudolf had given his life for it. Terrible remorse flooded her.

Then she sat up straight. *It's up to you now.* She could have sworn the voice was Rudolf's. She had to give his martyrdom meaning. She didn't know how to go about it, yet, but the thought would sustain her. Somehow Hitler had to be defeated.

The sun was fully up now, and the snow became blindingly white in the morning light. They had, Amalia realized, reached the summit. This was the Brenner Pass, the border with Italy. There was no border guard.

"Stop the car," she demanded in a terse whisper.

Andrzej searched her face for an instant, and Rudi said, "Why, Mutti? We're at the border. We must get on."

But Andrzej relayed the message to Michael Webern, who managed to pull over onto a narrow shoulder.

"What is it, Amalia?"

"We must leave him here," she said. "In Austria. Chris, open the door, please."

Her son climbed out, and Amalia followed him onto the windy summit. Then Andrzej emerged, and motioning Chris back into the car, walked up behind her. She was entirely unaware of him, however, as she stood gazing down into the mountain chasm, which for her, was all that was left of Austria.

"Amalia, you must listen to me," Andrzej said, his voice brusque as he placed his hands gently on her shoulders. "Surely, you can see it's all rock here! There's no place to decently bury him, even if we had a shovel."

She turned to face him, eyes flaming. "He died for *this* country, Andrzej! How can I smuggle him into another and bury him in some churchyard full of Swiss strangers? There must be a place . . ." her restless eyes raked the formidable terrain.

He followed her gaze for a moment, and then, taking her chin, forced her to look at him, "You know that I would do anything for you, Amalia."

She nodded slowly. "You even tried to die for him, Andrzej." She looked steadily into the serious eyes, so very different from the cheerfully irreverent ones she had first encountered. "I can never forget that. Why did you do it?"

"For you. It was the only thing left I could do. Rudolf's life was far more valuable than mine." How would she have felt had Andrzej died for Rudolf? Swamped with grief, she could hardly answer the question.

"I don't know what to do without him, Andrzej. I'm only half a person now. But I don't know if I could have lived with such a sacrifice from you. I'm very glad you are alive."

Andrzej removed his hands from her shoulders and gestured behind them. "There was a dirt track a ways back. But the most we can do is cover him with rocks."

"That will have to do. We'll come back someday," she said. "When Austria is free, we'll give him a proper memorial."

The wind whipped between them like icy sheets. Amalia stood desolately still and alone.

"Amalia," Andrzej said quietly, "of all the men I have known, he was the finest. The noblest. Surely his memory will dignify the place he's laid to rest, no matter where it is."

At this, Amalia began to weep, slowly at first, but finally in gasping sobs. "Is there no place for the good and the gentle in this world?" she cried bitterly.

At length, Andrzej pulled her into his arms. "We must see that there is, Amalia. We must fight for it, even if it means giving our lives, as Rudolf did."

Amalia straightened and, squaring her shoulders, looked out once again across the mountainous slopes of her homeland. "I'll be back one day, Rudolf," she whispered. "And so will your sons."

About the Author

G. G. Vandagriff lived and studied in Austria, where she became fascinated by its history and that of its former empire. She received her bachelor's degree from Stanford University in international relations, specializing in central and eastern European economics, history, and politics. Later, at George Washington University she received her master's degree in the same subjects. In 1972, her master's thesis foretold the downfall of the Soviet Union and the breakup of the Warsaw Pact. When she began researching her genealogy, she was astounded to discover that she was descended from individuals who had lived in the nations of central and eastern Europe as far back as she could trace them. She concluded that they were the "voices in her blood."

She began writing *The Last Waltz* while she was still in her twenties, researching and revising it between the publication of her other books: *Voices in Your Blood, Cankered Roots, Of Deadly Descent, Tangled Roots, The Arthurian Omen,* and *Poisoned Pedigree.*

Besides writing, research, and genealogy, G. G. enjoys traveling and playing with her grandson, Jack. She and her husband, David, are the parents of three children.